RISE OF THE GRANDMASTER

RISE OF THE GRANDMASTER

RISE OF THE GRANDMASTER™ BOOK ONE

BRADFORD BATES

MICHAEL ANDERLE

LMBPN Publishing
PMB 196, 2540 South Maryland Pkwy
Las Vegas, NV 89109

First US edition, December 2019
Version 1.05, January 2021

eBook ISBN: 978-1-64202-623-8
Print ISBN: 978-1-64202-624-5

THE RISE OF THE GRANDMASTER TEAM

Thanks to our beta readers

Crystal Wren, Mary Morris, Kelly O'Donnell, John Ashmore, Larry Omans

Thanks to the JIT Readers

Angel LaVey

Billie Leigh Kellar

Dave Hicks

Deb Mader

Diane L. Smith

Dorothy Lloyd

Jackson Hendricks

Jeff Eaton

Jeff Goode

Joshua Ahles

Peter Manis

If I've missed anyone, please let me know!

Editor

The Skyhunter Editing Team

CHAPTER ONE

A baritone voice blared from the speakers above the stage. "Do *you* have what it takes to be an adventurer?"

Tim bumped his shoulder into Xander's and leaned over to whisper to his best friend. He kept his eyes on the stage. "Can you believe this shit?"

"I know, right? Since when do college graduations have corporate sponsors?" Xander asked, scowling.

On the stage, a man in a neatly pressed suit started to talk about NPC Corp's new game, *The Etheric Coast*.

At least Xander understood how Tim was feeling.

It wasn't the game or the pitch that had him so upset. All he wanted to do was play *The Etheric Coast*, but he'd never be able to afford a POD for the full immersive experience.

Tim's parents didn't even have enough money to fly out for graduation, and they still had his brother and sister to put through college.

A smaller hand clamped down on Tim's and Xander's shoulders, and sweet breath brushed the nape of his neck as the owner of the hand whispered, "I didn't hear you two masters of industry complaining when NPC Corp updated the internet on campus." Sierra leaned back and pointed at Tim. "I remember *you* saying something like, 'Holy flaming shit balls, Xander! This is better than sex!'"

Tim turned around to look at the girl he'd failed to get up the courage to ask on a date for the last four years. Jet-black hair framed Sierra's light complexion, making her seem almost angelic.

How could he have been such an idiot? Had he realized too late that no internet in the world would ever be better than the woman sitting behind him right now?

Tim smiled, his cheeks burning. "I might have been exaggerating." He held his finger and thumb a pinch apart to demonstrate.

Xander copied the motion, being a little bit more generous with his measurement. "Not by much."

Sierra glared briefly at Xander, then turned her gaze toward Tim as if Xander had never spoken. "Oh, I don't think it's a cable issue." Her voice dropped to a conspiratorial whisper. "I've heard that finding the right partner can make all the difference with your connection."

Tim spluttered. If he'd been drinking, he would have sprayed liquid all over her lap. Had Sierra just hit on him?

If there was one thing Tim was sure he could get comfortable with, it was hot women hitting on him.

They were about to graduate, so this would probably be the last time he saw her. The girl he'd been crushing on for the last four years was sitting with him right now. All he had to do was make a move. What was it Xander was always telling him to do? Nut up or shut up?

It was time to nut up.

"Speaking of connections, what are you doing tonight?" Tim was barely able to stop himself from slamming his palm into his forehead repeatedly. Maybe it didn't sound as bad out loud as it had in his head?

"Not you." Sierra leaned back in her chair with a cocky grin on her face.

Nope. It obviously sounded just as cheesy to her as it did to him. Why was it things always sounded so damn cool in your head, but the second you said them, you realized they weren't nearly as awesome as you had predicted?

The grin on her face was what he chose to focus on. It didn't say, "Eww, gross!" Instead, her smile hinted that they might get to put that connection theory to the test if he expended a little more effort in.

Xander poked Tim hard in the chest, stirring him out of what was turning into a pretty decent daydream. "When are you going to learn, dude? She's just not into you."

Glenn nudged Tim from the seat on his left. "Probably 'cause of your micro-penis." He shrugged. "Word gets around."

His chance at getting Sierra's number went up in smoke…

"Fuck you," Tim growled, glaring at his two best friends. "And you. I thought you guys were supposed to have my back?"

Xander shook his head. "Sorry, buddy. Rule thirty-six, subsection B in the best friend manual states that it's incumbent upon you as a best friend to make sure your faithful coconspirator has no ego whatsoever."

"What does your magic rulebook say about throwing your friend under the bus in front of a girl he likes?" Tim grumbled.

Glenn pretended to open a book and thumb through its imaginary pages before stopping and pointing like he'd found a clue. "Right here! This passage clearly states you will always be better off trying to pick up girls without the help of your best friends."

Xander grinned. "See, man? The book never lies."

Sierra leaned forward again as the man on stage started winding things down. "I'll make the three of you a deal." She scowled at the three of them. "If the three of you can keep your mouths shut for the entire video, I'll come to your party tonight."

"Dude!" Glenn shouted.

"Right." Xander poked Tim again. "I dare you to say that we aren't the two best friends any guy could have?"

Tim wrapped an arm around his best friends' necks and gently crushed their heads against his own. "Don't screw this up for me." The look he gave them heavily implied their deaths wouldn't come quickly if they messed with his chance to see Sierra again.

They broke into peals of laughter, but as soon as the video began to play, his two best friends stopped instantly. Tim knew it was hard for the two Neanderthals to keep their mouths shut for more than thirty seconds. Shit, he hadn't been able to make them do it in four whole years.

Maybe beauty really could tame the beast.

If his two favorite assholes could keep their mouths shut, maybe he'd finally get to talk to Sierra for more than five seconds. Tim would only get to find out if his two amigos could keep up their end of the deal. Not likely, but hopefully, it would be good enough. He leaned back in his chair and watched the video, thinking about all the wonderful opportunities the future might hold.

A group of five players sat on the ground, gasping as they tried to catch their breath. It appeared items in the game had durability values, since all of the group's armor was ripped and torn. It was hard to tell for sure, but it looked as though a few of the blades actually had notches in them from being used.

Tim wondered if the items could be repaired or if they had to be replaced after the item degraded past a certain point. Everything about *The Etheric Coast* screamed reality. Dented weapons and armor just added another layer, and Tim forgot he wasn't actually there for a moment.

Each member of the party glanced at the yawning archway in

front of them, clearly unsure if they could—or even wanted to —continue.

One of the party members, a woman wearing flowing white robes, rose to her feet.

"Thank the bloody stars," the dwarf grumbled. "I was starting to think Jenn's mana would never regenerate."

Another woman in a tight leather ensemble purred, "Tell me about it. What kind of sick Dev thinks up a mechanic like that?" The player name over her head read LadyCat.

Jenn thrust her scepter into the air with a flourish. Her head bowed almost as if in prayer as she recited lines from the book in her off hand. White light streamed from the scepter, forming a glowing dome above the players.

With a flash, the light winked out, and a gentle mist started falling from the air above them. Each of the party members stood, letting the healing mist wash over them.

Tim watched in fascination as their wounds began to close and their health bars rose.

The party's weapons and armor still looked dinged and broken, but they were all slightly cleaner now. The overlay on the screen showed them at full health.

The healer fell to her knees, groaning. Tim could see that her mana bar was depleted. Was there some kind of blowback for pushing yourself too far?

A man moved away from the group toward Jenn. On his back was a bow almost as large as he was; an arrow from a weapon like that would be able to penetrate full plate armor. How strong did you have to be to use it?

The name displayed above the bow wielder's head was Jack. He pulled a vial of bright blue liquid from inside his vest and handed it to Jenn.

Jenn looked up at him gratefully and put the vial to her lips. As she rose to her feet, her mana bar continued to fill.

Tim watched her mana bar top out as she finished the last sip.

Tim wondered if the potion increased her natural mana regeneration, or if the blue liquid had the additional effect of continued restoration for a short period of time?

The rest of the group ignored the two as they walked back to the party. Everyone was too busy tightening the straps on their armor or putting the last few licks of the whetstone to their blades.

When everyone looked ready, a burly dwarf covered from head to toe in battered plate mail lifted his shield and turned toward the others. "Ready check," the dwarf growled.

Jenn had her book under one arm and her scepter held in front of her. "Ready, OakGut."

"Ready." Jack pulled the giant bow from behind his back.

LadyCat spun her daggers in her palms before slamming them home in the sheaths on her hips. "Ready."

The last man in the party was wearing a hooded robe, and his head was bowed in concentration. The entire group turned to stare at him.

OakGut kicked at the ground in front of him and sucked in a deep lungful of air before bellowing, "*Brixon!*"

Brixon bushed back the hood of his robe and flashed a warm smile at the surly dwarf. "Sorry, boss. I was just setting up some epic tunes."

The crowd laughed, and whatever the dwarf said next was lost in the roar of the audience.

OakGut smashed his axe against his shield, growling an oath to some forgotten god as he entered the archway. LadyCat followed him, dropping into a stealthy crouch as she crossed the threshold. Brixon and Jack entered next, and Jenn brought up the rear.

The camera pulled back as they entered the next room, revealing a large cavern. Giant stone pillars lined the circular space. There was something different about the columns. They almost seemed to be racks for gigantic casks of alcohol.

Tim looked at the top of the screen. *Is that a giant beer keg set up against the back wall?*

In the center of the room stood what looked like a simple, low-level goblin. His name was displayed in a fancier font that indicated he was a dangerous creature called the BrewMaster.

The little green man bounced from foot to foot with a giant smile plastered across his face. He had a metal brewer's stick in one hand, and a tiny keg strapped to his back.

Maybe this wasn't the boss. It was always possible he just made beer, but Tim's previous gaming experience screamed at him to pay attention.

Something interesting was about to happen.

The BrewMaster grinned at the adventurers, revealing rows of razor-sharp teeth. He pulled a small glass from a loop on his belt, then reached up to his shoulder and grabbed a hose. He pumped the device on his back twice, and beer streamed into the glass. The goblin drained the entire glass like a frat boy taking a shot before letting out a belch that shook the screen.

"Oh, that does hit the spot." The goblin started dancing from foot to foot again as he grew in size.

It was like watching someone Hulk out in a movie, except this guy had easily quintupled in size. He now looked more like a cave troll than a goblin.

Tim heard a couple guys off to his right start to chuckle. "Now *that* is a trick I have to learn. Drink a beer and grow three sizes."

Xander couldn't resist. "That's what Monica said after you went out last Friday."

Tim smirked as his best friend got punched in the shoulder. *I hope Sierra didn't hear that, even though it was hilarious.* No joke was good enough to put their deal at risk. He turned his eyes back toward the screen, praying Xander hadn't ruined his chance.

The keg of beer on the BrewMaster's back was now big enough for a grown man to drown in, and the brewer's paddle he carried had ugly-looking spikes poking out of it at all angles.

OakGut crouched behind his shield and sprinted forward to intercept the BrewMaster's paddle before it could plow into the rest of the group. A clang echoed across the cavern as the dwarf absorbed the blow on his shield.

"OW, BITCH!" The dwarf screamed in rage, shrugging off another attack before lashing out with his axe.

Every graduate in the auditorium heard the *whoosh* as the dwarf's steel sliced toward the goblin's unprotected leg. Tim braced himself, waiting for blood to pour from the gruesome wound, but the blade just bounced harmlessly off the BrewMaster's leg.

The BrewMaster poured himself another drink from the keg on his back, then tilted his head back and laughed before he drank it. He inspected his leg. "Not even a scratch. You should be embarrassed."

The BrewMaster swung his paddle, hitting the dwarf solidly.

OakGut flew through the air and slammed into the cavern wall. The surly dwarf tried to climb back to his feet, but his health bar dropped steadily.

Golden light streaked across the cavern and hit OakGut in the chest. A moment later, his armor glowed with the same golden radiance. A gentle mist rained down from above him, and his health bar started to climb.

The BrewMaster cackled, turning his gaze on the healer. "Would *you* like to sample my brew?"

Tim blinked when a soft, feminine voice spoke over the battle cries. "Special ability Do you want to party? activated."

The BrewMaster pointed his nozzle at the healer and blasted her with a stream of golden ale. Tim couldn't help but laugh as the woman was thrown from her feet and left soaking in a puddle of beer on the cavern floor.

If the possibility of a night with Sierra hadn't been on the line, Tim would have asked Xander how the game developers knew what his average Friday night looked like.

Glenn grabbed Tim's shoulder in excitement as the fight continued to play out.

Tim could almost feel the tension in the crowd. It was like everyone instinctively knew this was the moment the battle would be decided. He bit his lip as the BrewMaster stomped toward the healer.

OakGut bellowed a string of curses as his armor bathed the room in a golden glow, and the tank charged back into the fray. His axe flashed red before slashing the back of the BrewMaster's leg.

Maybe it was some kind of taunt skill.

Brixon launched a fireball at the goblin, and the crowd gasped in awe at their first glimpse of real magic in the game. The flames washed over the BrewMaster, but the magical fire seemed to have the same effect as OakGut's axe. Brixon scratched his head for a moment, then grinned. Deciding on another spell, Brixon started to chant.

The first of Jack's arrows bounced harmlessly away, and the second one left a small scratch. As far as Tim could tell, it was the first damage any of them had done to the boss. A quick look at the boss's health bar confirmed it. It might as well have been full.

The next few arrows had no effect, just like the dwarf's axe. All Brixton's spellwork seemed to do was damage the BrewMaster's clothes.

There had to be something the group was missing. Maybe they needed to break the keg on his back. Tim didn't know nearly as much about *The Etheric Coast* as he should, but he knew one thing.

Bosses *always* had a weakness.

Glenn might have ruined Tim's chances for a date when he cheered as LadyCat appeared on the screen again. The leather-clad vixen slid in behind the boss, twin daggers in hand.

She screamed in triumph as blades slashed into the BrewMaster's Achilles tendon and blood erupted from the wound. Tim wondered if she'd activated some kind of backstab bonus to land the critical hit.

A sigh rose from the crowd; they could all see what was about to happen. Cringing as though he could feel the blow, Tim watched as LadyCat dodged the first strike of the BrewMaster's paddle.

Her second attempt wasn't so successful.

The paddle hit LadyCat dead center, sending her flying across the room. Her limp body didn't move after it slammed into the barrels, shattering them.

LadyCat was now the second person on the team to end up drenched in goblin ale. The real question was, had she been impaled by one of the giant splinters?

Sierra pointed over Tim's shoulder at the BrewMaster's health bar. Something interesting was happening—the color of the bar changed from red to purple. Jack's next arrow sank into the Brew-Master's chest up to the fletching.

Breaking the barrels must have been what made him vulnerable. Nothing else had changed. If *The Etheric Coast* put unique puzzles into every boss fight, the game was going to be epic.

"Attack!" OakGut bellowed, axe flashing red again as he charged at the BrewMaster. This time his axe found purchase when it hit. Each strike carved chunks of flesh from the goblin's unprotected legs.

Two more arrows found their way into the goblin's chest, and a third lodged in the boss's throat.

A small tear in reality appeared above the goblin, flames poured from the opening like a waterfall of liquid fire. The Brew-Master fell to his knees, screaming as his steaming skin started to puddle around him.

The goblin wasn't the only one to collapse.

Brixon was on his hands and knees, looking as if he were about to throw up. Tim scanned the screen, searching for the reason, and noticed that his mana bar was depleted.

Not the smartest thing to do in a battle. Ending up on your knees like that at the wrong time would get you killed.

The BrewMaster tried to crawl away, but LadyCat popped out of thin air to put a stop to it. She planted a well-placed foot on the goblin's charred and steaming back forcing him to stay down. Each step she took further up his back elicited a squeal of pain from burned boss beneath her.

She dropped to her knees, pinning his shoulders in place and then reached down placing her daggers against the goblin's throat.

LadyCat stood in one fluid motion, pulling hard with both daggers to make sure they cut through the BrewMaster's leathery hide.

Blood sprayed from the Bosses throat, coating the cavern floor with blood. LadyCat jumped off the bosses body as his hit points rapidly plummeted toward zero. The BrewMaster's health bar started flashing from purple to red.

Tim wondered what the change of the health bars color meant. It was probably some kind of function to let the players know the BrewMaster's invincibility was down. That, or this was a burn phase and they had to kill the boss before all hell broke loose.

If the bosses invincibility returned Tim wondered if they could break the barrels themselves or if the team would have to trick the boss into doing it again? There were so many ways this could go he was excited to see how things turned out.

The more Tim watched the fight, the more he wanted to play the game.

The dwarf made sure they didn't get a chance to see what happened if the party didn't finish the fight in time. OakGut's axe was bathed in purple flames as he repeatedly hacked the back of the Goblin's neck.

The boss's health bar hit zero, and the party started to cheer.

11

Slowly, the BrewMaster's body disappeared. It was replaced by a giant golden chest.

The screen faded to black as the dwarf reached for the lid.

Tim read the white letters that flashed across the screen aloud. "Join NPC Corp today. Your adventure awaits."

"Adventure waits for no man." Tim chuckled. Wouldn't it be great if he could play videogames for money instead of having to get a real job?

"Or woman," Sierra countered.

Tim turned to look at her. "Are you into gaming?" he asked, wondering why he didn't already know that about her.

"Just a bit," Sierra replied casually. The look on her face dared anyone sitting around them to question her gamer cred.

Before one of Tim's idiot friends could say something to ruin the moment, the president of the university walked onto the stage, with a gaggle of professors and administrators behind him.

Tim turned back around.

One by one, the president called out the names of the graduating students, who marched past him and collected their diplomas as if on an assembly line.

Tim wanted to be excited, but all he could think about was that college was over. It was time to step into the real world. Being an adult came with pesky responsibilities like paying off his student loans...*and rent.*

His parents could also use the financial assistance, but he knew they'd never pressure him for it.

Maybe he was just grouchy because he had wanted them here for his graduation.

Tim understood that flying across the country when they were strapped for cash didn't make any financial sense. Raising three kids wasn't cheap, and it didn't get any cheaper when the first one went off to college.

If he could just find the right job, things would get easier for everyone.

Tim's brow compressed into a frown. *I have an interview this afternoon. Maybe I'll get lucky and have a chance to figure out the rest later.* He looked around the room. There was a solution to every problem, and if there was one thing he was good at, it was fixing problems.

Thinking about the old neighborhood didn't do him any good. All he wanted to do was help his family get out of there. "With your brain or a gun," he whispered.

Looking down at his diploma, Tim was happy with his choice.

"Snap out of it, big guy." Xander bumped Tim's shoulder to get his attention and pointed across the auditorium at Sierra's diminishing form. "Better do something quick."

Tim jumped on top of his seat and bellowed like the warrior had in the video. Everyone turned to look at him, and his cheeks burned with embarrassment at the attention.

He focused on Sierra. "I believe the lady owes me a date."

Sierra laughed lightly as she glanced at the growing crowd. "Since when did 'I'll show up at your party,' turn into a *confirmed date?*"

"Snap!" someone shouted.

The rest of the crowd oohed.

Tim's heart felt like it might beat out of his chest and sweat dripped from his forehead, but he couldn't chicken out now. When it came to love, you were either all in, or you were on the sidelines.

This was his moment, and all he had to do was claim it. Licking his lips did nothing to ease the dryness in his mouth. Tim knew he was running out of time.

He wouldn't freeze. Not this time.

Tim's smile started to grow as the words to his favorite Proclaimers song poured from his mouth.

Sierra was running toward him before he made it to the second verse. With a graceful leap, she landed on a chair in the row in front of Tim, then leaned across the gap and gave Tim a quick kiss. "I'll be there," she whispered.

Then, as fast as LadyCat had disappeared in the video, Sierra was gone.

The auditorium broke out in wild applause.

"*YES!*" Tim's fist rose above his head, just like his favorite character from the *Breakfast Club*.

Maybe today wasn't going to be such a bad day after all.

CHAPTER TWO

Tim's first job interview went well enough. The company called back an hour later with an offer. It was the amount of the offer that was the problem.

Seventy-five thousand dollars a year to work in the most expensive city on the planet? It just didn't make sense.

Tim was *all* about the numbers. Sure, after rent and basic living expenses, he would be fine.

Add in a student loan payment, and sending money home to his parents? He wouldn't even be able to afford his favorite streaming service.

What was the point of working your ass off if you couldn't even afford to spend a quiet night at home?

Biting his lip, Tim wondered how things turned desperate so quickly. Just two weeks ago, he'd passed his finals and was ready to leave college behind him for good. He was ready to grab the world by the short and curlies and make it his bitch.

That was until one by one all of his applications came back with the same simple response.

"We've decided to go in another direction."

With only one option on the table, it felt like the decision was already made. There was no way in hell Tim was going to put everything his parents had worked for at risk by not taking the job.

Unless he found a better option in the next couple of days, he'd do what he had to.

Maybe he should have been a banker. You had to give them credit. Whether the market was up or down, they always made money. But sitting in an office and talking home loans with people seemed duller than watching grass grow.

The market was where finance really felt alive. There was money to be made, both in long-term investments and in margins. Good traders knew how to work both ends of the system, and how to protect themselves from a sudden downturn.

Tim smiled as he started pulling off his smelly workout clothes. At least Sierra was still coming over. Didn't someone say the love of a good woman erases all wrongs?

That kiss! Oh, man, that fucking kiss.

Tim hadn't expected the song to work. His voice had sounded like a cat getting strangled by Gollum. But it had.

Not only had it worked, but she had kissed him!

Tim stepped into the shower and let the hot water wash over him. Oh, shit maybe it was time to switch to cold water. "I look like an old man who popped one too many blue pills," he muttered.

Laughing and cringing as the freezing cold water did its work, Tim finally felt like himself.

Things weren't so bad. So what if he couldn't afford much for the first few years? Eventually, he'd get a raise or move to another position. His prospects weren't nearly as bleak as he was making them out to be.

If he was really lucky, he might even get laid.

Stepping out of the shower, he swiped on some deodorant, then added a quick splash of cologne. He wanted to smell nice, not like one of those idiots who didn't know when to call it quits with the body spray.

We all knew that guy. Don't ever be that guy.

Sweaty palms, check.

Racing heart, check.

Tim looked in the mirror on the back of his door one last time to psych himself up for the party. "Looking good." He flashed himself the double guns before jumping from foot to foot like the BrewMaster had in the game. "Time waits for no man. You've got this."

The door handle felt cool against his sweaty palm. With a single motion, he twisted the knob and jerked the door open, then bounded down the stairs to join the party.

The music in the house was loud enough that Tim couldn't talk without shouting. Xander had three kegs in the corner, and Glenn was manning the bar on the opposite side of the room. The dance floor was full of people grinding.

It was one hell of a graduation party.

Ignoring all the inquiring looks he received, Tim scanned the crowd for Sierra. He didn't see her anywhere.

Someone bumped into his shoulder, and he looked down to see a red Solo cup full of beer. Tim took the drink without bothering to find out who had handed it to him and gratefully gulped down half of it, hoping it would calm his jangling nerves.

"Thirsty, huh?"

Tim spluttered as his eyes fell on Sierra's amused smile. "Thank you," he choked out eventually.

Sierra was rocking a low-cut tank top with jean shorts. Her eyes sparkled. "Careful, a girl's going to think you're a lightweight."

"Well, if you're that girl, you'd be right." Tim looked down at the floor with chagrin. "I've never been much of a drinker."

"Devoting all your time to something more sinister, huh?" Sierra teased.

"Between school and my part-time job in the cafeteria, there isn't a lot of time left to work on my keg stands." Tim pointed at the kegs and laughed at Glenn holding Xander up by the ankles for what seemed like an eternity.

"Well, no one spends as much time perfecting their craft as Xander does." Sierra laughed as Xander toppled over, then motioned for Glenn to lift him up again. "I bet Xander spent more hours drinking this semester than he did in class."

Sierra squealed when Tim shot beer out of his nose, splashing her.

Tim's mind raced in desperation as he tried to come up with a single word to say. He used his shirt to wipe his face and hide the flush creeping up his cheeks.

What the fuck do I do?

Well, discretion was the better part of valor.

Smiling sheepishly at Sierra, he continued like he hadn't just blown beer through his nose like an open fire hydrant. "Some people crave attention, but not this guy. In fact, if one person in particular could completely forget about the last thirty seconds, I'd be forever grateful."

Sierra looked up into Tim's eyes. "Hey, when did you get here?"

Just like that, she hit the reset button on their night.

Tim grinned. "I just came downstairs. Sometimes I like hanging out in my room with a good game or an even better book."

Sierra nodded as if she couldn't agree more. "Less of a chance of snotty beer projectiles hitting you that way."

They both cracked up.

There was something about Sierra that made Tim feel less awkward in his skin. It was like she saw who he really was and understood. No, it was more than that. It was like she not only understood who he was but embraced it.

"Can I get you a towel or something?" Tim asked lamely. He looked around for something to wipe her arm off with.

Sierra took the clean side of Tim's shirt and used it to clean off her arm. "I've dealt with worse." She let go of his shirt. "Let's just say my three brothers are a handful and leave it at that."

Reaching up, she turned Tim's head so he was looking at her. "So, what did you think about the NPC Corp video at graduation?"

"It sounds too good to be true. How do you get paid a salary to play a videogame?" Tim smiled wistfully, wishing solving his problems was that easy? "I mean, it has to be some kind of scam, right?"

Right now, it kind of felt like he was channeling his mom's voice instead of telling Sierra how he really felt. The woman was a gamer, so she'd understand. It wasn't like he didn't know you could make money in the game. He'd sold a few high-level items in NPC Corp's last game to buy his mountain bike.

There was a big difference between earning enough for a bike and paying all of your bills that way. The gulf between the two seemed almost insurmountable. Add in the expense of POD rental and a decent connection to the game, and it might as well have been a fantasy.

Fuck *that*!

Why was he spending all his time talking himself out of something he wanted to do? Instead, he should have been researching *The Etheric Coast* and NPC Corp to see if it was a feasible plan for his future.

"You should check it out." Sierra flashed a flirty smile at him that implied she had some kind of insider knowledge. "I think you might change your mind."

"I think you could change my mind about a lot of things." Oh, man, he was laying it on thick now. Time to dial it back a notch.

Sierra reached out and played with the sleeve of Tim's shirt just as Xander crashed into his knees, ruining the moment.

Xander used Tim as a ladder to pull himself up to his feet, then swayed from side to side, trying to focus on one of them. He ended up staring somewhere between them instead. "What are you two talking about?"

Tim reached out to steady his friend. *"The Etheric Coast."*

"The game?" Xander tried to focus on his friend. "Dude, put down the controller and look at what's right in front of you." Xander leaned in, grabbed Tim's face with both hands, and offered his friend the sage advice of a man who's had one too many. "She totally wants to bone!"

Ah, so that's what embarrassment feels like!

Glenn rushed in to place an arm around his wayward companion and tried to steer him away. "Sorry for the interruption, folks. I'd be more than delighted to take this guy off your hands."

Sierra looked down into her beer, blushing furiously.

Xander pulled away from Glenn. "Why do people think they can make it in a game when they can't even hack it in the real world?" Xander looked at Glenn. "It's fucking pathetic."

Glenn mouthed the word "sorry," as he hurriedly dragged Xander away.

Tim turned back toward Sierra, only to see her eyes misting. "Don't take Xander too seriously. He's still pissed because the last time we played the basketball sim, I beat him by fifty points."

Sierra set her beer on a table and started walking toward the door. "I have to go."

This was it. Did he let her walk out of the party and resign himself to a life of cubical purgatory, or did he take a leap and follow his heart? Maybe he wasn't ready to dive into the game just yet, but he knew he didn't want the night to end.

Was it too soon for another grand gesture? Maybe something slightly more subtle this time.

Tim scooted around to head Sierra off before she got to the door and held out his hands apologetically. "Hey, you don't have to leave. Xander can be a total dick sometimes." He met her eyes with a hopeful smile. "*I* don't think anyone wanting to be part of the biggest game launch in history is a loser."

Sierra's eyes were wet and sad. A small smile tugged at the corners of her lips. "I'm just going to call it a night. I've got some packing to do before I leave this weekend."

Tim felt like he could see the grains of sand sliding through the hourglass as he tried to save the evening. The last grain fell into the bottom, and his time was up. "Can I get your number?" he mumbled, unsure of what else to say.

Sierra laughed. "Sure, but it's going to be disconnected next month. I don't need it where I'm going."

Knowing his luck, Sierra was probably joining Doctors without Borders and flying off to save people in God-knows-where. Admirable, sure, but it really put a damper on his plans to get to know her better.

But they were still talking. All he had to do was keep the conversation by asking an insightful question.

When Tim opened his mouth to lay it all on the line, nothing came out. He tried again and managed to squawk out a single word. "Why?"

Why the fuck was it that when he needed to ramble like an idiot, he couldn't talk?

Sierra shrugged. "I'm one of the 'losers' going into the game." Her eyes hardened as they fell on the couch where Glenn had deposited Xander.

That was a glare Tim never wanted to be on the wrong side of.

Although, following her gaze, Xander was already being served a giant helping of karmic justice.

Glenn was perched over him, drawing something on his face with a Sharpie.

Tim tried not to laugh. It wouldn't be the first time Xander woke up with artwork on his face. A hundred dollars said it was a penis.

Sierra sighed and looked away. "I signed my contract yesterday."

Tim took a step back to give her a little personal space. "But don't they have a pain feedback system? I'm not sure I want to know what it feels like to die."

"I'm sure they dial the pain way down, but you have to be able to feel it." Sierra scoffed Tim's shock away. "I mean, it can't hurt *that* badly, or people wouldn't keep playing."

Tim took another sip of his beer. "If I ever get into the game, I'm going to put off dying as long as possible. In fact, I'd prefer to never die."

Sierra's eyes narrowed, then she punched him in the shoulder. "Don't be such a baby." She was grinning now, and Tim knew exactly how her brothers must have felt. "It's just a game."

Was it wrong to fall in love with someone after they'd insulted you?

Tim couldn't stop himself from laughing as he reflexively stood up taller. At least he'd managed to stop himself from pushing out his chest before he made a complete fool of himself.

Sierra was watching him intently. Tim shrugged. "Hey, just because I don't want to know what it feels like to be burned alive, it doesn't mean I'm scared to die."

Sierra patted him on the cheek. "I'm sure you'd be able to handle it, but first, you'd actually have to play." She looked at Tim's cup, obviously wishing she had a beer. "Plus, who'd want to die when you have to re-roll your character?"

Tim almost dropped his beer. What was Sierra talking about? When you died in most games, you didn't have to reroll unless you were on a hardcore server. "Did you just say you have to start over *every* time you die?"

His mind was racing. Having to start over every time you died seemed like a monumental waste of time and energy. It wasn't fun to start a new game again at level one, with no skills or gold. Part of the joy in videogames was taking risks and succeeding. Sure, there should be penalties for dying, but having to start over was extreme.

Sierra saw the look of panic on Tim's face and tried to reassure him. "Once you become an adventurer, the rules change. You don't have to re-roll when you die, but you also aren't guaranteed a paycheck anymore."

"And the POD fees don't go away." Tim knew there was a catch.

"They don't, but a good adventurer can make more than enough. Or so I'm told." Sierra touched Tim's arm to make sure she had his full attention. "*The Etheric Coast* is the first new game NPC Corp has launched in twenty years. Do you know how many millionaires came out of their first game?"

Sierra grinned like she had just beat the devil and had a fiddle of gold to prove it. "Enough of them that I could easily end up being one this time around." Her face flushed with excitement. "New servers, new economy, tons of opportunity." She winked at him. "If you're bold enough to take it."

"What if you're not?" Tim asked, his smile faltering.

What was he thinking? There were too many people counting on him. There was no way he'd risk his brother's and sister's futures just so he could play a game instead of sitting in an office.

Sierra grinned. "Then you can keep your head down and do whatever job you've been assigned by the corporation. In three years, you'll wake up with a nice little nest egg."

Tim frowned, it still sounded too good to be true. "I just don't understand how they can pay you enough to come out ahead."

"Their last game had a trillion-dollar-a-month economy. I think there's going to be enough money to go around." Sierra smiled. "As for your paycheck, what a lot of people don't know is that NPC Corp uses time-compression software. Your three real-world years are twenty-one years in the game."

Tim stuck his finger in the air in a eureka gesture. "I knew there was a catch."

"Think of how much you could learn in twenty years." Sierra's eyes danced with excitement. "Not to mention waking up debt-free."

"And hairless," Tim countered.

"I'd let you shave me from head to toe right now if you erased my student loans and gave me a hundred thousand dollars." Sierra made a mock frowny face and pretended she was shocked Tim didn't have the money. "No? Guess I'll have to let NPC Corp do it instead."

Try as he might, Tim couldn't stop thinking about a hairless Sierra. It was like the time she'd had to get stitches after being nailed by a softball and they'd shaved half her head. He probably should have talked to her then, but he'd been wrapped up in another romance. That was the thing with them; it seemed that it was never the right time, but that was about to change.

Change was good, right?

Sierra bent close to Tim, playing with the sleeve of his shirt as she looked up into his eyes. "You should really consider it."

"I might just have to do that." Tim leaned in for a kiss.

They broke apart a few minutes later.

Sierra looked into his eyes hungrily. "Don't forget to mention my name if you decide to check it out." Without another word, she turned and walked out of the door.

Tim watched her leave, then stared at the door for a few minutes. What was the harm in looking into whether he could support his family with NPC Corp and *The Etheric Coast*? Could it really be worse than a life without the amenities?

Tim rushed back up the stairs and into his room. He slammed the door shut and slipped into his chair.

It was a moment's work to fire up his computer and type NPC Corp into his URL. Before committing to anything, Tim had to be sure it was fiscally responsible. If he was going to follow the woman of his dreams, there was a lot of research to do.

Tim traded his beer for a cup of coffee and got to work devouring every scrap of information he could find about the new game and the company running it. If there was a way he could follow Sierra and still live up to his responsibilities, he *had* to take it.

What was it they said? When love was on the line, you had to be willing to risk *everything*.

CHAPTER THREE

The shiny monolith that was the NPC Corp recruitment office on campus featured black steel and mirrored windows. NPC Corp was your friendly neighborhood gaming company, and this was a college campus.

They should have built a castle.

Tim shook his head. Someone had definitely gotten fired for green-lighting this monstrosity.

While the building wasn't what he expected, NPC Corp was obviously doing something right.

A line extended from the front door and down the block. He'd walked past this building a million times, and had never seen a line as glorious as this. Maybe there was some kind of special event going on, with the launch being right around the corner.

Gamers were a greedy bunch. They tended to hoard nuggets of information about an unreleased game like prospectors from the 1850s. Being the first one to release a secret could net you millions of followers overnight, it was the kind of thing that made careers.

Then there was the subsection of gamers who would hoard any

tiny scrap of information they found, hoping it would give them a leg up on their competition.

Sometimes it was individual players, and sometimes it was an entire guild, but whatever secret they held would never see the light of day.

Who needed friends when you were the best in the world?

There was nothing wrong with wanting to get world firsts. People loved seeing their names next to discoveries, on PVP leaderboards, and definitely for clearing dungeon and raid content. Tim had never believed in treating gaming as a job, but if the money was right, it might be his job soon enough, regardless of his personal philosophy.

Tim believed playing games should be fun.

The best part about these huge games was that there was something fun for everyone to do. It didn't matter what you were into. *The Etheric Coast* boasted robust systems for crafting, housing, and combat. Apparently, you could even do the virtual snu-snu, if you were into that kind of thing.

In other games, Tim had always enjoyed the dungeons and the raids, but his secret passion was working the market. There was money to be made there. Sure, it took some effort watching the auction house for deals, but someone had to do it.

There were even people who logged in just to chat.

Tim planned on having some fun in the game, but fun would have to be placed on the back burner until he could make enough extra gold to send his parents money. Each day he would have to grind harder than everyone else. His singular focus had to be making enough money to send home.

He'd live in virtual squalor if he had to.

It didn't take long for a frown to tug at the corners of his mouth. When had he crossed the line from wanting to check this place out to scheduling an interview? God help him, he could already see himself inside the game. It wasn't just Sierra pushing him toward the job. Tim was slowly realizing it was something he desperately wanted.

But the numbers had to make sense.

People glared at Tim as he continued working his way closer to the door. He got it; no one liked a line jumper. Someone cutting in line was almost as bad as a double-dipper at a party. Everyone knew you were supposed to put the dip on a little plate instead of dipping in the big bowl with the same chip twice.

Today was different. He wasn't the line jumping asshole people wanted to hate. Instead, he was going to see how much the devil would offer for his soul. Tim chuckled as he watched the people in line.

Everyone here today appeared to be an underclassman.

Maybe they were just pissed that he might get to play the game. NPC Corp had a strict no-interference policy with students before graduation. The last thing the college wanted was to have all their paying students defecting to a videogame.

A sense of being in the right place at the right time washed over him. This was where he was supposed to be; he knew it. How in the hell was he going to explain this to his parents? It was their dream for him to become a successful businessman. When he told them he was giving that up to play a game, their hearts would be broken.

"Just another variable to take into consideration," Tim mumbled, lost in his thoughts.

Something smashed into his chest, sending him stumbling back a few steps. His eyes focused on the muscled arm he'd run into as the man it was attached to stepped out of the line. Fuck, the guy was huge. He might as well have been a grizzly bear.

Tim knew how well that'd worked out for Leonardo DiCaprio.

That didn't mean Tim couldn't take him. He just couldn't do it fairly. Who got to decide what was fair, anyway? Was it fair that this guy was twice Tim's size and trying to ruin his day?

Fuck, no!

But he also couldn't get in a fight right outside the place he wanted to work. This wasn't the neighborhood back home. This was a college campus, for God's sake. Here, you solved problems with your words. Words could be just as deadly when used correctly, but this time, he was looking to use the softer side of the English language to get out of a jam.

"Back of the line, asshole," Mr. I-Haven't-Had-a-Carb-in-Years barked as he planted his feet shoulder-width apart.

The motherfucker might as well have been a wall.

Oh, man, Tim could see it now. A quick kick to the boys, followed by a knee to his nose. Fight over, but so were his prospect of getting hired and seeing Sierra again. As much as Tim liked watching bullies squirm, now wasn't the time to make a stand.

Or was it? His fingers curled into a fist.

If he catches me, I'm spending a week in the hospital.

Forcing his fingers to unclench took more effort than he would have thought, but he refused to be the first one to break eye contact. Somethings were just so ingrained in his personality, he couldn't stop himself.

It also didn't mean he had to give in to his baser instincts. Walking away didn't make you a coward. There was a time to fight, and this wasn't it. Not every asshole who gives you the stink-eye deserves to be hit in the face, no matter how gratifying it would be.

The people in line pulled out their phones, ready to record the fight. Sometimes college felt a lot like high school. Tim let out a weary sigh; he had to try. "I'm actually running late for a meeting inside."

Tim motioned for Muscles to move to the side. "Do you mind?"

"The last loser I let past said he had an appointment. I had to force him out of line and send him on his way." He flexed his gigantic arms and took a threatening step forward. "I've been here for three hours, bitch, and no one is cutting in front of me."

The crowd cheered.

Fuck, if the rest of the people were on his side, there weren't a lot of options. Maybe I should just kick him in the boys and run for home. I could reschedule my appointment for later this afternoon. Maybe they wouldn't catch me on camera.

Or he could dodge around the goon and make a mad dash toward the door. The building had to have security guards; they wouldn't let him get pummeled to badly.

Was there a third option?

Tim didn't want to be immortalized on YouTube kicking some guy in the sack and running away. It was the kind of video future employers pulled up right before you got the call that they decided to go in another direction.

Tim imagined sitting in an HR meeting and trying to explain his actions.

He just couldn't do it.

"Listen." Tim tried to soothe him with his best we're really on the same side voice. "I really do have an appointment inside."

"Back." Muscles grinned as he took a step forward.

"Of." He closed the distance between them.

"The." He put his hand on Tim's chest and shoved him backward.

"Line." Muscles flexed at him again.

He'd tried doing things the right way, but some guys were just too damn stubborn to listen to reason. Was flexing your muscles supposed to scare him? Guys back home didn't flex if they wanted to hurt you, they just punched you. Telling someone you were going to hurt them before you did it just gave them a chance to get away.

Tim had never been much of a runner.

The crowd was cheering the bastard's antics, and it was making him bolder. Tim felt his hands clench into fists.

No.

He wouldn't lose his head now. He'd worked too fucking hard to get to this point to lose it all over some macho bullshit. All he had to do was wait for the security guard from the front door to get here. He could see him limping toward them from the corner of his eye.

The man wouldn't be able to help him in a fight. From the looks of it, walking to meet them was a struggle. He was at least seventy years old and had a cane in one hand. The growing scowl on the man's face was a pleasant development.

Maybe there was a way he could use this to his advantage.

Scenarios spiraled through Tim's mind. The easiest plan was to say something nasty to Muscles about Tim having enjoyed his time with his mother last night. The guy would hit him, and all he had to do was stay down. Getting the crap kicked out of him on his way to the interview was a surefire way to gain some sympathy from the hiring manager.

On the other hand, the security guard might get hurt. If this were a game, Tim wouldn't think twice about sacrificing the man to get what he wanted. Pixels didn't have feelings. A win was a win.

But this wasn't a game.

Muscles took another step forward with his hand extended to push Tim in the chest again. Every instinct Tim had told him to swat the limb away and attack. A bully never learned a lesson until someone put them in their place.

Instead, he took a step back, his decision made.

"I know I didn't stutter." Mr. Testosterone pointed his muscled arm toward the back of the line. "Turn around before you're too broken to enjoy what's inside."

Why was it so easy to start a fight, and so hard to get out of one? Tim pointed behind the brute. "Why don't we let Security settle this?"

"That's a great idea, loser. He's already bounced four people today." Muscles turned and shouted to the guard, pointing back over his shoulder at Tim. "This asshole's cutting in line."

The security guard's eyes flicked toward the man with a look of annoyance, and yet he still found a way to turn his scowl into a tight-lipped professional smile. The security guard shook his head as he stared at the burly man, giving Tim the impression this wasn't the first time he'd had to deal with him today.

The security guard locked eyes with the brute, making Tim rethink his stance on whether the man would be able to help him in a fight. When he was satisfied Muscles wasn't going to interrupt him, the security guard turned to face Tim. "Is there something I can help you with, sir?"

Muscles shoved Tim out of the way. "I told you, Grandpa. He cut in line. Just say the word, and I'll take care of this for you."

The security guard's smile turned into a frown. He jabbed a finger into Muscles' chest and got right up in his face. It wasn't the kind of fire you'd expect to see from an older man with a knee brace.

The security guard didn't even look worried as he jabbed him a few more times to get his point across. "Get back in line." He pointed toward the crowd of people. "If I get one more complaint about you, you're done here."

Muscles looked at Tim and the security guard. "Awwww, come on. I was just trying to help," he whined as he stomped back to his place in line.

The security guard turned back toward Tim and motioned for him to follow him. The man stopped once they were out of earshot of the crowd. "That's better." He stuck a finger in his ear and rubbed it around before pulling it out and looking at it. "How can I help you today?"

It was weird, but Tim thought the man's voice sounded familiar. He looked at the name pinned on the right side of his uniform. Jeffery Oak. The man had faint stubble on his face, but as far as Tim could tell, the rest of him was completely hairless. He had to know if the man was who he thought he was, but he also had to answer his question.

"I have an appointment with Christine." Tim tried his best to look professional, but he was afraid that ship had sailed.

The security guard pulled out his phone and flicked through a few images on the screen. He stopped on one and then held his phone up in the air, looking from the screen to Tim and back again. "Mr. Price?"

Tim nodded.

He cocked his head toward the door. "Right this way, please."

Fuck it. Maybe he hadn't left all of the old neighborhood behind after all. Tim turned and waved bye-bye at the muscle-bound jerk before catching up with the guard.

"Thanks for the help back there."

The guard laughed, flashing Tim his first genuine smile. "I'd kick him out of line, but frankly, it's easier for us to ban him after he comes inside and willingly provides us all of his personal information."

It reminded Tim of the cops sending out fliers for free tvs to people with warrants. They'd show up and get arrested. *Bet they wished they'd paid those parking tickets now.*

Tim laughed as the guard led him inside and past the giant screening room everyone was waiting to file into. Were all these people here just to watch a trailer? He wondered if it was the same one NPC Corp had played at graduation. If it was, these people were in for a treat—but not one worth waiting three hours to see.

Wait, was that where Tim had heard the guard's voice before? It couldn't be, but he had to know for sure. How did you ask someone if they played a surly dwarf in an unreleased videogame without sounding like you were totally off your rocker?

Jeffery used the card attached to his belt to open a panel next to the door. Once the panel had opened, a chin rest appeared in front of the screen. The man who might or might not have been a dwarven tank placed his chin on the scanner, and a green light mapped his face while a red one scanned his eyes.

Tim wondered what kind of place this was that they needed biometric security. Was there something valuable on campus, or were they making sure nobody could get out? It might not be wrong to say a steady diet of videogames and horror movies had made him a paranoid person.

The magnetic locks on the door to the left of the panel snapped open, and the door slid into the opposite wall with a hiss of compressed air. Tim didn't want to know how fast that door could close. NPC's security seemed like overkill. Then again, he wasn't the one with trillions on the line.

Tim followed the guard inside, and the door closed behind them. They were standing in a long, narrow hallway that was sealed at both ends. The only things that weren't white were the black panels located next to either door. He was starting to freak out. This corridor felt much more like it belonged in *Resident Evil* than at a gaming company. Maybe this had all been a mistake.

Jeffery repeated the sequence on the next door. When it opened, the guard moved out of the way.

"They'll call me to bring you back out when this is over." He gave Tim a warm smile and started limping back the way they had come. "Reception's on your left."

"Hey," Tim called to the retreating guard. "This is going to sound weird, but do I know your voice from somewhere?"

Jeffery smiled and gave Tim a wink. "Maybe you saw my video."

That was it. This old security guard *was* the dwarf from the video.

No fucking way! What did you say to someone who was obviously badass?

Tim started walking through the door and then paused in front of Jeffery and looked deep into his eyes. "They played the video at graduation. It was a huge hit. You have to tell me, is it worth it?"

Jeffery beamed. "Every damn second." He leaned close to Tim as if he wanted to tell him a secret. "But first you have to survive what comes next."

Tim watched open-mouthed as the old man limped away. "What in the hell does that mean?"

He didn't get a response. Jeffery opened the door at the other end of the hallway, leaving Tim to wonder about the wisdom of his recent life choices.

There was only one door open to him now, so he stepped through it and into another solid white corridor. The door hissed closed behind him, and the locks snapped into place with solid-sounding thuds.

Tim's hands were sweating, and his heart was racing. What in the fuck had he gotten himself into? Was he going to wake up in a bathtub full of ice missing his kidneys? He looked around.

Selling illegal organs would explain how NPC Corp paid their employees so well.

There was only one way out now, and it was forward. There was a ninety-percent chance the fucking dwarf was just screwing with him, but he had sure set the mood. If he ever stopped playing *The Etheric Coast*, he could probably get work in scary movies.

He'd be the perfect guy to look into the camera and say, "They went into the woods, and they were never heard from again."

CHAPTER FOUR

The solid white ceiling, walls, and floor did nothing to ease Tim's mind. It felt like he was in a hospital, or maybe a slaughterhouse. Each step forward was an exercise of determination.

Wasn't this what had happened in *Hostel*? One moment they thought life was great, hot chicks wanting to sleep with them. The next thing, they were strapped to chairs, with some guy bitching about how he failed med school while he's cutting their fingers off.

Tim made it to the corner. Bracing his back against the wall, he edged closer until he was in a position to peek into the room beyond.

His heart found a new level of overdrive as he leaned out just enough for a quick peek.

"BOO!"

Tim jumped back and hit the wall on the other side of the hallway before crashing to the floor. He scuttled back, his mind screaming. What in the fuck was this? Was this it? Was he really going to be killed by someone who said, "Boo?"

A blonde woman stepped around the corner, looking embarrassed. She held out a hand, offering to help him up. "Sorry about that, but Jeffery would have been so disappointed if I didn't try. I'm Christine."

So, they *were* just screwing with him. Well, at least he wasn't going to die. Two could play at *that* game.

Tim clutched Christine's outstretched hand and allowed her to pull him to his feet. "Pleasure to meet you, Christine. I'm Tim."

Christine looked him over for a moment before motioning for him to follow her. "Let's get started."

Tim smirked. She was probably wondering if he was mentally unstable. At least he hadn't failed the interview by falling for their joke. Wait, if Christine knew Jeffery, was she in the video too?

Christine moved out of Reception and down another hallway. "Normally I'd waste time with the whole spiel, but as you probably noticed, we're quite busy today."

She opened the door to her office and motioned for Tim to take a seat. "Before we can get started, you have to sign an NDA. To save time, I'll paraphrase it for you."

Placing a tablet in front of him, Christine scrolled to the bottom of the page, where Tim's name was printed. "It's two hundred pages of legalese to tell you one simple thing. If you fuck up and release information to the public, we own your ass."

"What do you mean by 'own my ass?'" Tim made air quotes as he said it. He wasn't comfortable with anyone claiming ownership over that particular part of his anatomy.

She eyed him, one eyebrow raised. "Just think of everything you see here today as classified, and we won't have a problem. *Capiche?*"

Not understanding at all, Tim placed his thumb on the screen, knowing he wouldn't be able to move on without signing.

The screen flashed green, and a man in a nurse's uniform walked into the room. Christine smiled warmly at the man. "Joe's here to take a blood sample."

"No one said anything about needles." Tim pushed himself as

far back in his chair as he could. It wasn't the prospect of pain that bothered him. He just didn't like thinking about something being jabbed into his flesh for the explicit purpose of sucking his life-force out.

"Ever have a friend with diabetes?" Joe asked. "That's what this little machine is. It just pricks your skin enough to generate a bead of blood."

Joe went to work on his finger, and Christine continued her speech. "This is just to make sure your body reacts well to our serum. Otherwise, there is no point in continuing the interview."

Tim wiped his finger with the cleaning swab, and Joe put his blood into the machine for testing. "How many people fail the test?" How shitty would it be to come this far just to get rejected?

"Less than one percent," Christine stated happily. "With each iteration of the serum, the number shrinks. Eventually, anyone who wants to will be able to play our games."

Joe gave Christine a thumbs-up as he started putting his instruments back on the tray. "See you for lunch later?"

"Not today, but I'll have time tomorrow." She turned away from Joe and locked her predatory eyes on Tim.

She looked at him like she hadn't eaten in days. He felt like a hamburger.

Christine handed Tim a tablet with a list of professions on the screen. "Normally we'd run you through a simulation to help you pick the profession that's best suited to you, but like I said, we're kind of busy today."

Tim scanned the list, looking for something interesting. There weren't a ton of options left, which was not surprising, with the launch of the game being so close.

How in the fuck was he supposed to choose?

Stable boy. *Hell, no.*

Chamber pot cleaner. *Fuck that.*

Blacksmith's apprentice. *Now that had possibilities.* He continued scanning the list, coming up with several decent options.

Where were all the standard questions? How could he pick one without knowing how much he'd get paid? This was the strangest interview he'd ever been to.

Christine tapped her nails on her desktop with impatience, drawing Tim's attention to the cat figurine next to her monitor. A quick look around her office confirmed it was the only personal effect in the entire space. Her name was Christine, she had a cat on her desk, and she knew OakGut.

Was this LadyCat?

Looking slightly annoyed at how long he was taking, Christine offered him a sly smile. "Anything I can do to speed this along?"

Tim's face flushed. He never went into a situation without knowing all the outcomes. He felt lost here. None of his research had prepared him for this. "It's just…" he paused, thinking about the proper way to phrase his question, "how do I pick a profession without knowing about compensation?"

Christine looked bored as she rattled off the information. "All standard contracts are for a three-year duration. The POD fee, your in-game quarters, and a daily meal will be provided for you by the company. In return, you are required to work eight in-game hours a day at your chosen profession. What you do with the rest of your time in-game is your business."

Christine watched the screen while tapping on her keyboard for a few moments. She turned her chair back toward Tim. "Our standard offer for a basic profession is seventy-five thousand dollars in student loan repayment and eighty thousand dollars in salary, to be paid at the time of your contract's fulfillment."

Tim was still trying to come to grips with the fact that the woman sitting across from him might be the leather-clad assassin from the game. Glancing at Christine, he tried to imagine her in the leather outfit. He shook his head to clear it; now was not the time to travel down that particular rabbit hole.

The numbers made sense. While it was less than he'd make in the real world in the same timeframe, he had several additional benefits. His student loans wouldn't accrue any interest while he was gone, and paying off a seventy-five thousand dollar chunk at once would lower his monthly payments significantly. Secondly, he wouldn't have to pay rent, buy food, or keep a subscription to any services.

The biggest problem with the offer was that he wouldn't be able to help his family now. In three years they'd be fine, but until he got out of the game, they would be stuck. Maybe there was a way he could negotiate a monthly payout.

Christine eyed him, one of her eyebrows curled in an expression that could only be a dare. "Please don't ask if it was me in that stupid video."

"I wasn't going to ask." Tim looked back down at the tablet and mumbled, "At least, not yet."

"What was that?" Christine tapped her cat figurine, ignoring Tim's protest. "Oh, fine, if you can't help yourself." She stood up dramatically. "It was me. I'm LadyCat."

"I knew it!" Tim exclaimed.

Christine opened a drawer on her desk and pulled out a plastic-sheathed screenshot of her character. With a flourish, she signed the picture, gently blew on the ink to make sure it was dry, then slid the picture back into the plastic envelope. She slid the picture over to him with a reverence normally reserved for a much holier text. "I'd hold onto it. Might be worth something someday."

Tim took the picture and slid it into the folder he brought copies of his resume in. He wasn't exactly sure what to make of their conversation so far. Did she want the recognition or not?

He decided it was better to be grateful. "I'll cherish it."

"I don't want to see it on eBay." Christine grinned as she dropped gracefully back into her chair. "Now, let's get down to brass tacks. As you can see, I'm a bit of a celebrity at the moment, and I'd like to enjoy it while it lasts." She leaned her elbows on the desk and steepled her hands. "To save time, if you sign in the next five minutes, I'll bump your salary to a hundred thousand dollars. Student loan repayment remains the same."

Tim felt a bit off-center. How was he supposed to think about what to do when he couldn't get her leather-clad image out of mind? "Can I have part of my salary paid out monthly to my parents?"

"Sorry, kiddo," Christine shook her head. "The money gets paid at the end of the contract, not during."

As much as he wanted to say yes, Tim couldn't hit the button. His parents needed help, and if he couldn't find a way to get them some money, he couldn't take the job.

Tim stood up and extended his hand to Christine. "I'm sorry to have taken up so much of your time."

She slapped his hand away. "Level with me. What's it going to take?" She tapped her screen a few times. "Bottom line it."

Twenty thousand dollars over thirty-six months was roughly five hundred and fifty dollars a month. It wasn't a ton of money, but given the way his mom could make a dollar stretch, it would be more than enough.

Tim screwed up his courage. "I've got a family to consider. Can you take the twenty thousand dollars you offered me and pay it out monthly?"

"Sorry, kid. Company policy." Christine looked resigned to the fact he wasn't going to sign, but she had one last trick up her sleeve. "You can always make additional funds in-game and have them converted into cash. With the right profession, you'll be able to accept crafting contracts." She tapped the screen. "Not every profession can do that."

It all came down to Tim's choice, and if he could make enough on the side to send home. "So how much more can I make?"

Christine was energized by his question. "That's up to you, and highly dependent on what profession and class you choose. You can make money by questing, adventuring, selling buffs, crafting... lots of different ways. You can convert all of it to cash. Like I said earlier, your room and board are covered, but in return, you won't be paid up front for the eight hours a day you spend working for us in the game."

Tim felt a grin creep across his face. "You said the standard contract? Is there a way to make more money by changing the terms?"

Christine looked like it was Christmas morning. "Yes. Clever boy. There are more ways to upgrade. I have a list of options and how they will change your payout." She pulled out another tablet and called up a list of options on it before sliding it across to Tim.

She wasn't lying. All of these were upgrades, but none of them saved him money. There were upgraded meal packages, lodgings, and even the ability to receive a monthly stipend of in-game currency.

Tim made it to the end of the list, then scrolled back the other way. He was surprised to find there were several options lower than the standard package. LadyCat had conveniently passed him the tablet with those options off-screen.

The lowest-tiered option came with lodgings in the slums and was guaranteed to be free of rats and lice. The room came with a bed, chamber pot, and a single stained mirror. The meal offered with the room was a single serving of stew with a hunk of hard bread.

At the lowest tier, he'd bank an additional thirty thousand dollars. Now that the numbers made so much sense, he'd be a fool to ignore them. Tim's parents would have to deal with his absence.

Tim selected the slum package. He was about to become a gamer.

Christine's monitor beeped. She looked at his selection and then stared at him. "Are you sure?" She shook her head in disgust. "The slums are pretty fucking gross." She caught herself. "Sorry, I meant that they wouldn't be *my* first choice of accommodations."

Tim shrugged, his mind made up. "It can't be that bad."

"Yes, it can, and worse." Christine leaned back in her chair.

"The slums are full of the worst of the worst. People go there to escape the law because the city guards won't follow them down there." She wrinkled her nose. "When it rains, some of the sewers pour out into the streets."

Nothing said "good morning" like walking through puddles of shit, but Tim could make it work. The extra money would be worth it. Now he just had to pick the right profession. Before he could commit, Tim had to make sure he understood how the system worked.

"I'm going to stick with the slums for now, but I have a few questions about professions." Tim smiled warmly at her. He knew she was in a hurry, but this was important.

"Be quick about it." Christine looked at the screen. "My commission for this meeting is plummeting rapidly."

Tim caught the subtext. This woman was slippery. "Can professions be upgraded like classes can?"

Christine watched him as if she were trying to make an internal decision about how much to share. "They *can* be."

Tim grinned. "Do *you* make more money if you upgrade them?"

"Aren't you a smart cookie?" Christine got up from her chair, walked over to her office door, and closed it. She sat back down. "There is a possibility to upgrade your job for NPC Corp in the game, but it's based on more than skill. You will also have periodic performance reviews."

It made a certain kind of sense. You wouldn't want to promote someone who was talented if they couldn't perform simple job functions. Just knowing there was a possibility he could make even more money without becoming an adventurer appealed to Tim.

Now he just had to figure out how to get the money out of the game and to his parents.

Tim nodded, already thinking about how fucking awesome this was going to be. "And in-game currency can be converted into real dollars?" Dollars he could send home.

"It can be, and the value is controlled by the players. People who want to buy in-game currency can place an order and wait for the fulfillment, or just buy the cheapest available. NPC Corp controls the market to ensure all transactions are secure."

There was one more thing Tim needed to know. "Can I set up external distributions from inside the game?"

Christine knew she had him now. "No. We can create them for you before you go in, or when we do your performance review."

It was risky, but anything sounded better than life in a shitty one-bedroom apartment without cable. At least in the game, Tim would have options. If he did this, he'd still be able to help his family. All he had to do was work harder than anyone else.

If there was one thing Tim wasn't afraid of, it was hard work.

Tim selected blacksmith's apprentice from the list of professions and made sure the housing was still set to the slums. When everything on the screen looked correct, he placed his thumb to the tablet and signed his life away for the next three years.

He couldn't have been more excited about it.

Christine scanned his final decisions. "Blacksmith's apprentice." She glanced at him. "You're a glutton for punishment, aren't you?"

Tim wasn't sure what she meant by that. He'd simply picked the profession he thought had the most potential for profit. There was always a chance he could learn to make weapons and armor, and Christine had mentioned something about crafting contracts. It seemed like the perfect choice.

After he got settled, he'd have to find Sierra in the game. There was something about that girl he couldn't get enough of.

Wait, hadn't she told him to mention her name?

Christine stood up to open her office door for him. "Someone will be waiting for you in Reception with your paperwork. Bring it with you on Monday, and we'll get you plugged in."

Like he was a battery.

Tim shook his head, banishing the thought. "Sierra's going to be excited when I tell her I signed up."

"She should be. The girl is our best recruiter. Sierra's already at the platinum referral level."

"Referral level?" What the fuck was that? Tim got a sinking sensation in his belly. Had she talked him into the game just to get a reward? It didn't seem like something she would do, but it didn't matter. Tim had made the choice because it made the most financial sense, not just to chase a girl.

Christine patted him on the back as she ushered him into the hallway. "It's all explained in the paperwork." She smiled joyfully as she closed the door in Tim's face.

Tim stared at it for a minute, wondering what had just happened. The entire experience had been surreal. He turned away from the door and tried to focus. There was a lot he had to get done in a short period of time. Next Monday, he'd be entering *The Etheric Coast*.

For the first time since being handed his diploma, Tim was excited about the future.

CHAPTER FIVE

As pumped as he was about his decision to play *The Etheric Coast*, Tim was worried about his parent's reaction. Putting off the call seemed like the only sane thing to do. Could he live in the game forever? Then he'd never have to explain why he'd turned down the job they would have wanted him to take.

With calling his parents firmly off the menu for now, Tim pulled up the student directory. It wasn't cyberstalking if you only sent one email, right? He didn't want to be a creeper, but he also didn't want to go into the game without at least attempting to see Sierra one more time.

No girl wanted to get strange emails from a random dude on the internet. Tim always thought chicks were kidding when they said people sent them dick pics all the time. It turned out his faith in humanity was dead wrong when it came to guys and pictures of their wieners.

Tim put together a quick email and added a snapshot of the photo Christine had given him. In the subject line, he decided to be clever.

No Dick Pics, Promise

Fuck, the smiley face was too much. It screamed, "Surprise! Here's a giant picture of my cock!" It was too late to change it now. Hopefully, Sierra would know it was a joke and open the email anyway.

Tim looked around the room and tried to think of a reason not to call his parents. It was hard to drop off the map when family was involved. If you went incommunicado for too long, they did crazy things like call Campus Security to check on you.

Imagine being so scared of your parents you hid in a videogame. As funny as that would be, it wasn't really an option. Being an adult *suuuucked* sometimes. Part of the deal was confronting your problems instead of hiding from them.

In his experience, hiding from your problems only made them worse, but it didn't mean you had to enjoy the days you faced them. Sometimes you just had to put one foot in front of the other until the day was over, or in this case, until the conversation was over.

What was the worst that could happen? It wasn't like his family was going to disown him because they didn't like the job he picked. They might be disappointed, but they'd get over it.

It was funny how simple life felt sometimes. It was a constant series of seemingly minuscule decisions. You basked in the triumphs and wallowed in the disasters of those choices. Sure, some of the things in life were out of Tim's control, but he'd always found he felt the most comfortable in those moments of pure insanity. When everything spiraled out of control, time seemed to slow down, until he found the perfect solution.

He was the eye of the storm.

Flipping open his laptop, Tim took a deep breath and opened a video call to his family back home. "DeeeBop, deeeDuuup." Tim hummed along with the tone as he waited for them to pick up.

Mom appeared on the screen first, and Dad shouldered in next to her. "Congratulations!" they shouted together as they threw confetti into the air.

Sometimes his parents were the best. "Thanks, guys."

"Love you." Mom poked Dad and turned back to the camera. "But we're both dying to know."

"What's next?" Dad cut in.

Oh, shit. Not even a little small talk first.

Tim could do this. Taking the job at NPC Corp made the most financial sense. All he had to do was explain it to them. He smiled into the camera. This was good news, and he didn't have anything to be ashamed of. "Two companies made me offers."

"Tell me one of them is close to home?" his mom pleaded.

Dad tried to shush her, and she slapped his hand away. "Well?"

Tim tried not to laugh; he was going about as far from home as a person could. "It's not close to home, it's actually on another planet."

His parent's faces wilted like flowers in the desert sun.

Man down, man down, Call the medic. He had just told the worst joke in fucking history, and his parents were devastated by it.

"Some kind of space thing?" Dad asked hopefully.

Tim didn't break out in hysterical laughter, but he couldn't stop smiling. At least his dad thought enough of him to believe he might have joined the Mars program, but Mom's scowl told him she'd already figured it out. "Tell me it's not that videogame everyone's talking about." She glared into the camera. "We didn't send you to that fancy university so you could play games."

She turned to Tim's dad, pointing a finger accusingly at their screen. "I thought he was over this stuff?"

"Honey..." Dad started.

She cut him off; she wasn't having any of it. When she turned back to the camera, she leaned in. "You should have focused on your studies more."

How was Tim supposed to respond to a statement like that without sounding like an ungrateful little shit? Just because he loved videogames, it didn't mean he didn't study. They'd had that particular argument more than once.

Tim took one more look at his mother's scowl and decided to throw caution to the wind. "I think graduating was a pretty clear indication I focused on my studies."

"Don't be smart with your mother," Tim's dad snapped reflexively. "Just tell us what you've gotten yourself into."

This wasn't like the time he stole a candy bar and hid under the bed to eat it. He'd been a stupid kid back then, first for stealing the candy bar, and secondly for forgetting to wash the chocolate off his face before going downstairs to dinner.

The memory stood out vividly. It was the kind of defining moment that shaped who he'd become.

Dad marched my ass straight back to the store, paid for the candy bar, and gave the guy an extra twenty in case I'd taken anything else he didn't know about. Then he handed me a bucket full of cleaning supplies and sent to me to clean the bathroom. Have you ever been in a convenience store bathroom?

Not a pleasant sight or smell.

Lesson learned. You had to think about your actions. Maybe it was okay for a beggar to steal bread, but it was never okay to steal just because you wanted something. The moment his dad marched him into the store was the first time it had dawned on Tim that his actions could affect other people.

But family was all he ever thought about. Every choice he made was to help them. "I've worked hard for the last six years, first to graduate high school with good enough grades to get into any school I wanted, and then to get the scholarship. I know about hard work."

The scholarship hadn't come until after Tim aced two years at the community college, and even *then*, it was only a partial scholarship. It had been enough to get him to the university, with his parents' help, and a lot of student loans. But *he'd* earned the opportunity by working his ass off.

Tim looked his parents in the eye proudly. "The entire time I was in school, I had one goal—to make things easier for my family. I'm going to do that, but I'm going to do it *my* way. This time, there isn't a mess for you to clean up, Dad. I got a job. It might not be the one you wanted me to have, but it's a dammed good one." Tim stared at the screen, hoping they would understand.

He was wrong.

"We didn't work this hard so you could throw your life away!" Tim's mom shrieked.

Tim's dad put a calming hand on her shoulder, but she brushed it off and stomped out of the room. He turned and faced the camera with a sigh. "You've always been a smart kid, Tim. Maybe too damned smart. If you think this is the right thing for you, I have to trust you." He winked at the screen when Tim's jaw dropped. "Just don't tell your mother I said so."

"Love you, Dad." The screen went blank as Tim disconnected the call.

Dad would help Mom come around. By the time Tim stepped out of his POD three years from now, all would be forgiven. He tried to put himself in her position. She'd had a dream for her oldest son, one they had sacrificed to help him achieve, and then he made a choice she didn't understand.

Deep down, he knew his mom was just scared because she wanted the best for him. Tim understood that feeling very well since he wanted the best for her too.

The laptop speakers blared. "You've got mail, bitch!"

Fucking Glenn!

By the time Tim finished adjusting his settings, he was pissed enough to sign Glenn up for a few bondage catalogs. It wouldn't be Tim's fault if they showed up at Glenn's parents' house instead of campus...

Oopsie.

Tim closed the laptop and then remembered what had started

all of this. He opened it back up and found a message from Sierra waiting for him.

Subject line: AWESOME!!!

You want to meet up Monday and go to NPC Corp together?

S

With every fiber of my being.

Maybe something slightly more subtle would be better? Tim didn't want to send her running in the other direction, screaming for the cops. Technically, they hadn't even gone on a date yet. He stared at the screen for a few minutes and decided on a simple reply.

Time and Place.

Sierra's response was almost instant.

Joe's 8:30

"Hell, yeah!" Tim leapt from his seat at the desk and did his best impression of Snoopy's happy dance.

Whenever he felt bad, the world seemed to have a way of making things better. It felt like the rain had stopped, and the clouds were parting.

"C'mere, sunshine," Tim opened his drapes to bask in the sunlight as a smile took over his face. "Time to make the future my bitch!"

CHAPTER SIX

J oe's Diner was the best breakfast spot close to campus. Kids
flocked there from six am until they closed at three in the
afternoon. Every table was full, and it wasn't just because the
food was amazing. The owner had a personal philosophy.

You never left Joe's hungry.

It was crazy to think this breakfast would be the last meal he
had for three years. Would food taste as good in the game? Fuck,
he hoped food in the game tasted good. He couldn't imagine
spending the next twenty years eating gruel with a wooden spoon.

It was too bad he couldn't take Joe's into the game, but since he
didn't have that kind of pull with NPC Corp, he'd have to settle for
shoving his face full of food there this morning.

Tim was determined to make this the best breakfast he'd ever
had, and that meant options.

His personal favorites included corned beef hash, potatoes or
hash browns, and biscuits and gravy, with a big glass of juice. If
there was room—and who was he kidding, there was *always* room
—he'd wrap the entire meal up with a double helping of home-
made apple pie a la mode.

He might gain six pounds after the meal, but he was pretty sure that when he came out of the game, no one would be able to tell.

If the thought of food wasn't enough to get his feet moving a bit quicker, there was the extra enticement of meeting Sierra. It was a shame they wouldn't get to spend more time out of the game together, but Tim was happy enough with their current circumstances. The way things stood now, he had over twenty years to win her over. Even Pepe Le Pew couldn't strike out with so much time on the clock.

Tim rounded the corner and came to a dead stop. Where was the line? Where were the people? Joe's hadn't been closed for a single day since he'd been on campus. Why was it closed now? He started to panic, but then he noticed a sign in the window.

He read the sign with puzzlement. "'Today is the first day of the rest of your life.'"

It most certainly was, but how could Joe know that? Was this some kind of *Inception*-level prank by Sierra? If it was, then how had she gotten Joe to go along with it? Maybe the sign wasn't meant for him, and they had just happened to pick a favorite campus hangout on the one day it was closed.

What were the chances?

Tim looked at the sign and then into the clear glass windows. To his surprise, Sierra was sitting inside. He waved stupidly, then cringed at his overenthusiasm. Sierra didn't appear bothered by his eagerness to see her. She detached herself from the seven people in the booth and waved at Tim in as she headed toward the door.

Tim counted four women and three men and wondered if those were her other recruits. He was missing something, he was sure of it. He just couldn't put his finger on what it was.

Sierra smiled at him as she unlocked the door and pushed it open. "Tim! You made it! Come in, there's a ton of food."

Tim stepped in and took in the lay of the land while Sierra closed and locked the door behind him. He'd prepared himself in case Sierra might not want to spend time alone with him. It wasn't the worst thing in the world if he meant no more to her than anyone else in the restaurant. At least he was guaranteed a good meal, and from the looks of it, some boisterous company.

There was a tug on the sleeve of his shirt. Tim turned around and was stopped dead by one look into Sierra's gorgeous green eyes.

Sierra pressed her body to Tim's. "I'm happy you're here."

Happy because he was part of her recruitment group, or because she liked him?

Tim didn't know why he was a fucking idiot who had to agonize over every little thing. His pulse quickened as Sierra's fingers lingered on his chest. "Me too?"

Sierra's green eyes danced with mischief. "I would have asked you to meet me somewhere more private, but I already had this scheduled with my recruits." She leaned her head against his shoulder and batted her eyes adoringly. "I hope you don't mind."

Tim opened his mouth to speak but closed it again before he fucked it up. Maybe she'd seen the disappointment on his face when he'd noticed the other people inside and felt sorry for him. Tim didn't care. It was never a good idea to question Lady Fortune when she smiled down upon you. Having a girl making something up to him was almost unreal.

Today *was* the first day of the rest of his life. Today was the day he walked into the game and got to become anyone he wanted. What he wanted right now was to not be afraid to take a risk.

Tim didn't have to be shy anymore, or awkward. He closed his eyes and leaned in to kiss Sierra. Her lips pressed against his, and his mind exploded. Why in the hell had he spent four years being too afraid to pursue this?

Wild applause broke out from behind them. Two of the guys stood up in the booth as they clapped. The ladies smiled with embarrassment and tried to get them to sit down. Joe came out of the back and looked around for the source of the commotion. His eyes settled on the two of them, narrowing slightly as he headed in their direction.

Sierra's cheeks burned a whole new shade of red. Tim wasn't sure why she was so worried. Joe was as friendly as they came. He'd never heard the man say an unkind word to anyone. It didn't stop Sierra from clutching his hand when Joe stopped in front of them.

Joe looked from Sierra to Tim and back to her again. "Who's your new friend?"

"This is Tim." She looked at the ground.

Tim looked from Sierra to Joe with growing confusion. Why was she so worried?

Joe put his hands on his hips, smug as a cat after licking a bowl of cream. "Oh, so *he's* the one."

"Dad!" Sierra slapped him on the chest and buried her face in her hands. "This is so fucking embarrassing." Sierra removed a hand so Tim could see her face. "I think I'm going to die."

Tim looked from Joe's smiling face to Sierra's. "Wait. Joe's your *dad*?"

Sierra didn't look up. In fact, it looked to Tim like she wished she were invisible. He'd felt the same way when introducing his parents to people, so he understood what she was going through. You never knew how someone would judge you, based on what your parents did for a living.

She didn't have to worry. He wasn't that kind of douche.

Joe stuck out his hand. "Got it in one."

"That is so cool. I love this place." Tim grabbed Joe's hand and gave it an enthusiastic shake. "Best breakfast in town."

Sierra lowered her hands, trying to determine if Tim was just screwing with her or if he really liked the place. She smiled at her dad and plucked at Tim's shirt. "Why don't we get you some food? Then you can meet the others."

Tim let Sierra lead him a few steps away, but then he turned around to look at Joe again. "Wait, did you say I'm 'the one?'" He grinned at Sierra. "Someone's been talking about me."

Sierra's eyes cast daggers at her father, and she tried to play it off. "Maybe."

Joe walked past them, heading back toward the kitchen. "Don't let her fool you. She goes on and on."

Sierra shrieked. "Dad!"

Tim laughed. He'd felt the same way when he introduced a girl to his parents. What was it with parents and the need to show every cute baby photo in the world to their kid's date? No girl wanted to see that crap on date one. Baby pictures required a much longer commitment.

He could tell Sierra was super-embarrassed, so he tried to change the subject. "Did you say something about food?"

She slapped him playfully. "Of *course*, the food would be more important to you than the people."

Tim steered them toward the large covered trays. "A man's gotta have priorities."

"Well, this girl already ate." Sierra smiled at him as she broke away and headed for the booth. "I'll save you a seat next to me."

It was like the lights went out when she walked away.

Why did he miss her touch so much? They hadn't even gone on a real date yet. There was just something about Sierra that drove him wild. It wasn't only lust, although he felt a ton of that too. It was like they'd met in another life. At least they would have the next twenty years to explore those feelings.

Maybe the introspection could wait until he finished some of Joe's famous pancakes.

Tim was embarrassed as he sat down with three plates of food. Thankfully, everyone else was done eating and just having coffee, or there wouldn't have been room for all his dishes.

Sierra eyed his plates with awe.

It was like she'd never seen anyone eat breakfast before.

If it was going to be his last day on Earth for three years, Tim was going to make this meal count. Screw what anybody else thought. He covered the pancakes in melted butter and pecan syrup. After inhaling a few bites, he looked up to see everyone watching him. Was there something he'd forgotten to do in his haste to do some serious damage to Joe's bottom line? Then it clicked.

The dark coffee played against his tongue with hints of toffee as he leaned back into the booth. "Hi, I'm Tim."

"He sure knows how to make an entrance," one of the guys joked.

Everyone laughed, but it was the special kind of laughter shared between close friends. Sure, the joke was on you, but there was no malice in it. He imagined it wasn't every day someone sat down at your table and ate half a stack of pancakes before introducing himself.

Sierra leaned her shoulder into him. "So, this is Tim. Apparently, he likes pancakes better than people."

Tim took another sip of coffee. "Dogs, too."

A few people laughed, and one or two looked like they didn't get it. Sierra smiled and took control of the conversation like a pro. "Okay, left to right, we have, Melonie, Sarah, Josh, John, Amber, Steve, and Petunia."

"Fuck you," the one called Petunia giggled. She extended her hand across the table to Tim. "My name's Cassie."

Tim quickly wiped his hand to make sure it wasn't covered in syrup before grasping hers. "I'm sure there's a story there, but I don't know if it's polite to ask."

"Stick around long enough, and you'll figure it out." Cassie flashed him a wicked smile before turning and chatting with Steve.

"She's a bit much, but she's my best friend." Sierra rolled her eyes in Cassie's direction.

"You've already met my two best friends." Tim grinned. "I think we both know I don't have any right to judge." He took a sip of coffee. "Plus, she seems kind of fun."

Smiling, Sierra chatted with the people across from them. Tim took that as his cue to get back to work on his pancakes. One plate of corned beef hash, three pancakes, and one biscuit slathered in gravy later, Tim looked up to see Joe coming toward their table with a giant cake.

His stomach groaned in protest.

"Just one slice," he mumbled, patting his belly. "We got this."

Joe placed the cake on the table and beamed at his daughter.

He was so proud of her. That was the reaction Tim had hoped for when he told his parents about the job. That particular conversation hadn't exactly gone as planned, but his parents loved him, just like Joe loved Sierra. Tim knew his mom and dad would do anything to make sure he was happy. It was just going to take them a minute to adjust.

Joe smiled, but his eyes started to mist over. "I promised Sierra I wouldn't do this, but I just can't help it."

"Dad?" Sierra questioned with just a hint of warning in her tone.

Joe started cutting slices of cake, pretending she hadn't spoken. "I'm going to miss you, Sierra. With your mom gone, you and this place are all that I have left. Three years is going to feel like forever, but I'm excited that you've found your place in life."

Tim slid out of the booth so Sierra could stand up. She pulled Joe into a hug. "I love you too, Dad."

"Can you love me and make me a millionaire?" Joe chuckled. "I'm tired of flipping pancakes."

"As if." Sierra put one hand on her hip and pouted. "We both know you're going to be flipping pancakes here until you die." Sierra poked him in the gut. "You love this place too much not to."

"I do, but it's not the most important thing in my life." He hugged her again before smiling at the rest of the table. "Let's have some cake."

It wasn't apple pie, but carrot cake was one of Tim's all-time favorites. You could never go wrong with cream cheese frosting.

People started making their excuses to leave as they finished eating. Tim didn't have anything left to do. Everything he owned was either in storage or in his backpack. For the first time in his life, he felt like a nomad.

It fascinated him to think that there were people out there who weren't comfortable staying in one place too long. They took odd jobs and traveled around the country, never staying put for more than a year or two.

New places and new people weren't Tim's thing. A solid internet connection and a few friends on a voice server was all he needed to feel connected to the world.

But he was starting to think there might be room in his life for one more. "Are you ready to go?"

Sierra held up a finger, indicating she needed a minute. "I'll meet you by the door."

Tim got up, took a quick spin to the last bathroom he'd need for three years, and then headed to the door. Sierra appeared a few minutes later. Her eyes were red, but she looked happy. Tim wrapped an arm around her waist, and they walked out of Joe's together.

CHAPTER SEVEN

The company building on campus handled their final paperwork. The entire process took less than an hour, then they shuttled the new employees off to NPC Corp South. It was the largest data center and POD facility in the southwestern United States. The online article he read mentioned it was NPC Corp's newest and most technologically advanced facility.

Unlike the building on campus, this place had zero frills. From the outside, the building looked like a warehouse being guarded by a private army. The shuttles pulled to a stop, and everyone stepped off.

Tim moved Sierra in front of him as they formed into lines. He wanted to make sure they didn't get separated when they were split into groups. Then they were led inside the facility.

Tim had read about the process of getting ready for the POD, but being here felt different.

Maybe it was the cold gray concrete floors, which made the place feel more like a prison than a gaming company. It made a certain kind of sense, though. Why spend money on aesthetics when no one was going to be there to enjoy them? They could drop the POD at the bottom of the ocean, and he'd still be in *The Etheric Coast* having a blast.

The next part of the process happened in a private room. There was a bathrobe on the wall, and below it was a pair of paper slippers. Next to the bathrobe was an open bin for his belongings. Tim placed all of his clothes and his backpack in the bin.

A panel on the front of the bin started blinking red. Tim looked down at the container and noticed a picture of a fingerprint. He placed his thumb on the panel and the bin snapped closed, then moved into a recess in the wall.

A shower nozzle on the far wall turned on, making Tim jump. Feeling a little silly for overreacting, Tim moved toward the water and stuck his hand out to gauge the temperature. "At least they didn't cheap out on the water heaters."

The water felt very good as it washed over his body. He fucking loved showers. Whenever Tim had a bad day or just needed a break, he always took a shower. Some people liked to walk to clear their head; he preferred to take a shower.

A chime sounded, stirring him from his thoughts as the water was shut off. Nozzles appeared on the sides of the small stall. Another nozzle descended from the ceiling at the same time a separate one came up from the floor.

After freaking out when the shower turned on, Tim thought he was handling the appearance of more random nozzles pretty well.

A female voice garbled through some hidden speakers. "Please close your eyes, and place your feet on the markers. Once you are in position, please place your hands on the handles located on either side of you."

When Tim grabbed the handles, the voice spoke again. "Depilatory spray will proceed in five seconds." Tim wondered what it was going to feel like to have no hair. He remembered with a chuckle the time they'd used Nair on Xander while he was passed out.

Xander should have appreciated how much bigger it made his junk look.

Tim closed his eyes and fought against opening his mouth as the spray hit his body. He might not have any hair after this, but there was always a hidden upside. At first he was worried the mist was going to be a high powered stream designed to wash his hair off, but it felt more like the misters outside a restaurant on a hot day.

The mist stopped, and Tim released the handles. He glanced in the mirror as he slipped on his robe. Not his best look. Tim actually preferred having hair, but he didn't feel nearly as bad about being bald as he would have thought. On the plus side, he didn't even have to clean out the drain.

With his bathrobe and paper slippers in place, Tim moved back into the corridor. It took a few minutes of searching, but he finally picked Sierra out of the crowd. Tim could have spotted those beautiful green eyes anywhere.

She tried to turn away as he approached, but Tim turned her chin so she was facing him and gave her a kiss on the lips. "Tim!" she squealed. "I look gross, like an alien!"

"You are beautiful. Ready to go on a magic carpet ride?" Tim almost choked on the words. Where did he come up with this stuff?

Sierra beamed at him, her bald head shining in the light. "Try to save the enthusiasm for when we're in the game." She tugged on his arm and led him down the hallway. "When I have my hair back."

Tim resisted the urge to run his hands over her head. "As you wish."

They walked arm in arm until they reached their separate rooms. Tim leaned in to accept her kiss. "See you soon."

Sierra pulled him in close and then pushed him away. "Count on it." She disappeared into her room, leaving Tim standing in the hallway alone.

He watched the closed door for a few moments, wondering how he had gotten so lucky as to have found a woman who shared his interests. Tim turned away from the door and entered his own room. It was bigger than he expected, with the POD in the corner. Two lab technicians were waiting for Tim inside.

This was the part of the experience he wasn't looking forward to. Getting naked in front of strangers wasn't really his thing, but you couldn't climb into the POD with your clothes on. With a shrug of acceptance, Tim slipped out of his robe and strode brazenly toward the technicians. This was the new, bolder him, after all.

A few moments into the process, it had become clear the lab technicians weren't interested in looking at him. They attached electrodes to different parts of his body once he was inside the POD and fitted him with a waste disposal unit and an IV.

Two new people entered the room, and the techs left. The woman approached the POD while the man stayed by the door. She leaned in and started checking the various connections. "Hi, I'm Doctor Rudinski. The guy standing behind me is here to make sure I don't touch you in any inappropriate places."

Tim looked down at his lower half, which was covered by the waste disposal unit. "Good luck with that."

Doctor Rudinski laughed. "Everything seems to be in order. I'm going to give you a light sedative. When you wake up in the game, you might be slightly disoriented."

Tim already felt disoriented. "See you on the flip side."

Oh, man, was he on a roll today!

Shaking her head, the doctor pushed down on the plunger. She watched Tim for a moment, then checked his vitals on the screen before turning to the man behind her. "This kid's going to handle the serum like a champ."

Tim tried to ask what that meant, but his tongue felt like it weighed a million pounds. Speaking was out of the question. He tried to lift his arm to get the doctor's attention, but it didn't move.

His vision blurred as the doctor patted his arm to reassure him. Why was he even worried? This was the best day of his life, at least until tomorrow.

Tomorrow, he would wake up inside *The Etheric Coast*.

CHAPTER EIGHT

Disoriented was the right word for it.

Tim's surroundings didn't help matters much. The floor was solid white, and in the distance, he could make out blotches of white like walls on the horizon. The rest of the space was solid black, making the floor seem to stretch to infinity in all directions.

Tim stood and took a deep breath. Was this some kind of loading screen? It reminded him of something console games did while they brought up the game in the background. Sometimes you could even run and practice attacks while you waited.

If he was in the game already, it was fucking awesome. He didn't feel any different than he had in the real world. Everything moved and bent the same.

Tim wondered why he even needed to breathe. Was there really air?

There was only one real question on his mind. He looked around to make sure no one else had popped into his loading screen, then pulled out the waistband of his jeans and looked down.

"Oh, thank God."

Everything was still the same down there. His jeans snapped back into place, and Tim started scanning the horizon, looking for any hint on what to do next. He wasn't comfortable with waiting around for things to happen to him. Tim liked to be the one pulling the strings.

The blank canvas surrounding him hadn't changed. Was he supposed to do something, or just wait? Tim tried to remember what he'd read in the paperwork, but he'd just glossed over most of it. What was with game companies and the thirty-page terms of service agreements? Who had time for that shit?

He just wanted to start playing.

Shaking his head, Tim wondered how long the game would take to load. He was sure it'd only been a minute or so, but those minutes turned into hours when you factored in the anticipation. He remembered how long it had felt between each birthday when he was a kid. After he'd gotten older, those special days had started to creep up on him.

While he'd always been a planner, he'd never been patient. Tim's whole life seemed to be a battle between the perfect plan and the need to get shit done. Maybe he could prompt the game to load faster?

Looking out into the void, Tim shouted, "Character Creation."

Nothing happened.

He tried again. "Load *The Etheric Coast!*"

The scenery remained the same. Tim looked around again, wondering if there was something else he needed to do. Shrugging, he picked a direction at random and started walking.

The ground felt real beneath his feet, but it was disconcerting to look out upon vast nothingness. He imagined this was how people had felt when they'd caravanned across the great open deserts of the past.

Slowly, an image began to form in the distance. Tim started to run toward it. Soon enough, he could make out what was in his path.

A door.

He reached the door out of breath and full of anticipation. The door was gray, with large, bright gold lettering at eye level. The weird thing was the door seemed to be floating six inches above the ground. Tim shook off his surprise paused to read the words. The Etheric Coast

This was fucking *it*! He was about to enter the game. Tim walked around the floating door. It didn't matter how the physics of the door and its sign worked inside the game, the rules of reality clearly didn't apply.

He exhaled. "Time to see how far down the rabbit hole *really* goes."

All he wanted to do was get into the game and figure out how to make money. Once he had a handle on the game systems and a plan to make enough gold to send home, he'd branch out into more adventurous activities. Tim didn't hesitate. He grasped the handle and opened the door. Inside was his room back on campus.

Tim did a double-take. "What the fuck?"

All of his furniture was present. Even his Mythica poster was on the wall. What was going on? He looked behind him. The vast whiteness of the other room was still there. Shrugging, Tim stepped through the door and into his room.

There had to be a reason the game took him to his dorm. Maybe it just a way to ease his transition into the world? The disorientation he'd felt was already fading. If he didn't clearly remember climbing into the POD, he would have sworn it was just another day on campus.

He sniffed, regretting it instantly. "It even smells the same."

Not that the smell was a good thing. Spinning in a slow circle, Tim enjoyed the nostalgia. There was a sense of stepping back into a moment from the past. Imagine how much money NPC Corp would make if they could replay the highlights from people's lives?

Tim wasn't here to relive the past.

"I'm here to enjoy the future." He slowly looked around the

room again, and a blinking light on his laptop caught his attention. Tim sat down at his desk and studied the screen. On the black background, there was a single line of text.

C:\Run The Etheric Coast

Just below it, the word <YES> was highlighted.

This was fantastic! Tim couldn't remember the last time anyone had launched a program using an actual command prompt. Now everything was just a double-click away, and ease of use was the new king. This was so much cooler than he'd thought it was going to be.

Tim took a deep breath and hit Enter.

A little eight-bit knight ran across the screen, and music that would have been right at home in a classic Nintendo game played from the speakers. When the knight reached the center of the screen, he pulled a giant key from his back instead of a sword. A small keyhole appeared on the screen, and the knight hefted the key above his head and inserted it into the keyhole. Jumping, the little knight grabbed the edge of the key to try to turn it.

The key wouldn't budge.

The little knight pulled himself on top of the key and started jumping up and down in frustration. The key jiggled, but it didn't move. Nothing seemed to be working for the little guy. The knight fell to his knees, heaving for breath, and slowly lowered himself back to the ground.

The knight rose from his crouch and dusted off his clothes. He looked directly at Tim, held out a hand, and made a turning gesture. When Tim didn't move, the knight pointed at him and back at the key. The look on the knight's face would have been priceless if it was someone else's IQ he was questioning.

Tim frowned at the screen of his laptop, wondering how he could help. It wasn't like he could turn the key himself.

Could he?

Tim smiled as his hand sank into the display. He turned the key, and the screen expanded to fill the entire wall. He pushed his chair back and watched in wonder as a list of options and tabs appeared on the left-hand side of the screen. On the right-hand side was a 3D rendering of his body.

Tim's eyes went wide at the sight of his almost-naked body. "At least they gave me a loincloth."

Looking at the options, Tim realized he had made it to character creation. This was always one of his favorite parts of the game. The first thing he noticed was that his race was set to human. There were three other races available to select, and each of them had different starting stats.

As a human, his base stats were set to twelve in every category, and he was given eight points to spend however he wanted. He could get any single stat to twenty, or he could increase multiple stats as he saw fit.

What he found really interesting was that there were only five stats he could change. Each stat had a general overview listed, but Tim knew from other games that you never truly got to min/max your stats until later on. A few points might not make a big difference in the endgame, but it could give him a leg up on the competition now.

Strength: Increases damage with melee weapons

Tim noticed that if he hovered his hand over the stat, an addition tooltip came up. When he read it, he had the distinct impression that one of the developers was fucking with him.

(Also helps you lift heavy stuff)

Maybe they just forgot to edit those out on their last pass before launch. Tim found himself cracking up as he went down the list.

Endurance: Increases health and stamina (you know, for when you have to run away _really fast_)

Dexterity: Increases proficiency with ranged weapons and daggers (for when you're not sure if you want to get stabby from a distance or up close)

Wisdom: Primary stat for healing skills. (Lets you see the

way things work before others. It doesn't mean you have to be a pompous ass about it)

Intelligence: Primary stat for magical DPS (Damage Per Second). (Yeah, it also makes it easier to learn other skills, but nobody likes a know-it-all.)

Oh, yeah. Someone was going to get in trouble for this stunt, but it was probably worth it. He hadn't laughed this hard in years. It was a long-standing tradition for developers to try to sneak in snarky little digs or homages to things they loved.

One thing it did let him know was that all the stats were going to be important. What good was getting the best loot if you didn't have the strength to haul it back to town? Of course, you had to worry about your main stats first, but there was always a synergy to be established.

Below the main stat bar were four sub-stats for perception, vitality, revitalization, and luck. The bar was grayed out, indicating he couldn't place additional points in those categories.

There weren't snarky tooltips for those, only standard definitions.

Perception: You will see the truth of things when others cannot.

Vitality: Increase health and health regeneration.

Revitalization: Increases mana and mana regeneration.

Luck: Increase the rarity of looted items. (Who doesn't love better shinies?)

Just when Tim thought the developers had let him down, they had slipped in a little fun. If things kept going like this, he was going to feel right at home in *The Etheric Coast*.

There were only two basic options to choose from. Tim had to pick between being a fighter and a mage. It seemed pretty generic, but you always started out with limited abilities and then gained power exponentially until endgame.

Endgame was where the real grind started.

Before he could even think about stat points or race, Tim had to decide between the two. What race and stats he picked might be influenced by his choice, so how did he want to play the game: as a fighter or a mage?

Tim had always loved the wanton destruction you could deal wearing heavy armor while you were out doing the daily grind, but he *hated* tanking in dungeons and raids.

DPS-ing was fun, especially when your name topped the charts. But was there any way to make additional money from it?

If Tim entered the game as a mage, there was always the chance he could become a healer. He might even be able to sell buffs on the side. Good healers were always in demand for groups, and eventually he'd be running content on the side of his day job for extra income.

Picking mage made the most sense for now.

Tim hit the button for his class and realized he couldn't select it without going in order. With the most important choice made, Tim backtracked to the first tab and looked over the different starting races.

Human, elf, half-elf, and dwarf. It wasn't the most robust list he'd ever seen, but this was day one. He was sure the list would grow.

The dwarfs were clearly fighters, so Tim dismissed that right away. Half-elves received bonuses for dexterity and endurance, making that the next race to cross off the list.

The elven race was intriguing. Elves received a boost to wisdom and intelligence. Both stats were raised to sixteen, but their strength and endurance were set to ten to counter it. Also, he would only receive four points to distribute.

Did Tim want to be an elf? He could boost his wisdom straight to twenty, making his healing spells more effective. However, his strength and endurance would suffer. Lower strength and endurance might mean he couldn't pick certain classes later on.

Maybe it would be better to stay human?

Tim looked over the races again before finally making a choice.

He settled on the human and was slightly disappointed when the pointy ears disappeared from his character. Every choice was a risk at this point, but at least no one else knew any more about the game than he did.

Tim agonized over it for a few more minutes before he finally pulled the trigger. He tapped the screen to add five points to Wisdom and three points to Intelligence. One last look over the choices he'd made and Tim was ready to get into the game and see how things worked.

Strength 12
Endurance 12
Dexterity 12
Intelligence 15
Wisdom 17

His perception, vitality, revitalization, and luck were all set at +1.

On the next screen, he selected mage from the options, which brought up a submenu of specialties available at level ten. This was where the real customization started. As a level-ten mage, Tim could select options including Ranged DPS, Melee DPS, Summoner, or Healer.

At level twenty, each of the specialties offered a class-change quest. It looked as if there were further specializations available at level forty, but anything above level twenty was grayed out and hidden in the interface.

Tim wondered what a mage would do as Melee DPS. Wearing robes would ensure one hit could wipe you out, but if you could add fire or ice to kicks and punches, it'd make you one hell of a brawler.

Maybe he'd be able to try it one day, but for now, Tim was going to walk a much different path.

Tim selected the healer tree and scanned the level-twenty choices.

Cleric: A devoted follower of the Goddess of light. A cleric

heals from the front of the battle, calling on the goddess to shield their allies from harm. Clerics wear heavy armor and carry a one or two-handed mace and a shield.

Hydromancer: Devoted to the path of the all-healing power of water. Hydromancers excel in group healing and cleanses. Hydromancers wear robes and are often seen using a book or a talisman, along with a scepter.

The healer in the video Tim had watched at graduation must have been a hydromancer. Having seen the spells in action, he knew just how powerful the class could be. It seemed like the class everyone might select after seeing the video.

There was also the possibility he could use hydromancy for other things, maybe in conjunction with his job at the forge.

Battlesworn: The battlesworn believe hurting your enemy is the best way to help your allies. Debuffs can reduce the amount of damage enemies can inflict and increase the amount of damage targets can take, and can be cast in conjunction with curses. Curses damage the target over time. All curse damage caused by battlesworn is converted into healing.

Shaman: Shamans call on the forces of nature and the spirits of their ancestors to heal their allies. They wear leather armor and tend to range around the center of the battlefield. Rumors are that grandmasters can even raise the dead.

It seemed like there was a lot to think about before he reached level twenty. Until then, he'd just have to focus on learning the basics.

This was going to be fucking awesome!

Tim also felt better about not having to make such an important choice right away. Sometimes it wasn't until you started playing a class that you realized you'd totally fucked up and had to start over. In a game like this, starting over would delay his plans to send money back home.

Leveling this way, he gained a small sample of universal skills, and then he'd be able to make an informed decision about what step to take next. It was exactly the way he liked to do things. It paid to have a plan A and a plan B.

Tim selected mage from the drop-down box and was moved to the character creation tab. On the right side of the screen, the 3D rendering of his character became available to interact with. He could spin it and zoom in to examine every angle.

On the left side of the screen were sliders. He could make himself taller, skinner, and slightly more muscular. There was also the option to make himself shorter, fatter, and bald. He adjusted the bars to make himself look as awful as possible.

What would Sierra think if she could see him now?

Tim laughed as he hit the Reset to Default button. He played around with the dials for a few minutes to make himself slightly leaner and add definition to his muscles. After pushing his height up to six feet, Tim got into the detail work. A little more tinkering and his hair was slightly longer, and he had the perfect five o'clock shadow.

The last tab Tim looked at was all about ink. Several thousand tattoos streamed past his vision as he scrolled through them. He'd never gotten a tattoo in real life but had always wanted one. Here he could do it, and it wouldn't hurt.

Eventually, he settled on a tribal lizard. It took a few moments to wrap the tribal tattoo around his bicep the way he wanted, but he finally got it. It looked like the lizard was resting its head on his shoulder, and its tail wrapped around his arm and trailed down the inside of his forearm.

Now he felt right at home. It was him, but a slightly more badass version. Tim looked over his choices and hit the Confirm button. His character spun in a circle and disappeared from the screen. In its place was a bar that said **Character Name:**

Tim thought about it for a moment. Should he stick with something simple like his own name, or go with something more ostentatious like "Detective Waffle?"

The truth was probably somewhere in the middle. He didn't

want to be one of those guys who took a fantasy name and butchered it just so they could have it. He'd seen enough Letsgolas and XLegolasX names to last a lifetime.

But did he want to just be Tim?

This was a new beginning. In *The Etheric Coast*, he could be anyone he wanted to be. All he had to do was type the name, and that was it. He gazed at the screen and thought about it. Naming your character was always the hardest part.

With the seconds ticking away, Tim felt like he was missing out on time in-game. Just how adventurous was he feeling? His hands started to shake as he tapped the keys. From now on, he would simply be known as…

Zero.

He hit Enter, and red warnings flashed on the screen.

Name taken.

What the fuck? Whatever. Someone had done him a favor. Who wanted to be called Zero for the next twenty years?

The more he thought about it, the more keeping his name the same made sense. It was easy to join a party if you wanted to group up and easy enough to say that people shouldn't fuck it up. Maybe later he'd get a title or the option to put in a last name, and he could add a little flair then.

He typed in his name and hit Enter. No red buzzers, no flashing lights. Maybe it had worked? In what world was the name Zero taken, and there wasn't a single person wanting to be called Tim? Maybe he simply made it into character creation before other people?

Screw it; he could ponder the intricacy of gamer tags later. For now, he'd be entering the game as Tim, aspiring healer and black-smith's apprentice. The 3D rendering he'd created started to spin, and everything faded to black.

CHAPTER NINE

"I think I'm going to be sick."

Tim whirled and jumped to the side as the man sprayed like a fountain.

The player fell to his knees, heaving. He looked up blearily, with vomit staining his lips.

A woman in a white gown rushed forward, placed a cloth around the man's neck, and led him away from the others.

A human male with ebony skin climbed onto a barrel. "Only one popper, huh?" He held a finger in the air and then put it in his mouth. "An auspicious sign if there ever was one."

He looked out over the sea of new arrivals and smiled. "Now, let's hurry this the fuck up. I've got beer to drink."

The name Jeremy was crudely scratched into the barrel he was standing on. His huge muttonchops made him look like a fierce warrior. The look was somewhat softened by his gigantic grin and even bigger afro. "Take a few moments to get accustomed to your new bodies. In a few minutes, we'll form a line and outfit you with clothes."

Clothes! Tim looked down, expecting to find himself completely naked. He was still wearing the loincloth his avatar'd had in place during character creation. At least he didn't look like a wayward extra from *Westworld*.

Plus, this wasn't just an avatar. For all intents and purposes, this was his flesh-and-bone body.

Relief swept over Tim as he flexed and moved his limbs. They sure didn't skimp on the reality factor. He took a few steps to test his balance and started scanning the crowd for Sierra.

A female dwarf sashayed over to a group of her friends. Tim watched her for a moment, wondering what Sierra had decided to play as. What if she was a dwarf? Or a man?

Tim laughed as he scanned the players milling about. Sierra didn't seem like the kind of girl who would consider a sex change, but gamers had a long history of playing the opposite sex in games. He decided to save the panic attack for if and when he had to cross that bridge.

People all around him were grinning like kids at Christmas as they pinched and prodded their new bodies. A few people pinched their friends as well.

Tim got it. It was a surreal feeling to be distinctly you inside someone else, but that wasn't the right way to look at it. For the next twenty-one years, this was going to be him.

He fucking loved it.

Could you get fat in a digital world? Was the food even good enough to get fat on? There were so many questions he wanted answered, but first he had to find Sierra. She'd be around here somewhere.

Tim's eyes settled on a pointy-eared beauty in the crowd. Her black hair and green eyes were a combination he hadn't seen on another player.

"Those pointy ears are kind of hot," Tim mumbled as he started walking in that direction. The first few steps he took felt slightly awkward, but by the time he'd reached the half-elven girl of his dreams, he'd gotten things under control.

The half-elf he hoped was Sierra turned toward him for the first time and smiled. It was hard not to stare at her. A band of white cloth covered her breasts, and she was wearing the same simple loincloth he had on. Tim's feet stopped moving, regardless of how much closer he wanted to get to her. The half-elf goddess was easily the most stunning woman he had ever seen.

Sierra almost seemed to float as she skipped across the cobblestones toward Tim. He couldn't take his eyes off her as she danced from one stone to the next. She stopped in front of him and twirled around. Her long black hair and the white wrapping that did just enough to cover her privates swirled around Sierra like she was in a tornado.

Giggling, Sierra came to a stop. "Isn't this awesome?" She pulled Tim into a hug. "I fucking love this game."

Tim grinned, having just thought the same thing a few moments ago. They were really inside *The Etheric Coast*. How cool was this? Not a car or factory in sight. The air here had to smell fantastic, right? Tim exhaled, then took a deep breath.

Did medieval cities really smell this bad?

Sierra brushed Tim's arm with her fingers. "It's so real. You feel real."

A shiver went down Tim's spine. "You, too."

Her skin felt exactly like he had imagined it would. He'd been worried the game wouldn't be as real as NPC Corp promised. As far as he could tell, he might as well have been back in his room with a girl who appreciated kinky cosplay.

"The people who developed *The Etheric Coast* really deserve a raise." Tim spun in a slow circle, taking in the few buildings he could see through the archway of the courtyard they were in. It felt like stepping back in time instead of into a game.

A centaur galloped through the square, Tim watched it until it was out of sight. Things were certainly different here, but this was going to be the adventure of a lifetime.

Was it wrong to want to ride a centaur? It was probably taboo to even ask. It'd be like walking up to a person at the supermarket and asking if they could give you a piggyback ride while you did your shopping.

Considering a regular job seemed to border on sacrilege now that he was here. *The Etheric Coast* was exactly where Tim belonged. He was sure of it.

Tim grabbed Sierra's hand. "Let's do this thang."

"I thought you'd never ask." She tugged him forward until they were in line with the other players.

Jeremy climbed off his barrel and was now sorting the players. "Fighters to the right, mages to the left." His bushy muttonchops moved as he spoke. "Don't dawdle, there's beer to drink and whores to fuck."

Whores to fuck?

"Don't even think about it." Sierra gave Tim the look all women got when they thought their men's eyes were lingering a moment too long.

Jeremy brushed between them on his way to the front of the line. "They have male whores too." He winked. "Equal opportunity and all that."

It was Tim's turn to give her the eye. He wagged his finger back and forth. "No hanky, no panky."

"Whatever, grandpa." Sierra laughed as she danced out of his grasp. "Male whores change everything."

"Aren't all men whores, sister?" A surly female dwarf pushed past them to get to the front of the line.

Tim and Sierra looked at each other and broke out laughing. Some people were just too much. The only sex he wanted to have in this game was with the woman in front of him, although now might not be the best time for it. Both of them had to get settled in the game, and there was plenty of time to make that leap when they were both ready for it.

Sierra pulled Tim out of the line. "Let me figure out how to send you a friend request so we can hook up tonight after we get settled."

She was clearly a fighter of some kind, so they'd be on completely different paths until group content was available. Maybe Tim should have taken that into consideration when creating his character. "Sounds good to me."

Tim wondered how you even pulled up the player interface as he watched Sierra staring blankly into the distance.

A screen appeared in front of him. How cool was that? Just thinking about the interface made it work. He thought about adjusting his combat options and notifications from the default settings, but it didn't make sense to fiddle with his setup before fighting anything.

Friend request from ShadowLily received.

Tim accepted the request, wondering if maybe he should have upped his character-naming game just a bit. Dismissing the user interface, Tim started to think about how long it would be before they got back together in person. At least they could always hook up for a quick beer at night, and maybe slaughter something together after work.

Determined not to let any of his time in *The Etheric Coast* go to waste, Tim placed his hands on Sierra's hips and leaned in for a kiss. Her lips were soft and tasted sweet. They indulged in each other for a moment before breaking apart.

Tim stared into Sierra's sparkling green eyes. "Never made out with an elf before."

"You still haven't." Sierra flashed him a flirty smile before bounding away. "I'm a half-elf."

Tim watched her go, wondering how he had gotten so lucky.

CHAPTER TEN

"One robe, one scepter, one book." Jeremy bellowed. Marching up to a man in line, Jeremy grabbed a scepter from the pile and shoved it into the player's hands. "They're all the same. Keep it moving."

Tim reached the barrels of robes and glanced at the different heights listed on them. He quickly found one marked for humans and picked the first robe in the six-foot barrel, then the first scepter he saw. Casting a side-eyed glance at Jeremy to make sure he wasn't getting the man's ire up, he picked up a spellbook and moved to the side.

Tim pulled up his user interface while the rest of his group was moving through the gear line. This was the perfect time to figure out how his inventory worked. The last thing he wanted to do was find a great item and have no idea how to equip it or store it.

Tim focused on the opaque screen hovering above him and started flicking through the tabs to find the right one. "It can't be too hard. It's just using the inventory."

The inventory screen was hovering in front of him, but how did he add items to it?

Tim put the scepter and the book inside his robe and tried to slide the items into one of the open squares in front of him. His bundled robe fell to the dirty cobbles.

"Motherfucker!"

There had to be a way to make this work. Maybe it was because he had tried to put three items into one inventory square? Tim picked up the spell book and tried to place it in the translucent square. The book landed on his robe again.

I'm starting to miss the days where I could just hit "I" on the keyboard and drag and drop stuff wherever I wanted.

Maybe he was making a mountain out of a molehill. Tim did that sometimes. It was easy to take the simplest of tasks and make it seem insurmountable. When he found himself making excuses not to get things done, it normally only took a moment of self-reflection to snap him out of it, or in this case, Jeremy chuckling behind his back.

I'm going to figure this shit out without any help from Chuckles.

Tim bent down to pick up his robe. He ran the thick, woven fabric through his hands. He could probably just put the robe on, but eventually, he would have more complicated gear. There was no way the game would require you to have a squire just to get dressed, so there had to be an easier way to do it.

Since he'd entered *The Etheric Coast*, everything had been pretty intuitive. Maybe all he had to do was think about where he wanted the item to go, and it would go there. What was the worst that could happen? His robe was already lying on the dirty cobbles. At least it wouldn't look to everyone else like he was just repeatedly holding his items out at arm's length and dropping them on the ground.

The robe disappeared.

Flicking his gaze to the right, Tim saw the item in his inventory. He quickly repeated the process with the spell book and scepter, then moved on to the next step. If all he had to do was think about an item he was touching to put it in his inventory, maybe it worked the same way to equip it?

Tim looked at the robe's inventory slot and thought.

Equip robe.

Nothing happened. Maybe now that was in his inventory, he could use the item in a more traditional way.

Tim wondered if he looked like an idiot to everyone else as he reached out into thin air, but he didn't really care. When he touched the square containing the robe, a list of item stats appeared to the right of it.

Simple Brown Robe: This item is good for keeping the sun off your back and the guards from arresting you for being naked.

Armor +1, Durability 5/5

To the left of the item was a small box hovering in the air.

Equip item <yes/no>.

Tim tapped the Yes button with his left hand and the robe appeared on his body.

"Eat it, bitches." Tim pumped his fist.

A system prompt filled his vision.

Tutorial Schmutorial: You don't need any help when it comes to figuring things out, even though using the game's inventory tutorial would have saved you a fair amount of time. Luck +1

Shouldn't the bonus be to intelligence? Or was the game insinuating he wasn't smart enough to figure the system out and he'd just gotten lucky?

Tim grinned as he dismissed the pop-up. It kind of felt like his best friend Xander was here, trying to make sure his ego remained as small as possible. Before moving to the next item in his inventory, Tim took a minute to make sure his pop-ups were disabled during combat and minimized until selected at all other times.

He didn't need the scepter right away, but he *was* interested in the spellbook. Hovering his hand over the item brought up information on the right-hand side of his HUD.

Novice Spells Volume 1: This book contains the spells flame burst, healing orb, and snare.

On the left-hand side of the screen was a familiar box.

Would you like to learn these spells now? <yes/no>

He was going to learn real fucking magic! Of course, he wanted to learn the spells right now.

Tim slammed his hand emphatically on the Yes button. Searing pain tore through his head, and he fell to his knees, gasping for air. Just as quickly as the sensation burned through his mind, it was over.

Learning new spells was going to suck donkey balls.

Surprisingly, when he stood back up, he felt perfectly fine, so learning new spells wouldn't be so bad. He just couldn't do it during combat unless he wanted to die. He also wasn't exactly sure how to use his new skills. Did he have to equip them, or did he just have to try to use them?

Tim looked over the crowd until his eyes rested on the player who had thrown up on entering the game. Focusing on the man, he thought about casting healing orb.

Nothing happened.

Tim slapped his forehead. *Of* course, *nothing happened! I don't have my scepter equipped.*

Tim equipped his scepter and tried again. This time he clutched the scepter in his left hand and held his right hand out in front of himself, palm open. The words of the spell rattled through his lips, and he felt the scepter acting as a focus for his power. A small orb of liquid formed hovering an inch above his extended palm.

He thought of his target, and the ball flew across the space hit the man in the face.

The man fell on his ass, spluttering curses. One of his friends helped him to his feet, and the two of them started looking around for whoever had thrown the water.

"My bad," Tim called as he waved. He put on his best apologetic smile. "Can you tell me if you feel any better?"

The man he'd healed shrugged off his friend's helping hand and stormed over to Tim. "What do you mean?" he roared. "Of course, I don't feel any better! You just threw fucking water in my face."

Oh, shit, not again.

Tim felt his smile falter in the face of the man's anger. "I can see how you might think that, but I assure you it was a healing spell." He tried his most disarming smile to see if it would help. "So, do you feel any better?"

The man took a step back, rubbed his wet face, and started grinning. "I do feel better." He patted Tim on the shoulder. "Little warning next time, yeah?"

Tim smiled back sheepishly. "I might also need some work on my aim."

The man wrapped an arm around his shoulders and started steering him toward his friends. "I'm Dean, by the way, and this is Matt."

At least he wasn't the only one using a normal name. "I'm Tim."

Dean let him go and moved to stand by Matt.

Matt slapped Dean in the chest. "I wish they'd get moving. I have a serious thirst."

Smiling at his friend, Dean dropped his voice to a conspiratorial whisper. "I bet you do." He winked. "It's that tavern wench from the brochure, isn't it?"

"I didn't pay to upgrade my room for no reason," Matt said, wiggling his eyebrows suggestively.

Dean laughed as he turned toward Tim. "So, where are you staying?"

Tim looked down at his feet before answering, wondering if he'd made the right choice. "In the slums."

Slapping Tim on the shoulder like they were old friends, Matt grinned incredulously. "Get a look at the balls on this guy!"

Dean shuddered. "If you ever want to see how the better half lives, come find us."

Tim accepted both their friend requests as their group leader Jeremy tried to get everyone's attention.

Jeremy smiled at the assembled players and started shouting. "All right, let's get this shitshow moving."

Tim wasn't sure why, but he kind of liked the guy. Sure, he was burly, and kind of in your face, but there was a friendliness to him, too. He was the kind of guy Tim wanted on his side in a scrap.

Jeremy walked them out of the courtyard and into a larger cobbled square. "We're going to take a small tour, and I'll be pointing out the inns. When we reach your inn, feel free to leave the group and get settled in your room. Work starts in the morning for everyone."

After moving into the center of the square, Jeremey paused, letting everyone orient themselves. Their guide made sure everyone was paying attention, then started his speech. "To the north, you will find the nobles and the castle. Those of you staying at the Gilded Heart Inn can head that way now."

A few people, including Dean and Matt, headed in a northerly direction. It must have been a trick of the programming, but the northern side of the city seemed to sparkle in the light.

Tim shook his head. It must just be his imagination.

Jeremy cleared his throat. "To the south, you'll find most of our middle-class and merchant families. Those of you headed to the Plushy Pillow Inn, follow the road south. If you don't know what direction south is, pull up your map."

A map? Of course, he had a fucking map. Tim almost face-palmed. Why hadn't he looked for it earlier? He pulled up his user interface and scrolled through the tabs until he found the map.

He was in the city of Promethia. The entire city was laid out in perfect detail. He could even zoom in and look at the storefronts. The square they were in had roads leading off in the four cardinal directions.

The one thing Tim couldn't do was look outside the city. There was a gate along the southern wall of Promethia labeled Level Ten. Could they not leave the city until level ten?

Tim spun in a slow circle, wondering what hidden secrets there were to explore. He couldn't gain ten levels by killing rats, so there had to be a quest chain hidden around here somewhere.

He even loved the name of the city. Promethia made a certain kind of sense. It was a new beginning, the dawn of man in an age of machines. Would the players be the champions of this world or its tormentors? Tim smiled as he scanned the map of the city. Finding out was going to be so much fun.

Tim put his map away as Jeremy continued talking. "Those of you who weren't ogling your maps might have noticed that to the east of us is the sea. You're going to find all your crafting trainers in that direction. It's also the only place in the city you can access the global market."

Jeremy looked around to make sure everyone was paying attention. "So, if you want to buy and sell stuff," He pointed toward the ocean and the piers. "You go that way."

Jeremy grinned as he looked over the group, which had shrunken by a third. "Come on, we've got a couple more stops to make." He headed west into the heart of the city. After about half a mile, Jeremy stopped in front of a sign hanging over a door.

Pointing to the picture of a pig tucked into a bed, Jeremey continued. "This is the Snoring Snout. They have good food and comfortable beds."

A man came out of the door, his stained leather apron billowing out around him. "Come on, folks, let's get you settled inside. I've got buttered rum on the burner and stew warming above the fire." The innkeeper held the door open. "Don't be shy."

If this was the regular package, maybe Tim shouldn't have taken the extra money. Staying here looked like a good choice. The Innkeeper was friendly, and it wasn't too far away from anything he might need in the city.

When the door closed, Jeremy turned around and looked almost shocked at the ten players standing around him. "Oh, my. Let's keep it moving, shall we?" He strode forward, searching his pockets.

Tim wondered if Jeremy had lost his notes and was now officially winging it. Not that he could knock him. Every college student had thrown a few reports together at the last second, so he was familiar with the process. Put on a brave face and hope no one noticed.

As they walked deeper into the city, Tim noticed that some of the cobbles in the street were cracked. The buildings here were also starting to signs of wear. It wasn't too bad. He'd seen worse back home.

Jeremy came to a stop once again. "Welcome to the Blushing Pony. You pretty much get what you pay for."

The players milled about waiting for the innkeeper to come out and greet them like the one from the Snoring Snout, but no one emerged from the inn. Noticing that his remaining players weren't going to enter the inn on their own, Jeremy opened the door and motioned for those staying there to go inside.

Jeremy closed the door and mumbled, "Like I said, you get what you pay for." He turned around and started to head back to where they had started.

"What about me?" Tim called.

Jeremy spun, looking startled. "Oh, yes. I almost forgot." He smiled warmly at Tim, but his eyes sparkled mischievously. "The world takes all kinds, doesn't it?" He pulled a small flask from inside of his robe and took a quick nip. "Come on, then."

Tim tried not to laugh as Jeremey slipped the flask back inside his robes. He might not have been the ideal employee, but he couldn't deny his guide had a certain flourish to him. He got the feeling their tour might have been accelerated a bit due to their guide's hurry to get back to his own inn.

Looking at the sky, Tim felt like it was getting darker. Jeremy was picking up the pace, but he couldn't take his eyes off the horizon.

Were those fucking rain clouds?

They passed another inn, but Jeremy didn't slow. Cracked cobbles quickly became the norm instead of the exception. Just how bad were the slums going to be?

Jeremy stopped just outside an archway. The two guards stationed on either side-eyed him suspiciously as he pointed through the arch into a section of the city that was darker than where they were now. "You'll find the Blue Dagger Inn down there." He waved cheerily and started to turn away. "Good luck."

Tim looked at the two guards. He couldn't decide if the two men were there to keep people out or to keep them from coming in. Was his new residence really that bad?

Not wanting to keep Jeremy from his drinking, but also not wanting to let the chance of making a friend with an inside track on the game go, Tim shouted at Jeremy, "Thanks for walking me all the way down here."

"Eat a fish," Jeremy delivered with a deadpan expression.

What the fuck? He couldn't have heard him right. It must have been some kind of error with the sound. "What did you just say?"

Jeremy pulled Tim in close and whispered to him in a conspiratorial fashion, "It'll catch on if enough people say it."

Smiling reflexively, Tim tried to wrap his head around Jeremy's new catchphrase. "I'm sure you're onto something."

The guide released him and gave him one last casual wave as he walked away. "Just remember, next time someone pisses you off, tell them to eat a fish." Jeremy chuckled. "You'll thank me later."

Tim probably wouldn't be using Jeremy's new catchphrase any time soon. "Eat a fish." He could just imagine the confused look on someone's face right before the fight broke out. Jeremy might have been a fun guide, but his new phrase could use a little work.

The guards' clenched their spears tighter as Tim peered through the archway. He tried to ignore them as he took in the lay of the land. The slums didn't even have cobbles. The road in front of him was just packed dirt.

This place was going to suck if it rained.

As if on cue, the heavens above the slums opened up. Tim turned and looked north and south.

Nothing but fucking sunshine.

Even the bay to the east was cloud-free; the only place it was raining was the slums. *Fuck it.* It didn't matter where he slept, or if his feet got muddy. It had been the right choice to pick the Blue Dagger Inn.

Now he just had to prove it.

CHAPTER ELEVEN

"What the fuck was that?" Tim cried as something other than mud squelched up between his toes.

New players should really be given some kind of footwear. Come to think of it, he'd seen a few people with boots. Maybe some kind of recruitment perk, or an upgrade? If Tim ever had the chance to enter another game, he was going to have to spend more time going over the details. It seemed that Christine had left a lot out during their initial meeting.

Tim trudged through the muddy streets toward the in. He hoped some of the puddles would clean the worst of the muck from his feet. At least there was a torch burning outside the inn. Most of the other buildings looked abandoned, or maybe they just couldn't afford torches.

The lone torch was enough to highlight the wooden sign over the door, which swayed gently in the breeze. When the light caught it just right, Tim could make out a drawing of a blue fist holding a dagger.

The front door of the inn was cracked. Tim peered through the gaps in the wooden slats, but the light coming from inside was too muted for him to see anything. *Fuck it.* Tim shrugged and stepped through the door.

At least it will get me out of the rain.

Tim closed the door behind him. There wasn't anything to wipe his feet on, so he left muddy footprints on his way to the counter.

Beyond the entryway was a large room with tables and chairs scattered around a giant fireplace. Five men were having a conversation at one of the tables, but otherwise, the inn was empty.

A balding, middle-aged man with rotted teeth tapped the counter to draw Tim's attention away from the men gathered around the table. "Greetings, traveler." The innkeeper smiled. "I'm afraid to tell you this is a private establishment. We don't have any rooms for rent."

Tim looked around the inn, noting the peeling paint and the stained floorboards. "Maybe you should rent more rooms." Just like in the real world, his mouth still had a habit of running away with itself. Still, this was a game, and Christine had sold him a room here. He wasn't leaving until he got one.

"I believe you know where the door is," the older man snarled at him before casting a look into the main room. Several chairs scratched the wooden floor as they were pushed back from the tables.

Why did he always find himself in these situations? He might not be able to fix the innkeeper's perception of him, but he wasn't going to sleep in the fucking rain. "I've got a reservation." Tim tapped the counter. "The name's Tim."

A brutish man with scars on his cheeks stepped forward. "Hey, Ernie. This asshole giving you trouble?"

Ernie sneered. "He says he has a reservation."

The other man started to laugh. "We haven't had one of *those* in years." His look was ice-cold when he turned his eyes on Tim. "We prefer to keep our business to ourselves."

Ernie pulled out a dusty ledger covered in cobwebs.

. . .

Tim's heart dropped. If the reservation book had cobwebs on it, his name couldn't be inside.

Dust flew from the pages when Ernie flipped the book open. Coughing to clear his throat, the innkeeper flipped to the last page with writing. His eyes went wide. "Will you look at that? The kid actually *does* have a reservation."

Tim let out a breath he hadn't known he'd been holding.

The brute shoved Ernie out of the way. "Let me see that." He looked from the name to Tim. "The boys aren't going to like it."

"The boys don't own this place." Ernie snatched the book from the brute's hands. "The boss said if anyone's in the book, we have to let them stay." Ernie took a key from the rack and tossed it to Tim. "Second floor, fourth door on your right."

The brute stepped in front of Tim. "Just remember, eyes, ears, and mouth shut." He locked eyes with Tim like a mongoose facing a cobra. "Got it?"

This wasn't the time to pick a fight or figure out what they were trying to hide. All Tim wanted to do was get cleaned up and track down Sierra. He reached up and patted the much larger man's chest. "Whatever you say, Chief."

There was his big mouth again. What was it about being in the game that gave him the confidence to be so brazen?

The man smiled and moved out of the way so Tim could pass. He looked at Ernie. "'Chief,' huh? I kinda like that."

"Praise the lady, kid! Did you really have to do that?" Ernie said, looking back at Tim. "Now we're never going to get him to stop calling himself 'Chief.'"

Tim smiled as Ernie started to laugh. "Oh, I'm sure I can come up with something much more disparaging if you give me a few minutes."

"Just get out of here before you get yourself in trouble." Ernie slapped his thigh and laughed harder. "Chief! Can you imagine?"

Chief might not have been very smart, but he was also the last person Tim wanted to tangle with. Granted, this was a game, so maybe he shouldn't base his opinion on looks alone. Maybe there was a way to scan players and NPCs.

Tim looked at the man he'd called Chief and tried to find out anything else he could about him.

Gaston The Sneaky: Level ??? assassin.

Yep, he'd turn Tim into another bloody stain on the floorboards.

Maybe he should just go to his room, then figure out what to do next. Tim left the two men in conversation and walked around the corner and up the stairs to the second floor.

When he reached the second floor, he received a quest prompt.

A den of thieves: The inn is clearly being used for something other than hosting weary travelers. Get to the bottom of the mystery.

Reward for completion variable upon results.

Well, that didn't give him much to go on. The reward could be anything. The entire quest might just be a colossal waste of time. Still, he hadn't received any other quests yet, or even a general direction to go in.

He accepted the quest. "Maybe I'll get a pair of boots?"

Tim opened the door to his room and peered inside. He reached through the doorway and tried to flip a switch, but the wall was flat. Of *course*, there wasn't a light switch. What was he thinking? Tim grabbed the small lantern hanging beside his door and stepped into the room.

With the door closed behind him, Tim felt a little bit safer. He walked around his small room and lit a few more lanterns. A knock on the door stopped him from seeing how soft the bed was. It also made him jump, and he pulled out his scepter. Maybe the brute from downstairs had decided Chief wasn't a nickname he actually liked.

A young girl shouldered her way past him with a bundle of

logs. Her much younger brother trailed behind her with a small handheld wagon.

Tim jumped out of the way. The kids clearly weren't in the mood for small talk.

After the rain, a fire seemed like the perfect thing. Maybe he'd be able to find some candy or something to tip them. It was the least he could do if they tended to his fire and chamber pot every day.

The girl lit the fire like an expert and then unloaded the rest of the wood from her brother's cart. When the young man didn't start moving right away, she slapped him across the back of the head. "Get moving, Dudley."

Maybe less candy for her.

Tim would have laughed, but it reminded him too much of his own childhood. Both children exited the room, then the girl reappeared with a pitcher of water and a towel.

She glared at Tim's muddy feet. "Get a pair of boots." She stomped out the door and slammed it shut behind her.

At least he wasn't the only one who thought new players should get boots. Tim took a seat on the chair by the fire and started cleaning his feet. It was a losing battle. The only way to get this much crap off his feet would be to take a bath. If baths were extra here, then he didn't have the money for one just yet.

Which brought him to the question. "What in the fuck do I do next?"

Tim brought up his user interface and saw that he already had a message from Sierra.

"I'm at the class trainer now and loving it. Maybe we can hook up tomorrow instead?"

He wanted to be angry, but Tim was kind of feeling the same way. He had a quest to complete and boots to find, after all. Plus, he had to stay in front of the curve to meet his goals. It didn't matter which curve it was: leveling, crafting, or healing. He couldn't afford to fall behind.

It was time to get to work.

The first thing Tim did was pull out his map. After fiddling with options on the side, he found the two places he was looking for. The healing and mage trainers were both on the north side of town. He selected the temple on his map and set a waypoint. From the looks of the building, it would be hard to miss, but why take the chance?

He opened the door and bounded down the stairs. Rushing past Ernie, he shouted. "I'll be back later."

It wasn't long before his feet were coated in mud again, and then he was back on the cracked cobbles on the outskirts of the city. Why wasn't it raining here? It was like the game developers had decided the slums needed rain to make them more depressing.

It took Tim a few minutes heading in a northerly direction before he found a fountain. He took the time to wash off his feet and the bottom of his robe. No reason to look like a total slob. Now that his feet weren't covered in mud and horse crap, Tim felt a little bit better about the afternoon. Bringing up his map again to reorient himself, Tim started walking.

It turned out he didn't need the map. The temple was huge—Roman Coliseum huge. It even boasted magnificent marble columns in front. Men in white robes with blue trim moved on the stairs of the temple, ushering people inside for healing.

A priest stopped to talk to a group, then they turned around and headed away from the temple. The man was pulling a small cart behind him with a boy lying inside. The kid moaned as they drew closer.

Not sure why they were being turned away, Tim called out to the man. "Why can't you go inside?"

"The priest told us they've taken enough charity cases for the day." The man continued moving his family down the road. "I guess we'll just have to try again tomorrow."

Maybe there was something Tim could do. He only had the one spell, but it might be worth trying. "What's wrong with your son?"

"The boy fell on his scythe running when he heard the lunch bell. Cut his damn leg pretty good." He rubbed his son's head affectionately.

"If you have a minute, I'd be more than happy to try to help." Tim equipped his scepter and called on the spell. The ball of water formed in his hand just like it had before. He aimed for the boy's bandaged leg.

The kid groaned when the water splashed him, then his face sagged with relief. His mother moved forward and started stripping the bandage from his leg. The wound had closed, but it wasn't completely healed yet.

Tim cast the spell three more times before he was satisfied that the wound was completely healed.

A notification appeared on his screen.

Skill Increase: Your Healing Orb spell has reached novice rank two. The Orbs you cast will now be one percent more effective and will require one percent less mana to cast.

Awesome.

It felt kind of good to use his spell on someone who really needed it. Tim dismissed his notification and took a step back as the boy's father tried to slip a small bag of coins into his hand.

Tim pushed the coins back toward the man. "I can't accept those."

A hand clamped down on his shoulder. "Take the offering," a priest hissed in his ear.

The family started bowing and slowly backed away. Tim kept the small purse of coins in his hand as he turned to get a better look at the man who had come up behind him.

The man's white and blue robes almost seemed to shimmer in the bright sunshine. His lips were turned down in a frown. "It seems you have a small affinity for the healing arts. Come inside, and we can discuss your future."

Tim turned to say goodbye to the man and his family, but they were already gone. With a shrug, he started up the steps behind the priest. He wasn't exactly sure what to make of the man just yet. He'd never met a healer who would turn away an injured child. Something felt off about this whole situation. There was only one way he'd ever get to the bottom of it.

He had to follow the priest into the temple.

CHAPTER TWELVE

Did that guy's robes just change color?
How much did it cost to get your hands on a set of those, and why didn't he have them already? Tim quickly inspected the man to see if he could find out more about what he was wearing.

Technicolor Robes of Wandering: +1 to walking speed. Also known to draw the attention of the people around you.

He let his gaze fall on the priest in front of him and tried to use the inspection skill again. This time the skill only came back with the man's name: Brother Egon.

It was more than he had known about the man a minute ago.

Tim looked around again, slowly realizing that everyone around him looked ridiculously wealthy. Without shoes on, he felt like a beggar instead of someone here to receive training. He didn't want to go inside the temple, only to realize he couldn't afford to pay for the temple's services.

Brother Egon didn't look like the kind of man who enjoyed having his time wasted. *I don't have any money.* "Just how much does this training cost?"

"His eminence has decreed that anyone with the talent will be trained, as long as they bask in the light of the Goddess Eternia." Egon made a symbol over his chest and looked toward the heavens.

The way Brother Egon had delivered the line made one thing clear. The man in front of him didn't believe training everyone was right. He only carried out the task because he was ordered too. Normally healers felt a calling to help others, but that didn't seem to be the case here.

Brother Egon turned around, giving Tim's bare feet a look of disgust. "Thankfully for you, Cardinal Jepsom, second only to his Eminence, has devised a work program for those of less fortunate circumstances to repay their debt to the temple."

Work program? Sounded like the kind of thing where you ended up paying four times the cost of the skill in labor. "What kind of work?" Tim looked at the men on their hands and knees, scrubbing the temple steps, and shuddered.

Fuck it. He could scrub stairs with the best of them if it meant learning a few new spells before anyone else could get them.

Brother Egon glanced at the men washing the temple steps. "Something befitting your skills." The priest glared at Tim. "Certainly you are skilled at something?"

Tim stopped in his tracks. "Why even offer me the chance to come inside? You clearly don't want me here."

"His Eminence makes the rules," Egon snarled. "The rest of us abide by them."

There was a story to be had there. Obviously, not everything was roses and sunshine inside the Temple of Light. Maybe that was why some of the poor were being turned away. There must be some kind of internal conflict brewing amongst the goddess' people.

He scanned the parishioners entering the temple again and realized he might be onto something. With all the wealth around him, it was hard to fathom the church not having the resources to help the less fortunate citizens. With no training, he'd healed the boy in a matter of minutes. Why did people have to suffer when a simple spell could heal them instantly?

"It's fucking bullshit," Tim mumbled.

"Did you say something?" Brother Egon continued walking deeper into the temple.

"The temple is magnificent. Your order must be very proud." Hopefully he had bought it.

Egon's persistent sneer softened into something that resembled a frown. "The Temple of the Goddess Eternia is the finest in the Four Kingdoms. This is where doctrine is created and the high priest resides."

The high priest must be their version of the Pope. He sounded like he might be ok. It was the cardinal Egon had mentioned who had Tim worried. Just how much did the high priest know about what was happening at the temple?

Tim followed Brother Egon through the winding halls until he lost all sense of direction. They finally stopped outside of a door cast in solid gold. A gonglike sound rang through the chamber, and two giant men moved out of the alcoves and flanked the door.

Placing their hands delicately on the door, the men began to push. Nothing happened at first. *Just how heavy are those doors?* As Tim watched, the two men strained against the weight. With a groan, the doors separated and started to swing inward on giant gold hinges.

When the gap between the two halves was wide enough for a man to slide through, Brother Egon started forward. Tim followed closely on his heels. As soon as they cleared the threshold, two men inside of the chamber started pushing the massive doors closed.

Fuck, Tim had enough problems getting off the couch to open a regular door. Imagine how pissed these guys would be if his Eminence had a fondness for delivery?

The doors thudded back into the frame, sealing them inside of the chamber. He refused to look back. This was a church, after all. What was the worst that could happen? Instead, he tried to focus on the room in front of him. Frankly, he was a little disappointed.

The entire chamber was solid white. It almost reminded Tim of the loading screen, except this room was carved out of white marble. Pillars rose on either side of him, vaulting the ceiling high enough that he couldn't see into the rafters.

Dark blue tapestries hung from the walls, matching the single runner leading from the door to a solitary chair. Tim would have called it a throne because of where it was placed in the room, but it clearly wasn't meant to be intimidating. It was more of the kind of thing he'd expect to find by the fireplace in his room than in this majestic temple.

The chair was occupied by a man in simple white robes with a platinum circlet around his bald head. There seemed to be a war raging on his face as the smile he wore fought to become a full-fledged grin. The best part was that the warmth of his smile reached his eyes. The man was genuinely happy to see them.

Before they made it halfway across the room, he rose to his feet. "Is this the one I heard about? The one who healed the boy on the steps of our temple?" His Eminence looked eagerly at the priest at Tim's side.

Brother Egon bowed his head in subservience. "It is, Your Eminence."

When Tim didn't say anything, Egon elbowed him in the side. The jab to the ribs must have been his subtle hint to speak. Rubbing his side, Tim looked at the high priest, not sure exactly how to handle the situation. What did you say when you met the man who held the key to your entire future?

Did you treat him like royalty, or just go with the flow?

"Hi, I'm Tim."

Oh, shit. Not exactly what he was going for, but it could have been worse. Much worse.

Quickly bowing his head, Tim added, "Your Eminence.

"Enough of the Your Eminence crap." The high priest waved his hand is if dismissing something distasteful. "My name's Paul. I'm pleased to meet you." He extended his hand.

Should Tim shake it, or was this more of a kiss-the-ring situation? He'd never been much of a kiss-the-ring kind of guy. Just because you had an influential job, it didn't make you more important than anyone else.

Reaching out, he clasped Paul's hand. A small zap, almost like the static electricity from a blanket, passed between them as their hands met. That was weird. Maybe Tim was missing something. He tried to inspect the high priest as they shook.

Paul?

If the man hadn't told him his name, Tim doubted his inspection would have revealed anything. Based on his experience in other games, Paul could probably crush him with his little finger. Not a heartwarming thought, but he seemed to be nice enough.

Tim let go of the high priest's hand and smiled as he looked around the room. "Thank you, Paul. Your temple is very inspiring."

Paul sat down. "The structure is inspiring, but it's not my temple. Everything we do, everything we accomplish, is in service to the Goddess Eternia." He winked. "Your little display outside makes you just the kind of person we are looking for."

Leaning forward in his chair, Paul watched Tim closely. "What made you help those people?"

Tim didn't even have to think about it. "The kid was hurt, and I had the ability to help him. Why wouldn't I?"

"Why, indeed?" Paul shot a glance at the priest before continuing, "You appear to have what it takes to become an acolyte in the Temple of Light. Would you like to join our order?"

It seemed wrong to refuse, but he didn't know enough about the priests to be sure if he wanted to join. Plus, he couldn't dedicate himself wholly to the church when he had a job starting in the morning.

"Your Eminence." Tim paused, feeling slightly silly. "Paul." He shook his head to compose himself. "I do not want to seem ungrateful, but for now, I am simply looking to advance my skills in the healing arts."

Tim felt Brother Egon's withering glare upon him and tried to ignore it, but if Paul seemed disturbed by his answer, he didn't show it.

"Each of us comes to the Lady in our own time." He stood back up from his chair. "If it is training you want, then it is training you will receive." Paul grinned and made the same ritualistic motion over his chest. "May Eternia's blessings shine down upon you."

The high priest's gaze hardened as he turned back to Brother Egon. "Tell Cardinal Jepsom to go easy on this one. I'd like to keep him around awhile."

"As you command," Egon bowed his head, "we obey."

"Stop that shit," Paul growled. "Just tell him what I said."

Bowing low, Egon turned away. "Of course, your Eminence."

Paul looked at Egon's back for a moment, then reached into his robe and pulled a letter free. His right hand moved through a complicated series of gestures and time to slowed to a crawl.

The high priest handed Tim the letter. "Deliver this for me." He tapped Tim's head with a single finger. "The location is on your map."

Quest: Deliver the high priest's Letter.

Success: Deliver the letter to the location indicated on the map.

Failure: Fail to deliver the letter for any reason.

Reward: The reward for this quest will vary based on completion results.

Accept the quest: <yes/no>

Tim accepted the quest, and as soon as he tucked the envelope inside his robe, time sped back up. Paul was sitting back in his chair, head bowed as he looked over some giant leather-bound tome.

Egon hissed, "Cardinal Jepsom doesn't like to be kept waiting."

Tim cast one last glance at Paul. What had he just gotten himself into? All Edmond Dantes had been tasked with was delivering a letter, and everyone knew how well that had worked out for him.

Turning away from Paul, Tim jogged to catch up with Egon. The doors to the high priest's chambers closed behind them with the finality of a prison cell.

CHAPTER THIRTEEN

ardinal Jepsom had a big hat.

After five minutes with the cardinal, it was the only nice thing Tim could say about him. He couldn't even tell you it was a nice hat or a particularly splendid one. It was just big, and tall. The cardinal probably wore the ugly thing because it made him look more intimidating.

Thankfully, it looked like their meeting was drawing to an end.

Jepsom motioned for Tim to follow him to the door. "We have a room set up for you to handle some of our most basic requests. If you can successfully heal ten supplicants, I'll find some boots for you."

Quest Received: Heal Ten Supplicants

Success: Heal all ten parishioners

Failure: Fail to heal any of the parishioners completely

Reward: Boots

Accept Quest <yes/no>

Tim accepted the quest. Boots sounded nice, especially when he was going to have to walk through the mud again. Still, he'd come here to learn, not for footwear. He wanted to know what it was going to take to learn a new spell, but if he didn't approach the cardinal the right way, he was pretty sure the man would make his life a living hell.

Lowering his eyes as Egon had done, Tim searched for the right tone of subservience as he spoke. "Cardinal, I hate to be troublesome, but the high priest implied that I might also receive training."

Cardinal Jepsom's smile drew tight. "You have to walk before you run, my boy." He opened the door to his chambers. "Once you've become proficient with your basic ability, we will teach you something new."

Tim had met people like Jepsom before. You had to make sure you locked in the details, or else they kept trying to take more. He needed to know exactly how long it would take to learn a new skill so he could start planning for the future.

"What level of skill is deemed to be proficient?" Tim lowered his eyes under the cardinal's withering glare.

I fucking hate this shit.

How did people stand it back in the Middle Ages? Today you didn't have to bow your head to anyone. For better or worse, we were all the same.

"Apprentice level one should show sufficient dedication," Jepsom snapped.

Before Tim could respond, Egon grabbed his arm and pulled him into the hallway. "I will show him to his room, Cardinal."

Jepsom's only response was to slam the door shut in their faces.

Brother Egon led Tim back through a series of hallways until they reached a simple wooden door. Opening it, he motioned for Tim to join him inside. "I'll send in your first patient. When you are done, send them back outside. If they offer you anything, place it in the donation box behind you."

Tim wondered if the donation box was part of a test. If someone gave him a gift and he didn't put it in the box, they might refuse to train him. Did that mean someone was watching him now?

Looking around the sparse room didn't reveal any cameras, but there wasn't electricity, so that made sense. Why did he keep looking for the trappings of technology?

There were probably other ways people could watch you before electricity. They had seers in all the stories, and if there was magic, someone could have a scrying table. Fuck, maybe they wouldn't even need one.

Not that Tim would ever let his actions be dictated by someone watching. He believed in being himself, no matter what the situation. Tim was more than willing to do a little friendly role-playing if it helped grease the wheels of fortune, just like he had with Jepsom. This was a game, right?

So donations would go in the box, and Tim would pray the cardinal would teach him something useful. Any new skill might give him a leg up on the competition and put him in a position to pick the perfect group, instead of having to accept whatever scraps were left over.

All he had to do was put in the work.

Egon left the small room, giving Tim time to look around. Outside of a few basins of water and supplies for bandaging wounds, there wasn't much to look at. There was a single bench in the center of the room where someone could sit or lie down.

A woman walked into the room. She stopped and stared at Tim, obviously questioning if she was in the right place. "Brother?"

Ahh, now he understood why she was so confused. He wasn't wearing one of the traditional robes. It would be like walking into your doctor's office and seeing a guy in a t-shirt and flip flops waiting to give you an exam.

At least my imaginary doctor had flip-flops.

"Hi, I'm Tim." Oh, my God, he'd done it again. Why did he always default to his name as a response in stressful situations?

She didn't care who he was. The lady just wanted to know if he could heal her.

"I must have entered the wrong healing chamber." She started to leave the room.

Tim would fail the quest if she left the room, but he couldn't just grab her. He pictured walking back to his inn without boots. "Are you here for healing?"

"Yes," she replied, turning away from the door. "It's my arm." Her left hand moved toward her right bicep, drawing his attention to her bandaged arm.

"Then you're in the right place." He flashed his best disarming smile. "I'm helping the brothers out while I decide if I want to join the order."

The woman let out a sigh of relief. "I'm Cressida." She took a seat on the bench and looked up at him expectantly.

"Do you mind?" Tim motioned toward her bandage. Cressida shook her head, and he moved forward to undo the bloodstained wrapping. "This doesn't look so bad."

"That's what I told my dad, but he insisted that I come to make sure the wound didn't get infected." Her shoulders slumped. "What a waste of a day."

"I know exactly how you feel." Although he'd picked up a couple of quests, Tim wasn't sure he was spending his time very efficiently. His hand twitched through the motions of his one healing spell. Each time he cast it, it seemed easier than the last.

The small orb of water hovered in his hand. Tim pushed the orb against the woman's arm, and the wound closed instantly.

He left her sitting there as he took one of the basins of water and a towel from the rack. Tim quickly wiped off her arm, amazed at the fresh, new skin, where moments ago there had been a deep cut. Cressida didn't even have a scar.

"How does it feel?"

Cressida bent her arm, then poked it a few times. Her face

scrunched like she expected the spot to hurt, but the smile spreading across her features said her arm was pain-free.

"Feels brand new." Cressida stood up. "Maybe this wasn't a waste of time after all."

"I hope not." Tim smiled gratefully as she passed him a small leather bag full of copper coins. Cressida left the room, and Tim slipped the coins into the donation box as the next parishioner walked in.

Tim groaned. "I need a nap."

The ninth parishioner left the room as Tim sagged to the floor. His mana bar was completely drained. Why did his head feel so fuzzy?

Slowly his mana began to regenerate. With each little uptick of the blue bar, he felt better. As his energy came back, Tim climbed to his feet. The next supplicant entered the room, and he motioned for the man to take a seat while he quickly checked on his pending notifications.

Skill Increase: Healing Orb novice rank nine.

Sure your healing orb is stronger now, but you're still a novice.

Was the AI screwing with him again? Tim didn't even care. He loved the snarky undertone the game had; it made him feel right at home.

A man in fancy robes sat down on the bench. He pulled up the hem, exposing his bandaged leg, and lay down with his back on the bench. The wrapping on his leg was stained brown, and Tim could smell it from where he was standing six feet away.

It was the kind of leg they would have cut off during the Civil War, but in *The Etheric Coast*, Tim could save it. Stepping forward, he cut away the man's bandage and almost gagged as the foul smell sucker-punched his nostrils.

"You should have come in earlier," Tim chided gently as he prodded the man's leg. He wasn't sure yet if examining and understanding the wound would enhance the effectiveness of his spell, but as far as he could tell, it didn't hurt anything.

"If I wanted a lecture, I would have stayed at home and listened to my wife complain about my leg," the man barked gruffly. "Like I don't have other things to do. She wants the fancy-ass house, but she also doesn't want me to go work." The man grimaced. "How in the fuck can I do both?"

At least Tim's quest didn't involve giving relationship advice. He wasn't qualified as a love guru, but he had just chased a girl into a gameworld for the next twenty years, so he knew a little something about going above and beyond for love.

He smiled at the man. He'd figure it out or he wouldn't. Love was a fickle mistress. "Well, let's just see if we can't get you back to her sooner than anticipated." Tim conjured his healing orb and splashed it into the wound.

The dark red tendrils of infection spreading from the wound faded slightly but returned as the water dripped off the man's leg. The wound remained open, even though it had started to draw closed around the edges.

This was going to take a lot of work.

Tim looked at the man's leg again as his mana regenerated. When he was ready, he cast Healing Orb again., but while the leg was healing, Tim wasn't doing anything for the infection. Even with his leg healed, if Tim couldn't cure the infection, the man would still die, just as if he'd never come to the temple. There had to be something more he could do.

Growling in frustration, Tim slammed his hand into the wall. What was he missing?

"It seems you've hit a wall," Paul said, entering the room. "Both figuratively and literally."

Tim's cheeks burned, but he looked the high priest in the eye. "I'm having a problem with the infection."

"Let me show you something." Paul smiled as he reached out and placed his hand against Tim's forehead.

The same spark Tim had felt the first time he shook Paul's hand passed between them again. He looked away from the high priest and focused on the man's leg. It was like he knew exactly what to do. His hands moved through the gestures of the spell as if he'd known them his entire life.

His new spell activated.

The man lying on the bench let out a sigh of relief as the infection disappeared. He stood up, testing out the leg.

Tim noticed the man was still favoring it slightly and cast another healing orb. The water splashed his leg, and he began to laugh. Spinning into a little the jig, the man continued to giggle as he tossed a coin purse at Tim and left the room.

Tim put the coins in the donation box and turned back around to face the high priest. "Thank you for teaching me the Cleanse Spell."

"You can thank me by taking care of what we spoke about earlier." Paul left the room just as Egon returned.

"I'd ask how you cured the last man, but it seems the high priest has taken a shine to you." Brother Egon glared at him. "As it stands, you've completed the cardinal's quest. Here is your reward."

Quest: Heal Ten Supplicants Completed
Reward: Old leather boots
You have successfully healed ten parishioners as requested. Despite receiving a little help, you've fulfilled the terms set out in the description of the quest.

"Just take the damn boots." Egon slammed a pair of worn boots into Tim's chest. "It's time to go."

Tim took a second to put the boots into his inventory and then equipped them. The leather boots molded perfectly to his feet. At least he didn't have to worry about finding the right size, but he still needed to find a pair of socks or else he was going to have some wicked blisters later. He took a few steps in his new boots, enjoying the feeling of not being barefoot anymore. While the boots didn't add to his stats, they were going to make the walk home a million times better.

Brother Egon didn't waste any time leading Tim through the halls. It dawned on him that maybe they had wanted him to fail the test. Then they could get more work out of him before they had to teach him anything. The entire quest might have been rigged from the beginning.

I'm going to have to remember the person giving the quest is just as important as the quest itself before accepting any future missions.

Tim could see bright sunlight through the wide-open doors to the temple. For some reason, he couldn't wait to get outside. The temple felt almost claustrophobic with all of the people near the entrance.

Or maybe it was the incense.

"Tim, do you have a moment?" Cardinal Jepsom called from beside the door.

Sweet relief was so close, but if he wanted any further training, he couldn't risk blowing off the second-highest-ranking member of the church. "I will always have time for you, Cardinal." Tim lowered his head and ground his teeth together to keep silent.

Jepsom put an arm around Tim's shoulders. "It seems the high priest has taken an interest in you." The cardinal leaned close, his lips almost brushing against Tim's ear. "Did he give you something?"

Thankfully his head was still bowed, or else the cardinal would have seen his eyes widen momentarily at the mention of the letter. No. He didn't mention the letter specifically. The cardinal was fishing for information.

Tim looked up and met Jepsom's eyes, his dislike for the man making it easier to lie to him with conviction. "No, sir, he just came to check on my progress."

The cardinal looked irritated. "Are you sure? I reward my friends very well."

Quest: Deliver the high priest's Letter

New possible outcome: Deliver the letter to the cardinal for an unspecified reward.

The cardinal might have followers, but Tim doubted very much if he had any friends. "I'm sure." He held the man's gaze.

"Very well." The cardinal shook his head as if banishing a dark thought. "Then you may go on your way." Tim turned to leave, but the cardinal grabbed his arm. "The offer stands. If you ever come into possession of information I might find useful, you know where to find me."

Cardinal Jepsom made the sign of the lady over his chest and began to chant as he walked deeper into the temple.

Tim stepped out into the sun and tilted his head toward the sky. The warmth felt amazing after being trapped inside the cold stone building for so long. Life was looking up. He had boots and a couple of quests to finish. Plus, he couldn't wait to see the look on the cardinal's face if the high priest found out what he was up to.

This was going to be epic!

CHAPTER FOURTEEN

Am I being followed?

Tim peeked over his shoulder for the third time since leaving the temple. It took him a second to locate it, but he finally saw the same hint of orange around the man's waist. The guy was pretty good at staying hidden, keeping at least fifteen feet back and a person or two between them at all times.

There was always a chance he was just being paranoid after the cardinal's last-second ambush at the doors of the temple, but Tim didn't think so. *The question quickly changed from am I being followed, to why, and what in the fuck am I going to do about it.* The why seemed pretty simple; there was only one thing he could possibly have that Jepsom wanted.

The letter.

Tim knew something was going on at the church, and the way the quest was delivered to him seemed different than what he'd experienced in most games. Whatever internal conflict was happening inside of the temple was about to bubble over.

Whoever Tim decided to deliver the letter to would gain leverage over the other, and while he felt like he was making the right decision, how many movies had Tim seen where the seemingly kindhearted person turned out to be the dastardly villain?

Maybe he should just read the letter.

What would the harm be if he just took a peek? Reading the letter might actually give him the information he needed to make the right choice.

Tim felt the weight of the letter in the inner pocket of his robes, but he'd never been one to give in to temptation. Doing things the easy way wasn't his style. He was more of the repeatedly bash your head against a problem until you had an epiphany kind of guy.

So instead of taking the easy way out and giving the letter to the cardinal like a good little follower, he was being followed by a man with bad intentions. He needed to come up with a plan quickly.

Flame Burst was Tim's only damage-dealing ability, and he hadn't used it yet. Getting into a fight with an untested ability wasn't very smart. He didn't know much about the game, but he was pretty sure he could use his scepter like a bat. Also, if the person was above level five, he might only stand a chance if he bashed them over the head from behind.

"My way doesn't seem very sportsmanlike," Tim mumbled as he picked up his pace.

Provoking a direct confrontation seemed like an easy way to handle things, but he could lose, and losing meant death in this game. Tim wasn't an adventurer yet, so losing also meant giving up all the progress he'd made in the game so far. He wasn't ready to risk his life after working all day to raise his skills. Leading the man away from the crowded streets and trying to kill him wasn't the only option he had.

What Tim actually needed was more people around him.

With more people around, he might be able to escape, or maybe even alert the city guards to the man's stalkerish tendencies. The guards were stationed at regular intervals on the north side of town. It was a plan with a lot of promise, assuming, of course, that Cardinal Jepsom didn't have the city guards in his pocket.

We all know what happens when you assume things.

If he couldn't go to the guards, and a direct confrontation would probably result in his death, what was he going to do? The idea hit him like a head-on collision between a semi-truck and a compact. All he had to do was keep walking.

He'd gone to a few of those free protection classes on campus. Sure, they were mostly for women, but sometimes it paid to be in the know. One thing they always stressed in any potentially dangerous situation was to find a campus police officer or one of the blue emergency beacons.

If neither of those options was attainable, your next best chance was to go into a crowded place. Apparently, shitty assholes who were likely to attack a woman were less likely to do it in the presence of other people.

But there was something else Tim loved about crowds—it was easy to get lost in them.

Tim pulled up his map and adjusted his course to head toward the ocean and the marketplace. One thing he knew about medieval cities and their counterparts in games was that the harbor would be busy, and the marketplace would be insane. Once he was in the crush of people, it couldn't possibly be too difficult to lose his pursuer.

The hardest part of Tim's plan was walking slowly when he knew there was someone behind him potentially wanting to do him harm. All he wanted to do was run. Every noise threatened to push his growing sense of panic over the edge. He was like a sprinter waiting for the starting gun to set him free, and yet he managed to keep the same slow pace he'd had since leaving the temple.

The marketplace came into view, and Tim stared at it in wonder. He'd never been to one of the great open-air bazaars that were famous all over the world, but he had been to the swap meet a time or two. The sprawling commercial quarter was something Tim would have never imagined in his wildest dreams.

The marketplace might as well have been its own city. Hundreds of booths lined the open thoroughfare. Shops and restaurants occupied both sides of the streets. Every building was filled to the point of overflowing. There had to be tens of thousands of people moving through the lanes between stalls.

Seeing so many people in one place was kind of a shock after the desolate streets of the slums. All of them were so packed together, it was hard to discern individual people from where he was standing. Looking down on the market from above was like watching schools of fish from a distance. All Tim saw were groups of color flowing down the streets.

The market was exactly what he needed to make a break for it.

A smile broke out across Tim's face as he quickened his pace. If he could get into the press of people and cause a distraction, there was a good chance he could get away. All he needed was a chance. Otherwise, he'd have to abandon his quest to deliver the letter until another time and head back to the inn, where he'd be safe in his room.

There was work for him to do at the inn as well, and Tim had the distinct impression that he was going to need a good night's rest before meeting the smith in the morning. Being a blacksmith's apprentice wasn't going to be easy, but it sure beat the hell out of cleaning up horse shit. Imagine signing up to scrape horseshit off the cobbles for the next twenty years!

At least those guys had one up on the guy cleaning chamber pots.

As he entered the market, Tim saw the man behind him try to close the distance between them. This was it; he had to act now. A man walked by carrying a crate of apples. Tim kicked out, catching the heel of the man's boot as he passed. The merchant bumped into someone on his left and then pitched forward, spilling the crate of apples all over the street.

People milling around darted forward, stealing the apples as the merchant swore and swatted at their extended hands. Tim spotted the same flash of orange again, only this time he knew what it was. The man following him had an orange sash tied around his waist. Not exactly discreet, but most of the citizens here wore at least one piece of brightly colored clothing.

Were the colors people had on representative of factions within the city? Tim marked the thought for further examination as he wove through the crowd. Reaching out, his fingers closed around the notched wooden barrel full of salted fish. Feeling a twinge of guilt, Tim yanked on the barrel and sent it tumbling to the ground.

The merchant cried out in shock and a few people screamed, thinking something sinister was afoot. Other people tried to grab a fish and dart back into the crowd. The merchant's screams of protest could be heard over the general din of the market, drawing the attention of the city guards. The two men started making their way toward the fishmonger's booth.

Time to go!

Tim's feet started moving again. The distraction wasn't worth shit if he didn't get away. Turning away from the chaotic scene, Tim continued deeper into the market. When he looked over his shoulder, he didn't see the man with the orange sash, but he didn't feel safe yet. He still had to make it out of the market.

At least he didn't have to worry about counter surveillance. In this world, there weren't any cameras or cell phones. His biggest problem was that he didn't have a change of clothes and couldn't afford one.

"Not yet, anyway," Tim mumbled through gritted teeth, casting another glance over his shoulder.

Tim decided he was all in on his desperate bid to escape. He'd do whatever it took to make it out of here, even if it meant bending his moral code. Stopping to look over a merchant's wares, he kept his eyes glued to the clothing next to them. When the merchant left to help a new customer, Tim stole a cotton shirt and a pair of simple woolen trousers.

Before the merchant could turn around, Tim had the items in his inventory. He started moving with the general flow of the crowd again. His gut twisted as he thought about what he'd done.

"Desperate times," Tim murmured, even as he swore an oath to come back and repay the woman for the clothes he'd stolen.

A few quick turns and surreptitious glances behind him later, Tim un-equipped his robe and equipped his new clothes. With his disguise in place, he reoriented himself and started working his way toward the nearest exit. Once he cleared the market, he could head to the north side of town and deliver the letter, and then he could get some rest.

It was always better to be safe than sorry, so Tim stopped at another stall and pretended to check out the wares while he watched the crowd behind him. The familiar hint of orange he'd grown used to wasn't there. Tim beelined for the exit, stepping back out into the main thoroughfare.

Tim took a deep breath, wishing for some fresh air, but only smelling the press of humanity that surrounded him. Being in the market pressed against so many people felt suffocating, but now he was back out in the open and totally exposed. He couldn't risk leading the man with the orange sash to where he was delivering the letter, so he started to form a plan.

There was only one way to be sure.

Tim darted into the alley on his right, sprinting a short way before ducking behind a stack of crates. His breath was thrumming in his ears, each beat of his heart thudding harder than the last. He wrapped his hand around the grip of his scepter and leapt from behind the crates, ready to attack.

"Graahhhhh!" He swung the scepter as hard as he could.

The alley was empty.

A lady walking past the mouth of the alley gave him a curious look, shook her head in disgust, and moved on. It was the same kind of look a person had on their face when they saw someone talking to themselves about the fairies while wearing a tinfoil hat. Tim didn't have a tinfoil hat, but he had just attacked the air like a little kid playing swords after Saturday morning cartoons.

Tim took a few calming breaths, laughter spilling from his lips as he placed his scepter back into his inventory. He must have looked ridiculous, jumping from behind the crate and slashing the empty air. At least the house he was looking for wasn't too far away.

Tim pulled up his map, and after a few dicey moments, he found a way to leave a transparent overlay in the top right-hand corner of his vision. Using that, he moved through a series of alleys and servants' passages until he arrived on the Street of Thorns.

"Not a very welcoming street name," Tim mumbled as he looked up and down the road for any hint of orange.

Nothing jumped out at him, so Tim quickly double-checked the waypoint on his map, then took off at a brisk walk. He reached the house in question a few minutes later. It was a massive building, much like the famous row houses of San Francisco, but with a much more Tudoresque appearance.

The craftsmanship of the building impressed him. It must have taken forever to attach each of the dark wooden shingles. Tim wondered what kind of money a contractor could make inside the game. Eventually, people would be able to afford land and build houses. Then they would want all the things houses needed, including the furniture they'd grown accustomed to from their cushy inn rooms.

A craftsman with the right entrepreneurial nature could make a killing.

But he wasn't here to admire the man's house. He was here to deliver a letter. Stepping up to the door, Tim fished the letter out of his inventory and looked at it for the first time. The name in scrawling calligraphy on the front was Lucy Briarthorn.

Not what I expected.

Served him right for assuming the letter was going to a man. Just because they'd stepped back in time, it didn't mean the developers had created a sexist world. So far, the only deity he knew of was a woman, and at least half the players were bound to be female.

Tim smiled as he grabbed the brass knocker on the door. Gone were the days of a boys' club for gaming. Women were an important addition to the gaming scene, not only as players, but on the development front. The sheer number of female developers working on the games he loved couldn't be ignored. It was a brave new world in the gaming community, and he was loving every minute of it.

Tim slammed the brass knocker down and waited. A minute or so later, a man wearing a pair of leggings covered with a simple woolen tunic appeared at the door.

"May I help you?" the man droned as he noted Tim's ragged appearance.

"I have a letter for Lucy Briarthorn."

The servant held out his hand expectantly. "Well, come on, I don't have all day."

"The letter is of some importance. I was directed to place it in the lady's hands myself." It was a lie, but after being followed, Tim wasn't sure he could trust anyone besides the high priest's intended recipient.

Scoffing, the servant started to turn away. "The lady of the house doesn't have time for the likes of you."

"Then it's a good thing the letter isn't from me." The man glared at him. "I believe the lady is expecting it." Tim wasn't sure what to do if he couldn't get inside.

A female voice called from the darkness of the entryway, "There's only one letter I'm expecting."

Tim held up the letter and flashed both sides so whoever was standing inside could see it, then he held his breath, hoping for the best.

"Show him to the study, Reginald. I'll be there in a moment."

Reginald grunted and motioned for Tim to follow him inside.

Maybe Tim would have been better off handing the servant the letter. The quest only stated he had to deliver it, not that he had to place it directly in the hands of the recipient. Something about ensuring the letter's safety felt right, though, and he'd done more than enough to have earned a few answers.

Tim didn't get hit over the head as soon as he stepped inside, so there was a good chance he wasn't going to get murdered. Letting out a sigh of relief, he followed Reginald through the house until the servant stopped outside a set of dark wooden doors. Smiling, Reginald flung the doors open with a flourish.

The study was bigger than Tim expected. It felt more like a library than an office. There was a fireplace dominating one corner of the room. Reginald headed in that direction to add a few more logs to the fire, giving Tim time to take in the entire room.

Spinning in a slow circle, Tim scanned the shelves of books. In some places, the shelves reached all the way to the ceiling, and there were ladders attached to shiny brass rails that could be rolled around the walls.

There was a treasure trove of knowledge here. He could almost feel the power radiating off of the books.

Lucy Briarthorn swept into the room like a vision from heaven. Her flowing silk robes seemed to dance against her skin as she moved. Long blonde hair hung to the center of her back. Tim couldn't decide if she was wearing makeup or not, but her face had an almost angelic shine to it.

Lady Briarthorn glided across the room. It wasn't that she floated exactly, it was more like each of her steps was so perfect, they flowed together. Lucy took a seat behind a desk made of black stone and motioned for Tim to take the open chair across from her.

Tim pulled the letter from his inventory and handed it to Lady Briarthorn. Reginald moved to stand behind him, placing firm hands on each of Tim's shoulders to make sure he couldn't get up without a fight.

Lucy simpered. "You must excuse me for the precautions, but the last person claiming to have a letter for me intended me bodily harm."

Tim almost laughed. "I think you must have me confused with a much more daring individual." The way she moved, he wasn't even sure if he'd be able to hit her, let alone kill her. That was assuming he could break free of Reginald's grasp.

Lady Briarthorn snorted. "True, you don't pose much of a threat, but there are other ways to kill a person."

Yeah, like poison.

He wasn't here to poison her, though, just to drop off a letter and get the hell out. "Paul asked me to deliver it personally."

Lucy slit the letter open with a dagger and began to peruse the contents. Her eyes lit up. "That sneaky little bastard."

Lady Briarthorn quickly scribbled a reply and sealed it with wax. She handed the letter to Tim. "Take this back to the high priest and tell him preparations are underway." Reaching into the desk, Lucy pulled out a small coin purse and tossed it on the table. "For your trouble."

Quest Received: Turning The Tables

You've successfully delivered the high priest's letter to Lucy Briarthorn, but she has another task for you to complete.

Success: She paid you upfront for the job.

Failure: Reginald hunts you down and removes a finger for every coin that's missing.

Accept the quest <yes/no>

Tim snatched the bag of coins off the desk. "You've got yourself a deal."

Lady Briarthorn stared coolly at him from across the desk. "You know the price for failure."

Tim nodded in acquiescence.

Lucy's deadly expression turned warm. "Then we understand each other." Reginald's hands released their grip on Tim's shoulders. "Reggie will see you out."

Reginald grabbed Tim by the shirt, hauled him out of the study, and closed the doors behind them. "I hate when she calls me 'Reggie,'" he grumbled, stomping down the hall in the direction of the front door.

Tim started to laugh; he'd had a few of the same experiences. With Xander as a best friend, you could be given a new and insulting nickname at any time. "Just like when people call me Timberino." He shook his head as if warding off a bad memory. "I hate that shit."

"Timberino. That's good." Reginald chuckled as they reached the front door.

"Just remember, I know your pet name, and you wouldn't want a secret like that getting around." Tim gave him a jaunty wave as he walked down the steps and out onto the street of thorns.

Tim pulled up his map and started looking for the quickest way home. *If I wake up early enough, I might be able to get my reward from the high priest before work.* As much as he hated to admit it, being chased through the market and delivering the letter was enough excitement for one day.

Tim had always fancied himself as more of a kill-the-monster-type player. He wasn't into all the cloak and dagger political intrigue shit. Too many people died playing those sorts of games. Tim glanced into the upper-right-hand portion of his vision and turned until the arrow on the map matched the way he wanted to go.

Once everything was aligned, he started the long walk home. "They really need to add quick travel to the game," he grumbled. "At least I have boots and a few spare coins."

CHAPTER FIFTEEN

*A*nother *week of this, and I'm going to be in the best shape of my life.*

Seriously, who knew not having access to a car or public transportation could make you so fit? In the future, Tim would probably appreciate it, but right now, his feet were sore from breaking in his new boots, and he was pretty sure he'd earned a few blisters.

You'd think they would have taken the horrible feeling of breaking in a pair of boots out of the game.

But it really wasn't his sore feet that were on his mind. Tim was still thinking about the clothes he'd stolen and how it might affect the person he stole them from. Sure, one pair of pants and a shirt might not be the end of the world, but if their business was just hanging on, losing a few items could be the tipping point.

Tim didn't want to be responsible for that.

Now that he had a little coin in his pocket, he'd have to stop by the market and make a small donation. They might not like what had happened yesterday, but at least it wouldn't cost them anything or take the food out of their family's mouths.

Even though the NPCs were just code, everyone he met in the

game felt like a real person. It made them more than ones and zeros. Tim didn't want to be responsible for fucking up their lives. The goal of the game was to eventually destroy the big baddie, not to become one.

The guards nodded to Tim as he ducked through the archway back into the slums. It was better than the shifty look they'd given him earlier, although he wasn't sure what he'd done to deserve the new status. A gentle mist started to fall from the sky as he made his way down the dirt path to the inn.

A man stumbled out of the alley on the right side of the road, clutching one hand against his side. Blood blossomed on his shirt as he fell to the ground. Tim started forward, then stopped, eyes frantically searching the mouth of the alley to see if anyone was coming to finish the job.

Turning away from the alley in a panic, Tim shouted toward the guards on the other side of the archway. "Help! We need some help down here."

One of the guards peeked through the opening. Not seeing an active attack, he went back to his post. What in the fuck was going on? Why weren't the guards coming to help? It didn't matter. He might not be able to fend off the attackers, but he could save the man's life.

Tim equipped his scepter and the words for casting healing orb tumbled from his lips automatically as he ran toward the injured man. The first orb splashed the man, and Tim started casting the second one as he knelt next to him. This time, he cradled the orb in his hand and pressed it to the wound on the man's side.

Lifting the victim's shirt, Tim watched the wound seal itself closed. He dropped the man's shirt into place and cast a furtive glance toward the alley. No one was running toward them with the intention of finishing the man off, but no one was coming to help, either. As he looked down at the unconscious man lying in the muddy street, one thought kept screaming through Tim's mind.

Now what do I do with him?

"Fuck," Tim grumbled. "Do I really have to do this?" Casting a forlorn look up and down the street and not seeing any help, Tim grabbed the man's forearms and started dragging him toward the inn.

He's not sleeping in my fucking room.

Tim yanked the stabbing victim up the steps to the wooden landing and shoved the inn's door open with one hand. Holding the door open with his butt, he pulled the man inside behind him.

"Ernie, I need some help over here," Tim shouted as he stared at the counter.

Ernie grimaced as he peered over the counter. "Kid, I don't know what you've heard, but we aren't in the body disposal business."

"He isn't fucking dead. Just help me get him somewhere more comfortable until he wakes up." Tim pleaded.

Ernie shook his head. "This isn't a charity."

Was everyone in this game just a worthless-self-serving piece of shit? Where was the compassion? Tim wanted to scream in frustration, but he knew it wouldn't help. He'd read about how ruthless things had been during the Roman Empire, and again when England rose, to claim the top spot but he had never truly understood how brutal those times had been.

A royal could kill a peasant and no one would bat an eyelash. Power ruled. Every single society in history had been ruled by the strong. Every tribe, every nation, was trying to explore and expand. Tim shook his head to clear it. There were more important things than world history lessons to worry about.

Gaston got up from his customary table. "What's going on?"

Ernie gave Tim a look that said, "Now you've done it." "The squatter's dragging in bodies."

Gaston gazed at the unconscious man on the floor, then looked up at Tim with a cruel smile on his face. "The first thing you should learn, kid, is that you never shit where you eat."

"Isn't that a sex reference?" The only time Tim had heard the expression used was in reference to not sleeping with a co-worker.

Gaston looked appalled. "Why would anyone ever mix shitting and fucking?" He looked like he might throw up.

Ernie shook his head. "You travelers are a weird bunch."

Fuck. As if Tim didn't have enough problems to contend with, these guys thought he was some kind of sexual deviant. The last thing he needed was to be hassled every time he came home. Hopefully, these two had enough going on they'd forget about tonight.

Gaston did a double-take at the man on the floor, then his entire demeanor changed. "Fuck me! It's Freddy." Rushing past the unconscious man, Gaston wrapped his hands in Tim's robes and slammed him against the wall. "What in the fuck did you do to him?"

Tim stared calmly back into Gaston's enraged eyes. He felt the cold calm of battle descending on him. It happened to him sometimes when a fight was unavoidable. It was like his brain knew and gave him a way to deal with the stress of it by turning off his emotions.

This time Tim fought off the cold clasp of the berserker and tried a much more diplomatic tactic. "I just saved his life and dragged him all the way here." Tim tried to break Gaston's grip on his robes but couldn't.

Tim glared at Gaston indignantly. "Let. Me. Go."

Ernie came around the corner and knelt next to Freddy. The innkeeper placed a hand on the unconscious man's throat to check his pulse. "Still alive."

Standing up, Ernie moved toward Gaston and placed a hand on the man's giant shoulders. "The kid did ask for help when he came in, so maybe he's not responsible."

"You better pray Freddy backs up your story," Gaston growled.

Tim brought his arm up and slammed it down on Gaston's wrist, breaking his grip on his robes. "If you gave two shits, you'd be out there looking for whoever did this instead of wasting your time on me."

Turning away from the two men, Tim headed toward the stairs. "And keep your fucking hands off of me."

"Kid's got fire," Ernie said, watching Tim stomp up the stairs.

Gaston grinned back at him. "He's starting to grow on me." Reaching down, Gaston pulled Freddy over his shoulder and carried him into the other room. "Just don't tell the kid I said it."

Tim smiled as he reached the top of the stairs. Things might not have gone as smoothly as he would have liked today, but at least he was making progress. Tim locked the door and leaned his back against it after he stepped into his room. Letting out a sigh, he heaved himself away from the door and sat in the room's only chair.

Now that he wasn't running panicked through the streets or about to be throttled by the largest assassin he'd ever seen, Tim noticed a notification glowing in the bottom right-hand corner of his vision.

He pulled up the notification tab and was bombarded by messages. One of the notices had a golden border around it. "Must be important."

Tim clicked the golden outline.

He was lifted into the air, and golden light swirled around him. It was like a drug that targeted all of his pleasure sensors at once and sent them into overdrive. His feet hit the floor, and the golden light vanished.

His legs felt weak after the wonderful sensation left him. "That's not addictive or anything." Tim already couldn't wait to do it again. Part of him wondered...if each level took longer to achieve, did the pleasure he received as a reward last longer?

"Fuck." The game had already turned him into the lab rat that hit the pleasure button until it died from starvation.

Tim shook it off and read the notification.

Congratulations. You have reached level two. Your vitality

and revitalization skills have been increased by one point. You have one unassigned skill point.

What should I put it in? If healing is what I want to do, I should probably focus on wisdom until I hit twenty points. Then I'll have to reevaluate.

Tim assigned his skill point to wisdom and looked over his enhanced character stats. Not too shabby for his first day in the game. Tim was sure some people had made it much farther than he had, especially if they were teaming up for quests. Part of him wanted to grin all night, but he couldn't risk a bad performance at work on his first day.

"Why am I so tired?" He stared into the dancing flames of the fire.

It didn't take long for Tim to realize he'd probably walked more in the game world today than he had in a long time. It was too bad he didn't have his FitBit on. He would have crushed his step goal for the day, or maybe even the week.

Tim quickly scrolled through his other notifications, hoping for a note from Sierra. *I wonder how her first day went?* He fired off a quick message, saying they should try to hook up sometime this week, then continued scrolling through the minor notifications until he reached the last one.

Healing Orb Skill increased to apprentice rank one: Congratulations, you are no longer the lowest of the low. You have one apprentice-level skill.

Healing Orb is now ten percent more effective than the base version and applies fifteen percent of the amount healed as a HOT (heal over time) over the next five seconds.

That's fucking awesome! Not only had he gained additional healing, but the additional healing over time bonus was epic. It would give him a few moments to scan the battlefield and to restore a little mana before casting again. Tim wondered just how powerful this spell would become at grandmaster level.

Dismissing his notifications, Tim stood up and headed toward the bed in the corner of the room. Instead of taking off his clothes, he just un-equipped them.

"Doubt they get dirty in my inventory," Tim said, looking down at the loincloth he was wearing. "Tomorrow I need to find a shop that sells boxers."

The bed was softer than he expected, and the sheets were clean. Despite all of Ernie's misgivings about having a customer in the inn, he was sure going out of his way to make sure Tim was comfortable. Thinking about the men downstairs reminded him that he had a quest to finish.

Maybe I'll get to it in the morning.

CHAPTER SIXTEEN

B*EEP! BEEP! BEEP!*

"What in the fuck is that!" Tim roared, swatting at the air in front of him.

Tumbling out of bed, he hit the ground with a thud. "Fucking game and its pain mechanics."

Tim rubbed his shoulder as he stood up. With the incessant beeping rattling his head, it took him much longer to pull up his user interface and turn off the alarm than he desired. Apparently, the system was designed to make sure he wasn't late for work, but he was going to need a much softer ringtone.

If he couldn't change the tone, each morning would become a tossup between having a heart attack and making it to work on time.

After walking over to the chamber pot, Tim un-equipped his loincloth. "At least taking this thing off is easy." He finished up and re-equipped all of his clothing. "Man, if I could do this at home, I'd save so much time."

With everything in place, Tim headed for the door. His belly rumbled as his hand closed on the handle. Hopefully, the food was good and hearty. He had the distinct feeling he was going to need all the energy he could get to make it through his first day. Slipping out of the room, Tim closed the door behind him and headed down the stairs.

As much as he hated to admit it, it was kind of nice being the only customer at the inn. Tim preferred things to be nice and quiet, especially in the morning. Entering the lobby, he turned toward the dining area, expecting to see Gaston and his crew, but their table was empty. Next to their giant round table was a much smaller table with a single chair.

The table must be Gaston's way of apologizing.

Tim gave the burly assassin's table a wide berth. Even though the men weren't there now, it didn't mean they weren't watching. It felt like a test. If he sat at their table, it was game over, but if he sat at the table they'd set out for him, he might get a little bit closer to finding out what was actually going on here.

There was a quest to complete, after all.

Sitting down in the chair seemed to be the cue Ernie needed to appear. The innkeeper slid a plate of what looked like grits with a melting chunk of butter in the center of the bowl to him. Next, Ernie slapped down a plate of sliced meat, then finished his breakfast presentation with a glass of something that looked surprisingly like orange juice.

Grits weren't a thing where he was from. Sure, he'd had them a time or two, but most restaurants in his area didn't even have them on the menu.

Speaking of menus…

"What's all this?" Tim smiled as Ernie finished setting down a wooden spoon and a knife.

"Sliced lamb, grits with butter, and a glass of rumpleberry nectar." Ernie beamed as he said the last word. "Nothing but the best after what you did last night."

It seemed rude to ask for a menu after Ernie had laid out his best fare, and it wasn't like he hated anything on the table. It must be the time he'd spent on the West Coast, but the cube of butter melting in the middle of the bowl screamed heart attack to him. Then he remembered he was in a game. Did cholesterol or calories matter here?

"What exactly is a rumpleberry?" Tim blurted as he started mixing the butter into the grits.

"It's a large orange fruit that grows on a rumple bush." Ernie tilted his head, examining Tim as if he were trying to figure out if he was dense or just screwing with him. "Don't they have rumpleberry bushes where you are from?"

Tim took a sip of juice, and a smile bloomed across his face. The sweet, tangy taste of fresh-squeezed orange juice lit up his mouth like a chandelier. "We have something similar where I am from, but the fruit grows on trees instead of bushes."

"Where you're from sounds like a very strange place." Ernie turned, heading back toward the kitchen. "Call if you need anything else."

"Thanks, Ernie." Tim waited for the man to disappear from view, then dug into the food like a starving dog.

How did I get so hungry?

Normally in games, you ate for buffs or to regenerate your health and mana at a higher rate. Here, it seemed Tim needed to eat because he was hungry. Could you starve to death in the game? While that was a chilling thought, it wasn't something Tim had to deal with today. Right now, he was going to do his best to pretend he was back at Joe's with a plate of corned beef hash in front of him.

Thinking about Joe's brought back memories of his final meal in the real world. It seemed like a lifetime ago. Fuck, it was a different world ago. In reality, it had been less than a day, but it was a day with no food and a whole lot of walking.

Tim worked through the giant bowl of grits and the plate of sliced lamb. The rumpleberry juice was a taste of home he hadn't been expecting. All things considered, the meal was pretty damn good, and he was full to the point of bursting. Tim shoved the empty bowl away from him and leaned back in the chair. Today was going to be a good day, as long as he got his ass moving.

A second alarm sounded, letting Tim know he needed to leave now to make it to work on time. He dismissed the alarm and started making his way toward the door. Pausing at the counter, Tim shouted back toward the kitchen. "Thanks for the great breakfast, Ernie." Not waiting for a reply, Tim opened the door and stepped out into the rain.

But it wasn't raining.

"That's a first." The rolling clouds above him seemed to take his thought as a personal assault as they let loose with an early-morning drizzle. Who knew living in the slums also meant it rained all the time? NPC Corp had conveniently left that little factoid out of the brochure.

The constant drizzle made Tim wonder who'd designed a system like this. Didn't poor people deserve a little sunshine? Walking toward the archway to town kind of reminded him of the animated Robin Hood movie he had loved as a kid.

"Sometimes the sun outshines the rain, but not in the slums of Promethia." Tim sang a fun little parody of his favorite scene from the movie.

The guards at the archway didn't even glance at Tim. Now that they'd seen him go back and forth a few times, he was a known commodity in the area, and not worth hassling. Who knew living on the west side of town carried such a stigma with it? Not that it mattered to him. Once things got rolling, he'd be able to upgrade to nicer amenities if he wanted too.

Most of the city must have been sleeping. The streets were almost deserted until he reached the market. Tim could see the men streaming over the docks like ants on a fallen doughnut. Merchants in their stalls called to potential buyers. The market felt as if it were alive, the thrumming heartbeat of the city.

Tim pulled up his map to zero in on his location and plotted a course to the smithy from there. His in-game clock told him he had just enough time to drop off a few coins for the damage he had caused and the clothes he'd stolen yesterday.

Quickly weaving through the stalls, Tim left the salted fish merchant two silver coins, then slipped another two coins to the tailor before disappearing into the crowd. It was most of his reward for delivering Lady Briarthorn's letter, and he hadn't even dropped it off yet.

I like my fingers to much to not drop it off.

The hair on his forearms stood up as he thought about Reginald standing over him with a pair of garden shears. "That will be four fingers, Timberino."

Maybe watching too much tv really did rot your brain. It certainly seemed to have an effect on the way Tim imagined things playing out. Did watching too many horror movies make him abundantly cautious or completely paranoid? The jury was still out, but for now, he had all his fingers right where he wanted them.

Tim came to a stop outside of the smithy and changed from his robes back into his shirt and pants. "Time to see what I got myself into."

The dark stone surrounding the smith's workshop made it stand out from the wooden buildings around it. Bright orange light bathed the interior, and Tim could feel the heat pouring out the door like an open oven during the holidays.

When Tim entered the building, it felt like his whole body was being blasted by a blow dryer set on high. He looked around, not exactly sure what he was supposed to do.

"You're late," a burly dwarf snarled as he rounded the corner of the forge. The dwarf's arms looked strong enough to rip Tim in half, and despite his silver beard, the man walked with the pep of a young man.

A thick leather apron and matching gloves bounced off Tim's

chest. The dwarf chuckled as he turned and headed deeper into the workshop. "Put those on so we can get started."

Tim glanced at the clock displayed in his user interface, noting that he was two minutes early for his shift. Saying something didn't seem like the right play here. Sometimes it was better to keep your mouth shut until you got the lay of the land. It only took him a few seconds to place the items in his inventory, and then he inspected them.

Apron of the Unburning: Fire Resistance +10

Gloves of the Smith: While wearing this item, your hands cannot be burned. Don't worry, though. The rest of you can still be turned into a crispy critter if you make a mistake.

The silver-bearded tyrant gave Tim a hurry-up expression. "Get a move on. The bellows aren't going to pump themselves."

Tim followed the dwarf to the forge and looked around in confusion. *What exactly do bellows look like?* "Uh, sir?" He wasn't even sure what to call his new boss. "Where do you need me?"

"First, cut the 'sir' shit. I'm not a knight, I work for a living. And two," the dwarf held up two fingers, "my name is Ironbeard." He glared at Tim. "Use it."

Turning away from Tim, Ironbeard pointed at a large metal device toward the back of the forge. "Those are the bellows."

When Tim didn't move, Ironbeard grabbed his arm and dragged him over to his station. "All you have to do is keep pumping until I tell you to stop." The dwarf jumped into the makeshift seat and pulled the bellows back before pushing them forward again. He eyed Tim, trying to decide if his visual instruction was enough for him to understand the job.

Ironbeard patted the leather-wrapped handholds. "If you can handle this, I might even let you give out a few quests later. I hate dealing with all those pesky travelers." The dwarf headed back toward the front of the forge.

Giving out quests sounded like nice easy work compared to

pumping the bellows. "I'm here to help in whatever way I can," Tim shouted after him.

The contraption in front of him was a huge thing made out of iron and leather. Ironbeard's demonstration hadn't left anything to question. Tim climbed into the wooden chair and put his feet against the braces. Pulling the iron rod towards him filled the bellows, and pushing the bar away emptied them.

Not exactly the kind of job you'd expect to hold after getting a degree in business, but it was the one he'd signed up for. Tim also wasn't sure if this was the normal setup. It seemed like the dwarf had made some modifications to make the system sturdier and easier to use for longer periods of time.

Just keep your mouth shut and do the work. You've got years to learn from the master.

He might only be pumping the bellows today, but at some point, he'd learn how to melt metal and forge it into something useful. Players were always going to need weapons, and farms always needed shoes for their horses and tack for their field animals. Apprenticing here meant he'd have a useful money-making skill to rely on.

Ironbeard's head popped around the corner of the forge. "Well?" he reprimanded.

Tim shrugged and got to work. It was almost like using a rowing machine except he didn't have an eight bit competitor to try and lap.. He worked the rod in and out, sweat dripping from his forehead after the first few attempts.

I'm going to need two bowls of grits tomorrow.

Three hours later, Ironbeard roared, "Enough!"

Tim flopped out of the chair. He stood for a second, but then his legs buckled, sending him to his knees. Sweat was streaming down his face, and every breath he sucked in felt like it was barely enough to keep him from passing out. Black spots swam across his vision, but at least the air was cooler by the floor.

"I can't believe you kept it up for so long, boy." Ironbeard clapped Tim on the back. "After the second hour, I kept going just to see how long it'd take you to break."

Laughing, Ironbeard walked toward the counter. "Take the rest of the day off, and maybe I'll teach you something useful tomorrow."

Tim climbed back to his feet like some kind of wounded crab flipping itself over on the beach. His arms wouldn't support his weight, but at least they'd stopped tingling. A groan escaped his lips, but he'd impressed the old dwarf enough to earn a bit of respect.

"Same time tomorrow?" Tim asked as he moved toward the door of the shop.

"Tomorrow?" Ironbeard mumbled as mulled it over. "As long as you can still lift your arms." He chuckled. "Otherwise, take the day off."

Tim started to leave, and Ironbeard shouted after him, "Don't get used to the extra time off. I plan on getting my money's worth out of you!"

Rubbing his arms to bring back some circulation, Tim stepped out into the sun. It felt good to be out in the light, and the cool breeze off the ocean danced across his skin. He'd expected the market to slow down a bit after the morning deliveries were finished, but if anything, the market was busier. Tossing a copper coin to a vendor, Tim grabbed a glass of rumpleberry juice and started his walk back to the inn.

Before going to deliver the letter to the high priest so he could turn in his quest, Tim needed to clean up. At least getting cleaned up would be easy. He quickly un-equipped all of his clothes and then quickly re-equipped them. At least his clothes were clean now. He giggled, thinking about what the NPC's must have thought when they saw all his clothes disappear and reappear almost instantly.

"Probably jealous." Tim shrugged. "They all have to do laundry."

A few minutes later, the familiar arch leading to the slums came into sight. The guards nodded to him as he made his way inside. For once it wasn't raining, but the clouds overhead rumbled, threatening to open up before he reached the inn. Tim started to sprint, hoping to make it under the awning before getting drenched, but he skidded to a stop when his eyes settled on the people milling in the street outside the inn.

Why in the fuck were these people here? The inn was always empty. Tim moved forward and started weaving his way through the crowd toward the front door. When he reached the door, Ernie pulled him inside and slammed the door shut behind them.

Taking a few deep breaths, Ernie glanced sheepishly at Tim. "It seems we have a small problem."

"That somehow involves me?" Tim hadn't done anything interesting enough in the game to draw a crowd like this to his location. He doubted most heroes got a welcome like this, so it had to be something else. If the cardinal had sent them, he would not have made it inside.

So what was going on?

Ernie gave him a halfhearted smile. "It seems word of your little miracle with Freddy spread through the slums. We haven't had an honest to goddess healer down here...ever."

Tim slumped against the wall, exhaustion from working the bellows finally catching up with him. "And they're all here hoping I can help?" He looked at Ernie with pleading eyes, hoping it wasn't the case.

"I hate to break it to you, kid, but there's no putting the cork back in the bottle on this one." Ernie smiled warmly at him. "But you don't have to do anything you don't want to."

A long sigh escaped Tim's lips before he could stop it. If the cardinal found out he was healing people outside the temple, he might not get any future training. If that happened, Tim might have to go to the academy to learn magic instead. There was a lot riding on his choice.

In the end, it wasn't a hard decision.

Tim kept thinking about his answer to the question the high priest had asked him after he'd healed the boy on the temple steps. *Why wouldn't I?* He wasn't going to let those people outside suffer just to follow the rules. If they needed healing, he would heal them.

Tim glanced into the dining room and saw Gaston's crew at their customary table. "I take it these guys wouldn't want a bunch of people coming in and out of here for healing."

Ernie wrung his hands nervously. "No attention is the kind we like best." His eyes sparkled as he thought of something. "We have an old storehouse at the side of the inn. I can have it cleaned out, and you can set up shop in there."

Lowering his eyes, Ernie asked, "If you want to help, that is?"

Tim clapped the man on the shoulder. "Give me a few minutes to get cleaned up, and I'll be right down."

Fuck Jepsom!

If these people needed help, they were going to get it. He'd still have to find time to get to the temple, give the high priest Lady Briarthorn's response, and collect his reward for delivering the initial letter. Hopefully, healing the people outside wouldn't take too long. He could probably focus on the worst cases and handle the rest tomorrow.

Cool water and a rag weren't nearly as refreshing as a shower would have been. Tim wondered if they had plumbing on the north side of town. After a week of using a rag to bathe, he'd probably pay good money to have someone dump a bucket of water over his head.

Say what you wanted to about the modern world, toilets and showers really made all the difference. Tim equipped his robe and scepter and headed downstairs. Ernie was waiting for him in the lobby.

"Just follow me." Ernie shoved the front door to the inn open and led Tim around to the side of the building, where at least twenty people were lined up outside the storeroom waiting for his arrival.

"This is going to take all day," Tim mumbled. "If this many people come every day, I'm going to need an assistant."

Ernie smiled. "I'm sure we can find someone to help." He led Tim past the line of people and into the shed's single room. "But not until tomorrow."

There was a table in the center of the room, but no water or towels for him to clean the patients with. Looking at his inventory, Tim didn't have the funds to bankroll the supplies he would need to make this room acceptable. Maybe if he finished a few more quests, he'd have enough coin to pick up a few things.

Ernie watched Tim expectantly. "Should I send the first person in?"

Tim couldn't think of a reason to refuse the man. Instead, he thought about all his favorite heroes, and how they had all started from humble beginnings and triumphed not only over the enemy but over life itself.

A smile spread across his lips. "Origin story," Tim mumbled.

Holy shit, *this is my fucking origin story.*

"What was that?" Ernie asked, looking confused.

Sometimes all you needed to be happy was a change in perspective. Sure, Tim was working out of a one-room shack hammered onto the side of a dilapidated inn, but the people living in the slums needed him. If he helped them, maybe they could turn this part of the city into something more than a slum.

Maybe Tim could help build something special.

Tim waved away Ernie's confused expression. "Send the first person in, and let everyone know they can't come in until the previous patient has left."

"You got it, kid." Ernie paused in the doorway. "Thank you for this."

"I'm not the most gifted of healers, Ernie, but I'll do what I can."

His first client came through the door shortly after Ernie exited the room. She was clutching one arm to her side. If he had to wager a guess, Tim would have said it was broken. He smiled warmly at the woman, and his real work for the day began.

"This might hurt a bit." Tim pulled the woman's arm straight, then cast healing orb. The bones snapped together, and the woman fell to her knees, screaming in pain.

Tim lifted her gently, watching her eyes for any other signs of pain. "How does it feel?"

The woman tentatively extended her arm, testing the range of motion slowly. A huge grin lit her entire face as she enjoyed the results of Tim's work. "It's perfect." She pulled him into a hug. "Thank you so much."

Tim backed up, shocked by her reaction. "Send in the next person on your way out." He'd never been great at dealing with gratitude, and he didn't know what else to say.

A frown tugged at the woman's lips, and she looked at the ground as she spoke. "I don't have much to offer you."

"Whatever you have to give is fine. If you don't have anything to spare, don't worry about it." Tim smiled at her, imagining the look on Jepsom's face if he found out people were being healed for free. "If you're injured, you are always welcome here."

She pulled out a handful of copper coins, looking at them wistfully before putting them in Tim's outstretched palm. "Thank you."

Tim plucked ten of the copper coins out of the pile and handed the rest back to her. "Send in the next person."

It didn't make sense to give her the money back. He should have taken the coins. This place needed a lot of work, and if he lost access to the temple for training, he might have to purchase spellbooks in the future. Still, taking all of the woman's money hadn't felt right.

What he needed to do was find some kind of balance. If he didn't make any money in the game, he wouldn't be able to send money home. It simply wasn't worth it to work his fingers to the bone, knowing that he couldn't accomplish the one goal he set out to tackle. There had to be a way to help these people and make money. All he had to do was figure it out.

Tim smiled wearily as the next person came in, still thinking about how to manage his time. Making money here wasn't the only thing he had to worry about. He also needed to level up. He couldn't do quests and run a temple of his own.

Soon there wasn't enough time for Tim to think about his problems. He lost himself in the work, healing one person after another until he collapsed to the floor in exhaustion.

Ernie shooed the rest of his patients away, telling them to come back tomorrow.

Sitting down next to Tim, Ernie handed him a little blue vial. "This should make you feel better."

Is this my first mana potion? It kinda felt like a milestone. Tim chugged the vial's contents and handed the empty container back to Ernie. "Thank you."

Ernie stood up and held out his hand, helping Tim to his feet. "Think of it as my thanks for everything you've done today."

Tim took Ernie's outstretched hand and grunted as the man pulled him to his feet. "You know, where I come from, people thank others with food. Lots of delicious food."

"I can make that happen. When should I expect you?" Ernie held the door to the shed open.

Tim stepped outside, enjoying the smell of the misty air after being trapped in the storage shed for so long. "I've got a quest to turn in at the temple. Shouldn't take too long."

Ernie closed the shed door and locking it before replying, "I'll have my daughter Gwenny set up a pot of stew and a loaf of bread in your room."

"That sounds perfect. Thanks, Ernie."

The innkeeper waved away the compliment. "What you're doing here makes a real difference. The people won't tell you how much because they're too proud, but the first woman you helped was about to lose her job at the bakery because of that arm. Now she doesn't have anything to worry about."

"Healing these people might seem like a small thing to you, but to them, it means the world." Ernie shook his head in wonder. "You don't even have the common sense to fleece them like the temple does."

Tim winked at Ernie. "Oh, I'll come up with a way for the people to repay me. It will just happen on a much bigger scale."

"Now you're starting to sound like an evil overlord." Ernie laughed at Tim's response. "Your good guy persona is going to take a hit if you sound too much like a northsider."

Tim started trudging up the muddy road toward the main part of town. "Don't worry, Ernie. I don't want the people working for me so I can keep them under my thumb. What I have in mind won't be evil. In fact, it might just be the kind of thing that levels the playing field."

"Don't go storming the castle!" Ernie started laughing as he ducked back into the inn.

If Tim was strong enough to storm the castle, he wouldn't be delivering letters. Maybe he was looking at the situation all wrong. He had more than one quest to pursue and an entire world to explore. Sure, things could have started smoother, but he was making progress.

Rome wasn't built in a day.

CHAPTER SEVENTEEN

The temple looked creepy at night.

Blue flames replaced the normal orange glow. The black shadows and flickering blue lights made the temple feel like it was underwater. Tim ascended the steps quickly, making his way to the front door.

A brother in the standard white robes with blue trim was waiting by the door to assist any parishioners. "How may the Goddess Eternia serve you?"

Tim wondered if he should just ask to see the high priest, or if he should employ a little deception. Even if he managed to talk his way around the brother in front of him, Tim wasn't sure he could find the high priest's chambers on his own. Honesty seemed like the best way to go.

"I'm here to see the high priest." Tim met the man's inquiring look. "He's expecting me." Okay, so maybe a little deception wasn't out of the question.

The brother by the door clapped his hands, and a young boy in a simple brown smock appeared. "Take this man to the high priest's chambers." He glanced at Tim. "We will let the high priest's personal guards decide what to do with him."

The boy motioned for Tim to follow him into the temple.

As Tim walked past the brother, he noticed that the man was smirking at him. Something wasn't right here. He felt like he was walking into a trap.

All of the passages looked the same to Tim. He wouldn't be surprised if the brothers deliberately walked in circles to obscure the route to the high priest's chambers. That or the temple had been built with the winding passages as a defensive measure. Thankfully for him, his life didn't depend on the answer tonight, and his guide was doing all of the heavy lifting.

The golden door loomed ahead of him as Tim entered the high priest's antechamber. Two burly guards pushed open the door as soon as they approached. The young boy gave a squeak of shock at the sight of open doors and ran back the way they'd come. It wouldn't be long before Cardinal Jepsom heard he was here.

Tim had to get the letter into Paul's hands as fast as possible. Darting through the gap in the door, he sprinted toward the high priest's chair. Two men stepped out of the shadows and blocked his path their halberds. Paul rose from his chair, lifting a single finger into the air, and the guards faded back into the shadows.

Paul smiled as he closed the distance between them. "I believe you have something for me?"

"I do." Tim reached into his robes and pulled out the letter. He placed the sealed envelope in Paul's hand and took a respectful step back so Paul could read the letter without worry.

The high priest seemed absorbed in the letter, so Tim took a moment to check his notifications.

Quest Completed: Turning The Tables

You have successfully delivered Lady Briarthorn's letter.

The good Lady Briarthorn already paid you for the quest, but at least you don't have to worry about Reginald cutting off your fingers anymore.

The high priest looked up from his letter. "I believe I owe you something as well." Paul handed him a small coin purse and a ring with a blue stone at the center.

Tim continued looking over his rewards as the high priest returned his attention to the letter.

Quest Complete: Deliver the high priest's Letter

You have successfully delivered the high priest's letter, and earned the ire of Cardinal Jepsom.

Reward: Ten silver coins and a ring of wisdom +1

Tim equipped the ring, noting that his wisdom had increased to nineteen. He was so close to twenty and the first bonus, he could almost taste it. Just a few more quests or a couple of levels, and he'd find out what the bonus was.

Paul wasn't done reading his letter yet, so Tim checked his last notification.

Skill increase: Healing Orb

You have reached apprentice rank three. Your healing orb is now twelve percent more effective, and the healing over time effect lasts for an additional second.

Not a bad increase, but the progress Tim received for healing people had diminished greatly once he'd moved from the novice to the apprentice rank. The amount of effort needed to move up seemingly grew exponentially as he leveled. Tim didn't even want to think how much it would cost to level a skill once he reached Grandmaster rank.

Paul tucked Lady Briarthorn's letter away and handed Tim a new envelope. His eyes danced with mischief as he spoke. "I'm afraid I'm going to need your services once again."

Quest received: Deliver the high priest's letter (again)

Success: Deliver the letter to Lady Briarthorn.

Failure:???

Reward: Free level-ten class change

Paul smiled at him. "I can't stress how important this is. Not just for me, but for the Goddess Eternia. To impress upon you the importance of this matter, I offer you an additional gift."

"Will you accept my quest?" Paul extended his hand.

The reward being offered was so good he couldn't help but feeling the risk involved with the quest might be more than he wanted to take on at the moment. Sure, things had worked out well so far, but that was mostly due to blind luck and a whole lot of running. Plus, if Tim didn't take Paul's quest, he only had one other option. The quest at the inn could turn out to be interesting, but it was probably going to end up being just as dangerous.

Fuck it. What was the worst that could happen?

Tim clasped the high priest's hand. "I won't let you down, Paul."

Paul nodded solemnly before releasing Tim's hand and shuffling back to his chair.

Tim followed him, wondering if the older man might have lost his marbles. He got his answer when Paul retrieved a small chest that was hidden behind the chair.

Paul opened the chest and rummaged inside. After shaking his head several times, the high priest finally nodded in approval. Closing the chest, he rose back to his full height and turned to face Tim. "Please accept this as a token of the Goddess Eternia's gratitude." He motioned for Tim to kneel.

Tim wasn't sure if there was a proper way to kneel, so he dropped his left knee to the ground and bowed his head slightly forward. It almost felt as if he were getting knighted until he felt the cold metal brush his forehead.

"Stand and receive the lady's light," Paul intoned, holding one arm out in front him and the other across his chest.

Tim rose to his feet as a searing white light engulfed him. His body rose into the air, then, soft as a feather, his feet touched the ground.

Holy shit, I feel fucking fantastic.

That was the thought roaring through his mind, but what he said was, "What was that?"

Paul smiled. "A small blessing from the Goddess Eternia. Long may we bask in the holy righteousness of her light."

Tim had to admit that whatever had just happened was pretty awesome, but he also didn't want to join a cult. At some point, he wanted to go out and adventure. Being stuck in the temple working for someone else wasn't his calling.

"Thank you for the blessing." Tim reached up, feeling the light circlet now resting on his head. It felt wrong to take it off and examine it after Paul had put so much effort into the item's presentation. He casually touched the circlet. "And for this."

The doors to the high priest's room started to open. "You might not be thanking me very soon." Paul frowned as he looked at the man entering his chambers unannounced.

Cardinal Jepsom stormed into the chamber, his face tight with righteous anger. "I demand an audience."

Paul looked at the open doors. "It seems as though you have one, granted or not." The high priest sat down on his chair. "Explain your intrusion."

Jepsom at least had the good sense to look worried by the tone of Paul's voice. "I'm sorry, Your Eminence. I did not mean to intrude, but I wanted to catch this imposter of the faith while you were present."

The cardinal glared at Tim. "It has come to our attention that this initiate is healing the citizens of Promethia outside of the temple." Jepsom frowned. "In some cases, he isn't even accepting payment. It's preposterous."

Paul looked at the man with open disdain. "Is it not our job to bring the lady's light to those who need it? To spread her word where it is needed most?" The high priest stood from the chair, eyes burning with rage. "Maybe you've grown too comfortable inside these walls. A pilgrimage might be in order."

Jepsom fell to his knees. "Your Eminence, I only strive to follow the rules you have set for this city. To make the temple a beacon that shines throughout the world."

"And to line your pockets." Paul's voice was filled with holy fury. "It would be wrong to presume I don't know everything that happens inside these temple walls." The high priest clicked his tongue. "But it isn't my place to judge you. Eternia will handle that. I can only hope to steer you away from folly."

Rising to his feet, Jepsom stared into the high priest's eyes. "There is no folly in banishing one who cannot follow the rules." The cardinal turned toward Tim, his grin dripping with malice. "I did tell you not to heal people outside of the temple, did I not?"

The high priest seemed to be on Tim's side, so there wasn't any reason for him to lie. "You did."

Paul shook his head in disgust. "And your punishment for this young man is to excommunicate him from the temple because he defied you?"

Jepsom smile was almost nauseating. "No, Your Eminence, for defying *your* rules. An example must be made."

This back and forth could go on forever. Tim didn't have time for it. At some point, he had to sleep, or he wouldn't be able to work the bellows tomorrow. Despite what Ironbeard had said, he was determined to be at work so the dwarf would know how important the job was to him. Without his job at the forge, he wouldn't be living up to the terms of his contract.

Tim needed this game, but what he might not need to be successful was access to the temple.

An idea started to form in his mind as the two men bickered. At some point, a confrontation between these two was inevitable. Jepsom wouldn't wait much longer to seize power, not if Paul was able to get messages out of the temple. Once the cardinal was out on his ass, the high priest could probably restore his privileges.

Now wasn't the time to get caught between the two men, not if he could avoid it. Tim dropped to one knee, looking up at Paul. "I'm sorry for the trouble I've caused Your Eminence. As long as our previous contract remains intact, I will gladly forego my access to the temple."

"You will?" Jepsom stared at Tim in disbelief. The look on his face made it clear that he never would have considered giving up the temple as an option.

Paul looked unhappy but nodded his acquiescence. "The terms of our arrangement will still be honored, but you can no longer train inside these walls."

The cardinal cut Paul off before he could continue. "No more unsanctioned healing or there will be repercussions."

Waving his finger at the cardinal, a smile returned to Paul's face. "But not by us. Tim is not bound by temple law, and we will not spend resources to stop him from helping the injured."

"But, Your Eminence!" the cardinal whined.

"Enough!" Paul screamed into the man's face. The two guards hidden in the shadows moved forward. "You forget yourself, Cardinal. The Goddess Eternia makes the rules, and I give voice to them on this plane of existence."

Paul poked Jepsom in the chest hard enough to make him back up a step. "So when I tell you the boy shall not be harassed or harmed in any way, you should consider those words may not be my own, but a command from the Goddess herself."

Turning away from Jepsom, the high priest strode back to his chair and sat down. "Now, get the fuck out of my chambers."

"This isn't over," Jepsom hissed at Tim, low enough to make sure no one else could hear him.

Tim dipped his head and then looked up, meeting the man's hate-filled eyes. "Thank you for your kindness, Cardinal. I'm sorry to have disappointed you." *Sometimes I just can't stop myself from twisting the knife.*

With a flash of his robes, Cardinal Jepsom stormed from the room as dramatically as he entered them.

"You've made a powerful enemy today." Paul looked at the doors as they started to close. "But you've also made a friend." He clapped his hands. "Vigo, see that Tim makes it out of the temple unmolested."

"As you command, so it shall be done." Vigo motioned for Tim to follow him.

Paul called out from behind them, "The future of Promethia is balanced on a razor's edge. I'm counting on you to make sure we don't get cut."

Tim followed Vigo out a door at the back of the chambers. No big deal, just the fate of the whole fucking world to carry around.

But who wanted a boring quest? Sure, he was delivering letters, but he was also spreading insurrection, or helping to quash it, as the case may be. Tim didn't know what he'd been expecting when he entered *The Etheric Coast*, but it sure wasn't this. Still, the longer he played, the more interesting things got.

If his first full day in the game was this much fun, he couldn't imagine how great the next twenty years would be.

CHAPTER EIGHTEEN

There were at least three people following Tim now.

Fuck, how had he landed himself in this mess? He'd been so careful when he left the temple, sticking to the main streets, then making a detour through the market to ward off any potential followers, and yet somehow, he was still being followed.

What's the worst that could happen?

He could get stabbed to death in the alley. Not a fitting end for a hero. Maybe he wasn't a hero, or maybe he should just be thankful they weren't trying to light him on fire.

Tim's heart was racing as he ran down the cobbled streets. Where were the guards? You'd think more of them would be out at night, but the streets were deserted. He might as well have been walking through a ghost town. Even the players seemed content to call it a night when the sun set.

A bright light bathed the street in a warm glow as someone exited a tavern. The roar that followed the man outside gave Tim an idea. Darting past the confused customer, Tim pulled the door open. As he stepped inside, he un-equipped his robe and re-equipped his shirt and pants.

Stepping up to the bar, he tossed down a few coppers. "Beer!"

The bartender sloshed an earthenware mug down in front of him, then slammed a red-hot poker into the beverage. "Steamed cider is what we've got."

Tim took a sip from the mug, then a much larger swig. "Then steamed cider it is!" He took another sip before turning toward the entrance and casually scanning the crowd.

The man with the orange sash swore as his eyes darted wildly around the room. Leaning back against the bar, Tim took another sip of the cider. *This is pretty good.* He kept his eyes moving but looked back just in time to see four men shoving their way to the back of the building.

I never even saw the fourth one.

After polishing off the cider, Tim licked his lips, savoring the taste of cloves and fall spices that lingered on them. All of his pursuers were heading out the back, so he'd leave through the front. Hopefully, the distraction would be enough to get him safely to Lady Briarthorn's house.

But what would happen to him once he delivered the letter? All the man in the orange sash would have to do is wait for him to leave. He might not have the letter, but they could still take him out. How was he going to get back to the inn safely? "Probably more running," he grumbled.

At least Ernie will have food waiting for me.

Tim's stomach growled as he exited the tavern and started running back the way he'd come. After a few minutes, he turned down another street and started making a slow loop back toward the Street of Thorns. Finally, when Tim thought his legs couldn't possibly run another step, the lady's house came into view.

Tim rushed up the steps and raised his hand to pound on the door, and it swept open.

Reginald ushered him through the door quickly, closing it behind him. "Hurry up, we've been waiting for you." The manservant grabbed the sleeve of his shirt and pulled him deeper into the house.

Lady Briarthorn didn't stand up as they entered. Instead, she simply held out her hand for the letter. Tim pulled the sealed envelope from his pocket and placed it in her hand.

She scanned the contents quickly and then looked up to meet his eyes. "It seems the high priest puts a lot of faith in you." She frowned. "I, on the other hand, do not."

Lucy Briarthorn stood and walked toward the fireplace to toss the letter into the flames. "Not yet, anyway." She turned away from the fire and watched Tim like a lion hunting a gazelle. "If you want to earn my trust, I have a task that needs to be completed."

"You mean being chased through the streets to deliver this letter wasn't enough to prove my loyalty?" Tim didn't even know what the two sides were fighting about. All he knew was that he liked Paul a metric fuck-ton more than Cardinal Jepsom.

Reginald moved from his post by the door, but Lady Briarthorn waved him back with a laugh. "I can see that you aren't without charm, but I need to know if you have steel underneath that pretty exterior."

She flipped a coin at Tim. "A gift from Paul. He said not to come back for your reward just yet."

Tim looked at the coin, which had the number ten on it. Maybe he could use this at level ten and skip the whole rigmarole that normally came with a class-change quest. It would put him way in front of the other players, and it made almost dying worth it.

Quest Completed: Deliver the high priest's letter (again)

Reward: Level Ten Class-Change Token

Level Up: You've reached level four and have two stat points to distribute. No one can say that you aren't an overachiever.

Title Granted: Two for One

This title doesn't provide any bonuses, but now you can be called Two for One Tim whenever you want.

Did that mean some titles granted bonuses? It was just like this game to bury the lead behind a ton of snark. Most players probably skipped the messages entirely and missed the subtle hints. Gaining two levels also meant he had another two stat points to distribute.

Once Tim got back to the inn, he could sit down and think about where he wanted to allocate the points. For now, he just wanted to ensure he made it back safely. Maybe he should just dump both points into endurance instead of intelligence or wisdom? Being able to run farther and faster than the next guy was his bread-and-butter move right now.

The skill was especially valuable when the guy chasing you had a knife.

Tim gazed past Lady Briarthorn into the roaring flames. Was this his fight? Did he really want to be involved? That was the crux of the issue. If he took this quest from Lucy Briarthorn, he would cement himself on their side of the fight.

This was his chance to turn back. All he had to do was say no, and Tim could show up to work in the morning and just be a normal citizen until he found something else to peruse. It would delay his plans, but restoring the slums was inevitable. Having Lady Briarthorn and the high priest on his side later might make all the difference.

Plus, Jepsom was a giant dick.

The cardinal's syrupy-sick smile flashed through his mind, and the decision practically made itself. "Tell me what you need me to do."

Lady Briarthorn extended her hand toward Tim. "Tomorrow night, I have a most unpleasant task for you. A man working with Cardinal Jepsom to steal funds from the Goddess' temple is in town. We need someone to take him out."

Murder.

"You want me to kill someone?" He'd heard that same speech from the gangs back home and managed to turn it down flat, every time. You shouldn't have to kill someone to be accepted.

Lady Briarthorn turned away from him and stared into the fire. "As distasteful as it is, the job needs to be done. I've heard you travelers are quite adept at killing."

Of course, we are.

Since gamers were little kids, they'd been conditioned to kill everything in the game that awarded experience. Killing in games might as well have been hard-wired into their DNA at this point, but this wasn't your average game. Things felt real here, and Tim wasn't sure if he could cross that line.

At least not with a human.

Line up some rabbits for target practice, or a goblin or two, and he'd be all for it. Sure, it was a game, and Tim knew he'd have to kill things, including people, eventually, but not so soon. He'd always preferred to let the others do the killing in games, while he did his best to keep his party alive. Right now he was a party of one, so he'd have to man up if he wanted to continue.

Jepsom had sent men after him twice now, and one thing Tim knew from experience was if you let a bully kick the shit out of you, it emboldened them for next time. It was a fallacy that bullies got bored when you gave up since every asshole wants a dog to kick around. Tim was tired of being the dog.

Maybe it was time someone gave Cardinal Jepsom a taste of his own medicine. "Just send me the details," Tim nearly growled.

Lady Briarthorn made a motion with her hand. "Done."

Quest Received: Fleecing The Righteous

"Dapper" Don Diego is waiting aboard the Mary Lou at the docks. Sneak aboard his ship and put an end to his nefarious ways.

Bonus for any recovered items or treasure.

Success: Kill Dapper Don Diego

Failure: Fail to Kill Dapper Don, or to recover any of the stolen items.

Reward: Ten percent of the take and a new weapon.

If Jepsom was the kind of prick Tim thought he was, ten

percent of the take might be an astronomical number—just what he needed to turn his new shed into a proper place to heal patients. With enough money, he could do more than make it suitable. He might even be able to rival the temple's services.

This quest chain seemed slightly advanced for someone at his level, but the game sure knew how to throw you right into the action.

Accept the quest: <yes/no>

Tim hit the Yes button and immediately felt the weight of his decision. He was about to kill someone for money. Sure, the cause was righteous. Holy, even, but did that make it right? Maybe Tim's biggest problem was he was thinking of all the NPCs as people, and not just monsters, or objectives to be fulfilled. It was one thing when you were behind the keyboard, but seeing what looked like a living, breathing person in front of you and telling yourself it was okay to kill them took some getting used to.

However, this was a game, and in most games, you leveled by killing things. Maybe he could find somewhere to practice his flame burst spell. It might not be enough to kill someone at such a low rank, but it would make a hell of distraction, and then he could crack him over the head with his scepter.

Tim followed Reginald to the door, completely lost in his own world. This was it—his first real mission. Hadn't he just been bitching about being a glorified messenger a few hours ago? Now that he had a real job to do, Tim was worried about that too. Maybe instead of worrying, he should lose himself in the role.

He was on a secret assassination mission for the Goddess Eternia.

How fucking cool was that?

Reginald opened the door for him, and Tim stepped out into the night. The streets were clear, but that didn't mean much. He was sure his tails would find him soon enough, and then it would be down to whether he could outrun them.

CHAPTER NINETEEN

Almost there.

Tim quickened his pace as the familiar stone archway came into view. He hadn't seen a soul since leaving Lady Briarthorn's house, and getting home was starting to feel a bit too easy. At least the guards were there, but he wasn't sure they'd actually try to protect him from an attack after the guards hadn't helped him with Freddy last night.

But having witnesses might deter someone from getting to close if they were still trailing him. Tim looked at the guards' stoic faces as the torchlight danced across them. *Might as well be statues.* Still, Tim gave them a jolly salute as he walked through the arch. If the plan he was hatching worked, they might need the guards on the *other* side of the arch before too long.

The rain started as soon as he stepped into the slums. Maybe there was something they could use all this water for? If this was the only part of the city with a constant supply of fresh water, they could use it for farming, or supply it to merchants and crafters. There were plenty of ways to monetize the excess water if they just put in the effort.

Ideas ran through Tim's mind like Olympic sprinters. There was a way he could make this part of the city great again, he just knew it. The people here worked hard, and they deserved to live in better conditions. If he could find a way to make that happen and pocket some coin while doing it, everyone came out a winner.

A grin stretched across his lips as the inn came into view. It might not look like much, but Ernie was ok, and Gaston was growing on him. Replace the door, give the building a fresh coat of paint, and the place wouldn't actually be half bad.

Tim started walking up the steps but paused when a voice called from the shadows, "Excuse me, sir." A man stepped out of the murky night, dripping wet from the rain. "Are you the healer they call Tim?"

He'd almost made it inside, but in a flash like lightning, his hopes for dinner and sleep had been thwarted. "I am."

"I hate to bother you, sir." The man looked at the ground, wringing his hands with nervous energy. "But it's my mother... she's too sick to walk down here."

The man looked up, his expression stuck somewhere between anguish and hope. "Do you think... I mean, would you consider... coming to our home?"

There was no way Tim could make a habit out of this, but if he was truly interested in healing these people and building this neighborhood up, he'd have to make the occasional house call. Plus, the man had a point. The sickest among them, or the most grievously injured, wouldn't be able to make it to his healing shed.

"What's your name?" Tim asked, reaching out and clasping the man's shoulder.

"Marvin, Marvin Tanner, sir."

Tim smiled at the man, hoping to ease his nerves. "I'm going to come with you, Marvin, but I want you to keep this between us for now." He held the man's gaze. "Can you do that for me?"

"Yes, of course. Whatever you need." He looked around as if

maybe Tim were playing some kind of joke on him. "Are you really coming?" He waited, mouth hanging open, eyes almost frantic.

"Lead the way."

Marvin let out a whoop of joy. "Thank you so much. This means the world to me."

Tim smiled at the man's back as he started walking down one of the side streets. "I'm more than happy to help." He thought briefly about what he'd said to the man moments before and decided to clarify. "Marvin, if someone really needs my help, it's ok to tell them to find me at the inn."

"Just tell whoever you send to take it easy on me. I'm new to the area and still trying to find my footing." It wasn't going to take much longer for him to relax. This side of town and The Blue Dagger Inn were already starting to feel like home.

Marvin glanced over his shoulder, his eyes filled with sadness. "Aren't we all?" He kept trudging down the muddy road. "Trying to find our footing, that is."

It was funny if Tim really thought about it. He'd felt the exact same way in the real world, always wondering what was coming next. Your whole young life was set up that way. You had to get to high school so you could get to college so you could get a job so you could buy more stuff. There was never any secure footing. In the real world, you were always racing to the next thing.

Despite only being in the game for a few days, things felt different here. Tim thought he knew exactly who he was and what he wanted to accomplish. He wasn't sure how he was going to get there, but he had time to figure it all out. Maybe his half-elven princess would have an idea or two about how he should proceed.

He'd been so busy today he hadn't even thought about checking his messages. How could he not have looked to see if Sierra had messaged him? She was the reason he was here, or at least, one of the reasons. Tim pulled up his user interface as he followed Marvin down the street.

No new messages were waiting for him, so he typed up a quick message to his girl.

This game's intense, huh? With work and the early quests, it's easy to lose track of time. Let's catch a drink sometime this week.

It wasn't his best work, and it definitely wasn't poetry, but the message didn't come off as sounding needy, which was a bonus. He wanted to be with Sierra, but he didn't want to smother her. They were both going to be searching for their own ways to conquer the game for a bit, but when they got together, the world better watch out.

With the message sent, all Tim could do was wait for a reply. He shut down his user interface and continued to follow Marvin deeper into the slums. Maybe his next purchase should be some kind of waterproof cloak. It only seemed to rain in the slums, but this is where he lived, so buying a cloak seemed like a prudent investment.

The streets grew even darker as the torches along the sides of the road grew farther and farther apart. There were more shadows than light on the street. Tim hadn't expected that the city could get much worse, but he'd been wrong. The people down here were living in what amounted to thatched huts.

Marvin stopped in front of a dilapidated one-story house. He opened the door and paused in the entryway to light a candle. Motioning for Tim to follow him inside, Marvin moved out of the doorway. "Mom's in the bedroom."

Water dripped from his damp hair, and Marvin's smile almost seemed like more of a leer in the flickering candlelight. "Thank you so much for doing this."

Tim smiled as he closed the door behind him. "It's no problem. I'm happy to help."

Turning away from Tim, Marvin led them deeper into the house. There was a closed door ahead, and candlelight flickered underneath the threshold. Marvin moved toward the door and knocked gently.

"Mother, we're here."

Tim couldn't make out the response, but Marvin must have heard something because he slowly opened the door. Moving into the room, he filled a glass of water by the bedside table, then made his way to the other side of the bed so Tim would have room to work.

This isn't going to take long, and then I can finally get some food and a nap before work.

"Ma'am, I'm just going to pull the blanket back. It helps if I can see the wound." Tim inched toward the bed and wrapped his fingers delicately around the blanket.

Tim pulled the blanket away, noticing a flash of orange before the pain blossomed in his chest. He couldn't breathe. What in the fuck was happening? Looking down, Tim was surprised to see the hilt of a dagger sticking out of his chest like he was starring in a horror movie.

But this wasn't a movie.

Tim stumbled away from the bed, trying to cast healing orb.

Marvin grabbed his arms from behind. "We can't have any of that." He laughed.

The man with an orange sash around his waist climbed from the bed, his bald, sweaty head shimmering in the light. Tim's eyes moved toward his sparkling golden earring as the man leaned over him.

Baldy placed one hand on Tim's chest and wrapped the fingers of his other hand around the grip of the dagger. Tim wanted to scream, he wanted to cry out, but all he could manage was a weak trickle of bloody spit.

"Fuck you!" Tim felt his lips moving, but no sound came out. He was too weak to stop what was about to happen. How could it end like this? He was just getting started!

"Not so smart now, are you, boy?" the man with the orange

sash gloated. "Death comes for us all, some sooner than others." He pulled the dagger free with a wet, sucking sound.

The man wiped the blade off on his robe before tucking it behind his back. Marvin let his arms go, and Tim collapsed to the floor. He couldn't speak, he couldn't move. The world started growing dimmer around him, then everything went black.

So this is what it feels like to die...

CHAPTER TWENTY

"Please take a number and find an open seat," a female voice cooed from the overhead speakers.

Speakers?

Where the hell was he?

Tim had just been in a house trying to help a sick woman. Tim's hands shot to his chest, patting every inch of it as he looked down to confirm what he was feeling. His chest was fine. There wasn't even any blood on his t-shirt.

But the man with the orange sash? It had seemed so real.

The Etheric Coast is a game, he reminded himself, and yet he couldn't stop looking down at his chest. *Fuck it.* He wouldn't feel right until he checked. Tim lifted his shirt and looked down at his bare chest. No ragged hole where a dagger used to be, so everything was fine.

Moving toward the little red dispenser, Tim took a number and found an empty seat against the wall. The entire room was empty. Hopefully, this wouldn't take too long. If he was going to lose two full days' worth of experience, he needed to get back into the game as quickly as possible. The ticket in his hand informed him that he was number one hundred and seventy-three.

A chime sounded, and the same female voice spoke. "Now calling number one."

Tim looked around the empty lobby. *This is going to take forever, and there isn't even anyone else here.* He started scanning the tables for a magazine, or anything that would help him occupy the time.

A door opened somewhere to his right, and a woman stepped out. She was wearing a black business suit, cut to fit her like she knew the tailor personally. "Just screwing with you."

She held out her hand. "I'm Barbara, your NPC Corp case-worker. If you're here," she opened her arms to encompass the entire lobby, "it means you have a little problem with dying."

Barbara turned away from him, opening the door behind her. "Why don't we head to my office and chat about it."

Tim started to follow her, then stopped. "Wait, are we still in the game?"

Barbara looked over her shoulder. "You're still plugged in if that's what you mean." She stopped at the third door on the left. "This is where players come when they die, or every now and then for a psychological checkup."

She lowered her voice. "Gotta make sure you don't crack."

After his recent brush with death, Tim knew exactly what she meant. It wasn't just that dying in the game could make you crack. It was that the whole experience felt so real. It would be easy to lose yourself in the game. Imagine building a fortune and watching it crumble; people killed themselves over things like that. Tim felt a million times better knowing the company was keeping an eye on their mental well-being.

Even if it was just to save their own asses.

Barbara stepped into the office, her voice drifting behind her. "You'll get used to your little visits here, although I've heard it can be quite a shock after being in the game for a while."

Tim entered her office and closed the door behind him. He

took a seat on the opposite side of the desk from Barbara, feeling almost like he was back in Lady Briarthorn's study. Looking up, Tim met her eyes. "So, what do we do now?"

Barbara's fingers tapped the desk as she watched Tim. "This is where I prepare you to roll a new character."

Tim flinched as if he'd been slapped. He had known it was a possibility, but it seemed so unfair. He didn't die in combat, so maybe there was some wiggle room. "Are there any other possibilities?"

"Humm, they told me to expect this, but they didn't say you'd be so darn cute when you asked about it." Barbara turned to her laptop and started typing. She tapped her finger on the screen. "It seems like it's your lucky day."

Tim's heart rate started to climb. This had to be good news, but he'd fallen victim to more than one game developer's broken promises. "I like the sound of that." He leaned forward in his chair, hoping for the best.

"Because you're under level five," Barbara snorted, clearly not impressed by how Tim had been spending his time in the game, "I can offer you the chance to be resurrected whole."

Tim started to grin as he leaned back in the chair. Being resurrected with all of his skills and items was more than he could have hoped for. "Can I ask you a question, Barbara?"

"You just did." She sat back in her seat, trying to suppress a giggle. "Sorry, I couldn't help myself. It was something one of my old teachers used to say."

She tapped the screen of her laptop a few times and turned back to Tim. "You can ask me anything you want. I'm your case-worker, after all. If you can't ask me questions, who else can you talk to? "

Turning away from her screen, Barbara refocused her attention on Tim. "What's on your mind?"

"When I die, normally I'd lose all my stuff, right?"

Barbara looked bored. "Yes."

"And this is the same for every player?" Tim's mind was already starting to ponder a way he could make money off the problem before she answered.

"Yes, unless they've reached level ten and become an adventurer." Barbara watched him with an appraising eye. "Or they manage to die before level five, like you."

Maybe there was a way he could start a bank using passwords so people working for NPC Corp could retain some of their wealth if they died. Tim was coming to the realization that it was pretty easy to bite the big one in *The Etheric Coast*. All he had done was deliver a few letters, and the NPCs had taken the time to lure him into an ambush and kill him.

Tim would have to be much more careful in the future. He'd also have to reexamine his philosophy on in-home visits, at least until he could protect himself, or hire someone else to do the protecting. Until then, all healing would have to take place in his shed. If you couldn't' walk there, you couldn't be saved.

Not a very classy motto, but one he'd have to live by for now.

Tim would also have to deal with the men who had killed him. There was no way he could let that slide. The man in the orange sash and Marvin had to be dealt with, but he needed a few more skills before he could think about putting them in the ground.

Still, Tim wouldn't feel safe until the two men had been dealt with. There was no way he could go to work every day and come home to heal people at night, knowing those two men were out there.

And how could he revitalize the slums if he couldn't even keep himself safe?

He'd find a way. This defeat was exactly what he needed to push himself harder.

Barbara was looking at him with an expression that told him she'd been talking for some time, and she knew he'd been completely tuning her out while his imagination ran wild.

Tim looked down at the floor. "I'm sorry, can you say that again?"

"I asked if you are ready to head back into the game now." Barbara looked at him expectantly, as if hoping for more than the slack-jawed expression she'd been greeted with last time she'd asked the same question.

Tim felt antsy; there was so much to do back in the game. Barbara shouldn't have had to ask him more than once. "I'm ready."

Barbara tapped a button on her desk, and the door to her office opened. "Try not to die again. As pleasant as this meeting was, I don't want to do it again soon."

Tim stood up and looked at the doorway. A black vortex of energy pulsed and thrummed where the hallway used to be. *What's with this game and doors?* He paused in the entrance to look down at his uninjured body. What he should have asked Barbara was if his resurrection was going to hurt.

"Only one way to find out," he whispered.

Tim locked eyes with the woman and jumped backward into the portal. *"Geronimo!"*

CHAPTER TWENTY-ONE

The cobbles under Tim's felt like a bouncy castle.

The sensation faded quickly, but now he knew why the other guy had thrown up. Five more seconds of that, and he would have been down on his knees, dry-heaving in the courtyard. Shit, he'd never die again, just to avoid the sensation of coming back.

Sure, it was cool jumping from Barbara's office right back into *The Etheric Coast*, but the hangover wasn't worth it. Tim remembered his first day in the game and decided to take his first steps slowly. He wobbled on shaky legs like a newborn calf, but then found solid footing.

Maybe this will help. Tim quickly cast cleanse on himself, followed by healing orb. Surprisingly, the cleanse took away the worst of his symptoms. If cleanse worked as well on real hangovers as it did on digital ones, he could probably make a fortune at the more popular drinking establishments.

Tim thought about the sales pitch for his new wonder cure. Imagine being able to get drunk and rowdy with the boys, only to walk outside and become instantly sober, so the old lady would be none the wiser. Or maybe your man didn't like it when you took a little nip when he was at work? No problem, Tim had a cure for that. Have a dungeon to take down, but spent too many of the wee hours trying to outdrink a centaur?

"Tim's got a cure for that too!" He chanted like a late-night car salesman on local tv.

A smile spread across his face as he pulled up his user interface. He was still level four, and all of his skills were intact. Even his coins were there. He wondered if the game just took his loot back from the NPCs. Tim's smile turned into a grin as he imagined the man in the orange sash trying to pay for a drink and realizing all his money was gone.

"It's like it never happened."

Tim closed his user interface and started walking out of the New Player Courtyard. He paused in the archway to watch the street for a moment, soaking in the warmth of the sun's rays. A woman walking by stopped across from him and stared at him with wide eyes like he was taking a dump on the street. It looked as if she was torn between running away and calling for help.

Tim spun around looking behind him, expecting the man in the orange sash to coming for him again, dagger in hand, but there was no one there. Looking down, he realized the front of his robe was covered in blood. It must have looked like he'd just been stabbed, or worse yet, that he'd murdered someone else.

The guards on this side of town might be more inclined to take an interest in my bloody clothes.

Tim quickly replaced the robes with the shirt and pants in his inventory. He wondered if the stains would come out of his robes if he re-equipped them, but now wasn't the right time to find out. Hopefully, the inventory swap would also get rid of the hole over his heart. Otherwise, he was going to need a new set of robes, regardless of whether the blood came out.

Screw it; he could afford a basic robe if he needed one. Tim walked out of the starting area and began making his way to the slums when his alarm went off. What the fuck? Wait, it was sunny out, but that alarm couldn't mean what he thought it did. A quick check of his user interface confirmed the worst.

He was late for work.

Tim took off at a sprint. His job at the smithy was the one thing he had going for him. He couldn't screw that up. Tim needed the job. It came with the perks of a salary and a place to sleep. He couldn't imagine spending the next twenty years panhandling.

The merchant stalls and buildings looked blurred as Tim raced through the streets. Tim's lungs were heaving uncontrollably by the time he skidded to a stop outside Ironbeard's shop. Hands on his knees, he sucked in air like a fish gasping its final breaths out of water. Black dots swam across his vision, but he didn't pass out.

Ironbeard's voice rang out as soon as he crossed the threshold to the shop. "You're late." The dwarf came around the corner carrying a red-hot sword in his hands. "And you look like shit."

Tim couldn't disagree. It'd been a hell of a night. He met the dwarf's hardened gaze. "Sorry." Not much of an apology, but it was all he could think of at the moment.

Shaking his head, Ironbeard chuckled. "I didn't expect you in today, but when you come to work, you have to be on time. Since I already have help in the back, you'll be working the counter."

Marching up to the counter, Ironbeard pulled out two giant sacks. One of them was filled with silver coins, and the other bag had copper coins spilling from the top. The dwarf set the bags down and watched Tim intently. "I'll give you the same speech I give everyone. I know how many coins are in the sacks, so don't get any ideas."

"I'm not sure I'm qualified to sell your wares." Tim looked at the items in the shop. He had no idea how to use most of them, let alone how much they were worth.

Ironbeard chuckled. "By the Builder, boy. I didn't know you had a sense of humor." He slapped his thigh, laughing in earnest. "Running my shop... I can't believe it."

A few moments later, the rumbling laughter stopped, and Ironbeard met Tim's confused look. "The coins are for quest rewards."

What was Ironbeard talking about? He offered people quests? How had he not know about this?

"The copper coins are for goblin rings since they're iron. And the silver coins are for orc jewelry, which is normally made out of silver or gold. Inspect the items, make the proper payouts, and put the items in the barrels."

Ironbeard watched Tim for any sign that he understood the instructions. "Can you handle that, or do you want to work the bellows again?"

Tim looked at the bellows and shuddered. "I can handle it." Walking over to the barrels, he peered inside. Both containers were about half-full of various rings, earrings, and nose studs. Many of them still had flesh attached, and all of them were covered in blood from when the players ripped them off the monsters' corpses.

Tim grimaced. "Who has to clean these?"

"I told you I'd be putting you to work later." The dwarf peered at Tim, laughter dancing in his eyes. "Next time, don't be late."

I should have taken the day off.

Picking earlobes and nose cartilage off of the rings and washing bloody jewelry wasn't a very appealing activity, but it was his job for now. "How much do I pay out?"

Ironbeard grinned, feeling like his apprentice was finally catching on. "Twenty-five copper for ten pieces of iron jewelry, and ten silver for a mixture of silver and gold from the orcs." The dwarf paused, stroking his beard in thought. "Make sure each group of ten orc rings includes at least one gold band."

The burly dwarf rubbed his hands together in anticipation of all the new metal he'd have to work with. "I pay more than the other merchants, so there should be plenty of takers." Ironbeard looked at the barrels and the coins and back at Tim.

"Don't look so worried. Everything will be fine," Tim smiled reassuringly at the Ironbeard's frowning face. "I have a degree in finance."

"Ah, so somebody told you that you were smart once." The blacksmith spat on the ground. "Good for you. Might as well be a piece of toilet paper for all the good it's doing you here."

Tim froze, eyes locking with Ironbeard's steel-gray irises. "Wait, there's toilet paper in Promethia?"

"Yeah." He looked at Tim as if he was as smart as a box of rocks. "How else do you wipe your ass?" Ironbeard shook his head. "Don't tell me you're still using leaves."

Heat crept into Tim's cheeks. "Let's not talk about it." Why in the fuck did he not have toilet paper? Ernie was going to have some serious explaining to do.

Trying to sound more confident than he felt, Tim turned and laid his hands on the counter. "I'll be fine up here by myself. Seriously, you don't have to worry."

"Says the guy wiping his ass with leaves." Ironbeard shook his head in disbelief. "Don't make me come up here. I've got other work I need to do today." He paused. "But if you really need me, I'll be in the back."

Not a ringing endorsement, but at least the dwarf finally left him alone. Now he could get started removing the orc bits from the rings they'd already collected. Since he'd end up cleaning all of the items, he might as well get ahead while he had some downtime.

Tim dumped the barrels out onto the floor. The smell coming off of the rotting flesh was enough to make him retch. It was a good thing he hadn't eaten since yesterday, or he might have made things worse. Nothing said fun like cleaning rings covered in blood, puke, and fleshy bits.

Picking up a nose ring, Tim ripped the cartilage off and wiped the ring down with a rag before tossing it back in the barrel. Then inspiration struck. *What if I can put the rings in my inventory, and they came out clean just like my robes with the mud?* If nothing else, it was worth a try.

Tim picked up another disgusting ring. Pulling up his user interface, he put the ring in his inventory, then pulled it out again. Resting in his hand was one blood- and cartilage-free ring.

This was going to make things a whole lot easier.

Now that Tim had a way to easily clean the rings, he was running into another problem. He only had two barrels, but three kinds of metal. It was an easy enough fix. All he had to do was track down another giant barrel. Looking around, he spotted an empty crate at the side of the room.

Tim grabbed it. This would be fine since there is a lot less gold to deal with. He carried the crate over and set it down next to the two barrels, then looked around for something to write on the crate with, and spotted a bit of charcoal. With penmanship of a surly third-grader, Tim scribbled the word Gold on the side of the crate.

With all the receptacles Tim needed in place, he started sorting through the silver and gold rings. It was easy to see the gold were vastly outnumbered by the silver. No wonder Ironbeard wanted to make sure he received at least one golden ring with the silver ones the players turned in.

Gold must be harder to come by, or maybe it's from some kind of elite orc. If Ironbeard needed more gold, maybe he should offer a separate quest just for the gold rings. The surly bugger might have to pay out a little more, but he'd come out on top in the end.

He wondered how much all of it was worth. The loot was probably worth more once the blacksmith melted it down to make something more useful out of it.

Looking up, Tim saw his first customer approaching the counter. "How can I help you?"

The player slapped his bloody hand down on the counter, splattering the surface with bits of blood and dark goo. When he pulled his hand away, there were ten iron rings on the counter. One of the rings still had an entire ear attached to it.

I'm not cleaning that shit up.

If Ironbeard was paying more than the other merchants, then he deserved better than rings covered in bloody bits. Reaching out, Tim pushed the rings back toward the player. "We're only accepting cleaned rings from now on."

The player sneered at Tim. "Fuck that! I want the same deal I got yesterday." He pushed the bloody pile back across the counter.

Tim shrugged as if he could care less. He wasn't going to tell this asshole the trick about putting the rings in his inventory. Let the bastard work for it. "It's fine. I just can't pay you the entire amount if the rings are dirty. I can offer you twenty copper, or you're free to find another smithy that will take them."

The player's face turned beet-red. "This is outrageous! You're trying to fleece me."

Tim smiled. "It's the same payout as long as you bring in the rings cleaned." He pushed the bloody rings back across the counter. "Or you can accept the reduced price."

Ironbeard hadn't told him it was okay to make changes to the terms, but if Tim was going to run the quests rewards, he was going to do it his way.

"I'm already here. Just fucking take the things." The player tapped the counter and then held out his gore-covered palm. "My money."

Reaching under the counter, Tim plucked twenty-five copper coins free. He placed five of them next to the sack and the other twenty in the player's hand. "Pleasure doing business with you."

"Whatever." The player stormed off.

"Another satisfied customer." Tim chuckled. He'd have to do a better job in the future. Ironbeard wouldn't like it if all of the players went to another smithy. Sure, the guy was a dick, but Tim's only job was to pay the coin for the rings. If he wanted to make things easier on himself, he had to tread carefully.

One thing that would make life easier was if I could put the whole pile of rings in my inventory at once.

"That just might work," Tim mumbled. He placed his hand over the rings. With a thought, he added the pile to his inventory, then put them back on the counter with another thought. All of them were clean.

Tim dumped the iron rings into the barrel and then got to work cleaning and sorting the rest of his gruesome pile on the floor. It didn't take long for him to get all of the rings cleaned and sorted. It was too bad he couldn't put the floor and counter in his inventory to clean them. Instead, he'd have to do it the old fashioned way.

Tim found a bucket and a brush and got to work on the counter. No one wanted to walk into the blacksmith's shop and look at a bloody counter.

It wasn't a butcher's shop, for fuck's sake.

When the countertop was blood-free, Tim moved to the floor. Ten minutes later, nobody would have been able to tell the floor had been covered in rotting goblin ears and nose cartilage.

The next player entered the shop and approached the counter as Tim put away the bucket and brush. "How can I help you?" he asked, turning around to face the man.

A radiant smile ignited on the player's face. He raised a hand full of grizzly trophies and got ready to slam them down on the clean counter.

Did people enjoy making the largest mess possible when they knew they'd wouldn't have to clean it up?

Tim held his hand over the counter, stopping the player from making more work for him. "We only accept the rings once they've been cleaned."

The player's face filled with righteous fury. "Fuck that."

Tim sighed. It was going to be a long day.

But once he trained the players, he would never have to deal with the issue again. Before the player could storm off, Tim grabbed one of the grizzly rings. "All you have to do is put the rings in your inventory and take them back out again." He demonstrated with the ring he'd just taken, then dropped it back into the player's hand.

The player looked at the clean ring in his hand. "Are you serious?"

Tim smiled. "Works on clothes, too."

The rings vanished and then reappeared in the player's hand, completely clean. "Far out." He set the rings on the table.

Reaching under the counter, Tim took out ten silver pieces and dropped them in the player's waiting palm. "Don't forget, this quest is repeatable. We'll buy as many rings as you can get."

The player looked at his hand, and the coins disappeared. He flashed a grin. "Thanks for the pro tip, bro. I'll be back for sure."

Tim waved as he left, then tossed the eight silver rings into the barrel and the two golden hoops into the crate. This wasn't going to be so bad, if the last player's reaction was anything to go by. It seemed not everyone knew about his handy little inventory trick.

Another day or two of this, and he wouldn't even have to explain things. Players would just turn in the rings free of filth.

Whose degree was worth toilet paper now, bitch?

CHAPTER TWENTY-TWO

"Time to clean those rings, boy," Ironbeard called as he stripped out of his thick leather apron.

"Already done." Tim pointed at the two barrels and his crate. Showing a little initiative with the rings might just be the kind of thing that softened the dwarf up to listening to his new idea. "Have you ever considered offering an additional quest just for gold rings?"

Ironbeard stopped in his tracks. "One thing at a time, lad. Did you say you cleaned all the rings already?" He looked around the shop for a giant mess but couldn't find anything out of place.

The dwarf approached the barrels and peeked over the rims. "Well, I'll be." Ironbeard turned to face Tim. He stared at him for a moment, tugging his beard in thought. It was the kind of well-practiced gesture the dwarf probably didn't even realize he was making.

"How?" The smith watched Tim intently. "I won't have any kind of dark magic in my shop."

Dark magic? It shouldn't surprise Tim that the game would have dark magic. There had to be villains, right? What *did* surprise him was that the use of such magic was so widely feared it could cost him his job.

If there was a Goddess of Light, there might also be one of darkness.

Tim smiled and leaned close to the dwarf as if he were going to tell him a juicy bit of gossip. Ironbeard's eyes grew bigger as he waited for the hook Tim had set. "I got the players to do it."

Ironbeard burst into laughter. "You sneaky son of a bitch! This is fantastic. Cuts the work in half." His smile turned into a frown. "How many clients did I lose with this new policy of yours?"

Reaching down, Tim pulled a small sack of coins from his purse. "None yet, but a few accepted my offer of a reduced rate for the dirty rings."

Tim dropped the small sack of coins into Ironbeard's hand. "Here's fifty copper and ten silver. You'll find that amount matches what's in the barrels and missing from the coins you provided."

It was hard not to feel good about the work he'd done today. Most of the players had been receptive. One or two might not come back, but that was a small price to pay for not having to clean the rings himself. As long as Ironbeard kept paying above the going rate, they'd be the first stop for any player with half a brain.

The dwarf moved to place his hands against each of the barrels, then picked up the two sacks of coins he'd given Tim that morning. His face scrunched as if he was working on a complicated math problem, then he grinned. "Everything seems to be in order."

Ironbeard pulled two silver coins from the pouch and gave them to Tim. "Only seems fair."

"Thank you." Tim pocketed the coins before the dwarf could change his mind. Strictly speaking, Ironbeard didn't have to pay Tim a dime. NPC Corp was taking care of his salary, room, and board in return for his labor.

The dwarf stashed the coin bags in his vest. "Now, you were saying something about offering a quest for just the gold rings. Do you really think players would go for it?"

Tim nodded. "I'm guessing the gold comes from some kind of elite orc. If the reward is good enough, players will group together to cash in. Plus, they'd get a decent payout for any iron or silver pieces they collected along the way."

Pacing back and forth, Tim tapped one finger on his chin. "Of course, it only makes sense if you can make use of the extra gold."

Ironbeard slapped Tim's shoulder. "One can always use more gold, boy!" Tugging his beard again, the dwarf looked at the barrels and the much smaller crate. "But the deal has to make financial sense."

Stepping to the counter, he pulled out a small book and started writing in it. Then he turned to Tim. "What if we did the same payout for the iron, but cut the silver payout to eight coins? I'll offer one gold piece for ten of the gold orc bands."

Tim thought about the adjustments and saw one glaring problem. "Can I suggest one change?"

The dwarf guffawed. "Don't hold back on me now, boy."

"Instead of lowering the payout for the silver rings, why don't we increase the number of rings needed? Say, twelve rings for ten silver." Tim grinned. "No one wants to earn less money, not if it just means looting a couple additional rings."

"All right. I'm adjusting the quests now." Ironbeard extended his hand toward Tim. "Keep making adjustments like this, and I'm going to have to teach you something."

Tim beamed at the dwarf as he clasped his hand. "Keep making those threats, and I might be tempted to learn."

Ironbeard slapped his thigh as he rumbled with laughter. "Get out of here. I'll be seeing you early enough tomorrow."

Giving his workspace one last glance to make sure nothing was out of place, Tim headed for the door. "See you tomorrow."

The sun hit Tim's eyes as he stepped out into the street, and the elated feeling he'd had moments before came crashing back down. Now that work was done, he was going to have to deal with the fact that two men had killed him, and he had to get ready for an assassination of his own.

It was going to be a busy night.

The first thing he needed to do was go to guards for help. They should take a murder in the city seriously enough. Where the crime occurred shouldn't be a factor—all of Promethia's citizens should be treated equally. Once the guards handled the matter, all he'd have to do was worry about was Lady Briarthorn's quest.

Not that her quest wasn't a problem.

Before he could worry too much about tonight's quest and how he'd handle his first attempt at combat, Tim had to figure out how to use his flame burst spell. He couldn't expect to sneak onto a ship full of people and take them all out using his scepter as a club. Clubbing people over the head until they died wasn't exactly stealthy.

Tim strolled through the market before heading back to the slums. Using the market to shake any unwanted followers was becoming a habit. At least this time, he didn't have to spill the merchants' wares all over the street to get away. Chances were he wasn't being followed. No one should be looking for him, since as far as Jepsom knew, Tim was dead.

Being dead came with the gift of anonymity, but that wouldn't last long. As soon as Tim held his next healing-shed session, Jepsom would hear about it. Then he'd have to be on his toes all the time. What he really needed was a group, or at least a half-elven warrior princess. He was pretty confident that with Sierra by his side, they could conquer anything.

The familiar arch leading to the slums came into view, and the same two guards were stationed on either side of the entrance. He looked at the men's metal breastplates and hardened leather greaves. Each of them carried a halberd, and also had a bastard sword strapped to his waist.

If these men were also hardened soldiers, they would be formidable foes in battle—just the kind of people Tim wanted to track down the asshole who had stabbed him. The man with the orange sash had to pay for what he had done, and Marvin needed to go down with him. *I mean, even in the gameworld, murdering people in the city had to be bad, right?*

Tim knew some games featured PvP as a primary source of combat or even just a fun diversion, but player versus player was different. He'd been murdered by an NPC in cold blood. It hadn't been a monster. He hadn't even left the city to go hunting yet. Players were out there passing him and making fat stacks, while he was getting murdered and falling farther behind the curve.

Just because he wanted something to be true, it didn't mean it was going to be. Maybe the guards were the game's way of making sure crime didn't take place openly in the streets. That kind of thing might be bad for PR. All citizens should be reminded that if you wanted to kill someone, do it indoors.

Trying to shake the cynicism from his thoughts, Tim focused on the guards. He might as well take the time to inspect them. Who knows, maybe under their names it would say, fuck off gamers, we've got better things to do.

With a thought, he inspected the two men.

City Guard: Barry, level twenty-five.

City Guard: Chris, level Twenty-five.

Yep, they could both flatten me in a heartbeat. Just the kind of help I need to make sure those bastards pay.

Tim slapped a hand against his forehead. He should have inspected Marvin last night. Maybe the inspection would have revealed something about the man that would have stopped Tim from following him into a trap. So far, his inspections hadn't revealed much, but Tim expected Marvin's would have said Sneaky Little Shit if his perception had been high enough.

He could still hear the fucker laughing.

Anger bubbled up inside him like a tar pit erupting from the earth. His hate wasn't bright and sharp, it was dull and full of darkness. Killing these men wouldn't be enough; he wanted them to suffer. They had to pay for what they had done, for making him feel the way he felt right now.

Weak.

Tim never wanted to feel that way again, and it wasn't right that he should have to. Who expected to be lured into a building to get murdered? It didn't happen to normal people where he was from, at least not on the regular. He'd thought he was safe in the slums, where the people cared about him, but instead, his assassins had used his willingness to help others against him.

It was going to be their turn to deal with the repercussions of their actions. Tim stopped in front of the guards. "Howdy, gentleman."

Chris's head turned toward him, but his body stayed firmly at attention. "Move along."

Barry smiled, taking one hand off his halberd to make a little shooing gesture.

Never one to be detoured by failing on his first try, Tim continued, "I'd like to report a crime."

"A fashion crime?" Barry chirped.

Chris smiled. "That's what happens when your closet is the city's rubbish pile."

The two men clinked their halberds together and had a good chuckle, probably thinking about how all their guard buddies would laugh along with them over pints at the tavern after work. It was always a letdown when the people you thought were there to protect and help you didn't come through for you.

Sometimes the world outside the game felt the exact same way. When their house off campus had been robbed, it had taken the cops over three hours to show up. The cops didn't even take fingerprints or pictures, they just handed him a statement for his insurance and a card to use if he had to add any other items to the list of stolen property.

What a fucking letdown. It's a wonder they ever catch anyone who doesn't turn themselves in.

Tim wasn't done trying, but he wanted to handle things the right way. Vigilante justice was all fine and good in the movies, but in real life, you had to let the cops handle things, or you went to jail too. If the city guards would help him, he was more than content to let the two men mete out justice as they saw fit.

Chris grinned at Barry. "Well, he didn't go away, so I guess he's going to tell us what's on his mind."

Barry smiled back. "I'm sure he has a fantastical tale."

Tim tried to keep his anger at bay. If the two men weren't being such colossal dicks to him, he probably would have been laughing at their antics. "Not too fantastic, just a murder to report."

Barry grinned. "Ohhhh, a murder."

Chris winked at Tim. "Probably just a bit of theater. Street trash trying to make a few coins." He waved away Tim's concerns as if they were of no importance. "You'd think with ingenuity like that, they'd be able to fix the damn streets."

Tim growled in frustration. "They stabbed him." He reached out to tap Barry's chest plate. "Right in the heart."

Barry took a scrap of cloth out his pocket and wiped away the smudge Tim's finger had left on his breastplate. "And you were there when this happened?"

"I was the one who got fucking stabbed." Oh, no. He'd done it. As soon as he told the guards it was him, their eyes rolled.

Chris looked at Barry, and they both broke out in peals of laughter. "But you're not dead, boy. You're right-fucking-here."

Barry grabbed Tim's arm. "Certainly not a ghost."

"I can prove it to you." Tim reached into his inventory and pulled out his bloody robes. He held out the garment so the men could see it. "They are covered in my blood."

"Blood?" the men asked together.

Tim turned the robes around, and they were clean. This was the one time putting something in his inventory had totally fucked him. At least the hole was gone, and he didn't need new robes. But how the hell was he going to convince the guards to help him?

Right now, they probably thought he needed to be locked up in the looney bin.

"Maybe one of you could come with me to where it happened?" Tim shoved the robes back into his inventory as he pled his case.

"Listen, kid, we enjoy a good gag, but now you're just wasting our time." Barry looked him right in the eyes. "I don't want to have to arrest you for disturbing the peace."

"Move along," Chris intoned.

Motherfucker!

He looked at the two men with despair gripping his heart. How could someone be considered dead if they were up and walking around without a mark on them? Tim understood the guard's point, but shouldn't there be something they could do? If not, then NPCs could just go around killing players without repercussions.

While he understood how it looked from their point of view, he was still pissed because they were being huge flaming assholes about it. He wished the curse of a thousand fiery chicken wings on them.

May their asses burn twice as badly as their mouths did.

He made the sign of the goddess over his heart and walked through the archway to the slums, leaving the two men behind him. A gentle mist started to fall. As much as he loved the rain, the mist stoked his anger. How was he going to get to the bottom of this without help?

Lady Briarthorn wasn't an option until he had earned her trust. He'd never make it back inside the temple to speak with Paul, not with Jepsom on the lookout for him. The guards would rather snicker and make fun of him because he couldn't prove that a crime had been committed.

A knife to the chest fucking hurt. He wasn't willing to just let it go.

So that left him with Sierra and the men back at the inn. Ernie seemed like he had contacts, and Gaston knew his way around a knife. Maybe the two men could help put his mind at ease. Or even better, take care of the problem for him.

Arriving at the front door of the inn made him feel a little better. At least inside these four walls, he knew exactly what to expect.

CHAPTER TWENTY-THREE

"Oh, good, you're here," Ernie came around the counter to greet him.

"I've got some ideas for the healing shed." The innkeeper started speaking again but stopped abruptly at the forlorn look on Tim's face. Ernie put an arm around the shocked-looking young man and guided him into the first available chair in the main room and.

Tim wanted to say something, but he felt so frustrated. He hated it when he couldn't do things on his own. Relying on others was something he was still getting used to, and the trust component was the hardest part. He'd brought these problems with him from the real world, and they were being magnified by the life-or-death nature of the game.

How could you trust someone when the smallest of screw-ups could cost you everything?

Ernie looked at him with concern, but Tim waved him away and took a sip of water to buy himself time to think. He was looking at this all wrong. This was an MMO at its core. It might be an overly simplistic explanation, but the rules probably still held true. Content was *always* easier to tackle in a group, and skilled groups normally geared up quickly, leaving the others far behind.

So, instead of trying to do this on his own, he had to trust his instincts and enlist the help of the people around him. "Ernie, I've got a problem."

Ernie sat down, scratching the stubble on his cheek absent-mindedly. He looked at Tim with the eyes of a man who had heard more than his share of sad stories. "I'm not going to like this, am I?"

Tim tried not to smile. Ernie probably wasn't going to believe what he had to say, let alone like it, but Tim was determined to tell him the truth. "Someone killed me last night."

The innkeeper's eyes widened. "You mean, someone tried to kill you."

Gaston stood up and dragged a chair over to Tim's smaller table. He spun the chair around and sat down with his arms crossed over the back. "What's all this about someone trying to kill you?"

Shaking his head, Tim replied. "Not tried, did. Someone killed me last night." He knew how it sounded. It sounded fucking crazy, but he had to tell them the truth.

Was it really so hard to believe he'd been resurrected when the world was full of magic?

Both men were looking at him as if he might have been bumped on the head. Ernie's concern was touching, but Tim didn't want it right now. What he wanted was for them to believe him. Someone had to. "It's a long explanation, but I can show you where it happened."

Wagging his finger, Gaston stood up, mustache dancing as he smiled. "You almost had me."

Tim was desperate. He needed these men to believe him if he was going to stand a chance going forward. If they heard some of the details, it might add credence to his story. "There was a man wearing an orange sash, and some guy calling himself Marvin."

Ernie seemed lost in thought as Gaston stood up and took his chair back to his own table. Some distant memory seemed to click into place, and Ernie's eyes sparkled with mischief as they locked onto Tim's. "There was a guy with long dark hair sulking around in front of the inn last night. I thought it was odd because he never tried to come inside, but the guy's name wasn't Marvin."

"Martin," Gaston growled. "Idiot didn't even have the brains to change his name enough for a proper disguise."

The innkeeper looked at Gaston, shocked by his simple acceptance of Tim's story after hearing about Martin. He still wasn't sure what to make of things, so he turned his eyes back to Tim. "Are you saying Martin killed you?"

Tim sighed, knowing it was his fault for not telling them the entire story from the beginning. "No! I'm saying that little shitweasel led me to a house by telling me his fucking mother was too sick to come to the inn. When I got there, Mr. Orange Sash stabbed me in the chest."

He took a deep breath to calm himself, but this was also where he could make his story believable. "It's only because of the Goddess that I'm still here." Tim hoped Eternia wouldn't mind him using her to explain his resurrection.

Gaston sat back down at their table. "I might be able to track those men down, but I have a feeling you have something darker in mind."

Ernie stood and planted his hands on the table. He starred at Gaston with an intensity Tim hadn't seen before. "You can't, Gaston. If you get caught, it's over for all of us, and we're so damn close," Ernie shouted at the burly assassin.

Twirling one finger in his mustache, Gaston leaned back in his chair as if he were about to tilt his hat down over his eyes and take a nap. "I owe him for Frankie." The assassin said the words slowly, leaving no room for discussion.

This was just the information he needed to get farther in his quest line. "So close to what?" Tim blurted.

Both men's heads snapped around, and both of them mumbled, "Nothing," and looked anywhere but at Tim.

Maybe Ernie had just given him a clue, or maybe they had a secret stash hidden somewhere in the inn. Now might not be the right time to go down that particular rabbit hole. There were much more pressing needs he had to address first, such as how the hell he was going to sneak onto a boat and kill someone.

Tim decided to pretend he hadn't asked the last question, since both the men appeared to be so uncomfortable about it. If Ernie didn't want Gaston to kill the men for him, maybe there was something he could teach him so Tim could do it himself. This was just the thing to take their minds off his attempt to pry into their business.

Tim leaned back in his chair, watching both men. "I'd never ask either of you to do anything that would put you at risk."

Tim focused on Ernie, and the man nodded to acknowledge his statement. Now that they understood each other, Tim shifted his gaze back to Gaston. "But there *is* something you can help me with."

Both men leaned closer, but it was Gaston who spoke. "Do tell."

"I get the feeling you're handy with a blade. Is there a way you could teach me a few tricks, so I can handle this business myself?" Tim smiled like he was offering them the best deal in the world. "You get to keep your hands blood-free, and whatever you don't want me to know about this place stays hidden."

"Not sure what you're talking about," Ernie chimed in on cue.

Gaston smiled as if he'd finally found a worthwhile opponent. "I might be able to show you a thing or two if you have the aptitude. Working with a dagger takes a certain amount of finesse."

The assassin's eyes went blank for a moment, then he frowned. "I might be able to teach you not to stab yourself in the leg. If you want to learn how to wield a blade properly, you're going to need more dexterity."

It wasn't much, but Tim had two stat points left to spend, and he still hadn't examined the circlet the high priest had given him. Before he made any hasty decisions, he needed to look over his stats.

A quick examination of the circlet revealed that it had added +1 to his wisdom, which was up to 20, explaining the extra point. Tim clicked on the wisdom stat, wondering what the bonus for crossing the threshold to twenty-one would be.

A small noticed appeared next to the stat. **As long as your wisdom remains above twenty points, you will receive a +2 bonus to perception.** He probably could have figured that out on his own by looking at his extended stats for perception, vitality, revitalization, and luck.

"Interesting." Tim tapped his fingers on the display. How would higher perception help him? There was no way to be sure until he needed to use it, but any increase in his secondary stats couldn't hurt.

The circlet pushing him up to twenty points made it easier to do what he knew was coming next. Wincing slightly, Tim assigned his two remaining points to dexterity. It was a stat he thought he'd never even touch, and now he was sinking his hard-earned points into it. He hoped this moment didn't come back to bite him in the ass later.

If I want to get justice, I'm going to have to take risks.

Ernie and Gaston were locked in conversation about how the assassin had to help Tim with whatever he needed done because there was no way the kid could do it himself without getting killed. Tim listened to them for a moment, then tapped Gaston on the shoulder to get his attention. "How about now?"

Gaston inspected him again. "At least now you're giving me a little something to work with."

Quest Received: Revenge They Say, I call it Justice

Success: Execute Marvin and the Man with the Orange Sash

Failure: This quest can only be accomplished if both individuals are dead

Reward: Increased Reputation with Ernie and Gaston
Accept Quest <yes/no>

Tim quickly accepted the quest. Now that his stats were high enough to learn something from the assassin, he was getting excited about tonight. That and the new quest were going to give him bonus experience for doing something he planned to do anyway. Never do anything for free when you could be getting paid was his new motto.

Ernie smiled now that Gaston was off the hook. "See? I told you the kid would be fine."

Tim looked at the Innkeeper. "There's something I need from you too."

"You mean besides a room, food, and my sparkling personality?" Ernie crossed his arms over his chest, knowing he had more work coming his way.

"Yes." Tim slammed his hand on the table. The man was still acting like this was a game, but those fuckers had stabbed him, and he wanted retribution. "I need you to track those bastards down, so I can make sure they don't hurt anyone ever again."

Ernie's frown grew deeper. "Excuse me for being the only one with the balls to say this, but doesn't killing people kind of go against your code as a healer?"

Tim's lips tightened into a thin line as a look of determination crossed his face. "The only code I have is the one that keeps me alive." He tried to stare through the man. "I'll do whatever it takes to make sure the people I care about are safe."

"Hear, hear," shouted Gaston.

"Fine. I'll find your killers." Ernie huffed. "Just don't go dragging any trouble back to my inn." He stood up from the table and headed to the kitchen. "I'll get you some food. If you're going to be training with Gaston, you're going to need the extra energy."

The burly assassin chuckled. "He's not kidding. You're in for a real treat." Gaston stood up, flipped his chair over his head, catching it by one leg on a single extended finger and balancing it there for a moment before setting the chair back on the floor.

Gaston picked up his drink and polished it off in a single gulp. "Meet me inside the red door when you're ready." He pointed across the room at a door Tim never noticed before.

Before he could say anything to Gaston, Ernie appeared with a flourish of his apron and began laying a feast on the table. Tim looked at the delicious food, thinking he might have just bitten off a little more than he could chew. Dexterity and hand-to-hand fighting, or his lack thereof, were exactly why he had chosen to play a healer.

"One step at a time," Tim mumbled, looking down at his grits. He took the first bite and felt his stomach began to settle. "You've got this." By the time Tim was done with his bowl, he almost believed it.

CHAPTER TWENTY-FOUR

D idn't red mean murder?
Or like they used to say in one of his favorite games, red meant dead.

Tim had read in some shitty horror fan mag how colors were used in films. Red was never good in movies. Just think about *The Sixth Sense*. He was always seeing red and then dead people. Who wanted to deal with that shit?

Of course, I'd much rather see dead people than be one.

Tim grabbed the handle on the door. Any trace of hesitation he'd felt about going down a darker path was banished as he thought about Marvin standing over him and laughing as he died. The motherfucker had laughed at him.

And those asshole guards weren't much better. Sometimes it felt like the entire deck was stacked against him, and that he'd never succeed. All he had to do in those moments was dig a little deeper. Everyone had a reserve they could dip into when they really needed that last little push. He needed that push now like a baby bird needed help out of the nest.

I mean, you never really know what you're capable of until you're well outside your comfort zone.

Going down a path that eventually led to killing another man was so far outside his comfort zone, it might as well have been Mars. Shit, they hadn't even colonized it yet, but if that Musk dude had anything to say about it, a colony on Mars was in humanity's future—not that landing a shuttle on the big red planet would make shoving his dagger into another person any easier.

But it sure would be cool.

The Mars thing, not the dagger. "Fuck." He babbled when he was nervous. Walking down the dark, creepy stairs behind the red door to learn how to kill people definitely had him on edge, but he refused to spend the next twenty years looking over his shoulder for hints of orange.

There was no doubt in his mind he'd picked the right teacher. That trick with the chair had been amazing. Gaston was huge, but he moved with the grace of a ballerina. A normal person couldn't move and balance the way Gaston did. Tim knew he wasn't on that level, but with the two extra points in dexterity, he wasn't useless, either.

Inside the door was a small landing that led to a rickety wooden staircase built into the wall. *Of course, the steps go down.* There weren't any torches lighting the wall, but there was the barest hint of an orange flicker of light coming from somewhere below him. The door closed behind him, sealing him in total darkness.

Tim froze. The last thing he wanted to do was walk into a trap. Maybe this was a test of some kind. He waited until his eyes adjusted to the dark as much as they could, then started down the stairs. The steps at his feet might as well have been black ice, and despite his hand touching the wall, he couldn't see his fingers. One step at a time, he went down.

Halfway down the stairs, he paused again. He could almost make out the faint trace of his hand against the wall. Was his eyesight getting better, or was the light coming from the bottom of the stairs helping more? As he tried to puzzle it out, a prompt flickered in the bottom right of his vision. He swatted it away, vowing to change his not-in-combat settings when he had the chance.

The prompt appeared in his vision again. "That's going to be annoying," Tim muttered as he opened the system settings and changed his commands to only show him messages and prompts when he asked for them.

Might as well see what was so important that it stopped me from becoming the guy killed before the opening credits of a slasher film.

Skill Received: Night Vision

Skill Rank: Novice rank one

It is now one percent easier for you to see in low-light conditions.

Not a bad little perk. Tim wondered if at the higher levels, you could see in total darkness. Imagine the fun you could have with that.

The best part about his new skill was the only thing required to increase it was darkness and a willingness to stumble around blindly until you leveled up. Cheap and easy; it was just his kind of thing, unlike those fancy burger places. Why would anyone pay twenty bucks for a burger when they could go to Five Guys and get the burger of their life for less than ten?

What the fuck was up with that shit?

Sometimes you just had to realize the world wasn't a logical place. People didn't always make rational decisions. They knew cigarettes killed them—fuck, the Marlboro Man died of lung cancer—but they still smoked. A good stiff drink might take the edge off, but a few too many, and your liver and kidneys were gone. Life was a wild, messy, endless clusterfuck.

And he freaking loved it!

Tim dismissed the prompt and continued down the steps until he reached a level surface. The tunnel in front of him extended for another fifteen feet, this time ending at a solid black door. No markings adorned the surface, and if he was in a George RR book, the room behind it would be full of human faces.

Thankfully he was in *The Etheric Coast*, and while there might be secret assassins who could wear other people's faces, he'd yet to encounter one. It didn't make sense to be afraid of things he'd never run into. Tim was afraid of cobras, which was totally irrational, but ever since *Rikki-Tikki-Tavi,* he'd been terrified. That didn't mean he got up in the morning looking for cobras everywhere. They weren't an American problem.

The philosophers of the world could spend a hundred years telling you what the color black meant. It was bad; it meant death. Witches wore black, and every bad guy in the movies had an all-black outfit hidden in the back of their closet. Over the years, Tim had learned one thing about black and white: they were just colors on opposite sides of the spectrum. Neither was evil or good, and history was full of assholes wearing white while committing atrocities.

"Fuck," Tim grumbled. Why couldn't he ever stop his mind from racing a mile a minute when he was nervous?

Colors. Who gave a fuck about what color the door was? What he needed to focus on was getting to Gaston and maximizing the small window of time he had left before he had to try to complete his quest. When he left the Blue Dagger Inn, Tim needed to be skilled enough with a weapon to kill a man.

Tim opened the black door and stepped into a well-lit training chamber. *Not what I expected.* He'd imagined some kind of underground fighting ring or a dirt-floored basement with bloodstains on the walls. He wasn't sure what to expect from his training session, except that he'd probably leave with a few bruises and enough knowledge to be mildly dangerous.

The room he was in standing in now was nothing like what he'd been expecting. Wooden training dummies lined one wall. In another section were targets set up at ten, twenty, and forty feet for practice with a hand crossbow or a dagger.

Speaking of weapons…

One entire wall was filled with knives, short swords, and ranged weapons. It was an arsenal fit for an armory. Tim wouldn't have been surprised if the weapons in this room were worth more than the entire block.

A smile broke out on his face. "At least I'm in the right place."

"That you are." Gaston stood up from a chair against the wall by the door. He finished his drink and flipped the cup so it landed on the seat of the chair he just vacated, not moving so much as an inch after hitting the seat.

"I want to show you something." Gaston pulled a lever by the door, and a ball fell from the ceiling. The chain snapped tight, and the ball spun and swayed from side to side. Sticking out of it were sharpened blades. They emerged at multiple angles, so there didn't seem to be any way to get close to the thing without risking being skewered like a kabob.

Gaston rushed forward, pulling two daggers from behind his back as he lunged at the ball. He flowed around the sharpened blades like water over a rock. The man spun with the fluidity of a ballerina and bent with the dexterity of a yogi. He kept up the deadly dance until the ball stopped swinging.

Moving forward, Tim peered at the chipped and dented wood. Somehow, Gaston had managed not to be hit by the ball's blades, but he had also done significant damage to the target. If this had been a person, the assassin could have killed him a hundred times over. Gaston was even better with a blade than Tim had dared hope.

"Don't tell me I have to do that?" Tim touched one of the blades and yanked his hand back as blood welled from the cut on his finger.

He quickly cast healing orb on his finger and looked at the assassin with more respect. Those blades weren't just for show.

Would he be able to do that one day? At some point, he'd have to make a choice. There was no way he'd have the time to focus on two classes, even if he was given the chance to learn a second one.

Splitting his time between the two would be counterproductive at best, and at worst, it would leave him way behind his peers. Players paid the most for the best and newest items. To get those, and the kind of payday he needed to accomplish his goals, Tim would have to focus on healing, but that didn't mean he couldn't learn how to poke holes in someone when he had spare time.

Gaston moved toward the door to pull the lever and raise the ball back up into the rafters. "Maybe we should focus on the basics first." He motioned for Tim to follow him over to the dummies.

"Since I can't deal with the problem on your behalf, I want you to have these." Gaston reached behind his back and pulled out a small bundle. In it were two daggers and a bandolier of throwing knives.

Tim looked at his newly acquired weapons with awe. Jepsom had made him heal people for hours, and Gaston was just going to give him two daggers and some throwing knives. Leaving the temple might not have been such a bad thing after all.

Simple Dagger of Dexterity: This was an average dagger before someone added a small weight to the back, improving the balance of the blade. +1 to dexterity.

Basic Throwing Knives: There's nothing special about these knives except that you have a lot of them.

The daggers were a huge bonus. Tim equipped both knives, enjoying the feel of the soft leather grips against the palms of his hands. Of course, the best part was the bonus to his dexterity, bringing the stat up to sixteen. It might have just been his imagination, but Tim felt more flexible.

Was that even a thing—feeling flexible?

Shaking his head to clear it, he looked at the burly assassin. "Thank you." He meant it. Tim had come down here not expecting much, and he'd already been given bounty beyond imagining. If he could use the daggers half as well as they deserved to be used, he might stand a chance in a real fight.

"So, what do I do now?" He looked at the dummy and back at the daggers in his hands.

"Try to stab the dummy." Gaston hit the dummy with his fist. "Get used to the feel of the blades in your hands and the resistance of each strike against the wood." He smiled as Tim took his first exploratory swing. "You'll find there are times to stab and opportunities for slashing. Knowing which to use and when will save your life."

Tim started bobbing and weaving. As he moved, he'd either or slash or stab with one of the daggers. He tried launching attacks with both hands, amazed by how well his left hand responded. He'd always been right-hand dominant and was in awe of ambidextrous people.

Gaston moved around him as he worked. Each time Tim did something the assassin didn't like, he corrected his form. Next he showed Tim how to reverse his grip on one of the daggers so the blade was pressed against his forearm. From there, he could slash or block with it. The burly assassin called a halt to their training and pointed for Tim to join him at the range.

Gaston pulled one of the knives from Tim's bandolier and showed him how to hold it. "Just remember, when you throw the blade, the end-over-end shit is just to catch the attention of the girls." The assassin pulled one of his own knives free, and with a casual flick of the wrist, the blade slammed into the center of the target.

"Holy shit! That was so fucking badass!" Tim blurted excitedly.

Whirling, Gaston pulled blades from inside his leather armor and threw them at the targets so fast Tim couldn't keep track of where all the knives were coming from, let alone where they were going. Finally, Gaston slowed, pulling what must have been his last blade free.

Balancing the slim knife in his palm, he licked the index finger of his other hand and held it up to test the air for a breeze. Tim held his breath as Gaston pulled his arm back and snapped it forward. The knife sailed forty feet through the air to land dead center in the target, where it quivered.

Smiling, Gaston turned back to Tim. "That's how you do it."

"Showoff," Tim groused as he helped Gaston pull the knives from the targets. "Let me guess: that's not how I do *this* drill either."

"Not if you want to hit anything." Gaston chuckled. "Now show me what you've got."

Tim pulled one of the knives out of his bandolier and held it out. Gaston clicked his tongue and adjusted his grip. When Tim looked at him for confirmation that his hold on the knife was right, Gaston nodded.

"Just throw the damn thing," Gaston growled, growing impatient.

Tim didn't want to overthink it, so he tried to mimic the motion the assassin had made when he threw his first dagger. The blade flew from his hand, and his heart rose in his throat as it neared the target. The knife dipped at the last second, catching the bottom edge of the target and spinning uselessly away.

"Not bad." Gaston clapped him on the back.

At least I didn't miss the entire target. So he either had to aim a little higher, compensating for the weight the blade dropping as it slowed, or he had to throw it harder. His throw hadn't been that far off the first time, so instead of trying to throw it harder, he'd just aim a wee bit higher.

Tim slipped the next blade from his bandolier and focused on the target. His breath slowed, and his field of vision narrowed until he could only see the spot he was aiming for. With a quick motion, Tim's arm extended, and the knife flew straight at the target. This time when the blade dipped, it struck the bullseye before bouncing harmlessly away.

"Maybe with a little more oomph!" Gaston chided, leaning

against the railing. "While humans are rather soft, they tend to wear things that make them much harder to kill."

Gaston was right. Even if the blade hit the target, it wouldn't matter if it didn't penetrate their armor. Without power behind them, the blades might as well have been something he tossed out to try to distract someone. What was he worried about, anyway? It wasn't like he was going to hurt the target by hitting it harder.

If he was going to throw the blade harder, he wouldn't have to compensate for the fall. If he did this right, the knife would fly straight and sink into the target. All he had to do was concentrate. His breathing slowed as he adjusted his feet. Tim focused on the bullseye and let rip with everything he had behind it.

Throwing so hard must have sent his aim off. The knife flew right past the target and sank into the boards behind it with a hearty *thwack*. He winced at the sound, already thinking about how he could make adjustments for his next throw.

Gaston slapped him on the back. "Now with a little less gusto, my overeager young friend."

"No shit." Tim quipped, giving the assassin a dirty look. Gaston laughed while casually plucking a knife from his own bandolier and tossing it at the target, looking Tim straight in the eyes. The blade sailed across the room and stuck perfectly in the center of the target. A bright smile lit Gaston's features, and he wiggled his eyebrows suggestively.

"Now you're just showing off." Tim chuckled at the assassin's antics. Had Gaston always been this funny, or was training together bringing out a side of the man he'd never seen? Until now, Tim would have told you the assassin would be more likely to slit your throat than shake your hand. Apparently healing Freddy had changed Gaston's attitude toward him dramatically.

Tim wanted to hit the target this time. Not so he could avoid another round of humiliation at the feet of a master, but because he wanted to. Deep inside, he wanted to be able to do this; he needed to. He also didn't want Gaston to think he was wasting his time. He was taking this very seriously. His life depended on how well he could use these skills.

Aligning his body to the target, Tim thought about his last few throws and what had gone wrong. This next attempt needed to be softer than the last one, but he still shouldn't need to compensate for the knife's flight toward a target that was only ten feet away.

Time seemed to slow down as Tim pulled the last blade free. The throwing knife felt heavy in his hand. He tossed it up and down a few times, working out the balance of the blade. He slowly curled his fingers around the hilt, then his breathing slowed and the knife flew from his hand. It struck the bullseye and quivered there, just as Gaston's blade had done earlier.

The burly assassin wrapped Tim in his arm, lifting him off his feet as he cheered. "I knew you had it in you." He set Tim down, beaming from ear to ear. "I've got one last thing to teach you before I want to see that spell of yours."

Gaston walked around the room putting covers over some of the torches, creating pools of dark shadows around the room. Gaston covered one last torch, and the man seemed to disappear. Looking around wildly, Tim tried to locate the assassin, but he just couldn't see him.

"I've got a feeling this is going to hurt," Tim mumbled as his legs were swept out from under him. He hit the ground with a thud and scanned the air above him for the next blow. Instead, a smiling face peered down at him.

"You're dead." Gaston extended his hand and helped Tim to his feet.

Gaston gently brushed off the back of Tim's shirt, then turned toward the room, extending his arms wide. "Shadows are an assassin's best friend. Strike from the dark, and fade to black."

He stepped into the shadows, disappearing almost entirely from sight. Tim could make out just the hint of his outline as he moved through the darkness. It must have been his perception skill helping him, but it didn't take Gaston long to lose him.

"Fuck." *I can't see shit in here.*

Tim frantically searched the shadows for any sign of the assassin. He turned slowly from side to side, vainly hoping that whatever Gaston did to him this time might hurt a little less than the last lesson. When the man didn't appear behind him, Tim turned to face the front of the room again, then spun and lashed out with a fist.

His hand sailed through the air, connecting with nothing. Tim stumbled forward, his balance complete thrown off by his wild swing. He had time to think about how stupid he must have looked before he felt a hand on his back. The simple shove sent him crashing to the ground,

He hit the wooden planks, a scream tearing from his mouth as a giant splinter sank into the palm of his hand. Gaston landed on his back, and four rapid punches slammed into places that must have been vital organs. He groaned. He rolled onto his back and looked up at the assassin.

"Maybe with a little less enthusiasm next time," Tim bitched as he pulled the splinter out of his hand and cast healing orb.

Gaston helped him to his feet. "Now it's your turn."

The assassin showed him how to use the darkness for cover and went over the points he'd hit on Tim's back. Even when attacking from concealment and behind the target, it was still important to hit something vital, or the fight could get out of control quickly.

Gaston called a halt to their training about an hour later. "I do have other things to do today." He smiled at his new apprentice. "But I still want to see this spell of yours." Gaston crossed his arms and leaned against the railing.

Tim put his new daggers back into his inventory and pulled out his scepter. He scanned the spell, instantly understanding how it functioned. His hand started moving through the casting when Gaston jumped in front of him. Tim faltered, then fell to the ground, clutching his head.

"That's mana burn, boy. You never want to stop casting in the middle of a spell." He helped Tim up. "Sorry to do that to you, but I didn't want the first time you used the spell in a fight to be the last time."

Tim glared at Gaston. "Yes, it's much better when the very first time I try to cast a spell, it causes me an immense amount of pain." Tim picked up his scepter. "Thanks for that."

"Maybe I was a little overeager in my instruction. It's not my fault you magic types are so finicky." He twirled one side of his mustache. "Also remember this if you are on the other side of a casting. Sharp knives being thrown at you can have the same effect as the surprise I just gave you."

"How about this time you just let me cast the spell, and we work on beating distraction in our next lesson?" Tim waited until the assassin nodded in acknowledgment and then tried casting flame burst again.

"Wait!" Gaston jumped in front of him. "This isn't a fire spell, is it?"

Tim looked up at Gaston from his place on the floor. Maybe he should just stay down here. You could cast while sitting, and he wouldn't fall nearly as far if the assassin interrupted him again. Although he was catching on. If you wanted to be a magical caster in this game, you had to have rock-solid focus.

"Of course it has fire. It's called 'flame burst,' for Eternia's sake," Tim shouted at Gaston as he disappeared into the shadows.

The assassin returned a moment later with two buckets of water. "What?" He shrugged. "If you haven't noticed, we're basically in a wooden box.

Tim smiled sheepishly. "I guess not being burned to death below the inn holds a certain appeal." Tim glanced at Gaston and pretended to start his spell before glaring at the man again. The assassin held up his hands in submission, and Tim focused on what needed to be done.

Words tumbled from his lips, and his hand moved through the

ritual gestures. He pointed his staff at the training dummy and flames erupted from the tip, washing over the wooden target.

Gaston rushed forward and doused the training dummy with water. "Not too bad. If you get overwhelmed, I'd definitely use that!"

Tim smiled as he looked at the singed dummy. The spell was much more powerful than he'd expected. Some of the monsters in this game would inevitably have fire resistance, and so would some of the players. Still, flame burst was a powerful tool. Maybe it was time for him to get some use out of it.

Gaston looked at his blackened training dummy and back at Tim. "Why don't we start focusing more on what you have to do tonight and less on burning down the inn?" Gaston put an arm around Tim's shoulders and led him back up the stairs.

CHAPTER TWENTY-FIVE

Ernie had left them a pitcher of rumpleberry juice and a plate of hardtack.

"The man might as well be a saint," Tim exclaimed, pouring himself a large glass.

"Or the Grim Reaper." Gaston chuckled. "Ernie is our master of poisons."

Tim sprayed his juice all over the floor. "Poison?" It made sense. Assassins normally had some kind of poison-covered weapon in most games. In a lot of them, the poison added a damage-over-time effect, but in rare occurrences, the poison could transfer some of the damage back to the user as life.

Gaston poured his own glass of juice and took a delighted sip. "Yep." He smiled devilishly. "But I'm sure the juice is fine."

Glaring at Gaston, Tim topped off his glass. "I'll be down in a minute." Grabbing a biscuit, he shoved it into his mouth and ran for the stairs.

So the assassin had a sense of humor that was low key funny. It was hard not to like Gaston, now that he was getting to see more of the man's personality, and a lot less of the "I'll slit your throat if you look at me wrong" vibe he'd given off when they'd first met. Plus, the burly assassin's display with the dummy still had Tim questioning his class choices.

I bet he could solo the BrewMaster.

But it wasn't like Tim had seen what a high-level mage could do yet, and he was pretty sure there was a cleric or two out there who had gone into DPS specialization. Master and grandmaster spells of any class had to be impressive, but the magic users might have had an edge, at least visually. Sure, it was cool to move like the wind, but imagine calling down meteors from the heavens, or summoning a dragon to fight by your side.

That was good shit! Far better than poking people with daggers.

It wasn't out of the question to believe a grandmaster of the healing arts could keep an entire army alive. Tim imagined standing above two armies fighting in the valley below him. The tide had turned against his men, and it was time for him to intervene. Calling upon the Goddess Eternia, Tim channeled her power through himself into his staff.

With a thunderous crash, he slammed his staff on the ground three times and screamed the final word of his spell. The clouds above them drew together, darkening as his magic flowed into them. Lightning arced, killing several of his foes, and then a gentle rain started fall amongst the men.

As their wounds began to heal, the tide of the battle turned in their favor. Tim fell to his knees as the men cheered their victory. Rising to his feet again, he looked out over the soldiers. The men turned to him, and Tim held his staff aloft in triumph. "For the Goddess!"

The men below picked up the chant, and it swept across the battlefield as they wiped out the rest of the enemy.

What a vivid daydream.

Entering his room, Tim shook off the thoughts of leading an army. Right now he was terrified of trying to kill one man, let alone thousands. He quickly finished the hardtack and his glass of juice. After a quick look in the mirror, Tim un-equipped his clothes and used his last bit of free time to go to the bathroom. If there was one thing he could live without having to do in the game, it would be taking a shit.

And toilet paper…

He was going to have to remember to ask about the fucking toilet paper. With his business concluded and his less-than-fun wiping completed, Tim slipped his loincloth back into place. He set the chamber pot by the door in the hallway, then went back to the table. Filling a basin with water, Tim wiped his body with a towel.

Truth be told, he was starting to smell a bit ripe and was really missing deodorant. If Ernie didn't have a shower, maybe there was a tub he could soak in, and some soap he could use to wash off the grime. He'd have to find out after he got back.

With the necessities out of the way, Tim sat down in front of the fire to collect his thoughts. Before he could sink too deeply into brooding about his quest, the notifications at the bottom right of his screen caught his eye.

Skill Granted: Small Blades

Rank: Apprentice rank one

You have mastered the basics. Ok, who are we kidding? You've learned from the hands of a master and benefited from his years of study. Don't worry, it's a long, slow climb up the rest of the skill tree.

Bonus: Attacks with blades less than eighteen inches long do five percent more damage. Dexterity requirement for weapons reduced by a factor of two.

Interesting. At some point, weapons would come with stat requirements, making where you put your stat points even more valuable. Sure, they were coming to him quickly now, but after level twenty, he'd bet things really slowed down. Imagine finding the perfect weapon for your class and not being able to use it because you put a point in a stat that didn't matter. He'd have to be even more careful of where he allocated his points going forward.

Skill Granted: Throwing Knives

Rank Apprentice rank one

Remember how horrible your second throw was? The system will, for the rest of eternity.

That seemed a little extreme.

Bonus: Your knives will be ten percent more accurate when thrown at a distance under twenty feet, and will do five percent more damage.

Learning from a master certainly had its privileges. Tim thought about how long it'd taken him to get healing orb to the first apprentice rank on his own and shuddered. There was a good chance that without Gaston's training, he would have died tonight. Now he felt as if he had a real chance.

Skill Granted: Sneak

Rank: Apprentice rank one

Your ability to hide in the shadows is almost legendary. You know, as long as you don't move and no one is looking for you. You shouldn't get too excited; chances are that if someone spots you, you'll probably end up talking to your caseworker again.

Bonus: Shadows cling to you like a second skin. Your ability to hide in them is increased by ten percent. When you aren't moving, characters searching for you must pass a perception check to see you.

Bet that perception check is pretty damn low.

Wow, the system was really starting to rub off on him. Now the game had him talking shit instead of being excited about his new skills. Everything he learned was at apprentice rank, and other people would probably spend a week getting to this point. Tim re-equipped the rest of his clothes as he read his last alert.

Skill Increased: Night Vision

Rank: Novice rank three

It is now three percent easier for you to see in low-light conditions.

I guess practicing hiding in the shadows comes with additional perks.

Looking over his newly acquired skills, Tim felt nervous, but there was light at the end of the tunnel. He could do this. Dapper Don Diego was going down. So what if Paul couldn't provide him any support and the guards didn't care that he'd been killed? He'd found everything he needed at his inn in the slums.

Those northsiders don't know what they're missing.

A smile tried to form on his face, but Tim only managed a weak upturn at the corners of his mouth. It was fine, he could do this. It was like anything else he'd ever wanted—he had to keep his eyes on the ultimate goal. Shit, soldiers were just normal people thrust into extraordinary circumstances. He'd seen *The Pacific*. Tim knew you only found out what you were made of when the bullets started flying.

He was pretty sure that when push came to shove, he wouldn't hesitate. If he was going to be in the game for twenty years, he had to take control. The last thing he wanted to do was be stuck handing out quests for Ironbeard while Sierra was off having wild adventures. He had to accomplish Lady Briarthorn's quest. His future depended on it.

Pulling one of his throwing knives free, Tim spun the blade idly in his hand. He'd learned it wasn't that hard to kill a person. It turned out people were pretty squishy. *Who knew?* If he could just sneak onto the boat and catch Dapper Don alone, it would be over quickly. Then he could call in the cavalry to loot the boat.

With a flick of his arm, Tim sent the knife flying. The blade thudded into the wall and quivered. Standing, he grabbed the knife, tucked it back in his bandolier, and headed out the door.

The time for fucking around was over. He was ready to roll.

Tim was downstairs in a flash and stepped into the main room a moment later. He saw the innkeeper huddled with Gaston at the central table. A few of his men lounged around them, drinking and chatting.

Tim almost felt bad about breaking the mood, but he didn't have long before he had to head to the docks and find the *Mary Lou*. "Tell me you have some good news for me, Ernie?"

The innkeeper frowned. "Seems Marvin's a bit smarter than I gave him credit for." Ernie shrugged. "He wasn't home, but I'll find him."

"Good." *I wouldn't have been able to take care of Marvin tonight anyway*. "And the man with the orange sash?"

Ernie looked at Gaston for help, but the big man just held out his hands as if to say, "This is on you." The Innkeeper frowned at the assassin but carried on regardless. "The man in orange has been a bit harder to track down. I have Freddy working on it. After you healed him, he's determined to do something for you."

Tim felt a shiver of emotion. It seemed these men really cared about what happened to him. They weren't just pieces on the board to be used. The man with the orange sash was dangerous, and he didn't want Freddy getting hurt because of him. "Tell him to be careful. That guy is a stone-cold killer."

Ernie finally smiled. "On that note, I did find the house you told us about and a considerable amount of blood in the back room."

Tim pointed at the ground. "I'm telling you...dead." He pointed at himself. "Then not so dead." He gazed at the two men. "And now I'm ready to exact a little justice."

Gaston chuckled. "Why don't you see if you can make it back from tonight in one piece?" He stood up and clamped a fatherly hand on Tim's shoulder. "When you wake up in the morning, you're going to know one of two things."

His hand tightened as he searched Tim's eyes. "You're either going to be ok with what you've done, or you're going to be sick about it."

"If you're going to be sick, try not to do it in your room," Ernie cautioned.

Gaston glared at the innkeeper, and Ernie mimicked zipping his lips. "Just know that if you need to talk about what you had to do, I'll be here for you."

If anything, Gaston's speech filled him with resolve. He could do this, and if he needed support, he had it. "If I need to, I'll come find you."

"Come find us anyway." One of Gaston's crew chimed from the table. "We'll be having drinks."

Gaston smiled. "If you're up for it. You'll be welcome to join us."

It felt good, being part of a group. There was a certain sense of accomplishment when things got done as a team versus on your own. "I'd be honored. I might even have to buy you guys a round."

"I'm going to hold you to that." Gaston clapped Tim on the shoulder and went back to the table. He picked up a small bundle and tossed it to Tim. "For tonight."

Tim started to open the package, and his first genuine smile since deciding to go through with this formed on his face. Inside of the bundle was an outfit made out of black cloth and leather, including a pair of boots, and gloves.

"Ok, so now I really have to buy you a drink," Tim mumbled as he looked at the gift he'd just received.

Ernie nudged him. "Don't leave us in suspense, boy-o. Try them on."

Tim equipped the clothes through the inventory system. Only one thought came to mind as he saw his reflection in the stained glass over the bar.

I look fucking awesome!

It was true. He kind of looked like Zorro without the hat and mask. Sneaking through the shadows dressed like this was going to be a cinch.

Tim glanced at the burly assassin, trying to keep his emotions in check. "It's too much. You didn't have to do this."

"Just think of it as my little way of helping you along the right path. Who knows, there might even be a place for you in our gang someday," Gaston rumbled.

"We'd have to check with the boss, of course." Ernie stared at Gaston as if he'd lost his mind.

Ignoring the innkeeper, Gaston slapped a meaty hand on Tim's back. "Don't worry, I'll put in a good word for you." He went back to his seat and sat down heavily.

Ernie put a hand around Tim's shoulders and started ushering him toward the door. "Remember to try to have a little fun tonight. It's ok to take pleasure in a job well done."

Was it really ok to feel good about killing someone? Should he ever cheer the death of another human? He thought about the videos he'd seen of the Towers falling, and bombs going off at marathons. Maybe some people did deserve to die. At least, in this case, it was just a game. No matter how real these characters felt, he wasn't killing a living person.

Tonight was all about making the right choices, and completing the lady's quest was the right way to go. He'd take out Dapper Don and get the stolen goods back to Lady Briarthorn. Eliminating the assassin got him one step closer to removing Jepsom from the equation and opening the temple for him to continue training.

And his percentage of the take should be a decent chunk of change.

The rain rattled on the overhang as he stepped outside. Tim thought about how badly he needed a cloak. Gaston had supplied the rest of his gear. At the very least, he could buy his own cloak. The market was on the way to the docks, so his walk home would be a good deal drier than his departure.

In life, there was always something to look forward to.

CHAPTER TWENTY-SIX

"I look fucking epic." Tim turned so he could see his entire outfit in the mirror.

Sure, he looked like the Dread Pirate Roberts in his black outfit, but without the mask, he wasn't as fearsome. That changed the second he put on his new cloak. Somehow the hood hung perfectly to keep his face hidden in the shadows, and the material was light enough that it didn't hinder his movements.

Now he looked more like the ranger Strider when Frodo first laid eyes on him. This getup was darker, though, just the kind of thing you would wear to jump out of the shadows and plunge a blade into someone. He wondered if people would treat him differently now that his outfit gave off a more dangerous vibe.

Tim loved feeling mysterious and dangerous, even if nobody else felt the same way as he walked past. None of the milling shoppers knew that under his cloak, he was armed to the teeth. Smiling as he turned to face the merchant, Tim pulled three silver from the pouch on his hip and handed them to her.

Three silver was probably too much for the simple black cloak, but could you really put a price on badassdom? Stepping back out into the crowd, Tim let them guide him through the merchant district. He doubted anyone was following him, but he was determined to be careful.

The last thing Tim wanted to do was draw unwanted attention, so he tilted his head down and let the cloak do its job as he put one foot in front of the other. Every now and then, he stopped and examined something from a stall, but he kept moving closer to his destination.

It might look odd to never buy anything. If anyone was watching him, it was a dead giveaway. Plus, he kind of looked like an assassin now, so more eyes might be on him than he was used to. Turning away from the street, he stopped at a fruit stall. He scanned the crowd briefly but didn't see anything out of place before his eyes fell on an orange fruit he was very familiar with.

"How much for a rumpleberry?"

The merchant took in Tim's appearance and hesitated for a second, then picked one up and tossed it to him. "Just a copper."

Tim pulled out a small handful of the dull copper coins. "I'll take a dozen."

The merchant put them in the bag, and Tim handed him fifteen copper coins. "If these are as good as the first one, they'll be worth the tip."

"Best rumpleberries in town." He waved away some imaginary naysayer. "Mark my words, you'll never have finer."

Tim thanked him again and faded into the crowd. He made a few more stops along the way, each time purchasing something small that he could give away or use. The point of the purchases wasn't so much what he was buying, but the time it gave him to scan the crowd for unfriendly faces.

No one stood out. The crowd was starting to thin as people made their way to the inns and taverns to enjoy their night. A normal person would be thinking about heading to bed at this hour, or maybe out looking for the special kind of company provided by a like-minded individual. Tim's purpose was much darker, yet he was excited as he edged closer to the docks.

Tim knew he'd have to get into a fight sooner or later. The best part of these games was the combat. Since he wasn't out killing goblins and orcs like everyone else, he was going to get his first taste of it against another person.

He just had to remind himself it was only a game. If he killed Dapper Don... No, *when* he killed Dapper Don Diego, the cops weren't going to come kicking in his inn-room door. This wasn't the real world. He shouldn't feel bad about slaughtering a few thousand lines of code.

Gaston and Ernie didn't feel like ones and zeros.

There was more to them. The two men had a flavor and depth to their personalities that made them feel less like characters and more like people. This wasn't like the games of old, where you had to skip over mountains of text to get to the exciting stuff. Here you didn't even have to skip a scene because you'd played the game before. *The Etheric Coast* was different.

This world was persistent.

The story never went backward. No one entering the game today would have the same experience he was having now. The game world changed and evolved as the players took control of it. Everyone's time in the game was unique. Sure, they might have to kill some of the same monsters, and maybe even go on duplicate quests, but there was so much more to it.

The Etheric Coast was alive, a living, breathing world of its own. In some ways, he liked it better than the real world. In others, he wished for home. They didn't have memory foam pillows or Joe's. He could really go for some fucking pancakes right about now.

Grits just didn't cut it.

It was funny; thinking about home completely banished the voice in his head that was telling him to turn back. He was fine with what he was about to do. All the mental handwringing and back and forth thoughts about doing things the right way, and he finally realized there was no right way. Not here, not in this place. There was a sickness in the Temple of Eternia, and it needed to be cleansed.

He would be the one to cleanse it.

His mission as an agent of change had started with Dapper Don Diego. The man was about to learn that working for Cardinal Jepsom had an expiration date. The cardinal might think he'd already won the war, but Paul was still fighting, and Lady Briarthorn didn't seem like the kind of woman who gave up. He'd picked the right side of the battle, so he had nothing to be ashamed of.

The cobbles under his feet shifted to wooden planks as he entered the dock area, which was so large that in most games, it would have been its own city. Tim moved through the sailors and deckhands as he followed the path on his mini-map. As the crowds on the docks thinned, Tim started using the shadows to stay out of sight.

He darted behind a pile of crates covered in old nets. The *Mary Lou* was nestled in a slip a few boats farther down the dock. Every inch of the way from here to the boat was dangerous. If he was going to succeed, no one could see him coming.

He sprinted between the dark spots like a pro using the joystick in an epic *Frogger* match. Two, three, four times he ran, hiding in whatever cover the shadows provided. Ducking, Tim wrapped his cloak around him and tried to slow his breathing and calm his rapid heartbeat.

Wouldn't it just be my luck to be found because I'm gasping like a fish?

Two men exited one of the nearby ships carrying lanterns and headed in Tim's direction. He felt the shadows receding, and tried to think of a story they might buy to leave him alone. In the end, it would probably come down to a bribe. A few silver coins might steer them to the nearest tavern and keep them out of his business.

A plan started to form in his mind. He'd just pretend to be

getting sick. Plenty of sailors returned from the tavern worse for wear. If they bought the ruse, awesome. If not, bribery was his next-best plan.

The light crept closer to where he was, and Tim hunched his back in preparation for playing the role of a lifetime.

"Not that way, you idiot." One of the men grabbed the other by the shoulders and turned him so he was facing the city instead of the open sea. "Not unless you want to meet Davy Jones."

The other man grumbled in response, and Tim sighed in relief as their lights started moving in the opposite direction. He waited for a moment, taking stock of where he was. There was no need to panic. Those men hadn't been looking for him. Everything was still going according to plan. He let out a deep exhale, and a sense of calm crept over him.

I'd rather be lucky than good any day of the week.

Tim made his next three moves without hesitation, ending up lying on his belly behind a couple of low crates and some kind of tub for cleaning fish. Nothing said "not fun" like landing in a pile of fish guts. Some of the slimy little fuckers might have even made it inside his shirt. At least the game cleaned his clothes when he un-equipped them.

With laundry off the table, he might as well focus on how to board the ship. There was a single ramp leading from the dock to the deck of the massive ship. Tim looked at the ramp and shook his head. Running up the ramp was a surefire way to get noticed, and came with a heavy possibility of being filled with holes soon thereafter.

Guess I'm going swimming.

Thankfully, the developers made getting in and out of his equipment easy. Tim didn't even have to worry about his clothes getting wet. He'd just un-equip them, swim toward the cargo net hanging off the side of the boat, and make his way toward the captain's cabin. In and out, no problem. A smile started to spread across his lips

This might be easier than I thought.

"Shut up, you worthless piece of shit!" a man called as he started dragging a second man down the ramp.

Three more men followed the one in charge, and one of them was wearing an orange sash. Tim's blood heated up at the sight of the man who had killed him. He wanted to run out and attack him but now wasn't the time. Despite his training with Gaston, Tim wasn't confident in his abilities to win a straight-up dagger fight against his nemesis, but he did feel confident planning, lying in wait, and springing from ambush to deliver a lethal strike.

"But I did everything you asked," Marvin pleaded as the man shoved him ruthlessly down the ramp.

Marvin's secret admirer had to be none other than Dapper Don Diego. Don covered the distance to the prone form of Marvin in a heartbeat. A savage kick lifted the beggar into the air and he hit the dock, whimpering as another blow thudded into his side. Marvin tried to roll away, but Don was faster.

Gasping for breath and standing gingerly on his kicking foot, Dapper Don Diego turned back toward the boat and shouted, "Did we not pay the man?"

"We did, indeed," the man in the orange sash replied off-handedly as if seeing Marvin getting the ever-loving crap kicked out of him was as normal as pouring himself a cup of coffee at breakfast.

"What good does that do me?" Marvin pleaded. "They know who I am." He clutched at Dapper Don's boots. "Why can't I just come with you?"

Don Diego kicked Marvin's hand free with disgust. "Juan Pablo, see that our friend here finds his way off the dock and make sure he doesn't come back, yeah?" Dapper Don winked at the man with the orange sash before reaching down to pry the coin purse out of Marvin's hands. "You should have just taken the money."

Juan Pablo kicked Marvin in the side, and a cruel smiled danced across his features. He picked the man up by the back of his pants and flung him toward the city. "Get up, you fucking maggot. It's time for you to become the hunted."

Don Diego looked down from the top of the ramp. "We don't have time for that. Just make it quick." He snapped. "I need you to find out if the cardinal has anything else for us to do before we shove off."

"Can't I watch him run?" Juan Pablo pointed at Marvin as he got up and started sprinting down the docks. "See? He wants to play."

"Be quick about it!" Don shouted at his henchman. "If we can catch the morning tide, I'd feel a lot better about things."

Juan Pablo strolled lazily after the quickly-disappearing Marvin. He looked like a man who had just had a big meal and was trying to walk off a carb coma. He seemed to savor every step as he continued down the docks in pursuit of his target. It was the thrill of the hunt. The only problem for Marvin was, Juan Pablo wasn't interested in catch-and-release.

After tonight, there might only be one name left on my list, Tim thought.

Dapper Don Diego pointed at the two remaining men. "See that he makes it back here on time." He sighed dramatically and disappeared from sight.

The two men started making their way down the ramp. "I don't know why we have to chase the bastard, it's not like he'll listen to us anyway," the first guard bellyached.

"Guy gives me the fucking creeps," the other man stated with all the diplomacy of a rhino snorting cocaine. "Let's go get a beer and say he gave us the slip."

"Now you're speaking my language." The two men laughed and headed off at a quicker pace.

Tim watched the two men leave, wondering how many were left on the ship. Sneaking up the ramp was still out of the question, but with Juan Pablo gone, he felt better about his chances. Seeing the two men together confirmed it was Jepsom who wanted him dead.

Who knew, this might even be fun.

Tim started un-equipping his gear lying naked in the remnants of the day's catch. Hoping most of the fish guts would wash off, he slipped his toes into the briny water, trying not to make a sound. Inch by inch, he lowered himself until everything but his head was submerged.

"I'm off to see a pirate, because of the horrible things he does." Fa-la-la-la-la.

CHAPTER TWENTY-SEVEN

There was cold, and then there was man-parts-trying-to-crawl-back-inside-you cold.

Yeah, big bodies of water got cold. He'd gone camping at Isle Royale in the summer. One of the highlights of the trip after hiking for three days was coming out on the coast. *All of us smelly fuckers ran straight for the water, and then we ran right back out.* It was freezing even in the middle of summer, but at least everyone had smelled better.

Taking a deep breath to ward off the chill, Tim pushed himself off one of the pylons and swam gently toward the side of the ship. He wondered if his ability to hide in the shadows worked as well if he was completely naked. The last thing he wanted was a video of him on the internet struggling to climb up the side of the ship as he took an arrow to the ribs and fell to his death.

At least in death, his balls would crawl back out from inside him.

He cursed the game developers for their twisted sense of humor. What good was an ocean if you couldn't surf and go swimming? Did the NPCs have a vacation spot with warmer water? He wondered what else Ernie might be keeping from him as he swam closer to the *Mary Lou.* By the time he reached the ship, he couldn't even feel the thick woven fibers as he pulled himself from the water.

Cursing silently, Tim inched out of the water as slowly as he'd lowered himself into it. Being quiet was even more important now that he was in enemy territory. Any sound he made might give away the presence of the world's first naked assassin. He tried not to chuckle as he forced his arms and legs into motion.

The exertion restored some of the feeling in his hands and feet, but now they felt like they were on fire while being jabbed full of little needles. Could you get frostbite in the game? Shaking away the thought of having only nine toes, Tim continued to pull himself up the hemp net. His teeth were chattering, but he was finally clear of the water.

He clung to the side of the ship, the wind whipping off the ocean keeping him from getting warm despite the effort it was taking to climb the side of the ship. A few feet higher up where the chances of getting drenched by an especially large wave were out of the question, Tim re-equipped his clothes.

The soft fabric felt rough on his skin, but it warmed him. Clothes made all the difference when you were trying to stay warm. He'd read stories about homeless people freezing to death in the winter, and thought no one should ever have to die like that.

Like a fucking human popsicle.

Right now, he was not quite turning into a popsicle but it'd take more than a hot shower to make his teeth stop chattering like a windup toy. When he got back to the inn, Tim would have to find out what the equivalent of hot chocolate was here, and then he wouldn't leave the fireside until he was sweating like a wrestler shedding weight for a match.

There would be plenty of time for hot drinks and rest later. By the time he left *The Etheric Coast,* Tim would have lived almost as much of his life inside the game as outside it. You could drink one hell of a lot of hot chocolate in twenty years.

Scanning the deck of the ship, Tim smiled in relief. There were plenty of shadows for him to hide in and not a lot of people roaming around. One man patrolled the bow of the ship with a lantern, and two others were keeping an eye on the stern. All he had to do was avoid the three men on guard duty, sneak into Dapper Don Diego's cabin, and take him out.

Easy-fucking-peasy.

Sure, if you were playing Agent 47. If you were on your first assassination mission ever, easy made you nervous. When things felt too easy, the hero normally got bamboozled. Tim climbed over the rail and moved into the first cluster of shadows he saw. No one called out; the alarm wasn't raised. Maybe he wasn't giving himself enough credit.

Tim watched as the guards with lanterns patrolled, but they didn't seem very interested in leaving their posts, which made Tim's job easier. Flitting from one shadow to another, Tim crouched as he ran across the open spaces. He made it to the mast, and finally he was standing outside the door to the captain's quarters. Tim took out one of his daggers and slowly turned the knob with his other hand.

When the knob turned, Tim's stomach dropped. Wouldn't the door be locked? He hadn't even thought about asking Gaston to show him how to pick a lock. Or maybe Don Diego was inside the room waiting for him?

Oh, shit.

It was too late to do anything but go for it. Tim swung the door wide and darted to the side of the entrance, then charged toward the back of the room. He slid to a stop, then backed up slowly, scanning every inch of the captain's cabin.

Dapper Don Diego wasn't here.

Tim closed the door. The last thing he needed was for some sailor to see the captain's chambers open as he stumbled back from a night on the town. At least he was inside the lion's den. All he had to do now was wait. Dapper Don would show up sooner or later. Tim would just have to hope that when Don Diego came back, he didn't bring company.

Moving to the side of the room that would remain hidden as the door opened, Tim tried not to think too hard about what would happen when Dapper Don finally came back. He hoped everything played out like it did in the movies. When people walked into a room, they never looked toward the door. Why would they, when all the furniture was arranged to minimize the dead zone the door created as it swung into the room?

He wasn't dumb enough to stand behind the door. If the captain flung it open and smashed him with the door, he might figure out something was up. Instead, he stayed a foot or so outside of the door's range. When the captain came in, Tim would leap at him as he turned to close the door. It wouldn't be a fair fight, but neither was pretending to be a sick old lady.

The seconds seemed to stretch into minutes, and the minutes felt like days. Waiting for the door to open was tense work. He'd only get one shot at this. Even if his caseworker respawned him, Don Diego would be gone. This was his moment, so he had to make it count.

A boot scrapped the deck outside the door. There was the clink of keys on a ring, then the scrape of metal on metal. The door rattled in its frame, and then again. "Motherfucker," the man on the other side snarled. "Must not have locked the fucking thing." The same rattle sounded as he fished his keys out again. The lock turned, and the door started to open.

Dapper Don stumbled into the room, swatting the door closed with his left hand while using his right to hold a bottle of amber liquid up to his mouth. He took several healthy gulps before weaving forward. He swayed from side to side, but a man with sea legs was no stranger to handling precarious balance issues.

Another few chugs from the bottle, and it clattered to the

floor. Diego stumbled, hit the edge of his desk with his hip, and made a mad lunge for his bunk. The side of his head caught the bedframe on the way down, and he landed on the ground in a heap.

Tim watched his unmoving body for a few moments before whispering, "He might have just offed himself."

It wasn't exactly the outcome he'd been looking for, but one dead pirate was as good as another. He pulled up his user interface and checked the quest, but it hadn't updated. *Guess he's still alive.* Tim closed the screen and watched as Don Diego took a breath. He'd spent so much time worrying about a fight that he hadn't prepared for the possibility that he might have to kill him in his sleep.

Stabbing someone while they were sleeping was next-level serial-killer shit.

But now it was worse. He wasn't going to stab someone who was sleeping, he was going to slit the throat of an unconscious man. It sounded like the start of a paranormal movie. Dude walks into the coma ward and starts introducing people to Mr. Mayhem, then the cops show up and blow him away. On the fiftieth anniversary of that gruesome night, a team of dedicated paranormal activists enter the property, never to be seen again.

It was time to make this a ghost ship.

Tim crept forward to make sure Dapper Don Diego wasn't faking. He pulled his second dagger free, then kicked Don in the boot. A small moan escaped his lips, and Diego's body went still again.

Tim was going to have to come up with a much better story to tell Gaston. Assassination stories were like fishing stories, right? The fish were always bigger and took way more effort to land, just like the stabs were always more precise, and no one ever saw you coming.

Kneeling, Tim straddled the captain's back. The man moaned again and kicked feebly. It wouldn't be long before Dapper Don came back to his senses enough to put up a fight. The last thing Tim wanted was for him to scream and bring the three guards.

He slipped the dagger in his left hand back into the sheath behind his back. Grabbing a fistful of Dapper Don's greasy black hair, Tim yanked his head back, exposing the man's throat. His palm felt sweaty, but his grip on the other dagger was secure. Now, if he could only remember what Gaston had told him.

Don't hesitate. It's better to cut deeper than to give them a scratch, and don't fuck it up.

Tim put the blade of the dagger against Don Diego's throat. When the cool metal touched his throat, the man started to squirm underneath him.

When Dapper Don couldn't get up, he swatted at Tim. "Hey, get offa me. This isn't funny."

Tim wasn't laughing.

"Paul sends his regards." Tim pulled Dapper Don's head back farther with a rough jerk and started to cut. *Don't hesitate.* With Gaston's voice ringing in his mind, Tim pulled the dagger across the man's throat with all the strength he had.

Blood spurted from Dapper Don Diego's neck, and he didn't cry out or move again. Looking down, Tim realized he'd nearly decapitated the man. He scrambled off of the corpse's back, not able to get away fast enough. He came to a stop when his back crashed into the wall.

Holy shit, he'd done it.

For better or worse, he was a killer. And what was with that line, "Paul sends his regards?" "What am I, a B-movie star?" Tim fought the smile trying to form on his lips. It didn't feel right to smile when there was a dead man a few feet away, but he was proud of himself. He had come through in the clutch.

Back against the wall, he waited for something to happen. There was no sense of overwhelming dread. He didn't throw up. On a scale of one to ten, he was probably riding an eight and a half or a nine. By all accounts, he was doing just fine. Tim wasn't sure what that said about him as a person, but as far as the game went, he was making progress.

It helped that Don Diego was a stinking shit-pile of a man, and working for the cardinal confirmed it. Not to mention the kind of men he employed and the tactics they used to get what they wanted. If these were the kind of people Jepsom planned to reward when he was in charge, Tim was glad he'd chosen to fight instead of sitting on the sidelines.

Slowly, he climbed back to his feet. His body was wired with adrenaline, making his movements almost jerky. Bending over the body, he picked up his dagger and wiped the blade on Don's shirt before sliding it back into its sheath. There was an option to loot the corpse, which was nice. Tim wasn't looking forward to scrounging around in the man's pockets. It was funny, which lines people chose to cross. The devs made it ok for Tim to kill him, but rooting around his corpse for loose change was too much.

Tim appreciated the developers' decision when all of Dapper Don's personal items appeared in his own inventory.

A red icon on the lower right-hand side of his vision drew his attention away from Diego. Tim opened the notification and realized that his quest had just updated. "They can do that?"

Quest Received: Fleecing The Righteous

Good job taking out the trash. Now that Dapper Don Diego has met his end, secure the ship before Lady Briarthorn's people arrive to claim your reward.

Success: Make sure the ship is free of guards or attackers before Lady Briarthorn boards the *Mary Lou*

Failure: If any of Lady Briarthorn's retainers die boarding the ship, your reward will be reduced to five percent.

Reward: Fifteen percent of the take and a new weapon upon successful completion.

An extra five percent of whatever was in the cargo hold might be worth the risk, but he'd have to kill the guards, and maybe find some way to secure the deck hatches so any men below couldn't make it topside and cause trouble. It wasn't impossible, but it would mean killing at least three more people. He had gone into tonight planning to kill one man, but now he was going to potentially kill four, and he had two more on his list for later.

His body count was growing faster than Bundy's.

It was logical to go after the single guard first. If he couldn't handle the man by himself, he'd never be able to take on two at once. Before he could worry about walking into his first real fight, he needed to find something to seal off the decks below. There was no way to know how many men were down there. Leaving the hatches open was just too big a risk.

Trying to ignore the corpse in the room, Tim looked for something he could use to block the door. There were two sets of shackles in the corner. Those might work if he could find some rope. Then he saw the sword lying against the wall. It was a beast of a thing. How anyone could lift it in battle, let alone swing it, was beyond his understanding.

As he got closer, Tim noticed that the edge of the blade was dull, and there were jewels set around the pommel. So the blade was mostly for decoration, the kind of thing an old warrior would hang above his hearth. Or maybe it was just the thing to block a door or a hatch, depending on how it opened. Tim put the massive sword and the sets of matching shackles in his inventory.

"I'm a fucking idiot." The palm of his hand made a thud as it bounced off his forehead.

The open inventory screen showed him exactly what he had looted from Don Diego. Among the items and coins the system had added to his inventory was a ring of keys, just the thing he'd need to lock people below decks and keep them out of the hold. Tim shrugged; it was worth a shot. Worst case scenario, he could go back to using the sword or the shackles.

Tim opened the door and poked his head out to scan the deck. Nothing had changed since he'd entered Dapper Don's quarters. He could clearly see the man with his lantern making his circles at the front of the ship and the other two in the stern. After slipping through the door, he closed it behind him.

The main entrance to the decks below was next to the captain's quarters. Tim peeked around the corner to make sure the guard at the bow of the ship was still in place, then pulled out the keys. He tried the keys one at a time, cursing when one didn't work. He'd thought the keys were loud when Don Diego had used them, but now each jingle might as well have been a banshee's scream.

The fourth key clicked the lock into place. Tim yanked on the handle and the door stayed firm. There was no reason not to be safe. Taking the giant sword out of his inventory, he placed it in the brackets over the hatch. If they broke the lock, the sword should keep anyone down there busy for a while.

With the hatch as secure as he could make it, Tim moved across the deck until he found a spot to watch the bow guard make his rounds. He completed the circular sweep every three minutes or so. He watched the man make the same loop four times before creeping forward. Tim pulled both his blades free and closed the distance to his target.

The light from the lantern swayed gently, casting shadows across the deck. When one more appeared, the man didn't think anything of it. Nothing ever happened on watch. He leaned over the edge of the boat and held out the lantern to scan the water below, then started moving to the next point.

Tim didn't know how the man missed seeing him, but he was thankful he had. Keeping his eyes locked on the target, he waited until the guard leaned over the edge of the boat again. Rushing forward, he sank both his blades into the soft spots on the man's back. The knives slid in to the hilt, and the lantern tumbled into the water below.

The man made a gurgling sound, and Tim realized he had been lucky enough to have punctured one of the man's lungs. He stopped the guard from falling over the side of the boat, laying him on the deck. While it would have been a convenient way to get rid of the corpse, it also would have made one hell of a racket.

How much time did he have before the cavalry arrived? His guess was not as long, so he needed to do this right. Tim had already wasted too much time watching this man circle the ship, and he still had to finish him off before moving on. "It's just a game," he mumbled as he slit the man's throat. Killing the monsters of this world was going to be a non-event after his actions tonight.

Pulling the body behind a stack of crates took some effort, but it was worth it. The last thing Tim wanted was for one of the guards to deviate from his route and stumble across their dead friend, not to mention the sword barring the hatch. He told the system to loot the body and moved toward the stern of the ship.

This was where things were going to get difficult.

Tim briefly asked Gaston about how to deal with multiple opponents at the same time, and the burly assassin had told him to kill one as fast as possible. Then you had one less to deal with than you did before. In theory, it was simple enough. If he could wait until the men were far enough apart, he'd be able to take one out before the other could react. He liked his chances in a one-on-one fight a hell of a lot better.

It might have just been a question of trusting his abilities. Hitting an unmoving wooden dummy was one thing, but killing two moving people was something else entirely. How could you feel confident in a fight to the death if you'd never been in one?

The rational part of his brain finally caught up to his panicked thoughts. He *had* been in a fight to the death. Sure, the man hadn't seen him coming, but if he had turned around, it would have been on like *Donkey Kong*. Maybe it was like when Harry Potter couldn't cast the Patronus charm until he knew he had been the one to do it earlier. Knowing you could accomplish something you thought was impossible gave you the confidence to do all kinds of things.

Tim didn't have a Time-Turner to fall back on, so he was going to have to go with real-world experience over a test run. So far his quest hadn't gone according to script, but he'd come out on top. By his count, it was Tim two, bad guys zero—unless you counted his unfortunate brush with death the day before. Then it was two to one.

Time to make his percentage a little higher.

Sneaking into position, Tim waited for the perfect moment. When the guard passed him, he launched himself from the shadows. The man managed to turn at the last second. His half-hearted defense wasn't enough to stop Tim's daggers from sinking into him, but the turn made it so he missed the vital spots he'd been aiming for.

The man's lantern fell to the deck as he screamed in pain. The guard started reaching for the sword on his hip, but Tim didn't give him the chance and slit his throat. Pounding footsteps forced him to turn and prepare the next guard. This man would surely have his sword out.

A flash of silver caught his eye and Tim rolled to the side, narrowly dodging the sword strike that would have slashed open his chest. The blade smashed into the deck, buying him the time he needed to get back on his feet.

He adjusted the dagger in his left hand so he could hold the blade against his forearm to slash or block. He kept the dagger in his right hand in a more traditional grip for thrusting. The guard started to circle him, his longer weapon giving him confidence. Tim knew the guard was forcing him toward his dead friend, probably hoping to screw up his footing.

When you were facing formidable odds, sometimes you had to do the unexpected. The dagger in Tim's right hand disappeared, and one of his throwing knives appeared in its place. He flicked his arm as Gaston had shown him, and the blade traveled between them and buried itself in the guard's leg.

Not what he'd been aiming for, but it would do.

His second attempt went much better, and the knife sank into the man's gut. With a bellow of rage, the swordsman brought his blade down in a vicious arc. It was the kind of suicidal blow that could cut a man in half.

If it landed.

Tim watched the blade coming at him. It was almost as if the sword were moving in slow motion. He wondered if this was how Gaston felt as he dodged and attacked the swinging death ball he kept in the basement. It was like his body knew exactly what to do.

Stepping inside the swing, Tim flipped the dagger from his left hand to his right and spun around the guard, kicking him in the back as he passed. The man hit the deck, screaming as the knives sticking out of him were pushed farther in. Not giving him the chance to strike again, Tim landed on his back, and his arm rose and fell six times in rapid succession.

He stood up and kicked the sword from the man's hand. His breath was coming in massive gasps. The world swam in front of him and then started to come back into focus as the oxygen reached his brain. Was there oxygen in-game?

No one had ever told him that fighting for your life was so draining. He'd been in more than a few fistfights, but those were normally over as quickly as they started. This was different. He'd been amped up, and now he was completely drained. His legs started to shake, and he hit the deck like a ton of bricks.

His entire body ached, and he hadn't even been hit. He could feel every bump and bruise, now that the action was over. Did soldiers always feel this way after a battle? It was a marvel they could fight for weeks or months at a stretch. He'd been in one little scrap, and he wanted to sleep for a week. Lying on his back, he looked at the gangway and saw Lady Briarthorn step onto the deck.

She spotted him and hurried in his direction. "Are you injured?"

Tim felt better at hearing the concern in her voice. He was happy to see that her eyes held the same compassion. "Just a little banged up. I'll be fine." Tim climbed to his feet, almost falling back down as the boat shifted gently against the dock.

Lady Briarthorn clapped her hands with joy as she beamed at him. "It seems as though everything is in order. I'll have my men take care of the thugs below." She turned away, heading toward the captain's cabin. "Stop by my house tomorrow. I'll have your pay and another job for you."

"I'll see you then." Tim sheathed his daggers and headed for the front of the boat. At least this time, he'd get to use the ramp.

Reginald was waiting on the dock with a few armed men. He eyed Tim as he made his way down the gangplank and waved him over. "You did good work here today. May the Goddess' light shine upon you."

"And on you," Tim intoned as he turned away. For now, his job was over. It was time to go home. There'd be time to think about what he'd done later, but right now, he really wanted the drink he'd been promised upon his triumphant return.

CHAPTER TWENTY-EIGHT

T he Blue Dagger Inn was a sight for sore eyes.

"Or in my case, sore-fucking-everything," Tim grumbled as he trudged down the muddy street. Rain had started to fall, but at least he had a cloak now, making the near-constant rain almost bearable.

Sometimes you had to find fulfillment in the small things in life. How happy you were was a matter of perspective. He'd spent plenty of amazing times in the beat-up old three bedroom house shared by six of his friends just off-campus. It wasn't the place or the cost of the drinks that made those memories special, it was the people.

One of the things that made Tim the happiest when he left for college was knowing he'd be able to help his parents relax. It was stressful putting three children through college, not to mention the cost of feeding them. He was here to make sure his parents never had to worry about a thing again.

Tim was doing this so he could boost his entire family's future prospects. So all of them could all benefit from how much his parents had sacrificed to get him here. He didn't want his brother and sister to be happy sharing a room; he wanted to give them the world. For now, he'd have to settle for getting them into a better school district. The rest would come with time, and only if his brother and sister wanted to put in the effort.

Nothing in life was ever handed to you. If you wanted to go to college, you had to put in the work. The same went for sports, or pro gaming, or even running a YouTube channel. The people who succeeded were the ones who worked the hardest to perfect their craft, whatever it may be.

Tim remembered watching Shannon Sharp be inducted into the National Football Hall of Fame, and finally realizing what some people give up to be great. In his speech, Shannon had said something like, "I woke up every day knowing someone was trying to take my job, and it pushed me to greatness."

He had been inspired by those words. The speech had reminded him that with hard work and determination, you could become anything you wanted. Tim wanted to make enough money to have a comfortable life and to make sure his parents didn't ever need a thing.

All he had to do now was apply a Shannon Sharp-like focus to his time in the game. The things he could build in *The Etheric Coast* would provide a better life for him and his family. It would give them the chance to succeed or fail based solely on their effort. If people were given a chance and a dollop of encouragement, Tim was sure that most of them would rise to the occasion.

But not all of them.

Some people would turn out like Martin. He wondered if Juan Pablo had tracked the sneaky little fucker down yet. Maybe he'd get lucky and Lady Briarthorn's men would cut him down, saving Tim the trouble of doing it himself.

Tim stepped onto the wooden planks of the inn's small porch. He tried to wipe the mud off his boots before opening the door, but he wasn't very successful. His fingers brushed the handle as he received an in-game message.

ShadowLily has sent you a message.

He was going to have to change his message settings. Sure, he had them suppressed in combat, but having a message pop into his field of vision when he wasn't fighting seemed crazy. Not to mention, who the fuck was ShadowLily?

Sierra.

He'd only used her in-game name once, and when he'd sent her the message earlier, he'd just done it from his friends list, which consisted of one person. Tim hadn't even glanced at the name, he'd just sent the message. It took a few minutes of playing with the setting, but eventually he moved his message notifications to appear with the rest at the bottom of his screen.

It looked like there was a pile of information for him to review, but first, he had to find out what Sierra wanted. He took a deep breath and opened the message.

Hey, I'm going to come check out your digs. I've never been to the slums. What were you thinking? See you in an hour.

An hour.

An hour was enough time to get ready for class, but not enough for the first time you'd seen your I can't believe she picked me girlfriend in days. Not when there was dried blood under your nails and all over your clothes. Fuck, he had to hurry.

Tim fired off a quick reply. **I can't wait. I'll tell Ernie you're coming.**

He opened the door, stepped inside, and closed it behind him. Gaston and his crew at their table cheered. Tim smiled at the men as Gaston rose from his seat, poured a glass of beer, and walked it over to Tim.

"You did well tonight," Gaston rumbled, thrusting the stein at Tim.

How would he know?

Tim pointed an accusatory finger in Gaston's face. "You were watching."

"I can't have my star pupil getting killed on his first mission, now can I?" He looked at the men at the table and leaned closer to Tim, whispering, "Wouldn't do much for my rep with the boys." He gave Tim a hearty wink before slapping him on the back and laughing.

Tim gazed at the man, feeling better about the night than he had moments before. "Speaking of the boys, I need you guys to be on your best behavior. I have a guest coming."

Ernie peered over the counter at them. "I won't have any of that in my establishment. You want to hire a lady of the night, you go to a brothel like the rest of Promethia."

"I dare you to call her a lady of the night when she gets here." Tim laughed at the men's flabbergasted expressions. "Guys, I swear she's just a friend of mine."

"But it's a lady friend," Gaston chided.

"We don't see too many of those around here." Ernie took a comb from his pocket and set to work straightening the tangled mess on the sides of his head.

Tim smiled at the two men's antics. "Don't get any ideas." He met Ernie's eyes. "So, who do I have to kill to get a bath and some fucking toilet paper?"

Gaston elbowed Ernie in the ribs as he came around the corner. "I told you he'd figure it out eventually."

"Figure what out?" Tim pressed.

Ernie swatted Gaston on the arm with a dishtowel. "See, he doesn't know a thing."

"Come on, Ernie, take pity on the kid. He's got a girl coming over." Gaston placed a hand on Ernie's shoulder. "Maybe it's time you give him the key."

"No, I couldn't," Ernie whined.

"It's time." Gaston chuckled.

Ernie still looked conflicted, but he reached into his vest and pulled out a silver key. "No one else lays a hand on this, not even your lady friend."

Tim took the key, wondering what the fuck was so special

about it. How great could a secret bathroom in this dump be? "I promise," Tim stated flatly as he took the key from Ernie's hand.

"Follow me." The innkeeper started walking down the hall.

Tim stopped and extended his hand to Gaston. "I couldn't have done it without you."

"I know." The burly assassin grinned at him. "You forgot about the man in the crow's nest, but I got him for you." He whispered, "Just don't tell Ernie, ok?"

"Your secret's safe with me, sensei." Tim beamed at the assassin, happy to be alive.

"It's nice to have such a receptive student after all these years." Gaston started heading back toward his table.

It came to Tim in a flash. "You know, my friend ShadowLily might benefit from your extensive knowledge. You should show her what's behind the red door."

"Do you think she'd appreciate it?" Gaston asked with a sparkle in his eyes.

"More than I did." Tim laughed. "Just don't make her face the murderball."

"Murderball." Gaston held up a finger as he contemplated the name. "I like that."

Tim left the assassin behind as he followed an impatient Ernie deeper into the inn. They made a few turns, and Tim realized the inn was much bigger than he'd thought. It was easily big enough for hundreds of guests. For some reason, he was the only one.

Must be the rain.

It also ensured he was the only person with a quest to find out what was happening at the inn. Obviously, this was a wicked den of thievery, but that wouldn't be enough to generate a quest. There was something else going on. Maybe seeing what was in this locked room would bring him a step closer to finding out the truth.

Ernie stopped in front of a solid-iron door and took a key out of his vest pocket. He placed the key in the lock, and gave it a hearty turn. The door opened a few seconds later, and Ernie led him inside.

The floor was tiled, something he hadn't seen anywhere else. In one corner was a bench with a hole in the middle of it, and a next to it was a roll of the cushy white stuff.

"Ernie, you've been holding out on me." He patted the man on the back as he stepped into the room.

The innkeeper walked in and headed to a device by the tub. He sparked something, and a small fire started. "Give it about ten minutes, and this should give you all the hot water you need for a proper bath."

Ernie headed for the door. "The Goddess knows you stink bad enough to need one."

"So my swim in the ocean didn't help."

"It might have if you hadn't gone swimming in blood right after," Ernie snapped as he closed the door behind him.

The man really didn't want to share his bathroom.

Tim looked around the room again and understood why. It took him a few seconds to un-equip his clothes. Knowing that they would come out of his inventory spotless was a good feeling. Freer now that he was nude, Tim made quick use of his new toilet. As he sat down, Tim swore he heard running water below him. Who cared? The toilet paper and bath were gifts from the Goddess.

The bath was calling him now. First, he needed to scrub off the muck, then he'd fill another tub and get clean. He got the water temp just right and climbed in. Dirt and blood made the water disgusting almost instantly. That was one thing he hated about baths—he always felt like he had to take a shower before and after.

What was the fucking point?

Since he didn't have the luxury of a shower, Tim was determined to take his bath in the shortest time possible. He didn't want to leave ShadowLily alone with Gaston for too long. He might come back to the common room and see them throwing daggers at apples on top of each other's heads.

The water was a rusty-brown color. Tim hopped out of the tub and drained it. He refilled the tub with extra hot water and found a bar of soap, and this time he washed himself. The water turned a little dirty as he got the last of the filth off, but he felt relatively clean. To make sure, he emptied the tub and repeated the process one more time.

"Ok, maybe this isn't so bad." Plus, it gave him the time to read the rest of his notifications.

Skill received: Back Stab

Rank: Novice rank seven

You are now five percent more effective when stabbing someone in the back. I'm not sure what that says about you as a person, but as an assassin, it seems like a good thing.

Tim chuckled. He wondered if there was someone writing these as events unfolded. The jokes seemed so tailored for him that it was hard to imagine them coming out of a database. He leaned back in the tub, letting the hot water pull all the tension out of his muscles as he continued reading.

Skill Increase: Night Vision

Rank: Novice rank five

It is now five percent easier for you to see in low-light conditions.

Skill Increase: Sneak

Rank: Apprentice rank three

Bonus: Your ability to hide in the shadows has increased by thirteen percent, and when you are unmoving, a character must pass a perception check to see you.

Skill Increase: Throwing Knives

Rank: Apprentice rank two

You almost missed your first throw completely, and your

second wasn't much better. Still, you managed to hit the target twice, so congratulations.

Bonus: Your knives are eleven percent more accurate when thrown at a distance under twenty feet and do six percent more damage.

Not bad for a night's work.

Tim was feeling pretty good about himself. He wondered if this was how other players felt after going out and hunting orcs and goblins all day. He was still questioning the developers' choice to make characters killable by NPCs and vice versa, although it added a sense of realism to the game.

Danger around every corner. Learn more on The Etheric Coast News Channel at five.

Tim pulled up his last notification. He'd have just enough time to dry off and get downstairs to meet ShadowLily. The last thing he wanted was for her to show up early and be stuck down there alone with those salty bastards. Who knew what kind of tricks thieves got up to when they were trying to impress a woman?

Skill Increase: Small Blades

Rank: Apprentice rank five

Bonus: Bladed weapons under eighteen inches long do ten percent more damage. The dexterity requirement for small bladed weapons has been reduced by a factor of three.

If he kept this up, he might be able to level these skills pretty far and use decent weapons, even if he focused on healing and willpower. Tonight had gone better than expected, and his share of the loot should be a tidy sum. He wouldn't find out how much he made until he met tomorrow with Lady Briarthorn, but it had to be enough to get his fledgling healing clinic off the ground.

Who knew, he might even get lucky and have enough coin to indulge in one of his side projects to make the slums a better place to live. A few small upgrades would make this side of town at least bearable, and whatever he accomplished now would pave the way for larger upgrades in the future.

Plus, once he got started building the community back up, he was sure more people would want to contribute.

Maybe setting his plan in motion would be enough for Ernie to start trusting him. Tim had already won over Gaston, and frankly, he'd thought the assassin was going to be the harder job. He didn't know what they were hiding here, but he was determined to find out. He had a quest to complete, after all.

CHAPTER TWENTY-NINE

"You have the most interesting friends," Sierra squealed as she dodged a blade thrown by Gaston.

Before Tim could scream at them to stop, ShadowLily tossed a knife at the assassin. At the last second, he plucked the blade from the air and fired it back so it planted itself in the boards at ShadowLily's feet.

"You're already getting better," Gaston roared with approval.

"Helps to have a great teacher." ShadowLily beamed at the burly assassin, her face flushed with excitement.

"At least tell me you weren't trying to skewer my lady?" Tim asked, taking a beer from Gaston's outstretched hand.

"Maybe just a little." He held up his fingers about an inch apart. "But what's a little skewering between friends?" Gaston winked at him.

"Look at where my next knife is aimed, and you'll know how much skewering you can expect from me in your future." ShadowLily pointed her knife toward Gaston's crotch, then made a grabbing gesture and a sawing motion.

Gaston couldn't keep the cringe from his face as he whispered to Tim, "If my mouth ever runs away from me, do me the courtesy of reminding me not to fuck with her."

"She already made that point." Tim slapped Gaston's back as he sprayed beer through his nose with laughter.

Ernie ran out with a mop. "You know, the beer is supposed to go in your mouth and down your throat, not in your mouth and all over the fucking floor."

"Speaking of beer." Gaston held up an empty pitcher.

"Go fuck yourself," Ernie snarled and stormed back into the kitchen.

ShadowLily looked at Tim and mouthed, "What's got his panties in a bunch?"

Tim shrugged and turned to Gaston. "What's up with Ernie? He seems more snarly than usual."

One of Gaston's crew got up, took a few pitchers with him, and headed into the kitchen. It appeared their night wasn't over yet. ShadowLily sat down at the table and took one of the mugs. Tim and Gaston took the seats on either side of her.

"You know how Ernie gets about visitors." Gaston smiled warmly at Sierra. "It's nothing personal."

Tim decided to change the subject before it brought anyone down. "Has Gaston offered to show you his murderball yet?" Tim asked as he took a sip of beer.

"Oh, I thought he was just being super-creepy when he said that." ShadowLily blushed. "I might have overreacted a bit."

"We worked it out in the end." Gaston smiled as he tilted his chair back and lowered his hat over his eyes.

"By throwing knives at each other." Tim scoffed.

"By training." The assassin yawned. "I can show her my murderball any time, but what I can't do every night is give you a gift."

Gaston's man came back with three pitchers of beer and two glasses on a tray. "Why don't you take this to your room and enjoy yourselves?"

ShadowLily planted a hand on her hip and stared at the men around her. "That's a little presumptuous, isn't it?"

"Or don't," Gaston replied lazily. "But it seems our innkeeper has departed for the evening, and the rest of us are awfully tired."

"Maybe your friends aren't as interesting as I thought." ShadowLily grabbed the tray and glared at Tim. "Lead the way."

He tried to take the tray, but she refused to let go. It was probably for the best since her higher dexterity would make sure they didn't lose a drop of the good stuff. He led her up the rickety staircase and into his room. It wasn't much, but he liked it just fine.

"Not what I was expecting," ShadowLily said as she set the tray down on the dresser. "The bed even looks comfortable."

Tim sat down on the bed and patted the spot beside him. "You could come try it out for yourself."

The half-elf smiled. "I hope you have impure thoughts in mind."

Tim stood up and bowed to her with a flourish. As he rose, he kept his eyes locked on hers. "Since the day I first saw you, I've had nothing but."

She giggled and launched herself at him. They hit the bed with a thud, and then they were kissing. Her clothes all came off at once, and his quickly followed. Being able to un-equip all your items in a matter of seconds was handy. Tim tried to close his inventory so he could focus on the woman below him but accidentally hit an item.

The shackles he'd taken off Dapper Don's ship tumbled out onto the ground. ShadowLily looked at them and smiled. "Nice try, tiger."

"It was a…" The rest of his thought was lost as she took him firmly by the back of the head and pulled him into her warm embrace.

"Let's worry about it later," she purred.

"As you wish." Tim sighed contentedly. Sometimes you really did get what you wanted.

CHAPTER THIRTY

Tastes great, no calories.

Something every girl loved to hear. It wasn't always true, but in-game, you could eat and drink whatever you wanted and never gain a pound.

How fucking awesome was that?

And the beer. It was so good that she didn't miss mixed drinks. Sierra had a feeling it wouldn't take some entrepreneurial gamer much longer to make a still. Then they could order whatever they wanted.

The Etheric Coast was pretty sweet. There was only one thing she missed from home, and it was her dad. Also, Tim had been shit at messaging her since they got into the game. Maybe she should just send him a message and take control of the situation, just to get the ball rolling. It helped that she really did like the guy. Sure, he was a little awkward sometimes, but in a cute way. He also seemed to care about his family, which was always a plus.

Now that they were in the game, she wanted to keep their potential relationship going. When they left the game, they could already have a lifetime's worth of memories together. Imagine getting to spend an extra twenty years with the person you loved. Sierra didn't know a single soul on the face of the Earth who wouldn't want to take advantage of that.

Sierra had just started typing Tim an in-game message that they should meet up when Cassie threw herself into the chair across from her with a dramatic sigh. "No one wants to play with me."

"They make machines for that." Sierra closed her message screen and looked at her friend.

"Not here. They've only got wooden paddles. Imagine the splinters." Cassie giggled. "But I was talking about grouping together with others to kill things."

That didn't make sense. Sierra had found a bunch of different people to group with relatively easily. All she had to do was talk with the people questing around her, and they started killing things together. She looked at her friend with an appraising eye, wondering what could have gone wrong.

"Why?" Sure, Cassie had made her character a little shorter than average, but all that mattered in *The Etheric Coast* was if she could kill things effectively. Maybe Cassie wasn't good at combat? Just because you could excel in one game didn't mean those skills carried over to another one.

"Mostly because I want to be a tank."

Sierra scanned her friend's gear, which was all leather. She didn't even have a shield. Cassie did have a rather wicked-looking stick that was bigger than her body, but that was about it. She could tell what the problem was: at first glance, you would think she'd just die, and then *you* would die, and no one wanted that.

But she'd played with her friend enough times to know she wasn't a pushover. "Where is the rest of your gear?"

"This is all I need. I'm an avoidance tank." Cassie looked satisfied with her choice, but Sierra was starting to doubt her sanity.

"What kind of tank avoids getting hit?" Sierra knew they had classes like that in other games, but she preferred to have a standard sword-and-board tank. Her friend was obviously having problems with her class selection, and it was impacting her grouping ability.

"I don't really avoid it. I kind of just redirect attacks." She blushed. "Right now, my class isn't that great, but there is a tanking tree based on dexterity, and I want to be the best at using it."

"I guess there is only one way I can sing your praises then." Sierra took another sip of the best beer she'd ever had. "We're going to have to go kill stuff."

"Do you really want to?" Cassie asked, not believing her good luck.

"Why not? I've never been much of a day drinker." Sierra stood up. "Let's go, girl."

Cassie linked her arm in Sierra's. "Lead the way, mistress of the dark. I will stand tall in the face of impossible danger as your champion!"

Tugging her friend toward the door, Sierra gave her a quick smile. "And shut the fuck up."

"Bitch," Cassie said between giggles as they walked out the door.

"So, what's the plan?" Sierra looked at the three goblins hovering over a deer carcass.

Cassie peered through the trees at the little green monsters. "I'll keep them busy, you poke 'em full of holes."

"It's not much of a strategy," Sierra grumbled.

Cassie grinned at her friend. "Try to keep up." With a battle yell, she jumped over the log they'd huddled behind and charged at the three creatures.

"Shit." Sierra dropped into stealth mode. Maybe they'd make it out of this if she could get one quick kill.

The goblins all pulled daggers from the cords they wore as

belts. Their faces shifted into tooth-filled grins as they looked at the small woman sprinting toward them. All three of them must have been thinking the exact same thing.

Dinner never ran toward them.

Cassie plunged into the middle of the pack, her bō staff deflecting two of the knives as she spun around the third. The goblins were all chittering and circling her, but the girl was fearless. She spun and dodged, using her staff to keep the goblins far enough away that they couldn't hit her.

"Is that all you got?" Cassie screamed at the creatures as they tried to circle her.

Sierra watched her friend in awe. While she might have been able to dodge as effectively as Cassie, she wouldn't have been able to take down all three of them by herself—at least not without getting cut a few times. Sierra used the shadows cast by the trees and the goblins' fire for cover as she stalked forward, looking for the perfect time to strike.

The goblin in front of Sierra lashed out, trying to hit Cassie. This was her moment. With the goblin distracted, she lunged forward and sank her daggers into the goblin's back. It fell to the ground, and Sierra ducked back into the shadows.

"Sniggly-figgly fits," one of the goblins shouted to the other.

The first goblin tried to crowd closer to Cassie while the second scanned the trees for Sierra. It didn't get to look for the half-elf for long. Cassie spun around the goblin trying to stab her and smashed her bō staff down on the other goblin's head.

"Pay attention to me, you little green bastard." Cassie hit him again before spinning and blocking an attack from behind.

The tiny tank moved around until she had both of the creatures facing her from the same direction. She kept her staff moving, prodding and pushing them to keep their focus firmly on her.

Sierra plunged out of the trees again, her blades quickly putting down another goblin. The third goblin turned toward the thief, screaming with rage. It gave up watching Cassie altogether and charged toward Sierra. The half-elf bent her knees, ready to fling herself away from the goblin's mad rush, when Cassie grabbed something from her belt.

The hook flew out of Cassie's hands and straight toward the goblin. It latched onto the creature's ankle, and she yanked on the chain attached to the hook, sending the goblin crashing to the ground. Sierra ran in and stabbed the goblin to finish it off.

"Don't forget to take their rings," Cassie said as she unhooked the goblin and started winding the small chain back around her unique weapon.

"Girl's gotta get paid," Sierra said, bending down and cutting the steel and silver rings free from the goblin's noses and ears. "Now let's see how you do against something bigger."

"Bigger?" Cassie asked nervously. "How much bigger?"

"Let's go for an orc this time." Sierra gazed at her friend, wondering how the five-foot-three girl would deal with a seven- or eight-foot orc.

"I've mainly been focusing on things my own size," Cassie explained sheepishly.

"Well, the dungeon bosses aren't pipsqueaks. They might be twelve feet tall, so you're going to have to get used to bigger enemies if you really want to tank." Sierra watched her friend, wondering how she'd take the news.

Cassie slung her staff over her back and secured it to some kind of strap. "I knew I'd have to face things bigger than me. Almost everything is bigger than I am. I just kind of thought I'd hit level ten and get my class change accomplished first. Right now, I'm basically a thief with a stick."

"Time to put that fancy-ass stick to use, isn't it?" Sierra asked, giving Cassie a wink.

"I can tell you one thing it can't do," Cassie replied, winking back. "Now, let's go find that orc."

"Or maybe a couple." Sierra knew her friend could handle this. She just needed a little more confidence.

"Let's not get too crazy." Cassie grinned. It was nice that her best friend had confidence in her, but Sierra had a penchant for running head-first into things, and Cassie didn't want to get dragged into another one of her adventures—although their joint quests always ended up being freakishly fun, even if it was just a two a.m. taco run.

"Crazy is as crazy does," Sierra said, making her voice sound like her favorite chocolate-loving shrimp-boat owner. "Now get tanking. I want to stab something."

"Holy shit, he's big." Cassie ducked behind the tree.

"The bigger they are..." Sierra started.

"Yeah, yeah. Do you keep those motivational quotes on a loop? If we start losing the fight, are you going to tell me to," Cassie made air quotes, "'hang in there?'"

"Only if he throws you off that cliff behind him." Sierra grinned at her friend like a madwoman. "Don't get thrown off the cliff, ok?"

"Easy for you to say. All you have to do is stand behind him." Cassie watched the orc as he tended the fire in front of the cave. The clearing was defined by the forest on one side and the cliff on the other.

Sierra tilted one of her daggers to the side in imitation of a gangster with a gun. "Tank life."

Cassie grinned back at her. "Now I get it. You're delusional."

"Maybe not delusional, but I *am* in a hurry to get back to town and take a bath. I've got plans to meet up with a certain someone, even if he doesn't know it yet." Sierra tapped the back of her dagger on her wrist. "Time's a-wasting."

"Did you see that this guy has the other three gold rings we need?" Cassie peeked around the tree again to confirm that. "There is a dwarf named Ironbeard who pays pretty well for them. His assistant even taught me a cool trick for how to clean the items in my inventory."

Sierra poked her head around the tree and took a peek at the orc. "Do you think three rings means he's some kind of boss monster? Orcs with one gold ring hit a lot harder than the ones wearing silver."

"Tell me about it." Cassie rubbed her shoulder. "But a girl's gotta eat, ya know?"

Sierra tucked her dagger back into its sheath and crouched to start circling to the opposite side of the clearing. "I'll wait for your signal."

"It's probably going to sound a lot like, 'Oh, shit I'm going to die.'" She glared at her half-elven friend. "When you hear me screaming for my life, it would probably be the perfect time."

"I'll try to make an appearance before you reach the 'Oh, shit, the orc threw me over the cliff' stage of the fight." Sierra stuck out her tongue and blew a raspberry at Cassie before disappearing into the shadows.

"Bitch," Cassie hissed after her.

It wasn't like Sierra had picked this role for her. She'd wanted to be a tank. Tanks ran head-first into danger. It wasn't the danger that bothered her so much; it was the chance of dying before reaching level ten and having to start all over again. "Ladyballs," she mumbled. "Grow a pair."

This motherfucker wasn't going to know what hit him.

Cassie walked around the tree, all five-foot-three-inches of her standing as tall as she could. Pulling her bō from her back, she walked boldly up the path to the cave and the massive orc standing in front of it. The biggest orc they'd seen yet rose from where he had been sitting by the fire and picked up a giant sword.

"Holy fuck, the blade's as big as I am." Cassie glanced toward the trees, cursing Sierra for making her do this.

But she'd picked this. In the face of certain death, tanks had to be brash. They had to swagger, or the DPS got skittish.

Looking up at the orc and his massive blade, Cassie paused in the middle of the clearing and spun her bō in a circle before placing it behind her back in a Bruce Lee manner. She held out her other hand, keeping her fingers about an inch apart. "I've seen bigger." Then she made the classic "bring it on" gesture Morpheus had used on Neo the first time they'd fought. "Let's see if you know how to use it."

The orc charged across the space between them, sword held above his head with both hands. He bellowed in rage as he bore down on Cassie, who had yet to move. The space between them dwindled faster than a man with a case of severe shrinkage. When the orc was fifteen feet away, he leaped into the air, muscles bulging as he brought his sword down to split the stupid girl in half.

Cassie watched as the orc jumped. She hadn't been expecting it, but there was more than enough time for her to recover. She spun out of the way, keeping her balance. Was it wrong that she was impressed by how far the big fucker had jumped?

She would have thought having all those muscles would weigh him down.

As the orc struggled to pull his sword out of the ground, Cassie went to work with her bō staff. She hit the orc with a rapid series of blows to the ribs. He seemed to shrug them off, still struggling to remove his sword from the ground and not paying an ounce of attention to her, which was pissing her off.

Not to mention that when he finally got the sword free, the orc would have a huge advantage.

Because of his size and the length of the fucker's sword, Cassie might never get close enough to hit him again, so she had to make him angry enough to stay focused on her now. That way, when Sierra made her move, the orc wouldn't turn around and kill her before Cassie could gain control.

Cassie stopped slamming her staff into the orc's ribs and spun in a fast circle, putting all her strength into the swing. Her staff smacked into the back of the orc's knees, and he stumbled to the ground.

Before he could turn around, Cassie thunked him on the head as hard as she could. Her staff bounced off the orc's grayish skin with a loud *crack*. The beast let go of the sword and whirled. He managed to catch Cassie with a backhand, sending her flying through the air as he turned back to his sword.

Now would be a great time for Sierra to appear.

Cassie hit the ground four feet from the edge and skidded toward certain death. Her slide stopped, and she looked down at her boots. The balls of her feet were on solid ground, but her heels were hanging over the edge. She never would have heard the end of it from Sierra if the orc had succeeded in throwing her over the cliff.

Note to self: tank the orc with your back away from the cliff.

Pulling his sword free from the ground, the orc screamed in triumph as he charged toward Cassie. Not ready to back down, Cassie started her sprint, hoping to meet his charge farther from the edge. Just before they would have collided, Cassie threw herself to the ground and slid under the orc's blade, coming to a stop behind him.

"*Mouthbreather!*" Cassie screamed as she rushed at the orc. Her staff crashed down on the back of his head, but it only seemed to piss him off.

The orc spun and brought his sword down from above. Cassie held her staff with both hands, lifting it above her head to block the blade. The orc smiled, knowing his sword would cut through the girl's staff and kill her. Then he could go back to dinner, with a little extra meat for the pot.

Sierra kept moving around the orc. She hoped her friend's staff would be able to deflect the blow, but she was pretty sure Cassie was about to die. When she died, Sierra had two choices: run or fight. She saw the look of determination on her friend's face and knew she would fight.

The sword hit the center of the wooden staff, and a metal clang rang across the open space.

"That's right, bitch. It only looks like wood." Cassie casually tossed the orc's blade to the side before hitting him again.

Sierra took that as her cue and leapt out of the shadows, her daggers poised for a kill. The blades sank deep into the massive orc's back, just under his ribs. She pulled the daggers free and plunged them in again. The orc tried to swing at her, but Cassie used her hook and chain on one of his arms to draw the swing off-center. Sierra didn't miss her chance. Lunging inside the orc's extended arms, she cut upward, almost like a prizefighter throwing an uppercut.

Only this uppercut came with a foot of steel behind it.

Her blade tore through the orc's throat. The half-elf dodged the spray of blood and ended up standing next to her partner. Sierra nudged Cassie's shoulder. "I think you might be getting the hang of this."

"Except for being terrified of getting cut in half the whole time, it was kind of fun." Cassie bent down and pulled her hook free. She tucked the weapon back into her belt, replacing it with a small knife to cut the orc's rings free.

Cassie slipped the rings into her inventory with the rest of the items they'd collected. "I'll turn these in to Ironbeard in the morning. Come and find me, and I'll give you your half of the bounty."

"Sounds good. Let's get back to Promethia. I've got a man to hunt down." Sierra grinned, thinking about the look on Tim's face when she just showed up.

"Stalker much?" Cassie sniggered as they started the long walk back to the city.

List of Tim's Current Stats and Skills
"Tim" Level four magic user

. . .

Primary Stats

Strength 12

Endurance 12

Dexterity 16

Intelligence 15

Wisdom 20

Secondary Stats

Perception 3

Vitality 2

Revitalization 2

Luck 2

Notable Gear

Circlet of Wisdom +1

Simple Dagger of Dexterity +1 (X2)

Level Ten Class Change Token

Skills

Small Blades: Apprentice rank five

Throwing Knives: Apprentice rank two

Sneak: Apprentice rank three

Night Vision: Novice rank five

Back Stab: Novice rank seven

Cleanse: Novice rank one

Healing Orb: Apprentice rank three

Flame Burst: Novice rank one

Open Quests

Fleecing the righteous

Revenge they say, I call it justice

CHAPTER THIRTY-ONE

Lightning parted the dark night like Moses parted the sea.

Tim looked into the dark swirling mass and thought about what had happened since he entered *The Etheric Coast*. Things hadn't exactly gone to plan, or maybe they had, but they certainly hadn't gone the way he imagined them.

Getting murdered wasn't part of the plan.

But that hadn't stopped the man in the orange sash from killing him, or the crazy visit to his caseworker that resulted in his resurrection. Tim's rise from the grave would have gone largely unnoticed if the high priest hadn't told everyone in the city about it. He was already on the bad side of Cardinal Jepsom, but now he was Public Enemy Number One.

That wasn't all bad. Since entering the game, he'd met some interesting people he was starting to consider friends. Gaston the master assassin and Ernie the innkeeper were NPCs, not to mention his boss Ironbeard. The surly little motherfucker was all heart under his gruff exterior.

The best thing by far was ShadowLily. He'd finally talked to the girl of his dreams and followed her into the game. Tim hadn't been wrong about his intuition. The whirlwind of their first few days in the game was coming to an end, and Tim knew it wouldn't be long before they were spending all of their time together.

When you find the right one, you just know.

There was only one aspect of the game he hadn't fully embraced yet, and those were his roles as assassin and healer. He loved the healing, and despite himself, he kind of liked the sneaking around and stabbing things. He'd like the stabbing part better if the people he was killing didn't feel so damn real.

Sometimes the quest picks the player, and you have to go along for the ride.

Tim smiled at the sky. He'd always loved the rain, and in the slums, it rained every day. Taking a sip of his beer, he stepped back inside the Blue Dagger Inn. There was plenty of time to watch the rain, but right now, what he was hungry for was another taste of adventure.

"Any last words?" ShadowLily purred, throwing knife pointed at Tim.

"Tangerine," Tim replied with a gulp.

ShadowLily swayed as she shifted her balance. It couldn't have been easy standing on the backs of the two tall dining chairs. In fact, Tim was pretty sure if he tried the same exact feat, he would have slipped and cracked his head open. The last thing he wanted was to visit his caseworker again so quickly. How did you explain to someone that you died trying to balance on the back of two chairs with a knife in your hand?

Almost seemed like natural selection.

"'Tangerine?' What in the fuck does that even mean?" One of the chairs started to tip, but she adjusted in the nick of time.

"It's my safe word."

ShadowLily scoffed. "Losers don't get safe words. Plus, it's in your best interest to just take it like a man. If my legs get tired, my aim might be off." She wobbled a bit just to emphasize her point.

Tim put the tin teacup on his head. "Maybe that's not how it should work. Maybe losers need access to more safe words." He smiled up at her unconvincingly. "I mean, we're the ones getting shafted."

"If you don't enjoy the taste of defeat, you should probably stop betting on things." ShadowLily grinned at him. "Unless you want to go double or nothing and risk finding out if I can do this on one leg, just close your eyes and let it happen."

"You know, this is starting to sound like a weird sex thing," Tim continued hurriedly, trying to distract her. "So, a lady walks into an inn with two chairs, a knife, and a teacup. Can you see where this is going?"

"One leg, it is." Her arm snapped back to throw the knife.

Tim ducked, and the teacup clattered to the floor. His hands came up to shield him. "Two legs. If you insist on throwing the knife at me, please use both your legs."

"I insist." She held out her knife, making a hurry-up gesture. "Now stop being such a baby." When he didn't move as fast as she wanted, ShadowLily dropped her voice, making it sound slightly husky. "It puts the cup on its head."

At least she didn't ask me to put the lotion in the basket.

ShadowLily swayed before steadying herself on the backs of the chairs. "Stand up and take it like a man."

"And now we're back to the sex jokes," Tim groused as he grabbed the fallen teacup and stood back up. Cursing for getting into this mess in the first place, he put the cup on his head and his back against the pillar. It wasn't like he could say no now. He'd lost the bet fair and square, and his most important needs as a man could still be satisfied if he were missing an eye.

Tim looked at ShadowLily, who was swaying on the back of the two chairs twenty feet away. "Fine, but only one throw."

"You owe me two." She grinned. "Like I said, stop making bets if you can't pay the piper."

Normal couples just bet each other sex stuff, why couldn't they be more like that? "I was just hoping I could pay you in another way." He tried to hit her with the 007 charm.

"Oh, you'll be doing that too." She flipped the knife into the air. The blade flew slowly end over end until it started to fall. She plucked the knife from the air, her legs never even trembling with the effort of maintaining her balance. "And don't even try to pretend like you don't enjoy it."

How is she a better James Bond than me?

Although, Tim had to admit he did enjoy it. Whatever *it* was, as long as he was doing *it* with her somewhere secluded, *it* was the best thing ever. One of the best parts of being in a new relationship was the sexual honeymoon, but normally it didn't include throwing knives. Throwing bladed weapons at someone you're having carnal relations with seemed like the kind of thing that ended up on the five o'clock news.

He could see it now on Promethia News Tonight.

Our last story of the evening takes place in the slums where a young man was killed by his girlfriend. When asked about why she did it, her response was, "My foot slipped."

"The endless enjoyment I derive from your body isn't up for debate. It's how much I enjoy mine being hole-free, that is." Tim smiled holding out his hands in a "don't kill me" gesture. "Isn't there another way we can settle this?"

"Just close your eyes, and don't move." ShadowLily licked a finger and held it up to test the air, as Gaston had done. "It will all be over soon."

"This is starting to sound more like an episode of how to catch a predator." Tim closed his eyes and leaned against the wooden pillar. The real question was, how much did he trust her? If the answer was "with his life," he was doing the right thing, and he had nothing to worry about.

Thwack!

The sound of the first blade hitting the wooden pillar a foot above his head made him jump. Somehow he managed to catch the teacup before it hit the ground. With his eyes still closed, he put the cup back on top of his head and tried to think happy thoughts.

Note to self, never gamble with a half-elf when death is on the line.

He took a deep breath and froze. The last thing he wanted was for ShadowLily to claim he moved and have to suffer through this again. Having knives thrown at a cup on top of your head was just as moronic as those idiots who shoot each other while wearing bulletproof vests. He had always laughed at them and thought it might be a blessing for humanity's gene pool, but here he was with a cup on his head.

The sound the knife made when it pierced the metal was like a bell going off inside his head. Tim dropped to the ground and grabbed his ears before turning to stare at the cup pinned to the pillar. The knife had gone directly through the center. Damn, she was good; he'd been wrong to doubt her. Now that ShadowLily was working with Gaston, her abilities had grown by leaps and bounds.

ShadowLily let out a scream of triumph and tackled him to the floor. "Told you I could do it."

Tim managed a weak smile. "I don't know why I ever doubted you."

She kissed him. "Remember that next time I ask you to do something crazy."

Tim wrapped his arms around her and crushed her body against his. "Next time, can the crazy thing be us throwing knives at someone that isn't either of us?"

"Depends," ShadowLily whispered an inch from his mouth.

"On?" Tim didn't know what it depended on, but as long as she didn't have to cut off one of his extremities, he'd do it.

"On how well you do that thing I like. After all, that was the second part of our bet."

"Oh." Tim started to grin. "I think I've got that covered." He laced his fingers through her hair and pulled her head down so he could kiss her again.

"You've got a room for that." Ernie walked past them, yanking the tin cup free from the pillar. "And I'll be billing you for this."

They broke into giggles as they rolled apart. Tim was just starting to daydream about what was going to go on in his room when the worst thing in the world happened. Tim's alarm for work went off. He had exactly enough time to clean up and get there without being late. Dismissing the alarm, he climbed to his feet before helping ShadowLily up.

"I've got to get ready for work." Tim made a sad face. "Can we get together tonight?"

"You still owe me, don't you?" ShadowLily winked at him. "Besides, I have things to do today. You're not the only one with responsibilities, you know. I hope you don't think when you're gone that I just sit around and pine for you until you come back."

"Shame." Tim grinned like a fool. "That's what I do when you're gone."

Blushing, she gave him a quick kiss. "Whatever. I've got stuff to do." She took her knife from Ernie and slipped it back into place. She walked toward the door. Halfway there, she stopped and turned. "I'll see you tonight."

Tim waved to her and thought about how much fun tonight was going to be. Ernie cleared his throat and pointed at the mess they'd made. Tim quickly straightened the chairs and tables they'd knocked over. When he looked up, the innkeeper was staring at him.

"That's one hell of a woman you have there," Ernie said.

"You don't have to tell me."

"But she isn't a guest of the inn, and we can't have her coming around all the time." Ernie frowned. "The boss wouldn't like it."

"Then maybe I should talk to the boss. I'm sure we could iron something out."

The innkeeper wrung the towel in his hands. "Maybe."

Gaston strolled into the room. "I'm sure you'll meet him soon enough. Until then, your lady is welcome here, as long as you keep her out of our business."

"Shouldn't be too hard." Tim turned toward the burly assassin. "Since I have absolutely no idea what you're up to."

"Trust me, it's better that way." Ernie looked relieved.

Gaston took a seat. "You know as well as I do that the kid could help us." He leaned back in his chair and put his feet up on the table.

"The boss said no," Ernie snapped. "No one else gets involved." He glared at the assassin before knocking his boots off the table. "Or do you want to be the one who tells the boss we failed?"

Gaston looked aghast but covered it up quickly by rolling a cigarette and lighting it. "I think we can make do on our own." He took a deep drag and blew out three perfect rings. "For now."

"Well, now is all we ever have to worry about, isn't it?" Ernie sighed as he pointed at Tim. "Don't you have somewhere to be?"

"Oh, shit." Tim ran for the bathroom.

"I had a case of the oh, shits once." Gaston hollered after him. "I'll never eat another dockside shrimp taco again."

Ernie shook his head in disgust. "There is a thing called over-sharing."

The assassin took another long drag from his cigarette. "I find it's easier to let other people tell you when they've heard too much. You never know when someone might want to hear all the juicy details."

Ernie slid a dish under Gaston's cigarette right before he ashed it on the table. "I for one could do with fewer details from you, especially if it involves the words 'dockside' and 'shrimp tacos.'"

"Just be thankful you weren't in the room with me." Gaston stubbed out his cigarette and stood up. "Guess I better take another look at our little side project." The assassin walked toward a door at the back of the room. "We all know how the boss gets when he has to wait."

Ernie pulled a vial from his pocket and tossed it to Gaston. "Give this a try. A few drops on your blades should make a difference."

"Nothing makes an assassin smile like a new poison to test." He slipped the vial inside his shirt and stepped through the door.

"Goddess, protect him." Ernie prayed as he stared at the closed door.

CHAPTER THIRTY-TWO

Juan Pablo moved from shadow to shadow before ducking into the alley.

Fuck.

Had he missed him again? Martin's antics were starting to grow wearisome. The chase was fun, but only to a point and only when he controlled the outcome. The sun had come up, and if he didn't return to the Mary Lou shortly, Don Diego would be furious. He'd seen the captain kill a man for tracking mud across the deck, and the last thing he wanted was to find out how the captain would react if he failed to deliver Martin's head as promised.

How had he disappeared so quickly? The smallest scuff of metal on metal reached his ears, and Juan Pablo let out a sigh. "Of course he went into the sewers. Isn't that where all rats go to hide?"

After bending down, he pried the sewer grate out of place and slid it to the side. Someone else could put it back if they cared so much, but he didn't have the time. He stepped onto the ladder and placed his hands and feet on the side to use it more like a slide. He couldn't let Martin get too far in front of him. If he lost the fucker down here, he'd never find him again.

He hit the ground twenty feet below just in time to see a flash of light heading down one of the tunnels. Brushing off his hands, Juan Pablo started to jog after the retreating glimmer of light. A few moments later, he was close enough to hear Martin humming. *He thinks he got away. This should be easy.*

Staying low to the ground, Juan Pablo increased his speed and closed the distance between them. He was about to launch into a full out sprint when he heard a voice call out. Then it happened again. The third time the voice sounded, he thought he finally understood what was being said.

Papa?

What kind of man makes his family live in the sewer? Still, the captain hadn't said anything about killing Martin's family. Maybe he would give them a chance to live. It all depended on Martin. He waited for the light to grow dimmer but made sure to stay in earshot in case there were other people he might have to contend with.

The idiot's daughter prattled on endlessly about her day. It was the most annoying drivel Juan Pablo had ever been forced to listen to. If he had to hear about how Daisy got stung by a bee at the park and cried again, he was going to vomit.

Fuck it, he was going to kill them now.

Juan Pablo pulled his trusty dagger free. They'd been through this dance together hundreds of times. Each time his blade sung him a new song. The sounds of death always fascinated him, and today would be no different.

Sixty feet away.

Forty.

Twenty.

A new voice joined the mix. "Where have you been? I thought you'd never come home."

"Things didn't exactly go to plan." Martin paused. "I wasn't sure if it was safe."

A female snorted in frustration. "When are you going to start listening to me! These get-rich schemes of yours are going to be the death of us."

"Of course, you're right. It's just that we were so close to being able to leave the sewers, and I fucked it all up." Martin sounded defeated.

Juan Pablo pulled the sheet hanging over the opening away and stepped into the room. "She is right, you know." He paused while everyone spun around and stared at him. "These get-rich-quick schemes really *are* going to be the death of you."

Martin pulled his wife and daughter behind him. "I'll come with you. Just don't hurt them."

"No." Juan Pablo stepped farther into the room. The little girl's sobs only heightened his rage. "If you didn't want them involved, you shouldn't have come back here."

Martin fell to his knees, hands extended in front of him. "Please! They didn't have anything to do with this." Tears streamed down his cheeks as he begged for everything he held dear.

Juan Pablo smiled at the man, a cruel gleam in his eyes. "You can choose one."

"One what?" Martin asked, too terrified to choose.

"Pick one, and I'll let them go." He kneeled and looked Martin in the eye. "Or I could kill both of them?" He stood up, testing the tip of his dagger against his thumb. "The choice is up to you."

Martin looked at his wife. Her face was calm and detached as if she'd expected something like this to happen all along. She smiled at him and nodded her head. Kneeling, he took his daughter's hand. "Baby, I need you to go to Daisy's right now and stay there until we come to get you."

"But I don't want to go," the little girl cried.

Martin's wife pulled their daughter close, giving her a kiss on the cheek. "Just go, baby. We'll be right behind you."

It was touching. The kind of thing that would make most men rethink this line of work, but there was something broken inside of him. He knew what the feelings were, but he just didn't feel them. Sometimes when he went to work with his blade, he almost felt something. It was that feeling, however brief, that drove him.

Murder was the only way his mind escaped the void.

There was this empty pulsating blackness right where his heart should have been. Sometimes he was happy that he didn't feel the way other people did. Their lives were messy and full of chaos. His was defined by one thing: when he wanted to do something, he did it. There were no half-measures or days off; he was relentless.

But even the most relentless got tired.

Getting back to his bunk on the *Mary Lou* was all he wanted. The hunt, as exciting as it had been, didn't really fill him with a sense of achievement. He liked it better when the hunted fought and kicked and screamed. Maybe if he killed the wife first, or even just cut her, Martin would grow a pair and come after him.

The little girl slipped past him and ran for all she was worth. Juan Pablo didn't have time to indulge in his work. Letting the girl go was probably a mistake. If the couple tried to fight him, they might be able to buy enough time for help to arrive. He took another step forward and stopped again.

The sight before him repulsed him to his core.

If there was one thing he'd ever truly felt, one thing he desired, it was to live. He'd never go down without a fight. Who would just let someone kill them? Life was never so bad you wouldn't fight for every last damn breath of it.

These two must not have shared his desperate desire for life. Juan Pablo closed the gap between them, crossing the room with slow, steady strides. It was the walk of an executioner. Martin and his wife continued to pray, their words growing louder as Juan Pablo drew nearer.

A chuckle escaped his lips as he listened to the familiar refrain. *Protect us from evil, save us from the darkness, we devote ourselves to you.* He'd heard it a million times, spoken to thousands of different gods. The one thing all of his victims had in common was that their prayers were never answered.

A cruel grin spread across Juan Pablo's face. "Ask your god to save you, and we will see just how much you mean to them." His dagger claimed her life first, then his. When it was all over, he felt the same as he had before it all started.

Empty.

Why would it be any different this time? Shrugging, Juan Pablo cleaned off his dagger and looked around. Not seeing anything of value, he pulled the curtain into place and headed the way he'd come.

The *Mary Lou* didn't look right covered in Lady Briarthorn's men like ants on a fallen bit of toast. Those bastards were scurrying over the decks, taking away their hard-earned plunder. Don Diego wouldn't have gone down without a fight, which meant he was probably dead. If the captain was dead, he was stuck in Promethia. What in the fuck was he going to do?

Jepsom.

It wasn't as if he could call the man a friend, but he was the only person he knew. He'd probably have to humble himself to the bastard. Men like Jepsom never felt respected unless you groveled, as if a few words said while kneeling changed the way a man thought about you. But he would play the part; he had to.

He was a survivor.

Juan Pablo turned away from the ship that had been his home for the last twenty years and strolled down the docks with the same casual stride he entered. There was no reason to hurry. He found that when the future was uncertain, it was always better to take your time.

Let the rabbits run their race, the tortoise always wins.

CHAPTER THIRTY-THREE

"That was a good day's work, lad." Ironbeard tossed Tim a silver coin.

Still trying to catch his breath from working the bellows, Tim mumbled, "Days' worth?"

Tim stood up. It would have been more impressive if he could have stopped his chest from heaving like the bellows he pushed all day. Hell, after eight hours of pumping the dwarf's forge, he would have settled for just one normal breath.

"I think that was more like a weeks' worth of work." Tim eyed Ironbeard and tried to stand taller.

The dwarf's massive shoulders rose and fell as he laughed. "You want extra time off, you're really going to have to impress me. As for saving me the trouble of having to hire another guy, well, that's what the coin is for."

"You want time off to cavort with your new lady friend, you are going to have to work harder." Ironbeard raised one bushy eyebrow. "Otherwise, you can canoodle after work." Laughing, he slapped Tim on the back on his way to the front of his shop. "If you have the energy."

"That's low, and how did you know I had a lady in my life?" Tim looked at the dwarf, appraising him with a new eye. The man was shrewder than he let on.

"It's written all over your face, kid. Only those who are stupidly in love get that look." Ironbeard peered into the barrels of metal they'd collected that day. "My guess is you didn't get a whole lot of sleep last night."

"Does Mrs. Ironbeard know you like to daydream about my love life?"

The smithy smiled. "*Mr.* Ironbeard seems to enjoy my impure thoughts very much." He poked Tim in the chest with one stubby finger. "Those thoughts never include you. I like a man with a little more beard and a whole lot more meat on his bones."

"Maybe on one of these extra days off you give me, we could take you and the Mr. out for dinner." Ironbeard hadn't exactly promised him any time off. In fact, the dwarf had said no, but that didn't stop Tim from trying. The weekend seemed so far away.

"Nice try, kid." The smithy shooed him toward the door. "Isn't there a lady waiting for you somewhere out there?"

Tim slipped the coin into his inventory and wondered what he had to do for a vacation day. "So if working the bellows, helping you secure more silver and gold than any of your competitors, and finding a way to eliminate cleaning said rings doesn't earn me a day off, what's it going to take?"

"Sure, you've made a few improvements since you arrived, but this is a 'what can you do for me now' world." Ironbeard looked at his shop and back to Tim. "But you've done more than any apprentice I've had, so that has to be worth something."

The dwarf tapped a finger on his chin. "Maybe it's time I taught you something useful. Any fool with strong arms can pump the bellows, but not everyone can shape metal to their will."

Ironbeard ran his fingers through the mountain of iron rings. "Tomorrow, we're going to melt this down and make bars." He glanced at Tim skeptically. "Think you can handle it?"

"Handle it? It's the reason I'm here." Tim gave the air a wild fist-pump. "All I want to do is learn how to make something cool." Tim looked at the smithy's shop, thinking about the future. Learning how to craft things from metal would be a great way to supplement his income.

Ironbeard looked at him with a wisp of a smile tugging at his craggy cheeks. "Maybe there is a hint of steel in your veins. We'll find out tomorrow." The dwarf dropped his voice. "And don't be late."

"It was only one time." Tim kicked himself mentally. It wasn't like he chose to be late. He had been kind of dead at the time. The dwarf thought that excuse was worth about as much as the horse shit mushed between the cobbles on the street outside.

"Death is no excuse for being late," Ironbeard said, shaking his head at the ridiculous excuses his apprentices came up with. Death was a new one, of course, because you couldn't really use that for a night off.

"Being late is also inconsiderate." The dwarf's voice dropped into the familiar pattern he used when he needed to berate his students at the academy. "One should always strive to be early, especially when keeping their job is important to them." He pointed at the door. "I don't want to see your ugly mug until tomorrow."

Tim started walking toward the exit, but he couldn't resist taking one last parting shot at his boss. "Says the guy with more hair on his face than on his head." He kept moving, but a smile formed on his mouth as Ironbeard's laughter filled the shop behind him.

One of these days, the dwarf was going to count on him. Maybe Tim could even help him expand his business. Paying top rate might mean Ironbeard had more rings than he knew what to do with. Maybe with a few more forges and apprentices, the surly little bastard could grow this place. With the right plan, they could do some amazing things. They were well on their way to cornering the metal trade already.

Didn't the day always feel better when it was time to punch out? It didn't matter what you did for a living. When the clock hit *time to get the fuck out of here*, it was always the best part of the day. Nothing made work seem worth it like putting your feet up at the end of the day and relaxing with a good meal.

Plus, if you were young and lucky enough, you might even work a really great shift. People always hated the one in the afternoon until nine at night shift, but Tim loved it. Whatever he needed to do, he could get done in the morning. Normally that was studying his ass off so he could work all night, but it also let him catch the parties as they were getting good and gave him a little pocket money.

Now he just had to adjust his schedule to Ironbeard's, but it still left him plenty of time for adventure. Not to mention, Tim was long overdue for a visit to Lady Briarthorn's manor. ShadowLily was off doing something until later and sitting at the inn waiting for her didn't sound very appealing. Plus, he wanted to find out how much his share of the plunder was.

Tim had no idea what was on the ship, but if Jepsom had been stealing artifacts from the temple, they had to be worth a lot. At the very least, it should be enough to start fixing up the healing shack and to get one of his pet projects started. How much money he had would determine what he could accomplish, but anything he did to start improving the slums would lay the foundation for more good things to come.

Eventually, the slums would become a desirable location. Before he could make that happen, Tim had to find out what was going on at the inn. He couldn't make his central hub inside of the building unless he knew Ernie and Gaston weren't criminals.

Relatively speaking.

They were a thief and an assassin, after all. If everything was on the up and up, all of them would be in jail, Tim included. Or maybe they didn't put people in jail for murders here. Promethia seemed more like the kind of place they'd execute their problems.

Tim was starting to learn that the gameworld didn't feel as black and white as the real one. Morality was a fluid concept in *The Etheric Coast*. It was perfectly acceptable to be a thief or an assassin. He was slowly coming to grips with the fact that he needed to treat this more like a game and less like real life. He didn't want to spend the next twenty years feeling like a bad person for doing his job.

Plus, if he were being honest, Tim kind of liked his job. Even when it required killing.

Maybe that said more about his personality than he wanted to look into, but this *was* a game. No one in the real world died when he slaughtered lines of code. Sure, the characters felt real, but they weren't—although the longer he stayed inside the game, the harder it was to tell the difference. The real world was starting to seem like a dream.

Tim couldn't help his family if he didn't find a way to be successful. Working for Lady Briarthorn was certainly helping him level. Despite his conflicted feelings over the tasks she assigned him, Tim was pretty happy with where he was in the game. He was making progress, and it felt like things were falling into place.

Tim ducked into the market as part of his normal routine. He moved around the stalls and changed outfits from his casual pants and shirt to his assassin's garb from Gaston. People made room for him as he pushed his way deeper into the crowded thoroughfare. Maybe his all-black outfit was a look he should save for when he was prowling at night. More attention was the last thing Tim wanted right now. But when you looked this good...

Garnering a little attention was inevitable.

Laughing, Tim continued perusing the market. There wasn't a person on the planet that would laugh at his own jokes as much as he would. No one could make him feel special like himself. He wondered what a psychologist would say about his behavior. It was probably some deeply rooted serial-killer-type character flaw. Or maybe this was more like him trying to diagnose himself on WebMD. Didn't matter what you looked up, you were dying from cancer every fucking time.

Got too many farts, dead of cancer in three months.

That was the kind of panic he was trying to avoid. Outside of Juan Pablo and Martin still being on the loose, everything was fine. Better than fine, really. Being with ShadowLily kind of made him feel like he had only been watching the world go by in black and white and now it was in color. She was that amazing, and she was all his.

Tim kept replaying last night's in-room adventures in his head. He was so distracted by the replay in his mind, he almost walked right past Lady Briarthorn's manor. Her house was even more impressive in the afternoon light. The sun glinted off the high stained-glass windows, and the wooden shingles gave the home texture you didn't find on the exterior of many modern homes.

The door opened as Tim walked up the stairs, and Reginald stepped out to greet him. "It's good to see you again, Timberino."

"Right back at you, Reggie." Tim grinned as the man slapped him on the back and led him inside.

Last night must have been even more profitable than I thought if Reginald is treating me like a long-lost friend.

Lady Briarthorn was waiting for them in the study. She stood up, walking around her desk. "It's good to see you again, Tim."

Her gown was made of white silk and blue flowers, and it was the most gorgeous thing he'd ever seen. It was like stepping onto the Hollywood red carpet and seeing your biggest crush. Or maybe it was because of the lady inside of it?

Tim's mouth fell open. He forced his jaw closed as he moved his eyes up to hers. There was something he should be doing right now, but for the life of him, he couldn't remember what it was. He wondered why she didn't wear a gown like this every day, and then he realized he hadn't even said hello. It was right there on the tip of his tongue, but it wouldn't come out.

She'd rendered him speechless.

Tim closed his eyes, and a half-elven face with a lustful smile and a twinkle in her eyes came into focus. Seeing the woman he really cared about was all he needed to come back to his senses. He gave a slight bow as he took Lady Briarthorn's extended hand in his own. "The pleasure is all mine, I assure you."

"So kind of you to say." She shook his hand and moved back around her desk to sit.

Tim wasn't sure what to do, so he took a seat across from her and watched as she gathered her papers on the desk. It seemed rude to interrupt her while she was clearly gathering her thoughts. Tim hoped this wasn't like when his parents gave him bad news. They always fidgeted around first. Sometimes it's better to say something and get it over with.

Just rip the fucking band-aid off.

Lady Briarthorn set the papers aside and focused on Tim. "First, I want to thank you for the work you did last night. Your actions helped save many of my men's lives. We also recovered all the holy artifacts Jepsom stole to fund his revolution."

She leaned back in her chair, looking apprehensive. "I know we promised you fifteen percent of what we recovered, but some of the items are priceless holy artifacts that can't be sold. I've come up with a number that is by no means close to what you were promised, but will make you very rich, and let us keep the items in the temple where they belong."

He knew the full amount of the reward was too good to be true. Fifteen percent of priceless would be enough money to buy the entirety of the slums and then some. He wanted to be mad and rage, but calm washed over him. This quest had been vital to his progression. He'd survived his first real fight, and spent the night in the arms of the woman he was falling for. His life felt like the first sip of ice-cold lemonade on a hot summer's day.

But he still wanted to get paid.

Lady Briarthorn wrote a number on a piece of paper and pushed it toward him. Tim picked up the thick piece of parchment and looked at the writing. The number one thousand had been hastily scribbled on it. But one thousand what? A thousand copper coins were a hundred silver and ten gold. A thousand silver coins would be a hundred gold, which was much, much better. With a hundred gold, he could do a lot of good.

Tim didn't even contemplate the fact that the number could mean a thousand gold. The number seemed too ridiculous to fathom. "Copper, silver, or gold?" He tried to play the part by looking at the sheet with skepticism.

While taking a sip from a glass of wine, Lady Briarthorn eyed him over the rim. "I hope you don't think so little of me that you would assume I meant anything but gold."

If he'd been drinking, Tim would have sprayed the liquid all over her stunning dress. Instead, he managed to gulp once, before sitting back in his chair and pretending that he hadn't just won the lottery. "A thousand gold will suffice. I'm sorry if my question offended you. I'm not used to working so closely with a woman of your stature."

His brain raced as he thought about everything he could do with a thousand gold. Maybe he could even cobble the street from the archway to the inn. No more muddy boots would be a hell of a nice start. With dry boots, he might even be inclined to meet with a few of the locals and come up with a realistic plan for several of the ideas he'd been bouncing around in his head.

Not to mention an upgrade for the healing shack. He could paint it and get a real table for his patients to sit on. He'd make everyone feel like they were getting the same service they would if they stepped into the temple. When it came to healing, everyone deserved the best care possible.

Lady Briathorn let out a most unladylike giggle. "What you mean is, you've never worked with anyone as filthy rich as I am."

Her smile remained in place as she watched the fidgeting youth in front of her. "No insult was given if none was intended. Your funds have been deposited in the bank." She passed him a sealed envelope. "This is everything you will need to access them."

She rose from her seat, dress swishing slightly as she moved to the corner of the room. After picking up a gnarled staff, she headed back toward Tim. "Paul thought this might be an appropriate weapon for you."

Tim took the staff from her. It didn't look like much, but some of the best items didn't. Moses had an old walking stick, and he parted the Red Sea. It only took a few seconds for Tim to put the staff in his inventory so he could examine it properly.

Staff of the Life Tree: Thousands of years ago there was a tree that could heal anyone who ate from its fruit. Sadly, these staves are all that are left of the once glorious tree.

Intelligence +1 Wisdom +2

Special Ability: Gift of the forest.

While in combat, you will regain 1% of your available mana every five seconds.

Fuck, yeah!

This staff was some next-level shit, not because of the stat boost, but because of the special ability. Getting mana back meant Tim could cast more spells. More healing made life easier for the entire group. This was fucking epic.

Lady Briarthorn nodded to him with approval. "And your final reward."

Quest Completed: Fleecing The Righteous

You successfully put an end to Dapper Don Diego and his nefarious activities. The Goddess Eternia is grateful for your assistance and has upgraded the rewards you received for this quest.

One Thousand Gold

Staff of the Life Tree

A notification popped up in his lower right-hand vision. Lady Briarthorn was moving back to her desk, so Tim opened it.

3x Level Up: Somehow, you did it again. While other people toil endlessly killing monsters, you take four lives and seemingly level at will.

You have reached level seven and have three undistributed skill points.

Tim leaned back in his chair, almost unable to process how lucky he was. He knew what he did in service of the goddess was important, but this seemed like a bounty for a king or a knight. His mind wandered toward the skill points, but he couldn't go down that rabbit hole right now. Lady Briarthorn probably had other things to do besides watching him sit there and zone out.

Plus, with ShadowLily in the mix, he'd probably be doing more healing than fighting. If his friends could only see him now, hiding behind his girlfriend, leeching all of her experience while tossing out the occasional heal. Who knew when he went to sleep last night that he would wake up a lion? All he needed now was three more ladies, and he'd have his own pride.

He started grinning before realizing he was an idiot. Keeping up with one woman was enough. He didn't know how a man could deal with more than one relationship at a time; it'd be too complicated. Life was so much easier when you focused on and were grateful for what you have instead of always reaching for the next best thing.

The grass isn't always greener.

Lady Briarthorn cleared her throat to reclaim Tim's attention. "I also have a matter of some importance I'd like to discuss with you."

So far, his quests had gone well, and he was ready for his next one. Who knew what kind of rewards were on the horizon this time? "I'm listening."

"It has come to our attention that several of the men Cardinal Jepsom appointed to stations inside of the temple are less than holy. We'd like you to make an example of these men, so the right-eous can flourish while the wicked wither and fade to dust."

Quest Received: Lancing the Corruption

Three of Cardinal Jepsom's top staff have been very naughty boys. Your job is to seek them out and eliminate them for the threat they pose to the goddess' reputation. See the indicated locations on your map.

Jonathan Duncan can be found at his mistress' estate

Steven Sylvester will be at the Lamppost Inn with his favorite working girl

Frederick Bohanna can be found at the Stiff Tart, being punished by his lover

Success: Eliminate all three targets

Failure: Fail to kill any of Cardinal Jepsom's henchman

Reward: A new robe

Accept Quest <yes/no>

Tim accepted the quest. He was too far into this chain to give up on it now. If the robe he received was anything like the staff, the quest would be worth it, even if it took him a few days. Completing this quest might also be the thing that pushed him to level ten. Then he could use his reward to select his first advanced class.

Lady Briarthorn stood up and extended her hand. "If there is nothing else, I do have other business to attend to today."

Jumping to his feet, Tim hurriedly grabbed her hand, giving it the briefest of shakes. "Of course. I'll be back when the job is done."

"May the goddess shine her light upon you," Lady Briarthorn intoned.

"And on you," Tim replied.

She pointed toward the door as she took her seat. "Reginald will escort you out."

Tim stepped out the door and waited for Reginald to lead the way. He could have found his own way back to the front door, but it seemed more proper to wait and follow the man. Reginald opened the front door, and Tim stepped out. He quickly descended the steps, trying to build enthusiasm for his long walk home.

"Happy hunting," Reginald called before slamming the door shut.

He wasn't exactly going hunting, though, was he? Maybe it would be easier if he thought about it like that, but he didn't want to become detached from what he was doing. If he had to kill people instead of monsters, he was determined to make sure he felt it. It should never be easy to take a life, even if you thought the person deserved it.

Maybe especially when you thought they deserved it.

People did all kinds of things when they felt they had the moral high ground. The problem with drawing lines in the sand was there would always be people on both sides of the line. He preferred to let people make their own choices as long as they weren't harming others or their property. What someone did was their business.

When it came to making choices, Tim was fine doing his own thing. No one was going to force him to drink the fucking Kool Aid.

Not that Tim would mind if someone slipped cyanide into Cardinal Jepsom's wine, but he doubted the game would make things that easy for him. He could feel the momentum of their eventual confrontation building like the crescendo of a symphony. Eventually, he'd have to face the man himself. Would he be strong enough? Could he bring friends? Tim didn't know the answers now, but he did know that it would be one hell of a boss fight.

CHAPTER THIRTY-FOUR

"Give that back, you little shit!"

Ernie yanked an iron skillet out of the hands of a small reptilian creature standing on two legs. The thing hissed at Ernie, then let go of the pan and pulled a dagger from its belt.

"Mineeee." The creature almost sounded fierce.

Ernie took a step back, raising the pan in front of him like a shield. He'd be able to swing it, and with a little force, he might be able to crush the thing's skull with one hit. Tim would be able to heal the innkeeper if he got injured, so they should come out of this encounter relatively unscathed.

Tim started to call out to Ernie but stopped as another of the creatures slunk out of the kitchen with a bag over its shoulder. Seeing his friend with a knife out, the other lizardman dropped the sack and pulled its own dagger free as it snuck up on Ernie from behind.

There was no way to know if the master of poisons could fight like Gaston, so Tim had to act quickly. The only thing he had going for him was that no one in the room had noticed him yet. Tim wanted to keep hidden as long as he could. There weren't exactly shadows inside of the inn, but there were a lot of tables and chairs to use for cover.

Ducking low, Tim started to close the distance to the lizard thing creeping up behind Ernie. He pulled one of his throwing knives from the bandolier. He wasn't sure if he could hit the creature from twenty feet away; he'd never tried a throw from that distance before. Instead, he kept quiet to get a little closer, but the lizard man had other plans.

The first creature must have received some kind of signal from his companion because it started herding Ernie toward the other one. Whenever Ernie tried to look away, the creature would slash at him with his dagger making sure the innkeeper's attention was fixed on his attacks.

The bastard was setting Ernie up to get stabbed in the back.

There wasn't time to get closer. Tim fought off the rush of panic that swelled. He knew he could do this; all he had to do was be logical about the throw. He shifted the knife in his hand, slowed his breathing, and stood up. His feet slipped into the perfect position for the throw without his even thinking about it

He exhaled and threw the knife for all he was worth.

The blade sailed through the air. The creature was far enough away that it gave Tim time to worry that he'd totally fucked up. At the last second, the blade dipped in the air before it slammed into the creature's chest. The reptilian man-thing fell to the ground and let out a strangled cry.

Ernie spared a quick glance over his shoulder, turning back in time to get his pan up to block a stab aimed at his belly. "What in the fuck are you waiting for?" the innkeeper roared.

Tim hadn't even thought about throwing a knife at the other creature. In his mind's eye, he could see Ernie braining it over the head with the pan. He grabbed another knife from his bandolier. The confidence of knowing he could make the throw settled his nerves.

This time, he let it rip.

The knife flew across the room and sank into the lizard man's side. Ernie brought his pan down on the thing's skull, cutting off its cries. The innkeeper sat heavily on the ground, the pan falling from his limp fingers. He looked completely exhausted and more than a little defeated.

"Fucking kobolds almost had me. I'm getting too old for this shit." With a weary sigh, he climbed back to his feet. He looked at the pan on the ground with the expression of a man who was staring at a vast gulf, wondering how he'd ever get across.

Tim knew how Ernie felt. Sometimes he didn't even want to get up from bed to retrieve something on his desk, which was four feet away. He'd toy with the idea for hours, torturing himself about how lazy he was being, but at the same time, not caring enough to get up. Until he did. That was the thing about Tim: he always came through in the clutch.

Sometimes it took a little prodding.

Ernie looked past Tim toward the front door. "Gaston, what took you so long? I've been dealing with these things for an hour."

Tim ignored Ernie's bitching and didn't acknowledge the assassin. Ernie had called these creatures kobolds, and that meant something to him. It was hidden in his videogame-soaked youth, waiting to come out, but he couldn't put his finger on it.

Bending down, Tim looked at the lizard-man. Well, it wasn't a lizard-man, not exactly. The things stood on two legs and didn't use their tails to help them move. Their faces didn't remind him so much of a lizard as a... Oh, fuck, it couldn't be. But with the scales and the face, the kobold couldn't be anything else.

The creature in front of him wasn't a lizard-man or any other kind of hybrid. He remembered them now from damn near every dungeon-crawler and fantasy RPG he ever played.

Kobolds were fucking dragons.

At least they could be if they lived long enough. What Tim remembered most from the games he played was that kobolds hoarded gold and trinkets in preparation for the return of their god or another dragon. Did that mean there was an actual dragon somewhere? Tim looked at the innkeeper as he pulled his blade out of the kobold's chest. "Someone's got some 'splaining to do."

Ernie sat in one of the chairs while looking at the two kobolds. "I guess we can't keep it secret much longer anyway." Ernie looked around as if he wished he could be anywhere but where he was. "There's a dungeon under the inn."

"No fucking way," Tim exclaimed. His first dungeon and he didn't even have to leave the inn.

"Way," Ernie said with a chortle. "Problem is, we can't get to it. The tunnels are infested with these little fuckers. We've been slaughtering them for weeks."

He looked at the kitchen and the bag of items on the ground. "But now they're getting bolder. We have to do something, or the slums will be overrun."

Tim's first instinct was to jump in and help. The slums were his home now, and he was making plans for their future already. He couldn't let anything happen to this area or the people living here. Ernie knew that, and he was willing to use the potential destruction to get his help. This might be his only chance to get to the bottom of what was going on here and complete his quest. In the end, Tim knew he'd help even if he didn't get the information, but he was willing to make Ernie squirm for a while as he tried to finish the quest.

"I kind of liked this place, but I can always find another inn," Tim said with a bit too much nonchalance. He moved to the other kobold and pulled his knife free. After standing, he cleaned the blades by putting them in his inventory and taking them back out, then replaced them in his bandolier before heading toward the door.

"Let me know how things work out." He waved casually over his shoulder to the two men and continued walking.

"You wouldn't just leave." Ernie was flabbergasted. "We need your help."

This was his chance to find out what was happening here. He hated having to play this game to get the innkeeper to fess up, but sometimes you had to be ruthless if you wanted the truth. He was starting to think of Ernie as a friend, and the only thing standing between them now was how much the man was willing to tell him. If Ernie wanted his help, he needed to tell Tim the truth.

"Actually, I *can* just leave. ShadowLily has her own place. I can crash there until this blows over." He watched the innkeeper for a moment. "I'm learning it's best not to get involved in things I don't fully understand."

Tim glared at the Ernie. "And I don't understand why this is happening, so I refuse to get involved."

Ernie cradled his head in his hands. His shoulders slumped, and when he spoke, his voice came out ragged and broken. "It's hard for a man to admit he's made a mistake, especially when he's ashamed." Sobs shook him. "Shame is a tricky thing. It can drive a man to the brink of madness."

He looked up at Tim, his eyes red from where he rubbed the tears away. "A few years ago, I had a bit of a drinking problem and a fondness for dice."

Ernie was doing his best to sink into the chair and disappear. No one liked talking about their biggest failures, and drinking mixed with gambling didn't lead to a happy ending. "I won't recount all the sordid details. Let's just say I ended up owing money to the wrong person."

Tim watched Ernie, and a mixture of feelings rushed through him. Part of him felt bad for the man, and the other part wondered why the innkeeper would do something so stupid. "Let me guess: the man you owe money to is this boss you and Gaston keep referring to."

All of the pieces were falling into place. Ernie didn't want to work for the boss, but he was terrified of him. "How did Gaston get roped into all of this?" Tim watched Ernie's face.

The innkeeper looked up. His cheeks were still wet from

crying. Tim could tell how heavily what had happened weighed on him. It was the kind of burden some men couldn't take, but Ernie still found a way to get up every morning. "I was the leader of our guild and owned the inn. Gaston worked for me, so it was a package deal."

"So now you're forced to work for this boss?" Tim hated the idea of being forced to do anything. "Or what, he kicks you out of the inn?"

"Or kills us," Ernie whispered.

Tim had problems envisioning a man so powerful that he could kill Gaston. He moved like water. If Tim were up against the assassin on his best day and Gaston's worst, he wasn't sure if he'd even be able to hit him. If the boss was powerful enough to have Gaston worried, maybe violence wasn't the way out of this issue.

"Fuck, Ernie! How bad *are* you at dice?" Tim didn't mean to shame the man further. He knew that for all addicts, there was a rock-bottom. What you did after hitting the bottom was what defined the rest of your life.

Tim was familiar with all kinds of addictions. One of his guilty pleasures was watching the show *Intervention*. Part of the pull was that it showed you how much people could hide from themselves. It reminded him to take stock of his actions before making any big changes. Not that being honest with himself was Tim's specialty. He could look at a bag of Doritos and tell himself he wouldn't eat the whole thing.

But he always did.

Gambling was kind of like eating for him. He tried to set himself a hard out. Sure he could eat four stacks of pancakes at Joe's, but he only had two. It was hard to wave away that third stack covered in syrupy goodness, but unless he wanted to adopt a new workout plan, a man had to know when to call it quits.

And then have the fortitude to stick with the decision.

Tim never did anything without a plan, and gambling was no different. He always set a budget for losing and a hard out for when he was up. The last time he'd gone to Vegas, he'd brought a hundred bucks to play five-dollar blackjack. Lose the hundred, and he was done. Triple it, and he'd get up and walk out. In the end, he'd doubled it and then blown every last cent on fourteen-dollar Coronas at the club trying to pick up girls.

You can't put a price on memories.

Ernie managed a weak smile. "I'm actually pretty good at dice." His face fell as he thought about where his confidence landed him. "As it turns out, I'm a shit drinker, though."

Tim laughed and clapped the innkeeper on the shoulder. If you could still joke about your mistakes, there was a chance you could conqueror them. Humans have this notion that people should never make mistakes, that they should be perfect.

Chill the fuck out, people. Not everything is end-times extinction event stuff.

Losing the inn and landing yourself and your friends in indentured servitude was pretty bad, but there had to be a way to fix it. Tim looked around the empty common room and imagined it full of people drinking and laughing. The streets outside were cobbled, and the rainwater was harvested for plants and profit. It was a nice dream, but all of it centered on the inn.

"How much do you owe him, Ernie?" Tim hoped it wasn't everything he had. There was no way he could risk all his gold to get this place back. Now that he knew exactly what was on the line and what the innkeeper had been hiding, Tim felt better about the situation. Ernie's honesty already bought him Tim's help, but there might be more he could do.

"Fifty gold." Ernie hung his head, sobs shaking his chest. "It's more than this place would make in three years." Ernie looked around the empty common room. "Back when we had customers."

Fifty gold was a debt Tim could cover. If he could get control of the inn, he could start working on the rest of his plan. It was risky, and Ernie might hate having him as a boss worse than the one he had now, but it could work.

Not that Tim wanted to keep the inn forever.

If Ernie could stay away from the dice, they could work out a plan for repayment. Once Ernie paid off the debt, Tim would hand the deed back to him. The last thing he wanted to do was screw someone he considered a friend out of his life's work. Ernie would get his inn back, and things might start to feel a little more normal around here.

Plus, was there any better feeling than helping someone help themselves?

Everyone needed a helping hand at some point. Asking for help was humbling, or at least Tim had always thought so, but you couldn't solo your way through life. Every successful person had people around them contributing to what they accomplished on a daily basis, even if it was just with the little things so they could focus on the big picture stuff.

Tim always appreciated it when opportunity wasn't just handed to him. He liked to prove his worth, to put the work in, and he loved it when he was pushed to do a great job. When you did things right and put in the effort, the results would always be worth it.

Just like the look on Ernie's face would be when Tim placed the deed to the inn back in his hands.

Ernie shook his head. "Malvonis won't just want what he was owed originally." He leaned back in his chair and released a weary sigh. "There will be interest, and he'll still want whatever's in the dungeon."

The innkeeper's shoulders slumped. "And we can't even make it to the fucking entrance."

"I see you've introduced our guest to the company." Gaston kicked one of the kobolds in the side before sitting at the table. "And your incredibly tight lips seemed to have parted considerably in my absence."

"The kobolds are out of the bag." Ernie snickered.

"I wish we could put them back in." Gaston looked at Tim. "Any bright ideas?"

"Hey, man, I just found out about all of this." Tim held out his palms facing Gaston. "Before we can do anything, I think I'm going to have to meet with this boss of yours."

Tim shifted his gaze from one man to the other, sensing their hesitation. "Come on, guys, it can't be that bad."

Gaston's eyes locked onto Tim's like a falcon's circling its prey from above. "Just remember, whatever deal you make, you have to be able to honor it. Otherwise, Malvonis will put you on the board, and every assassin in Promethia will be hunting you."

Being hunted by endless streams of assassins didn't sound fun. "I'll keep that in mind." Tim gulped. "But I'd still like to meet him."

"Don't go sticking your neck out for me, kid." Ernie looked into Gaston's eyes, pleading for help. When it didn't come right away, he continued, "There's no reason for you to go down with the ship. Get out while you can."

The burley assassin shifted uncomfortably under Ernie's gaze. "Maybe it's for the best that you leave. You don't want to be here when those things overrun the place."

Tim looked at the two men, not believing what he was hearing. "Come on, guys, at least let me try to help." Tim watched the two men. "I've got an idea."

"Oh, fuck, now we're really in trouble." ShadowLily took a seat at the table next to Tim. "And guys…" She looked at Ernie and Gaston. "When I asked to redecorate the room, adding dead lizard-men to the floor wasn't the motif I was going for."

"It was kind of a spur-of-the-moment decision." Tim laughed at the repulsed look on her face. "But we're open to suggestions."

Ernie frowned at the two of them. "You should take this more seriously. People are going to die."

Tim met Ernie's eyes. "An idea can turn into a plan pretty quickly."

"Food turns to shit pretty quickly," Ernie snapped back.

"Your idea better turn into a plan in the next few seconds." Gaston looked toward the front door.

"Trust me. It's going to be fucking epic." Tim said sagely.

He might have been overstating things a bit. So far, he'd only decided to talk with Malvonis and help Ernie and Gaston stop the kobolds from overrunning the slums, but if they could get to the dungeon and defeat it, he might be able to accomplish even more. The framework was starting to come together, even if the details were all a little hazy. Still, he felt almost as if something else were guiding him, like the goddess was telling him to roll the dice.

Bet Ernie used to tell himself the same thing.

It was a sobering thought, but sometimes you had to take a risk. Tim had the money. Even at a hundred gold, he could afford to buy the place. But Tim had the feeling the gold wouldn't be enough, and Malvonis would still want whatever was in the dungeon. While Tim was sure they could find a way to the entrance, he wasn't so sure they could win.

Maybe ShadowLily had someone on her friend's list that could help. Preferably someone who liked to carry a big-ass shield and hurl taunts at anything that tried to kill the rest of them.

Yes, things were starting to come together, and his idea was starting to gain some traction.

Now Ernie was also looking at the door. "You wanted to meet the boss."

Something hit the inn's front door so hard it rattled in its frame.

Gaston stood up and headed toward the door. "Here he is."

CHAPTER THIRTY-FIVE

Jepsom hated the sight of the man in front of him, but not nearly as much as the smell.

All great men were burdened with such problems. Why should he, the cardinal of the Goddess Eternia, be any different? Making the sign of the goddess over his chest, he mumbled a quick prayer and a request. "Bless me as I walk within your light."

He looked at Juan Pablo, who was kneeling before him. The man was a brute and a savage, but even the wicked had a purpose in this world. How could the righteous exist without the flames of anarchy driving the people into their loving embrace?

This man was a tool, nothing more, yet every tool had a purpose.

"Our loss at the docks was a heavy one." Jepsom sneered at the man.

Juan Pablo kept his head bowed. "Yes."

"With Don Diego dead, that loss falls on your shoulders." Jepsom circled the kneeling man. "And correct me if I am mistaken, but you are not a man of wealth, correct?"

Juan Pablo seemed to sink even lower. "You are not mistaken."

"Then tell me how you plan to make this right."

"I am but a soldier for you to command." Juan Pablo knelt until his forehead was touching the ground. "Use me as you wish."

It was nice when the cattle knew their place. It made things so much easier. Not to mention, this smelly oaf had eliminated their biggest problem. With Paul's champion returned to the light, the time was finally right for him to make his move. There was only one thing Jepsom needed to do first.

I just have to get rid of that bitch and her followers.

Thankfully, the goddess had supplied him with just the tool for the job. "There is something you can do for me." Jepsom smiled cruelly at the man's head, thinking about how easy it would be to stomp it into the tiled floor. Maybe he should just kill him now. The man was more of a loose end than a warrior of light. "Maybe even more than one."

"My blade is yours to command."

Of course, it is.

"Next time you come here, I expect you to smell better." He launched a kick at Juan Pablo's ribs. His foot thudded into his side, flipping the man onto his back. He quickly flopped himself back over, scurried to his original spot, and placed his head against the floor.

That was very good.

"Lose the orange sash and get some new clothes, something befitting a servant of the Goddess Eternia." He thought about kicking him again, but he was pretty sure the man understood his point.

"Once you don't smell like you spent the night rolling in horse shit and are properly attired, there is a task I need you to carry out." A cruel smile lit Jepsom's face. It held all the malice of a blood moon, and blood was exactly what he was after. "A certain lady has overstepped herself, and I need her knocked down a few pegs."

Juan Pablo kept his forehead against the ground, trying his best to ignore the dull ache in his ribs. "From the goddess's lips to your mouth, your will is my desire."

Reaching inside his robe, Jepsom pulled out a list of names. "Take this and go."

Standing, Juan Pablo grabbed the list. He didn't bother to look at it. Instead, he tucked the scrap of parchment inside his vest as he prepared to leave. "Thank you for your faith in me."

"It is Eternia who has faith in you." Jepsom's smile grew warmer like when he delivered his sermons to the masses. "Now go and show her that her faith hasn't been misplaced."

The man almost ran out of his chambers. Jepsom's nose wrinkled. The smell seemed to want to stick around. He moved to a brazier and lit a stick of incense. At least his nostrils wouldn't have to be assaulted by the smell of unwashed bodies for much longer.

It seemed as though the Lady had smiled on his ventures. Yes, she took away with one hand, but with the other, she offered new opportunities. Juan Pablo was the perfect scapegoat. If he managed to kill a few of the names on his list before getting himself dispatched, Jepsom would consider the outcome a win.

"Lady Briarthorn will not be my undoing." He raised a clenched fist into the air. "I swear it to the goddess that she will be dealt with in a manner most fitting."

A cruel chuckle escaped his lips as he locked the door. Turning back toward the room, Jepsom picked up a glass of wine and sipped. All he had to do now was wait for the smug smile the high priest had been wearing at their last meeting to disappear. That was when he'd know his plan was working.

It wouldn't be much longer; the path to ascension was open. He could just reach out and take it. Soon, when people looked at him, it would be with respect instead of fear. What else could they do? When Paul was dead, only one man would be strong enough to replace him. Soon he wouldn't be just Cardinal Jepson, he would be the high priest of the Goddess Eternia.

Kind of had a nice ring to it.

CHAPTER THIRTY-SIX

Malvonis must have been half-giant.

Tim thought Gaston was big for a thief, but the man walking into the inn had to stoop just so he could make it under the door. He must have been at least seven feet tall, but he wasn't thin and wiry like a lot of taller men. Malvonis was built like a diesel truck.

Gaston disappeared completely when the massive thief stepped in front of him to remove his cloak. With a frown, the man formerly known as the biggest thief ever took his boss's cloak and hung it on the rack before pointing in the direction of the main room where everyone was seated.

Malvonis shuffled forward, and with every step, the frown on his face grew deeper. His eyes moved to each person in the room as if he were mapping out their positions in case of an attack. Tim watched the man come closer, wondering what kind of mental damage someone must have to even consider getting in the thief's way.

The two dead kobolds on the floor claimed Malvonis' attention. With slow, deliberate steps, he moved toward the two corpses. As the enormous thief stepped into the light, Tim noticed that his bottom incisors were long enough to poke out through his lips, and he knew he'd been wrong about the man's heritage.

Malvonis wasn't a giant, he was a halfbreed. From the looks of it, he was half-orc and half-human. Tim wasn't sure what the man's orc heritage would do to his stats, but he expected that the half-orc would be stronger than he looked.

And he looked plenty strong already.

It wasn't every day you ran into a half-orc. Tim wasn't sure until now that halfbreeds even existed in *The Etheric Coast*, but he'd seen enough pictures of them in other games to know what one looked like. If he had to put money on it, he'd wager that he was staring at the real deal right now.

Ernie moved around the room lighting the lanterns hanging from the posts. Now that the room was fully lit, you couldn't miss all the little differences. Outside of the teeth, Malvonis also had a few other abnormalities. His head was wider than a normal man's. His skin looked tougher and had a green sheen to it. The real kicker was how little his bald head did to hide his pointed ears.

Ernie finished with the lamps and motioned for Malvonis to take his seat while he went to grab another chair for himself. "I wasn't expecting you so early," the innkeeper said, sounding frazzled.

"Oh, I never like to go to places at the same time. Makes it a little too easy for your enemies to lay traps." Malvonis sat, and the chair creaked underneath his bulk. "As for this place, I hope to never return."

Malvonis frowned, making his tusks jut out even farther. "But until you get me what I need, I'm forced to return time and again." He looked from Ernie to Tim. "Is it just me, or does it only rain in the slums?"

"It's not just you," Tim replied, hoping he sounded calmer than he felt.

Calm wasn't how he felt, though. Ernie dashed about like a mad man attempting to tidy things up as he brewed some tea, and Gaston kept looking at him and making the slit-throat gesture. Tim wasn't sure if Gaston meant shut the fuck up or if he was implying that he'd be dead soon. Shit, the gesture might even be code for he was about to try to kill Malvonis and wanted help.

"It's brutal on the hair." ShadowLily leaned back in her chair as relaxed as could be.

It might have been bravado, or she honestly might not care. Tim hadn't asked what her level was. For all he knew, she could be level ten and an adventurer already. If she'd made the change, her death wouldn't matter. She could be resurrected, but it also meant that from this point forward, the only money she'd see from her time in the game was what she made.

NPC-Corp didn't offer end-of-contract payouts for adventurers.

The company preferred people who wanted to stick with the program. That meant working eight hours a day, five days a week, at whatever profession you chose. For Tim, it was back-breaking labor behind the bellows. For others, it could be serving drinks. It didn't matter what you did as long as you did it for the entire term of your contract.

That was how you got paid.

Getting paid was what this was all about. Going back to the real world debt-free was going to be amazing. He didn't even have to join the Armed Services for free college. All he had to do was work for Ironbeard. Seemed like a fair trade-off. At some point, he might make the leap to being an adventurer, but right now, he liked the security and future his job provided.

Malvonis rubbed a huge hand over his bald head as he scowled at the half-elf. "Not a problem I'm familiar with."

ShadowLily giggled. "I guess not."

"I guess not," the half-orc rumbled. "I guess not." He said it loud enough to make Tim wince and slapped his giant thigh with a meaty fist. "That's fucking rich. Isn't it, Ernie?"

"Very rich," the innkeeper replied hastily.

Malvonis reached inside his vest and pulled out a dagger that might as well have been a sword. He slammed the blade into the solid-wood table, and the point stuck out through the bottom. Tim wondered just how strong you had to be to jam a knife through two inches of wood in one try.

Note to self: the half-orc is strong as fuck.

Wrenching his dagger free from the table, Malvonis locked eyes with ShadowLily. "Poking fun at me has serious repercussions." He pointed the blade at her. "I'd think real careful-like about what you say next."

She laughed. *Oh, my God, she fucking laughed at him.*

"Or what? You're going to write me a sad song about how you're bald?" She pulled out a knife of her own. "Get over it."

Rumbling, grating laughter bubbled up from deep inside of Malvonis like a volcano ready to spew. He brayed like a donkey in heat. "Forget what I said. I like her." He slipped his dagger back inside his vest.

Ernie rushed in with a cup of tea and a plate of cookies. Malvonis watched the innkeeper take a sip of the liquid before accepting the cup. "So, have you collected what I require?"

"Not strictly speaking," Ernie said while wringing his hands.

"It's a yes or no question." Malvonis took a sip of tea and a bite of a cookie before setting them down again. "Yes, you have it, or no, you don't."

"We don't have it," Ernie said as his shoulders slumped.

The smile Malvonis had been wearing disappeared and was replaced by a vacant expression. The very look of man set to do dark work. "Just when I was starting to think you wouldn't be the most disappointing part of my day."

Tim turned his head for a second and almost missed what happened next.

Malvonis finished speaking and almost seemed to blur. Ernie flew backward like he'd been hit in the gut by a battering ram.

Gaston was next to the innkeeper in an instant, his hand coming away red with blood as he plucked a knife free.

"Why?" Gaston screamed, eyes simmering with rage.

"I'm not in the business of supporting failures. Ernie had a job to do, and he didn't fucking do it." Malvonis stood up and advanced on Gaston. "Now that job falls to you." The half-orc bent to pick up his knife. He wiped the blade on Ernie's pant leg and tucked it away as he stood up. "Don't let me down."

Gaston kept his hands pressed against the wound in Ernie's stomach as Malvonis continued toward the coat rack.

Things hadn't gone as expected, not even close. Tim had wanted to talk business. Instead, he'd watched helplessly as a man he thought of as a friend was used for target practice. Tim cast healing orb and flicked the ball at Ernie. He walked toward the brute, hoping that the single application of his spell would be enough to stop the bleeding until he could heal the man properly.

"Excuse me, sir?" Tim said, taking Malvonis' cloak from the rack and holding it out for him.

"Sir? Kid, I'm no knight." He shrugged into his cloak. "About as far from one as you could get."

It took a moment for what the half-orc said to sink in. Tim was still getting used to how the same words could mean completely different things simply based on the time and place you used them.

"I'd like to buy the inn from you," Tim blurted, not sure if he'd get another chance to ask before the half-orc disappeared out the door.

"Not for sale." Malvonis shuffled toward the door. "Not that this shithole is doing me any favors."

"Then it's a matter of price?" Tim called.

The half-orc froze in the doorway. "Gold fixes a lot of ills boy, but I've also got obligations."

"You want something from the dungeon?" Tim watched as the giant turned, wondering if he just crossed a line that he couldn't come back from.

Malvonis stalked forward. "What of it?" He looked at Gaston, clearly wondering if he should kill them all.

"What if I could get whatever it is for you and offered you a reasonable price for the inn?" Tim tried to sound confident, but it was hard to do when the man in front of you could crush your skull like an overripe tomato.

"I might be persuaded into a bargain if you can get what I want." He smiled like a Great White about to take a nibble from an unsuspecting swimmer. "There is also the matter of interest on the gold Ernie borrowed from me."

It was a wrinkle Tim hadn't expected, but he'd gone too far to give up now. "Throw his interest into the deal, but I want Ernie and his men free from any further obligations to you."

"My, my, I hope you have deep pockets." Reaching out, he plucked the fabric of Tim's shirt. "From the looks of it, your ambition far exceeds your station."

"And I'm sure everyone you've met on your rise to the top told you that you'd be the most feared thief in Promethia one day." Tim stared defiantly at Malvonis. "Where I get the money and how I acquire the item is my business. It only becomes an issue if I fail to deliver."

Malvonis grinned with all the charm of Cheshire cat. "And you're fine with the price of failure?"

He didn't need to say what the price was. Ernie was bleeding out on the floor because he'd failed to get this man what he wanted. Gaston was going to be next. Neither of them could come back if they died, and Tim wasn't ready to lose them just yet.

"I won't fail." Tim hadn't failed at anything in the game so far. He'd been close more than once, but this was just another chance to prove himself.

"I've heard that before and said it more than a few times myself." Malvonis frowned. "You're asking me to put my reputation on the line, and I don't know you." The half-orc considered it for a moment. "Retrieve the dungeon heart and add two hundred gold. Do that, and the inn and its men are yours."

Tim balked at the number but remembered something. This was just a game, and everything was open to negotiation. "Seventy-five gold and the dungeon heart." He wasn't going to let this dick make him beg while he tried to rob him blind.

"A hundred gold." Malvonis waved away the amount as if it were trivial. "And the item." Looking down at Tim with a smug expression, Malvonis extended his hand. "The choice is yours."

Tim looked up at those tusks, hoping that he never felt them ripping into his flesh. "I'll need a week."

"Three days." Malvonis tilted his hand back and forth, trying to prompt Tim into action.

"I need a week." Tim took the man's giant hand in his own and gave it a firm shake.

"Deal." Malvonis turned to open the front door to the inn. "See you in seven days, kid." He stepped into the rain and pulled up the hood of his cloak before heading up the road.

Tim yanked the door shut and hurried to Ernie's side. The innkeeper reached up, clasping his hands. "What did you just do?"

"I think I just gave us a future." Tim pulled his hand free and went to work. The damage was worse than he thought, but Ernie was going to make it.

CHAPTER THIRTY-SEVEN

*D*ing, ding, ding.

"Giving him a bell was a fucking mistake," Gaston snarled at Tim as he stood up from the table.

"How else are we supposed to know if he needs anything?" Tim replied with a chuckle.

"Any half-assed healer would have made sure he didn't need the bell in the first place." Gaston slammed the door as he left the room.

Tim turned to ShadowLily and shrugged. "He's obviously never tried to heal anyone who basically had a knife thrown through him like a bullet."

"Don't be dramatic." ShadowLily smiled as she spun a throwing knife on one finger. "He didn't throw the knife through Ernie."

"Only because it bounced off his ribs." No one understood how hard healing was. It wasn't like the bones and organs just fixed themselves because he had magic. Tim had to put some serious thought into getting the best results.

To be fair, the bones kind of did fix themselves, but his spells did seem to work better if he put some thought behind them.

ShadowLily tucked her throwing knife away and plucked one of her daggers free. With a scream, she slammed it onto the table-top. The dagger didn't even make a big enough dent to stick in the tabletop. She looked at her dagger and then under the table before turning back toward Tim. "Malvonis must have rigged the table."

"Or he's just that strong." Tim sat next to her, pushing the dagger back across the table. "And he's fast. I didn't even see him move before Ernie was flying across the room like some kind of Jedi mind trick."

"It's no wonder they're all so afraid of him." ShadowLily put her dagger away. "Kind of makes me question your sanity."

Tim wasn't expecting that response. Outside of having to get to the dungeon and beat it, things had gone pretty much to plan. "Well, I was kind of hoping you could help me with something?"

"If you're asking for money, I don't have nearly enough." She frowned. "You're not asking for money, are you?"

Tim smiled. He'd never even considered asking her for money. It was kind of a personal pride thing for him. Never spend outside of your means and be happy with what you have or work harder to get something new and shiny. All it ever took to give him a solid reality check was to see someone struggling with even less.

If they could make do, so could he.

"I've got the gold covered." Tim took a sip from his drink. "It's the dungeon I'm worried about."

"You've got the gold covered?" She looked at Tim like she'd never seen him before. "Mind telling me how, Daddy Warbucks?"

"I recently came into a little money." Tim wasn't sure how much to tell her just yet. He knew he could trust her. Shit, his heart was already calling for him to bend the knee, but he also had to be careful. Tim had seen more than one relationship fail when it came to money.

"A hundred gold isn't a little bit of money. I have ten gold, and I could maybe round up another five if I called in every favor someone owed me. You're talking about giving away a hundred gold like it's nothing."

It wasn't nothing, and he wasn't giving it away. Tim had a vision of the future, and the inn was the first step.

"It's an investment." He knew that wasn't the answer she was looking for, so he stumbled on. "I helped the temple recover some relics, and the reward was more than I expected."

ShadowLily watched him as she tried to make sense of everything he just said. "So, you completed some unique quest, and landed a major windfall." She was smiling. "That's awesome. I hope there are more quests like that scattered throughout the game."

"I get the feeling there will be." Tim couldn't help but smile back at her. She didn't even ask how much he made from the quest. This was a woman he needed to keep around as long as possible.

"But you said you wanted this place for an investment? I just don't get it. Sure, Ernie and Gaston are awesome, but this place is in the slums. You could do so much better."

"Yeah, but what if the slums weren't as slummy?" Tim thought about what it would mean for people if he just cobbled the streets. It'd make it easier to travel, and if you had to enter the city proper, you wouldn't be covered in mud.

If he really wanted to make this work, he might have to invest in some of the other properties. The last thing he wanted was to make the slums shine so someone could come in and force these people out. Maybe his scheme was going to be more complicated than he thought.

"So, you're going to gentrify the slums?"

"Kind of." Tim thought about what he wanted to accomplish and how he wanted to do it. "Except I don't want to raise the value and force people out. I want the same people who are working their asses off to be the ones reaping the benefits."

"To make the slums really thrive, you're going to need a trading kiosk." ShadowLily looked a little crestfallen. "And I've only seen those in the market."

"A problem for another day. Right now, we've got more important things to work on."

"Yeah, like how we are going to get to the dungeon when Gaston couldn't?"

"That's where my favor comes in. I was hoping you knew someone who decided to be a tank."

ShadowLily's face went kind of slack, and Tim realized she must have gone into her menu to look for someone. He took a moment to open his own interface. He had a few stat points to allocate. Right now his stats looked good, but they would change, based on whatever weapons and armor he equipped. For now, he was satisfied wearing his assassin's gear, but he knew eventually he'd have to make a choice.

Strength 12
Endurance 12
Dexterity 16
Intelligence 15
Wisdom 20

With his staff equipped, Tim's intelligence would go up by one, and his wisdom by two. He'd also lose the plus-two to his dexterity stat when he unequipped his daggers. At the moment, his ability to fight seemed more important than his healing, so placing the points into dexterity might be the way to go.

There was no way to know how valuable stat points would be in the long run, but over time, dedicating them to a single stat might give you a benefit over someone who diversified. How big that benefit would be was anybody's guess.

With the quest he had in front of him, the smart money was on sticking them in dexterity, but they might have a tank joining them. Whoever that poor bastard was, he wasn't going to be happy getting hit and not getting healed effectively. I can't risk losing the tank, by being ineffective.

He looked at his stats again and allocated his three skill points. Tim let the choice marinate for a moment and hit the confirm button. *Not too shabby.*

Checking the rest of his stat sheet, Tim noticed that his secondary stats had also received a boost.

Perception 4

Vitality 3

Revitalization 3

Luck 3

Maybe every few levels or so, you were just given points? Or maybe it was how you played your character. The vitality bonus could have come from his work with Ironbeard and the revitalization bonus from casting. The increases to luck and perception might have happened with his recent conversations.

One thing Tim was certain of, he was going to have to pay a little more attention to his stat sheet.

Tim dismissed the stats and glanced across the table at ShadowLily. It looked like she had news, but maybe not the best. "What's up?"

"I found a tank." ShadowLily smiled weakly across the table. "She's not exactly traditional."

"'She?'" Tim asked before he even thought about it. There was no reason a woman couldn't play a video game as well as a man or better. In this world, everyone's stats meant the same thing. Being taller or bulkier might give you an advantage in looks, but when it came to gameplay, it didn't mean all that much.

Maybe it was okay that he reshaped his vision of a massive hunk of metal just soaking in the damage. Instead, it might be a woman holding up a shield big enough to protect her whole body. Tim didn't care how they looked or what gear they chose. He only cared if their tank was effective.

"I know it's a little different." ShadowLily almost seemed apologetic.

Tim held up his hand to stop her. There was no reason to apologize. There was nothing wrong with being different as long as you were good. Sometimes it was fun to challenge people's perceptions. Tim had decided long ago that you should never feel bad about who you are. Life was much more fun when you embraced your quirks. If anything, being inside *The Etheric Coast* gave them all a clean slate to be whoever they wanted.

"My question should have been, is she good?" Tim waited for ShadowLily's response. His entire plan would rise and fall on how good a tank their newest addition was.

"Cassie can hold her own." ShadowLily smiled. "It's not her ability to be badass I'm worried about. It's the way she's choosing to go about it."

Tim made a "come on, give me the bad news" gesture.

"Cassie is an avoidance tank." She sat back, looking worried after spitting out the dreaded word "avoidance."

"Isn't the whole point of a tank to stand there and soak up the damage so the DPS can do their thing?" Tim was starting to get worried now.

"No. The entire purpose of the tank is to keep the bad guys focused on them so the DPS can do their thing. *How* they keep the enemy's attention is up to them." ShadowLily gave him another weak smile. "I'm sure she can handle it."

Her smile didn't fill him with confidence, but he didn't know anyone else, so he was willing to give it a try. "Tell her she's in." His girlfriend beamed at him, and he knew he'd made the right choice. "Why don't you have her meet us later tonight?"

"Why wait? I bet she could be here in a few minutes." ShadowLily looked angry. "Unless you weren't serious about giving her a chance?"

Tim smiled at the woman of his dreams. "I'm a hundred percent committed to giving Cassie a tryout. With you and Gaston dealing damage, all she has to do is make it easy for you. Who knows? She might even work out better for us than a traditional tank."

"How so?"

"If Cassie doesn't take a lot of damage, I might be able to help the two of you fend off the horde of kobolds." The more he thought about it, the more he liked the idea. He could help them kill the kobolds until Cassie took a hit, then he'd switch to his staff to heal her before returning to the killing field.

"That would be kind of nice since we're still short one person for a full group." ShadowLily shrugged. "Unless you have someone else coming to join us."

"I'm sure we'll find the right person eventually, but I think we can handle this with just the four of us." Tim smiled, but his mind was already thinking of what kind of roles they needed to be fulfilled to round out their group.

"Whatever you say. You're in charge of this little mission." She got up from the table. "I'll go meet up with Cassie to fill her in and see if she needs any gear before we get started."

"Awesome. Let's plan on meeting here at eleven and spend an hour in the tunnels before calling it quits. We can do more tomorrow."

"Let me guess—you've got another one of your super-secret temple missions to take care of?" ShadowLily looked at him appraisingly. "If I didn't know any better, I'd say you were trying to get rid of me for some other reason."

Tim thought he saw the tiniest hint of jealousy in her eyes. It was a good look on her. There was something to be said for being wanted by the person you were falling for. He looked at the quest, and it didn't say anything about having to solo. "If you want to come along, I might be able to take care of more than one part tonight."

She pretended to think about it for a moment, but Tim knew she already had an answer. "I think I'll keep it a girl's night, but don't think I won't come with you one of these times."

"It's a standing offer. If I ever head off for a quest, you are always free to join me." Tim smiled, closing the distance between them. He gave her a quick kiss on the lips, then a much longer version. "I wouldn't be able to do this without you."

ShadowLily slapped him on the chest as they broke apart. "Don't you forget it!" She turned to the door. "And don't be late. One of us has to be up for work in the morning."

"See you at eleven." Tim gave her one last wave as the door closed before turning around and bumping into Gaston.

"Did you say you needed some help?" the burly assassin asked, eyes pleading for the answer to be yes.

"I think I'm fine," Tim replied. He wasn't going to give Gaston the easy out he was looking for. Someone had to stay here and take care of Ernie.

"You hear that, Ernie? The kid needs help with something!" Gaston shouted. "We'll be right back."

The assassin put an arm around Tim's shoulders and ushered him to the door. "Let's get the fuck out of here before he starts chasing us around with that bell."

CHAPTER THIRTY-EIGHT

"I wonder how long he'll ring that bell before getting out of bed?" Gaston laughed. "He's going to be so pissed."

"Well, he *did* just get stabbed." Tim looked at his burly companion. "It couldn't have felt very good."

"A mere flesh wound." Gaston's smile turned more serious. "That's the trick of magical healing. The body recovers instantly, but the mind takes a little longer to catch up. So, tell me, fearless leader, what kind of trouble are we getting into tonight?"

Tim was shocked. He hadn't thought Gaston would be allowed to help him on his quest. That he was just using this as an excuse to get away from Ernie. If the assassin wanted to help, Tim wouldn't turn it down.

"There are a few things I have to take care of." He shared the list of names with Gaston.

Gaston looked at the names, and when he reached the end, he frowned. "I can help with the first two, but I'm not allowed at the Stiff Tart anymore."

There was a story there, and Tim wanted to hear it. "You have to tell me more."

"Let's just say there was a misunderstanding involving a pineapple." Gaston shivered. "And I'm not going to be welcome there anytime soon." His frown disappeared. "Not that it wasn't totally worth it."

Knocking two of the names off the list would be amazing, and with Gaston's help, he just might be able to do it. Tim was sure Gaston could kill both men without breaking a sweat, but there was no way the game would make things that easy for him. In almost every game he'd played, you had to contribute to the kill to get a share of the reward. At the very least, Tim figured he had to participate in his own quest. Otherwise, it felt like cheating.

"Which location is closest?" Tim asked. He just wanted to get this done so he could meet up with their tank in time to get some sleep before work in the morning. The faster he wrapped up this quest, the more time he could spend focusing on the dungeon.

"The Lamppost Inn is closest, but I think we should go to the other address first. The houses there have a little more room between them. Should make things easier for us." Gaston looked at Tim and waited for him to make the decision.

"Lead the way, Gaston. I'm looking at this as a learning opportunity. It's not often you get to watch a master at work." Tim followed the assassin as he walked down the street.

"Grandmaster," Gaston corrected. "I might not be a full grandmaster yet, but I've sure enough earned the title."

Tim bowed dramatically. "Then the honor is all mine."

"Fuck you," Gaston growled.

"Sir, I am aghast that you would use such language." Tim laughed at the confused look on his face. "Starting to wonder if you would have been better off staying with Ernie?"

"At least this way when I stab someone, no one will complain." Gaston tied his hair back in a ponytail before glancing back at Tim and noting his concerned expression. "You know, because it's a quest and not for fun."

"Oh, I thought you might have been talking about stabbing me for giving Ernie that bell." Tim wasn't quite sure how to take Gaston yet. Did he really stab people for fun?

"I could always change my mind." Gaston grinned like the Joker. "But not tonight. Tonight we have darker deeds than stabbing our friends to handle." He put his arm around Tim's shoulders again and led him toward their destination.

―――

"Fuck, you're heavy." Tim huffed as Gaston climbed onto his shoulders.

"But I'm also strong enough to pull you up after me," Gaston fired back as he reached the top of the wall surrounding the estate.

Tim jumped, caught Gaston's outstretched hand, and let the assassin pull him up. A moment later, both of them hit the neatly trimmed grass of the estate's inner courtyard. No guards called out shouts of warning. In fact, the estate's grounds looked deserted.

They were in.

Now all they had to do was find Jonathan Duncan and get out of there before anyone noticed them. Tim looked up, ready to ask his burly companion what was next, only to see Gaston sprinting across the yard in a low crouch. The assassin went from one inky-black patch of darkness to another like a ghost.

"Little warning next time." Tim jogged after Gaston. This was his quest, after all. Shouldn't he at least try to keep up? Tim started sprinting, trying to follow the same path as the assassin. Every time he moved, Tim expected a guard to call out or an arrow to spear him from some unseen archer.

As he reached the last tree before the house, it dawned on Tim that there might not be any guards. How many people did you really want in the loop of your infidelity? Loose lips sank ships, and the only way two people could keep a secret was if one of them is dead.

Could they really be this lucky?

Gaston circled the house until he found what he was looking for—a trellis of ivy ran up the entire back wall of the house. The assassin glanced in both directions before jumping onto the trellis and ascending. The burly assassin reached the top and pulled himself onto the second story balcony before waving Tim up.

With the coast clear, Tim followed Gaston up the trellis. The entire time he was climbing he wondered why anyone would have one of these on their home. Sure, it looked awesome, but it made things much easier for people of a criminal nature to break in.

Tim joined Gaston on the second-floor balcony just in time to watch his teacher pick the lock. Picking locks was a handy skill Tim was going to have to learn if he had to keep sneaking into places. There was a part of him that longed to put these assassination missions behind him so he could focus on what he really wanted to do.

Healing.

In Tim's heart, he was a healer through and through. He wanted to control the ebb and flow of the battle by keeping his teammates alive, not by sneaking into houses in the dark to stab people in the back. Not that there was anything wrong with rolling an assassin; it just wasn't his cup of tea.

Most of the time in life, just like in games, you had to pay your dues before you got to the next level. The inn, everything he wanted to accomplish in the slums, all of it was possible because of his work for Lady Briarthorn and Paul. Without their help and their gold, Tim wouldn't be in a position to do much more than kill orcs.

With their help, he was in a position to create a dynasty.

For him, the choice was simple. He'd keep his head down and do the work, and when he was ready, he'd reap the rewards of his labors to get back to doing what he liked best.

Gaston opened the door and peered inside the house before motioning for Tim to follow him. When they were both inside, Gaston closed the door and led them deeper into the house. When they entered the hallway, the assassin held up a finger to his ear and pointed to their left.

Now that Gaston pointed out the noise, Tim couldn't get it out of his head no matter how much he wanted to. Coming from the room next to them was the unmistakable sound of two people going at it. Part of him wanted to laugh. It almost reminded him of being back at the house on campus. Thin walls and twelve room-mates made for some incredibly interesting breakfast conversations.

Gaston grinned as he opened the door leading toward the noise. The assassin stuck his head into the gap he made and froze. Ever so slowly, he pulled his head back and edged the door closed. Looking at Tim, he held up two fingers and motioned to either side of the door.

Guess there are a few guards here after all.

Tim motioned for Gaston to go back the way they had come in. There was another terrace outside the bedroom. The gap between the two was about seven feet, and they'd have to be able to jump across in a single leap from a standstill. If they could handle the jump and get through the other door quietly enough, they might not have to fight the guards.

After Tim climbed onto the railing, he wobbled a bit. He waited until he felt centered, then flexed his knees and sprang forward with everything he had. The open space below him passed by in an instant, but it took long enough that his heart was hammering. After clearing the rail on the other side, he hit the balcony and rolled.

The noises coming from the bedroom stopped.

"Did you hear something?" a female voice asked.

"Just the sounds of your delight," a man growled. "There is nothing to worry about, Maria. I've got two men at the gate, and another two outside this room. You're as safe here as if you were sleeping in the palace."

"Wouldn't that be something. I heard the sheets smell like rose petals."

"You're my rose petal."

She giggled, and Tim heard kissing noises. They were about to forget the world again, and Tim was going to take advantage of it. Gaston casually jumped across the gap and landed as softly as a cat on the other side. The assassin pointed at the white fabric billowing in the breeze.

The doors were open.

Probably trying to cool the room, like they had done a hundred times before. Only this time, Tim and Gaston were there to take advantage of their lax security. Creeping forward, Tim caught the sight of the woman's back as she moved on top of his target.

How in the hell was he going to knock her out and kill Jonathan Duncan without the guards noticing?

Tim looked back at Gaston, only to see the man smiling as he watched the two in bed. "Perk of the job." He grinned and reached into a small satchel tied to his belt. His hand came back out with a throwing dart.

With a flick of his wrist, Gaston tossed the dart, striking the woman on the back of her neck. Her back arched and she cried out as if in ecstasy before slumping on top of the man.

Tim rushed forward. There wasn't a lot of time left before the man completely freaked out. Already the man was shaking Maria, saying her name with greater and greater urgency. He was about to lose it, and when he did, the guards would kick in the door, giving them a new set of problems.

Tim's daggers seemed to appear in his hands as he crossed the space at a run. His target didn't even look up as Tim plunged the blades into him. A scream tore from his target's lips, and the door to the room slammed open. The two guards stormed in, brandishing their swords.

"Check on Duncan," one of the guards shouted as he faced the two assassins.

The other guard started moving toward the bed as Tim backed away. "No need to check on him. He's never getting up again."

The first guard let out a throaty war cry and charged at Gaston. The assassin simply ducked under the wild swing and cracked the guard on the back of his head with the handle of his dagger, sending the man to the ground in a heap.

Watching his companion go down so easily seemed to take all the fight out of the remaining guard. His sword clattered to the floor. "Please don't kill me."

Gaston hit the man on the temple. "The thought never even crossed my mind."

Tim looked at the assassin. "One mark down. One more to go." Tonight couldn't have been going any better if it had been scripted.

Gaston beamed at his friend. "Let's get a move on. The night is young, and if you want your second kill, there is still a lot to do."

CHAPTER THIRTY-NINE

Cassie waved at ShadowLily as she came through the door. It was good to see her friend in better spirits than she had been the last time they ran into each other. Maybe Cassie already knew she was there to entice her into tanking more.

"So, you couldn't get enough, could you?" Cassie asked ShadowLily as they sat at the bar.

"You know me. I'm never satisfied with a one-time performance of anything."

"Let's start with a beer, then." Cassie pointed toward the waitress and held up two fingers. She turned back to the half-elf with a smirk on her face. "And some food. You look like you need to eat."

"As delightful as that sounds, I kinda had other plans for us tonight." ShadowLily lifted one eyebrow to the sky in a flirty manner.

The waitress set down their beers, and Cassie flashed her a smile before the woman moved to the next table. "Do tell." She took a sip from her mug, eyes watching ShadowLily intently.

Leaning in close enough for people to think they might be

more than friends, ShadowLily whispered to her. "I might have found a dungeon."

Cassie sprayed beer all over the table. "A dungeon? You're fucking shitting me. No one's even seen one yet."

Eyes from around the room turned toward them, and Shadow-Lily gave her friend a death stare as she leaned back in her chair. Then she grinned at her, playing off her earlier statement as a joke. "Yeah, but wouldn't finding a dungeon be cool?" she said loudly enough for the people around them to hear.

A quick glance around the room as ShadowLily sipped her beer confirmed that most of the patrons had already turned back to their conversations.

Tossing a silver coin on the table, ShadowLily stood up and motioned for Cassie to follow her. "Let's go somewhere quieter so we can talk."

"My room's upstairs." Cassie stood up and started walking toward the stairs.

Damn, her room was pretty nice. It made Tim's look like a flophouse from some kind of gritty crime drama. Cassie's bed was of the four-poster variety, and she even had her own bathroom. It wasn't quite as nice as her quarters, but ShadowLily had been upgraded for recruiting her friends into the game.

Outside of the gold she split with her friends, the upgraded quarters were the biggest bonus she received. Funny how she had the nicest inn room in the world, even came with its own concierge, but all she wanted to do was go back to Tim's room and rock his world until they broke the legs off his rickety bed.

But right now, Tim had other things to worry about. "Have you decided if you are going to make tanking your permanent class yet?"

Cassie watched her friend closely and looked for any sign of what she wanted to hear. After a moment she decided to tell her the truth. If Sierra didn't want her in her group because of her tanking style, that was fine. She'd find a way to deal. "I'm fully committed to being a tank."

ShadowLily beamed at her. "That's exactly what I wanted to hear." Looking her friend over, one last question came to mind. "Have you upgraded any of your gear yet?"

Cassie looked at the floor. "Not really." When she glanced up, her eyes brightened. "But I did turn in those rings, so I have a little bit of money. Not to mention your half of the proceeds."

ShadowLily reached out to Cassie's outstretched hand and closed it around the coins before pushing it back to her. "Let's use those to try to find you some upgrades."

"Shopping is kind of my specialty." Cassie put the coins back in her inventory and rested her hands on her hips. "So, do you really know where a dungeon is?"

"We think we do." ShadowLily grinned at her friend. "But to find out we have to fight our way there. That's why I sent the message and am here now. We want you to be our tank."

Cassie smiled from ear to ear. "This is exactly how I imagined all my conversations going when I picked tanking. I have to say, it's a very satisfying feeling."

"Don't get too smug yet. There are a few risks involved." ShadowLily looked at her friend, trying to downplay their situation a bit. "Tim kinda made a deal with a shady gangster and if we don't get what he wants." She paused to make sure she had Cassie's full attention, then ran a finger across her throat.

"Can NPC's in the city even kill players?" Cassie looked appalled by the notion.

"Apparently they can." ShadowLily took her friend's hand. "So, you still interested?"

"It's not like I had other plans for tonight, and what kind of self-respecting woman turns down a shopping trip with her bestie?" Cassie linked her arm through ShadowLily's "Let's hit the market."

"How can I help you, ladies?" the merchant asked while moving around the counter.

"We're looking for something kind of unique," Cassie said as she moved farther into the shop.

"Unique? Oh, I like the sound of that, providing you have the gold to cover the cost." He pulled his hat from his head with a flourish and bowed so low that as he stood back up, the hat in his hand brushed the ground. "Allow me to introduce myself. I am Waldorf, master armorer."

"It's nice to meet you, Waldorf." ShadowLily looked around the shop at all the bulky suits of full plate and chainmail. "I'm looking for something my friend can use."

Waldorf frowned as he looked at Cassie. "It'd have to be custom-built, but we've built suits of armor for many a young man before. This won't be too much of a challenge."

Cassie frowned at him. Just because she was small didn't mean he should be comparing her to boys. "Actually, I'm not looking for a full suit of armor. I just need something to protect my forearms and shins. Something I can move in."

Spreading his arms wide, Waldorf indicated the entirety of his shop. "My good lady, does it look like we sell anything like that here?" He scoffed. "If you want something classless, go see that damn dwarf."

"Do you think he means Ironbeard?" Cassie asked ShadowLily.

"He's the only dwarf you've mentioned." ShadowLily put her arm around her friend's shoulders and led her out of Waldorf's shop. "Plus, this man clearly lacks the proper artistic vision to be great."

"I have vision!" Waldorf shouted after them.

"Yeah, on how to lose customers," Cassie snapped as they made it to the door. She took ShadowLily by the arm and led the way to

Ironbeard's store. "Can you believe those asshats? That was the third one who basically laughed at us."

"Let's hope our next stop does the trick." ShadowLily smiled. "Then if we need to get upgrades, we'll know where to come first." They continued walking through the crowded thoroughfares, feeling slightly better with each step they took away from Waldorf's shop.

Ironbeard's shop didn't look like much from outside. It was a simple stone building with a large wooden door. The door was open, and you could see the orange firelight flickering within. Unlike all the other shops they visited, this seemed to be a working smithy, not a store full of finished items.

Cassie led the way inside. "What's up, Ironbeard?"

"By the goddess, girl, you're back already? I swear you are going to bankrupt me." Ironbeard started pulling coins from the pouch under the counter.

Cassie held up a hand to stop him. "Believe it or not, I'm here to buy something this time."

Ironbeard let the coins fall back into the bag. "Music to my ears. Truth be told, I was kind of getting tired of people thinking I only exist to hand out quests."

"Sounds like the same luck we've had trying to find someone to make Cassie some armor," ShadowLily quipped. "You wouldn't believe some of the things people said."

"That's only because those other fools have never seen a warrior woman in action. They can be fearsome to behold." Ironbeard winked at their shocked faces. "It might surprise you to find out that some dwarven women go on to find great renown on the battlefield."

"I've never given much thought to the dwarven women before," Cassie admitted.

"Not many people do. Not until they see a line of axes and shields charging across the battlefield ready to crush the life out of them." He grinned, thinking about a memory from the past. "Once you've seen something like that, it's hard to forget."

"They sound amazing," ShadowLily said. "Kicking ass and taking names."

"It's who we are as a people. The gender of a dwarf never decides their station in life, only hard work and determination." Ironbeard clasped his hands together. "Now, tell me more about what you're looking for."

Cassie looked at her friend and received a subtle nod. "I need something to protect my forearms and shins, so I can use them to turn a blade away. But it has to be flexible enough that I can move."

"No heavy plate or chainmail." The dwarf ran a hand through his dark-silver beard. "Unless of course, you're strong enough to lift it."

Without warning, the dwarf grabbed a massive hammer from his workbench and tossed it to Cassie. She caught it in one hand and held it up in front of her with a shocked look on her face. "What the fuck?"

Ironbeard looked over the goods on the bench. "So, strength isn't a problem, but flexibility is," he mumbled as he started taking notes. "What do you plan on doing with this armor?"

Cassie dropped the hammer back on his bench. "Tanking, mostly, but not taking a lot of direct hits. I just need to be able to deflect attacks with more than my staff."

"Humm." Ironbeard looked at his notes and grabbed a tape measure. "I have a few ideas, but I'll need some measurements and time to come up with a few samples."

"Time is kind of a factor for us," ShadowLily said as she moved around the store glancing at the items.

"Always is with you adventurous types." Ironbeard started taking his measurements. "I'll have a few things ready in the morning, but the final project might take a little more time."

"Do you have anything she can use right now?" ShadowLily looked at the racks of armor.

"I've got some bracers that might do the trick, but nothing for her legs, I'm afraid." He looked at Cassie with a sheepish smile. "There isn't a lot of demand for armor in your size."

Ironbeard moved over to one of the racks and plucked a couple of items off it. "These will do nicely, and will only cost you a gold coin." He handed Cassie a pair of iron bracers she could use to protect her forearms. "Now, your custom pieces are going to be more expensive, but they will all be made from scratch to your exact measurements. I'd say the final cost will be somewhere around ten gold, or maybe a little more, depending on the material cost."

"Seems a little pricey?" ShadowLily stopped looking at the dwarf's wares and locked her eyes on him. "You wouldn't be trying to take advantage of us, would you?"

Ironbeard smiled back warmly. "Making the sample isn't free, and neither is the final product. If you don't have the gold, you can always find another armor smith."

Cassie reached into her coin purse and pulled out eleven gold coins. It was almost all the money she had in the world. She dropped the coins into his waiting palm. "Just don't let me down."

The coins vanished. "Of course not. One thing you'll learn about dwarves is that we never break a promise when it comes to a deal. Our word is our bond."

Cassie shook his hand. "Then I'll see you tomorrow." She put the bracers in her inventory before equipping them. Her arms felt a little heavy, but she'd be able to move well enough.

ShadowLily and Cassie gave Ironbeard a friendly wave before linking arms and marching boldly from the store. Tonight hadn't gone as expected, but as soon as they got to the slums, things would get better.

CHAPTER FORTY

The Lamppost Inn was a gorgeous three-story building built out of light-colored wood. Bright lights streamed from the massive windows, and roaring laughter spilled through the door every time it opened. There wouldn't be any sneaking in and out of the inn; it was packed to the gills.

Tim looked at Gaston. "Any ideas?"

The assassin frowned up at all the bright light. "If we could climb up the building next door, we could jump to one of the balconies and enter." He shrugged. "Doesn't do us a lot of good until we know which room he's in."

"Agreed." Tim looked at the windows, wondering what they could do next. "I'm guessing we wouldn't make it too far if we started kicking in doors and shouting our target's name."

Tim pulled up his inventory and switched into his normal pants and shirt. "I'll head inside and hope an opportunity presents itself."

"You get busy thinking, and I'll get busy drinking." Gaston grinned at him like Nicholas Cage in *Face Off*. "Killing is thirsty work."

Tim slapped his burly companion on the back. "I guess I'd seem rather ungrateful if the first round wasn't on me. Drink up while you can. Later, there will be work to do."

"Now you're speaking my language." Gaston pulled the door open and a wave of noise crashed over them.

Tim moved into the inn, imagining how the Blue Dagger would feel with this many people inside. One thing was certain, he'd miss the quiet the place afforded him now. There was something to be said for coming home and being able to relax in silence. Sometimes a little bit of quiet was all he needed to get his head straight.

There wasn't an ounce of silence to be found here.

Someone was playing some kind of raucous jingle on stringed instruments, and some idiot with a lute was trying to play along but couldn't match the rhythm. On one side of the room, there was a stage with women putting on a cabaret show right out of the Wild West, and on the other side of the inn were men doing the same thing.

Thinking back to his first day in the game, Tim smiled. He knew exactly what the Lamppost Inn was. Sure, it was an inn and a bar, but it was also a brothel, or at the very least, it gave you the impression that it was. Maybe this would make things easier. A plan was starting to form in his mind, although it would be risky.

Especially if ShadowLily ever found out.

He smiled as he paid for the first round. As long as Gaston could keep his big fat mouth shut, things would go fine. "I've got a plan."

"A good one?" Gaston took a sip of his beer.

"Guess I won't know until I try it." Tim set his beer down and made his way to the side of the room filled with buxom women in red and black corset tops and black garter belts.

"Just don't do anything I wouldn't do!" Gaston called after him before turning back to the bar and ordering another drink.

From the stories I've heard, that doesn't take much off the table.

Tim sniggered at his own joke as he made his way to the side of the room with the frolicking dancing girls. He moved around the crowd until he found one of the women that didn't seem to be garnering as much interest from the men. Never having done this kind of thing in real life, Tim wasn't exactly sure how you initiate the process. Maybe the same awkward way he did when trying to pick up a girl at a party.

The plan was to get her alone and ask her to tell him where the target was. Enough gold should get her talking, but it also meant he had to proposition a working girl. ShadowLily wasn't going to like that. What woman would? What else could he do? The time was starting to get away from him, and they still had to get back to the inn and meet their new tank.

"Excuse me, Miss," Tim said as he approached the woman.

"Fuck off," she snarled, turning to glare at him.

The attitude explained why she was alone.

Tim took a step back, watching her warily. There was a kind of beauty to her face. Sure, it was long and angled, but her hair was cut perfectly to minimize the effect. Looking at her again, he couldn't figure out why she wasn't more popular. Unless, of course, it was her greeting.

"I was wondering if you'd like to accompany me upstairs." Tim gave her a halfhearted smile. Was getting a hooker up to her room supposed to be so hard?

"I said, fuck off." She waggled her finger in his face.

A plump older woman in the same corseted outfit laid a hand on the woman's shoulder. "Liz, that's no way to treat one of our guests." The woman beamed at Tim. "Now, take this man to your room and offer him a large discount for being such a bitch."

Liz's face paled as she watched the woman, and with a great deal of effort, she lifted her hand, extending it daintily to Tim. "Would you care to accompany me?"

Tim looked at the two women, feeling uncomfortable. He was of the opinion that no one should be forced to do something they didn't want to when it came to sex. No is a word that only has one meaning. Thankfully for Liz, he wasn't going to be a normal client. The last thing he wanted was to have sex with her, but he couldn't show that now, not in front of her boss. So, Tim played the part of smitten customer.

Reaching out, he rubbed her hand gently with both of his before kissing it lightly. "The pleasure would be all mine." Even playing the part for a moment made his stomach turn.

Looking slightly revolted, Liz forced a smile on her face as she turned toward the stairs. "Follow me." She dropped his hand as soon as her boss wasn't looking and pointed toward the stairs. "Follow me."

"Go get her, you dog!" Gaston shouted from across the room.

Tim felt his face flush. Hopefully, his companion knew this was just a ruse. The last thing he wanted was for Gaston to go back to the inn, talking about how much fun they'd had at the whorehouse. If Gaston opened his mouth before he had a chance to tell ShadowLily, she might use him for target practice.

It wasn't like it would be an easy conversation anyway. Imagine trying to convince your girlfriend that you went to the whorehouse and up to a hooker's room because you had a quest. This wasn't *Leisure Suit Larry*, this was his life. He didn't want to ruin it by picking a battle he couldn't win.

On the plus side, he was going in with his eyes open, and no interest in indulging in Liz's companionship. Hopefully, he could get her to talk. If he couldn't, maybe he could buy her silence while he looked for a woman with looser morals in the selling-out-her-coworkers-department.

Liz led him to the third floor and down a long narrow hallway. She paused outside a door. and took a deep breath as if preparing herself for what was to come before she thrust the door open.

"Please come inside." She stepped back and motioned for Tim to enter the room first.

Stepping into the room, Tim couldn't help but be a little jealous. One corner of Liz's room was dominated by a huge four-poster bed. It looked like the kind of thing you could fall into and never find your way out of. The floor was covered in a hodge-podge of rugs, except for a small space by the window that had a claw foot tub.

The room was also about five times the size of his place at the Blue Dagger. He guessed it made sense since this was more of a workplace than sleeping quarters. You needed to have a certain amount of space when you worked from home. Sometimes it helped to have a designated area to get shit done, one where Xander wouldn't spill beer all over your homework.

Because that excuse held about as much water as "My dog ate my homework."

Instead of sitting on the bed, Tim found a comfortable chair and took a seat. Even the chair made him not want to get up. *How come her furniture is so much more comfortable than mine? I'm going to have to talk to Ernie about sprucing things up.*

"Can I get you something to drink?" Liz asked as she closed the door and moved toward a few bottles of amber liquid on a stand.

"I'm fine, actually." Tim wasn't fine; his heart was beating fast. This was the worst idea he ever had, and he needed to abort immediately. It was funny how being alone in a room with a woman that wasn't his girlfriend made him more nervous than when he laid everything on the line to bargain with Malvonis.

Liz took off her gloves, setting them on the table. "Straight to business, then?" When Tim didn't say anything, she continued. "The rate's twenty-five silver. A gold if you want to stay the night."

"What if I wanted something else?" Tim asked before he could stop himself. If she wasn't watching him, he would have slapped himself. It sounded like he wanted to do something kinky instead of buying information.

"Depends what you're into." Liz frowned. "I don't do the weird shit. If you want something crazy, you have to ask for Lorena."

"What if I didn't want anything?" Tim asked casually.

"I swear to the goddess, if you're wasting my time, I'll have Hank toss you out on your ass," Liz fumed.

Well, at least the women working here had some kind of protection. Not that he was interested in being introduced to Hank. Having to kill the bouncer would make things more difficult. "What if I paid you for the night, but all I wanted was a little information?"

Liz poured herself a drink. "Information costs more than sex."

Tim leaned back, a smile twitching at the corners of his mouth. At least she was open to the idea of being bribed. Now he just had to find out what she wanted. "And the cost?"

"You haven't told me what you want yet." She walked toward Tim and stopped in front of him, then trailed a finger down his chest. "It'll stay between us, I swear."

Tim grabbed her wrist, moving her hand gently away from him before getting up from the chair to create some space between them. "I need to know which room Steven Sylvester is in."

Liz finished her drink with a practiced flip of the wrist before returning to the bar. She poured herself another measure of the amber liquid and gulped it before setting the glass down with a trembling hand. "What business do you have with him?"

Tim noted the hardened expression in her eyes, but there was something else. A hint of fear or maybe loathing. There was always the chance Liz was afraid of what would happen to her if anyone found out she had squealed.

But if she was scared of him, revealing his plan might get her to open up. "I plan on personally introducing him to the goddess." He watched her face, hoping he'd made the right choice.

"Good. He fucking deserves it. You should have seen Jolene last week. Bastard covered her in bruises from head to toe. What kind of sick fuck does that?" Liz started to pour herself another drink.

"So, you'll help me?"

Liz took a small sip before setting her glass down. "I will, but I need your help with something as well."

Tim felt like time was slipping through his fingers. He still had to get back to the inn and take their new tank for a test run before he could go to bed. Then it was off to work. At least while he was at Ironbeard's, he had plenty of time to think. By the time he left work tomorrow, he'd have some kind of plan in place.

"What do you want?" Tim watched her, hoping whatever she asked for was reasonable.

"Oh, honey, you really do need to learn how to negotiate." She smiled. "I want out. Out of this hellhole."

"So, you don't like working here?" Tim was kind of surprised. You would have thought the NPCs in the game would love the jobs they'd been assigned. It wouldn't have mimicked life perfectly, but he'd never played a game where the NPCs hated going to work.

"Would *you*? All those ugly fat fuckers pawing over me for a few lousy coins. I can't stand it anymore, but I signed a contract." Liz frowned at the floorboards. "And they make sure you never earn enough to buy yourself out of it."

Tim felt for her. No one should be forced into this kind of job. If you liked it, awesome. If you didn't, no one should be able to force you into a sexual encounter. "And when you're free? What will you do then?"

She looked around the room, taking in each inch like it would be the last time she ever saw it. "I'll figure something out."

Tim noted the look of determination on her face. This was someone willing to do anything to get out of their current situation. Liz was motivated and would work twice as hard, knowing her only other option was to come back here.

Tim wanted to help her, but the cost couldn't be too high. "And your contract?"

She bit her lip, looking into his eyes with a vulnerability he hadn't seen before. "Ten gold." Her resolve hardened. "The price for the room number is ten gold."

He had the money, of course, but it was a devil's ransom for a room number. There was so much he could do with ten gold, yet it seemed a small price to pay to get Liz out of a life she hated. When you saved someone's life, you also had an obligation to protect it.

Sending Liz to the streets as a homeless beggar didn't seem like much of a reward. If she couldn't find a job or housing, she'd probably end up back in the same exact spot. Maybe there *was* something more he could do.

"My friend Ernie runs an inn. I might be able to get you a job there."

"I won't go back to doing the same kind of work." Liz looked like she was on the verge of tears.

Tim reached out to comfort her but stopped. The last thing Liz probably wanted was another man she didn't know pawing at her. "It's not that kind of place. ShadowLily would never allow it."

He flashed his best aw-shucks smile. "I was thinking more along the lines of waiting tables or cleaning. It's not easy work, but it's honest, and no one would ever touch you there."

"Sounds too good to be true." Liz frowned at him. "Like I show up for a job and next thing you know, I'm being shipped across the ocean to some asshole who likes women who look a little different."

By the goddess, maybe this game was a little too realistic.

But you had to have villains to have heroes. Otherwise, they'd all just be running around patting each other on the back and singing Kum-by-fucking-ya. Tim reached inside of his coin purse and thought about the amount he wanted to take out. Ten gold coins appeared in his hand as he pulled it free. He put the coins in Liz's outstretched palm. "This is your freedom. If you want the job, come to The Blue Dagger Inn. No strings attached."

Liz looked at the coins in her hand and back up at Tim. Tears leaked from the corners of her eyes, but there was a smile trying to fight its way free. She pulled him into a ferocious hug. "Thank you."

Tim hugged her back, happy he could do his part to pull one woman out of a lifestyle she detested. "You're welcome." He hugged her until he felt the shaking stop, then shifted so he could look at her. "The room number?"

"I'll take you there myself. It will look less suspicious that way." She started running around the room, stuffing items into a bag. "Let me just get my stuff together first. I want to get out of here before all hell breaks loose."

Liz finished packing and put the two overstuffed bags by the door. "Let's go." She grabbed Tim's hand and led him down the hallway.

Another one of the girls passed them, and Liz turned to Tim. "See, I told you all the hallways look the same."

The woman snorted as she continued down the hall, clearly not impressed with her co-worker. As soon as the woman turned the corner behind them, Liz grabbed his hand and pulled him into a run. "Claudia can't be trusted so you're going to have to hurry."

Liz stopped in front of a large wooden door, the kind that normally led to a suite of rooms. Did you ever notice that as houses or hotel rooms got fancier, so did the doors?

Pulling a key from some hidden pocket of her skin-tight garments, Liz slid it in the lock. "Give me at least five minutes to get out of here before you do anything rash."

Tim grinned at her. "I'll do my best, but no promises."

Liz walked down the hallway. "Then I'll see you when I see you."

Tim took a deep breath and turned the key.

The door didn't creak as he slowly pushed it open. Glancing inside didn't reveal anyone standing in the entryway. Tim pulled out the key and slipped into the room. He closed the door behind him before switching back to his assassin's garb for the dexterity bonuses.

A rush of adrenaline filled his system. With each step, his heart hammered a little harder. Was this why serial killers did it? For the thrill? Not that he was thrilled, exactly. The feeling was more like being terrified to the point of having a heart attack.

Each step could give him away, and he'd be in another fight for his life.

Tim forced his breathing to slow, and his heart rate started to improve. Maybe breathing was the key? He heard a woman's giggle followed by a man's grunt to his left. Unless there was more than one couple up here, he knew where to go now. The woman's laughter sounded again, pulling him deeper into the suite.

The double doors to the bedchamber loomed in front of him. He could hear the man and the woman now. They weren't saying anything important. Every now and then, she'd squeal as if Steven Sylvester was tickling her or pinching her. The only choice he had to make now was if he wanted to wait until they were fully engaged before entering the room.

I've seen enough old-man ass tonight to last me a lifetime.

Kicking the doors open with a flourish would certainly be dramatic, but seeing another naked man tonight wasn't on his list of things to do. Plus, he didn't have one of those handy darts Gaston had used earlier, so he'd literally be killing him during sex.

I guess it wouldn't be worse than stabbing a man while he was unconscious. Tim shrugged. Assassins didn't get paid for observing the niceties; they got paid for killing.

He turned the handle slowly, and there was a small click as the lock opened. The conversation didn't stop. If anything, the proceedings in the room beyond seemed to be growing in intensity. If he waited much longer, his only choice would be to kill them while they tried to perfect the horizontal mambo.

Pushing the door open, Tim stepped into the room. The couple on the bed didn't notice him, so he took the time to close the door and lock it. The two people on the bed dove under the sheets, and the woman started to giggle again.

"I'm going to get you," Steven growled.

"No, I am too pure for the likes of you."

Tim was almost tempted to hear where this was going, but he

didn't have all night. "Mind hurrying this up a bit? Some of us have other places to be."

The sheet flew back and Steven roared, "How dare you! This is my private suite."

"Mr. Sylvester, I presume?" Tim pulled his daggers free.

Steven cowered back, finally realizing Tim wasn't some overeager townie here to rob him. "We can work this out. Whatever you're being paid, I can double it."

"Sorry, but it seems your usefulness to the goddess has been greatly overrated. Please give her my regards when you see her." Tim pulled his arm back, not sure how the heavier dagger would fly compared to one of his knives. A little more strength should be all he needed.

The blade of the dagger glittered in the flickering candlelight. Tim flexed his arm, and the blade leapt across the room in a flash. He watched the dagger fly in a deadly arc before sinking to the hilt in the center of Steven Sylvester's chest.

I guess practice does *make perfect.*

The woman screamed, but an icy glance from Tim cut her off. He moved forward with purpose and pulled the dagger free. Steven Sylvester's body slumped, and he noticed a familiar icon in the bottom right-hand corner of his vision. The quest had updated to reflect that he'd killed the right man.

He wiped the bloody dagger on the sheets before replacing the weapon in its sheath. Without a word to the woman, he left the room. Once he was outside the closed double doors, Tim let out a breath he didn't realize he'd been holding.

This wasn't exactly what he expected to be doing in the game. Sure, sometimes in games, there were bandits and bad humans you had to fight, but normally that stuff came after you spent a few days killing your way up the food chain. Hopefully, once order was returned to the temple, he could finally start slaughtering monsters instead of people.

Not that some people weren't monstrous enough to deserve his special brand of attention.

The NPCs in this game felt so much like living breathing people that Tim was having a hard time remembering he was in a game. Maybe that was the trick? All he had to do was remember the men he was killing were bits of code designed for that very purpose.

If Tim could start making the distinction between how he'd deal with problems outside of the game and how he would do it if he was behind his keyboard, then maybe it wouldn't feel like murder. It wasn't like he could level by walking around and hugging everyone.

Not unless he was trying to level up his creep factor.

Tim hurried out of the suite and down the stairs. As he ran, he switched from his assassin's garb back into his shirt and pants. The inventory in this game was so fucking awesome. He didn't even have to pause in his rush. One second he was dressed in black, and the next he could have been any of the men downstairs. The system worked so well that it might have been magic.

Tim motioned for Gaston to join him. The burly assassin set down his half-empty beer, tossed a few coins on the table, and headed for the front door. At least the first part of his night had been a smashing success.

Now it was time to see how bad a bargain he'd struck with Malvonis.

CHAPTER FORTY-ONE

"Hey, you're the cute guy from Ironbeard's shop," Cassie said, looking at Tim from across the room.

ShadowLily laughed. "Cassie, this is Tim. Tim this is my friend Cassie, the tank."

"Doesn't look like much." Gaston snorted, turned toward Tim, and asked, "You sure about this?"

Tim looked at Gaston then back to Cassie. The assassin was right; she didn't look like much, but Tim knew that didn't mean a damn thing in games. It was all about your stats and your personal ability. ShadowLily wouldn't have recommended Cassie if she didn't think the girl was up for the job. So, was he sure?

Sure, as a man riding in a boat patched with duct tape.

But in his short time on this planet, Tim had learned one constant: the things he didn't know vastly outnumbered those he did. That was why you had to be able to rely on other people.

But the world also turned on a much simpler phrase: "Beggars can't be choosers."

They didn't know any other tanks, and recruiting someone this early in the game was hard to do. Half the people you ended up playing with wouldn't stick around. Another twenty percent were probably just flat-out terrible at the game. The only real way to know how someone could perform in an intense group setting was to bring them along and see how things went.

Tim winked at Gaston. "What's the worst that could happen?" Taking his seat at the table, Tim smiled warmly at their group's newest acquisition. "Happy to have you, Cassie."

"What did I just get myself into?" She looked at Tim and ShadowLily before frowning at Gaston.

"We've got a kobold problem," Tim said. "And we need your help getting past them."

Cassie stood up, grinning from ear to ear. "I'm sure we all have other stuff going on tomorrow. Let's do this." She pointed at Gaston. "Just tell Muscles over there to stay behind me."

Gaston flexed one of his massive biceps. "It was nice of her to recognize them, don't you think?"

Tim stood up. "I think you'd better stay behind her."

"Hide behind the lady and stab things." Gaston thought about it. "Doesn't feel right, but I'm not opposed to it."

"For this to work, we all have to do our part." Tim switched into his healing gear. "I'm going to focus on healing unless we don't need it, then I'll try to DPS where I can."

It felt weird being back in his healing ensemble after spending so much time in his new leather outfit, but the gentle breeze up his robes was rather refreshing. Plus, he'd finally get to try out his new staff.

"You got a pocket healer." Cassie grinned at ShadowLily. "This is going to be a cakewalk."

The half-elf looked at her friend with apprehension. Cassie had a penchant for getting overexcited. "Let's just take things slow and see how it goes."

Tim pointed at ShadowLily and touched his nose. "I like her idea."

"Bunch of babies," Cassie whined.

Gaston coughed into his hand. "I'm with Tiny. Might as well see what she's got."

Cassie looked like she was about to jump across the table and smash Gaston across the face. He just glanced at her with a knowing smirk, clearly enjoying the attention. Someone had to take control of the group or things were going to spiral out of control. It might as well be Tim since he had the most on the line.

He held up a hand and waited until everyone looked at him. "This is how things are going to happen tonight. We are going to head into the tunnels and take things slow. Gaston will use his stealth to scout ahead, and we'll take on the groups we think we can handle."

When he scanned his team's faces, none of them looked particularly happy. "Part of becoming a group is learning how to play together. It takes time. We start slow, and after we gain confidence in each other and our abilities, we'll be able to tackle harder content."

"But we've only got a week," Ernie said, entering the room with a tray full of beer. "So don't go too slow."

Each of them grabbed a beer from the tray. Tim took a thoughtful sip. "I feel like we need a name for our group."

"Normally, you don't earn a name until you've accomplished something." Ernie admonished Tim. He pulled a couple of vials from his pockets and handed them to the two thieves. "Little something for your blades."

"Okay, the name can wait." Tim held his beer over the center of the table. "To tonight's success!"

Five glasses clinked together, and everyone took a sip. It was a proper toast before heading off to battle. Tim was ready to see what they could do.

Ernie moved to the black door at the end of the room. "Just knock three times when you want me to let you back in." He swung the giant iron door open.

Tim peered inside. "Of course, there are stairs."

"How else would we get to caverns below the city?" Gaston clapped him on the back. "We shouldn't have to worry about much until we're farther in, but I'll scout ahead."

Tim turned back to the two women. "Cassie, lead the way."

"At least one man's not afraid to hide behind me." She flashed a quick smile at Tim as she moved past him and down the stairs.

ShadowLily gave him a quick kiss on the lips. "It'll be fine. I've seen her in action."

"Right behind you," Tim said before turning back to Ernie. "Expect us in an hour or so. This is just a test run."

"You got it, boss." He started closing the massive iron door as Tim stepped inside. "Just remember, three knocks."

Tim heard the door shut behind him with a sense of finality. It was the kind of sound that said you were never coming back from this godforsaken hole in the ground. Instead of panicking, though, he focused on the woman in front of him. She was moving down the stairs with purpose. Taking heart in ShadowLily's confidence, he bounded after her.

They reached the bottom of the stairs, and Cassie gave them a glance to make sure they were following before she moved forward. Tim walked behind the two ladies and took in the details of the cavern system.

The walls weren't smooth, but they did look shaped. Either there used to be an underground river here, or something else made a path.

A big fucking something.

The roof of the cavern had to be at least ten feet above his head. If he stood in the middle of the path with his arms outstretched there was at least five feet of clearance on either side. Not a path made by kobolds, not unless they had an army.

Fuck, I hope they don't have an army.

A smile broke out on his face. Maybe an army wouldn't be so bad, as long as they could take them on in small-enough groups. *Think of the experience we could earn.* Then again, a cavern full of

344

kobolds charging at them in retaliation for killing their friends sure seemed like an easy way to die.

Gaston appeared out of thin air. "Around the next corner, there is a group of five of them. Might be a scouting party of some kind."

"Cassie, you're up." Tim pointed toward the corner. "Group of five ahead."

"I've got this." She rounded the corner, letting out a fearsome battle cry and charging straight at the kobolds.

Tim watched in horror as she plunged into the group of monsters. Taking on all five at once wasn't what he'd had in mind. Gaston and ShadowLily were standing back from the fray, watching their tank attack the kobolds.

"Why are you waiting?" Tim called.

"Just letting her build agro," ShadowLily replied as she pulled her daggers free.

As nervous as Tim was, he could understand the logic behind her thoughts. There was nothing worse for a tank or a DPS than having the boss change targets. He'd seen it happen in more boss fights than he could count. That was the thing with DPS; they always had to be on top. Fuck the mechanics of the fight. Topping the leaderboards was all that mattered.

It looked like he was in luck, though. His new team was thinking ahead and willing to give her a few seconds to get all of the little buggers focused. He just hoped their new tank didn't end up full of little holes before the two assassins started doing their part.

Cassie's staff spun like a tornado. She moved quickly, easily blocking a dagger from behind, but she didn't stop there. Using the momentum of her blocked attack, she twirled around, bō staff blurring as she waited for the next attack. Her movements picked up speed as she furiously blocked attacks from all sides.

Weaving as she dodged blades and the movement of Cassie's feet almost made it look as though she were dancing. The kobolds were all totally focused on the whirling dervish in their midst. Tim cringed as a few of the attacks got close enough to leave a scratch. Without thinking, he readied his healing orb spell, waiting for the inevitable.

One of the creature's knives bounced of Cassie's forearm, and Tim let the healing orb fly. It splashed against her arm, and he gave a little cheer. "Direct hit."

"I've kind of got a lot going on here. I don't need you throwing water balloons at me." Cassie snarled as she fended off the next wave of attacks.

Tim noticed a glint of steel under the torn cloth on her arms. She had some kind of armor on under her clothes. That made him feel a lot better about their chances. "Sorry. Thought you'd need a little refreshment."

Before Cassie could respond, ShadowLily and Gaston darted forward, taking out two of the kobolds with their daggers. The other three creatures seemed to notice the thief and the assassin for the first time and started jabbering at each other. They tried to get around Cassie to run farther into the caverns, but she kept the creatures positioned in front of her, her movements focused on keeping the kobolds' backs to the rest of the group.

Two more kobolds fell to the group's blades. The last one gave up all pretense of trying to fight and made a mad dash to the side of the cavern, attempting to make it around Cassie. Her staff just missed its back leg as it ran up the cavern wall and dropped to the floor behind her.

"Don't let it get away!" Tim cried. If the creature summoned reinforcements, it might be more than they could handle.

Cassie's hand dipped to her waist as she pulled a hook free. She spun it around her head, letting more of the chain out as she did, then, with a well-timed motion, she let the hook fly. Tim watched as the hook and chain sailed across the open space. Somehow the hook found the creature's ankle, and it fell to the cavern floor with a squawk.

The kobold continued to scream as Gaston rushed forward to

end it. The assassin looked up after sinking his dagger into the kobold's back, his head tilted as if he heard something.

Turning back toward the group, Gaston shouted. "We've got company." He beat a hasty retreat to the tank. "There are ten of them this time."

"Ten," Cassie said, looking a little pale. "This is going to hurt."

"Not if I can help it," Tim shouted. "See if you can pick a few off with your throwing knives before they reach us. Cassie, you take control of the rest while they get to work."

"It's not much of a plan." Gaston laughed as he watched the Kobolds charging toward them.

"No plan survives contact with the enemy," Tim shouted above the din of rushing kobolds.

"Sounds like something said by a shitty planner," ShadowLily snarked as she let her first throwing knife fly.

The blade missed the rushing kobolds a few feet to the left. Tim looked at her, ready to give her a little of her own medicine, but stopped at the look of determination on her face. ShadowLily's second blade flew across the open space and sank into the chest of one of the creatures.

A quick scan of the battlefield showed that Gaston had dispatched two on his side, leaving seven for the rest of them to deal with. Cassie ran forward to meet the charge. Tim almost felt bad seeing, the smaller woman bound into a group of knife-wielding kobolds, but she'd proven herself more than capable.

Tim watched as she dove into the group, staff swinging faster than before. Despite her amazing moves, there wasn't any way Tim knew of to avoid seven attacks at once. He cast healing orb, determined to be ready for a real injury.

Two more of the kobolds fell under the group's daggers, and Cassie handled the remaining five with ease. She was smiling now, and he was starting to feel a little useless. Maybe it would be better for him to remain a DPS until they reached something more challenging.

Cassie cried out as a blade slashed across her back. Somehow she managed to parry the next attack, but she was in trouble. Tim let the spell go and the orb of healing water flew toward her as Gaston took out the offending kobold.

Her swings were slower now. Two of the kobolds blades bounced harmlessly off her forearms, but Tim could tell she wouldn't be able to keep it up much longer. His orb hit her in the back, and the effect was almost instantaneous. Cassie started to move with purpose again as ShadowLily took down another of the mean little fuckers.

Cassie was firmly in control now, herding the other three around to make it easier for Gaston and ShadowLily to finish them off. Tim cast a few more healing orbs in her direction, mostly just to feel like he was part of the fight and not just watching a *Twitch* stream.

One by one, the remaining kobolds fell. Cassie stood there panting from the exertion. Gaston had a cut on his arm that Tim healed as he joined the rest of the group.

ShadowLily was grinning from ear to ear. "That was fucking awesome." She pulled Cassie into a hug. "You kicked ass."

"Only because Mr. Water Balloon saved my ass," Cassie said, patting her wet clothes.

"It's called healing orb," Tim said, trying to sound offended. "I can't help that it gets you wet."

"Getting wet has never been my problem," Cassie said with a grin as she watched the water dripping off her clothes. "It's too bad your healing spell doesn't repair clothes."

"No, but your inventory does," Tim told her.

"Now it just sounds like you're trying to see me naked," Cassie quipped.

"Maybe it's not just him who wants to see," ShadowLily said with a laugh.

"Ugh, you just made it weird." Cassie motioned for the boys to turn around. A few seconds later, she called, "All clear."

"See? Good as new," Tim replied. He was feeling great about how things had gone so far. "How about we tackle a few more groups before we call it a night?"

"I'm in," Gaston said as he spun a throwing knife on the tip of his finger.

ShadowLily grinned at Tim. "You're the one with work in the morning. If you think you can handle it, then I'm in too."

"Then let's make it quick," Cassie said. "Our fearless leader needs his beauty rest."

"Fuck off," Tim groused. "And let's get started."

CHAPTER FORTY-TWO

"The cardinal sends his kind regards," Juan Pablo whispered. Pulling his blade free of the man's chest, Juan wiped it off on his target's shirt. These men were unworthy of the hunt since none of them ran. All of them had called on the goddess to protect them, and she had not. He wondered if in the next life, they would find peace, or if there was no next life for these Western fools.

Now that this poor excuse for a hunt was finished, it was time to make it look like a robbery. Juan Pablo stalked around the room, turning over furniture and emptying drawers. He took a few items that looked expensive. He didn't think the guards were very good investigators, but even the dumbest guard might not think it was a robbery if nothing was stolen.

Hopefully, Jepsom would have something more entertaining for him soon. Killing old men as they slept wasn't his way. He liked it when they ran, when there was a chase. Sometimes his little rabbits even surprised him by fighting back. Those were days to remember, days to be thankful for.

There hadn't been a lot of those days since Dapper Don had

been killed. The cardinal was an insufferable asshole. Often when the man was talking, Juan Pablo thought about sinking his dagger into him. The look of surprise on his face would be worth it, even if he died shortly afterward.

There would come a time when he wouldn't be able to suffer the groveling. He had enough money now that he could hire a boat to take him back home.

So why am I still here?

Revenge. It was that simple. He wanted to kill the man who'd ruined his life more than he wanted to see the cardinal in a puddle of his own blood. There were rumblings in the temple that the boy he'd killed was still alive. That the goddess had brought him back to life.

More bullshit.

He'd seen the life slip out of the man's eyes before he'd left the dilapidated room. It was more likely the temple was using someone who looked like him to build the religious fervor of their following. It would be simple enough to do. Outside of the high priest, not very many people had interacted with the man.

Juan Pablo shook his head. "Faking a resurrection is some next-level shit."

He'd never understand these people and their convoluted ideas of religion, but he would find the man the high priest had carrying out his orders. It was the least he could do for the memory of a life burned to ashes.

Taking a final look around the room, Juan Pablo jumped out of the second-story window and hit the ground, rolling with the impact. He came out of the roll and walked down the street as casually as a man could. He wasn't in any hurry to return to the temple, but his feet pulled him in that direction, regardless of his desire to stay away.

"Two of my top associates have been killed," Cardinal Jepsom raged.

Jepsom kicked the man kneeling in front of him. "And you." He sneered. "You only managed to kill one of the targets on your list."

"Just give me more time, Your Holiness," Juan Pablo said through gritted teeth. Every part of him wanted to grab the asshole's leg the next time he kicked him. From there, he was pretty sure he could snap the cardinal's neck before anyone interrupted them.

"Time! Time is something we don't have." Jepsom walked around the man in slow, deliberate circles. "I have a new task for you."

"Name it, Your Excellency, and it will be done."

"Of course, it will," Jepsom snapped as if the thought of someone not following his orders never even occurred to him. "I need you to stick to Frederick like glue. Wherever he goes, you go."

The cardinal paused his relentless circling. "When Lady Briarthorn's assassin shows up, gut him like a fish."

Juan Pablo risked looking up, and as soon as he saw the cardinal, he wished he hadn't. The grin on the man's face didn't hold a shred of sanity. He'd totally lost his mind. Juan Pablo had seen this all before. He'd worked for men dancing on the edge of insanity, and it never turned out well.

Refusing Jepsom wasn't an option, but it was even clearer to Juan Pablo that he couldn't risk staying much longer. Lowering his forehead back to the floor, Juan Pablo intoned, "Your will flows through my hands. It will be done."

"Then go!" The cardinal kicked him again. "The sight of you makes me sick."

You're not the only one.

Pushing up from the ground, Juan Pablo considered making his move now but discarded the idea. It'd be better to attack him outside of the temple if he wanted to live. There were plenty of people who relied on Jepsom for their power here, and more than a few would try to avenge him if they lost it.

Even if he *was* a giant prick.

Turning away from the cardinal, Juan Pablo marched toward the doors with a sense of purpose. He had a job to do, and at least for the moment, that job would keep him away from here.

CHAPTER FORTY-THREE

"Time to see if you're not totally worthless," Ironbeard said with a twinkle in his eye.

Tim couldn't help but think of his grandfather as he watched the dwarf. Grandpa was always full of little digs, but behind them was a person who wanted you to get the most out of life. He was the kind of man who pushed you hard so you would push yourself harder. Nothing great was ever built by someone who didn't put in the work was one of his favorite sayings.

Not that he would judge someone for slacking. He couldn't do that without being the world's biggest hypocrite. There were plenty of times he should have been studying, but instead he stayed up all night playing games with his friends.

On top of Tim's penchant for late night shenanigans, he might also win an award for pulling shit together at the last minute after he'd procrastinated for weeks.

He got the work done, but he never dedicated as much time to it as he should have. When you wanted to be great at something, you didn't get there without a lot of sleepless nights and a ton of effort.

Effort and repetition were the keys to success. Then there were the times when you just had to get shit done.

Using the tongs, Tim pulled the mold from the coals of the fire and placed it on the bench. After setting the metal tongs to the side, Tim put on his Unburning Gloves and grabbed a small chisel and hammer.

As he moved around the mold, he tapped in the spaces Ironbeard indicated. On the last tap, all four sides of the mold fell away, revealing a perfect bar of silver. The dwarf moved forward to examine it. He looked it over for a moment and, snorting his approval, grabbed a stamp and his hammer.

With one quick stroke, Ironbeard put his mark on the silver bar. That was enough for Tim to know he'd done a good job. The dwarf would not have signed his name to inferior work. Feeling pretty good about himself, he started to smile.

"I wouldn't start grinning yet, boy. We've got ten more of these to finish before you can go."

Ten.

Ten seemed like an insurmountable number. He'd made four iron bars before Ironbeard let him try the silver. His first three bars came out wonky, and he'd had to melt them down and start over. His fourth bar finally earned him the approval of the old dwarf, and he'd hoped for an early exit.

Leaving early wasn't in the cards.

Ironbeard laughed at the crestfallen look on Tim's face. "Don't be such a sourpuss. You can pour more than one at once, you know." He moved over to where he kept the molds. "I'd start with five at a time."

A customer entered the store, and Ironbeard headed to the front to see what they wanted. He paused in the doorway to the smithy. "Just take your time. Same rules apply—anything that doesn't make the grade has to be redone."

"Easy for you to say," Tim mumbled.

Of course, it was easy for Ironbeard. He'd put the work in,

slaving in front of the forge day after day until he could make bars of any kind in his sleep. Not only that, but he could now shape metal into a variety of incredibly useful things. No one became a master by sitting on the sidelines.

Tim walked over to the mold station and started laying out the pieces he'd need to make five bars at once. As he put the first mold together, he chided himself for getting angry. Hadn't he just been the one bitching about how greatness required effort? What kind of man would he be if he wanted to be great without doing a damn thing?

A foolish one.

Tim put the finishing touches on his molds and moved them to the coals. With the molds set, he started measuring the silver rings he would have to melt down for five bars. The silver went into the cauldron and he headed for the bellows. Maybe one day, he'd be good enough at this to have someone pumping the bellows for him.

The next twenty minutes passed in a blur of sweat and heat. His arms were shaking from the effort. Tim let the bellows go and peered into the cauldron, to see the silver melted and the impurities in a puddle in the middle. Careful not to waste any of the silver, Tim scraped the mess away with an iron spoon.

Then he repeated the process.

Now when he looked into the cauldron, everything was uniform in color, which was exactly what he wanted. Using the pulley system, he moved the cauldron above the first mold. All he had to do was pour the silver out slowly until the mold was full and move to the next one. Tim focused and lined up the spout so it was over the mold before he started to pour.

As the silver was cooling in the molds, Tim returned to the bench to get his next five molds ready to go. With his next set of molds in place, he measured out the silver and dumped it into the cauldron before turning his attention to the bars he'd already made. One by one, he pulled them from the embers and moved them to the workbench.

Four of the bars were perfect, but one had a blemish in it. Maybe a small air bubble had gotten trapped, or it was possible that he dripped sweat into it. Whatever the case was, he knew Ironbeard wouldn't listen to any whiny bullshit. There wasn't room for excuses in the dwarf's shop, there was only perfection. Nothing moved out the door until Ironbeard was satisfied it was the best.

In business, your reputation was everything.

It was a good lesson to learn and one that needed to be reinforced more often. Tim didn't even struggle with his choice as he put together a sixth mold. He placed it in the embers with the other five and started working the bellows. Once he was satisfied that the impurities were gone, he added the misshapen bar to the cauldron and went back to work.

An hour later, he was sitting at the bench, looking at ten perfect silver bars. Hopefully his surly companion would agree with him about the quality. He was ready to take a bath and start making plans for their nightly excursion into the caverns below the inn. They'd done well on their first attempt, but they had to push harder.

There was no way for Tim to know how hard the dungeon would be to clear. It could have a lockout timer, or just be ridiculously long. The last thing he wanted to do was wait for the last few days and have to scramble around like a crazy person in the hopes of evading Malvonis long enough to finish.

Half-orcs weren't known for their patience.

Ironbeard walked into the back of the shop toward the pile of ten bars. He picked up each one, examining it meticulously before setting it aside. When he was satisfied with all of the bars, he turned to Tim. "How many did you have to make twice?"

Tim was expecting more of a job well done and not a question about how many times he failed. "One of the bars came out a little funny, so I poured it again."

"Just the one?" Ironbeard asked, raising his bushy eyebrows.

Tim was insulted until he realized the dwarf was trying to give him a compliment. There was a tone of disbelief in Ironbeard's voice, as if he'd never had an apprentice do so well on his first try.

Tim just shrugged. He wasn't very comfortable with compliments. "Yep."

"And if on your second batch you had another bar, would you fix it, or try to pass it off so you could go home on time?"

"I'd fix it." No one liked to stay late at work, but when there was a problem, you had to buckle down. It wouldn't be as bad in this case because he'd also be learning something new that could potentially earn him a living down the line.

"Good." Ironbeard favored him with a rare smile. "A smith is only worthwhile if their product is consistent." He waved an arm around, indicating the shop. "And my consistency is excellence."

Tim knew exactly what he was saying. Nothing in his shop went out the door unless it was perfect. There wasn't a bargain bin or a place for cast-offs. Anything that wasn't perfect got melted down. It was the kind of thing you wished every business did, instead of a normal business where they try to force the cheapest product on you at the highest price.

Nodding his head, Tim said, "I understand."

"By the goddess, I believe you do, boy." Ironbeard slapped Tim on the shoulder, almost making the boy stumble. "I'm putting you on bar duty for a while, and once I'm satisfied, maybe I'll show you how to swing a hammer."

Tim started to smile. He was finally getting somewhere. Sure, maybe in a month or two, he might only be able to make a crude sword, but in a year or two, he might be able to make the highest-level adventurer swoon.

"Whenever you think it's time, I'm ready to learn."

Ironbeard watched Tim as he ran a hand through his big, bushy beard. "That time is coming, but it isn't today. Today you're done, so get out of here before I put you back to work."

"See you tomorrow." Tim didn't wait for a response. He switched out of his gloves and apron and into his regular clothes as he ran out of the shop. If he made it back to the inn early, he could take a bath before anyone else showed up.

There was something to be said about staying clean in this game. It took effort with all the work he did, but at least he didn't have to pay someone to clean and repair his clothes. As he stepped outside, Tim noticed the breeze coming off the ocean had a tang to it. It might as well have been a whiff of the freshest mountain air after being trapped in the forge all day.

Tim turned toward the market. He didn't think anyone was following him, but the man in the orange sash was still out there somewhere.

He had to be careful.

CHAPTER FORTY-FOUR

The water was hot.

At least that was something. If he couldn't take a shower, he'd settle for a hot bath. If nothing else, it scrubbed the sour smell of dried sweat from his skin. It also provided him some time to relax away from the rest of his team. Even the leader of a motley crew needed a few minutes to himself to decompress.

A bath was also the perfect place to check on his stats. He'd dismissed the notification window before bed, but now that work was done, he might as well get ready for tonight.

He was still level seven, so he didn't have any stat points to allocate yet, but he did have one skill that received an upgrade.

Skill increase: Healing Orb

You have reached apprentice rank four. Your healing orb is now 13% more effective and applies 16% of the original spell's healing as a heal-over-time bonus. The HOT is now applied over six seconds.

Tim was looking over his skills, wondering which one was likely to level next, when he saw one at the bottom he didn't remember getting. The spell was called "snare." He'd never used it, but it was the kind of thing that might come in handy. He put a mental checkmark next to the spell and hoped he'd remember to use it in one of their upcoming fights.

Killing monsters didn't seem nearly as fast a way to level as completing quest lines. Thankfully, he had two quests outstanding that should provide him with a decent bump in his progress. Finishing both of them might get him close to level ten, and then he'd have some tough decisions to make. What class would he chose, and would he become an adventurer?

Tim dunked his head in the water and started to scrub behind his ears. As he surfaced, Tim realized someone was pounding on the door. "Never a moment's peace," he mumbled before looking at the door of the bathroom.

"What!" Tim bellowed. This was the only time he had to himself for the entire day. All he wanted was to be left alone for a few moments.

Ernie ran into the bathroom. "We've got a problem!"

Tim shook his head. Couldn't the problems wait until tomorrow? From the look on the innkeeper's face, they couldn't. "Lay it on me, Ernie."

"There is some woman out here saying you promised her a job." Ernie stared at Tim, face flushed with anger.

Oh, shit.

"I might have made an offer to someone." Tim thought about dunking his head under the water to avoid what he knew was coming.

"Now?" Ernie stared daggers at him. "With all we have going on?" He moved toward the tub. "And I'm not exactly comfortable with a woman of her profession in my establishment."

Now wasn't the time to remind Ernie that the inn was about to become his. "You have something against barmaids?"

"No, I've got something against hookers. The Blue Dagger has never been that kind of place." Ernie stomped his foot. "And I want to keep it that way."

Tim stood up, holding out a hand for a towel. "Liz was looking for a change of professions, and she provided me with invaluable information on a quest I was completing for the temple."

Accepting the towel from Ernie, Tim quickly dried off and re-equipped his clothes. "I'm sorry, Ernie. I should have talked to you first. I might be buying the inn, but this is your place."

Ernie watched Tim with an appraising eye. "Don't hire anyone else. I don't even know how I'm going to pay her." He looked exasperated. "It's not like we have a lot of customers."

"Just give her a room and make sure she's fed. I'll take care of the rest until we get the inn running again." Tim clapped the man on the shoulder. "And I'll make sure not to make any more decisions about the inn's future without talking to you."

"Fine, but no more funny business." Ernie frowned. "Not until you get what Malvonis wants and get the deed to the inn in your hands."

"Thanks, Ernie." Tim opened the door so the innkeeper could exit first and followed him into the hallway.

"Don't thank me yet. This could all turn to shit." Ernie moved toward the main room.

"Well, at least one of us is staying positive," Tim snarked as they moved into the tavern.

Liz was sitting at a table with her bags on the floor at her feet. She looked different than the night before, maybe because she wasn't wearing a corset and her hair was tied up in a no-nonsense ponytail. She wasn't smiling, but it wasn't like she'd had the warmest introduction to the place.

"Hey, Liz. I'm sorry for the confusion." Tim sat at the table. "I left for work this morning and forgot to tell Ernie you were coming."

She tapped her nails on the table. "I'd be mad, but at least I'm out of that shithole." She looked around the inn. "Although this place looks like the other inn made me feel."

Tim glanced at the unpainted wooden walls and the scratched floor. "We're currently under renovation."

"So, what? You don't have any customers? How am I supposed to live?" She looked from Tim to Ernie. "How long do you think these renovations will take?"

Tim winked at Ernie. "We've got about six days to get everything sorted out."

"Five and a half, really." Ernie looked worried. "Not that I'm counting."

"Don't worry, Liz. Ernie is going to set you up with a room and board until we get things rolling again. I know it's not much of an offer, but it's the best I can do right now."

She looked around the room. "This place could really use a woman's touch."

"That's what I've been telling them." ShadowLily appeared out of nowhere and her eyes locked onto Tim's. "Who's your new friend?"

Tim felt the icy grip of despair wrapped around his heart. "Our newest hire."

Liz stood up, watching ShadowLily warily. "I'm Liz."

"ShadowLily," the half-elf replied stoically. "How did you two meet?"

"Funny story..." Tim's voice trailed off.

Gaston strutted into the room and took a seat at the table. "This is going to be good. Ernie, bring me some popcorn."

"If you want popcorn, you can make it your damn self," snapped the innkeeper.

"Now I'm starting to see why this place is so popular." Liz chuckled.

ShadowLily thrust a finger into Tim's chest. "You didn't answer my question. How did you two meet?"

Tim looked at Gaston quickly, realizing no help was going to be coming from that corner. Ernie couldn't help him, and Liz was kind of the source of the problem. What in the fuck was he going to do?

"So, you remember last night when you went out with Cassie, and I went with Gaston?"

ShadowLily lifted her hand and twirled her index finger in the universal gesture that meant hurry the fuck up.

"I kind of had a job I needed to do, and Liz helped me." Tim finished lamely.

"Helped you how?" ShadowLily crossed her arms and glared at him.

"With the information, of course." Tim looked at Liz, hoping she'd back him up.

Liz was smirking at him, her eyes filled with amusement. "As much as I'd like to throw him under the bus, Tim was honorable." She rolled her eyes. "I know. I couldn't believe it either, a man who kept it in his pants." She gave a tense smile at the half-elf's growing frown. "But the reason I'm here now is he offered me a job."

"Did he?" If looks could kill, ShadowLily's would have sent Tim six feet under.

"Not that kind of job." Tim held up his hands as if to ward off an incoming punch. "Liz is just going to be helping out around the inn until we get things rolling." Tim looked at Ernie. "Right?"

"I have a firm policy of not messing with women that carry small bladed weapons. Tends to keep all my man parts just where I want them." Ernie rose his bushy eyebrows in a way that let Tim know this was payback for not talking to him first.

Tim swiveled toward Gaston, eyes pleading for help.

"I just let you get the information. I didn't think you'd offer her a job." The burly assassin shrugged. "Not that I'm complaining." He sent a friendly wave at Liz. "She's a good deal better-looking than our current server."

Liz's smile disappeared. "Listen, if it's that big of a deal, I can just go."

Tim looked around the room. Ernie looked exasperated, ShadowLily was still fuming, and Gaston looked as if he didn't have a care in the world. When it came down to it, though, it was really his choice. He was responsible for Liz after he helped her out of her contract. At the very least, he owed her a place to stay until she found something better.

Tim pointed at Liz as she started to stand up. "You're staying." He turned to ShadowLily. "I made her a promise when she risked her livelihood to help me. She deserves a chance."

ShadowLily seemed to think about it for a moment but nodded her head as she came to some kind of decision. Striding across the room, the half-elf extended her hand. "Hi, I'm ShadowLily. Welcome to the Blue Dagger."

Liz took her hand and gave it a firm shake. "Thank you."

Tim felt an unsure smile spreading across his lips. It looked like everything was settled, at least for now. He knew from previous experience that he'd probably catch an earful later, but for the moment, the turbulence was over, and he'd come out the other side just fine. It also meant it was time to get to work. All they needed now was Cassie.

"Ernie, why don't you show our newest employee to her quarters?" Tim pointed at ShadowLily, then himself. "We can start ironing out a plan for tonight."

Liz got up from the table and followed Ernie from the room with her bags. Tim watched her go and wondered if he made the right choice. When it came right down to it, he didn't know much about her. He'd always been a pretty decent judge of character, but inside the game, the rules were different.

It was easier to hide.

As he took a seat at the table, Tim made the decision not to worry about it. Ernie was distrustful enough of strangers that he knew the innkeeper would keep an eye on her. That made things easier for Tim. All he had to do was focus on making it to the dungeon. Once they could get a look at what waited for them inside of the dungeon, everything would get simpler.

He looked up from the table and his thoughts before he motioned for the others to sit as he started going over his plan for the night. The two thieves nodded along as he spoke. All they were waiting for now was Cassie.

Where in the hell was she?

CHAPTER FORTY-FIVE

"This is Sparta!"

Cassie kicked the last kobold in the chest so hard it flew across the cavern and hit the wall with a crunch. The creature tried to stand, but Gaston stabbed it before it reached its feet. As the burly assassin stood up, the group eyed each other, smiling. They were making real progress tonight.

The best part was, the kobolds from the night before hadn't respawned, so the group didn't waste the first hour killing the same monsters. The party was farther into the maze of caverns than Tim would have thought possible. There was no way to know for sure, but they had to be getting close to the entrance of the dungeon by now.

"We have to be getting close." Gaston echoed his thought as he wiped his daggers on the kobold's filthy smock.

"As long as there are more of them, this experience is amazing." Cassie twirled her bo staff before slipping it into the harness on her back.

Tim hadn't even thought about checking his own experience gains since they entered the caverns again. Last night's experience

367

was enough to get him close to another level. By the time they cleared the dungeon, he might even be level ten.

Then he'd be able to use his free class-change token. Although he wasn't sure what he wanted to play yet, a few of the classes really stood out for him. It was going to be a tough decision when he had to make it. Once you made that choice, there was no going back.

Tim couldn't worry about his class choice now. They still had work to do, so, it fell on him to get the group back on track. "Gaston, scout ahead and let us know what's going on."

"I could use some company. These kobolds are sneaky little bastards when they want to be."

ShadowLily nodded toward them. "I'll go."

"I guess I'll just wait here then," Cassie said, starting to pout.

"Yeah, must be tough always being left behind with the healer." Tim chuckled. "It will give us time to talk about your new armor."

"Now he wants to talk fashion accessories." She stared at ShadowLily. "Where did you even find this guy?"

"I was volunteering at the mental hospital, and he just had the cutest smile." ShadowLily moved next to Tim and pinched his cheek like an annoying relative. "Now he's all mine."

"Love at first insanity." Cassie laughed. "Got it."

"Hey!" Tim sputtered. "That's not how it happened."

"You tell it your way, I'll tell it mine." ShadowLily gave Tim a quick kiss on the lips and disappeared into the shadows.

Throwing his hand up, Tim stared at Cassie. "See what I have to deal with?"

Cassie sniggered. "At least she's hot."

"That takes a good deal of the sting out of it." Tim smiled as he thought about the first night he'd spent in bed with his half-eleven girlfriend. "And she kicks major ass."

Cassie looked around the cavern, taking in the scattered corpses around them. "You can say that again."

Tim nodded. It sure was nice to have Gaston and ShadowLily

around. They made mincemeat out of just about anything. All he had to do was stand back and heal the odd scratch. Every now and then, he used his flameburst spell to make sure they didn't get surrounded, but otherwise, he mostly watched the battle.

It was kind of nice to be in the back; it made Tim feel more like a general. When they were in a fight, he controlled the ebb and flow of the battle by shouting out orders. Normally shouting orders at your girlfriend was a sure-fire way to end up castrated with your man parts thrown out of a window on the side of the road, but ShadowLily took it well.

As long as they were in combat.

He wasn't dumb enough to shout at her any other time. Maybe it was something he learned from his parents. Tim could count on one hand the number of times he'd heard them raise their voices in anger at each other. At him? Well, that was a whole different story.

Gaston reappeared. "We've got a problem."

"A big fucking problem," ShadowLily added as she popped out of stealth.

A big horrible smelly problem was the last thing they fucking needed. The clock was ticking, and it wasn't like he could ask for more time. Malvonis seemed more inclined to rip your arms off than to let you weasel out of a deal.

"Don't leave me in suspense." Tim knew there was a tidal wave of shit coming his way, but if any group could handle the situation, it would be his group of misfits.

"They've built defenses around the entrance to the dungeon." Gaston looked worried.

Tim wanted to feel more concerned about the fact Gaston was worried, but he chose to focus on the positive. The assassin had just told him they'd found the entrance to the dungeon. The news was almost too good to be true.

He had to be sure he heard him right. "So, you saw the entrance?"

"Of course, that's all you'd think about." ShadowLily smacked him in the chest. "Not the more than twenty kobolds hiding behind wooden barricades."

"Twenty?" Tim coughed. "Wooden barricades?" None of that sounded very positive, and the most kobolds they'd faced at once still stood at ten. "Any ideas?"

"I thought you were the idea guy." Cassie pointed at the thief and the assassin. "Just like they go stabby-stabby, and I take all the hits."

"Do you really want to get hit by twenty of them?" He chuckled at the dour look on Cassie's face. "I'm a good healer, but even I can't cure ten knife wounds at once."

"What the fuck are we going to do?" ShadowLily growled. "We have to get past them."

"Maybe we could try to lead some of them away." Gaston shrugged, knowing it wasn't much of a plan.

"But if they all charged..." ShadowLily looked at the floor. "We might need some more help."

Tim thought about it for a moment. He didn't want anyone else to know about the dungeon, not unless he was forced to reveal it. When he owned the inn and had control of the dungeon, he could make some real money. People would pay to get in there, or at the very least, he could conquer it once a week and use the loot to help with his other projects.

"We can't bring anyone else in on this. Our situation is precarious enough." He turned toward Gaston. "Do you think Ernie could make us anything? Like a poison gas, or something we can use from range?"

"Even if he can, he won't be able to do it tonight." The assassin kept his eyes focused, but Tim was afraid he might have let him down.

"Shit." Tim looked at his group, desperation washing over him. Permanent death until you registered as an adventurer was a real hindrance to getting shit done. In other games you could just go in and idle while you figured out the mechanics of the fight.

Their group didn't have that luxury, and Gaston couldn't respawn.

Rushing heedlessly into a fight they couldn't win was reckless and stupid. He needed time to come up with a plan, but he couldn't do it without seeing what was waiting for them up ahead.

Tim switched into his assassin's gear and looked at Gaston. "Show me."

"You sure?" the assassin asked.

"I can't plan a strategy if I don't know what I'm up against." Tim dropped into stealth mode. "Let's go."

"I'm coming too," ShadowLily interjected.

"Don't worry about me, guys. I'll just stay in the creepy cave surrounded by dead bodies until you get back." Cassie took a seat in the middle of the cavern.

Tim wanted to laugh, but he couldn't risk breaking stealth until he'd seen what was up ahead. Gaston led the way until they reached a bend in the tunnel. He stopped there and pointed around the corner.

Creeping forward, Tim tried to control his breathing. His nerves tried to get the better of him as the other room came into view. The last thing he wanted was to be responsible for killing his friends. Even if they could run all the way back to the inn before the kobolds caught them, would they be able to hold the door against twenty of them?

Inch by inch, he moved around the gentle bend.

Tim came to a stop, all the air seemed to have rushed out of his lungs. Gaston and ShadowLily might have been understating things just a bit. Sure, there were only twenty kobolds they could see, but they were entrenched behind barriers and had two small towers with archers. Beyond the kobold's defenses, he could just make out two giant stone doors.

The only place those doors could lead was the dungeon.

If they could take out the archers, they would have a chance. None of them had any useful ranged abilities. Tim didn't fancy their chances with throwing knives versus kobolds with bows. Plus, if the warriors charged, they'd be too preoccupied to get the archers, and the group would become fish in a barrel.

Tim tried to commit the layout to memory, but he realized he didn't have to. There had to be a way to screenshot or something. Opening his user interface, he searched through the options until he found a picture application. He snapped a couple pictures of the entire layout and some of just the towers.

This was exactly what he needed to come up with a plan. When they came back tomorrow, he'd have thought it through. Tim wasn't willing to risk his team unless he knew they could win. Just because he had a ticking clock hanging over his head, it didn't mean they all had to feel the Grim Reaper's cold embrace.

Tim trudged back toward his waiting friends. His steps felt heavy, but he knew they would find a way through this. As he reached the waiting thieves, he said, "Let's go."

When they were out of sight of the kobolds' defenses, the three of them dropped out of stealth and walked back to Cassie. She was sitting in the middle of the cavern and looked zoned out. Tim wondered if he looked the same way when he had his user interface up. Glancing at their tank again, Tim decided he'd make sure to only dip into his menus in private from now on.

ShadowLily reached out, touching Cassie's shoulder. "It's time to go."

Cassie made a motion with her hand as she closed out of her user interface. "What, already?"

Extending his hand to help her up, Tim flashed a weak smile. "We've got some planning to do."

Cassie started walking back to the inn, and the others followed her out of habit. "That bad, huh?"

"It sure would be easier if we had some ranged firepower." Tim looked at the cavern walls as if the roughhewn stone would somehow give him the answer. When one didn't materialize, he focused on putting one foot in front of the other.

It always felt this way in games. Being a ranged class was normally easier. You could avoid a ton of the pitfalls that plagued melee classes. But if you needed healing as a ranged class, sometimes you were out on an island and didn't get nearly as much attention. Tim shuddered as he thought about staying out of the red indicators on the ground and hearing one of his friends, screaming *"MORE DOTS."*

The easiest way out of this was to try to recruit someone to the team with a ranged class, but he wasn't ready to do that yet. They were so close, and he was sure they could handle this on their own if they just thought about the right way to approach it. Plus, did he really want to share the dungeon loot with some rando who wouldn't stick around?

Sometimes gaming could be frustrating when all you wanted was to rip through some content quickly but kept hitting roadblocks.

This wasn't going to be a fucking roadblock.

Not if he could help it. The stairs leading up to the inn appeared before them, and the crew made it to the top and back inside.

"How'd it go?" Ernie asked, his face lined with worry as he sealed the door behind them.

Gaston sat down heavily and lifted his hand to call for a beer. "One last hurdle to overcome."

Cassie took a seat next to him. "But it's a damn big hurdle."

Ernie looked at Tim. "Surely it can't be that bad."

Tim frowned at the defeated look on his team's faces. "Actually, there was something I needed to talk with you about." Putting on a brave face, Tim grinned at the innkeeper, trying to reassure him. "How do you feel about poison gas?"

"It can be a bit tricky." Ernie grimaced as a memory from his past came back to haunt him. "Once it's released, the gas is an indiscriminate killer. It will drop friend and foe alike."

"So, what I'm hearing is you can make it, but we need to be

careful." Tim patted Ernie on the shoulder. "How much time do you need?"

Ernie looked at Tim, clearly wondering how he'd gotten roped into making the gas without saying he could. "At least a full day, but probably a day and a half."

"That will take us into the weekend." ShadowLily looked at Tim. "Doesn't leave us a lot of time for the dungeon."

"If Ernie can help us get past the entrance, I think we'll have plenty of time. It's going to be one hell of a grind, though."

Cassie took a beer from Liz. "Well, I, for one, didn't have any other plans, so I'm ready to go."

Gaston stood on his chair. "Facing death with a chance for epic rewards might as well be the assassin's credo. I'm in."

ShadowLily looked at the others before taking Tim's hands in her own. "You don't even have to ask. I'm with you." She leaned forward and gave him a kiss. "We're in this together."

Tim returned the kiss and looked at his friends—his team, his group—and smiled. Things were coming together. One final push and they'd get to see the dungeon. It didn't hurt that the extra time Ernie needed would give him time to complete his other quest. Despite how bleak things had looked before, he could see a break in the clouds starting.

It was almost time to bask in the sun.

CHAPTER FORTY-SIX

"Happy Transcendence Day!" Ironbeard cheered.

Tim looked at his boss and couldn't help but smile. He'd never seen the grumpy dwarf happier than he was right now. "What's Transcendence day?"

"It's the day we celebrate the Goddess Eternia. Did you know she used to be mortal just like us until she transcended into a God?" Ironbeard looked around the shop to make sure no one was paying attention. "All of Promethia takes the day off to celebrate."

"Then why are we working so hard?" Tim wiped the sweat from his eyes. "Shouldn't we be drinking beer or something?"

Laughter bubbled up from deep within the dwarf's belly. "You can drink beer on Monday with everyone else, but you should enjoy some of the festival this weekend."

"Aren't you starting to congratulate people early if the holiday isn't until Monday? Tim couldn't help but grin back at the dwarf. He'd never seen his boss so elated.

"I like to get started now, so Monday can be a recovery day." Ironbeard chuckled. "You'll understand what I mean when you get a little older." He slapped Tim on the back. "Which also means I expect you to show up Tuesday morning ready to work your ass off."

It took Tim a second to realize that he had just scored an extra day off. Having the extra day made getting through the dungeon and not dying on one of Malvonis' blades a real possibility. If Ernie could come through with something special, they would be set.

"I'll be ready to work," Tim promised.

"Just know that you can still pump the bellows with a hangover and a bucket." Ironbeard chuckled. "Now get the fuck out of here so I can start celebrating properly."

"You don't have to tell me twice." Tim walked out of the shop, thinking about how to spend the next three days. Tonight he had something to take care of, but the rest of the time would be dedicated to getting through the dungeon.

Walking through the market before heading back to the slums was his go-to move. He stopped to buy a few rumpleberries and took his time at some booths, looking over the wares before exiting the market at a different location than he had the day before.

"Look at this, Chris. The dead have risen." Barry pointed at Tim as he approached the archway to the slums.

"Well, it *is* almost Transcendence day. Maybe he's next on the list for godhood." Chris snickered.

"Nice to see you," Tim snapped as he walked past them. It wasn't his fault that he died and came back to life. Not that these two assholes would have cared if he died and stayed dead.

"You don't have to get upset about it," Barry called after him.

"But if you do end up dying again, come and tell us straight away." Chris turned away from the opening, a cruel smile dancing across his face.

Despite how mad the two guards had made him, Tim understood how it must have looked to them. They probably thought he was just some crazy person begging for attention. His clothes weren't bloody, and he didn't have any injuries. How would he have ever been able to convince them he'd just been murdered?

Not being able to prove it, didn't make the man with the orange sash any less real. The bastard was still out there somewhere.

As it started to rain, Tim looked at the rolling clouds and let a few sprinkles splatter against his face. He wasn't sure if he'd ever feel safe until he knew the man in the orange sash was dead. Not to mention, he still had Cardinal Jepsom hanging over his head.

It was never a very good idea to make powerful enemies.

If the cardinal hadn't been such a threat, Tim would have been content to simply adventure with his friends. As it was, he needed eyes in the back of his head just to feel safe. Since he didn't have a spell for that particular affinity, he was on edge all the time.

Seeing people lined up outside of the healing shack didn't make him feel any safer, but he still had to help them. Between work and his mad dash to clear the caverns, he'd been ignoring the people who truly needed his help. He felt ashamed that he'd let anything stand in the way of helping them. All he'd wanted to do from the second he'd entered the game was to be a healer.

And a fucking good one.

Instead of heading for the door and the sanctuary of his room, Tim went to the people waiting outside. Ernie still had the doors locked as the renovations went on inside, but Tim didn't need a private room to heal. He could do it right here on the street.

Stepping in front of the shack, Tim called the first person forward. It didn't take long for him to work through the small group. He healed a burn, a cut, a broken wrist, and a turned ankle before the last person stepped forward.

"Tell me what happened," Tim asked as he looked the woman over for any sign of injury.

"It's my son. He fell on his back." She broke into sobs. "I don't have any way to get him here."

He thought about it for a minute. It could be another trap. They were so close to getting what Malvonis wanted that he couldn't risk going with her. An arm wrapped around Tim's waist, startling him from his dark thoughts.

"I see you still have a golden touch when it comes to the ladies," ShadowLily purred into his ear.

Tim turned to hug her and whispered into her ear, "It's just, the last time I went to heal someone, they tried to kill me."

"Well, I'm here now. Tell the poor woman we'll help her." ShadowLily smiled reassuringly at him. "We've got this."

Tim turned toward the woman, who was watching them with tears streaming down her cheeks. "Lead the way."

This had better not turn out like the last time.

An older woman ran out of the house as they approached. "Maria, is this the healer?" She ran past the woman they were following before Tim could say a word. The older version of Maria grabbed his hand and started yanking him toward the house. "Please, you have to hurry."

Tim didn't know what to do. This entire situation felt like a trap, creating a sense of urgency so he would rush into the house despite the danger it presented. He looked desperately at Shadow-Lily as the woman pulled him along.

"I'll check it out." His girlfriend ran past them and into the house and came out a few minutes later. "All clear."

Knowing that the house was clear of threats, Tim stopped resisting the older woman's tugging and ran for the door. "Where is he?"

"He's on the couch." ShadowLily's face twisted into a grimace.

Tim looked at Maria. "What's his name?"

"Marco."

The boy must have been in bad shape for her to still be crying, and ShadowLily's face didn't give him a lot of hope. Tim turned away from her and rushed past Maria's mother to the boy waiting on the couch. He wasn't a doctor, but Tim knew there was something wrong right away. The boy was deathly pale, but he didn't see any blood.

Kneeling next to the child, Tim brushed a strand of black hair out of his face. The kid's eyes flittered open. "Please help me."

A ball of healing water appeared in Tim's hand, and he splashed it on the child's chest. Marco groaned as the spell took hold. Next he applied his cleanse spell to the kid, hoping to rid his body of any infections caused by internal bleeding. Slowly and methodically, Tim continued to heal Marco until the boy fell into a deep sleep.

After standing up, Tim turned to find the mother staring at him. She looked at the pale, unconscious form of her son and started to cry. "Is he..."

Closing the distance between them, Tim put a reassuring hand on her shoulder. "No, Marco is just resting now. When he wakes up, he should be fine."

Tim glanced at Marco one last time. He hadn't healed many serious injuries yet, so he had to make sure the boy was ok. "If anything else happens or he doesn't feel better when he wakes up, come get me."

Maria fell to her knees and pressed herself against Tim's legs. "Thank you."

Bending slightly, Marco's grandmother peeled Maria away from Tim's legs. "Thank you, sir. I have no idea what she promised you, but we don't have very much money."

Tim had the benefit of being flush with gold for the time being, so he didn't need to survive on the offerings of others. Still, it set a bad precedent to do anything for free. His dad always told him if you're good at something, you should be paid for it. Just like if your friend is a plumber, you shouldn't invite him over to get free work done on your house.

Tim took the older woman's hands in his own. "Whatever you can spare is more than enough."

She reached inside her coat and pulled out a small bag of copper coins. The older woman looked at it, clearly unsure of how many to give him before just holding out the entire bag. "Thank you for your mercy."

Tim accepted the bag and quickly looked inside. There were twenty copper coins, and he took out five of them and handed the rest back to the older woman. She was clearly shocked to have gotten anything back, which made him feel even better about what he was doing.

"You're welcome." Tim took both her hands in his. "If he needs anything, please let me know."

Maria pushed her mother out of the way and pulled Tim into a warm embrace. "Marco wouldn't have lived without your help. If there is anything you need from us, all you have to do is ask."

Tim had never been a person who was comfortable with compliments. Nothing made him more uncomfortable than people heaping praise on him just for being himself. It was rare that he walked into a situation hoping he'd get something out of it. If it was in his power to help, he would.

"The payment you provided was more than enough." Tim felt his cheeks starting to burn with embarrassment as he looked between the two women.

Maria led them back to the front door. "Our offer still stands. If you ever need help, please let us know."

ShadowLily smiled at the women. "I'll make sure that he does."

They started walking back to the inn, and Tim nudged ShadowLily with his shoulder. "Thanks for protecting me back there."

"What, from the two harmless ladies?" She giggled. "I think you're selling yourself short."

"Anyone could have been in there, and you rushed in without a second thought. Not everyone would do that."

"Every now and then, I don't mind playing the sidekick." She bumped her shoulder into his. "But don't get used to it."

Tim smiled. ShadowLily was the real deal. It wasn't just her rocking bod that had him all spun around in circles; it was all of her. The simple question was, if you stripped away the great sex and the adventures, would he still want to be with her? If the answer was yes, it was a relationship worth taking to the next level.

He only hoped she felt the same way.

Tim grabbed one of ShadowLily's hands. "So, I've got a job to do tonight. Care to tag along?"

"What kind of job?" ShadowLily asked as she pulled him closer.

"The kind that involves infiltrating a kinky sex club and assassinating someone." Tim gave her hand a squeeze.

She dropped his hand and slapped Tim's shoulder. "Doesn't that go against your code as a healer?"

"I'm not a doctor. I don't follow a code," he said with all seriousness as he looked into the stormy sky. "But I have a quest to complete, and the last time I went out with Gaston, I came back with Liz."

"Well, we can't have another incident like that, now can we?" She laughed. "But don't get me wrong. You piqued my interest as soon as you said kinky sex club."

"Oh, the lady doth protest too little. I'm guessing she has a kinky sex club skeleton hidden in her closet." Tim laughed until he imagined ShadowLily in skintight latex, and he had to recite football stats in his head to avoid an unwelcome swelling in his pants.

"Maybe you'll find out tonight." She gave him a sly wink. "What's the name of this place, anyway?"

"The Stiff Tart," Tim said with a smile. It was a kind of a silly name, but it got the message across.

"Sounds like the kind of place where you're supposed to be my bitch," ShadowLily growled huskily.

"Guess we'll find out tonight." Tim slapped her ass and started sprinting to the inn.

"You'd better run!" ShadowLily smiled as she chased him.

CHAPTER FORTY-SEVEN

The Stiff Tart didn't look like much.

It was just a door set into a solid stone wall. There were three candles around the door, one on top and a single candle to either side. All of the candles had pink glass over the flames, casting the door in a wash of wavering pink light. There was a metal slat at about eye level in the door, and Gaston assured him that the password he'd provided would work.

Tim started to walk forward, but ShadowLily grabbed his arm. "Maybe I should handle this part."

"Whatever you say, Mistress." Tim lowered his head and moved to stand just behind her like a heeling dog. You never knew when someone was watching.

"Now you're learning." She pointed to where he was standing. "Stay." Turning away from Tim, she marched boldly up to the door and knocked three times.

The metal slat opened, and two very intense blue eyes stared out at them. "Password."

"Upstanding Citizen," she spat with disdain.

The person behind the door didn't say a thing, but they slid the metal opening closed with a thud. ShadowLily thought about turning around to look at Tim, but she just stood there glaring at the door as if she could open it through sheer force of will. Her frustration started to grow, but then she heard bolts sliding on the other side of the door.

The solid steel door slowly opened, and more pink light drifted onto the cobbled alley. The man who appeared was covered from head to toe in leather, with only his eyes visible. He stepped to the side, making sure they had plenty of room to enter.

ShadowLily turned and snapped her fingers at Tim. "You can move now."

"Thank you, Mistress." Tim moved forward but stopped just behind her again.

ShadowLily strode through the entranceway with Tim at her heels. All of the candles and torches inside were covered with the same pink glass that gave the hallway the feel of being submerged in some kind of bubble bath.

She moved to the end of the hallway and stopped at another door. Gaston had only given them the password for one of the doors, so if the second door required something else, they were totally fucked. The first door slammed shut behind them, and she heard the bolts sliding back into place.

Without any indication from the man waiting by the first door, the second door opened. A dwarven female stared up at them. She had curly brown hair and was wearing some kind of bra that left her nipples exposed. The dwarf gave them a long look before motioning for them to enter.

"I'm going to need a drink," Tim said as he took a look around.

ShadowLily spun and slapped him on the chest. "You do not have my permission to speak, worm!" Tim quickly masked the shock on his face and demurely lowered his eyes.

"My apologies, Mistress," Tim said as he stared at her boots.

"Just don't let it happen again." She looked at the dwarf. "Breaking them in is always such a chore, isn't it?"

"Bar's over there," the female dwarf stated in a surprisingly deep voice.

"We're in the market for a more private experience, and maybe someone to share it with us," ShadowLily purred as she ran a finger through the dwarf's hair.

"I don't do normals." The dwarf swatted ShadowLily's hand away. "But you should talk to Rick. He'll get you taken care of." She pointed at a man wearing suspenders and the smallest set of shorts in the world.

"Thanks," ShadowLily said with feigned disdain as she moved away. She watched the guy named Rick for a moment and thought about how his shorts were smaller than the ones worn by basketball players in the seventies. One wrong move and Rick would have a ball hanging out like a Christmas tree decoration.

She strutted toward Rick, aware that more than a few of the patrons around the room were watching her. There was no way she could look behind her to see if Tim was still playing his part. One wrong move and the people here would sniff out their little deception.

Despite herself, ShadowLily was kind of having fun. It wasn't every day she got to dress up like a sexy dominatrix. Roleplaying in bed could be fun if both people were into it, not that she'd be into doing this every night.

Being a dominatrix was too fucking demanding.

The last thing she wanted to do was spend her time telling Tim what to do. It seemed like more of a chore than a turn on. But the clothes, she liked them quite a bit. Kind of made her feel empowered. She had control over her body, and no one else could say a thing.

For now, she was content to play her part and see what happened next.

Stopping in front of Rick, ShadowLily put a hand on her hip. She waited for a moment, but the man completely ignored her.

Rick flicked his eyes toward her and went back to talking to his other guests as if she didn't exist. Tim watched the insult and wondered how long it would take for ShadowLily to lose her temper. The answer was not long.

Tired of waiting, ShadowLily grabbed the riding crop out of the hands of the man Rick was talking to and slapped his chest with it. "I'm tired of waiting, you worthless prick."

Rick rolled his eyes as he turned to face her. "No reason to get testy." His gaze moved down her body and back up to her eyes. "I was just finishing up some business." Rick gave the people he was speaking to a casual nod and they all found somewhere else to be.

His attention quickly returned to ShadowLily. "Welcome to the Stiff Tart. Here your darkest desires are our deepest pleasure to fulfill."

She snorted as if what he was saying to her was of little to no importance. "I require a room for myself and my bitch." She pointed at Tim and gave him a quick wink before turning back to Rick. "We'd also be interested in procuring additional companion-ship for the evening. I was told you can help with that."

"The room costs a gold coin, and the girl is included if you so desire." He made a motion over his head, and a line of ladies marched over from out of nowhere. "We also have men if that's your thing."

"A man would be better," Tim said, remembering that his target preferred male companionship.

The riding crop flashed out, catching Tim across the shoulder. He winced in pain and clutched his bruised arm. He looked up at her with the same kind of fixation Renfield gave Dracula before looking back at the floor.

ShadowLily tapped Tim with the crop a few more times before grabbing his chin and forcing his head up. She gave him a hard kiss on the mouth before pushing him away. "You're right. Maybe another man is exactly what I need."

Rick made another motion and the ladies disappeared, only to be replaced by a line of well-oiled man-flesh.

She walked forward and trailed her riding crop across their chests until she stopped, seemingly at random. "This one will do."

"Antonio. He is one of my finest." Rick smiled at the man almost longingly. "Please show our guests to Bungalow Seven."

"As you command." Antonio motioned for ShadowLily to follow him. "Right this way, Mistress."

Turning toward Tim, she commanded. "Pay the man!"

Tim opened his inventory and pulled out a gold coin. He tossed it to Rick and lowered his head again to follow his mistress to Bungalow Seven.

"Bungalow," as it turned out, was a loose term. The room was four pillars draped in swaths of pink silk. It gave you a sense of privacy from the other patrons, but nothing was completely hidden. Her first thought as she walked toward it was that it was kind of like being behind a screen or inside a tent.

People would be able to see their outlines but not much else.

Antonio held open two of the hanging silk sheets and ushered them into the space. Now came the tricky part. How did they handle Antonio? They couldn't have him running back to Rick after they asked their questions.

A look around the room revealed a bed and a large X made out of foot-thick wooden beams. The X had manacles on it, and there were also sets on the corners of the bed. Several objects placed around the room could also be used for restraint or pleasure.

Turning away from Antonio, ShadowLily moved to Tim's side. She leaned in close with her cheek gently brushing his. "What do you think about tying him to the X?"

Tim closed his eyes in case Antonio was watching. "Great idea." Then he tried to kiss her.

ShadowLily jerked her head away and smacked Tim with the riding crop. "Down, dog. *I* decide when you get to kiss me."

"As for you." She pointed the crop at Antonio. "I want you over there now."

"Yes, Mistress." Antonio moved to the X.

It didn't take her long to get the manacles in place. The muscle-bound masochist wasn't going anywhere until she set him free. All she had to do now was find a gag.

Tim stood up, relief etched on his face. Now that he didn't have to pretend to be her bitch anymore, he could help out. A few moments later, Tim slipped a gag in Antonio's mouth.

"Is this really what you've been doing in the game so far?" ShadowLily asked as she watched Antonio's eyes moving between them.

Tim shrugged. "Actually, this is my first quest that involves a place like this. The last time, I just had to sneak onto a boat."

"At least we got new outfits." ShadowLily grinned.

"And one of us looks hot in them." Tim checked her out again, hoping she might put the outfit back on when they got back to the inn.

"You don't look so bad yourself." She slapped his ass, causing him to jump.

Tim rubbed his sore right cheek as he leaned closer to Antonio. "You might have guessed by now we aren't your normal clientele."

Antonio's eyes were panicked as he looked between them. Tim stepped closer, his face mere inches away. "What we need from you is information." When he didn't move, Tim tapped him on the forehead. "Nod if you understand."

The man chained to what might as well have been a medieval torture device nodded his head vigorously.

"Good." Tim smiled. "Now that we have an understanding, I have one question for you." He waited until he was sure he had the man's entire focus. "Where is Fredrick Bohanna?"

Before removing the gag from Antonio's mouth, Tim pulled two gold coins out of his inventory. "Something to ease your conscience." When Antonio nodded, Tim pulled the gag free.

"That guy's a no-tipping prick. If you wanted information on him, all you had to do was ask." Tim slipped the coins into one of

Antonio's pockets. "There is a door against the wall out there. You'll need my key to get in."

"Where is your key?" ShadowLily looked at Antonio's outfit, not seeing anywhere to hide a key. The two coins Tim slipped into his pants bulged the tight leather to point it looked uncomfortable.

"Back pocket."

She reached behind him, feeling around for a second before she found a small slit in his tight leather shorts. Pulling the key free, she flashed it at Tim before tucking it away.

"You've been very helpful, and I hope you understand why we have to leave you tied up." Tim slipped the gag back into Antonio's mouth. "As soon as we're done, we'll let you go."

Antonio shook his head from side to side, struggling against the gag. "Wait," he cried, finally spitting out enough of the cloth to speak. "He has somebody with him."

ShadowLily frowned. "What kind of somebody?"

"I don't know. Never saw the scary fucker with him until the last couple of days. He looks like some kind of bodyguard, but he wears this garish orange sash. I get the feeling he would be just as likely to kill you as fuck you."

"Thanks, Antonio." ShadowLily put the gag back in place before slipping an extra golden coin into the other side of his shorts. "But we still can't have you talking until we get back."

She started walking out of the enclosure but realized Tim wasn't following her. "What's wrong?"

He looked as pale as a ghost. "The man with the orange sash is the one who killed me. This just got a whole lot more complicated."

"Well, it's a good thing you brought me to uncomplicate things." She grabbed his hand and tugged him forward. "Let's go get some payback."

CHAPTER FORTY-EIGHT

No one keeps anything pleasant behind a locked door.

With everything that was allowed to happen out in the open at the Stiff Tart, you had to be up to some very dark shit if you needed to hide behind a locked door. It wouldn't be long before they found out exactly what Mr. Orange Sash was doing here with Fredrick. Maybe he simply had guard duty, but there was always the chance he was waiting for them.

ShadowLily slipped the key into the door and turned it. Tim held his breath as the door swung open. When the man who killed him didn't lunge out of the opening and stab his girl, he let out a sigh of relief. All of their plans would be ruined if she died, not to mention that he was totally getting used to her half-elven look.

Right now, their biggest concern was that they didn't really have a plan. At the very least, he would have liked to know the layout of the rooms they were entering, but he didn't think to ask Antonio what was waiting ahead. With the door open, they couldn't go back and ask him now.

They were going to wing it, and winging it wasn't one of Tim's specialties. He liked to plan, and if it all went to shit, at least he had some idea of where things went wrong and how to fix them for next time.

As ShadowLily stepped inside, she changed into her thief's gear. Tim was kind of sad to see her outfit disappear. Despite how much he'd made fun of this place in his head, he loved looking at her ass in those pants. Maybe what these people were getting up to wasn't so bad. No one was forcing them, and consenting adults could do whatever they wanted with each other.

And if it meant she was going to wear those pants again, he'd come back here as often as she wanted.

Following ShadowLily's lead, Tim switched into his assassin's gear and equipped his knives. Since there were going to be at least three people in the room, helping with the attack seemed like a better choice. He could still cast a healing spell, it just wouldn't be nearly as effective with his decreased wisdom.

Tim sent a silent prayer to the Goddess Eternia. It never hurt to have help from on high on your side.

He closed the door behind them and flipped the latch to lock it again. If all the workers had keys, it wouldn't keep them out, but the closed door might buy them enough time to carry out his quest. He gave ShadowLily a quick nod before they both dropped into stealth.

Moving down the long, dark hallway was creepy as shit. The only light came from a single torch at the far end. Next to the torch were an empty chair and a closed door.

Why was the chair empty?

Tim spun to see the dagger coming at him. There wasn't anything he could do to block the strike. Instead, he threw himself out of the way. His back hit the wall, and he crumpled to the floor, looking at the thin red line cut across his chest. That was close.

Too fucking close.

The man in the orange sash stood over him with a haughty sneer twisting his lips. "I thought I killed you already."

"Dapper Don probably thought the same thing right before I

cut him down," Tim said with all the bravado a man lying defenseless on his back could muster.

"You ruined a good thing for me with the captain." Juan Pablo pointed his dagger at Tim. "I've been fucking stuck here, working for that asshole Jepsom just so I could find you." His sneer turned into a smile. "With your death, I can finally leave this shithole and sail home."

"Or maybe you'll never get the chance." ShadowLily dropped out of stealth and threw one of her knives at him.

The man in orange dodged the blade easily enough. "You're going to have to do better than that if you want to take out Juan Pablo." He pulled a knife from inside his vest and sent it flying toward her.

Tim couldn't see past his nemesis, but he knew the knife hit her because she screamed in pain. One knife wouldn't be enough to kill her, but Juan Pablo was already reaching inside his vest for another blade. Tim clutched desperately at his dagger as he climbed back to his feet.

ShadowLily wasn't going to die today.

Juan Pablo heard the movement behind him and turned to face Tim. The two men stood staring at each other, Tim with his daggers at the ready and Juan Pablo with a single long knife in his hand.

ShadowLily wasn't screaming anymore, and there was no way for him to tell why without getting past Juan Pablo first. Tim had to help her, and this motherfucker wasn't going to stop him from doing it. Juan Pablo had to die and die quickly.

"Your little bitch isn't as quick as she thinks." Juan Pablo sneered at him as he waved his blade in slow, methodical circles.

"Oh, she's more than quick enough to deal with the likes of you. You just got lucky." Tim snapped back with a confidence he didn't feel.

"That growing pool of blood says differently."

Tim pretended to try to look around him to get a better view of

ShadowLily, knowing the bastard wouldn't miss the opportunity to take him out. He wasn't wrong. Juan Pablo lashed out with his knife, and knowing the attack was coming almost wasn't enough to save him. His fight against the man in the orange sash almost ended right there.

Against all odds, Tim got his dagger up and turned the attack away. While he missed getting stabbed, he couldn't avoid the shoulder that slammed into him a moment later. His back crunched into the wall a second time, but he managed to stay on his feet.

Not that it did him a lot of good. He stumbled away from the wall and felt a throbbing pain in his arm.

Oh yeah, that's what it feels like to be stabbed.

Pain lanced down his arm. Shit. It felt more like the pain was ripping through his entire body. Juan Pablo smiled at him as he pulled the dagger free. Blood poured out of the open wound, and the dagger Tim held in his left useless hand fell to the tiled floor and bounced away.

Tim stared at the gold teeth in the pirate's smile, knowing that the last thing he was going to see in this world was that bastard's happy face. The tip of Juan Pablo's knife lowered, and Tim felt the tiniest prick of the blade on his belly. There was only time to do one thing, and if he was going to die, he wouldn't do it without a fight.

"I'm going to do this slow, so you'll remember me in the next life." Juan Pablo gloated as he slipped the tip of the blade farther into Tim's stomach.

"Fuck you!" Tim spat, as he slammed his dagger into the pirate's side. Sure, the move drove the fucker's dagger farther into his own stomach, but the wound he dealt the man with orange sash was worse.

Juan Pablo lurched to the side, then looked at the knife sticking out of him with surprise etched on his face. He plucked the dagger free and tossed the blade aside just as ShadowLily appeared behind him.

Both of her daggers ripped into Juan Pablo's back. She ripped the blades free and plunged them in again before kicking him toward the door. The man in the formerly orange sash hit the wall and collapsed to the ground. Blood pumped out of the five massive holes in his body before his chest stopped moving altogether.

ShadowLily turned away from the rapidly cooling corpse with a smile on her face. "He's not getting back up."

"Grrghh." Tim coughed up blood.

"Oh, shit." ShadowLily knelt beside him, clutching his hands. "You have to heal yourself."

Tim didn't respond, and his face was pale. She'd never seen someone go into shock, but she imagined this is what it would look like. His hand was clammy, and he wouldn't open his eyes. She dropped his hand and slapped him hard.

Tim's eyes fluttered open. "What the fuck?"

"Heal yourself, damn it!"

Tim's hand moved through the familiar gesture, a ball of water forming in his palm. He splashed it against his arm and formed another for his stomach. The pain was starting to fade, but the memory of the attack was still with him. Maybe fighting wasn't really his thing, after all. Life seemed so much easier when he was standing in back of the battle.

Switching from his assassin's gear into his healing robes only took a second. Once he had his staff equipped, Tim repeated the spells.

"Save a little of that juice for me," ShadowLily said as she slumped against the wall.

"Oh, shit. I'm sorry." Tim felt foolish even as he cast a healing orb on ShadowLily. He'd been so focused on himself that he completely forgot she was hit. He pressed the spell directly into her wound, and she let out a sigh of relief as the spell surged through her.

"Are we done yet?" she asked, exhausted.

Tim pulled ShadowLily up from where she had been leaning against the wall. "Not yet, but this part should be much easier."

"Let's hope so." She walked back over to Juan Pablo's corpse and took a knee beside it. A moment later she stood up, brandishing another key. "This should get us through the door."

"Good thinking." Tim switched back into his assassin's gear and looked around for his missing dagger. He found it a few seconds later and placed it in his inventory. When he took the blade back out, it was as clean and sharp as the day Gaston had given it to him.

"Maybe this time we should have a plan?" ShadowLily smirked at Tim.

"I thought I was the only one who liked plans." Tim motioned toward the door. "Unfortunately, we have no idea what we are going to find in there, so we're just going to have to improvise."

"I can handle that if you can?" She slipped the key into the door. "But maybe you should still go first."

"You wound me." Tim placed his hand over his heart. "And here I was thinking I had brought my most fearsome protector."

"You're not dead, are you?" ShadowLily hissed as she turned the key.

"Ask me how I feel about it in ten minutes." They dropped into stealth, then Tim pulled on the handle and stepped into the room.

ShadowLily entered behind him. From the sound of flesh slapping, they didn't need to be too cautious. Tim shook his head as he crept into the room. These assassination quests weren't the kind of missions he'd planned on getting into when he'd walked into the temple.

I mean, how often do you go to a place of healing and leave with a quest to kill someone?

It didn't feel right to sneak around killing people, and he sure as hell wasn't going to make this his profession. Tim would leave the killing to people with fewer scruples while he focused on healing. Everyone loved a healer. No one loved a guy that snuck into bedrooms to kill people.

That was a fact.

Still, there was one more name on his list. If you couldn't commit to seeing a job through, you shouldn't take it on. There was something to be said for finishing the job. How many people had he met that said they were going to write a book but never made it past chapter one, let alone finished the book?

That was the thing with the arts; everyone thought they could do it, but it was just not that easy.

Some people had loads of talent and others could learn to do something as a skill, but no one person could do everything perfectly. Tim couldn't paint for shit, but he could make the numbers in his Excel sheet sing.

Not that either of those things mattered now.

Moving farther into the room, Tim realized Fredrick's lover was another man. Well, love whoever you wanted to love. If you found another person in this world who completed you, you should hang onto them and not be ashamed.

That being said, he had always imagined his first time walking into a situation like this, it would be two women on the bed in front of him.

A smile crept onto his face. Sometimes the difference between reality and fantasy was just too big a gap to bridge. Plus, this wasn't like his dreams of finding two women going at it, only to be invited to join. He wasn't going to be joining this rodeo anytime soon. Instead, he was here to make sure one of these men found an early grave. It really didn't matter now.

Tim motioned for ShadowLily to stay put as he dropped stealth and walked casually toward the bed. "I'm looking for Fredrick Bohanna."

The men rolled apart. One of them looked up with rage burning in his eyes. "Who in the fuck are you, and where is that slimy bastard who was supposed to be guarding the door?"

"Juan Pablo is no longer with us." Tim ignored the bluster as he pointed his dagger at the other man. "You work here?"

He just nodded his head.

"If there is a bathroom in here, I suggest you go to it now." When he didn't move, Tim roared, "Get the fuck out of here!"

The man leapt from the bed, his ghost-white ass cheeks bouncing as he ran for a door at the back of the room.

Fredrick Bohanna didn't look nearly as concerned. He lit his cigarette with a taper from the candle and stared defiantly at Tim. "So, what, you're here to kill me?"

Tim pulled one of his throwing knives free and hurled it at the man. It stuck in the headboard not an inch from Bohanna's cheek and quivered. "Something like that."

"Well, you're going to have to try a little bit harder than that I'm afraid."

This meeting wasn't going how Tim expected. "You're not afraid to die?"

Fredrick laughed. "Why would I be? I am one of the goddess' chosen. I'm working directly for the next high priest."

"It seems the current high priest doesn't agree." Tim pulled another knife free. He took his time, slowed his breathing, and let it fly.

The dagger sailed smoothly and at the last second twitched to the right, leaving the smallest of cuts on Fredrick Bohanna's cheek.

"Like I said, you'll have to do better." He tossed the sheet to the side and stood up. "Can you?"

Tim didn't know what was happening, but he could feel something going on. It was like the man was pulling all the magical energy from the room in preparation for a catastrophic attack.

Gritting his teeth, Tim pulled his daggers free. "You'd be surprised by what I can do."

Lightening started to form on the tips of Fredrick's fingers and a cruel smile grew on the man's face as he prepared to kill the interloper where he stood. His hands came up, ready to unleash the spell, but his smile faltered.

ShadowLily appeared at his side, dagger covered in scarlet blood up to the crosspiece.

Bohanna's spell fizzled, and he looked at her in disbelief. "But I am one of the chosen."

"Not anymore." Tim plunged his dagger into the man's heart.

They stood there for a moment, looking at the body on the ground. Neither of them knew what to say. Tim knelt to loot the corpse but didn't find anything except a few pieces of jewelry. He quickly added the items to his inventory.

ShadowLily bumped the end table, and Tim heard the clinking of coins. He stood up as she tossed the bulging sack at him. Plucking three gold coins from the bag, he tossed them toward the bathroom and handed the bulging purse back to the woman of his dreams.

"Thanks for all your help. I really couldn't have done this without you." Tim glanced around the room to make sure no one else was going to pop out to attack them.

She pocketed the bag of coins. "And don't you forget it." ShadowLily gave him a sly wink. "While I liked the Stiff Tart, next time you want to buy me a kinky outfit, all you have to do is say something. We can skip all this drama and get to having fun."

Tim liked the sound of that a lot better than he liked hearing her scream in pain. He wrapped his arm around her waist as they started walking toward the exit. "Oh, I for one could do with a good deal more fun and a hell of a lot less almost dying."

"Yeah, but tell me the truth." She paused to look directly into his eyes. "It was worth it just to see me in those pants, right?"

Tim put the back of his hand to his forehead and pretended to swoon. "My life would not have been the same without it."

"Watch it, or you might not get to see my ass out of those pants ever again."

Things were getting serious. He pulled her closer and winked. "Give me some sugar, baby!"

"Let's just get out of here so I can live up to my end of the deal." Her clothes blurred as she switched back into her ultra-sexy outfit.

Tim let her get a few steps in front of him. "Never mind, I don't need a super-cool chainsaw hand as long as you own those pants."

ShadowLily turned, a smirk on her face, and one eyebrow arched so high she might have been trying to get the goddess' attention. "Eyes up, mister. I've got other assets that need attention."

Tim looked into the most beautiful eyes he'd ever seen. "Yes, Mistress." They entered the club again with him trailing behind her.

CHAPTER FORTY-NINE

"What is all this?"

Tim looked at the table covered in food and the bar next to it. There were people milling around, making little plates and sucking down glasses of some kind of turquoise liquid. He'd never seen anyone besides Reginald in Lady Briarthorn's house, so walking into a party was a bit of a shock.

Reginald looked around the room at the guests and back at Tim. "Why it's a party in your honor, of course. You've returned to us the victorious hero again."

Who knew stabbing people was heroic?

"I don't feel like much of a hero." Tim frowned at the gathering, wondering how quickly he could get out of there.

"Nonsense." Lady Briarthorn emerged from the crowd. "You've dealt a harsh blow to the usurper and returned to us unscathed. Isn't that what heroes do?"

She tilted her glass and finished her drink with a practiced flick of the wrist. "Come join me in the study, so we can take care of business."

Reginald bumped his arm. "Don't mind Lady Briarthorn. She's not much for parties either, but she has to keep up appearances."

Tim, on the other hand, loved a good party, but only if it was with a bunch of his friends. Despite his constant bitching about their shenanigans, he missed his two best friends. *They should really give this a try. Xander would love it.*

Tim followed the lady of the house back to her study. When the door closed behind him, he instantly felt better. One thing he'd learned in the game was that it didn't take much to kill him, and being surrounded by people he didn't know made him edgy.

He didn't wait for permission to be seated. Instead, Tim plunked himself down in his normal spot. Ceremony had never really been his thing. There was something to be said for just getting shit done, and his rush to get this meeting over with had nothing to do with ShadowLily waiting in his room, wearing pants that might as well have been painted on.

Lady Briarthorn folded her dress under her as she sat. "I know what we've asked you to do is weighing heavily upon you, but when the goddess calls us to action, we must be brave, we must be driven, and most of all, we must succeed."

She steepled her fingers as she watched Tim closely. "You've never let us down, even when the task was a bloody one, and rumor has it that you are still tending to the needs of the people in the slums."

"The people there need help. I do what I can." Tim felt kind of embarrassed about the whole thing. He wasn't some great hero or someone going above and beyond. He was just doing what he hoped someone would do for him given the chance.

"And humble." She smiled warmly as she looked at him. "All traits that are praised by the goddess." She stood back up and moved to the corner of her room. Bending at the waist, she opened a chest on the ground and pulled out a luxurious white robe trimmed with turquoise blue and a bag of coins.

"May I present to you your rewards for a job well done?"

A prompt appeared in his vision.

Quest Completed: Lancing the Corruption

You have killed all of Cardinal Jepsom's top aides. The pretender's rebellion against the high priest has been significantly weakened by your efforts. Every soldier has to do their part, and you have done yours admirably.

Rewards: Robe of the Everlasting and ten gold coins.

Tim quickly added the money to his inventory and examined the robe.

Robe of the Everlasting:

This robe has continually popped up throughout Eternia's history. It was originally worn by Thaddaeus the Loved over two hundred years ago. The robe turned up again during the reign of Malicious the Mad before being lost to history. Now it's yours. Don't fuck it up.

+3 to Wisdom

Special Ability, River of Souls: Become one with the souls of the dead, boosting your mana recovery and lowering the cost of your spells by 5% when activated.

Tim slipped the robe into his inventory. "This is incredible. I don't know what to say."

"I believe 'thank you' is the customary response." Lady Briarthorn said as she returned to her seat. "But we can dispense with the pleasantries. They aren't required between friends."

Friends?

Tim didn't think they were friends, but they were definitely on friendly terms. Normally, he would have been worried about someone using that term to try to butter him up for a favor, but Lady Briarthorn didn't ask for favors. She dished out quests and paid handsomely for their completion.

"I'll say thank you just the same."

She nodded her head in acquiescence. "The high priest has requested that you return to the temple at your earliest convenience."

"For my next quest?"

"Paul doesn't always tell me why, just what he needs done." The lady let out a dramatic sigh. "I would assume that your successes with me have made you an invaluable part of his plans, so I would expect it to be a working visit and not just a thank you."

Tim wondered what was going to happen next. Was it time to take out Jepsom once and for all or was there more to do before Paul wanted to make his move? Taking out the cardinal wouldn't be easy. The man had his own guards, and after seeing Fredrick summon lightning to his fingertips, there was no way to fathom what kind of hidden abilities Jepsom might have.

Tim stood from the chair. "I should let you get back to your guests."

Lady Briarthorn rose and gave him a perfunctory smile. "The trials of the highborn are never-ending." She motioned toward the door. "I trust that you can find your own way out?"

"I can, and thank you for not making me stay." It was a party in his honor, after all. When Reginald had originally told him, the thought of having to make a speech had entered his mind and almost sent him running back out the front door.

"Please, the other nobles are just here for the free food and drink." She leaned over her desk and whispered in a conspiratorial fashion, "And the gossip. Most of them don't care who you are or what you've accomplished."

She led him out of the office. "But I care." She started to walk back toward the crowd but stopped for a moment. "I'll have Reginald box up some food for you to take back."

"That isn't necessary." Tim noticed that their conversation was drawing attention to him.

"Of course, it is. A good host never sends their guests home hungry." She snapped her fingers, and one of the servers appeared before her. She whispered to the man before looking at Tim. "Reginald will meet you by the door."

Tim moved through the rooms, trying his best not to meet

anyone's eye. The last thing he wanted to do was to get embroiled in a conversation he couldn't extract himself from. He made it to the front door and stepped outside to enjoy the fresh air. That was one thing he didn't miss about parties. When you had thirty or forty people in a house, it got hot and stuffy quick.

The night air was crisp and refreshing.

Tim jumped when the door opened and Reginald popped out with two giant bags full of food. "Oh good, I thought you had left." He handed the bags to Tim. "The lady hopes you enjoy the spread."

"I'm sure it's better than anything I've eaten since coming to Promethia." He smiled at the man. "Try not to have too much fun."

"This is the easy part. Trying to wrangle a hundred drunk nobles into their carriages when the party is over is the real job." Reginald grimaced, thinking about what the night had in store for him. "Would you like me to call a driver for you?"

Tim thought about it for a second and tossed the idea aside. Once Reginald was back inside, he'd just put the food in his inventory and enjoy the walk back to the inn. Sure, it was kind of far, but he had a lot to think about before he got back. If Ernie had been successful with his poison gas, he wanted to get an early start.

Not wanting to waste time on the way back to the inn, Tim pulled up a translucent version of his user interface so he could look at his notifications while he walked.

Skill received: Dodge

Rank: Novice Level One

You might not have known you were doing it, but you managed to not get stabbed in the face more than once. Keep avoiding attacks to increase this skill.

You are now 1% more likely to successfully dodge an attack.

Skill Received: Infiltrator

Rank: Novice Level Three

You've used subtlety and wit to sneak into places you shouldn't. Never mind that you left Antonio tied to that post for

hours. Continue talking your way into places you shouldn't go and wearing disguises to increase this skill.

When trying to infiltrate, you receive a 5% bonus to conversation modifiers and your disguises are 5% more likely to be overlooked if they have flaws.

Skill Increase: Sneak

Rank: Apprentice Level Two

Your ability to hide in the shadows has increased to 11%. Try not to move too much, or you might get shot full of arrows.

Skill Increase: Healing Orb

Rank: Apprentice Level Seven

Your healing orb is now 14% more effective and applies 17% of the original spell's healing as a heal over time bonus. The HOT is now applied over six seconds.

Skill Increase: Small Blades

Rank: Apprentice Level Three

You might have learned at the hands of a master, but you still have a long way to go before you'll be considered skilled. Attacks with blades under eighteen inches long do 7% more damage. Your dexterity requirement for small blades has been reduced by three.

CHAPTER FIFTY

"And *kaboom!*" Ernie shouted as he threw a small vial across the room.

The jar sailed across the wide dining hall and slammed into the back wall. An unimpressive cloud of green vapor wafted up from where the glass shattered. Ernie watched the results of his throw with a wide grin. The gas lingered in the air for about ten seconds before dissipating.

"Doesn't last as long as I'd like, but it should be damned effective if you throw it into a crowd." Ernie looked at the expectant faces.

"That's it?" Cassie sounded worried.

"How effective?" ShadowLily questioned as she gave Ernie a skeptical look.

Stepping forward, Tim put a comforting hand on Ernie's shoulder. "If our poison master says it will kill the kobolds, then it will."

Sure, the gas didn't look like much, and Tim had no idea how effective it would be, but he knew Ernie wouldn't send them to their possible deaths with an ineffective bomb. Ernie needed this to work as bad as the rest of them. At least, he did if he wanted his old life back.

"The only problem I see…" Tim glanced at the woefully small supply of vials, "is that we don't have many chances to make this work. Every throw needs to count."

"Then you better let us handle it." Gaston pointed to himself and ShadowLily. "Each of us can take a tower."

It was a good plan, and exactly what Tim was going to ask them to do. He looked at the six vials and thought about what would happen once they took out the archers. The rest of the kobolds would swarm Cassie. She was good—better than good with her new armor—but she wouldn't stand a chance against twenty of those little fuckers.

But what if they could thin the herd with a few well-placed bombs? Tim looked at the vials and frowned. He bit his lip as he worked out what to do. Scenarios for what would happen if their initial attack failed ran through his mind. They were running out of time before Malvonis would return to claim his prize.

"Uh-oh. I know that face." ShadowLily smirked. "He's got a plan."

"Not another one." Cassie shook her head and smiled at Tim's bewildered look. "What? I hear things."

"Don't worry, you're going to like this one." Tim smiled at Cassie. "It's just going to take a little extra finesse."

Tim turned his gaze on Ernie. "Do you have any more of these vials?"

The man shrugged. "I've got a whole storage room full of empty ones."

"Good, because we're going to need to practice. When it's time for the real thing, every throw has to count." Tim turned slowly and met everyone's eyes. "This is what we are going to do." He laid out his plan for the team.

"It could work." ShadowLily beamed at the group.

"Sure has a lot of moving parts," Cassie said, looking grim. "I don't want to end up as a kobold throw-pillow."

"No one does." Gaston peered around the circle of faces, chuckling. "But isn't this why you became adventurers? Death breathing down your neck, new and scary enemies, and a chance for epic loot?"

Tim gazed at Gaston, wondering if the assassin might have a screw or two loose. Dying wasn't high on his list of things to do, at least not until he officially declared himself an adventurer and could come back without losing all his stuff.

"Let's see if we can avoid death's cold embrace until we're done with the dungeon." He smiled at his team. "Then you have my permission to die as you see fit."

"Inspirational as always," ShadowLily snarked.

"A good leader knows how to motivate the troops." Gaston nudged Tim.

Cassie looked at all of them like they were nuts. "When we all die, the first thing I'm going to do when I come back is give you all a hearty 'I told you so.'"

Tim was grinning like a fool now. "As long as we understand each other." He nudged Cassie with his shoulder. "Now let's get to fucking work."

Did your chest always feel this tight?

It felt to Tim like the cavern was smaller than before. Every advantage lay with the defenders. The kobolds had towers and archers. The space shrank even further the closer you got to the door, so if attackers came with numbers, they wouldn't mean much.

Not that they had numbers on *their* side.

It was the four of them against a horde of the tittering little bastards. Their plan was to take out the archers and live through the assault that followed. The group would be able to handle it as long as they had a little luck on their side.

Tim wasn't a fan of trusting anything to luck. Having a plan and working hard always produced better results. They had a plan, but it hinged on perfect execution by every single team member. It reminded him of an older MMO called *Wildstar*. It was the only raiding MMO he'd played where healers didn't have a resurrection spell. One mistake, and you were done for the entire fight. The stakes were high.

These stakes were higher.

One problem this morning and they were dead. Do not pass go. Do not collect two hundred dollars. There wasn't a jail in *The Etheric Coast*, at least not one he knew about. The only thing that would happen to them was true death. Re-rolling a new character now would put them so far behind that it might be impossible to catch up.

How would he send money home if he couldn't make it past level ten?

Not to mention that Gaston wouldn't be coming back. Tim would never forgive himself if he led the burly assassin to his untimely death. He looked at the cavern and the two towers with archers, and for the first time in a long while, he said a prayer. Only this time, instead of talking to God like he normally would, he spoke directly to the goddess.

"I've never tried this before, but if you are listening, if you do care, please see that we make it through this." He felt kind of silly, but the words and the emotions behind them were real.

Moving back to the entrance of the tunnel, Tim looked at his team. "Time to get into position."

ShadowLily and Gaston gave him grim nods before dropping into stealth. Cassie was watching him, her eyes slightly frantic. Tim placed a comforting hand on her shoulder.

"When you first showed up and said you were a tank, I almost laughed." She frowned at him, but Tim smiled. "This last week, you've not only proven that you're up to the task, but I'd like to think I've gained a new friend."

"Yeah, but us being friends doesn't mean I'm not about to get pumped full of arrows like an old lady's pincushion," Cassie retorted.

Tim couldn't help but laugh. There was a certain sense of gallows humor required to do what they were about to do. "True, but if you do turn into a pincushion, know that I'll feel bad about it."

Cassie grinned. "Asshole."

Tim gazed at her for a moment, not envying what she was about to do. "Are you ready?"

"If we wait any longer, my panties won't be white anymore." She grinned at the grossed-out look on his face. "Cause I'd shit myself, not because of the other thing. God, you men. A lady talks about her vagina, and all you think about is five days of the month. Get over yourselves."

"Just let me know if Gaston needs to check you for skid marks," Tim said, recovering quickly but not with his finest work.

Cassie glared at him with the hatred of a thousand burning suns. "Fuck off." She stalked around the gentle bend of the tunnel.

"That's the positive attitude that makes you such a great team player," Tim shouted after her.

The tank held up her hand and extended her middle finger, still walking.

This was it. There was no turning back now. Cassie would start the fight, and they would either win or die. Tim smiled nervously as he dropped into stealth. His ass cheeks were clenched too tight for any accidents. Maybe that was the key to not pissing or shitting yourself in fear during battle. All you had to do was clench so tight nothing could come out even if it wanted to.

He started to follow his tank, and with each step, he mumbled, "Goddess protect her."

As for Cassie, she had bigger balls than he did. She walked into the center of the cavern as if she didn't have a care in the world. One of the kobolds blew a horn, and the rest of them jumped into action. Archers manned the towers; it looked like there might have been more of them than there were on their last trip.

Tim's eyes darted around wildly as he tried to count them. Maybe they needed to abort until they found a fifth party member, someone with some ranged expertise, preferably of the magical variety. They had sharp and pointy pretty well covered at this point.

He shook his head and gritted his teeth. Stopping now wasn't an option, not unless he wanted to be ripped in half by Malvonis.

There were ten archers in each tower now, and what appeared to be twenty more lined up on the steps leading to the dungeon's entrance. Forty kobolds all told. It was an army against the four of them, but they had a few tricks of their own up their sleeves.

Cassie moved into range of their bows, strutting as confidently as if she were walking up to the bar to order a pint. She planted her feet, pulled the staff from behind her back, and roared, "Come on, you fuckers. I don't have all day."

Bold, yes. Suicidal, maybe, but on a badass scale of one to ten, it was a fucking eleven.

The kobolds started to titter amongst themselves just before they launched the first volley of arrows. Cassie handled it better than Tim would have. She stood there for a moment as the arrows shot high into the air, then started running. The space she'd just vacated looked like it had run into a jumping cactus with a serious axe to grind.

"Is that all you've got!" she screamed at them.

This time, the tower on the left shot first, and the tower on the right waited for Cassie to start moving to loose their own volley. She managed to roll away from the arrows, but even as she climbed back to her feet, the next batch of arrows was falling.

"Any time now," she shouted, an edge of panic in her voice.

The armed kobolds in front of the giant door let out a war cry and started to charge. That was the cue Gaston, and ShadowLily were waiting for. They had to make sure all of the fighters were committed before they sprang their trap. If this wasn't all of them, their careful planning wouldn't mean shit.

Tim watched as his teammates appeared and lobbed their first vials at the towers. Green mist billowed up where the vials shattered. Their next vials flew in right behind the first, catching the kobolds standing further back.

With their poison bombs away, the two dropped back into stealth and ran toward Cassie. The warrior kobolds hadn't even noticed their protection from the towers had been eliminated as they ran blindly forward with their eyes locked on Cassie.

"Fucking balls of steel," Tim muttered as he dropped from stealth. There was no way he would be able to stay as calm as she was with certain death charging at him.

Tim threw the first of his vials, and it landed just in front of the charging horde. The stupid little fuckers ran through the green mist undeterred. His next vial landed in the middle of the pack. A few of the kobolds fell to the ground as the double helping of poison hit them.

Cassie spun her staff like she was in Bruce Lee movie and screamed at the remaining kobolds bearing down on her.

Only five of the creatures made it through the mist. Two of them died as Gaston and ShadowLily appeared behind them, and the remaining three crashed into Cassie as she did her best to turn their savage sword strikes away from her body. Their tank moved the annoyances around until two more fell to ShadowLily and Gaston from behind.

Cassie's staff cracked into the last kobolds' skull, sending it to the ground with a thump. Gaston planted a foot on its back before it could wriggle away and pierced its heart with his dagger.

The burly assassin eyed his companions. "Well, that couldn't have gone much better."

"Watch out!" ShadowLily slammed into Gaston, sending them

both to the ground as a bolt of magical energy flew over their heads.

Tim looked up to see a kobold with a staff and shiny baubles hanging from its neck step down the stairs. Perched on the creature's head was the skull of a larger animal. There was no way to tell for certain, but Tim suspected the creature was some kind of shaman.

Blue light started to pool at the top of the shaman's staff. With a growl, it pointed the staff at Tim and a bolt of magical energy shot out. Cassie jumped in front of the bolt, catching most of it on her staff. The tank flew backward as if she had been hit by a truck, and her body rolled limply across the ground until it came to a rest.

Cassie wasn't moving, and the shaman was pointing his staff toward Tim again. He jumped out of the way as the energy sailed past. The magical attack hit the ground, ripping chunks of stone out of the rough surface. He looked back to make sure he wasn't about to be vaporized before running toward Cassie.

Tim kind of felt like a medic in a World War Two or Vietnam movie. Fuck the danger, his only job was to save her. He knelt over Cassie and summoned healing orb as the battle raged behind him. At this point he didn't care if he died, as long as he saved her.

He hit her with the healing orbs again and again. When she didn't move, he put his hand above her heart and pushed the spell directly into her.

A minute later, he crumpled against her in exhaustion. Tim's mana pool couldn't keep up with the demands he was placing on it. Tears of frustration streamed down his cheeks. How could this have happened? He was right here, healing her almost the instant she went down. There was no way she could be dead.

Fuck, had Cassie really just died to save him?

"Why would you do that?" Tim cried, covering her body from the battle still raging behind him. Leaning forward, he placed his head against her chest, hoping to hear something. Anything. Right now, he would settle for one ragged, whispery breath.

"Goddess, I know I am new to this world, and that I don't have the right to ask you for anything, but please don't let her die."

A hand tapped him on the back and he turned, his eyes swimming with tears. ShadowLily gazed into them as tears of her own started to fall. "She's gone."

"No!" Tim screamed as the realization hit him. He'd let her down, but not only that, he'd let all of them down. The group didn't have a chance of making progress in the dungeon without a tank.

He called on his magic, funneling every last bit into the spell. The orb in his hands grew until he needed both hands to hold the spell together. When his mana ran out, he dropped the orb onto Cassie's lifeless body.

He stared at her, expecting a miracle, but nothing happened. "It can't end like this. It can't." Tim rested his head against her chest again and wondered how he could have failed so badly. His only job in the group was to keep them alive, and he'd totally FUBAR'd it. Tears streamed down his face and sobs shook his body. He'd never felt like such a failure in all of his life.

He looked up from Cassie's body as white light filled his vision.

Before him stood an ethereal figure. Her blue robe moved around her as if she were underwater, but her clothes were dry. She lifted one arm, and white light shot from her fingertips into Cassie's body. Their tank's chest spasmed, and her entire body shook as if Cassie was having a seizure.

Tim kept his eyes fixed on Cassie as her chest started to rise and fall again. This time, the tears trickling down his face were from joy. It seemed that in *The Etheric Coast*, miracles still happened.

The Goddess Eternia, more beautiful than words could describe, stared at him. "You have called me, and I have answered. There may come a day when I ask for a favor in return."

"You have but to name it," Tim mumbled as he cradled Cassie in his arms.

"Remember this moment and what will be taken from you should you refuse." The white light grew until he couldn't see six inches in front of him and the goddess was gone.

"Tim, she's gone. We have to go back to the inn and figure out what to do." ShadowLily's hand was on his shoulder.

"I'll help you carry the body." Gaston sounded shaky as he stepped forward.

Cassie's eyes flickered open, confirming what Tim already knew. "It seems the rumors of my demise were greatly exaggerated."

"What in the actual fuck?" ShadowLily dove at her friend and engulfed her in a bear hug.

"Ugh! I might actually die if you don't let me breathe." Cassie tried to peel ShadowLily's vice-like grip off her.

"Just shut up and take it." The half-elf pulled back, grinning from ear to ear. "We all thought you were dead."

"She was," Gaston said, voice shaky. "I've never seen anything like it."

Cassie looked at Tim. "Would have been nice to know you had a resurrection spell in your bag of tricks."

Tim looked at her hands extended in front of him palms toward Cassie, in a "pump your brakes" gesture. "I don't have a resurrection spell. The Goddess Eternia saved you."

Their little tank stood up, patting her arms and legs. "Everything feels ok, but why would the goddess help me? I've never even set foot inside the temple."

He didn't know how much he should share with the group. Owing a favor to the goddess seemed like a private thing. "I asked for her help, and she came." His voice was filled with awe. He'd asked for help, and the goddess had delivered. It really was a miracle.

Cassie looked at the shocked faces around her. "Well, what are we waiting for? Let's see if this was all worth it."

"Damn well better be," Gaston rumbled.

"I second that." ShadowLily looked around the cavern at the forty-one kobold corpses littering the floor and the towers. "On the plus side, at least we don't have to clean this up."

"Nope. Just loot and scoot." Tim said, bending over the shaman's corpse.

"Loot and *what?*" ShadowLily laughed.

"And scoot." Tim looked at her confused face. "You know, grab the loot and get the hell out of here."

"Nobody says that." Cassie intoned. "There is 'tank and spank,' but not 'loot and scoot.'"

"I don't see that particular terminology catching on anytime soon," ShadowLily said with a grin.

"Don't be a hater," Tim snapped as he picked over the shaman's corpse.

Gaston pointed toward the stairs, and as they turned to look, the giant doors slid open, revealing a dark swirling vortex. The way into the dungeon was open. All they had to do now was be brave enough to find out what was inside.

CHAPTER FIFTY-ONE

"Are you sure you're ready for this?" Tim watched Cassie for any signs of fatigue.

"Death is just a frame of mind," Cassie said as she adjusted her armor. "At least with you around."

"Well, try not to do it again. I'm pretty sure your resurrection was a one-time deal." Tim frowned at the others. "No more dying."

"Hey! Gaston and I didn't die. That seems to be a tank and a healer problem." ShadowLily grinned at the two of them.

"Just wait until you see who has agro if it happens again," Tim said with a laugh.

They were all feeling a little twitchy after their battle with the shaman. Tim also felt lucky. If the goddess hadn't intervened, there wouldn't be any way for them to beat the dungeon. At least not before Malvonis showed up and ripped out their spleens. As it was, the entire group was whole and healthy.

The same couldn't be said for the kobolds.

"I think we stick with the same plan as when we scouted the cavern. Gaston, that means you are on point. Watch out for any traps, and if you see potential enemies, come back for the group. Don't try to engage them alone."

The assassin gave him a saucy salute and disappeared into the shadows.

Tim reviewed the rest of his team and sighed. "We made it."

"Did you doubt we would?" Cassie asked.

"Only for a moment." Tim looked at his boots. "I guess I won't truly be relieved until we are out of here."

"With the loot." ShadowLily smiled at them. "A good thief never leaves without the loot."

"Plus, I need some upgrades. Anything with defense against magical attacks would be a great start."

"No shit." Tim grinned. "We can't have you dying every time you take a hit."

"That only happened once." Cassie smirked at him. "And everything worked out fine in the end."

All three of them froze when they heard a noise. Tim was holding his breath, ready to heal Cassie for all he was worth. ShadowLily gripped her daggers tighter, and Cassie dropped into a defensive stance.

Gaston appeared a moment later. "It's all clear up to another door."

"That's odd," Tim mused out loud. "Normally dungeons have a few trash mobs."

"Maybe that was why the caverns outside were full," Shadow-Lily replied, sounding hopeful.

"Doubt it," Cassie said.

"To be fair, there were quite a few traps between here and there, but I'm pretty sure I disarmed them all." Gaston shrugged. "There is no way to be sure, though.

"Pretty sure?" Tim raised one eyebrow as he looked at Gaston.

"Traps were never really my thing. I've always been more of a stab-and-run kind of guy." The assassin pretended to brush a bit of dust off his shoulder. "But I'm pretty confident I got them all."

"Time to move out, then." Cassie moved to the front of their column as they walked further into the dungeon. "Just keep your eyes open for anything Gaston might have missed."

The group continued down the stone hallway, and Tim couldn't help but think of *Raiders of the Lost Ark*. With every step, he was waiting for a giant ball of stone to roll from out of nowhere and crush them. He kept his eyes moving over the floor, the walls, the ceiling. If something was off, he was determined to find it before it killed them.

They rounded one corner and then another. The first trickle of relief was just starting to creep down his spine when he noticed a faint blue outline around a stone in the middle of the path where Cassie was walking. Her next few steps would put her on top of it.

"Stop!" Tim shouted.

Cassie took another two steps forward before turning around. "What?"

Tim watched with growing horror as their tank's heel brushed the highlighted tile. There was a small clink like a chain being cut in half, and Tim ran forward. Cassie must have heard the same noise because she sprang back toward the group. The two of them collided and crashed to the ground in a heap.

Tim looked up in time to see a giant pendulum swing out of the wall. If it had just been a rod of metal, it would have crushed a person, but this particular pendulum was sharpened like something straight out of a horror movie. It swung back and forth at regular intervals, but that wasn't the biggest problem they had.

The biggest problem was the ten more that had dropped down the entire length of the hallway. Each looked to be swinging on its own clock. There appeared to be enough room between the blades that you could pause, but one step either way, and you were going to end up in two pieces.

Like those weirdos who cut eggrolls in half.

He snickered. You knew you were really missing food when you compared your friends getting cut in half to the monsters who did it to egg rolls. *I mean, come on. We all know when we see four halves that we only received two eggrolls, you cheap bastards.*

Gaston smiled at the rest of the group. "Guess I missed one."

"Guess you get to go first," Cassie said with a grin of her own as she stood up.

"As the lady commands." Gaston set off at a run.

Tim held his breath as the assassin rushed toward the first pendulum. The blade moved away just as he reached it. He paused and stepped forward. Each move had to be perfect, and it was rinse and repeat until he was standing at the end of the hall.

"So easy, even *you* might be able to do it," Gaston shouted back to the party.

"So easy, I'm about to put my boot up your ass," Cassie mumbled as she stepped to the front of the line.

It took Cassie three times as long to reach the other end, but she did it. ShadowLily stepped up next and made it across nearly as fast as Gaston. That left Tim standing there alone watching the blades as they swooshed across the hall, ready to bisect him.

"I swear, if I get out of this, I'll never cut anything in half again," Tim mumbled as he walked toward the first blade.

The air movement created by the pendulum as it passed him was enough to make his clothing ripple like he was standing in a stiff breeze. There was no doubt in his mind that a single hit would be enough to send him right back to his caseworker.

Tim wasn't ready to see her again just yet.

He took a deep breath and stepped forward. "Fucking frogger and the pendulum."

Instead of cars and shit, he was dodging big ass blades of death. He moved, stopped, and moved again. Each time he stopped, he thought it might be his last. One step in any direction, and you might as well put sliced Tim on the kobold dinner menu.

The last blade caught the fabric of his robe, sending him flying toward the wall. Tim's shoulder crunched into the stone, and he started to fall right into the path of the returning blade. This was it

—killed twice before he reached level ten. He had to officially be the worst player in the game.

Cassie yanked him forward just before he got a new haircut. "Try to be more careful. It's not much of a group without our fearless leader."

"I thought I was the leader," Gaston rumbled.

Cassie patted him on the back. "Nope, you're just the eye candy."

The burly assassin looked at their tank with a lopsided smile. "'Eye candy.' I like the sound of that."

"It's a bit derogatory, don't you think?" ShadowLily asked. "Reducing a man to a shirtless hunk of beef."

"Only if he doesn't like it." Cassie eyed Gaston. "But you do like it, don't you?"

"In my experience, a lady with a discerning eye is never wrong." Gaston looked at Cassie again as if he might have missed something the first hundred times he'd done it.

Tim slapped a panel on the wall, and all of the pendulums stopped swinging and began to retreat into the walls. "Or maybe not so discerning after all."

"Don't get mad because we wanted to see you run the gauntlet," Cassie said with a laugh. "It all worked out."

Tim pushed past them to the front of the group. "Maybe I should go first for now."

No one tried to stop him, so he kept walking. His eyes roved all over the walls and floor, but he didn't see any other faint outlines. Eventually, the hallway ended at another set of giant doors. Written on them in giant letters were two words.

The Gatekeeper.

It looks as though they had made it to the first boss. There was no information on bosses in *The Etheric Coast*, unless you counted the video they had seen of the crew fighting the BrewMaster. That meant they had to wing it and they couldn't die.

Surely the development team would have taken their lower levels into consideration when designing the dungeon.

Based on the forty-plus kobolds out front and the shaman who had attacked them, Tim wasn't holding his breath for a fair fight. He looked at each member of the group and met all of their eyes in turn. They appeared to be ready to go. Stepping away from the group, Tim placed his hand on the door and shoved it open.

The room beyond the doors was massive, just the kind of thing you would expect for a boss fight. Tim looked around to see if there was anything they might use for cover or against the boss, but it was just a wide-open space with another set of doors at the back. The room was so empty he started to wonder if they were in the wrong place.

The rest of the party filed into the room behind Tim, and the doors slammed shut. He tried to force the door open, but there wasn't a door anymore. They were sealed in the room with no way out but forward.

"Well, that makes things simple." Cassie pulled her staff from her back and strode to the center of the room. "Get ready, bitches."

Gaston bumped his shoulder into Tim. "I like her."

"As if you have a chance," ShadowLily chided as she dropped into stealth.

"Never underestimate a determined assassin." Gaston grinned as he watched Cassie stride forward.

Tim started casting healing orb. He had a feeling the calm before the storm might be coming to a rapid close. As if on cue, stones began falling from the ceiling, and a low rumbling sound filled the room. Whatever was coming for them was coming fast and from above.

A giant dropped from the ceiling, landing in front of the doors they needed to get through. As he rose from a crouch, the Gatekeeper roared in challenge from both of his mouths. Tim stared in wonder at the giant's two heads.

It was bad enough the first boss they had to face was thirteen feet tall, but the fucker had two heads as well, not to mention two axes that were as tall as Tim. At least the developers had made the two heads easy to distinguish. One was bald with jewelry, and the other had long hair.

"Hungry," the bald head snarled.

"Snack," the other one growled and pointed at Cassie.

"Enough for two." The first head laughed.

"I'm going to use her leg as a toothpick." The two heads of the Gatekeeper laughed together.

Cassie stood still watching the two-headed giant with icy detachment. "If you want a piece of this, come and get it."

Tim smiled as he watched her interaction. It never stopped impressing him how well she handled the danger. Maybe certain people were just born to be tanks. Having people constantly trying to kill and maim him didn't sound like much fun to Tim. He just wanted to stand in the back and keep the others alive.

Right now, he was in an enviable position. The Gatekeeper was focused on Cassie, and the other two were in stealth mode. He had no idea how they were going to stop the bastard though. If Cassie took a direct hit from either axe, he wouldn't be able to save her.

Tim just hoped Cassie was as good at fighting the boss as she was brave.

The giant rushed forward, one axe sweeping low to cut her in half and the other coming from overhead. Cassie jumped over the first blade and rolled out of the next attack. The two heads roared in frustration as the tank ran between the Gatekeeper's legs and disappeared behind him.

Tim watched in horror as the Gatekeeper locked all four eyes on him. Apparently, Cassie was too much of a bother, so the giant decided to settle for a much easier target. Tim didn't have any defensive spells. Flameburst might singe the bastard's eyebrows, but it wasn't going to be enough to take him down.

Tim started to slowly back away, but stopped when he bumped

into the wall. The giant took a lumbering step forward, having forgotten about Cassie.

Not a good idea.

"Hope you weren't planning on having kids!" Cassie swung her staff up between the giant's legs with all the force she could muster.

Falling to his knees, the Gatekeeper cried out in pain, but Cassie wasn't done with him yet. Her staff cracked into the back of one of his heads. She reared back, ready to strike again, but the giant spun with one beefy fist up and backhanded her.

Cassie flew across the room and hit the ground in a heap. Tim released the spell he'd been holding in his hand, and the healing orb flew across the room. Sprinting after the spell, Tim started casting again.

This felt a little too much like when the shaman took her out for his comfort. As he ran, Tim kept repeating to himself, "Please don't be dead."

His first healing spell found Cassie as she pushed herself up on one elbow. The second spell hit her before she could stand back up. Tim took in her bloody lip and determined face. She was about to head right back into the fight. One more orb would bring her back to a hundred percent. His fingers started twitching through the motions as he watched her eyes get bigger.

"Oh, fuck." Tim knew he'd screwed up by turning his back to the boss.

A giant hand closed around him, and he was lifted into the air. The world spun, and Tim found he was being held above the two heads and looking into their open mouths. Being eaten alive wasn't something he wanted to experience, but his arms were crushed against his sides so there was nothing he could do.

"Squishy." The brown-haired head laughed.

"He's turning red. I like eating the red ones." The bald one cackled.

Tim looked at the two mouths full of razor-sharp teeth and

wondered if this is what a seal felt like right before a shark took a bite of him. He tried to squirm, but all it did was excite the giant.

"Motherfuck, grrhhh." *I'm not Stretch-fucking-Armstrong.*

He was only about a foot away from their mouths now. Out of the corner of his eye, he could see Cassie bashing her staff against the giant's legs, but the Gatekeeper wasn't going to be distracted from its freshly-caught snack.

He could smell their breath now, and it reminded him of the time the family dog had rolled in shit and he'd had to give her a bath. Why was it that dogs rolled in the stinkiest thing they could find? He'd never understand it. Then he started to wonder what the Gatekeeper had eaten to make his breath smell this bad.

Was his last thought really going to be about dog-shit breath?

With death staring him in the face, Tim kind of expected that ah-ha moment where the universe opened itself up to him and he'd learn all its secrets. Instead, all he could think about was how he let everyone down.

Inches from the Gatekeeper's teeth, Tim heard a scream. It took him a moment to realize it was his own.

The arm holding him up started to waver, and Tim looked down to see a ragged tear in the bald head's throat. His screams of terror turned into laughs of joy. He wasn't going to die, or at least not just yet. The fingers around him started to loosen. Then it dawned on him just how high above the ground he was.

"Oh, shit." The giant's grip loosened enough that he tumbled free.

He bounced once off the slack face below and tried to get his feet under himself as the ground rushed up. The hard-tiled floor didn't give an inch when he slammed into it. Tim groaned, but at least he was alive. A pair of hands slid under his shoulders as someone started to drag him away.

It was a funny thing now that he was out of the fight. He felt like he was watching a stream back in the real world. Cassie moved around the Gatekeeper, keeping his attention focused on her. It was easier to do with one of the heads out of commission. The remaining head seemed to have control of both legs, but the arm that had been holding Tim in the air hung limply at his side.

Cassie crouched and made her back as flat as possible. Gaston appeared a second later and ran straight for her. He planted a foot on her back before she lifted herself and he flung himself at the giant. Gaston flew toward it, daggers in hand like something out of a Greek legend.

The twin blades slammed right into the Gatekeeper's eyes. Gaston let go of the daggers, and, placing one foot on the giant's chest, he kicked himself into a flip before landing smoothly ten feet away. The Gatekeeper took two stumbling steps forward and crashed to the ground.

A face so beautiful it might have been an angel's appeared in Tim's vision. "Thought we lost you there for a second."

"I'm happy you didn't. Getting eaten alive is in my top three horrible ways to die." Tim cast healing orb on himself and instantly started feeling better.

"What are the other two?" ShadowLily asked as she helped him to his feet.

"Drowning and being burned alive." He smiled at her sheepishly. "Personally, I hope to die in my sleep as a contented old man."

"Ah, I always wanted to die during sex," Gaston said with a laugh as he joined them. "If you're going to punch your ticket, it might as well be doing something you love."

Cassie slapped him on the arm. "Gross."

Their group stood in a semi-circle over the Gatekeeper's corpse. They'd done it. The first boss of the dungeon was down, and they could keep moving forward. Once they completed the dungeon, he could give Malvonis the dungeon heart and reclaim the inn for Ernie.

Then the real work could start.

CHAPTER FIFTY-TWO

Cassie pouted. "Let's get to the loot already."

Tim smiled at his feisty little tank. "Don't let me stop you."

He hadn't even thought about what to do with the loot yet. Tim figured they'd just split the coins and dish out the rest on a need versus greed basis. Their party was small enough that there shouldn't be any real squabbles, and they definitely didn't need a loot council. That stuff was just for larger raid parties.

And only because people tended to bitch when they wanted something and didn't get it.

Tim had always been a firm believer in gearing up the tanks and healers first, then the best DPS. Having a tank that could soak up more damage before dying and a healer to keep the group alive tended to make things easier for everyone. No one liked to go into a raid or dungeon, slamming their heads against a boss for months.

Cassie knelt over the corpse of the Gatekeeper. A moment later, Tim received a notification that five gold, thirty-two silver, and fifty-five copper coins had been added to his inventory. Not a bad haul for one boss, but now he wanted to see what items the Gatekeeper left behind.

"Well, that was anticlimactic." Cassie stood up and tossed an old-looking key toward Tim. "This was all he had."

"Maybe we just get loot at the end of the dungeon?" Tim said as he inspected the rusted key.

There didn't seem to be a chest on the ground or anything, so the key must open the path to the next room. Tim didn't mind delayed gratification, but he could imagine that not getting loot from each kill might feel tedious after a few bosses.

"I guess we better keep moving, then." Tim frowned at the two-headed giant's corpse.

ShadowLily patted him on the back. "I hope it's worth it."

So far it didn't feel worth it, but it wasn't like he had a choice. His deal with Malvonis required that he go on, regardless of loot. He looked around the room one more time to make sure he hadn't missed a chest. Sometimes developers put them in weird places.

Why, he'd never understood.

After working hard as a team to bring down the boss, distributing the loot should be the fun part. Some of his best memories in games were boss kills. Everyone had to execute, and after you died a few times with the boss's health under ten percent, everyone gets a tiny bit antsy. Then, when you finally bring the fucker down, you cheer like you won the Super Bowl.

He was sure he'd feel that elation when they finally cleared the dungeon and saw the rewards. If nothing else, at least he wouldn't have to worry about Malvonis waiting in the dark to kill him. Sometimes being alive was its own reward.

The door at the far end of the room had a single keyhole, so it seemed pretty obvious what he needed to do. Tim walked to the door and slid in the key. There was no way to know what was waiting for them on the other side, but as long as he didn't immediately get his face ripped off, it couldn't be too bad.

He took a breath and turned the key. The door opened into a

small antechamber, and in the center of the room was a chest. A smile spread across his face as he was prompted by a system message.

You have successfully defeated the Gatekeeper. You have three days until your lockout expires. Next time you enter the dungeon, you will be automatically moved to this waypoint to continue your adventure.

This game was fucking awesome.

Not only could they take a break and not have to trek all the way back through the dungeon, but there was also a big chest full of loot. Or at least he hoped it was. Tim stepped out of the way so the others could see inside the room.

"Cassie, care to do the honors?"

"Hell, yeah." Cassie ran to the chest. As she placed her hand against it, she let out a little squeal of delight.

"Boots with decent stats." She touched the chest again. "They're bound to me, though." She looked at Tim with a bashful expression. "Maybe loot is individualized instead of one giant chest for everyone."

"Only one way to find out." ShadowLily marched forward and placed her hand against the chest. "Gloves, and not bad ones, either."

Tim glanced at Gaston. "It's only fair. You made sure I didn't turn into the Gatekeeper's lunch."

Gaston walked toward the chest and laid his hand on it. "Not too shabby." He held out a bandolier for his throwing knives. "I could put this to good use."

Now that it was his turn, Tim felt hope welling inside him. Wasn't it always that way when you had a random roll? Everyone hoped for the best item possible, but the odds were never in your favor. That was what *The Hunger Games* got wrong. Just like when you bought loot boxes, you normally just got shit on.

Tim placed his hands on the chest, and a smile cracked the corners of his mouth. "Boots for me as well." He quickly replaced his boots with the new ones from the chest. They were simple boots made of soft white leather. They didn't have any special abilities attached to them, but they provided Tim with an additional +2 to willpower.

Normally he wouldn't get overhyped about boots without a set bonus or some kind of special ability, but he remembered coming into the game without shoes. Just walking to the inn had hurt his feet, and it had taken him forever to get them clean again. Any upgrade, even a small one to his footwear, felt pretty damn good.

Not to mention the effect loot had on the group. Everyone was smiling and trying on their new gear. The chest was just the thing to give them the morale boost they needed to keep going. If they could get one more boss done, they could take a break and continue in the morning, still with a full two days to clear whatever was left.

He was happy with their progress so far and anxious to keep going. He looked around at all the grinning faces. "Ready to see what's next?"

Cassie moved to the doors on the other side of the antechamber. "Maybe this time you should let me go first."

Tim waved his hand at her. "By all means."

Cassie shoved the door open. The next part of their adventure was about to begin.

CHAPTER FIFTY-THREE

"What in the hell is that?" Tim asked as he peeked around the corner.

ShadowLily leaned around him. "Looks like a giant fucking wolf."

"Dingo ate my baby," Cassie chortled from behind.

"This dingo looks like it could eat all four of us," Tim replied as he moved away from the corner.

"It can't be that bad." Cassie moved forward in a crouch, taking Tim's vacated spot. She peeked around the corner. "Or maybe it can be."

Tim didn't envy Cassie. Going up against a wolf of normal size was intimidating, but this wolf's head had to be four feet off the ground. If it stood on its back legs, it would be taller than Gaston. It wasn't so much a wolf as a dire wolf.

Cassie backed away from the corner and looked at Tim. "So, what's the plan?"

"Give it nose-bops," Tim said mischievously.

"Aren't dogs supposed to love those?" ShadowLily replied with a laugh.

Tim shrugged. "Guess Cassie will let us know."

"Come on, guys. This is serious." The tank frowned.

"Same plan as usual then. Cassie, you're the bait. Gaston and ShadowLily, you do the killing, and I'll try to stay out of the way."

"Spoken like a leader of men," Cassie growled as she pulled her staff from behind her back. "Why is it that generals just stand in the back?"

"Too important to lose." Tim snickered. "Now go give our little buddy a nose-bop with your stick."

"I've got somewhere else I'd like to shove this stick," Cassie grumbled as she snuck around the corner.

ShadowLily and Gaston dropped into stealth, and Tim waited for a count of ten before he rounded the corner.

A snarl was the only sound he needed to hear to know the wolf had spotted Cassie. The giant wolf had its head lowered and its teeth bared in warning. There was a massive ridge of fur down the beast's spine as the snarl turned into a growl. Salvia dripped off its jaw as its back legs tensed to charge.

Cassie stood her ground, looking small compared to the beast. "Bring it on, Fido!"

With one last growl, the wolf jumped, clearing the twenty feet between them in a single leap. Cassie rolled to the side, lashing out with her staff as she climbed back to her feet. She caught the wolf in the side, but it didn't seem to notice.

Spinning with quickness and dexterity that can only be obtained by an animal with four feet, the wolf lunged at her. Tim cried out and tossed a healing orb in Cassie's direction, but he didn't have to worry because her staff came up in time. The wolf's jaws snapped closed on her staff instead of their tank's throat. The beast tried to rip the weapon out of her hands, but Cassie held on for dear life.

The last time Tim had seen an animal shake something so violently was when his dog got a new toy. She'd pounce on it and pick it up, shaking the toy from side to side as if she expected the guts to come pouring out.

Only this time, the toy was Cassie.

Gaston and ShadowLily appeared almost simultaneously as they each plunged their daggers into the wolf from opposite sides. The mighty beast yelped and released Cassie's staff as it turned to snap at the new attackers.

ShadowLily screamed as the wolf sank its jaws into her arm. The creature started to shake her as she stabbed it with her other blade. Gaston roared and jumped on the wolf's back before plunging his daggers in its hide. The wolf let out a howl of fear and rage, shook Gaston free, and slumped to its belly. A soft whimper escaped its throat, then it was still.

Rushing forward, Tim healed ShadowLily, then cast a couple of wayward heals at the rest of the group to take away any niggling injuries they might have. Satisfied that the group's health was in order, he turned his attention back to the giant wolf.

For some reason, Tim felt worse about killing the wolf than the people he'd assassinated. Maybe because the wolf wasn't really bad, unlike the people he killed. It could also be that it was like a giant dog, and he couldn't imagine someone stabbing a dog. He doubted he'd feel the same way if it was a bear.

Please don't let there be a bear.

Coins appeared in his inventory as Cassie looted the body. When she turned to face them, Tim gave her a halfhearted smile. "I told you a solid nose-bopping was the key."

"That fucker almost ate my whole face. He didn't deserve a nose-bopping." Cassie looked at the toothmarks on her staff. "Let's just hope there aren't more of them."

But of course, there were.

Three wolves and some kind of flying insect later, they finally reached the door leading to the next boss fight.

The Beastmaster was inscribed on the giant door.

"Explains the wolves," Cassie said as she read the inscription.

"That flying thing was intense." ShadowLily shuddered.

"Let's just hope the Beastmaster doesn't have another one." Cassie rubbed her shoulder. "Those pincers fucking hurt."

Tim lobbed a healing orb at her. Cassie glared at him as the water splashed her shoulder. "Hey, just making sure you're topped off."

"I'm not a drink." Cassie mocked as she placed her hands on the door. "Everyone ready?"

One by one, the group nodded. Satisfied with the results, Cassie pushed the door open. She looked back once to make sure the rest of the party was really ready before she strode boldly into the room. Tim trailed behind the group, taking in the lay of the land.

There was a rocky outcrop on one side of the room, and what appeared to be a small stream carved into the floor on the other. Tim didn't know what the two features meant yet, but he was sure they would be important during the fight.

"Mind the water and the rocks," Tim shouted to the group.

"I'll do my best," Cassie said, turning her head from side to side as she looked for the boss.

The doors at the end of the room opened, and another giant wolf ran into the room. Trailing behind it was an orc decked out in furs. He had a giant crossbow hanging from his back and two or three knives strapped around his waist. The Beastmaster looked at Cassie standing alone in the middle of the room and let out a rumbling laugh.

Big mistake, fucker.

If there was one thing that pissed off his fiery little sparkplug of a tank, it was people not taking her seriously. He got it. On the surface, she didn't look like much of a warrior, but underestimating her was a big mistake. Tim knew from experience that she was damn good at her job and fearless to boot.

The Beastmaster called to his wolf, and it returned to his side. He petted the beast affectionately as he watched Cassie. His eyes flickered in Tim's direction for a moment, but he didn't seem very impressed. Leaning down, he whispered something to the wolf and stood back up.

Reaching for the giant crossbow on his back, the Beastmaster growled. With his weapon in hand, he extended one finger in Cassie's direction and shouted, "*Attack!*"

The wolf bounded forward as soon as the Beastmaster's command was finished. The group had their hands full facing the wolves on the way to the boss. Now they had to fight a wolf and the Beastmaster at the same time.

It wasn't going to be easy.

Tim was watching Cassie with a healing spell ready to go when a crossbow bolt slammed into his leg. How the fuck had he forgotten about the boss? He splashed the spell he had ready for Cassie on the hole in his leg. The spell helped, but having a bolt tear through your leg still hurt like a motherfucker before the healing started.

Time slowed to a crawl as Tim watched the battle. Cassie was trying to maneuver the wolf so it was between Tim and the boss. He looked at his torn and shredded leg and focused on healing it. Another bolt flew past his head, breaking his concentration. It was time to move.

"Persistent little fucker," Tim growled as feeling started to return to his limb.

The Beastmaster moved around the room, trying to keep his line of sight to Tim clear. The orc had a smile on his face as he slipped another bolt into his crossbow.

Why *wouldn't* the fur-covered pale-green bastard be smiling? Everything was coming up Beastmaster.

Gaston flashed in from nowhere and cut the wolf's exposed

hamstring. The animal spun on three legs and sank its fangs into Gaston's arm. The assassin cried out in pain even as he plunged his other dagger into the wolf's eye, killing it instantly.

"No!" the Beastmaster shouted as he swiveled away from Tim and put Gaston in his crosshairs.

The crossbow fired just as ShadowLily pushed it up, and the bolt flew over Gaston's head into the rocky outcropping behind him. The orc backhanded ShadowLily and she fell to the ground, one of her daggers clattering to the stone floor. His knife moved down for a killing blow.

"Not today, fucker," Cassie snarled as she kept the strike from cutting ShadowLily in half. Sparks flew off her staff as the weapons ground against each other.

Tim climbed back to his feet, but his leg was still a little shaky. He could worry about himself later. Right now, he had to make sure Gaston could get back in the fight. Cassie and ShadowLily seemed to have things under control now that they only had to deal with one target.

But why the water and the rocks?

Tim got the feeling something was about to happen, and whatever it was wouldn't be good for them.

The Beastmaster let out a shrill whistle as he tried to fight off the two determined ladies. Cassie's staff bounced off one of his shoulders, but the orc hardly seemed to notice. He growled an obscenity and slashed in a wide arc with his dagger to create some space.

Tim continued to heal Gaston as the assassin moved to join the fight. *This was it, they had him now.*

As Gaston drew closer, the Beastmaster reached into his pouch and threw a handful of something in front of him. The team backed off, choking as green mist spread out in a circle. Their clothes seemed to be smoking.

What in the fuck?

Then it clicked. *"Get in the water!"* Tim screamed as he ran toward the stream carved into the floor.

He sure hoped he was right about the stream. Otherwise, he might have just killed his entire team. Tim sprinted for the water, firing healing spells as he went. This was the first time he really got to use cleanse in a battle. The spell felt clumsy to his fingers, but it was keeping his party alive.

With one last look to make sure everyone was going to make it, he threw himself into the stream.

The water was cold, and he came sputtering back up to the surface. The Beastmaster was picking up his crossbow. He'd have a couple free shots at them as they climbed out of the stream. With his aim, that meant at least one of the party would probably die unless Tim could do something. Tim only had the one offensive spell, and he called on it now.

Flames roared from his fingertips.

It looked much more impressive than it was, but his flameburst spell was enough to make the Beastmaster fumble the crossbow. Tim was just starting to congratulate himself when he heard a shriek from above.

He looked up in time to get his hands in front of his face as a giant falcon slammed into him. The talons shredded his arms and the beak took a chunk out of his cheek before the bird flew off in search of another target.

He'd never considered himself the prettiest guy on the planet, but he was sure the hole in his cheek had knocked him down a peg or two. There was a reason Two-Face didn't make the cover of a lot of magazines. Tim began healing himself and turned to find out if his companions were faring any better.

Cassie was going toe to toe with the Beastmaster as Shadow-Lily ducked in behind her, slashing at anything the boss left exposed. Gaston had a throwing knife out as he tracked the circling falcon.

Gaston's arm reared back, and the blade flew.

A single feather fell from the heavens. The Beastmaster roared so loudly the room seemed to shake.

Gaston turned away from his kill and rushed back to the boss. The Beastmaster slowly backed toward the rocky outcropping. Tim didn't like it one bit. If he had designed the game, there would be one more monster in there. A ton of big and scary things lived in caves.

The Beastmaster's back was nearing the opening when he growled again, but this time the tone was different. Tim started to yell a warning, but there wasn't enough time. A huge grizzly bear emerged from the cave. Standing on its back legs, it bellowed a challenge at the group. The bear landed back on all fours and the Beastmaster climbed on top, pulling a spear from somewhere.

The motherfucker was riding the bear like a horse.

"Kill the boss first!" Tim screamed at the group as the grizzly charged forward.

Tim knew what this was, or at least he thought he did. What was happening now felt just like a classic enrage scenario. It was a race against time to see who died first, the four of them or the Beastmaster.

Cassie deflected the spear but took a claw in the shoulder. Her bo staff clattered away, and the bear reared up to crush her. As the bear's giant front paws came down, ShadowLily pulled Cassie to the side but ended up with a spear in her arm for her trouble. The grizzly shoved ShadowLily to the ground and chased the fleeing tank.

Gaston. Where in the fuck is Gaston?

Tim rushed forward to heal his favorite girl. He knelt by her side and focused on closing the wound from the bear's paws first. Who would have thought *The Revenant* would provide training for healing bear attacks? He kept the healing flowing as he turned to follow the battle.

Cassie reclaimed her staff, but the bear tore it away in a single strike. The Beastmaster had risen, ready to spear her through the heart, when Gaston finally appeared.

Rushing forward, the assassin ran up the back of the bear and stabbed the Beastmaster in the back. The orc fell from his perch and Gaston followed him to the ground, landing heavily on his body. Tim watched as the burly assassin's arm rose and fell as he stabbed the Beastmaster like some kind of psychotic sewing machine. There was no way the orc could live through that.

The bear let out a cry of sadness and ran back to the cave without doing any more damage to the group.

The party was torn and bloody, but they'd beat the second boss. Now it was time to collect their loot and take a break. They'd come back tomorrow and finish off the dungeon or die trying.

Tim looked at his soaked and battered companions and smiled. He had the best team in the world, and they were making better progress than he'd expected. It wouldn't be long now before they could put this dungeon and Malvonis out of their thoughts completely.

"Who would like to do the honors?" Tim asked as he looted the Beastmaster for the key. He barely even registered the gold as it came into his inventory, but he thought it looked about the same as last time.

"You do it." ShadowLily winked at him. "It was your idea to jump into the water. It saved all our asses."

"About that." Cassie frowned at Tim. "How did you know it would work?"

Tim thought about coming up with some bullshit explanation about how he'd played a lot of games where the environment around you during a boss fight gave you clues, but instead, he told them the truth. "I didn't. Frankly, when I jumped in, it was a coin toss."

"You risked our lives on a guess?" Gaston growled.

"An educated guess," Tim squeaked. "There was no way I could heal you of that acid damage. I knew there had to be a way to neutralize it."

Gaston clapped him on the back. "Death by the unknown is better than melting, I guess."

Tim felt a little shudder run through him as he thought about the scene from *Who Framed Roger Rabbit*. Melting by acid didn't look like a pleasant way to go.

Tim took the key from his inventory, walked to the door of the antechamber, and slid it into the hole. The double doors opened, revealing another chest in the center of the room. He reached the chest and bent slightly to place his hand on the lid.

Belt of Wisdom +2

Another generic item, but better than anything you could buy from a shop at this level. Tim thought about it for a moment and realized maybe he'd been expecting too much from the dungeon's loot.

At lower levels in any game, the loot was pretty standard. You didn't normally get big set bonuses and cool effects until higher levels. The last thing developers wanted to do was waste time creating cool items you'd throw away after a few levels.

Tim added the belt to his inventory, then equipped it. Looking down, he noticed it was cord like friars used to wear, rather than an actual belt. It was pretty cool-looking, and he'd never turn down extra wisdom as long as he was healing.

"Nice belt," ShadowLily said as she shouldered past him to put her hand on the chest. She grinned as she stood up. "Nice, I scored a hood. Now I'll look like a proper rogue."

Cassie came forward next. "Not too shabby." She pulled out a new bo staff and twirled it. "It's a little bit lighter than my last one, but it feels solid."

Gaston sauntered up to the chest last. "Another bandolier." He shrugged. "I guess the luck of the goddess isn't with me today."

"If you end up with a third one, I promise to buy you something nice." Tim grinned at the man, thinking about how they couldn't have done this without him. Tim always hated it when he walked away with a bunch of vendor trash. You could only equip the one item, and if the item was bound to you, it couldn't even be given to another player.

"I think freedom from Malvonis will suffice as a reward." Gaston winked at him. "But if a nice bottle of whiskey happened to find its way to me, I wouldn't complain."

"Whiskey, it is." Tim wrapped an arm around the big man and turned him back the way they'd come. "Now let's get out of here."

The black swirling vortex that greeted them at the dungeon's entrance was now right outside the antechamber door. Tim looked at the others and stepped in. A moment later, he reappeared in the cavern outside the dungeon. They were almost done; he could feel it, but pushing on now would be a mistake.

All of them needed a break and a chance to go over their spells and upgrades, but tomorrow they would end this.

Thank the goddess.

CHAPTER FIFTY-FOUR

"Damn, that feels good," Tim said with a sigh as he slipped into the hot water.

As much as he loved showers, he was starting to get used to this bath thing. Maybe it was because even though he was fully healed, his muscles were still stiff from the battles. And maybe when he saw The High Priest, he could ask if he had a spell to help with that. Or maybe he just needed to find out what CBD was called here.

The hot water soaked into his sore muscles as he pulled up his stats. Things looked a little different after he acquired his new loot, took down two bosses, and turned in his quests to lady Briarthorn and Ernie.

Tim had almost forgotten about his quest to kill Juan Pablo, but the innkeeper hadn't forgotten. As soon as they returned from the dungeon, he handed Tim his reward. The reward had consisted of an increased reputation with Ernie and Gaston. He felt like he was doing a pretty good job of boosting that already, but a bonus never hurt.

He wondered if he could see his reputation with certain individuals anywhere. He fiddled with his user interface for a bit but didn't see anything right away. Shoving the unhelpful screens to the side, Tim focused on what he really wanted to see.

Tim had gained a level and had plenty of notifications to go over.

His stats had taken a pretty good bump from all his new gear. When he was fully decked out in his healing outfit, his stats had really gone up. Apparently almost getting killed a lot had done wonders for his luck. It reminded him of the beginning of *Gladiator* when Russel Crowe looked at his second and said, "Still alive." He was still alive, mostly because of other people saving his ass.

As the healer, it probably should have been the other way around. He'd also increased in ranks in his spell usage, and received a new skill rating.

Skill received: Appeal to the goddess

Rank: Novice Rank One

You asked the goddess for help, and she granted it. Now you owe her a favor, but it can't be that bad, right?

You may use this skill once a month. The goddess may choose to ignore your pleas for help. She is quite busy, after all.

To increase this skill, continue to shine in the goddess light and act upon her will when she calls upon you.

That was a weird fucking skill.

Although the goddess had saved Cassie's life, so it could come in handy. Did shining in the goddess' light just mean to keep doing what he was doing? So far, he felt pretty good about his standing with the temple, but he'd have to remember to ask Paul about it when he had the chance.

All in all, their little dungeon run and his quests for Ernie and Lady Briarthorn had moved him along quite a bit. Not to mention the level he gained. Now he just had to get his last available skill point allocated so he could head upstairs and see if ShadowLily would put on her kinky club outfit for him again.

The gear he was getting made Tim's Wisdom stats soar, but

maybe he was focusing on one stat too much. If he was mostly going to be healing now, he might as well try to get his intelligence up to the first baseline at twenty. Then if he was still relying on his daggers to get him out of trouble, he'd work on his dexterity.

Tim put the point into intelligence and confirmed the change before dismissing the window. He felt better about his time in the game now that he was doing more healing and less stabbing. If things kept progressing like this, he was going to have a lot of fun. The only thing he had to worry about as far as the temple was concerned was the next mission from Paul.

He probably should have been more worried about the next boss in the dungeon, but the team had proven they could adapt and work well with each other. All Tim could do now was trust that they'd learned enough to win. Being killed by the boss or getting murdered for not defeating it ended up with the same result.

They'd all be dead.

Or at the very least, he'd be dead.

Tim dunked his head in the water and pushed his long hair back when he came up. Why was he thinking about dying when all they'd done was kick ass? Sure, the goddess had helped them over their first hurdle, but the team had done the rest on their own. If anything, he should feel excited about tomorrow.

Tomorrow was the day everything changed and their future began.

CHAPTER FIFTY-FIVE

"I'm never going to get used to that feeling." Cassie bent over, clutching her stomach.

"It's not that bad," Tim said, stepping out of the vortex.

"Kind of tickles," Gaston sniggered as he stepped into the antechamber.

"Whatever," Cassie growled. "Let's get moving."

Despite yesterday's close calls, Tim was feeling good about today. All of them had slightly better gear than the day before, and they were coming together as a team. It didn't matter if you had the best players in the world. If they couldn't work together, you were destined to fail.

Stepping forward, Tim placed the key in the lock and pushed open the doors to the next phase of the dungeon. He took one look inside of the next room and started to back away.

"Spiders. Why is it always fucking spiders?"

He'd played enough games as a kid to know that in every version of every fantasy game, there was always a level or a dungeon full of spiders. The last thing he wanted to see in *The Etheric Coast* was a huge, mutated spider. It was one thing to see the monstrosities on the screen, but quite another to face them in real life.

Shit, every time he watched *Arachnophobia*, it gave him chills, and ninety-nine percent of those were just little spiders. Even the biggest one he wouldn't be afraid of now, not with this team, but in games, the biggest ones might be four or five feet tall. More like *Eight-Legged Freaks* than anything resembling a real spider.

"Don't tell me our leader is afraid of a few webs." Cassie poked him with a finger.

Tim jumped. "It's not the webs that concern me. It's what put them there."

Peering into the chamber, Gaston frowned. "He's right. This is going to suck." He held up two fingers like they were fangs and made a plunging motion.

Gaston's imagery didn't help calm Tim down. He'd almost been eaten alive, but being paralyzed in a web until the spider's poison liquefied your insides so it could suck them out was quite another.

"Why are men such babies when it comes to spiders? They aren't that scary." ShadowLily looked into the room with a smile. "How bad can it be?"

Tim pointed toward the head of a dire wolf poking through some webbing. "You'll have to tell me when we run into the spider big enough to kill that thing."

"We don't know it was just one," Cassie chided.

"Is that supposed to make me feel better?" Tim whined as he looked into the room for any sign of one of the spiders.

"Time to grow a pair." Cassie grinned at him as she stepped into the hallway.

"Just try not to touch the webs, they act like sonar for these things." Tim kept his eyes on the ceiling as they moved further along. "And don't forget to look up."

Cassie froze in the middle of the wide hallway. She used her staff to point out the black body against the white webbing. The spider didn't look like much now, but its legs were curled in so you couldn't get a real feel for the size from this far away.

Tim looked at the bloated black body, and the first thought to run through his head was, *It's a fucking giant black widow.* Venomous, used webbing to trap prey, and scarily fast for a spider. He hated the fucking things. From where he was standing, Tim guessed the center of its body had to be at least two feet around. That meant with its legs extended, the thing was easily going to be bigger than a German Shepherd.

"Why couldn't it be fucking zombies," Tim muttered to himself. "Everyone loves killing zombies."

Cassie pulled the hook and chain from her belt, and Tim watched in horror as she sent it sailing toward the spider. The hook slammed into the back of the spider, and it screeched as it dropped to the ground. Cassie pulled the hook back and dropped into a fighter's crouch.

The spider moved from side to side, keeping what felt like a hundred eyes on them. Then it rushed straight at Cassie with its pincers flexing and poison dripping from its fangs. When it was ten feet away, it leapt onto the wall and kept running. From five feet away, it sprang toward her, legs extended far enough to the sides that there was no escape.

Tim held his breath as Cassie's staff came up. He hoped it would be enough. He wasn't sure how well his cleanse spell worked on spider venom, but he was sure he'd find out soon.

Cassie's staff slammed into the fat center of the spider, and it damn near burst as she flung it into the wall. Its eight legs thrashed as it tried to get back up, but a throwing knife slammed into the red mark on its belly, ending the spider's squeals of pain.

"See? They aren't so bad." Cassie looked back at Tim with a haughty "I told you so" expression.

Tim pointed into the corridor behind her and the four spiders that were eyeing them now. "You were saying?"

"Don't be such a drama llama." ShadowLily threw one of her daggers, taking out a spider.

A second later, one of Gaston's daggers downed another one.

Cassie charged forward to meet the remaining two, but one got around her. The spider leapt for the ceiling and scuttled toward Tim. Throwing knives sparked off the stone ceiling as the spider ran past ShadowLily and Gaston. Tim felt pressure in his chest as he started to panic. One of his nightmares had finally come true.

He cast flameburst as the spider jumped toward him and the blackened corpse slammed into his chest, sending him to the ground. He felt icy pain running up his left arm and looked down to find one of the spider's fangs buried in his forearm. He pulled the fang free and began casting cleanse.

"At least I get to test it on myself first," he mumbled as he cast the spell again. As he cast cleanse a third time, the spider venom was wearing off.

Tim stood back up and looked at the group. "Not quite as effective as I'd hoped."

"Effective enough to keep you alive." ShadowLily gave him a quick kiss. "Let's keep going."

Cassie took charge as they continued moving down the hallway. They faced two more groups of spiders before reaching the final door. Cassie stood at the door and scraped away the webbing so she could get a better looked at the name carved there. The webbing stuck to her hand, and she pulled it away in disgust.

Tim stepped forward. "Let me." His flameburst spell might not be the most effective thing in the world, but it would easily burn away the webbing. The webs caught fire and shriveled, leaving Tim staring at the name on the door. He stepped back so everyone could see who they would be facing.

The Cursed.

"Well, that's not ominous or anything." It also didn't give them a lot of information. The Cursed could literally be anything.

He frowned at the door, trying to guess at what might be

waiting for them inside. There was no way to know for sure, but it would have something to do with spiders. Maybe it would be a giant fucker like when Harry Potter followed the spiders. Tim took two things away from that scene: never trust Hagrid's sense when it comes to monsters, and never, ever fucking follow the spiders.

Only this time, they didn't have a choice.

He took one last look at his group and shoved the door open.

The room in front of them was a giant circular cavern. Spider webs clung to the ceiling, walls, and even the floor in spots. Besides the webbing, there was only a giant stone column that extended from the floor all the way to the ceiling. His first thought was it might be something to hide behind if spiders tried to slow them down with webbing. There wasn't any way for him to plan their attacks when they didn't even know what the boss looked like. Tim glanced at Cassie and nodded. "Lead the way."

Cassie tapped her bo staff on the ground and took her first step into the room. "Don't fail me now."

The thief and the assassin dropped into stealth. Tim proceeded slowly, making sure to give Cassie some space. The giant doors closed behind him, and a sense of dread at the incoming fight settled over him. He took a few deep breaths and reminded himself of how successful they'd been up to this point.

If anyone could pull this off, it would be them.

A few stray stones fell from the ceiling, and Tim looked up as the biggest spider he'd ever seen dropped to the floor. But it wasn't just a spider. Sure, the thing had spider legs and a spider body, but its top half was the torso of a woman. The damn thing was just like a centaur, but with a spider's body instead of a horse's.

"And I thought I had nightmares before," Tim whispered as he watched the Cursed move to the center of the room.

There was no way to deny that if the rest of her had been legs instead of a spider, the elf torso attached to the giant spider body would have been hot. She had long black hair, and her skin almost had a purple tone to it. The chainmail armor the Cursed had on told you she meant business, but so did the massive two-handed sword strapped to her back.

The Cursed looked at them with a cruel sneer on her face. "It's not often delicious morsels walk so willingly into my lair." She pulled the sword free, rearing up on her four back legs. "My spiderlings will be very happy when they feast upon your corpses."

Cassie laughed. "If they were back that way, they won't be eating again."

"Oh, there are more," the Cursed chided. "There are always more."

"Right now, I see only one ugly bitch, so I'm going to start there." Cassie ran forward, looking woefully small against the six-foot-tall spider legs of the Cursed.

Cassie's first attack bounced harmlessly off one of the black legs. Her second and third attempts were no more effective. The Cursed's giant two-handed sword missed her by a hair's breadth as she rolled away. Standing, Cassie turned just in time to be toppled by one of the other legs.

The Cursed cried out in delight as she rushed forward to stomp Cassie to death.

Tim cast healing orb in her direction, but no amount of healing would help if Cassie was split in two by that giant fucking sword. He watched nervously as Cassie rolled around, dodging three strikes at once. The fourth leg pierced her stomach, and the sword rose into the air as Tim bit his lip.

This was it. With Cassie down, they were totally fucked.

The sword started to descend and Gaston appeared, slashing at one of the Cursed's hind legs. The leg tumbled away, twitching as it hit the ground.

Moving so fast it was almost a blur, the Cursed pirouetted on its remaining legs, bringing her massive blade around in an arc to cut Gaston in half. He saw the blade and managed to bring his daggers together to block the strike, but the force of the blow sent him flying across the room and into the wall, where he fell limp.

Tim started casting healing orb like it was going out of style. Cassie got the first one and Gaston the second. The Cursed ignored the assassin and rushed toward the downed tank. Tim started running to intercept the spider, but ShadowLily got there first.

His girl dropped out of stealth and tore a hole in the Cursed's bulbous body. She danced away from the legs and disappeared again, this time taking a piece out of one of the boss' front legs.

The Cursed yelled in a language Tim didn't understand and started climbing the walls. Soon she disappeared in the webbing covering the room. Smaller spiders descended from the ceiling, and a quick count revealed there were at least five of them.

"Adds!" Tim cried out for everything he was worth, just like he had in the days he'd spent behind the monitor in his room.

He cast another healing orb at Gaston and saw him twitch awake. Cassie was back on her feet and running in their direction. Tim looked at the team to make sure they were topped off and prepared himself to deal with at least one of the spiders.

"Cassie, let's start working our way back to the pillar."

"Are you serious?" she snarled as she stepped up to meet the charging spiderlings.

"It wouldn't be here if we weren't going to need it." Tim pulled Gaston to his feet.

Cassie took out the first spider with her bo staff. "Let's go." She charged into the spiders, creating room for the rest of them to get behind her. Now they could back toward the pillar while they dealt with the rest of the adds.

Gaston picked two off with throwing knives, and ShadowLily took out another with a cast of her own. There was only one left, *but where the fuck was it?*

Tim readied flameburst before he even looked up. The flames shot from his hands as the spider crashed into him. He pushed the charred corpse to the side, careful not to get bitten again. Standing up, he brushed burnt bits of spider off his robes.

Worst barbeque ever.

The group continued trudging toward the pillar as they worriedly scanned the room for more spiders, but they saw no additional spiderlings. They reached the stone column just as the Cursed exploded from the webbing on the ground.

"Take cover!" Tim shouted and dove behind the pillar of rock.

Gaston and ShadowLily appeared next to him, but Cassie didn't make it. Tim poked his head around to see their tank getting covered in webbing. If they hadn't come back to the pillar, it would have been all of them trapped there, and this mad quest of theirs would have been over.

Still, they wouldn't be able to win this fight without a tank. Cassie was going to hate him, but he had to make a move now, or all of them might be joining her sooner rather than later. Tim watched until the Cursed stopped hurling webs at the tank and ran to Free Cassie.

There was only one quick and dirty way to do it.

Flameburst ripped through the webs like he'd splashed gasoline on a fire. Before the spell stopped, he was casting healing orb at her.

She emerged from the smoking remnants with her clothing only slightly singed. "Let's not do that again."

"Then hurry up and kill this bitch." Tim waved her away like an aristocrat would one of his servants.

ShadowLily whispered in his ear, "You're going to pay for that later."

"Only if we live." Tim cast another healing orb at Cassie as she charged at the Cursed.

Knowing she couldn't damage the boss with her staff, Cassie employed a defensive tactic. She kept the legs and sword as busy as she could. Tim could tell the Cursed was starting to get frustrated, but Cassie just kept dodging and smacking her as if she didn't have a care in the world.

Gaston appeared under the spider's belly and slashed it open.

He tried to dance out of the way, but one of the legs pierced his arm. The Cursed reared back to finish him off, but ShadowLily ran up her back and sank her daggers deep into the human torso. Gaston rolled free of the legs as they started to close in on themselves.

The Cursed was dead.

FUCK, YEAH!

Tim ran forward, healing Gaston as he did. The hole in his arm started to close as Tim pumped more power into the skill. By the time he reached the assassin, he was as good as new.

"We did it." Gaston grabbed Tim by the shoulders and shook him like a rag doll. "We fucking did it!"

Tim extracted himself from Gaston's grip and smiled. "Was there any doubt!" Tim roared back as something slammed into him, sending him crashing to the ground.

ShadowLily rolled on top of him. "You did it." She kissed him on the lips.

"Get a room already," Cassie said as she walked past them to lay her hand on the Cursed.

"This is a room, although it is rather large. And I'm not sure if I'm into people watching or not," Tim snarked.

"Gross," Cassie spat as she stood up with the key in her hand. "Why don't you try using this so the rest of us can keep our breakfasts down?"

Tim pulled ShadowLily into a deep kiss before rolling back to his feet. He bent over to help her up and turned toward Cassie. After three quick steps, he plucked the key from her hand. "Don't mind if I do."

At the final door of the dungeon, he slipped the key into the lock. Tim paused for a moment, letting the feeling wash over him. He wasn't going to die, and his plans for the slums were about to come to fruition. Everything he'd been working so hard for was just in his grasp.

The key clicked in the lock, and the doors swung open. Sitting inside of the room was a chest more elaborate than any they had encountered so far. Tim glanced at the group. "Anyone want the honor?"

Gaston grinned. "As long as we get Malvonis the dungeon heart, I don't care who goes first.

"Just open it already." Cassie beamed at him. "You deserve it."

"We all deserve it. I'm so impressed right now." Tim couldn't stop grinning as he looked at his team.

"Enough with the speeches. I want to see the loot," Cassie clamored from behind him.

Tim placed his hand on the chest and felt his smile growing. This was the best reward so far, mostly because he didn't have a set of gloves yet. The gloves with +2 wisdom went into his inventory without a second thought. Reaching back into the chest, he also took the dungeon heart for Malvonis. The last thing he got access to in the chest was a market kiosk.

Not only could Ernie reopen the inn, but people could list items for sale and buy them just like they were at the market. They'd get a small cut of every transaction. This one item could be worth a fortune. It was better than all the gold in the world as far as Tim was concerned. It was like compound interest, the gift that kept on giving.

Cassie stood up with a very roguelike hood on her head. "I'll take all the free armor I can get." She held out her hand, showing off a new ring. "Not to mention +1 resistance to all magical attacks."

ShadowLily Twirled a new set of daggers in her hands. "Badass!"

Looking over a new pair of pants, Gaston smiled. "Just my size."

A black portal appeared against the far wall, with the swirling vortex that was their ticket out of the dungeon. Tim took one last look around the room. "Let's get the fuck out of here. Drinks are on me."

CHAPTER FIFTY-SIX

They entered the inn like Caesar returning to Rome after a victory.

Tim ran toward Ernie with a grin so wide it threatened to split his face open like Gallagher using a sledgehammer on a watermelon. "We got it." He held up the dungeon heart in his fist.

"No." Ernie looked at him with disbelief and maybe a twinge of hope. He spied the dungeon heart in Tim's hands and knew that the kid wasn't lying. "You actually did it."

Tim motioned the rest of the group over. "No, we did it together. Without your poison, we wouldn't have made it into the dungeon, and without Gaston's awesomeness, we would have been finished."

He pulled Cassie and ShadowLily close. "Not to mention our tank and my favorite exterminator." Tim let them go and shouted, "Now let's get some drinks."

Liz came from the back with a tray full of beers. "I heard the celebration and figured these were in order."

Gaston leaned over to Ernie. "I like this one."

Ernie elbowed him. "Your biggest problem is you like them all."

"Only the good-looking ones." Gaston rumbled with laughter.

Tim took two beers from Liz. "Thank you." Turning, he handed one to Ernie. "Set up the meeting with Malvonis, and I'll go to the bank and grab the gold we need."

To the rest of the group, he said, "Try not to celebrate too much. We've got one more thing to accomplish before this is over."

ShadowLily spun her new daggers. "I'll be ready."

"Maybe be a little less confrontational than last time," Ernie chided.

"I'm not making any promises. If that half-orc fucker goes after Tim, I'll kill him." She slammed her daggers back into their sheaths. "But I can try to be civil first."

Tim grabbed ShadowLily around the waist and gave her a long kiss. "I love it when you get all protective."

"Ughhh. Save that shit for when I'm drunk enough to stomach it." Cassie finished the rest of her beer and motioned for Liz to bring her another one.

"I'll be back." Tim took one last look at the party he'd assembled before ducking out of the room. Walking down the rainy streets of the slums, his only thought was, *How did I get so lucky?*

It felt weird having that much gold in his inventory. Thankfully, you'd never be able to tell just by looking at him. It wasn't like he had two giant sacks of clinking coins over his shoulders. Being in *The Etheric Coast* made things of that nature a hell of a lot easier.

Like laundry. He'd never have to do that shit again.

Even the raindrops coming down as he entered the slums didn't bother him. Life was looking up. Malvonis would be out of their hair, and the inn would be back in Ernie's hands soon enough.

With the market kiosk he'd looted, there was no doubt in his mind they'd make the hundred gold back pretty quickly. At least, they would if he could turn the inn back into a hotspot. Shouldn't be too hard. There wasn't another tavern in this entire section of the city.

On the walk back, he'd also decided to apply all the money they made from the kiosk toward Ernie's debt. The faster he could give him back the building, the better. Then he could look into other real estate while putting his plan in place. The continued proceeds would make a pretty nice safety net for him when and if he decided to become an adventurer.

The adventurer title still scared him. If he decided to go that route, he'd be giving up his guaranteed income for a chance to make more. It was a frightening proposition when you had to bet on yourself. At least he knew success or failure would be his alone.

But he had promises to keep.

His family wasn't exactly poor, and with him out of school and away from home, there was one less mouth to feed. That didn't mean his family was living high on the hog, either. Tim wanted more than anything else to make sure his parents didn't have to slave away into their golden years.

It was almost time for them to get ready to enjoy the later part of their lives, including what their children were accomplishing. Tim didn't want them just scratching by, he wanted to see them flourish. He'd love to help them move into a newer house and get rid of their ten-year-old car. They deserved it, if for nothing else than giving him the chance to succeed.

That opportunity wasn't something every child received. Some kids came home, and their parents didn't even ask about home-work. Not Tim's parents. They made sure his work was done before he went out to play or vegged out with videogames. Mom and Dad had put healthy meals on the table and made sure he worked out.

He knew it wasn't always easy for them, and he hadn't always shown his appreciation when he was younger, but now that he was entering the real world, or a close approximation of it, he understood what they had sacrificed to give him a leg up. They gave up a lot of their dreams to make sure their kids could have theirs.

That was love you couldn't buy.

The inn appeared in front of him. Tim shook the rain off his cloak as he stepped through the door. One look inside, and all of the happiness drained from him.

Malvonis had Ernie pressed against the wall dagger at his throat. "Where is it?"

"I told you, he'll be back with it soon." Ernie pleaded as he struggled to get free.

Gaston was sitting in a chair, nursing a nasty-looking cut over his eye. ShadowLily stood in front of him with daggers out, scowling at the half-orc's back. Cassie looked just as enraged, but there was nothing they could do. One wrong move and Ernie was dead.

Tim flicked a quick healing orb at Gaston and walked calmly into the room. "Would you mind putting my innkeeper down? I get a little twitchy when people hold blades to my friends' throats."

"You've got poor taste in friends." Malvonis snarled as he drew a single drop of blood from Ernie's neck.

"Where I come from, a man makes his own choices, and he lives with them." Tim sat down in a chair and motioned for Liz to bring two beers. "On the plus side, once our business is concluded, you won't ever have to see him again."

Malvonis pulled his dagger away from Ernie's neck and slipped it back inside his cloak. When he turned, there was a smile on his face that said, "See I can be reasonable, and I was never really going to hurt him."

He sat down across from Tim and threw his feet on an empty chair. "Do you have what I want?" The half-orc's voice was calm, but his eyes danced with the threat of violence.

Tim's heart was racing, but he took a sip of his beer, pretending like he was having a drink with a good friend. "That depends." He set his beer down and wiped his lips with the sleeve of his robe. "Did you bring the deed?"

Reaching inside of his cloak again, Malvonis pulled out a worn leather binder and tossed it on the table. His tusks twitched. "I brought it."

"Do you mind?" Tim picked up the document without waiting for an answer. He motioned Ernie to his side. "Is everything in order?"

Malvonis tapped his dagger on the table. "No honor amongst thieves, eh? When I tell you I'll do something, it's done." He sneered at Ernie. "Always."

Ernie took a step back but didn't drop the document. After folding up the paper and slipping it back inside the leather envelope, he set the package on the table again. "It's all there."

Tim watched Malvonis closely. He couldn't help feeling as if the joke was on him, and as soon as he handed over the dungeon heart, the bastard would just kill all of them. There wasn't anything he could do to banish the feeling, so he pushed forward.

"And I have your word that Ernie and his men will be left alone?"

"As long as they stay out of my business, I'll stay out of theirs." He slammed a giant fist into the table, making everyone jump. "But I've been about as patient as I care to be. Live up to your end of the deal, or I'm going to start cutting."

"Fair enough." Tim's voice might have squeaked, but all things considered, he felt like he was holding it together pretty well in the face of almost certain death. "Here's your gold." He set two large sacks on the table.

"And the dungeon heart." Malvonis' eyes bulged, and his grip tightened around the hilt of his dagger.

Tim pulled the Dungeon Heart from his inventory and set it on the table. Malvonis' eyes sparkled with glee as he picked the object up. Standing, Tim extended his hand to the half-orc. "It seems our business has come to a close."

Malvonis tucked the heart into his vest and picked up both coin sacks in one giant hand. With the other, he gripped Tim's hand and gave it a bone-crunching squeeze. "Stay out of my way, or I'll kill every last one of you."

Smiling through the pain in his hand, Tim kept his eyes and face worry-free. "As long as you don't come back to my inn, we won't have a problem."

"Is that a threat, boy?" Malvonis growled as he pulled Tim closer.

"Just a friendly reminder of the terms of our deal." Tim pulled his hand free. "I believe you were just leaving."

"I believe I was." Malvonis pulled on his hat as he walked toward the door. He moved slowly to let them know he didn't give a shit what they thought.

When the door to the inn closed, Ernie bolted it. The strength left the man's legs, and he sagged against the door. "I really hate that fucker."

Tim shook his hand, hoping to return some of the feeling to it. "Tell me about it. For a second there, I thought he was just going to kill us and call it a day."

"I'm surprised he didn't." Gaston took a sip of his beer. "Malvonis isn't known for his self-restraint."

Tim shrugged. "I guess the heart was that important to him." He felt a niggling doubt in the back of his mind. It was never a good thing when a bad man got something he wanted. It almost felt like his decision to give up the heart was going to come back and bite him in the ass.

No one looked like they wanted to celebrate anymore, and he wasn't going to try to force a festive mood on the team.

But he also wasn't going to let them leave without a little something to look forward to.

"Tomorrow night, I'm going to take everyone out so we can talk about the future. Drinks and food are on me. I don't know a lot of places to go yet, so I'm going to rely on the locals to point us in the right direction."

"I know a few places," Gaston said with a grin.

"Nobody wants to eat their dinner off a stripper's ass." Liz smacked the burly thief on the back of the head.

"I've got an old friend at the Drunken Butler," Ernie said, wiggling his eyebrows. "I'll get us a big table."

Liz looked at Ernie in shock. "I've been trying to get in there for a year."

The innkeeper shrugged. "It helps to know the owner."

Tim slapped Ernie on the back. "Awesome. Get it set up, and I'll be there."

"Better bring some extra gold. I'm feeling awfully thirsty." Gaston smiled and walked in the direction of the stairs leading to his training room.

Cassie gave Tim a high five. "I'll be there." She stopped to give ShadowLily a hug and headed for the front door.

Liz locked the door behind her. "I guess I'll see you tomorrow." She gave them one last wave before walking up the stairs to her room.

Ernie picked up the deed to the inn and handed it to Tim. "We couldn't have done it without you."

"Just wait until you hear what I have planned." Tim smiled at the look of horror on Ernie's face.

"Maybe we should take a break first." Ernie gave him a baleful look. "Or at the very least, sleep on it." He waved at them as he walked toward the kitchen.

ShadowLily gave Tim that look that could only mean one thing. "You know, I could use a bath."

Tim smiled back at her. "You know, I was thinking the exact same thing."

Baths were actually kind of fun when you had company.

CHAPTER FIFTY-SEVEN

Cardinal Jepsom looked at the abomination in front of him with a sneer.

He hated the thought of using such a man—half a man, really—for his purposes, but the cardinal had no other choice. A man walking through the desert took water where he could find it. Jepsom was, for all intents and purposes, lost. The only card he had left to play was with this monstrosity.

The thief was half-orc, half-man. It made him fearsomely strong, but not the kind of person he could be seen associating with. Not if his plan to become the next high priest was going to work. All his carefully laid plans had been dashed like a boat against the rocks of the harbor. Now he was grasping at straws, willing to take risks he never would have considered years before.

Only the bold become legendary.

"Do you have it?" Jepsom's voice was lower than a whisper, as if he didn't dare put a voice to his desire in case it blew away like a grain of sand in the wind.

Malvonis reached into his cloak and pulled out the glowing

orange and red heart of the dungeon. "I do, but the price has gone up."

Licking his lips nervously, the cardinal couldn't take his eyes off of the prize in front of him. "What is it that you want?" He had to stop himself from trying to take the heart by force. His dreams were so close. Just a few minutes more.

"One thousand gold," Malvonis said flatly as if there could be no further discussion on the matter.

"You will have it." Jepsom reached for the heart.

"When I do, you can have your prize." Malvonis started to put the dungeon heart back inside his cloak.

It was all the cardinal could do not to cry out in dismay. "Wait here." He walked to a door at the back of his chambers, turned the handle, and stopped. He couldn't just give in. If the freak wanted more gold than they'd originally bartered for, then he wanted something else from him as well.

"Since you've taken upon yourself to change the terms of our deal, I will do the same. There is a new assassin in the city, one who has caused me quite a bit of discomfort of late." He frowned as he thought about the three men he'd lost in as many days.

"I'll give you five hundred gold now and the rest when you've located and killed the man." Jepsom locked onto the brute's beady little eyes with his own. "Find him and kill him, and I'll consider our deal complete and give you the rest of your payment."

Malvonis smiled. "I'd be honored."

"Fuck your honor. Just kill the bastard." Jepsom opened the door and disappeared inside.

He returned a moment later and tossed two small sacks at Malvonis' feet. "I trust you know someone who can convert these to coins."

Malvonis opened the first bag and peered inside. A collection of precious stones glittered in the torchlight. He quickly checked the other bag before tucking them both into his vest. "This will do just fine."

The half-orc stood up, refusing to kneel in front of the cardinal for a moment longer. "My boys will find him, and I'll handle the deed myself. You can count on it. My word is my bond."

Jepsom sneered at Malvonis. "I'll settle for results."

Malvonis reached into his cloak, pulled out the dungeon heart, and tossed it to the cardinal. "I'll send you a letter when it's done." He looked around the temple. "This place makes me kind of uncomfortable."

Waving the orc away, Jepsom kept his eyes on the heart. When he heard the door close, the cardinal looked up to make sure the room was empty before he returned his eyes to the one thing that mattered. This was it—his moment. Everything hinged on his ability to contain the power within the heart.

A sheen of sweat lingered on his forehead. It was no small task to grab the future by the balls. Once you did, you had to hang on for dear life, but he was ready. His time being second fiddle to that bastard of a man was over. The temple and the goddess' eternal love would be his. All he had to do was seize the prize.

Cardinal Jepsom shoved the heart into his mouth and began to chew. He felt a warm sensation rush down his throat as he swallowed, and suddenly there was power inside of him waiting to be set free. A strangled cry escaped his mouth as he was lifted into the air. White light exploded from his body, and he fell to the ground.

Dark laughter bubbled from inside him as he rose to his feet. "Yes." The power coursed through his veins. "Yes!"

They will submit or they will burn. Such is the way of the world.

CHAPTER FIFTY-EIGHT

"E rnie, I don't know what to say. The food was fantastic," Tim gushed.

"The Drunken Butler is one of the best restaurants in Promethia. I used to come more often, but recently, it's been out of my price range."

ShadowLily lifted one eyebrow in question. "Income took a hit when Malvonis took over, huh?"

"You've seen my client base at the inn. Bunch of freeloaders," Ernie snapped and finished his beer.

"I resemble that remark." Gaston beamed around the table as he held up the pitcher and signaled the waitress.

Tim looked at Ernie, his face suddenly serious. "Don't worry too much, Ernie. The Blue Dagger is going to be so full soon, you're going to need to hire a whole new staff."

"And hopefully keep the one staff member you already have." Liz lifted her glass toward the innkeeper.

Ernie clinked her glass. "Only seems fair since you've basically been working for free." He smiled. "But we've been closed for so long that people might not even remember us."

"Oh, I don't think that will be a problem," Tim intoned sagely. "Not with what I have planned."

"Here we go again," Cassie chided. "When our fearless leader gets something stuck in his head, let's just say it's better to get out of the way."

A man in a white chef's coat appeared at their table with two pitchers of beer. He set the pitchers down and looked at Ernie. "It's been a long time."

Ernie jumped up and pulled the man into a hug. "Indeed, it has." Ernie kept one arm around the man's waist as he introduced him to the table. "This is Wyatt. He got his start at the Blue Dagger."

"All of Ernie's friends are always welcome at my place. Without this guy's help, I would have never been able to start this restaurant." He looked at all the customers. "I better get back to the kitchen. I just came by to say I've comped your meal, and I hope you stop by to catch up sometime."

"More beer, then," Gaston roared. "Free beer is the best beer."

Cassie elbowed him. "It wasn't like you were paying anyway."

Tim gazed at Wyatt and Ernie. They were obviously very old friends. It was good to see that Ernie had someone in his life who appreciated him. Seeing the chef's reaction to the innkeeper let Tim know he had judged the man correctly.

Tim stood and went over to shake the chef's hand. It seemed rude not to thank him for such a kind gesture, and one kind gesture deserved another. "The food is fantastic. Thank you for having us."

Wyatt waved away the compliment. "It was my pleasure."

"At the very least, let me leave a generous tip for the staff." Tim pulled out four gold coins and slipped them into Wyatt's hand. "Make sure everyone has a great night."

Quickly tucking the gold into his coat, the chef smiled at him. "Happy Transcendence Day."

Tim crossed his fingers over his heart. "May the goddess' light shine down upon you."

"Enough of that crap. More beer." Gaston roared as he finished another glass.

"I can see you have your hands full." Wyatt beamed at Ernie. "Some things never change."

Ernie pulled the man into a hug. "And some things do. Thanks for taking care of an old friend."

"Anytime you need anything, all you have to do is ask." Wyatt patted him on the back and headed for the kitchen.

They all sat back down at the table. When everyone had a beer in hand, Tim decided the time was right to bring up his next plan. "So, I noticed in the system menu that there is a guild tab."

"Are we really going to form a guild?" Cassie asked.

"I don't see why not," ShadowLily replied. "Normally, there are bonuses for guilds, and it would probably help with recruiting later on."

"Oh, I was just worried about the name. You know a cool name can make or break a guild's rep." Cassie grinned across the table. "I vote for the Fearsome Four."

Gaston laughed, earning himself a nasty glare from Cassie. "Fearsome Four is an absurd name. I want to be called the Flying Violinists."

Liz sprayed her beer over the table as she started laughing. "Why?" she asked between sputters.

"Because no one would know what it means. A name like that garners interest." Gaston sat back, eyeing the table. The burly assassin had a smile on his face, but his eyes dared anyone to take a shot at him.

ShadowLily nudged Tim. "It was your idea. I'm sure you have a suggestion."

Tim looked around the table, wondering if his name for the guild would go over better than the last two had. I mean, people had to like it better than Gaston's name, at the very least. "Since we are based out of the Blue Dagger Inn, I thought it would be cool to do a play on that and called ourselves the Blue Dagger Society."

Tim waited for them to laugh, but instead, they looked thoughtful. Ernie smiled and gave him a thumbs-up. Liz gave him a subtle nod.

ShadowLily went one better and pulled him into a kiss. "I love it."

Cassie made a retching sound. "That was for the kiss, not the name. Just show me where to sign."

"I guess the name has a certain appeal. Not as good as the Flying Violinists, but it seems I've been outvoted." He clinked his glass against Tim's. "I'm in."

Tim went into his menu and created the guild. He sent invites to everyone at the table and smiled as they accepted them. This was it, the foundation for everything they were going to do in the game. The group was primed for success. All they needed to do was find a fifth member for their team, and they'd be ready to conquer *The Etheric Coast* together.

While they were looking for that elusive fifth member, Tim would find someone to help him purchase more of the properties by the inn. He'd get them fixed up and rent them out to the shop owners. Once he had the cobbles in place and the market kiosk driving people to the inn, this section of the slums would become a gold mine.

The recurring income should be just the thing he needed to be able to send a constant stream of money home to his parents. Depending on how much Tim could make, he might even be able to give up his job and become a full-time adventurer. He knew that was the path ShadowLily was on, and he didn't want her to do it without him.

And how many grandmasters had made it there by not taking a few risks? None, that was how many. You didn't get to the top of any profession without taking a chance or two. Only this time, he was playing with his future on the line.

Those student debts wouldn't pay themselves, no matter what the politicians promised, and leaving the game without a guaranteed income scared the shit out of him. Being scared wasn't going to stop him from making the right choices. Turning the slums into his little money-maker could set him free to follow his dreams.

Tim looked around the table at all the smiling faces, and it dawned on him that he didn't know what the rest of them wanted from their time in the game. For their group to be successful in the future, he had to find out what motivated each of the party members. The last thing he wanted was for the group to feel like they always had to follow his lead. He was sure all of them had their own agendas.

He'd found a way to get Ernie his inn. Maybe he could help the rest of them. All Tim had to do was put the time in. Taking a sip of his beer, he sat back and thought about how bright the future looked.

One day, the people of Promethia would hear their names and run to the window to get a glimpse of them as they passed by. The players and NPCs would all know the name of their guild. Together, they were...

The Blue Dagger Society.

List of Tim's Current Stats and Skills.

"Tim" Level eight magic user

Primary Stats
  Strength 12
  Endurance 12
  Dexterity 16
  Intelligence 16
  Wisdom 30
  Perception: 5

Vitality: 3
Revitalization: 3
Luck: 5

Notable Gear

Circlet of Wisdom +1
Simple Dagger of Dexterity +1 (X2)
Level Ten Class Change Token
Boots of Wisdom +2
Robe of the Everlasting: Wisdom +3
Belt of Wisdom +2
Gloves of Wisdom +2

Skills

Healing Orb: Apprentice rank nine
Dodge: Novice rank two
Flame Burst: Apprentice rank three
Cleanse: Apprentice rank seven
Appeal to the Goddess: Novice rank one
Infiltrator: Novice rank three
Sneak: Apprentice rank two
Small Blades: Apprentice rank six
Throwing Knives: Apprentice rank two
Sneak: Apprentice rank three
Night Vision: Novice rank five
Back Stab: Novice rank seven
Flame Burst: Apprentice rank three

Open Quests

Tim has been directed to seek out the High Priest for his next quest.

CHAPTER FIFTY-NINE

"What kind of guild name is this anyway?" Cassie shouted as she took cover behind a boulder.

Tim pressed his back against another of the large rocks surrounding the farm. "You said you liked the name. What's wrong with the Blue Dagger Society?"

"That was before people started singing *The Reaper* to me everywhere I went," the tank snapped as she peeked around the boulder.

"It's not my fault idiots don't know the difference between the Blue Oyster Cult and us. And I'm sure people have shouted way worse things at you." Tim grinned at the exasperated look on her face. "Plus, once I get the shirts made, you're going to love it."

"Shirts? You're making shirts?" Cassie shook her head. "We'll be laughingstocks."

"Hey, you don't have to wear it, but they are pretty cool. It's this skeletal hand cut off at the wrist holding a blue dagger. Then there's blood running down the edge with a single drop at the tip."

Tim couldn't help but laugh as he thought about the shirt that inspired the design. When he was a kid, he went to a military

470

surplus store with his friend. He found a shirt of a skeleton cutting a guy's throat in the water, and the shirt said Navy Seals, a cut above the rest.

He wondered what the guys at the printing shop thought when they saw the Navy Seal shirt. Their expressions couldn't have been as priceless as the seamstress' face here when he ordered the guild's new design. "The lady I found to make the shirts thought it was crazy, but she's a whiz with a needle."

ShadowLily popped out of stealth. "Maybe we should talk about this later. You know, when our deaths aren't on the line."

"I second that," JaKobi agreed, as he ran a hand down the front of his bright red robes.

"New guys don't get a vote," Cassie snapped.

"My name's JaKobi," he grumbled.

"Ah, I almost forgot we brought along our new sparkplug," Tim snarked.

ShadowLily patted their newest member on the back. "Don't mind these two. They're just on edge. We've been through a lot these last few days."

It was true. Over the last few days, they had beaten their first dungeon, and Tim had taken out the man in the orange sash, not to mention all the work the guild accomplished at the inn and on his healing shack. Add in his full-time job, and this adventure was the most relaxing thing Tim had done all week.

Although the look on his girlfriend's face told him he was too hard on the new guy. It was tough enough being judged on your skills. Every group he'd ever joined had its own way of doing things, and when it was different than a player's norm, it took them some time to get used to things. So he decided to save the shitty jokes until they were better friends.

Otherwise, their newest recruit might just think he was a dick.

"JaKobi, you ready to show us what you've got?" Tim tried to look reassuring, but after the hard time he'd given the guy, he wasn't certain he pulled it off. "I'm sure you'll do fine."

The mage held out his palm, and a little blue ball of fire appeared in it. "I'm as ready as I'll ever be." JaKobi looked around the landscape and noted the lack of monsters. "What are we even here for?"

Gaston appeared behind their newest member. "The bounty, of course."

JaKobi jumped, and the fireball in his hand spluttered out. He glared at the assassin. "Stop doing that."

"When it stops being entertaining, I'll let you know." Gaston turned his gaze on Tim. "It's almost time."

"Time for what?" JaKobi asked as he looked around worriedly.

The ground shook. Tim imagined this was what it felt like when a herd of buffalos ran across the plains. A buffalo would have been an easier kill, and they also didn't burst from the ground with giant razor-sharp claws.

Large chunks of dirt flew in all directions as the monster they'd come to hunt dug its way out of the field. A head appeared in the hole, and the beast's nose twitched as it scented the air.

Tim glared at Cassie and mouthed, "What the fuck?"

Cassie shrugged her shoulders. "The Bounty Board did say 'giant.'"

Peeking around the rock he was hidden behind, Tim took one look at the gopher and shook his head. "When you told me it was a giant gopher, I thought it'd be like ten times as big as a normal one, not a hundred."

"Well, the contract wasn't specific but it did say it was a quest for a group of five." Cassie grinned. "We've got five. What's the big deal?"

"Oh, I don't know. The two-foot-long claws on the end of its massive fucking paws or those sharp-ass teeth." JaKobi grimaced before pressing himself against the rock and doing his best to be invisible.

"I'm with him." Tim laughed.

ShadowLily smacked him on the shoulder. "Don't be such a

baby. All you two do is stand in the back and splash people with water. I've got to get up close to that thing."

"The work of a master assassin is never done." Gaston winked at the party before setting his eyes on Tim. "Same plan as usual?"

"Sounds about right." Tim smirked. He was tired of working all week and ready to let out a few of his frustrations. "You two drop into stealth. Cassie will get the beastie's attention, and we'll do our part from range."

"See? Nothing to worry about." Cassie adjusted her latest additions from Ironbeard's shop before pulling her bō staff from her back. "Just say the word."

Tim walked to JaKobi and put a comforting hand on his shoulder. "It'll be fine." He shifted his gaze to Cassie. "Go do your thing."

Cassie snorted and twirled her staff around in a way that would make Bruce Lee jealous. She took a quick peek around the boulder to check the positioning of the giant gopher, then stepped from behind the rock as if she didn't care about the giant furball of death waiting in the recently-tilled field.

"Hey, you overgrown hamster!" Cassie shouted as she strutted out alone onto the field. She banged her staff on the ground like she was signaling lunch at a farmhouse. "Come and get it."

The gopher's head snapped toward the tank, and his beady little eyes lit up. Pulling itself the rest of the way out of the hole, the giant shook the dirt off. It pawed at the ground and prepared to charge. Its bluster didn't mean much to their tank. Cassie stood up straighter, determined to meet the hulking monster head-on.

With a battle scream that would make any dwarven warrior jealous, Cassie charged at the gopher. Tim watched as the beast took her in, but then it did something unexpected. The fucking thing turned and dove back into the hole.

Tim wanted to chase the rodent down there, but he'd seen *Caddyshack* and knew better than to screw with a gopher on its own turf. The hole was only slightly larger than the gopher itself, not a lot of room to maneuver in a fight. Then a single thought hit him in the head like a ninety-mile-an-hour fastball.

What if the gopher wasn't running away?

"Shark!" Tim screamed at his tank.

Cassie stopped running. "What?"

"You ever see *Tremors*?" Tim began casting a healing orb. This was going to hurt.

Cassie's face went blank for a second and then his bizarre references hit her. "Oh, shit." She started to run as she scanned the empty field for something solid to stand on.

The gopher exploded from the ground like a Great White stalking a seal. Chunks of dirt exploded around it as Cassie was sent flying.

Tim watched as she turned her body in midair and managed to land on her feet. "Well, that's new." She was always sent flying by these giant bosses, so maybe their tank had earned some kind of tumbling or recovery skill.

The monster-sized rodent twitched its cute cheeks. *Yeah, they were cute if you could get past the big-ass teeth ready to rip you apart.* Its eyes roved the ground, looking for its target. It wouldn't be long before it found Cassie.

Not that their little tank gave the beast a chance. She roared as she crossed the distance between them in a single leap. Her staff crashed into the gopher's head, and the gopher spun and used one of its paws to bat Cassie away. The tank flew through the air again, but this time she didn't quite manage to get her feet underneath her.

"This feels more familiar." Tim leapt into action and cast healing orb. Cassie was still climbing to her feet. They needed to buy her more time. "Light 'em up, JaKobi!"

When no burst of flame hit the gopher in the back, Tim turned to look for the mage. He found him huddled against the boulder, shaking like a leaf in the wind. "Well, at least we figured it out before a more serious battle," he muttered.

Cassie got her staff up in time to deflect the gopher's claws, but the force of the blow sent her sliding backward, her heels digging into the freshly-plowed earth. The gopher tensed its back legs, ready to pounce, then Gaston appeared and slashed a deep wound into one of them. The creature spun to attack the new threat, exposing its flank to their team's thief.

ShadowLily screamed like a warrior princess straight out of the age of Vikings. Her daggers sank into the gopher's back, and she used them like ice axes to climb the monster. Her body bumped the gopher's as it tried to shake her off, but she didn't let go.

Cassie used her hook to secure one of the beast's legs, and Tim finally remembered the spell he'd never used. His fingers moved slowly through the snare spell, but he managed to activate it. The gopher's movements slowed, and a split second later, Gaston took full advantage of the situation.

Ducking under the gopher, he slit its belly before rolling out the other side. The monster hit the ground, but ShadowLily wasn't done yet. She reached the giant creature's neck and thrust her daggers in. Blood sprayed from the wound, and its whiskers twitched once before the gopher fell on its side.

Tim rushed forward to make sure none of his party got crushed. He rounded the gopher's body to see the three of them standing there smiling. At least no one had been seriously hurt. He tossed a couple of healing orbs in their direction, erasing any scratches or bruises they might have picked up during the fight.

"See? Bounties can be fun." Cassie pointed an accusing finger at Tim. "And if we hurry, there might be time to do one more."

ShadowLily looked at the corpse. "I don't see any scorch marks. What happened to JaKobi?"

Not wanting to throw the poor guy under the bus, Tim shrugged. "Guess he got knocked out of the fight early."

"'Cowering behind the boulders' is a much more accurate description," Gaston chided.

"Hey, not everyone is cut out for this kind of thing," Tim countered. "It can be a big shock if you've never done it before."

"Hey, guys." JaKobi came around the gopher's corpse. "I'm sorry I let you down. I think I'll just head back to town." He turned away from the group with his head hanging low.

Tim was impressed he had the guts to come over and talk to them after what happened. It took courage to look into the eyes of people you let down. Being able to admit you made a mistake and own up to it was something not everyone could do.

JaKobi might not have been ready for the big leagues yet, but there was potential there. Who knows? Maybe the kid just needed them to give him one more chance. Tim never minded giving someone a chance to prove they could do better. He looked at ShadowLily and she gave him a subtle nod.

"Hey, wait up." Tim ran around the gopher to catch up with JaKobi. "We're going to do another bounty if you want to come."

The fire mage looked like he was stuck somewhere between crying and being furious with himself. "Why? I'm just slowing you down. You're better off without me."

True, at least for that last fight, but Tim hated seeing someone with potential struggle because they didn't believe in themselves. Maybe all he needed was a little push. There was always the chance he'd expected too much out of a new addition to the group. Most players were probably avoiding the stronger bosses until after they hit level ten and became adventurers.

Now Tim just had to find a way to phrase his response so he didn't sound like he was offering JaKobi charity. "If you don't want to come, that's fine, but I really want to see what a fireball looks like in action."

"They do look kinda cool," the fire mage replied without looking up. "As long as I actually cast one."

Now they were getting to the heart of the problem. The kid just needed a little confidence. "I'm willing to give you another shot. All you have to do is want it."

JaKobi's lips almost twitched into a smile before they gave up. "All right. I'll come, but don't expect too much."

Tim was already thinking of all the ways he could get the mage involved in their next fight without a lot of risk. It wouldn't be too hard. I mean, who wouldn't love throwing fireballs at everything?

"Oh, I've got a plan." Tim thumped him on the back. "Don't worry about a thing."

ShadowLily appeared, and both men jumped. "You know it's never a good thing when he says that."

Cassie trotted up. "It really isn't."

"I don't know." Gaston snickered. "All of his ideas sound bat shit crazy, but his plans always seem to work."

JaKobi looked from one face to the other. "Is that supposed to reassure me?"

"Didn't you just hear them," Tim blustered. "They said my plans always work. So like I said, you have nothing to worry about."

"Is he for real?" JaKobi asked the party.

"He's mostly full of shit, but he's not lying about his success rate." ShadowLily bumped her shoulder into Tim's.

"Except for that one time I died," Cassie snarked.

Tim smirked at their tank. "Hey, it's not my fault you got all heroic without any magical protection. And if I remember correctly, you were only mostly dead."

"Mostly dead," JaKobi croaked. "How can you be 'mostly dead?'"

"Never mind." Tim waved away his cinematically brilliant reference as if it were of no importance. "The point is, Cassie's still with us, and we haven't lost a battle yet."

"And we throw really good parties." Gaston smiled. "If for nothing else, stick around for the beer."

JaKobi grinned. "I do like beer."

"Who doesn't?" Cassie started to lead the way. "Now, there's just one last thing you have to tell me." She paused dramatically. "What in the hell kind of name is 'JaKobi?'"

The fire mage shot a look at the group that said he'd explained this so many times, it hurt him to do it again. "My real name is Jackson, and my favorite *Star Wars* character is Obi-Wan. I used the name in my first online game, and it just kind of stuck."

Tim patted their newest member on the back. "JaKobi-wan, you're my only hope."

CHAPTER SIXTY

"So what I want you to do is throw a fireball at it." Tim made a throwing gesture.

JaKobi looked incredulous. "But won't he run right at me?"

Cassie grinned at him. "That's kind of the point."

Tim tried to pull JaKobi's attention back from their crazy tank. "Don't worry about her, she just doesn't understand how getting hit by everything isn't what most people want to do."

Ignoring Cassie's stuck-out tongue, Tim continued. "But all you have to do is fry this fucker. We'll handle the rest." He tried to give JaKobi a reassuring smile, but there was no way to know how it came off. "Don't worry. We've got your back."

JaKobi stood and tapped his staff on the ground. His red robes streamed out behind him in the blustery weather. He looked briefly at the party, then walked toward his position.

Tim noticed JaKobi's free hand was shaking, but he was still moving forward. It took a lot of courage to be scared but keep going. Most people couldn't do it. Being able to act when you were terrified was the very definition of what made a person courageous.

It was a good thing no one could see JaKobi's legs since they were wobbling like those of a newborn calf taking its first steps. He looked across the clearing at the Hobgoblin and his five minions. *Was he really going to do this?* As far as he knew, Tim was setting him up for some kind of payback because he'd failed so hard at the last fight. He would throw a fireball at the Hobgoblin, and the rest of the group would run off and leave him to die.

Tim didn't seem like the kind of guy who'd leave him hanging.

At some point, you had to trust that you'd made the right choice when you picked a group. They hadn't kicked him out after one mistake like most people would have. This was his chance. All he had to do was throw a fucking fireball, and they might keep giving him chances until he figured out how not to shit himself in battle.

JaKobi's fingers twitched through the spell he'd used thousands of times in practice but never in a real fight, and the blue orb of flame appeared in his hand. Before he could talk himself out of it, he threw the ball of fire at the Hobgoblin.

A wild cheer rose from behind him, and he realized the group was congratulating him. Then a roar erupted from across the clearing, and JaKobi knew his fireball had hit his target. Without thinking, his fingers moved through the spell again. A new flaming ball appeared in his hands, and he launched it at one of the regular goblins.

The little fucker jumped out of the way, but JaKobi was warming up to the task now. He called on his spells and continuously rained fire on the enemy as if he could command the stars to fall from the heavens.

Cassie ran past him and unleashed a battle cry as she charged the Hobgoblin. JaKobi wasn't sure, but it sounded like she screamed, "Suck my balls." He hoped that was in reference to the fire he'd been flinging, but these days, you never knew for sure.

It was kind of nice standing in the back of the battle, sending bursts of flame wherever he thought they were needed most. Plus, with Cassie out there, his chances of getting hit by anything were relatively small.

His staff clattered to the ground, and JaKobi looked at his arm and wondered what the hell had happened before he saw an arrow sticking out of it. A moment later, the pain hit.

"Son of a bitch!" JaKobi yowled.

Tim ran to him. "Don't worry. It hurts more when I pull it out."

What?

Did he say "pull it out?"

"You'll be fine." Before JaKobi could get away, Tim ripped the arrow out of his arm. A second later, he slammed a healing spell into the wound, then he picked up JaKobi's staff and handed it to him. "Get back to work."

JaKobi tested his arm and it worked fine. Getting hit wasn't so bad if you had a healer. Sure, it hurt, but it wasn't the end of the world. Why waste so much time being worried when kicking ass was so much more fun?

The biggest problem JaKobi had now was that he was just too fucking stationary. He had to figure out a way to cast and move. There was only one way to find out if he could.

JaKobi started to run.

His spell fizzled as he tried to cast it, but he wasn't out of the fight yet. After a little trial and error, he figured out he could cast the spell and run with it for about five seconds. Any longer than that and the fireball disappeared before he could throw it.

With his new ability to run for a brief stint after casting, JaKobi found he could stay just in front of the goblins' arrows. The thief, the assassin, and the tank were engaged with the massive Hobgoblin, so it was up to him to pick off their ranged opponents. He'd already brought one of the archers down, but there were four left.

A second goblin caught on fire and ran around. The flames only burned faster because of his antics. *Guess goblins never heard of stop, drop, and roll.* JaKobi hit him with another blast to make sure he was out of the fight, then he got moving. He kept his eyes up and waited for the next goblin to show itself. It didn't take long.

And then there were two.

JaKobi was warming up to his role now. The roars of pain from the Hobgoblin indicated he didn't have a ton of time to do his part before the fight was over. The fireballs flew from his hands like bullets from a semi-automatic weapon. He grinned as the next goblin fell victim to his fiery wrath.

JaKobi scanned the battlefield in search of his final target. Where in the hell was the last goblin? He turned slowly and tried to figure out how he missed it or if one of the others got him. A cheer went up as the Hobgoblin went down. When he looked back, the scared look on his party's faces told JaKobi something was wrong. Instead of asking if he was about to die, his fingers twitched through a spell he'd never used before. Flame shield roared to life behind him, but not soon enough.

The first arrow made it through before the spell took effect. A shot in the arm had felt bad, but an arrow through his hamstring hurt worse. JaKobi fell to the ground and turned to look for his attacker.

Flameshield destroyed the arrow aimed at JaKobi's chest. All that was left of the projectile was a trail of smoke hanging in the air. His biggest problem now seemed to be that the spell only had enough juice to stop one attack, but there was a goblin with a sword running straight for him.

JaKobi tried to stand, but his leg wouldn't support him. He could only scuttle backward like a three-legged crab. Each time he moved, the arrow bumped the ground and he cried out.

The goblin seemed to get more excited by his squeals of pain. He tried to call on the flames to protect him again, but his mind was too scattered to cast the spell. His next attempt at flame shield winked out of existence before even being touched.

The goblin gibbered some curse JaKobi couldn't understand and lifted the sword above his head.

It's been nice knowing you. He watched death coming at him, but the only thought running through his mind was that the little green bastard was smiling. JaKobi closed his eyes, not wanting the last thing he saw to be a sword splitting his head open. He grimaced. It wouldn't be long now.

CLANK!

When JaKobi opened his eyes, Cassie was standing behind him. She had somehow turned the blade away with her staff before the goblin could split JaKobi's skull. The others were rushing ahead to finish the goblin off, but there was no need. Cassie had the little bugger occupied, and he was ready to end this.

JaKobi shoved all the pain in his leg into a little box and locked it away. Then he felt the flames surge to life in his right hand. "Get out of the way."

Cassie didn't need to be told twice. She hit the goblin, shoving the creature a few feet away before diving to the side. Flames washed over the little green bastard, reducing him to ash in a matter of seconds. With the last threat to their party dead, the pain rushed back in.

Fuck that hurt, but at least he wasn't hiding behind rocks anymore.

With Tim's face above him, the pain hit him hard. *What was Tim's fascination with ripping arrows out?* A nice cooling sensation took the pain away as Tim worked to close the wound. At least he had someone to help. Healing potions were still out of his price range.

JaKobi propped himself up on his elbows and a grin spread across his face. "That was fucking awesome!"

"Dude gets filled with arrows like he tried to hug a porcupine, and he's smiling." Cassie shook her head.

"Big improvement." Gaston snorted.

ShadowLily held out a hand to help the fire mage to his feet. "Hey Mikey, I think he likes it."

"Guy's a natural." Tim grinned as he enjoyed his girlfriend's reference to one of the most epic science fiction films ever. Before splashing another healing orb on JaKobi's leg, Tim asked, "How do you feel?"

JaKobi looked into the smiling faces of his group and felt like he finally found a home in the game. "So, what's next?"

Tim wrapped an arm around the fire mage's shoulders, and together, they walked back in the direction of the city. "First, we're going to turn in these bounties, then we'll drink."

Taking a few arrows for the team should earn me a drink or two.

JaKobi grinned, but his expression turned serious as he looked at the group's leader. "The real question is, did I do enough to make the cut?" His voice wavered as he finished speaking.

This was it—the moment of truth. He'd totally failed during the first fight, but he'd redeemed himself during the second. Now that he had some experience, he was starting to warm up to the idea of becoming an adventurer. How hard could it be when he'd be surrounded by these fearless veterans?

Tim took his arm off JaKobi's shoulders and considered the question for a moment. "I think you're doing great, but it's not only my choice. Why don't we do a few more bounties tomorrow, and then the guild will vote on it?"

Not quite the answer he wanted. "Sounds good to me." JaKobi felt betrayed by his voice as he heard the hint of disappointment that had crept in. A vote was the best he could expect after his epic fail with the giant gopher.

"He's got my vote," ShadowLily chimed in as she gently nudged Tim in the ribs.

"Mine too," Cassie chortled. "Did you see when he lit the goblin on fire? It was fucking awesome!"

"I don't see why not," Gaston said with an easygoing smile.

Tim didn't hesitate. "I guess you're in. One more reason to celebrate tonight." He leaned closer. "Welcome to the Blue Dagger Society."

JaKobi had never before felt like he belonged anywhere, but with this group, he felt like he could finally be himself. He couldn't stop smiling. "I'm in a guild." *No one back home would ever believe it.*

CHAPTER SIXTY-ONE

Malvonis was fucking tired.

Tired of working for the cardinal, tired of not being respected, tired of every fucking obstacle that stood in his way. It wasn't as if he'd decided to have an orc for a father. As if any child could pick who their parents were.

"Shunned" was the word Malvonis used when describing how others treated him, and that was the nice version. Reviled, despised, and disgusted was probably closer to the mark. That was why he chose to spend his life in the shadows and hidden away under his cloak, only stepping outside when there was work to be done.

But things weren't getting done, and he was growing upset.

It wasn't good for the people around him when Malvonis lost his temper. He liked to think it was his orc nature that made him this way, but the truth was he just had a disposition for violence. Not to mention a hair-trigger when it came time to mete out justice for life's constant disappointments.

Say one thing for his father, he'd beaten him until Malvonis understood his place. There wasn't an orc alive who didn't reject him, and the humans merely tolerated him. He'd never been treated like an equal, not by either fucking race. So he made his own way in the world and carved out a place for himself amongst the thieves.

Since leaving home, not one damn thing had been easy.

Spend a few nights sleeping in the gutter after getting robbed, and you started to realize it was better to be the one doing the robbing. Violence in the face of resistance had become his first, second, and third option. It was the mark's choice if they didn't want to give up the goods.

Malvonis' life lessons didn't end there. He'd learned not to beat around the bush when it came to blows. There was no point in hemming and hawing or pushing someone around. If you were going to act, it had to be with everything you had, and a knife ended a fistfight rather quickly.

Years of study with the blade made him a master, his size and strength made him fearsome, and his intelligence set him apart from most assassins. In a perfect world, he would have been an asset, maybe even employed by the crown, but not here. Here, he was just gutter trash, no matter how much he accomplished.

Promethia could burn for all he cared.

But where would he go then? There wasn't a place for him in this world, yet he chose to live. Clawing, fighting, and scratching his way to some semblance of a normal life. It might not have been the life he wanted, but it was a damn sight better than sleeping in those huts in the forest.

His men only followed him out of fear, but fear he could work with. And the ladies wouldn't be beating down his door with invites to dinner any time soon. So when it came down to it, his life's purpose was whatever job he was working, and his current project was frustrating the shit out of him.

Malvonis turned his head and scanned the alley again. There hadn't been so much as a rat running across the dirt-stained cobbles in more than an hour, but he had patience. The first thing you learned when everyone tried to kill you on sight was to be mindful of your surroundings and wait for the perfect time to strike.

There were two men hidden behind a crate about fifteen feet away from the entrance Malvonis was watching. He'd been staring at the two men since he arrived outside of the den. It was an easier task than most. As far as thieves went, these two were just about worthless. They were more concerned with the bottle of rum they were passing between them than watching the alley.

No one expected to be attacked at home. Home was where you were supposed to be safe. Nowhere was safe for Malvonis, so he made damn sure that anyone who screwed with him felt the same way. He'd asked the leader of this den for information. The man had happily accepted his gold, but he hadn't delivered. It is said that there was no honor amongst thieves, but there was a brotherhood.

Or so he'd been told.

The only thing Malvonis cared about now was making an example out of the bastard who stole from him. You couldn't let a thing like that slide, or every two-bit street hustler and their momma would think it was open season on his assets. Maybe it had been too long since he reminded the herd of who was in charge of this city's underground. After tonight he hoped no one would need another reminder.

Going back to the cardinal with his hat in hand seemed like a good way to meet the goddess in person. Despite his distaste for this world, Malvonis wasn't ready to move onto the next life. That meant he needed to find out something, something about the man who killed the cardinal's men.

So far, he hadn't found shit.

His man came out of the entrance to the thieves' den and started walking down the alley. He looked briefly up to where Malvonis was crouched on the roof and shook his head. So Brax thought he could take his gold and not deliver. Tonight the slimy little bastard would learn the error of his ways.

He crept across the roof until he was above the two men on guard and prepared to jump. He pulled out his twin daggers, Tooth and Nail, before stepping onto the railing. He gauged the distance again as he leapt from the roof into the open space.

A three-story fall goes by in a blink.

It's not like the movies where everything slows down. In reality, you hit the ground much sooner. By the time he exhaled, his daggers had sunk into the two men. With three hundred pounds and three stories of force behind them, the fight was over before the men could do so much as squeak.

Who knew it was so hard to make noise when you were split from your skull to your belly button?

He pulled his blades free of the remains, moved around the crate, and walked toward the door. He thumped on it with the butt of his dagger until a man pulled it open.

"Piss off. We're closed."

He grabbed the doorman with his left hand and sank his dagger into his stomach. The look of surprise on his face was epic. You really couldn't replicate the look of a man who'd had a dagger shoved through his gut. He pulled the blade free and flung the screaming man into the alley behind him. The thief hit the opposite building with a sickening crunch that silenced him for good. The sound his bones made when they snapped was almost enough to bring a smile to Malvonis' face.

"Jerry, tell that guy to fuck off and close the door already," a man shouted from inside.

"Jerry can't come to the door right now," Malvonis growled as he stepped into the thieves' den. "He's got a bad case of 'I'm too dead to fucking move.'"

Five men sitting around a card table stood up as a sixth man strutted into the room. Brax was all swagger and bluster, but there was fear in his eyes. Fear was good. Fear was something to exploit.

"I told your man that I haven't found anything yet." Brax hedged for time as his men spread out in a semi-circle.

"And yet, the gold I paid you wasn't returned." Malvonis spoke slowly as his eyes moved from one man to the other.

Brax wiggled a finger in the air. "Tsk tsk, tsk. That's not how this works, and you know it. You pay me to try to find the information. If I can't, or it doesn't exist, I still get paid."

"You expect me to go back to the cardinal without an answer?" That would be as useful as going to the city guard and admitting all of his crimes.

The information peddler had the gall to laugh. "Who you do business with is your own choice. As far as I'm concerned, I've held up my end of the deal."

"By what? Getting drunk and playing cards? I thought you knew enough about me to be smarter than that." Malvonis frowned across the room. "Or have you forgotten the last lesson I taught you?"

Brax's haughty smile faded. "I haven't forgotten. This time I brought more men."

Malvonis took the statement as his cue that talking wouldn't produce any further results, at least not without a demonstration. He slipped his daggers back into their sheaths and reached for his throwing knives. The blades flew from his hands faster than most men could see.

Five seconds later, Brax's crew was lying on the ground with blood slowly pooling around their rapidly cooling corpses. Malvonis walked past the dead men, drawing closer to Braxton with each step. The man looked around the room in disbelief, his mouth hanging open like a fish on a hook.

"The cardinal needs to know who this man is, and you're telling me that with all of your contacts, you couldn't find out a single fucking thing?"

Brax backed up until he hit the wall. "It's like he's a ghost. No one's ever heard of him, let alone seen the bastard. Are you sure he even exists?"

Malvonis pulled one dagger free from a nearby corpse, relishing the feel of the cool grip against his sweaty palm. "Oh, he exists." Without further hesitation, he stabbed the information peddler through the chest, pinning him to the wall. "But you no longer do."

"May you suffer the same fate when the cardinal finds out you've got nothing." Brax spat a wad of bloody phlegm on Malvonis and laughed. "If his temper is anything like yours, I'll be seeing you in hell soon enough."

With a roar of rage, Malvonis pulled his dagger free and cut off Brax's head. "I guess we'll find out."

The half-orc gave a sharp whistle, and two of his men entered the building. "Search this place. Bring back anything of value or any information you might find."

The two men looked at the destruction their boss had rained down on these men and nodded their heads faster than a flock of chickens heading to the feeding trough. Without saying another word, Malvonis pulled up his hood and stalked back out into the night.

He had another appointment to keep.

CHAPTER SIXTY-TWO

The healing shack was back up and running full tilt.

Tim even had an assistant now. She made sure that those with the most serious wounds were seen first, and that he always had clean water and towels on hand. He looked around the small room and had to admit it was better than anything the temple offered.

The light blue paint on the walls added a touch of serenity to the place. He also had some kind of vertical garden against the far wall. The extra oxygen and clean air was a real treat after being in the temple's stone confines. Ernie even had the floor redone. New tiles covered the entire room.

In short, the place was awesome.

And awesome was good because Tim had been spending an inordinate amount of time in the confines of the healing shack. It seemed word had spread that there was a healer in the slums, one that didn't charge more than you could afford. People were eager to find out if the news was true and kept showing up in droves.

He didn't mind the extra work, but he also had other responsibilities. He was the head of a guild now, and it wasn't like their group didn't have other things to do. Most of them still had to reach level ten. Out of the human companions in their party, only ShadowLily had achieved that goal so far.

Luckily for Tim, that meant she was off working on her class change quest with Cassie, which gave him the time to focus on his healing skills. He was just starting to realize how much effort it would take to become a grandmaster of one skill, let alone an entire discipline such as healing.

The only person who hadn't won in the deal was JaKobi. He was stuck outside the shack posing as Tim's guard. At least he didn't have to worry about being attacked; people tended to back off when the threat of being burned alive was on the table.

Tim moved through the patients as fast as he could. Before he knew it, the sun started to dip on the horizon. Tim poked his head out of the door. "We're going to wrap it up for the day."

JaKobi was used to this by now. He turned away from the door to face the people waiting in line. Walking down the two steps so he was amongst them, he started handing out little blue cards. These would let them move to the front of the line, except for any emergencies. It wasn't exactly fair, but it was better than a fuck off and come back tomorrow at the back of the line.

"I'm sorry he couldn't see you today," JaKobi said as he handed out the cards. "Please understand the healer has many commitments, including a full-time job."

"Why doesn't he make this his full-time job?" a man called out.

JaKobi locked eyes with him. "Considering you can't afford to be healed at the temple, one would expect you to be a little more grateful."

"Maybe I would be if I wasn't going home in pain," the man groused.

A ball of flame appeared in JaKobi's hand. "I can make it so you don't hurt ever again if you'd prefer."

The man started to back up, holding his arms out in front of him. "I didn't mean nothing by it. Honest, I swear."

"Good." JaKobi smiled as he extinguished the flame. "Then we can keep this little incident between us, and you can come back tomorrow."

"Whatever you say." The man took off at a run.

"You forgot your ticket," JaKobi shouted after him, barely able to keep a smile off his face.

JaKobi handed out the rest of the little cards and turned to find a man in a light blue robe standing behind him. He jumped back a step, his flame shield roaring to life.

Tim poked his head out of the crack in the door he'd been watching through. He trusted JaKobi enough to let him be his guard, but he was still evaluating him. While he might have handled the abrasive man differently, Tim was happy to see that the fire mage controlled the situation without incinerating anyone.

If he knew one thing about fire mages, it was that they tended to be temperamental.

The man who snuck up on JaKobi was lucky to have escaped without being burned. Tim was happy the mage showed some restraint because the man he nearly turned to ash was a delegate from the temple.

Tim turning from the door as he spoke to his assistant. "That will be all today, Judy." The plump older woman smiled when Tim slipped a silver coin into her hand. "See you tomorrow."

She slipped out of the door to avoid the brewing confrontation and hurried down the street. Now that Judy was safe, it was time for Tim to figure out what was going on. He stepped onto the small patio.

Tim looked at the wall of flames and then spoke directly to their newest recruit. "JaKobi, do you mind?" The flame shield winked out of existence a moment later.

"Sorry, boss. He startled me." The fire mage shrugged his shoulders and started moving to his normal post by the door.

The healer from the temple looked a little stunned at their

interaction but found his voice a moment later. "May I have a moment of your time?"

Tim moved back to the door and held it open. "Of course."

He didn't know if this was a messenger from Paul telling him to hurry the fuck up and get to the temple, or if this was one of the cardinal's minions trying to kill him. If he had to put money on it, this was one of Jepsom's goons.

Once the man entered the shack, Tim turned toward JaKobi, giving him a subtle nod. "Care to join us?"

The fire mage looked at him with a questioning expression but moved from his position by the door into the shack. "Don't mind if I do."

"Be ready for anything," Tim whispered to JaKobi as he walked by. His guard gave him a worried smile but moved to stand at the back of the room where he could easily keep an eye on the proceedings.

The fire mage had come a long way in the last couple of days. He'd spent their first fight together cringing in terror, but eventually found himself and even led the attack in their second battle. Now he was positioning himself to watch their visitor and the door at the same time. It seemed that giving the kid a second chance was all he needed to come out of his shell.

The rest JaKobi did for himself.

Tim stuck out his hand in greeting. "I'm Tim."

The healer gave Tim's hand a perfunctory shake. "Dunstin." The man looked around the room. "How quaint."

Had to be one of the cardinal's men if he was such an asshole. "What can I help you with, Dunst?" There was his big mouth getting him in trouble again. Tim tried not to smile as he heard JaKobi snicker behind them.

"Dunstin," the healer corrected. "I've been sent by the highest authority in the temple to remind you that healing outside the temple is forbidden. You must stop all healing-related activities at once."

Tim pretended to consider it for a moment and then started to smile. "No, I don't think I will."

Dunstin looked flabbergasted as if he never considered the possibility that someone would refuse to follow his orders. What was it with these pricks? They served the people, not the other way around. Tim turned his back on the man, effectively dismissing him, and started cleaning up the room.

"The cardinal demands," Dunstin blustered, "that you cease these illegal activities at once!"

Tim faced the man, whose smile was slipping from his face, and fixed him with the cold, merciless eyes of a psycho killer. "I have two problems with what you've said so far. The first is that the cardinal is the highest authority in the temple. He isn't. You have a high priest for a reason."

He took three quick steps forward and poked his index finger into the man's chest. "And the second is thinking I give two shits what that bastard Jepsom thinks. I serve the goddess. It is her will that guides me."

"Paul saw these people needed help, and now they have it." Tim glared at the foppish little asshole. "If there's nothing else, you can see yourself out."

"Don't think this will go unpunished. The cardinal is not a forgiving man." Dunstin glared at him. "I wouldn't be surprised if the next time I saw you, you were clamped in irons."

"I appreciate your concern, Dunst, but I think I'll be just fine." Tim made a shooing motion. "Now run back to your master and find out how happy he is that you failed your mission."

The healer glared at Tim and started to reach inside his robe. His hand stopped when the smell of something burning caught his attention. The hem of Dunstin's robe was on fire. The man let out an undignified squawk and ran for the door. JaKobi's and Tim's laughter followed him into the street.

"Try not to burn him too badly." Tim chortled as he watched the healer running back toward the arch.

"He's a healer. He'll be fine," JaKobi replied as he canceled the spell.

"He'll also be back, and with help." Tim frowned as Dunstin scuttled through the archway and out of the slums. "Let's go back into the inn."

"Good, I could use a beer." JaKobi pulled a key out from around his neck and locked the door.

Tim watched the archway for a little bit longer. If the cardinal suspected he was still alive, he might know Tim was the assassin. If that was the case, the next time they came for him, it would be in force. Jepsom's empire was crumbling around him, and Tim was the author of his woes. It made sense to lash out at the one target he could hope to kill. But it wouldn't happen today.

For now, he was still alive.

CHAPTER SIXTY-THREE

"Just kill him already!" Cassie roared.

ShadowLily dropped behind the smelly fish monster and stabbed it in the back until it died. "We'll be here all day if I don't do this right. My quest is to kill twenty of them by stabbing them in the back."

"Well, these fuckers are bigger than me and are carrying tridents. I can't even get close to them, so keeping their attention is a real bitch," Cassie fumed. "It's just so damn frustrating."

ShadowLily grinned at her best friend before kicking the body over and looting it. "But you can't say I don't take you to all the nicest places."

Cassie frowned at her slime and fish gut-covered boots. "I think we have very different ideas about what defines a," she made air quotes, "nice place."

"You mean you'd rather be somewhere else?" ShadowLily stood and looked into the ocean cave they'd entered. Her quest for the class change to rogue was going well so far. After this part of the quest, she only had one last thing to accomplish.

Not that the game had told her what that one thing was.

The class change quest had to be done step by step. Each part of the quest only revealed itself after completing the previous step. In this case, it meant she had to kill fifteen more of these fish people by stabbing them in the back. While she could do it solo, having Cassie around made it a million times easier.

"Why can't quests ever be like, go to the pub and drink six pints of beer?" Cassie groused.

ShadowLily smiled at her. "I swear to the goddess that if your class change quest involves drinking beer after I had to do all this, I'm going to be so pissed."

"Don't get your panties in a twist. It's not like you won't get to drink the beer with me." Cassie tried to wipe some of the fish-men's slime off her staff but only succeeded in covering her gloves in the sticky substance. "I'm never eating fish again."

"Just imagine how much sushi one of these could make." ShadowLily started walking deeper into the cavern, avoiding the seawater that covered half the floor.

"Yeah, nothing says fun like eating half-human, half-fish sushi." Cassie made a barfing sound. "I think this game is trying to make me a vegetarian."

"I'll get you a veggie and fruit platter as soon as we get back." ShadowLily quickly put her armor in her inventory before reequipping the clean version. "Now, let's go kill some fish-heads."

"At least they don't talk. Imagine if they were parrot-heads." Cassie did the inventory trick with her own outfit and weapon before stalking farther into the tunnel.

ShadowLily watched from stealth as her friend took the lead. She hated to admit it to herself, but she was never really sure this was going to work out. Whoever heard of an avoidance tank? It seemed like those classes were always getting shunned because one hit to them by a raid boss at end game was almost always catastrophic.

And while they hadn't made it to the end game yet, she was impressed by how well Cassie had handled the bosses in their first dungeon run. The girl was amazing when it came to being fearless. There was no way in hell ShadowLily would volunteer to be a tank in this game.

She preferred life in the shadows.

One of the fish-men jumped out of the water, covering Cassie with brine. It looked like the drinks, and maybe a spa treatment, were going to be on ShadowLily tonight. If they even had spas in *The Etheric Coast*. Slowly it dawned on her that she didn't know much about the city they lived in and what amenities it had to offer.

She was too busy kicking ass to go on a walking tour of Promethia.

Cassie moved the fish-man into position and set ShadowLily up for the easy kill. Their system was working pretty well, but things felt too easy. Tim was always telling her that nothing in games was easy. If things felt too simple, the developers were trying to lure you into a false sense of security.

And then, *whamo!*

The big baddie pops out and wipes the entire group. They hadn't run into anything scary yet, but ShadowLily knew Tim was right. Something huge and evil wouldn't be too far away.

The next fish-man fell to her blades, and she started to wonder what kind of sick developer came up with these creatures. Fish heads with bulging eyes and mouths full of razor-sharp teeth stuck on human bodies. It was like some psycho killer from a movie who sewed the heads of animals onto people's bodies.

She wondered if their back story involved pissing off the goddess or if some asshole decided to get freaky with a really big fish. Whatever happened, there was a race of hybrid fish-men that they were slowly exterminating.

Three fish-men later, they ran into a solid wall. ShadowLily frowned at the wall and peered into the water. There was no way to deny it—the current moved under the wall and hopefully into another chamber.

"Looks like we're getting wet." The thief looked at the water again and wished there was a different way. Jumping blindly into what might be fish-men infested water and trying to swim into another room seemed reckless.

Cassie took one look at the dark water and rounded on her. The tank's face was redder than a woman who couldn't get her hands on the new Popeyes' chicken sandwich. "I'm not jumping in there. We have no idea where in the hell it goes, and I can't breathe underwater."

"I thought you had big lady-balls?" ShadowLily snarked. "A little swim never hurt anyone."

"A little thing called drowning still makes you dead." Cassie looked into the dark swirling pool. "Seriously, tell me we don't have to do this."

"We don't have to do this." ShadowLily checked her quest and saw she needed two more kills to complete it. This was the only location marked on her map, so she had to keep pushing forward. "But I do."

Without waiting for her friend's rebuttal, she dove into the water and started swimming with the current. Maybe it wasn't her brightest plan. Cassie was right; they had no idea where this tunnel went. She was pretty sure the fish-men weren't worried about oxygen like they were, so she really could die. At the same time, she knew games were created to give you a way to win.

She just hoped there wasn't some magical breathing device she was supposed to find before taking the plunge.

There was no way to tell if she was going the right way. It had already been dark in the cave, but underwater it was pitch black. All ShadowLily could do was follow the current and hope that when she needed air, there was something besides solid rock above her.

There was a noise from behind, signaling that Cassie had

decided not to make her do this next part of the quest alone, despite her fears of drowning. ShadowLily hoped she hadn't killed them both by taking a leap of faith. Her vision started to swim as her chest grew tighter in the search for oxygen. It reminded her of trying to hold her breath and do laps in the pool back home.

Only in her pool, the penalty for failure wasn't death.

Just when she thought she'd totally fucked up, there was a faint light ahead. Nothing made a drowning person swim harder than seeing potential salvation. She pushed her body faster, knowing the only way out was forward. Her lungs burned. It wouldn't be long now before her body forced her to take a breath.

Then it was all over.

When her head broke the surface of the water, she spluttered and gasped. Before even looking around, she floated on her back, just sucking in as much of the sweet, sweet air as she could.

Cassie breached the surface a few moments later, and after a few lungfuls of fresh air, she looked relieved.

"Still alive," ShadowLily intoned serenely as if she were just floating down the lazy river with a margarita in hand.

"No thanks to you," Cassie retorted as she climbed out of the water. "The real question is, how are we going to get back? Swimming against the current is going to be a problem."

Her tank was right. Getting back out was going to be a real bitch. Unless the tides turned, they couldn't make the swim. The good news for them was the water seemed to be from the ocean, so the current should change at some point. If *The Etheric Coast* even had tides. Things didn't always work the same way here as they did back in the real world.

ShadowLily swam to the edge and pulled herself up onto the rough cavern floor. "I'm sure we'll be fine."

"Easy for you to say. If I die, I have to start over," Cassie grumbled.

Looking at her friend, she did her best Tim impersonation. "But I have a plan."

"It never makes me feel better when he says it either." Cassie climbed out of the water. "Normally, a plan from your boy toy means I get the shit kicked out of me for a while."

Pulling Cassie close, ShadowLily grinned at her. "But never a dull moment, eh?"

"I could use a few more dull moments." She pulled her bō staff from behind her back. "Now, let's go find something to hit before I lose my temper."

"You got it, boss," ShadowLily snarked as she followed a stomping Cassie through the cave.

They continued walking, and the spaced-out torches gave them just enough light to see. In the distance, there was a brighter light. With every step, the tension grew. They hadn't seen one of the fish-men since swimming through the underground channel and nearly drowning. It couldn't be long now before one of the creatures burst from the water to attack.

Their eyes were adjusting to the brightness now, but it wasn't sunlight. There seemed to be a room at the end of the tunnel lit by thousands of candles. Wax dripped down the rocky walls and puddled on the ground. They walked further into the chamber and could just barely make out what was at the end: a giant throne made out of the bones of a whale.

And it wasn't empty.

It must have been the leader of the fish-men, or at least the leader of this cavern full. He towered above the two men at the bottom of the throne. If she had to guess, ShadowLily would have said he was a good foot taller and at least fifty pounds of muscle heavier than them. This next battle wouldn't be as easy.

The king of the fish-men stood up from his throne and stared down at the two women. "You have killed many of my school. For that, there must be retribution."

Cassie turned toward her friend. "I think he just threatened us."

"Well, we did kill quite a few of his people." ShadowLily grinned at the tank.

"So, business as usual?" Cassie twirled her bō staff and glared at the king.

ShadowLily pulled her daggers free. "I don't see why not."

Without a word, Cassie charged at the throne. The two guards sprang into action, moving to intercept her before she could reach their king. The little tank spun and dodged their attacks, giving ShadowLily the chance to pounce from stealth.

The rogue-to-be took out the first fish-man without an issue. The second one realized the thief was the bigger threat and turned to face her. Cassie thunked him on the head for his troubles. When the creature spun back around to ward off Cassie, ShadowLily plunged her daggers into him from behind.

A quest update appeared in the lower right-hand corner of her vision.

Kill twenty Fishmen from behind: Complete

Update...

...New quest received.

Kill the fish-men's king and take his necklace back to your class change representative to complete your quest.

Cassie looked at the two dead fish-men and turned to look at ShadowLily. "So do we get to kill the big guy now or what?"

The thief grinned back at her. "Looks like we do."

The king of the fish-men let out a fearsome war cry, drawing the duo's attention before he pulled out a massive trident from behind the top of the throne. At the base of the three points was a glowing blue jewel.

Tim wasn't the only one who played enough games to know the jewel was important. It either gave the king additional protection, or it performed some kind of elemental attack. Her guess was it had something to do with water.

The king jumped from the throne and landed behind them, effectively boxing them into the cavern.

"Guess he doesn't want us to get away," ShadowLily muttered before dropping into stealth.

"It's not like we can swim out of here with him chasing us. Trapping us in the cave again seems like overkill." Cassie gritted her teeth as she moved to face the king.

The first blast of water hit the tank right in the chest and sent her flying into the throne. She hit the bones and bounced down a few of the steps. Thankfully the king seemed less worried about her and more interested in finding the thief who disappeared.

The giant fish-man turned his trident toward the ceiling and let off another blast of water. As the droplets fell from the cavern's roof, they revealed ShadowLily sneaking up to him from behind. He swung the trident in a slow arc, ready to blast her.

Cassie had seen about enough from the smelly fish-headed fucker. Flipping back to her feet, the tank growled and started running. Why did all these assholes think they could turn their back on her?

The king's arm made a horrible snapping sound as her staff slammed into the limb and shattered the elbow. The trident fell from his hands just before he could blast ShadowLily into next week.

Not willing to die so easily, the king pulled a dagger from his belt and slashed at Cassie with his one good arm. It was easy enough for her to dodge the attacks now that she only had to worry about them coming from one direction. She kept the king's attention focused on her so ShadowLily could get to work.

The rogue didn't disappoint as she stabbed her daggers into the king's scaly back. The king of the fish-men wailed in pain, but ShadowLily silenced him a moment later. All of her training with Gaston had prepared her for this moment. The bulbous-headed bastard didn't stand a chance.

It almost seemed unfair having higher skills than someone at her level would normally have, but that didn't stop her from taking full advantage of them. She made sure the king was dead before moving to examine his body. The only two items he had on him were the necklace and the trident. She tossed the trident to Cassie and took the necklace for her quest.

"What do you want me to do with this?" Cassie looked at the weapon in her hand.

"Keep it or sell it. I just wanted to give you something for helping me out." ShadowLily watched her friend, hoping the little bonus would make her happy, but it wasn't gratitude she saw on Cassie's face. The look her friend was wearing was different somehow, it might even be described as devious.

The tip of the trident rose as Cassie pointed it at ShadowLily. "Might as well see if it works."

Oh, shit!

"This is for a day spent in stinky-ass fish guts." Cassie let a blast of water fly.

ShadowLily tumbled across the cavern floor and came up spluttering. "If you didn't like the gift, all you had to do was tell me," she snapped.

"Oh, I like it just fine," Cassie started to raise the trident again. "It's going to be a hit at pool parties. Super Soaker *this*, bitches." She shifted aim away from ShadowLily and sprayed an arc of water across the cavern walls.

The thief watched her for a moment then smiled. "I think I just figured out how we get out of here."

Cassie frowned. "Have I told you how much I hate it when you sound like Tim? Sure his ideas work, but they seem sketchy at best."

"Are you really saying you don't want to use the trident to shoot us back through the underwater passage like a rocket?"

The tank looked at the water and then back to her best friend. "No, I don't think I'm saying that at all." Her frown turned into a shit-eating grin. "Let's do this."

Once in the water, they straddled the trident like a broom. As the weight of the metal and their gear pulled them under the surface, Cassie activated the trident, and they launched forward like a cork from an extra bubbly bottle of champagne.

If they hadn't been underwater, they would have screamed in joy.

CHAPTER SIXTY-FOUR

"I'm surrounded by incompetence!" Jepsom raged.

He looked around the room at all his disciples' upturned faces. "Every fucking one of you is worthless."

Jepsom pointed at one of the men whose name might have started with an H. "I asked you to stop that street preacher, not to incinerate him in front of a crowd." He shook his head. "Have you ever heard of discretion?"

"And you!" The cardinal rounded on Dunstin. "How hard is it to get some street healing hack to disappear?" When he snarled, the man shrank away in fear. "And if I understand the situation correctly, not only did you not resolve the issue, you scurried away like a roach from the torchlight."

"He had a fire mage with him," Dunstin pleaded.

Smack!

The chamber echoed with the sound of Cardinal Jepsom's open hand making contact with Dunstin's cheek. "If I wanted excuses, I would have sent whatever the fuck his name is." Jepsom pointed at the man he just chastised. "But I wanted it handled, so I sent you."

"I apologize for failing you." When Dunstin wasn't slapped

again, he took it as a sign to continue. "Tell me what to do, and it will be done."

Jepsom cracked the insolent bastard on the head with his staff. "I told you what to do, and you fucked it up." He took a deep breath to center himself. "It seems that if you want something done, you have to do it yourself."

Jepsom reached down and placed a healing orb against Dunstin's skull. "I will have need of you again. Try to be less disappointing in the future."

"As you command, Cardinal." Dunstin hurried to his feet.

The cardinal looked out at the waning members of his band. The only three men Jepsom trusted to get things done had been killed. There was still no word on who had assassinated them, but they had to be good if they also took out Juan Pablo. The man was a brute, and no one had been better at killing than him.

Now all Jepsom's hopes of finding the assassin rested on the shoulders of an even worse brute. If the half-orc shit didn't come through, he would have his head on a stick, goddess be damned. It was bad enough his own men were so incompetent that he needed to rely on outside help, let alone the help of a half breed.

The cardinal locked his eyes onto Dunstin's. "I have a task that even you might be able to handle. Find Malvonis and bring him to me."

Raising his staff again to deliver another blow, Jepsom sneered. "Do you think you can accomplish the task I've set before you?"

"I can and I will, Your Eminence." Dunstin turned and left the room.

Jepsom looked at the rest of his followers. "I'm not the high priest yet, but it is only a matter of time." He smiled at the men standing in front of him. "When I take over, all of you will be promoted. Do not forget what we are working for."

The cardinal made the sign of the lady over his chest. "You are dismissed. Go and tend to your duties."

The priests filed out of the room, and Jepsom smiled. If he

could nip a few of these problems in the bud, he might still have a chance to pull off his coup. The Dungeon Heart had given him power, but he had to use it wisely. The last thing he wanted to do was tip his hand early and give Paul a chance to stop him.

This healer in the slums was troubling, though. He'd already dealt with one healer down there, and now there was another one in the same spot. The slums hadn't had a proper healer in over fifteen years, and now they were springing up like wildflowers after the first rain of spring.

If the man refused to bow to Jepsom's commands, he'd have him locked up. A few coins in the right pockets and the city guard could make someone disappear more quietly than any of his men were capable of.

Jepsom moved to his desk and started to write a letter to his contact at the city guard while he waited for that idiot, Dunstin, to return with the half-breed.

Malvonis entered the chamber with his head held high.

Jepsom hated him for that simple act of defiance. This was his chamber, and anyone entering it should bow their heads as a show of respect. He looked at the half-orc from where he was sitting at his desk on the dais above him. The fucker would learn to respect him, or he'd hire someone to remove the half-breed from the equation.

Although, maybe he needed more men with backbones. Too many of his followers just rolled over and exposed their bellies at the sight of him. If you couldn't trust a man to stand up for himself, how could you ever trust him to stand up for you?

If getting out of this mess meant giving the half-breed more leeway than he was comfortable with, so fucking be it. Maybe Jepsom's curse didn't have to be that he was surrounded by those with weak minds and even weaker hearts. How was he supposed to build an empire when the servants the goddess provided him weren't up to the task?

All of the goddess' servants had crosses to bear. It mattered not that his was heavier than most.

It was too bad his personal burden saddled him with worthless supplicants. Maybe once he took the temple from that blithering idiot Paul, he could find some worthy men to stand before the people and spread his message. It was high time the priests of the temple were recognized as better than the common man.

Who else could heal the masses?

Who else could bring them into the goddess' warm embrace?

There was no one more dedicated to the success and grandeur of the temple than Jepsom. He wanted the goddess' house to shine above all others. The high priest should have power that rivaled the crown's. Who else could the crown call on when its army marched to war? Without him and the healers he commanded, there might not even be a Promethia standing here today.

But there was no way he could rule a kingdom if he couldn't get the simplest of tasks accomplished.

"Tell me you've found the assassin," Jepsom sneered.

Malvonis met the cardinal's eyes. "All I can confirm so far is that it wasn't someone local."

Why was he surrounded by halfwits? "How do I know you're not just taking my gold and spending it all on cheap beer and whores?" Cardinal Jepsom put down the document he was reading and focused his full attention on the half-orc.

Malvonis plucked a small leather pouch from his belt. He tossed it casually on the desk, where it landed with a wet thump. "Because I've taken the left thumb of every would-be assassin in Promethia. None of them took credit for the deed."

The half-orc motioned to the sack. "Trust me when I say none of these men were lying."

"So the thumbs of some peasants are supposed to make me feel better? If all I wanted was to feel good, I'd go to The Tart for a blowie, or maybe I'd visit your mother." The cardinal picked up the leather pouch and threw it on the ground. "What I wanted were results."

"Do you think I wanted to come here with nothing?" Malvonis growled. "Do you know how many men I killed to stand here today? Of course, you don't." He turned away from the cardinal, upset with himself for losing his cool.

Malvonis slipped a mask of composure over his face as he turned to face a fuming Jepsom. "The killer isn't in the city, and if he is, no one's ever heard of him."

The cardinal's hand came down on his desk hard enough to crack the thick mahogany surface. "Not good enough." Goddess save him, he was surrounded by worthless assholes.

Jepsom sneered at the abomination but decided to turn a negative into a positive. "If you can't handle the task I've given you, maybe there is something else you can do for me."

As much as it pained him to do so, Malvonis lowered his head in submission. "Tell me what you need done."

"There is a man in the slums healing the peasants for less than what the temple charges. While I'd prefer for him to simply disappear, that would raise too many questions. I'd like you to visit with him and impress upon him the severity of this matter." Jepsom smiled. "Forcefully, if possible."

The cardinal's eyes danced with excitement. "But not dead. At least, not yet."

Malvonis smiled at himself. This was a job he knew he could handle. It would be worth doing just to keep the cardinal off his back. "And where can I find this healer?"

"Some closed-down inn called the Blue Dagger." Jepsom sniggered. "Have you ever heard of such an absurd name?"

Malvonis shook his head. Thankfully Jepsom seemed to take his movement as acquiescence and didn't notice how badly the words shook him. "I'll track him down and deal with the situation as you've asked. Anything else I should know before I nip your little problem in the bud?"

Jepsom leaned back in his chair and steepled his fingers while he considered how much he should tell the half-breed. "I've dealt with one upstart in the slums already. If the rumors can be believed, this might be the same man. No one makes a fool out of me and lives long enough to do it again, especially not some entrepreneur too poor to find a decent place to live."

The cardinal moved away from his desk and down the steps to face Malvonis. He stared into the creature's almost human eyes. "Find this man, and you might find the answer to your assassin problem."

Malvonis tried to keep the shock from registering on his face. The kid he'd sold the inn to was a healer, but could he also be an assassin? It didn't make a lot of sense, but he was used to people not being what they looked like on the surface. He'd promised Tim he'd stay away from the inn, but it wasn't like the cardinal would take no for an answer.

"I'll find him and impress upon him the seriousness of his situation." Malvonis' hand rested on the hilt of his dagger. "I'm sure after our little talk, you won't have any further issues."

"I hope not." Jepsom turned away from the vile creature and walked back up the steps to his desk. "The last place you want to end up is on my shit list. I might not be able to track down this assassin, but I know exactly where to find you."

Malvonis grinned at the cardinal and refused to be cowed. "When that day comes, don't expect me to roll over and take it." Without waiting for a response, the half-orc spun on his heel and left the room.

Jepsom watched him leave, wondering if Paul had to deal with as many insufferable people as he did? Why was it that when you truly needed something done, there was never enough time? Events had clearly spiraled out of his control, but all it would take to get things on track were a few minor course corrections. It wouldn't be long until he was back on top with the station of high priest firmly in his grasp.

If this healer in the slums was truly an enemy of the temple, he'd have no choice but to use his influence to make sure the man disappeared. There wouldn't be a public trial, but he would be convicted of crimes against the temple and thrown into the city's dungeon. Problem solved, and all it cost him was a little extra gold.

Thankfully gold was the one thing Jepsom wasn't in short supply of.

CHAPTER SIXTY-FIVE

"Chug it. Chug it. Chug it," ShadowLily shouted with the rest of the bar.

Cassie finished the beer and slammed down the mug. "That's ten, bitches." She smiled blearily at ShadowLily as she tried to stand up. Her feet got tangled with something and she crashed to the ground.

"Who tripped me?" Cassie slurred as she looked around the room. "And why is everything all spinny?"

ShadowLily crossed her arms over her chest and glared at her friend. "I told you I'd be pissed if your class change quest involved beer."

"Don't be a hater. I'm your bestie." Cassie climbed to her feet, swaying from side to side. "It's not my fault my class has a cooler quest than yours."

ShadowLily put an arm around Cassie's shoulder and steered her toward the door. "So what's next on the list, killer?"

Cassie leaned against her best friend for support. Her eyes went blank as she pulled up her user interface and tried to focus on the text.

Taking One For The Team:

Now that you've made sure your team is safe by drinking all the beer in sight, it's time for you to earn your keep. Head to the Rusty Spoon and sign up for the first available fight. It's time to put your tankiness to the test.

Enter the ring and take the first three hits before fighting back.

Cassie grinned at her friend. Why was ShadowLily so tall? "I've got to go to this place and get punched." She shared the location of the Rusty Spoon. "But I'm going to need some help getting there."

"Your quest doesn't sound nearly as fun now." The rogue smirked at her friend. "Let's get your ass-beating out of the way so we can call it a night."

"One more beer, Garson!" Cassie roared. "If I'm going to get beat up, I need my pain medication."

ShadowLily took the beer from the bartender and handed it to her friend. "Are you sure about this? I'm guessing they won't let you into the ring if you can't stand up."

The little tank sucked down half the beer, tossed a silver coin on the counter, and headed toward the door. She made it exactly four steps before falling flat on her face.

"Sumofabitch, motherroofer," Cassie slurred as she pushed herself up.

"Don't worry. I've got you." ShadowLily picked up her friend and half-carried, half-dragged her to the door.

The cool sea air hit Cassie in the face like a punch. The pungent odor almost made her puke, but the cold breeze helped more than the smell hurt. Why did you always get so hot when you were drinking? She wished she could walk by herself, but the beer and her spinning vision made standing on her own an impossibility. ShadowLily might have been carrying her now, but by the time they got to the Rusty Spoon, she'd be ready to fight.

Not a rewarding quest for her best friend, but at least they didn't have to deal with slimy fish guts again.

The twenty-minute walk took them twice as long as it should have. Cassie's head was throbbing, and while her balance was coming back, she was now dealing with a rebellious stomach. What she really needed to get through this was another beer.

That was the problem with drinking. Once you'd gone too far down that particular rabbit hole, the only way out was to keep consuming more and keep the pain at bay by staying loose. Unfortunately, even in her groggy state, Cassie knew payback for tonight's shenanigans was going to be a real bitch.

She didn't have days to nurse a hangover. All Cassie had was right now. If that meant drinking a few more beers so she didn't pass out and have to try this again tomorrow, so be it. Just one more drink was all she needed. Anything was possible.

The Rusty Spoon came into view, and even with her blurry eyes, Cassie could tell the place was a dive. The building had a rusted brown exterior, but she had no idea where they got the spoon part. Frankly, the fucking place sounded more like a restaurant down by the harbor than an underground fight club.

ShadowLily held open the door for her. Cassie was just as disappointed by the inside as she had been by the outside. A few tables were scattered across the open space in front of her. There was a bar at the back with a lonely bartender holding down the fort.

The bartender had a mustache. She fucking hated mustaches. People always seemed to think they looked better with them, but only a few men could pull them off. Tom Selleck and Burt Reynolds might have worn lip fuzz well, but most people just ended up looking like Joaquin Phoenix.

Never be Joaquin with a mustache.

Cassie sidled up to the bar and wondered where she was supposed to find someone to fight. "Yo, 'stash, give me a beer."

ShadowLily held up a finger. "Make that two. I'm going to need one if we are hanging out here."

The bartender glared at them. "We're all outta beer."

"What kind of shitty bar is this anyway?" Cassie groused. "I'm supposed to come here for a fight, and not only is there no one to hit, but I can't get a fucking beer."

Mr. Stash's look softened. "So, you're looking to get a little rough and tumble?"

Cassie slapped her hand on the counter. "From the looks of it, the last time this place got rough and tumbled was when the goddess still walked this plane."

"Looks aren't everything," the barman smiled. "But if you are looking for a fight, you're in the right place." He reached under the bar and pulled something out.

A section of the floor slid to the side, and the noise of a thousand screaming voices poured out of the opening. The echo of flesh hitting flesh could be heard over the crowd. Someone down there was getting the crap kicked out of them. Cassie peered into the space, but all she saw were stairs.

"Stairs." She shook her fist like a cop in a black and white movie when their nemesis got away. "I'm in no condition to handle the stairs." Cassie gave ShadowLily a pleading look. "Maybe we should just go home."

"And have to do this all over again tomorrow?" The newly minted rogue wrapped an arm around Cassie's waist and dragged her toward the opening. "I don't fucking think so."

"Fine." Cassie shoved her off. "I can do it myself."

The stairs seemed to swim before her. *Moving fucking steps make everything so much harder.* She took them slowly, pausing on the first step until her vision cleared enough to take the next. Finally, her feet touched the bottom, and Cassie looked around to see what kind of trouble she'd just gotten into.

There was a giant ring painted in a washed-out rust color in the center of the room. The walls of the ring were just over waist-high on a man. Not high enough to keep you in if you had a mind to run away, but high enough that if you got hit, you wouldn't flop out into the crowd.

Women in shimmering silver dresses were bringing drinks to the crowd, and men with numbers stuck onto the brims of their hats were taking bets. It didn't take her long to figure out where to sign up for a fight. There was a big sign hanging in the corner with an arrow that pointed down toward a tiny desk.

Only a couple people bitched when Cassie bumped into them. For the most part, she just received sour stares and a few unhelpful shoves. Ignoring the haters, she continued pushing her way through the crowd. All of them were just jealous she was about to make one of their fighters her bitch. Anyone who thought they could stop her could fuck right the fuck off.

Cassie swayed just a bit as she approached the counter. She didn't think this was the kind of place that cared if you were drunk or not, but she tried to keep from listing to the side as she stood there.

"I'd like to sign up for the first available fight." Her eyes didn't want to focus, but she could worry about that when she was in the ring.

The man behind the counter tipped his cap back so he could get a better look at her. "Are you sure? The next guy up is a real bruiser."

"Just put my name down in your little book." She turned to ShadowLily and gave her a look that said *what in the fuck, I thought I was pretty clear.*

"It's your face, darling," the man muttered as he scrawled something on the paper.

"It might be your face if you call me darling again," Cassie snapped. "Now, where can I get a beer?"

"Better drink it quick. You're up next." He pointed past him toward a bar at the back of the room. "Good luck."

Cassie pushed her way through the crowd toward the bar. When she reached the counter, she slapped her hand on it. "I need a beer, and I don't have a lot of time."

A girl in some kind of sparkly crop top set a beer down in front of her. "That will be a silver, honey."

She tossed the coin on the bar and took a sip from her beer. "What's with all the cutesy nicknames?"

ShadowLily grinned. "Just wait till you see what they called you on the betting board." She poked her friend in the ribs. "Half-pint."

"Fuck, no one wants a half a pint of anything," Cassie grumbled as she glared across the room at the man who took down her name.

"With ten to one odds against you, I'll clean up if you win." ShadowLily showed Cassie her betting sheet. "I put a gold on you. Don't let me down."

"You do realize I have to let the guy hit me three times before I can even fight back, right?" Cassie smiled as she waved down one of the men taking bets and put a gold on herself. Hopefully, betting on your own fight wasn't frowned upon.

"I thought all the extra beer was so you wouldn't feel a thing." ShadowLily tipped her friend's cup back to her lips. "Drink up."

"Maybe I can win if I just throw up on him?" Cassie giggled and then let out a huge belch.

ShadowLily wrapped an arm around the tiny tank's shoulders and moved them toward the ring. "How about a little less throwing up and a little more kicking ass? You're out there representing the guild. Let's make sure you get a win."

That was the thing with joining a guild; you couldn't be a dick to anyone because your actions reflected on the entire guild. Not that she wanted to be mean to people, but sometimes you just wanted to talk shit. Shit-talk built fucking character.

Cassie smiled as the man at the side of the ring motioned for her to enter. There hadn't ever been a good fight that didn't have a little trash talk to start. People are still quoting Ali. *Float like a butterfly, sting like a bee.* It was one of the greatest sports quotes of all time, mostly because he backed it up.

That was the thing with trash talk; it only worked if you could also walk the walk.

She wasn't too worried. The fighters leaving the ring as she entered didn't look very tough. They were about Tim's size, and Cassie was pretty sure she could take their fearless leader out without breaking a sweat. All she had to do was take three hits, and then she could let loose. The beer should help diminish the pain she'd feel tonight, but she'd be sore as hell tomorrow.

Cassie moved to her mark and waited.

An announcer stepped into the ring. "Tonight, for your viewing pleasure, we have a fight that will be burned into your memories forever. In this corner, we have Half-pint, here to take on our champion."

Champion? Oh, fuck. I'm totally screwed.

The announcer pointed to the other end of the ring. "Now it's my sincere pleasure to introduce the destroyer of jaws, the purveyor of destruction, *SMASHHHHHHHHH!*"

Everyone in the crowd chanted "Smash" over and over until a massive man jumped over the railing and into the ring. He looked at Cassie with eyes as hard as granite as he sneered. Smash turning his back on his opponent and flexed his arms, and the crowd went wild. A lady in the front almost swooned.

He was obviously the crowd's favorite, and while she was confident she'd survive a few hits, those hits were going to be a lot harder to swallow because of the man's size. Cassie kind of felt like David Spade when he got into the fight with Chris Farley in *Tommy Boy*. Her face wasn't going to hurt so much "here or here" as it was going to hurt all the fuck over.

Getting hit by one of those fists would feel like it was a four by four.

Nothing in her quest said she had to take the full force of the blows. It just said she had to let him hit her three times before she could fight back. As an avoidance tank, she couldn't just dodge them. The entire point of the exercise was to get hit, but maybe she could spin with the hits to minimize the impact.

She sure hoped so.

The announcer looked at Cassie. "Are you ready?"

Cassie wiped the sweat from her forehead and tried to focus her eyes. "As ready as I'll ever be."

Turning away from Cassie, the announcer pointed at Smash. "Are you ready?"

Smash just flexed and growled.

The announcer made his way to the side of the ring and climbed on top of the railing before he looked at both of them one last time and roared, "Fight!"

Smash played to the crowd for a moment before fixing on Cassie. "Sure you're up for this, little girl?"

"You probably get asked that a lot," Cassie snarked. "Not a lot of second dates, I'm guessing." She held up her hand with her fingers about an inch apart.

"That big mouth of yours won't save you here." Smash started lumbering forward.

Probably shouldn't have egged him on when I have to let him hit me.

"Fuck," Cassie grumbled as she started to circle with the much bigger man.

Smash didn't waste any time. He moved quickly with his fist cocked back to end the fight in one blow. Cassie tried to move with the punch, but her brain and her feet weren't aligned. Instead of turning her body so she rolled with the hit, she ended up ducking under it.

Smash's fist caught the back of her shoulder and sent Cassie tumbling to the ground. She rolled a few feet until she hit the barrier. Thankfully, the big oaf was more interested in the crowd than following up his attack. He walked around the ring with his arms held high as if hitting a girl a third his size was a major accomplishment.

A groan escaped Cassie's lips as she stood back up. Her adrenaline was doing its best to counteract the alcohol in her system. So far her vision had cleared the tiniest bit, but that didn't help her shoulder feel better.

Tomorrow was going to be a shitty day.

Smash finished his victory lap and came toward her again. Cassie's feet didn't betray her this time as she rolled with his next punch, making it more of a glancing hit than an actual strike. She would have congratulated herself on the move but getting hit still hurt, whether you took the full force of the shot or not.

The big fucker wasn't done with her yet. His fist smashed into her side, lifting her from the ground. There hadn't been a way to dodge that shot, at least not that Cassie knew of. She lay on the dirt floor thinking about her life choices.

"Whatever possessed me to become a tank?" she mumbled to herself as the crowd cheered for Smash.

"You say something to me?" Smash growled from across the ring. He leaned against the rail as if he didn't have a care in the world. Grabbing one of the patron's beers, he took a swig before handing it back.

Now that Cassie didn't have to get hit, she was pretty sure she could avoid all of his attacks. This fucker was about to learn the meaning of "the bigger they are, the harder they fall."

"Only that you hit like a girl. But I'm not surprised after what we talked about earlier." Cassie held up her hand again, insulting his manhood. Why guys always fell for that shit, she didn't know, but if you wanted a man to shut up, all you had to do was accuse him of having a small dick.

Smash roared like Cassie had just told the world's best mom joke on the playground before he rushed forward to end the fight. He opened his arms wide, obviously thinking to crush her against him until she gave up, but the last thing she wanted was to be pulled against his big hairy man-chest.

Two tree trunk-sized arms closed on thin air as Cassie dove through Smash's legs. She came to a stop behind him and spun on her knees while inflicting her first hit of the match. Cassie's tiny fist slammed into the family jewels, but what would have brought a normal man down only seemed to enrage the hulking brute.

Before Cassie could move out of the way, one of Smash's massive feet slammed into her stomach. The kick sent her tumbling across the ring until she crashed into the wooden barrier. Tim was right; she did end up getting thrown through the air a lot.

One of the many perks of being tiny.

Trunks For Arms grabbed Cassie, lifting her in the air like a girl with her first doll. "You're going to pay for that, bitch." He pressed her tighter against him, attempting to crush the air from her lungs.

"I already am." Cassie grimaced. "Not sure what you had for lunch, but your breath is fucking atrocious." She tried to look defiant but she was worried the fight was almost over.

Cassie took a deep breath right before Smash tightened his arms again. Now she knew what it felt like when an anaconda got hold of you. Getting the air crushed out of her didn't feel much better than when she thought she might drown following Shadow-Lily through the underwater cave.

Sure, the ride out had been fun, but the thought of drowning just sucked.

Cassie stared up into Smash's smiling face and couldn't wait to wipe the idiotic look from it. She started wiggling around, trying to get free, but it was fucking impossible. All her actions seemed to do was make the asshole excited.

Smash grinned at her. "I knew deep down you really liked me. Maybe after you wake up, you'd like to come to my room? I'll show you why they *really* call me Smash."

Her skin started to crawl. The thought of sleeping with this hulking ass-clown made her want to puke. There wasn't any way she could wriggle free, but that didn't mean it was over. If the idiot had just kept his mouth shut, she might have lost, but now she was determined to make him pay.

Cassie tried to push herself away from him and managed to get an additional inch or two. Then she craned her head back. *This is going to hurt.* She snapped her head forward, ducking her chin to her chest as she did so.

Crack!

Blood splattered across Cassie's forehead as it slammed into Smash's nose. She didn't give him time to recover. Instead, she reared back again. Her head snapped back three more times before the asshole let her go.

Smash had his hands up, clutching his broken nose and massaging his jaw. He was groaning, but that wasn't going to stop her from ending the fight right now. This time she wasn't throwing an off-balance punch into his balls. Instead, it was a full-throttle kick to the man-parts.

Smash went down in a heap. Before he could get his shit back together, Cassie slammed her knee into the back of his head and followed with a kick to the face. The big fucker was down for the count. She'd done it. The fight was over.

The crowd went nuts.

The noise hit her. Now that the fight was over, she couldn't keep her intoxication at bay. Cassie stumbled toward the edge of the ring. She paused for a moment, watching the crowd spin around her like images in a kaleidoscope, then puked all over the floor.

A moment later, an arm wrapped around her waist, and ShadowLily pressed a cold cloth to her head. "Let's get you back to the inn."

Cassie looked around, not really seeing the ring. "I won, right?"

"Yep, and you readjusted his nose and the babymakers." ShadowLily laughed. "It was one hell of a fight."

"You'll have to tell me about it tomorrow." Cassie sagged against her. "I'm not sure I'll remember all of it."

"I'm sure the bruises will remind you." ShadowLily helped her friend outside and whistled for a cart.

They climbed into the open one-horse cart, and Cassie sunk into the cushion. "Can't you just call your boy toy to fix me up?"

"Tim's more than a boy toy. At least, I think he is." ShadowLily looked away from her friend, unwilling to watch her reaction to what she was about to say next. It scared her to say the words out loud, like saying them might destroy everything.

"He might be the one," ShadowLily whispered.

When her friend didn't say anything smart, the rogue looked at her. ShadowLily was afraid of the incredulous expression Cassie might be wearing, but if you couldn't share your feelings with your best friend, what was the point of having one? Her eyes moved over Cassie's face, and she let out a sigh of relief.

The tank had fallen asleep.

CHAPTER SIXTY-SIX

"Come here for a moment, lad," Ironbeard grumbled. Tim put down the last of the bars he'd been working on and moved to stand by his boss. Ironbeard wasn't really a let's talk kind of guy. Mostly Tim liked that the dwarf showed him how to do something and then left him alone. It gave him time to think and to come up with more of his wacky plans.

"What's going on, boss?" Tim pulled off his gloves and set them on the counter.

The smith stroked his beard for a moment, thinking about how to phrase what was on his mind. "I just wanted to say that I've heard what you are doing in the slums, and I'm proud of you."

Not exactly sure how to respond, Tim mumbled, "Thank you."

"The real question is, what in the hell are you doing working here when those people need you?" The smith took a look at the bars Tim had made and shrugged. "Not that I don't appreciate the help."

Tim wasn't exactly sure how to say it. Did the NPCs know about the contracts they signed? He decided to just go with it.

What was the worst that could happen? "The contract I signed to pay for my food and lodging requires me to work. I decided to work with you because I thought learning a skill would be beneficial."

"But why do it at all? None of those bastards at the temple are hurting for gold." Ironbeard poked his head into the front of the shop to make sure no one had wandered in. "Your inn room couldn't possibly cost that much."

Tim smiled. He didn't even know what his inn room would cost if he had to pay for it. "Unlike the temple, I only charge what people can afford for my services. I make a little money, but not the kind you could retire on tomorrow."

The dwarf watched him for a moment, trying to decide if Tim was telling the truth. He seemed to be skeptical about someone not charging an arm and a leg for healing. "Well, I just wanted you to know it's a good thing you're doing. I was actually thinking of giving you some time off every day so you could do more healing."

Ironbeard wagged his finger in Tim's face. "But only if you use the time for healing the needy."

"I might just take you up on that offer." Tim's face grew serious. "I still want to learn more about the work you do here, so I'll promise to use the extra time for healing if you promise to teach me something new every couple of weeks."

"You've got a deal." Ironbeard stuck out his hand.

Tim clasped the dwarf's hand. "So, does this new deal of ours start today?"

The dwarf clapped Tim on the back. "You little shit." He grinned. "Go ahead and get out of here, but if I ever need healing, I expect it to be free of charge."

"Never do anything for free that you can get paid for." Tim laughed at the expression on Ironbeard's face. The dwarf was stuck somewhere between rage and acceptance. "I'm just kidding. If you ever need healing, I'll be happy to do it."

"Good, because I was about to change my mind about letting

you go early." He watched Tim as he walked out of the smithy. "Still might if you start slacking off."

Tim left the little shop and headed into the market. He hadn't noticed anyone tracking him since the man with the orange sash died, but it paid to be cautious, especially with Jepsom's representatives making new threats.

Thankfully, he'd taken the lesson his death had taught him to heart. He now carried several different pants and shirt combinations with him. As long as someone didn't see him change clothes, it would be hard for anyone to track him. Tim made his first wardrobe change and continued out of the market.

He thought about using some of his extra time to go and see the high priest, but he really wanted to make it back to the inn. Ernie had found someone who worked in real estate for him to speak to, and Tim wanted to lock up some deals before he made any changes to the slums. If he didn't own the properties, the only people benefitting from the gold he spent would be whoever owned the properties.

Not that the rejuvenation effort was only about making gold, but if someone was going to make gold off of his labor, why shouldn't it be him? The last thing Tim wanted was to make his part of the slums so nice none of the residents could afford to live or work there.

At least most of the buildings near the inn looked like closed commercial properties and not homes. He wouldn't feel like shit for buying an empty building and turning it into something nice. Once he owned a few other properties, he'd get the cobbles put in and place the market kiosk in the inn.

People listing items on the kiosk would save money by not having to travel as far to list them. Hopefully, the money they saved would be spent at the shops lining the street as they left. All he had to do was fix up the buildings and get the right kind of shops in, and he was sitting on a money-generating machine.

If Tim could obtain enough in-game currency, he could afford to send some home to his parents and have enough left over to make a payment on his delayed student loans. Then he could become an adventurer without worrying that he was letting everyone down. Sure he might lose his payment from the company, but if he played his cards right, there was a chance he could make more by taking a risk.

Not exactly a risk when I have five back up plans, Tim thought to himself as he continued walking.

He did wonder if he could keep his job with Ironbeard once he became an adventurer, but he'd worry about that afterward. What he needed to find out now was what the rest of the group wanted. Gaston was an NPC, and he'd been helpful, but they couldn't drag him around forever. The man had to have some kind of life outside of helping them.

Tim was a hundred percent sure ShadowLily was going the adventurer route, and Cassie was probably on board. JaKobi might not be ready to make the decision yet.

Tim would feel a million times better if he knew he would be taking the plunge with a full group already in place.

The only way to find out what everyone wanted was to ask them, something he'd neglected to do for far too long. Some leader he was. All he'd done so far was follow his own agenda, assuming everyone was on board with it. Things had worked out so far, but he had to do better. Friends deserve to feel like they are being included in the group's decision-making, not given orders by the world's worst boss.

Not to mention his girlfriend. There wasn't a woman in the world who would put up with a man who was constantly telling them what to do. At least, he'd never met a man or woman who enjoyed being nagged. ShadowLily was quickly becoming the most important person in his life, and her feelings and desires mattered to him. Tim couldn't say when it had happened, but somewhere along the line, he'd started considering what she would think before he did things.

That was the thing with love. *Once you were in it, you realized that when you made the other person happy, it made you happy.* It was a true partnership when both people in the relationship were selfless. Take care of each other, and everything will turn out fine.

He'd been slacking on his end, and it was time to change that.

Tim smiled as he neared the arch. Two familiar guards were standing in the archway watching something. Last time Tim had seen the guards take an interest in the slums, someone had been stabbed. He didn't get the same vibe right now, so he wondered what was up.

"What do you think those people are doing gathering around the side of the inn?" Chris asked his partner.

"I don't know. Maybe they are trying to guess the airspeed of a swallow." Barry elbowed Chris in the side.

Tim stepped up and peered between them. "Actually, I think they are waiting for me."

"Oh, get a load of this guy, Chris. Thinks he's the duke of the slums," Barry sniggered.

"Duke of the slums." Chris slapped his knee. "That's a good one. I was just going to ask him if he'd started some kind of cult we need to be worried about." Chris looked at Tim. "Anything you'd like to confess?"

"You mean besides the cult I started, and the fact I know how fast a swallow can fly?" Tim stepped between the men before walking under the arch to enter the slums.

"No one knows how fast a swallow flies. That's the whole fucking point!" Barry shouted after him.

"See how he didn't respond to you" Chris poked Barry in the ribs. "Maybe he really *is* duke of the slums."

Tim gazed into the sky as a light rain started to fall. When he'd first entered the game, he'd hated that it always rained on him when he came back to the inn. Now he was starting to like it. The rain let him know he was close to home.

Nothing felt as good as being at home surrounded by the people he cared about.

CHAPTER SIXTY-SEVEN

"You worthless piece of shit!" Cassie raged.

Tim chuckled as the mug she threw at him was incinerated by JaKobi's flameshield. "If you needed healing, you should have come by the shop."

"I've been hungover and in pain all day." Cassie waved her hand. "Couldn't you have just splashed me with water before you left?"

Tim was pretty sure if he'd splashed her with water while she was passed out, it would have been a lot worse than a thrown mug.

"If I'd known you were hurt, I would have. You two must have crashed right before I left." ShadowLily hadn't come to bed, but Tim had found the two of them draped over the couches downstairs when he had walked out. He looked at ShadowLily, hoping she would help extricate him from the situation.

"Don't look at me." ShadowLily gave Tim a sly smile. "I can't deal with her when she's being dramatic."

Cassie stood up and started pacing back and forth. "Dramatic. Dramatic! I've been stuck by the toilet all day, but lover boy could have fixed it in an instant." She turned and scowled at the healer.

Tim laughed as his healing orb hit Cassie in the face and forced her to stop her tirade. He tried not to gloat because being hungover was the worst. "You were saying?" Tim quickly cast root on her before she could charge him and then followed it up with Cleanse."

"What in the hell was that?" Cassie raged as she wiped off her face.

"Feeling better?" Tim asked hesitantly as he moved toward ShadowLily for protection.

Cassie's glare could have melted the paint off a car. "Maybe, but that was uncalled for."

"Splash me with water. Don't splash me with water. I'm confused now." Tim looked at JaKobi, and the fire mage just shrugged.

ShadowLily gave him a quick kiss. "Go take a bath. You stink."

"Is that what the smell is?" Cassie grinned. "I thought Ernie was making a new concoction."

Tim walked past Cassie on the way to the bathroom and whispered. "You might want to consider taking a bath yourself."

The swift kick to his ass almost sent Tim sprawling. The extra points he'd put into dexterity really saved him from looking like a total fool. He spun around and looked at Cassie's defiant expression before deciding that he was better off accepting the payback for his comment.

He laughed, thinking about Cassie waking up with an inked-on mustache next time he found her passed out on the couch. She reminded him of his little sister, and he'd never let his sister get away with kicking him in the ass. That was the thing with payback; it was a merciless bitch.

Tim was tempted to run back to Cassie so he could mess up her hair, but he wasn't quite willing to risk it. Instead, he continued to the bathroom. Ah, the hell with it. He couldn't resist taking a parting shot. "If that smell doesn't go away, everyone will know it wasn't just me!"

Dodging the second mug she'd thrown at him in under five minutes, Tim ducked around the corner. A moment later, he popped his head back out, hoping Cassie didn't have another mug in hand. "JaKobi, let the people waiting for healing know I'll be with them soon."

"You got it, boss." The fire mage stood and walked out the entrance.

Tim closed the bathroom door behind him, happy to be alone for a minute. He turned on the water to fill the bath and smiled. Scratch that. His bath would be a million times better if his sexy half-elf seductress was in here with him. There were some activities that were more fun with a partner. Taking a bath was one of them.

Tim walked out of the inn with ShadowLily by his side. She came to help out with security when she didn't have anything better to do. He was lucky to have her since security wasn't a fun job. It normally meant standing around for hours doing absolutely nothing. It was nice to have her and even better for JaKobi, who'd get to spend the afternoon grinding experience to catch up.

Their fire mage was a little behind the curve but moving up quickly. Dude became highly motivated once he found his place after doing bounties with them. If Tim were honest with himself, JaKobi might pass him if he didn't get back to business soon. Between his two jobs and trying to get the slums going, he'd fallen behind his companions. At least he didn't have to worry about his class change quest. Not having to spend a week grinding missions was going to be nice.

JaKobi was leaning against the door of the healing shack. Tim gave him a quick nod and pointed behind him at his girlfriend. "Thanks for keeping an eye on Judy and the shack, but ShadowLily decided to give you the afternoon off."

JaKobi stepped in front of Tim before he could enter. "You might want me to stay for a few minutes when you see who's inside."

Doubt started to burrow through his mind. "Another of Jepsom's men?"

Before the fire mage could answer, ShadowLily cut him off. "You didn't tell me the cardinal sent someone here. How are we going to keep you safe if you don't give us all the details?"

Tim looked at JaKobi and quickly realized he wasn't going to get any help from him. He turned back toward ShadowLily and smiled sheepishly. "It slipped my mind."

"Weak." ShadowLily pulled Tim close. "I don't want you dying on me, so you have to tell me what kind of trouble you're getting into."

JaKobi smiled at the two of them. They were on the border of being so cute he wanted to gag, but secretly he hoped to have the same kind of relationship one day. "The trouble seems to be of the half-orc variety."

Tim's face went pale. "Malvonis is here?"

"Didn't give me a name." JaKobi shrugged. "Just showed me a big knife and said he'd be waiting inside."

"Where's Judy?" Tim looked around, hoping to see her outside.

JaKobi worked his mouth like he was sucking on something sour. "She said not to worry about her, that she had work to do." He made air quotes. "I'm not leaving because some asshole with a knife wants to harass the boss."

Turning away from the mage, Tim looked at ShadowLily. "Go get Cassie and Gaston, but stay outside until I call for you." He turned to face the door and nodded to JaKobi. "You're with me."

"You got it, boss." The fire mage stepped forward and pushed open the door.

Tim walked into the shack first and was pleasantly surprised not to see Judy cut to ribbons. Malvonis was sitting in a chair by the wall, eating something that looked suspiciously like grapes. He had a smile on his face that made his tusks stick out a bit farther than normal.

Judy had finished getting the towels and the water ready and was about to step outside. "Tell your friend he'd better be picking up his own damn seeds."

Tim looked at her stern face and the pits on the ground. "JaKobi, do you mind?"

The fire mage lifted one eyebrow in question, and when Tim gave him a subtle nod, he started casting a spell. With one wave of his hand, the scattered seeds on the floor burst into flame. All that was left of them were tiny wisps of smoke.

Tim watched Malvonis but didn't see any hint of surprise, although he was pretty sure JaKobi's spell got the message across. The half-orc now knew Tim had a fire mage on his side who was good enough to incinerate several targets at once. The message also said, don't fuck with my place, or you might be next.

"Judy, I'm going to have a word with our guest. When you see him leave, send in the first client."

"Of course, sir." Judy flashed Tim a brief smile, scowled at Malvonis, and closed the door.

Malvonis stood up from the chair and tucked the remaining grapes inside his cloak. "You've got a nice little racket going on here, but the cardinal wants it to stop."

"So Jepsom sent you after his man failed to get the answer he wanted?" Tim moved to stand in front of the sitting thief. "I thought we had an understanding about you not coming back here?"

"When I took the job, I didn't know I'd be coming back here." Malvonis gave Tim a sly smile. "Can't we just make this easy on each other? The message from the cardinal is simple: Stop healing, or things will get worse."

A ball of flame appeared in JaKobi's hand. "Is that a threat?"

"Call it a friendly suggestion." Malvonis shrugged his massive shoulders. "If this situation was going to come to violence, I wouldn't have announced myself. I find that killing goes much easier when the person you are trying to murder doesn't expect it."

Tim held up his hand to silence JaKobi's reply. "Consider your message delivered. Kindly tell the cardinal I'm not interested in his offer."

The half-orc's smile disappeared. "He won't be pleased with your answer."

"Then he can take it up with the high priest, whose blessing I have." Tim was starting to get worked up, but he'd be damned if he was going to be the first one to lose his temper. "I actually needed to see him, so I'll just fill him in on Jepsom's messengers in the morning."

Malvonis held up his hands in front of him in a slow the fuck down gesture. "Seems as though I've found myself in the middle of a political squabble I'd rather not be a part of. Being on the bad side of either of those men isn't good for your health. Despite what you might think about my profession as a whole, it's much safer than playing politics."

"Tell me about it," Tim groused as he thought of everything he'd done in the game so far. All of it, every little thing he'd been through, was because of Cardinal Jepsom's ambition. "I'd much rather the two of them worked this out themselves, so I could stop looking over my shoulder for who was going to try to kill me next."

"Not going to happen any time soon," Malvonis grumbled. "I don't know what you did to piss that guy off, but he's got a real hard-on for you now."

Tim shook his head in disgust. His life would be so much easier if Jepsom simply disappeared. "I get the feeling the cardinal's support inside the temple is waning. Might be a good time to pick the other side."

If Tim could get Malvonis out of the picture, his life would sure as hell be a lot simpler. Shit, if he could get him to fight for the high priest instead, he might not even have to fight with Jepsom himself. In a perfect world, he'd be able to orchestrate the whole thing, but inside *The Etheric Coast*, he didn't have that kind of pull.

"I don't pick sides. The only thing I do is take a job and see it through to the end. If coming down here and roughing you up gets me square with that evil bastard, I'll do it." Malvonis eyed Tim, making sure his hand didn't stray toward his dagger. "But I'm just as inclined to call it a day as long as you help me out."

JaKobi extinguished the fireball he'd been holding. "Why would you do that?"

Malvonis shook his head, clearly asking himself the same question. "Normally, I wouldn't, but the cardinal just wanted the message delivered. He doesn't want you dead." He scratched absentmindedly at a scar on his arm. "At least not yet."

Looking around the shack, the half-orc started to smile. "People working for the cardinal have a way of disappearing. I'm not keen on joining their ranks."

"I might have disappeared a few of them." Tim wondered if he'd said too much. "But I'm sure the cardinal is much more efficient at it than I am."

The half-orc started walking toward the door. "As long as you're okay putting on a show, I'll just leave. After I tell the cardinal I've roughed you up, I think I'll take a vacation until the rest of the temple's drama is sorted out."

Tim looked at JaKobi. "Tell the others to stand down."

Grinning, Malvonis stepped out of the way so the fire mage could leave the room. "You had people ready in case I attacked. Smart, very smart." His tusks jutted out when the half-orc's mouth opened in a grin. "I think I'm starting to like you, kid."

"I don't like taking chances." Tim looked at the half-orc, and despite Malvonis' change in tactics, there was no way he could trust this man not to come back and kill him if the cardinal asked him too.

Anything Tim said to the thief right now might as well be said straight to the cardinal. "So, what's your plan?"

Malvonis grabbed one of the pots full of water. Turning away from Tim, he kicked open the door and stormed out. Before walking down the steps, he threw the pot back inside, where it shattered, splashing water everywhere. "And don't you forget what I fucking told you!"

The half-orc pulled up his hood and stalked toward the exit of the slums. Tim watched him go, wondering just how much trouble he was in. If the cardinal sent Malvonis to kill him in the future, there was a good chance he'd end up dead. Getting to level ten and becoming an adventurer was looking more appealing by the second.

Tim pondered his options, realizing there was really just one question he needed to ask. How long would it be before the cardinal took the next step? He had to see Paul and find out what it was going to take to end this. Tim had finally reached the end of his rope with that bastard. Jepsom's threats had to stop; he had more important things to worry about. It was time to turn the tables and let the cardinal find out what it felt like to be powerless.

Judy looked into the healing shack to make sure nothing else had been destroyed and started cleaning up the mess. He made a mental note to give his assistant a hearty bonus at the end of the night.

Turning away from the mess, he looked at the members of his guild. "We'll talk as soon as I finish healing these folks."

"That's fine, but none of us are going anywhere." ShadowLily frowned at Malvonis' back as he slowly continued on his way to the arch.

"I knew there was a reason I kept you around." Tim kissed ShadowLily on the lips.

"I was thinking it was because of the great sex and my sparkling personality, but now we've gotten to the truth of the matter. You just like my knives." The half-elven thief pulled out her blades and spun them on her palms.

"As long as you aren't throwing them at me." Tim immediately thought about the time he'd had a teacup on his head. He'd never be dumb enough to make that bet again.

"You two make me wanna barf." Cassie chuckled. "Now that the drama alert is over, I'm going to finish my bath. Scream really loud if you need me before then."

Tim smiled at the thought of a naked Cassie jumping out of one of the windows with her staff in hand, ready to save them all. If that ever happened, he'd have to get her picture put on a coffee mug.

Gaston ignored their byplay, focusing his attention on JaKobi. "Do you know how to play Kill the King?" He wrapped an arm around the man's shoulders and started leading him to a little table set up outside of the door. "Why don't I show you?"

If JaKobi was smart, he'd keep his coins in his pouch. Rule one was to never play cards with Gaston if you wanted to leave with any of your gold.

Tim looked at the gathered faces and said to the first person in line. "I'm sorry for the delay, ma'am. Please come inside, and I'll get you fixed right up."

Judy helped the older woman up the three stairs and into the shack. This was what it was all about. He was a healer, and these people needed him. There was no way he would stop when they deserved a fighting chance to thrive. Like a flower growing in the cracks of a sidewalk, life would find a way.

His job was to make that life a little more bearable.

CHAPTER SIXTY-EIGHT

"I need a beer," Tim called as he entered the inn.

Ernie smiled at the young healer. "And some food, if I'm not mistaken."

Liz came out of the kitchen carrying a tray covered in bowls with little silver lids and loaves of hard, crusty bread. Another night of stew. Tim grimaced. But hey, at least the food had gotten better since Liz started. Not that she did the cooking, but she was helping Ernie vet new cooks to take over the kitchen.

To be fair, the reason the chefs were making so much stew was because she wanted to create a baseline to judge them by. If they all cooked different meals, how people voted might depend on the person or the day. Now they'd had one meal from each of the cooks, and the guild could put in their votes for who they liked best.

Each dish seemed better than the last to Tim, but he was getting sick of stew. He might love a bowl of the stuff, especially on a cold and rainy night, but not for every dinner for two weeks in a row.

It was a little much.

The bowl in front of him smelled divine. It was the first time someone had made more of a cream base than a traditional stew. He felt like he was eating a steak version of chicken and dumplings with potatoes instead of dumplings.

That was the thing with food, Tim might not be able to cook it or to describe it very well, but he sure as hell knew how to eat it. He ripped off the heel of the bread and dipped it into his bowl. When it had soaked up enough of the sauce, he ate it ravenously.

Tim looked up after finishing his bread and noticed that everyone else in the room was watching him. "What?" he mumbled as he ripped off another chunk from the loaf.

"We've all been waiting to find out what in the fuck Malvonis wanted, and you haven't even looked at us." ShadowLily sat next to him. "So, what's up?"

Tim set down his bread and covered the bowl of stew with the lid, knowing full well by the time they were done talking, his dinner wouldn't be hot anymore. "Jepsom sent him to tell me to stop healing people outside the temple."

Taking a sip of beer to clear his throat, Tim continued, "Malvonis was annoyed when he found out the high priest and Jepsom weren't on the same page when it came to my healing. I'd say he left because he wanted to avoid pissing off Paul, but I don't think the bastard does anything unless he wants to. That means we probably haven't seen the last of him."

Tim polished off his beer and motioned for Liz to bring him another one. "On the plus side, if we end up in a confrontation with the cardinal and have to take him out, our potential Malvonis issue disappears." Tim looked around the table at the shocked faces. "Just saying."

"Makes sense to me. Why fight when you can get two of your enemies to wipe each other out?" JaKobi tapped a finger on his chin in thought. "It's kind of brilliant, really. Like when the Sith use the trade federation to get shit done."

"You know, not everything can be tied back to a *Star Wars* movie plot." Cassie glared at the fire mage.

"Just try me," JaKobi fired back, grinning ear from ear.

Tim smiled at the fire mage. He couldn't help it. JaKobi's love of all things *Star Wars* was infectious. He was just about to try to trip him up when ShadowLily elbowed him in the ribs.

"Let's not get off-track," ShadowLily looked at the two of them. "What we decide to do next is important."

"Speaking of important." Tim deflected answering whatever her next question was going to be by asking one of his own. "I've been meaning to find out what everyone's plans are after they hit level ten and complete their class change quests."

"Maybe we should worry about the super-assassin the cardinal hired to rough you up." Cassie looked at Tim incredulously. "Priorities, man, priorities."

"Not much I can do until I go see the high priest. I'm not sure the five of us are strong enough to take out the cardinal even if we wanted to, not that I would even try without Paul's blessing."

JaKobi snorted. "Too bad Jepsom doesn't feel the same way about taking you out."

"Tell me about it," Cassie grumbled.

"You should see the high priest tomorrow." ShadowLily looked at Tim, her face etched with concern. She put one finger over his lips before he could speak. "Before work."

"I was afraid you were going to say that." Tim groaned. "I'm going to take the rest of this food up to my room and get ready for bed." He mock-glared at his girlfriend. "Apparently, I have an early-morning appointment."

"There are some perks to going to bed early." ShadowLily picked up her own bowl and headed for the stairs. "I'll see you up there."

Tim knew she was being flirty to try to keep his mind off what might happen tomorrow. Going to see Paul wasn't without risk. He'd already been banned from practicing at the temple for defying Jepsom's orders. Going back inside might mean his death if the wrong people found him before he made it to the high priest.

He started walking toward the stairs but paused and turned to face the members of his guild. "Remember to think about what you want out of your time in the game. I want whatever we do next to benefit all of us."

JaKobi nodded. "You've got it, boss."

"I'm already doing what I want. The only thing that would make it better is more money." Cassie smiled. "You've really gotta quit your job so we can do bounties during the day."

"That would be kinda awesome." JaKobi smiled, thinking about all the loot they could earn.

"So, you both want to be adventurers?" Tim thought about how easily they'd made the choice and how hard he was struggling with his.

"You don't?" Cassie asked in disbelief.

Tim almost laughed at the look of shock on her face. "I didn't say that. It's just that I need to have a few things in place before I can take the leap."

Cassie huffed. "Better get on it. We're all waiting on you."

Tapping his spoon on the lid covering his soup, Tim sighed. "You're going to have to wait a little longer—and don't make that face. We've done tons of cool stuff so far."

"Yeah, but think about all the stuff we're missing out on while you're at work." She elbowed JaKobi in an attempt to get him to agree with her. "Right?"

The fire mage grinned. "Yes, we've done lots of cool stuff."

"Pussy," Cassie said as she poked JaKobi in the ribs hard enough to make him grunt before she turned her attention back to Tim. "Seriously, think of all the stuff we could do if you didn't have to work."

Tim had come into the game with a plan. He was here to make enough gold to send some real-world currency home to his family and pay off his student loans. Until Tim knew he could accomplish those feats as an adventurer, he had to keep his options open.

It felt like he was being pulled in one direction, and he had no idea if the game was manipulating him into becoming an adventurer or if it was something he truly wanted. Tim felt alive when they were out running bounties and conquering dungeons, but he couldn't let that excitement overrun his pragmatism. Sometimes you had to stick with boring and reliable.

But you also had to be willing to risk it all if you wanted to succeed.

Was he willing to put his future on the line by dedicating all of his time in-game to making more money, or was he going to stick with the basics and come out with a guaranteed payout? It was hard to put all your effort into a dream that might not pay out in the end.

But he wanted to be an adventurer badly enough to dedicate himself to his dream completely.

The hardest part for him was knowing that he was doing it for the right reasons. He didn't want the fame that followed some of the gamers when they finally called it quits. Tim only wanted this to work because of what it could mean for his future.

Gaming was something he loved, and making money at it would be the ultimate job. Working together with a team to take down the biggest baddies in the game was something he lived for when he was behind the screen. Now that he was on the screen, did he really expect those feelings to be different?

Part of him was dead-set on staying firm and doing the job he'd been assigned, but the other part of him, the part that fed his imagination, was already setting things up. Tim's work in the slums wasn't bringing in any money yet, but it would, and with a safety net in place, he felt a lot better about making the switch from worker to adventurer.

Tim smiled as he realized he'd become lost in his thoughts while JaKobi and Cassie were waiting for an answer to her question. He decided to play it off for now and mark them down for a more serious discussion later. "You know me. I've got to plan things out before I make a decision."

"By 'plan,' he means shout out orders and pray that everything doesn't turn to shit in an instant," Cassie said drolly to JaKobi.

"Whatever Tim's doing seems to be working. I'm more concerned about these guys from the temple showing up and trying to take us out."

"Well, there is always something to look forward to." Tim turned away from his friends and walked up the stairs.

Cassie shouted after him, "We have very different ideas about what to get excited about."

"I don't know. If I was heading upstairs to ShadowLily, I'd be excited too." JaKobi said with a smile.

Cassie elbowed him in the ribs. "Don't be gross. Save that shit for your guy friends."

The fire mage held up his hands in surrender. "I was talking to Gaston."

The assassin picked up his soup and left the room without saying a word. Ernie and Liz followed him out, leaving JaKobi sitting alone with Cassie. "Isn't this soup delicious?" he stammered.

Tim smiled at himself as he watched the two of them from the landing on the stairs. Once he realized Cassie wasn't going to pick a fight, he continued up the stairs to his room. The Guild was becoming more than a group of adventurers. They might even be more than just friends.

To Tim, the guild members already felt like family.

CHAPTER SIXTY-NINE

The streets of Promethia were almost empty this early in the morning.

Tim thought about the traffic around campus in the morning and realized he didn't miss it at all. There was something to be said about some good old fashioned peace and quiet. Not to mention the lack of cars. The air seemed to smell sweeter, but that could just be the game enhancing his experience.

Walking to the temple wouldn't take too long, and it felt much better doing it with boots on. His first day in the game, Tim had made the trek without shoes, and he was happy he'd never have to do that again. Who would have thought finding footwear was such a big deal?

He slowed down as he came to a spot where he could look between the buildings toward the market and the warehouses. Peeking out behind the large structures was the harbor and the docks that helped make this city flourish. Men and women were already working hard on the docks and in the market. They moved like ants swarming over a piece of fallen fruit, setting up stalls, displaying their wares, and loading and unloading boxes from the ships.

The market was the one place that was truly alive all day long. The workers and the shoppers might change, but it was always busy. It was exactly the same kind of environment he wanted to create in the slums. Why shouldn't there be somewhere else to shop?

Especially when the gold that shopping brought in went straight into his pockets.

His stomach did a little flip as the temple steps came into view. It wasn't easy to walk headfirst into what might be a trap, but Tim had to speak to Paul. Thankfully there were people making their way inside for healing or prayer already. Tim hoped he could slip in with the crowd and then find one of the acolytes to take him to the high priest. He might be able to find Paul's chambers on his own, but there was a better chance that he'd end up lost for hours in the temple's winding halls.

Tim ducked his head down as he started up the steps. Jepsom didn't have as many followers as he used to, but he still had eyes and ears all over the temple. He joined the others in line and continued shuffling up the steps until they reached the temple doors.

The inside of the entrance was just as grand as Tim remembered from his first trip. Pillars held up a vaulted ceiling; the place felt as if the roof were in the heavens themselves. It still mystified him to this day how men could use stone in such a way. There was a certain amount of craftsmanship slowly lost in the real world.

When was the last time someone built something that truly inspired people? Tim would have loved to see the look on people's faces when the churches and chapels were built in the middle ages. Imagine coming from a village where you still had thatched roofs and seeing something like the Sistine Chapel or the Notre Dame Cathedral.

It would have been life-changing.

Kind of like deciding to enter *The Etheric Coast* was for Tim. Outside of the game, he would have been stuck in an office crunching numbers and hoping to make a wealthy client even wealthier. Here he was leading the fight against a usurper inside the temple and trying to build something from scratch.

There was something to be said about living in a world where the only thing holding you back was your desire to be successful. Inside the game, people were still completing world firsts. There was a whole new land of opportunities to explore here. Things that no other person had discovered were waiting to be found.

Promethia was literally brand new.

Tim thought about how connected they were back in the real world. You could get in touch with anyone at any time from anywhere in the world. It was nuts, and yet people still seemed to spend more time alone.

Come into *The Etheric Coast,* and you could only send in-game messages that might as well have been physical letters to other players. If you wanted to talk to an NPC, you had to get off your lazy ass and go find them. And for Tim, sending in-game messages kind of broke his immersion. Now that ShadowLily was with him almost all the time, he didn't check his messages as often as he should.

This was his home now, and he would be here for a long time. Whatever he had to do to make the game feel real, he was going to do it. Tim felt like he was LARPing at a Renaissance festival. Only when he went home, he didn't have to get ready for school in the morning.

Now that Tim was well inside the temple, he started to look for one of the younger members the church used for runners. He spotted one across the room and made his way to the boy. The kid, dressed in a simple brown smock, was standing off to the side, waiting to be called to task by one of the brothers.

Plastering a confused smile on his face, Tim approached the boy. "Excuse me, good sir. I was wondering if you could help me?"

The boy looked shocked at being addressed directly. "I can escort you to one of the brothers if you need assistance."

"I do so hate to be a bother." Tim kept his smile in place as he looked around the temple. "It's just that the high priest asked me to meet him here, and I have no idea how to find his chambers."

Now the kid looked slightly panicked. "The high priest?"

"Yes, do you think you can help me track him down?" Tim tried to put just the right note of hopefulness in his voice.

"I can find one of the brothers to escort you." The boy started to turn away from Tim.

"That won't do at all." Tim stopped the boy from turning and slipped a gold coin into his hand. "Let's not waste a brother's time with this. If we get there and he doesn't wish to see me, surely his guards will turn me away at the door."

"I don't know if I should," the kid stammered.

Tim looked directly into the boy's eyes. "I promise you that I have an appointment, and he will be happy to see me." He looked from side to side and lowered his voice to a conspiratorial whisper. "But there are others here who might not be as excited by my intrusion."

The acolyte thought about it for a moment, then reached out to grab Tim's hand. "Follow me." The kid was wearing a look that said it wouldn't be his fault if the guards tossed the man out on his ass.

It took the kid about fifteen minutes to get Tim in front of the giant golden door of the high priest's chambers. They'd passed a number of brothers in the hallway. A few of them stared at them curiously, but none tried to stop them. A few times, he'd held his breath, waiting to be stabbed in the back by one of Jepsom's men, but the attack never came.

The golden door started to swing open, and Tim looked at the boy. "Thanks for your help."

He watched as the kid ran off without saying a word. Maybe he had better places to be, but Tim got the feeling the runner he'd sequestered didn't want to be seen here, at least not with him. With the door open, he walked forward. There was no reason to stand on ceremony. It was time to find out what Paul had in store for him.

The high priest stepped down from his simple wooden throne and walked toward Tim with his hand extended. "I'm happy to see you. When you didn't show up right after Lady Briarthorn's party, I was worried something might have happened to you."

Tim shook Paul's hand. "It's good to see you." He let go and made sure to look the man straight in the eyes. "Nothing has happened to me yet, but Cardinal Jepsom has sent a couple of men down to the slums to stop me from healing."

One of Paul's eyes twitched, and his cheeks turned red. "He *what?*"

"He sent some priest named Dunstin to see me, and when I told him to fuck off, he sent Malvonis." Tim felt the fury coming off of Paul in waves and thought he'd better de-escalate the situation. "But we were able to handle it."

"Sending a brother is one thing, but retaining outside help is something else entirely." Paul turned away from Tim, walked back to his throne, and sat down. "Apparently our efforts to stop the cardinal have only made him bolder."

The high priest let out a heavy sigh. "I hoped removing his top three associates from the temple would be a firm enough reminder of who was in charge, but it seems he has taken my actions as just another slap on the wrist."

Paul shook his head in disgust. "I believed there was still a way to return Cardinal Jepsom to the goddess' light. He was a good man once, not that you could tell by looking at him today. Something has to be done about him," Paul said as he wrung his hands with worry.

Tim wondered if this was going to be the moment he finally got the kill quest. There was no doubt in his mind that destroying Jepsom was the final step in this chain. Every single thing he'd done had brought him closer to this moment. All he needed was for Paul to say the word.

"What do you need me to do?" Tim watched the high priest, his anticipation making him twitchy.

"I think it's time we ended this. Cardinal Jepsom's time amongst the living must be brought to an end. May the goddess have mercy on his soul."

Quest Received: Wrath of the goddess

It's time for you to end Cardinal Jepsom's time on this plane, but it can't be done inside the temple. Paul has scheduled an event to honor the cardinal. It will be held in seven days, and you will be given a copy of the itinerary.

Your reward will be determined by the results.

Accept Quest: Yes/No

Tim quickly accepted the quest.

Paul stood up and extended his hand. "The goddess thanks you." Paul pulled a book that had a faint golden glow around it from his robes. "Her appreciation isn't without benefits." He handed the book to Tim.

The leather binding was hand-stitched, and the golden glow had to be coming from some kind of magic infused into the book. Tim wasn't sure what he was being handed. It could have been a bible, or maybe a weapon for his off hand. He accepted the book and reviewed the flowing script on the cover, which read *Healing Storm*. Was this a spell book?

Thinking back to his first day in the game, Tim opened it. Power seemed to flow through him and he was lifted into the air. When his feet touched the ground a moment later, he knew the spell completely. A prompt appeared in his vision.

Skill Granted: Healing Storm

Rank: Novice Level One

The Goddess Eternia once pointed her hand toward the heavens and bathed an entire city in holy rain. You might not be able to heal a city yet, but a group of five players shouldn't be a problem.

Healing Storm is an AOE (Area of Effect) spell that can heal up to five party members as long as they are standing within the spell's radius.

It was his first AOE spell. As long as everyone crowded together, he could heal all of them with one spell. The mana cost might hurt after a bit, but it saved Tim the trouble of casting separate healing orbs on each person. It would be a real lifesaver, especially in a situation where everyone was taking damage at the same time.

If Tim was able to level the spell up enough, he might even be able to heal through some of the boss' status effects. No more jumping into the river to get rid of the acid. Just keep killing, and he'd be able to keep you alive.

That was his job, after all.

"Paul, this is more than I deserve," Tim mumbled, still not quite believing his luck.

The high priest shook his head from side to side. "For all that you've done in service of the goddess, you deserve it. I trust that when the time comes to carry out this last task, you won't hesitate?"

Tim had to think about it for a moment. He'd waffled about the killing thing for too long. This was a game, and he was a hero. Stamping out evil wherever he found it was part of every hero's journey. No one ever shouted, "Hey that Lancelot is a real looker, too bad he's shit with a sword." One of the biggest parts of being a hero was the ability to take down the game's most vile enemies.

Jepsom certainly counted as vile.

He wondered why it had taken him so long to come to grips

with killing the NPCs. It probably had something to do with the NPCs in this game feeling so real. It wasn't like he could walk through his neighborhood back home and smite people for bad attitudes or not trimming their grass.

He'd leave the grass-measuring homicides to Dennis Rader.

Here in *The Etheric Coast*, the people felt just as real as the ones back home, but they weren't. He didn't have to feel bad about killing an NPC as long as he was on the right side of things. It also helped that Jepsom was a giant ass. He might have a problem killing an innocent man, but the cardinal was anything but innocent.

Tim looked into Paul's searching eyes and spoke with resolve. "You can count on me to handle it. I won't let you down."

"May the goddess' light shine upon you," Paul intoned. "I'll do my best to spread the word to our people that they are not to interfere with any healing taking place in the slums. Mentioning that the healer working there has been blessed by the goddess herself and is to be left alone should be a sufficient story to accomplish that goal."

Shaking the high priest's hand again, Tim couldn't help but grin. This was really going to piss Jepsom off, and angry people made mistakes. "Thank you so much, Paul. I'll have to get with my team, but I think we might be able to handle this quickly."

"Then go into the world and spread the light of the goddess to those who need it most." Paul made the sign of the goddess over his chest and called for one of his guards to lead Tim out of the temple.

Tim looked back once to see Paul sitting on his throne, head bowed in thought or prayer. It couldn't have been easy to condemn one of his own to death, but sometimes you had to cut out the rot before the infection could spread. Hopefully, having the blessing of the goddess eased the high priest's mind.

Tim stepped into the sunshine and felt a sense of determination. This part of his journey was almost over. After he finished his quest for the temple, he'd be able to move onto something else. Maybe they could find a new dungeon to explore, or another quest chain meant for a group instead of just him.

Whatever the future held, Tim had the feeling it would be fucking awesome.

CHAPTER SEVENTY

"Come on. Let's go," Cassie whined.

"But Tim should be back in a couple hours, and I want to know what happened at the temple." ShadowLily leaned back in her chair and propped her feet up. She hoped Cassie would get the point.

"That's why we have to go now." Cassie put her hands on her hips. "You know as well as I do that as soon as lover boy gets back, we're going to get roped into some crazy scheme."

ShadowLily grinned at her best friend. "I do know. Why do you think I'm trying to rest right now?"

Cassie kicked ShadowLily's feet off the chair and sat across from her. "If we leave now, I'm sure we'll be back before he gets here." She knew no such thing, but getting the last step of her class change quest done was too important for whole truths.

"Do you really think we'll be back in time?" ShadowLily's expression said she hoped what Cassie said was true, but she was also just really tired of sitting around.

"Of course, we will. Remember how quick the last part of your class change quest was." Cassie smiled reassuringly. "We got this."

"Fine." ShadowLily turned away from her wily little friend and looked at the fire mage. "JaKobi, can you handle guard duty later?"

He looked at the book he was reading. "I don't know. My schedule's kind of full." He held up the book to make sure she saw it.

"I hope that's a joke." ShadowLily stood up and walked toward him. "What are you reading, anyway?"

"*History of Ragnus the Burner*. Apparently, he was a grandmaster fire mage who snapped and started burning people alive as sacrifices to the Shining God." He set the book down. "And yes, it was a joke. I don't mind staying with Tim while you knock out Cassie's quest."

Cassie blew a raspberry at JaKobi from across the room. "Don't pout because I didn't ask you to come."

"Don't worry. You can pay me back by helping with my class change." The fire mage beamed at her affectionately.

Cassie stood up and grabbed her bō staff from where it rested against the table. "See, Tim's in good hands. Let's go do this thing."

ShadowLily tapped her fingers on the back cover of JaKobi's book. "Do you think there is more than one God in the game right now?"

"There could be, but this is from at least five hundred years ago." JaKobi laughed at Cassie's exaggerated hurry the fuck up expression. "When we have some time, I can talk to one of the mages in the great library. I'm sure they would know if the people of *The Etheric Coast* worship multiple members of the divine."

"What does it matter?" Cassie whined. "Let's get a move on. We don't want to be late for lover boy's triumphant return."

"It matters because if there is more than one god, there could be repercussions for helping one of them." ShadowLily frowned. "I've never read a story where there were multiple gods who lived amongst each other in harmony."

"But that wouldn't have anything to do with us." Cassie

motioned toward the door. When ShadowLily didn't move, she grabbed her hand and started pulling.

"Says the lady resurrected by the goddess." ShadowLily let Cassie drag her toward the door. "JaKobi, if you think you can make it back on time, I'd love to find out the answer."

The fire mage grinned as he watched ShadowLily struggle in the doorway, waiting for his answer. He'd never felt as important as he did right now. Having someone wait on your very words felt oddly satisfying to him. "I'll follow you out." JaKobi tucked the book back into his inventory and headed for the door.

ShadowLily gave him a wave and let Cassie pull her outside.

"I thought you said this would be easy," ShadowLily wheezed out between gasps.

"It was easy until they started chasing us." Cassie grinned like Nicholas Cage in *Face Off*. "But we've got this."

ShadowLily jumped over a fallen log and picked up her pace. "Tell me again how we got this?"

"You're acting like it's my fault. How was I supposed to know the cool-ass jungle hidden inside a cave would be filled with giant lizard-men? This isn't my fault; the quest is marked solo. Why would I plan on running into a shit-ton of monsters? All I did was follow the quest arrow on my map." A branch hit Cassie in the face and scratched her below the eye.

Cassie wiped the blood away but kept running. "Never a healer around when you need one."

"We could have had one, but you didn't want to wait," Shadow-Lily snapped.

A group of lizard-men with shields and swords appeared on their left, forcing the two women to turn right and keep running. Cassie got the distinct impression they were being funneled farther into the jungle when all they wanted to do was leave and come back with a full group. She looked behind her one more time to confirm they were still being chased.

Cassie's grin disappeared. She was pretty sure the lizard-men could have run them down by now if they truly wanted to. The bastards had to be seven or eight feet tall. The lizard-men also had huge tails that they used like third legs to run even faster. While Cassie considered herself pretty fast, this was like Michael Phelps trying to outswim a Great White; it was never going to happen.

Not to mention, if the fuckers weren't trying to catch them, they might be in real trouble.

She kept running though because facing off against fifteen of the giant green-skinned monsters with just the two of them was suicide. Cassie hadn't completed her class change quest yet, and she was pretty sure the goddess was done handing out favors. It must be tough being a goddess. The number of people constantly hounding you for help had to be overwhelming.

What Cassie wanted right now was a get the hell out of Dodge. If this was Monopoly, the lizard-men wouldn't be allowed past go, but this wasn't a board game. There was no way to know what would happen if they were caught, although she doubted it would be pleasant. Instead of hoping things would work out for the best, Cassie pushed her legs to move a little faster. Eventually, she'd run out of endurance, but she wasn't going to give up.

Giving up just wasn't in her.

Cassie had spent most of her life being told she was too small. Sure it came in handy when they wanted her to be on top of the pyramid or to stand in front for a photo, but it sucked when they were picking teams. It didn't matter that she could drop dimes on the basketball court or kick the shit out of a soccer ball. People saw her and thought, "She's too small to be good."

She didn't let the haters bring her down in the real world, and she sure as hell wasn't going to let some overaggressive lizards do it to her now. When the moment they were too tired to keep running came, she'd turn and fight. Those green fuckers wouldn't know what hit them.

ShadowLily was already starting to slow. Her higher dexterity was nice for fights when she needed to dodge and get stabby, but for cross-country marathons, it wasn't the stat she needed.

It was almost time to make the choice. If she had to decide between getting shot in the back by arrows or hacked apart by swords while running away, she'd rather go down swinging. Cassie glanced at her friend, hoping she wouldn't be the cause of ShadowLily's first death after becoming an adventurer.

"I don't know about you, but I've done about all the running I can." Cassie lunged to the left to avoid a branch, but quickly corrected her course as another group of lizard-men appeared out of thin air to keep them on track.

Cassie couldn't shake the feeling that they were being herded toward something.

ShadowLily tried to smile, but her chest was heaving so hard, it looked more like a grimace. "I'm not missing the heals as much as I'm missing Tim's ideas. I could really go for one of his crazy plans right now."

"Me too." Cassie gulped for air. "But if you tell him I said that, I'll have to kill you."

"Might not be alive long enough for you to get the chance." ShadowLily pointed at a giant hole in front of them.

"Fuck!" Cassie screamed as she skidded to a stop.

There wasn't anywhere for them to go. Lizard-men stepped out of the dense foliage, creating a path that led to only one place: the fucking hole. The giant fuckers who had been chasing them filled the gaps between trees. They raised their shields and slowly marched forward. Cassie felt like she was in the movie *300* and was about to get kicked into the well.

If she was going to die, it'd be on her terms.

"You should stealth and see if you can get out of here," Cassie whispered as she pulled her staff from behind her back. She'd been playing around with her new trident, but the weight of the tip threw off her movements. For now, she was sticking with her old tried and true bō staff.

"And let you have all the fun?" ShadowLily's bravado might have been faked, but it sure as fuck made Cassie feel better.

"This is Sparta!" Cassie roared and charged toward the line of shields.

Her bō staff clanged harmlessly off the solid iron shields. Despite Cassie's best efforts, she couldn't land a single hit against the well-organized lizard-men. They snarled fiercely as they used their shields to push them toward the precipice. It reminded her of riot police trying to clear a street.

There was only one place the two of them were going.

ShadowLily tried to dart through a gap in the shields, but it closed quickly, and she was slammed in the chest by one of the shields. The lizard-men waited for her to stand up before herding them toward the hole again.

"You know, the Spartans kicked their enemies into the well, right?" ShadowLily tried to smile, but her eyes had the look of a trapped animal.

"They also had abs of steel," Cassie retorted.

ShadowLily took a step back. The lip of the hole was only twenty feet away now. "What in the fuck do their abs have to do with anything?"

"If I'm going to die, I want to do it thinking about being surrounded by three hundred men whose abs I could scrub my clothes on."

"Gerard Butler, I've got a new role for you to consider." ShadowLily grinned. "It's playing a washboard in a film titled *Cassie Does Laundry.*"

"I'd fucking watch the shit out of that." Cassie looked over the edge of the pit as they shuffled backward. It wouldn't be long now before they had to put up or shut up.

"So, do we make one last attempt to get out of here, or are we going to Thelma-and-Louise this shit?" ShadowLily slipped her daggers back into their sheaths and held out her hand.

"We ride together, or we die together. Bad girls for life." Cassie thumped her chest. "Just know that I'm totally the Will Smith of our group."

ShadowLily took Cassie's hand in her own. "Well, I do have funny ears."

Looking into her best friend's eyes, she paused when her heels hit the edge. There was nothing behind them but darkness. One more step and they might be dead. The lizard-men moved forward with their shields raised to shove the two women over the edge, but they took the final step themselves.

Chittering laughter filled the air as the women's screams descended into darkness.

CHAPTER SEVENTY-ONE

Where in the hell was everyone?

Tim looked around the inn's main room and saw Ernie and Liz talking to a man at the bar. The rest of the guild was gone. Even JaKobi, who never seemed to leave the inn, was absent from his normal spot at the bar. The Blue Dagger Inn hadn't been this empty in forever. Even on his first day in the game, Gaston had been here with his crew.

Speaking of Gaston's merry men, Tim hadn't seen them in a while. It reminded him that Gaston had a life outside of helping them. He'd have to find out how long the assassin was willing to continue lending them his services. There was always the chance Gaston would want to go back to doing his normal day to day operations now that the inn was safe and Malvonis was off their backs.

Ernie saw Tim standing in the entrance and walked around the bar to come and meet him. "We're waiting on JaKobi to get back before we open up the healing shack." The innkeeper shook Tim's hand. "Until then, Lady Briarthorn sent someone to speak to you about real estate."

"And my two girls? Where did they get off to?" Tim watched the man at the bar, trying to gain his measure. He was speaking to Liz in a well-mannered way that earned Tim's approval.

"They left in a hurry. Something about Cassie wanting to finish her quest before you came back and ruined her chances for the evening." Ernie sniffed him. "I'd suggest a bath before your meeting, but I know you're in a hurry."

Tim wafted air toward his nose. It wasn't as bad as normal. Leaving the smithy early did wonders for his aroma. "Thanks, Ernie."

The man at the bar stood up as Tim approached and extended his hand in greeting. "Randolph Applebottom, at your service."

"You can call me Tim." He shook the man's hand and motioned for him to join him at a table. "Sorry about my appearance. I just came from my job at the smithy."

Mr. Applebottom waved away his apology. "I understand you are in the market for some real estate?"

"I am." Tim leaned back in his chair. "Lady Briarthorn seems to think you can help me in that regard."

"I should certainly think so. There aren't many people who can do what I do. Working in real estate is more of an art than a science, and I am a very good artist." Randolph tipped his glasses down so he was looking at Tim eye to eye. "Tell me what I can do for you."

Tim tried not to like the man. Mr. Applebottom certainly seemed proud of his real estate prowess, but despite his best efforts, Tim found that he was enjoying his company. "I'd like to find out how much the buildings surrounding the inn are selling for, and what it would cost to repair them."

Randolph smiled. "Acquisition should be easy enough. The crown has been trying to unload most of them for years. As for fixing them up, I'd expect that to take a big slice of your budget." He dropped his excited tone for one more conspiratorial. "How big a budget do we have to work with?"

That was the question, wasn't it. He had a pretty good chunk of gold, but how much was he willing to risk? If his ideas to revitalize the area didn't pan out, he could be losing all the money he'd planned on sending home to his family. If it did work out, he could be set for life.

Was he willing to bet the farm on one roll of the dice?

"Tell me what you think you could accomplish with five hundred gold." It wasn't all his money, but it was enough that if Tim lost it, it would hurt quite a bit.

"I should be able to acquire most of the properties, but it won't be enough for the renovations." Mr. Applebottom looked at Tim with an appraising eye. "How would you like me to proceed?"

"Let's worry about securing the properties for as little as possible, and then we can talk about the cost of renovations. We'll start with the buildings closest to the inn and move outward."

Mr. Applebottom stood and extended his hand. "It seems I have a lot of work to do."

Tim rose and shook the man's hand. "Just keep me up to date, and tell me when I need to make the funds available to you."

"I'll have my banker create an account that we can use for the purchases and to conduct the renovations." He smiled from ear to ear. "Every couple of years, some young entrepreneur comes along and tries to turn this little wasteland into something special. I hope it works out for you."

"Me too." Tim walked him to the door.

Now that he had the place pretty much to himself, he headed for the bathroom and took a quick bath. Despite how much he'd enjoyed bathing since he entered the game, he'd have to talk to one of the contractors about installing a shower. Sometimes taking a bath was just too much work.

Like right now, all he wanted was to take a quick shower to get the grime off before going to his second job. But instead of a three-minute shower, Tim had to go through an entire process. As he filled the tub, he wondered exactly how much adding a shower would cost.

On the plus side, at least he had access to toilet paper now.

The whole crap-and-piss-in-a-bucket thing left a lot to be desired. That was something they left out of Victorian movies. It wouldn't have been nearly as romantic if you watched people duck into stairwells to take a shit. No wonder there was always someone scrubbing the floors in those manors.

How was it that the Romans had worked out plumbing but the rest of the world used chamber pots?

It was one of the questions you had to ask when you studied history. Maybe people had just gotten to the point they were so busy killing each other that plumbing was the last thing on their lists to worry about.

Every single history book seemed to skip over the famine and struggles of the poor during those days. Now we had a different system. We lifted up our poorest members of society just enough that they see what they were missing out on, while our CEOs raked in the cash.

Not that Tim had anything against making oodles of money.

When it came right down to it, he wanted to make as much money as possible. Not to buy fancy things, but to be in a position where the day to day concerns of how to pay for things went away. Once that happened, he could focus on living life instead of worrying about which bill was more important.

He'd been raised to work hard and to save. He would never buy anything on credit unless it was a car or a house, and both those things together shouldn't be more than fifty percent of his total income. At least business school had taught him how to manage his money. It was a skill that would come in just as handy in the *Etheric Coast* as it did in the real world. Of course, he'd never earn a cent just sitting in the tub.

Tim hopped out of the bath and dried off before equipping his healing outfit. He stepped out of the bathroom and back into the inn's common room. JaKobi was waiting for him, looking a little flushed.

"Sorry I was late." He shrugged in a manner that said it couldn't be helped. "ShadowLily asked me to look into something, and I lost track of time."

JaKobi was kind of a bookworm. If she sent him to do research on something, it was no surprise he'd zoned out. It happened to the best people from time to time when they found something new that captivated their interest.

Tim remembered the first time he'd stayed up all night playing *Final Fantasy*. He'd walked out of the basement as the sun was coming up. His dad was making coffee in the kitchen and gave him a quizzical look before asking, "Were you down there all night?"

The answer, of course, was yes, although Tim didn't confess. Sometimes a little white lie and a long, sleepless day at school were better than losing access to the game. But that was the thing with passion. It didn't matter what you loved, when you loved something and were driven to be the best, you put your heart and soul into it, even if it was just playing a videogame.

When a person got wrapped up in something they loved, time was just a number.

Tim smiled and waved away JaKobi's excuse. "The way I see it, you made it here right on time."

The fire mage looked relieved. "Whatever you say, boss. You ready to head to the shack?"

He wasn't ready, not really. What Tim really wanted was a nap. Working two jobs wasn't for the faint of heart, and if you counted leveling and running his fledgling guild, Tim had three jobs. It was a lot to bear, but if he put in the work for the next couple of years, he'd be able to enjoy the rest of his time in-game.

Three jobs were nothing if it meant retiring in style at forty.

People said to find something you love and you would never

work a day in your life, but that wasn't true. Tim loved a lot of things, but anything could feel like a grind. Some days he was sure even Brad Pitt woke up saying, "They want me to play another fucking crazy person?" But when you truly loved something, the passion always came back. There was a certain amount of energy that filled him, and he was ready to take on whatever the day presented.

Tim was ready to embrace the work.

"Let's go." Tim smiled as he stepped into the light drizzle. Things were really starting to come together. If he could get a little lucky, his future was going to be bright. Not just *his* future, but the futures of everyone in the Blue Dagger Society.

Judy had all the people who needed healing lined up. Any injury that needed immediate attention was at the front of the line. After that came anyone he hadn't seen yesterday, then anyone else who showed up.

Tim beamed at the plump older woman's efficiency. "Thanks, Judy. You're doing an amazing job as usual." He pulled out a small purse with thirty silver coins in it. "I believe I owe you a little something extra for the other day."

"It's my pleasure to help." She smiled. "I left a few of those cookies you like on the table in there. Let me know when you're ready, and I'll send the first person in."

"I'm ready now, Judy." Tim made his way into the shack, stuffed a cookie in his mouth, and got ready for his first patient.

The man who came in had a steel rod through his arm. It almost looked like one of the long spikes they hammered into the ground when putting down railroad tracks. Tim hadn't seen or heard any evidence of a train since he'd entered the game, so he wasn't sure what the man had been up to. Sometimes it was more polite not to ask how the injury happened, so he didn't.

That didn't stop his mind from creating stories about what may have happened to the man as he directed him to take a seat on the table so he could get a closer look at the injury. Tim motioned for JaKobi to join him. "Mind holding him down?"

JaKobi came over from his position by the wall and helped the man lie down on the table. The fire mage put his hands on either side of the metal rod and used his weight to push down on the man's arm. "I can tell you from experience that it hurts like hell when he rips it out, but you'll be fine."

"Rips it out—" the patient stammered.

"Trust me." Tim wrapped his fingers around the steel rod and yanked with everything he had. Blood sprayed out of the wound, and the man screamed in pain. Trying to keep his laughter in as the man used a combination of swear words that would make his favorite fictional vampire blush, Tim healed the wound.

The man thanked Tim profusely as he stood up and tested out his arm. He placed a small bag of coins in Tim's outstretched hand. "Thank you."

"It's what I'm here for." Tim smiled warmly at the man and motioned for Judy to escort him outside.

The older woman ran back into of the room, slamming the door shut. Her face was etched with fear. "There are guards coming down the street—a lot of them."

Knowing that he hadn't done anything wrong, Tim wasn't too concerned about the city guards making an appearance, although it did feel a little odd considering how much effort Barry and Chris put into not crossing the archway.

"Why don't we step outside and find out what they want?" He put a comforting hand on Judy's shoulder. "I'm sure everything is fine."

Judy's pale face didn't inspire him with confidence. He was torn on the subject of law enforcement. In games and fantasy movies, there seemed to be two kinds of guards. There were the evil men and women who worked for a man like the Sheriff of Nottingham, and there were good knights like the ones who worked for King Arthur. There didn't seem to be a lot of ground between the two.

Being a college student with a fondness for beer and parties, Tim had met both kinds of officers. He preferred the laid-back version. Unless there was theft, violence, or murder, Tim's philosophy on law enforcement was the least interaction he had with the law, the better.

Tim liked the number of his total yearly encounters with the cops to rest around zero.

Not having any idea what to expect, but not holding out a lot of hope after meeting Barry and Chris, Tim shot a quick glance at JaKobi and whispered, "Don't do anything stupid."

The fire mage had a pretty level head, but anyone who dabbled in fire magic had a short fuse. Something about working with fire made them temperamental. Tim didn't know what JaKobi's buttons were yet. It was best to not take a chance and give him simple instructions to follow.

Tim stood on the small patio and waited to see where the guards were headed. It didn't take long to see they were coming straight for the shack. There were twenty men, led by what must have been a commander of some type. You could always tell who was in charge by who had on the biggest hat. Or in this case, a hat with a giant feather sticking out of it.

All twenty men had swords on their hips and spears in their hands. They were wearing some kind of hardened leather breast-plates, but no other armor. It wasn't the kind of crew you sent to get healing, and none of the men looked injured.

Things were about to get interesting.

"How can I help you today, gentleman?" Tim strode forward, making sure all of the guards' attention was focused on him.

Most of the people waiting for healing suddenly realized they had better places to be as the commander started to speak. "In the name of the crown, I have come to arrest the healer known as Tim."

This had to be fucking Jepsom. The asshole didn't know how to accept no as an answer.

"I'm Tim." He gave JaKobi a quick nod, and the fire mage wrapped an arm around Judy's shoulders and led her off to the side. "Can I ask what I'm being accused of?"

The commander bristled. "Crimes against the temple. The cardinal has provided us with information regarding your illegal healing practice. We are here to take you in."

Tim kept his smile in place, but his mind was racing. With twenty guards, he didn't stand a chance at getting out of this. Plus, he really didn't want to hurt these men. Making an enemy of the crown didn't sound like a very good idea.

"When I spoke with the high priest this morning, I was under the impression that I had his blessing." Tim kept his eyes focused on the commander. "But maybe the cardinal knows more than the man in charge of the goddess' affairs."

The commander paused for a moment. "Please come with us. If what you say is true, I'm sure we'll have this sorted out shortly."

"I hope so. Those people were waiting to be healed, and you've sent them away in pain." Tim turned to JaKobi. "Find the others and tell them what happened."

"We'll come for you as soon as they get back," JaKobi promised, his eyes ringed with orange light.

Tim stepped forward and immediately found himself surrounded by ten men on each side. The commander marched back to the front of the procession and led them into the city. Whatever was happening here wasn't good. If Jepsom was looking to separate him from his friends, he'd done a masterful job.

The cardinal was quickly becoming the one man in the world Tim didn't have any reservations about killing. In fact, the thought of Jepsom's death brought a smile to his face. Tim arched his shoulders back and kept his chin held high. If anyone saw him, he wanted them to know he wasn't afraid.

There was only one person who needed to be worried about

their future right now, and these armed guards might be taking Tim directly to him. He had the feeling that when he got to his destination, Jepsom would be there to gloat. Tim, determined not to give him any satisfaction, continued to march as if this was his personal guard and not his prison detail.

Sometimes you just had to roll with the punches.

CHAPTER SEVENTY-TWO

A t least Tim wasn't in shackles.

That was the only good thing he could say about his experience. Being escorted from the slums by twenty armed guards seemed like a little much to him. It was the kind of display that was intended to make a point. Jepsom was letting him know just how big a pain in the ass he'd become.

Once he was delivered to the man in charge, Tim would simply explain that the whole situation was a giant misunderstanding. Whoever heard his case had to know that he had the full support of the high priest and that charges from the temple wouldn't stand. Any logical person would have to let him go.

The procession entered a massive courtyard. In its center was a ten-story tower surrounded by smaller buildings on each side. One of the buildings looked like barracks, but the other had guards stationed outside of the door. The tower itself didn't seem big enough to house many prisoners, although it was rather tall, and the solid gray stones made it look very imposing.

As the gate closed behind Tim, the twenty armed guards went back to whatever their duties for the day were. Only the head of his escort remained. He took Tim by the arm and led him to the tower.

Tim didn't see any other prison cells and started to think that maybe the prison was actually below his feet. Being in jail was one thing, being trapped underground in the dark was something else. Starting a new character didn't seem like a bad option when the only other choice was to rot in the dark.

A small shudder of fear made his shoulders tremble. Then he pushed the fear aside and focused on what was right in front of him. If there was any chance of him getting out of this before he saw the inside of a cell, he had to keep his wits about him. Succumbing to the fear of imprisonment now wouldn't do him any favors.

The man who was sent to collect him signaled to a guard by the tower, and the man opened the door for them. Tim went inside first and stopped in the wide circular chamber, unsure of what to do next. The door slammed shut behind him, and the bolt latched in place with a sound of finality that made Tim aware of how badly this could go.

His captor led him to a small desk. The man behind the desk looked to see who had come in and smiled warmly at the officer. "Ah, Captain Reynolds, what brings you to us today?"

Captain Reynolds stood stiffly as if there were a rod jammed up his ass that forced his spine to stay rigidly straight. "I've secured the package for the sheriff. Please inform him that it was done without incident."

"I should hope so. I've never seen a full detachment sent to collect one man. Rather unorthodox, if you ask me," the man at the desk stated flatly.

The captain looked like he was about to answer when a man with a large belly strolled out of a room at the far side of the tower. "That's why nobody asks you anything, Richard."

"Just seems like overkill, Sheriff. I mean, look at him. He's a healer. What was he going to do?" Richard sounded petulant.

"Oh, I'm sure there is much more to him than his profession." The sheriff's eyes roved over Tim. "Or maybe there isn't. It's not my job to question my orders, only to carry them out."

"If there is nothing else, Sheriff, I'd like to return to my post," Captain Reynolds stated in a very matter-of-fact voice.

Tim got the impression the captain wasn't a big fan of the sheriff and wanted to leave as soon as possible.

The sheriff's eyes moved away from Tim and focused on the captain. He extended his hand to the man as a knowing smile lingered at the edges of his mouth. "Thank you for your service, Captain Reynolds. I'll make sure to let your commander know that your performance was satisfactory."

"Thank you, Sir." Captain Reynolds spun on his heel and left the room.

The sheriff turned to Richard. "Send a message to Davros. Our newest acquisition will need to be shown to a cell."

Tim had been watching the proceedings silently, but he couldn't hold his tongue a moment longer. "A cell? Shouldn't there at least be a trial first?"

The sheriff let out a long rumbling belt of laughter. "Did you hear that, Richard? He wants a trial." All the humor faded from his features, and the sheriff's eyes turned hard. "This is where they send people to disappear. There will be no trial. A judgment has already been made, and you will suffer for your sins."

All Tim could think was, *Please don't let me be the next Edmond Dantes.*

Richard frowned. "With all that's going on, Sir, is this the right time to be adding another prisoner?"

"We certainly have the space." The sheriff smiled.

"But with the unexplained deaths, shouldn't we keep him locked in the tower?" Richard almost pleaded.

Unexplained deaths? As if being in prison wasn't bad enough, now he had to worry about something else. The last thing Tim wanted to do was get embroiled in a quest chain at the prison. He didn't have time to figure out this mystery. There was a man of the cloth that needed to meet his demise.

"Oh, I think he'll be fine with the rest of the population." Glaring at Richard, the sheriff slowly nodded his head. "And I don't want to hear anything else about it."

"I'd like to hear more about it," Tim cut in. "If you have men suffering from some kind of illness, maybe I can help."

The sheriff turned his dark, soulless eyes on Tim. "Please join me in my office for a moment." He pointed to the room he previously exited, and from the tone of his voice, Tim knew it wasn't a request.

Tim followed the sheriff into the tiny room and took a seat as he noted the placard resting on the desk, proclaiming it the property of Sheriff Jon Hobbs. Jon's massive belly brushed against Tim as he squeezed around the desk before finally falling into his seat.

This might be Tim's only chance to get a word in, so he decided to go for it. "I think there has been some kind of mistake."

"A mistake? Oh, I don't think so. The cardinal was very clear in his instructions." The sheriff tapped a letter on his table. "He wanted you removed from the equation, and here you are." He opened his hands as if to say, "See, it's simple."

"But I've committed no crime. The healing I've done was sanctioned by the high priest. When he finds out what happened, there will be hell to pay." It was all bluster, but it was the only card Tim had to play.

"Oh, I think not. By the end of today, everyone will have forgotten about you." The sheriff had a sickly sweet smile on his face. "That is what I specialize in—making problems disappear."

Tim scoffed at the notion of him disappearing. "If you wanted to be discreet, you shouldn't have sent twenty men to round me up." Tim noted the little tick above the sheriff's right eye. He'd scored a point. "When my friends find out I'm here, they will come for me."

"We've got plenty of room." Jon Hobbs was back in control

now. Being threatened seemed to harden his resolve. "Now, let's get to the business of the day so I can get back to mine, and you can start commiserating about your poor life choices."

The sheriff stood and pointed at a poster on his wall. "The rules are simple. No fighting, no stealing, no bullshit." He tapped the poster. "We count on the prisoners themselves to enforce these rules. The only time you will see any of my men is when it's chow time or when we're dropping in some fresh meat."

Jon had a cruel smile on his face as he pointed at Tim. "You're today's catch."

Tim didn't like the implication that he was fresh meat. Fresh for what, the grinder? He tried to keep his face calm as the sheriff continued his spiel.

"Twice a day, we bring in food, mostly hard biscuits and stew, but every now and then, we splurge, and you get a potato." The sheriff smiled at Tim as if getting a potato should be every man's fondest wish.

I'm totally fucked.

Jon grinned. "I knew you were a potato man." He winked at Tim. "Just between you and me, we might be having them for dinner in honor of your arrival. The other prisoners will be thrilled."

Tim shook his head to clear it. Why was the sheriff giving him the normal "hope you are a model prisoner" shtick when there might be an illness inside of the prison? Didn't he have the right to know?

Raising his hand to interject, Tim spluttered, "So what about these deaths?"

Sheriff Hobbs took a seat. All the good humor he'd been showing while trying to ruin Tim's life drained from his face. "It's true. We've had something mysterious happening in the dungeon, but I'm not sending any of my men to investigate it."

The sheriff leaned his chair back and rested his hands on his belly. "Frankly, no one's going to miss a few inmates. The only thing I'm worried about is making sure whatever is afflicting them doesn't spread outside these walls."

Something didn't feel right to Tim. This man seemed awfully relaxed, considering there might be some kind of plague brewing under the city. He thought about his trip over here and all of the men he encountered. None of them seemed sick. Was there a chance these men were infecting the prisoners on purpose?

There was no way for Tim to be certain of what was happening. The one thing he did know was that he wouldn't be getting out of this today. For all of his bluster, he was going to be thrown in the dungeon. The last thing he wanted to do before they tossed him in was make the sheriff upset.

"But these are my worries." Jon Hobbs leaned forward, eyes locking onto Tim's like an owl hunting a mouse. "All you have to worry about is following the rules."

"No fighting, no stealing, no bullshit," Tim chanted. "I won't be a problem."

Sheriff Hobbs stood up with a smile on his face that didn't reach his eyes. "See that you aren't. Those boys down there aren't the forgiving sort if you know what I mean."

Tim was pretty sure the sheriff meant that if you got caught stealing down there, it was the last thing you'd ever get caught doing. Watching *Sons of Anarchy* had only taught him that he didn't want to be in prison, not how to deal with it once you were tossed in alone.

"Follow me." The sheriff squeezed past Tim and out into the tower again. He pointed at a man waiting by the door. "This is Davros, and he'll be escorting you to the dungeon. Don't give him any shit, or by God, there won't be another potato served for a month."

Davros stayed just outside of the tower and motioned for Tim to join him. "Right this way."

If he could cast snare on the sheriff and flameburst at Davros, he might be able to make a run for it. Tim's fingers started to twitch through the emotions of snare when he saw the five men training in the yard. There was no way he could take all of them on and win. If he lost, it would only make it harder for his friends to get him out.

Just when things had been going so well, Jepsom had managed to take him off the board before he could do the same to him. Not only was he going to be trapped here, but the clock was ticking. He had seven days to plan and execute the cardinal. Tim wasn't going to be able to do that from inside the dungeon.

"Did the sheriff tell you the rules?" Davros asked as he took Tim's arm to lead him across the courtyard.

"Yeah, no fighting, no—"

Davros cut him off. "Ignore all that shit. Some of these guys are going to test you. If you don't stick up for yourself, you're going to spend the rest of your short life naked and afraid."

He yanked Tim to a stop. "Just don't do it at chow time because the guards will break everyone's skulls, not just yours."

Tim wasn't sure what to say, so he settled for a simple, "Okay."

The dungeon was sounding worse by the minute. First, there was something going on with a disease, and then there was the chance he'd have to win a few fights just to stay alive.

This is why he was getting into real estate and out of being a political assassin.

Tim didn't want to have anything to do with politics and fighting with powerful people. Let the other players have their power. All he wanted to do was make a nice living. It'd be amazing to wake up one day knowing he'd never have to worry about money again.

Not that Tim wanted to live the millionaire lifestyle. He wasn't into flashy things. All he wanted was a nice home to call his own and to make sure his parents could take care of his brother and sister without stressing out. If he could do that, he'd consider himself rich in more ways than one.

Davros opened the gate to a set of stairs leading under the tower. "Sorry about the smell. There isn't a lot of ventilation."

"Might be why the prisoners keep getting sick," Tim quipped before he could stop himself.

"We didn't have any problems before the sheriff went to visit his sister on the other side of the mountains. When he came back, things changed." Davros shrugged, knowing there was nothing he could do about it. "I'd say the sickness is more of a byproduct. The inmates had these marks on their…"

"Ah, Davros, fresh meat for the grinder," a guard inside a second gate called as the two of them approached.

"Sure is, Stan. Make sure he gets in safely. They say he's some kind of healer." Davros motioned for Tim to join the guard inside the gate.

Tim paused before going in. He wanted to know what Davros had been about to tell him, but the man's reaction to the other guard gave him pause. At the last second, he turned his question into gratitude. "Thank—" All the air rushed out of Tim's lungs as Davros' fist slammed into his belly.

"Just remember what I said." Davros shoved Tim toward the entrance.

Lesson number one, don't thank the guards for shit. Tim snickered as his stomach relaxed and it became easier to breathe. Not that the air in here smelled very good. He turned toward the gate, taking one last breath of fresh air before following the guard inside.

The smell inside the dungeon reminded Tim of the time he'd walked into a room with mold. They weren't kidding when they said that stuff could kill you. Inhaling black mold was toxic in all kinds of ways. He imagined he was being walked into Mold Central. Next thing you know, shit was going to spiral out of control like in *The Andromeda Strain*.

Part of him wanted to believe it was mold or something to do with the dead not being removed from their cells fast enough, but he just couldn't do it. People didn't get funky marks on them from disease. Yes, they could get sores, but marks sounded like something was biting the prisoners.

Stan locked the gate and took a lantern from beside the door. "Let's go."

Tim followed Stan down a set of winding stairs. They reached the bottom four minutes later. Here there was another door, but this time the lock was on their side. Stan put his keys in the lock and opened the passage.

"In you go." Stan made a little shooing motion.

Tim stepped inside the door and jumped as it slammed back into place. This was it, for better or worse; he was inside the dungeon. There was a mysterious illness, and maybe some kind of monster down here.

What could possibly go wrong?

CHAPTER SEVENTY-THREE

"How long has it been?" Cassie asked as she slumped against the wall of the pit.

ShadowLily slid down the dirt wall and sat next to her friend. "Since I sent the message or since we've been down here?"

"Whichever one gets us help first." Cassie used her heels to dig furrows in the ground as she thought about their situation. ShadowLily's class quest had been so easy, it had given her too much confidence in her own. She couldn't stop beating herself up for getting them into this mess. There was no way out of the pit unless the lizard-men let them out.

"It's been three hours since I messaged Tim and JaKobi. I haven't heard anything back." ShadowLily frowned. "And that has me worried. Tim might not be Johnny-on-the-spot with his messages, but he always responds."

Taking a calming breath, the half-elf leaned her head against Cassie's shoulder. "What could they possibly be doing?"

"You've really got it bad, huh?" Cassie asked with a grin. They might be trapped, but it was always the right time to poke fun at your friends.

"What do you mean?" ShadowLily asked as she sat up straight.

Cassie was grinning from ear to ear now. It was dark at the bottom of the pit, so she wasn't sure her bestie could see it, but she was sure ShadowLily would hear it in her voice. "You're so in love with Tim that even while we're stuck in a pit waiting to be eaten by hungry lizard-men, all you're thinking about is if he's okay."

"Oh, shit."

"Oh, shit, indeed." Cassie laughed. "You're in the love zone."

"Better than *The Twilight Zone*?" ShadowLily snarked before gently leaning the back of her head against the wall of the pit. "When did this happen?" Then, in a more panicked tone, "Do you think he feels the same way?"

"Girl, you've had him locked up since day one. Only way you're getting rid of him now is if you burn him off like a leech." The tank hopped to her feet and started pacing the pit. She hated being still, and that was why she couldn't wait for them to become adventurers. No more of this going-to-work shit. They were going to be epic.

ShadowLily would have smacked Cassie if she could see her. "Gross."

"It's true. He's stuck on you like gum on the bottom of your shoes." Cassie smiled again. "And we all know how hard that shit is to get off."

ShadowLily was starting to come out of her shock. "There should be a law against people spitting their gum on the sidewalk."

"The first execution in what has been dubbed by some on social media as the bubble gum disposal act will air live tonight at nine." Cassie started to giggle. "Problem solved. No one is going to risk spitting that shit on the sidewalk ever again."

"At least *The Etheric Coast* is safe from those horrible criminals. They don't have gum or sidewalks here." ShadowLily extended her hands out and brought them together like she was a giant crocodile. "Imagine how those lizards would look with a mouthful of gum."

"That shit would go viral on Twitter for sure. People would look at one another at work and be like, hey, did you see that video where the lizard was trying to chew gum?" Cassie brushed off the seat of her pants. She had a thing about being dirty; she didn't like it one fucking bit.

Gazing up into the darkness, Cassie shouted, "Hey, lizard-for-brains." She took a deep breath and then belted, "Any chance we can hurry this the fuck up?"

No one responded to her shout, and Cassie slammed her fist into the hard-packed earth of the wall. "I wish they'd just get it over with. This waiting around shit is killing me."

ShadowLily patted the ground next to her. "Why don't you try to get some rest? When they come for us, we're going to need our energy."

Cassie sat down and cuddled against her friend. Her mind was spinning, and she was worried they might not actually make it out of this. Despite the parade of random thoughts circling her mind, the little tank's eyes started to close. All that running must have really taken it out of her.

Orange light flickered through the darkness, stinging Cassie's eyes.

"Why in the fuck is it so bright?" Cassie looked at ShadowLily, and a chorus of drums sounded from overhead.

The drums had the effect of putting her on edge, but not as much as the giant cage the lizard-men had lowered into the pit while they'd been sleeping. The cage was made out of bent branches tied together with thick green vines. Stuck out in a circle around the cage were five torches.

After sleeping in the dark for so long, the lights seemed impossibly bright. "You think the green bastards would have a little more respect for the two finest ladies they've ever laid eyes on," Cassie groused as she blinked.

ShadowLily walked over to the cage to inspect it. "I think we're supposed to get in.

"No way." Cassie scrambled to her feet. "There isn't a horror movie out today where climbing into a cage had a happy ending. Shit, even in the Disney movies, getting in a cage normally means someone is trying to eat you."

ShadowLily looked at the lip of the pit fifteen feet above their heads. "It's not like we have a choice. Unless you've thought of another way to get out of here?"

"It's not like anyone could think with all that racket." Cassie motioned above them, indicating the relentless sound of the drums. She joined ShadowLily by the door. "Let's just do it."

"I'm happy you said that. That way, when this all turns to shit, I can blame you. I always find it feels better not to be the one who fucked up." ShadowLily opened the door to the cage and stepped inside. "I can't believe the boys back at the inn never messaged us back. There is going to be retribution, but not until I get an ice-cold beer."

"Shit," Cassie blurted as she joined ShadowLily in the wooden cage. "I haven't checked my messages since we got up." It took her a few seconds to get her user interface open and another brief moment before her messages displayed in front of her. There was one new message from JaKobi.

We're on the way.

The timestamp on the message indicated it was from four hours ago. Either they'd never made it here, or they were waiting in a pit just like them. Maybe they should not have asked for help. Adding more deaths to her conscience wasn't going to make her feel any better. Against so many lizard-men, their entire guild working together might not have survived the first wave of battle.

"JaKobi sent me a note that said they were coming." She closed the cage door. "I don't think they made it."

"And you didn't get anything from Tim?" ShadowLily asked worriedly.

"Nope, but I'm sure he's fine. Probably too busy working on one of his harebrained schemes to check his messages." Cassie looked around and wondered when their ride to the surface would begin.

"I hope you're right." ShadowLily looked morose as the cage jerked violently. Once they were moving, the cage settled, making it easy for them to stand without falling over. Getting to the top after falling on their asses wouldn't give the right impression.

The cage continued to rise smoothly as if they were being pulled up by a winch of some sort. The drums continued to get louder as they drew closer to the surface. Finally, they were lifted above the pit. Both women gasped as they looked at the scene below them.

They were in a wide-open clearing. The jungle's thick grass had been chopped or flattened. There was a throne inside the bottom half of a giant lizard's jaw. The teeth rose over the chair like an arch with spikes. Sitting on the throne was an enormous lizard-man. The chieftain's arms and legs were painted vibrant colors, and he wore a headdress made out of colorful feathers.

The chieftain only kept Cassie's attention for a moment. She could deal with one giant bastard, but what she couldn't deal with were the hundreds of lizard-men gathered in the clearing.

Was this some kind of celebration? If it was a celebration of some sort, the question quickly became, were they the guests of honor or dinner?

The cage was lowered to the ground, and the door opened by one of the lizard soldiers. He pointed toward the throne. When the two of them didn't start walking, he nudged them forward with the tip of his spear.

"We get it already." Cassie slammed her open palm down on his spear. "If you touch me with that thing, I'm going to kick your fucking ass."

The lizard-man's tongue flicked out around his teeth, and there was a sound coming from his throat that might have been laughter. He pointed over their heads again and lifted his shield to give them another push in the right direction.

Cassie glared at their captor. "Try it."

ShadowLily put a calming hand on Cassie's shoulder. "We've got bigger things to be concerned about."

"But kicking his ass would make me feel so much better." Cassie turned to see what could possibly be worse than being surrounded by hungry-looking lizard-men.

It didn't take her long to see what ShadowLily was worried about. Standing at the base of the throne were Gaston and JaKobi. Both men had their hands tied in front of them. It didn't escape her attention that each of them had been assigned their own guard, while the sexist lizards only assigned a single escort for the two of them.

"Chauvinist fucks," Cassie grumbled. "Just let me go *mano a mano* with one of these green bastards, and they'll learn not to underestimate a woman."

"Maybe we can worry about satisfying your ego after we're safe." She kept her eyes locked on the throne. "Tim's not here. Where in the hell is he?"

"Working on a secret plan?" Cassie sure hoped that was what Tim was doing. Right about now, they could use one of his great ideas to get the hell out of here.

They stopped at the base of the throne as the chieftain watched them. "Coming into the hidden forest is a death sentence. The four of you will be sacrificed to appease Havithor, the Great Worm. With your lives comes peace and prosperity for our people."

Cassie spat on the ground. "I desire a trial by combat." It was worth a try. That shit always worked in the movies.

The weird laughter chittered from all around them. The chieftain walked down the steps toward Cassie. Stopping in front of her, he smiled. "I will grant one of you the right to face our champion. Win, and all of you shall be spared. Lose, and all of you will become willing sacrifices to the Great Worm."

Cassie stood as tall as she could. Her eyes shot daggers at the chieftain. There wasn't an inch of back-down in her. "Bring it on, Puff. I need a new pair of boots."

The chieftain chuffed his laughter. "Wouldn't you prefer one of your champions to take your place?" He pointed at the two men with their wrists bound in front of them.

Gaston nudged JaKobi's shoulder. "He doesn't know how bad he just fucked up."

"Right. One time I asked Ernie for a small serving, and she thought I was making a joke about her. My arm hurt for a week. That lizard just implied a woman wouldn't stand a chance against their champion. Cassie's going to wipe the floor with him."

The chieftain followed the two men's conversation before turning his confused gaze on Cassie. "So it will be you who faces Drago?"

"Drago's about to be my bitch!" Cassie scanned the crowd. "Which one of you is it?" she shouted in defiance.

The chieftain walked back up the steps to his throne. He lifted his arms and the drumming stopped. "The sacrifices have asked for the right to fight our champion, and I have granted them the opportunity." He snickered before looking across the clearing. "I call on Drago the Destroyer to represent the clan."

A cheer rose from the crowd and they scrambled to line the clearing, leaving one path to a hut set at the far edge. The drums started to play again, but this time their rhythm was different. This time the drums summoned their champion to war.

Cassie heard them shouting the name "Drago" over and over. She wasn't sure what all the hype was about. Looking around the crowd didn't show her a lot of difference between one lizard-man and another. Unless Drago was some kind of freak, she'd be fine.

A large gray shape came out of the hut. At first, she thought it was a massive sculpture, something to show them just how badass their champion was, but then she realized it was him. The giant lizard-man had to walk out of the hut sideways. As he turned to face them, he rolled his massive shoulders.

Drago was easily twice as wide as the rest of the lizard-men, and Cassie wouldn't have been surprised to find out he was at least nine feet tall. The massive beast shrieked into the sky, and the drums started to play faster. The lizard-men near the hut formed a circle.

The chieftain looked at Cassie with a smug smile etched on his features. "Our champion awaits."

Cassie pulled her bō staff from her inventory and twirled it. She cast a withering look at the chieftain and did her best Samuel L. Jackson impression. "I've had it with these motherfucking lizards in this motherfucking game."

With one last look at her friends, Cassie stalked forward to meet Drago in the circle of champions.

CHAPTER SEVENTY-FOUR

T hankfully, there were torches in the dungeon.

Tim forced a nervous smile on his face. Sometimes in life, it paid to be grateful for what you had and not be concerned with what you wanted. Being trapped down here without a single torch would have been infinitely more miserable than it was right now.

After what Davros said, Tim had been expecting to be ambushed by the other prisoners the very second he entered the dungeon, but he hadn't seen one of them yet. He wasn't sure exactly what he envisioned, but it had been more like the scene in *The Chronicles of Riddick* than the silent welcome he was receiving now.

He moved deeper into the dungeon without revealing anything new. The walls were made out of roughhewn stone blocks, and the stones didn't always match. Either some of them had been replaced over the years, or they used stone from multiple quarries to make the dungeon. Despite the general smell of dampness, the stone walls and ceiling appeared to be dry.

A long, raspy moan echoed down the hall from somewhere in the darkness.

It was the kind of sound you'd hear in a ghost movie right before something came out of the walls and chased you down. Tim realized that there could be ghosts in the game. Almost every type of fantasy game had some version of the undead in it. Who else were the clerics going to smite with their holy light?

That being said, he generally wasn't scared of dark and creepy places. He was more of a "have to see it to believe it" kind of guy. At least, that was what he liked to tell himself, but if you put him in a cemetery late at night, added a little fog to the ground, and something brushed against him, he'd run away faster than everyone else.

You gotta be realistic about these things.

Tim pulled his staff out of his inventory and readied his *flameburst* spell. If he rounded a corner and a bunch of people tried to rob him, there were going to be a few crispy motherfuckers down here.

Hell, yeah, he was ready to rumble, baby!

Instead of a corner at the end of the hall, there was a dark wooden door. Tim grabbed the thick iron ring and pulled the door open. Another moan filled the air. This time it sounded more like a man getting a limb cut off in a civil war movie than a ghost. He forgot all about being worried and rushed into the room to help in any way he could.

Four men were huddled around a bundle of straw on the floor. A fifth man was lying there, and that was who was making the god-awful sound. The other men seemed to be trying to hold him down as he writhed in pain. One of them had a rag and a bucket of water and was washing the sweat from the sick man's forehead.

"What's going on here?" Tim asked.

Two of the four men jumped away from the man on the floor, making the sign of the goddess over their chest. The other two looked at Tim with their jaws hanging open in shock. From the looks on all of their faces, they didn't expect to get out of the room alive.

Now that he'd given all of them a heart attack, Tim tried to sound friendly as he spoke. He pointed at himself. "New arrival. Sorry if I startled you."

"That bastard Hobbs is still bringing people down here? Jordan, I told you we needed to try to kill that fucker the last time he was down here."

"Simmer down, Henry. That was five years ago. It's not like killing Hobbs would do anything but make it harder on all of us. You know damn well they'd just find an even bigger asshole to takeover."

Jordan turned to look at Tim. "If you haven't heard yet, there's something going on down here, and I'd say dollars to doughnuts the sheriff is behind it."

Henry motioned for the other men to take his place by the man on the floor. "The sheriff has never been anything to us but uninterested. As long as we don't kill each other, he's never given a shit about us."

Tim took a step forward. "Do you mind if I take a look at him? I'm a healer by trade. There might be something I can do."

"I told you the goddess would provide," Henry said, making Her sign over his chest before motioning Tim forward.

Leaning down, Tim started to examine the man's arms and legs. "One of the guards mentioned some of the afflicted had marks on them. Have you seen anything like that?"

"There's something on the back of his neck. We've never seen anything like it before," Henry chimed in as he bent down to help roll the injured man over.

The moan that escaped from the man's mouth broke Tim's heart. He'd always been fine with being in pain himself, but he hated seeing others in pain. There was something about seeing someone hurt that made him want to help them. He probably should have tried to be a doctor back in the real world, but who had time for all the extra classes when there was beer to be drunk?

The marks on the back of the man's neck weren't like anything Tim had seen before either. All he could say for certain was that he was fairly sure they weren't dealing with a vampire. There were three marks at the base of the man's neck. He took the wet rag and wiped the crusted blood away, but still couldn't make sense of them.

Tim looked at the men gathered around. "I'm not sure what happened to him, but I might be able to help." He motioned for the men to step back and started casting cleanse.

On the fourth cast of the spell, a foul-smelling white pus leaked from the wound on his patient's neck. The man on the ground let out a strangled cry, then his body went still. Tim watched him for a few moments, afraid that he might have killed him. He splashed a healing orb against him and hoped for the best.

The four men in the room were staring at him. One of them had a look on his face that said, "If he's dead, so are you." Doing his best to ignore them, Tim kept his eyes locked on the man he'd healed. His chest had started to move, but he wasn't awake yet.

At least I didn't kill him.

When his eyes fluttered open, the men in the room jumped back from the body like they'd seen a ghost. Or maybe they were worried about zombies. Oh, shit, did this game have zombies?

Tim held out his hand. "Water. I need water."

Henry ran out of the room and came back a moment later with a skin that had the stopper removed. Tim took it from him and leaned over the man on the ground to help him drink. Maybe the goddess really did have a hand in all things. It was starting to feel like he'd been sent here to help these men. It wasn't like the saints from the real world got there by tending to the affluent.

They were considered saints because they'd helped everyone.

Not that he thought of himself as a saint, or even saintly. It took a certain kind of selflessness to reach that level of divinity, something he didn't have. Yes, he had a strong desire to help people, especially those less fortunate, but Tim also liked his things and his alone time.

That part of him he would have to give up to become saintly wasn't something he was ready to part with just yet. Plus, his life was already pretty awesome. He was in a new reality with the woman he loved. Here he could heal people and lead a group. Back home, he would have been the lowest man on the financial totem pole in a giant corporation.

One of the forgotten.

Tim extended his hand to the man he'd healed and pulled him into a sitting position. "How are you feeling?"

"Better now that I'm awake." He looked at the five men huddled around him. "Thanks for not leaving me to die."

Jordan leaned down next to him. "None of us knew what to do, Tony." He stopped talking and pointed at Tim. "Hobbs arrested this healer, and he saved you."

"Fucking Hobbs," Tony mumbled. "Hate having to be grateful to that bastard for anything."

"Then don't be." Tim smiled at the man. "I hate that fucker too."

"From the goddess' lips to my ears," Tony said with a smile. He looked around the room, and his smile quickly faded. "Do we have anything to eat?"

Henry slapped him on the back. "Of course, this crazy fucker wakes up, and the first thing he asks about is food."

Jordan helped Tony to his feet. "I'm sure we can wrangle some-thing up. If not, it's almost chow time." He pointed at Tim. "The new arrival means potatoes tonight."

Tony shuddered. "I swear to the gods it's a good thing we found another use for those potatoes, or I would have gone nuts by now. But the goddess has her ways." He elbowed the man next to him. "Doesn't she, boys?"

Tim laughed out loud at the men's antics, wondering what

exactly they did with their potatoes. He actually loved potatoes. There were so many ways you could make them: baked, twice baked, smashed, mashed, or fried. They always tasted awesome, and they were one of the cheapest fillers you could buy, although a steady diet of spuds did sound horrible. There had to be something he was missing.

Did Sheriff Hobbs think he was Penn?

That crazy comedian had eaten nothing but potatoes for three months. Sometimes you gotta do what you gotta do to lose weight, but restricting your diet like that would break Tim in a week, if he made it that long. He needed real food, even if it meant having to exercise.

Henry wrapped an arm around Tim's shoulders. "Plus, we have to introduce fresh meat here to the rest of the boys."

Looking at each of the men in turn, Tim felt like they might just be screwing with him. At least his first day in the dungeon wasn't going to be filled with running away from hordes of hungry sex-starved men in fear. He might even be able to spend his time here doing something useful. "Is there anyone else who needs healing?"

Jordan smiled. "Oh, I'm sure some of the guys will take you up on that offer. We don't usually get visits from the healers down here." His gaze narrowed on Tim like a grandma spotting her favorite yarn on sale at the hobby store. "Maybe with you here, we can finally get to the bottom of what's going on."

"Any chance you're up for helping us?" Jordan extended his hand toward Tim.

Quest Received: Something Wicked this Way Comes

There is something strange happening in the dungeon. The guards and the sheriff are calling it a mysterious illness, and yet there are rumors that the illness is caused by some kind of attack. Your job is to find out the truth and put an end to whatever is going on.

Accept Quest: Yes/No

Tim accepted the quest. If he was going to be trapped here for a few days, he might as well get some experience out of it. There was always a chance his friends would find a way to get him out of here earlier, so he could always abandon the quest chain or come back and do the quest later.

There was also a part of Tim that didn't want to be too involved. He didn't want anyone to die, but he certainly didn't want to make life more comfortable for criminals. Although, with how he'd been spirited away, it was more than likely at least a few of these men were down here for doing the right thing.

Not all of them could be innocent, though, not with the prison right in the city. Somebody would have surely noticed the dungeon filling up without any criminals being tried. If working through the monarchy was anything like working through the government, maybe no one took the time to notice. The sheriff could have a nice profitable side business going right under the kingdom's nose.

Innocent or not, something was attacking these men. Tim believed, at the very least, every prisoner needed to be safe from physical threats. Being eaten or fed on seemed to meet his threshold for demanding justice. No one was going to be eaten while he was here.

Criminals or not, he wouldn't stand for a monster feeding on these men.

The five inmates led him down a long hallway. There were branches going in multiple directions, but they continued in a straight line. At the end of the hallway was another wooden door, although this one was open and you could hear boisterous shouting and singing coming from beyond.

Tim stepped into a large common room. With all of the raised mugs, he might as well have stepped back into the Blue Dagger. Sacks of potatoes lined one wall, and against another, there was some kind of contraption that must have been a still. They were making alcohol out of the potatoes.

No wonder these guys got fucking excited about potato night.

Given how the rest of the prisoners were acting, he would not have thought there was a sickness down here. Tim took a few steps into the room and craned his neck to see what everyone was looking at. On the floor in the center of the room was a black cloth with a man lying on it. He started listening to the songs being sung and realized this wasn't a party, but a funeral.

"If you'd been arrested yesterday, Khris might still be with us," Henry said as he handed Tim a drink. "As you can tell, everyone contributes their potato rations to the still. The fuckers upstairs think we love to eat the damn things, but we use them to make vodka."

Tim took a sip of his drink and coughed so hard tears leaked from his eyes. He looked into Henry's smiling face. "Strong stuff."

"The stronger, the better I say." Henry clinked his glass against Tim's and wandered off to join the proceedings.

The shot of potato vodka in Tim's belly was warming him up nicely. He kept his eyes moving around the room. It was kind of like being invited to a massive house party when you only knew one person. Clinging to the person you came with like a flotation device was frowned upon. At some point, you had to branch out and mingle or go home.

Going home wasn't an option, so Tim had to talk to a few people. He'd had problems breaking the ice with other college students, but now he was about to do it with thieves, rapists, and murderers.

Tim chuckled for a moment. Technically, he was a murderer and a thief, so as long as none of the guys down here were rapists, he might be in okay company. It was funny how that line differed in the game. Killing for the right reasons in the game could make you a hero, but back in the real world, it only made you a serial killer.

Even *Dexter* lived with the fear of getting caught.

But Tim's favorite serial killer only went after the bad guys. Dexter always reserved a little extra time to make sure his victims knew he was there for a reckoning, just like Tim believed there was a special place in hell for rapists and the people who hurt children. Hopefully, one where men like Dexter killed them a hundred times a day.

Tim looked around the room's tall stone walls and dirty floors and muttered, "This dungeon is too good for those worthless fuckers."

There were some crimes that Tim considered so horrific you shouldn't be let out. In his mind, rape was the worst crime, and seeing people get off with such light sentences had always rubbed him the wrong way. The person who was raped didn't get a redo after a few years in a box. They had to deal with their wounds for the rest of their lives.

It just didn't seem fair. Lock those fuckers up in a jail that only housed other rapists and call it a day.

Tim was startled out of his thoughts when Tony touched his arm. He almost jumped but managed to stop himself at the last moment. "What's up?" He tried to smile, covering his freak out so smoothly they should have called him "Iceman."

Tony watched him for a moment and then flicked his eyes to the man standing next to him. "This is Baron. He's in charge of our merry band."

"Merry might be too nice a word for it," Baron said in a baritone voice that could have competed with James Earl Jones for top honors. "We're mostly just trying to survive."

"Ah, it's not that bad." Tony pointed at Tim. "Tell him how you saved my ass."

Taking another sip from his drink, Tim coughed again. Between gasps, he managed to choke out the word, "Healer." Ok, so maybe his smoothness wasn't at peak levels today.

Baron grinned. "It's vile stuff, but it's the best we can do." He motioned for Tim to join him in the corner where there was a little less ruckus. "So tell me honestly, have you ever seen anything like this?"

"No, and I've seen a lot of stuff." Tim didn't think the wound was from a weapon. The only logical explanation was something supernatural, but he couldn't think of anything offhand that left those kinds of marks on someone's neck.

Back home, he'd been a horror movie nerd. He had a personal rating system for scary movies. There was a "fuck no" pile for movies that were so bad you wondered why someone had invested in them. That pile of movies never got watched again and normally ended up in the trash.

No way he was donating them to perpetuate the cycle of shittiness.

The next pile was the "I watch those while doing other stuff" grouping. This included movies that had barely escaped the "fuck no" pile, but also a few that hadn't earned the right to be in the "watch with reverence" stack.

So when Tim said he'd seen a lot of stuff, he meant it. He'd seen every harebrained idea out there, and all the classics, not to mention however many billion seasons of the Winchesters hunting down just about everything. Even with all his knowledge of the macabre, he still couldn't figure this out.

There were plenty of things out there that liked to snack on humans, though. The undead wouldn't have left anything behind, vampires normally hit the major arteries, and werewolves just kind of fucked people up, they didn't necessarily eat them. There was always the chance it was paranormal since all kinds of things feed on people's essence.

There was no way to know what they were dealing with unless they could catch the thing in the act of feeding. At that point, they'd either know what it was and be able to stop it, or they'd be next up on the menu.

"Anything you can do to help us stop another one of these attacks from happening would be greatly appreciated." Baron looked at the men in the room. "These might not be the best men in Promethia, but they are my friends."

"Do you know if any of the other victims had marks on their necks? I wonder if they have to be attacked a few times to end up like Tony or if it only has to happen once." Tim turned away from the crowd to focus on Baron's response.

"We haven't checked anyone who hasn't gotten sick. The first sign seems to be moaning in their sleep. After a few nights of that, they get a fever, and then they die. The guards come and collect the bodies." Baron looked lost in thought.

"How many men have died?" Tim took another sip of his drink, preparing himself for the answer.

Baron took a long swallow from his own cup. "At least fifteen, maybe more. Sometimes people like to be alone down here. We can't keep track of everyone."

"When there is the time we should round everyone up so we can check their necks." Tim ran a hand through his hair, brushing it behind his ears. "Then maybe we can find something that links them together. Anything could be important. Where they sleep. Are they alone? Maybe even what they eat and drink."

"If we can figure out how these men are being targeted, we might have a chance of stopping this thing." Baron looked at the men mourning the loss of a friend. He took a sip from his drink, and a sad smile spread across his face. "Let's let the men have the night. We'll get started first thing in the morning."

Tim found a quiet corner with a little bit of straw he formed into a bed. He covered it in his cloak and sat down. He continued nursing his drink as he thought about what he had to do here. Then he realized he also had to be ready to take care of the Jepsom issue if his friends busted him out.

He pulled out the information Paul had given him and started looking it over. His mind kept wandering to the more immediate problem of staying alive long enough to escape, so he set the file aside and rested his head against the wall. It was always easier for him to think with his eyes closed.

He'd find a way to get through this. Tim wasn't ready for his story to be over just yet.

CHAPTER SEVENTY-FIVE

Big motherfuckers make more noise when they fall.

Cassie grinned as the thought circled through her mind. The quest she was on wouldn't have led her to this cave if there wasn't a way for her to win, and the way out was walking toward the center of the clearing now. When she beat the overstuffed lizard, they would be out of here and back to the inn before you could order a pizza.

Why is thirty minutes or less still not a thing?

Circle of Champions was an apt description, but cage match would have been closer to the truth. There was a thirty foot dome of vines being slowly lowered over the area they were going to fight in. The dome might be in place just to make sure the contestants couldn't run, but Cassie had the feeling the vines might be strategic as well.

Not that Drago needed an extra strategy to beat her. Big lizard smashes small girl might be the headline on the news at eleven, but not if she could help it. A much more rewarding story would be her kicking Drago's gray-skinned ass back into the egg he was hatched from.

ShadowLily, Gaston, and JaKobi had their hands bound in front of them and were standing off to the side to watch the battle. Guess the lizard king wanted to make sure they didn't try to run if she lost. No one would walk willingly into a worm's maw, but that was their only option if she didn't come through.

They didn't make sunscreen strong enough to ward off lava.

Everything was riding on Cassie, but she was used to that. As a tank in games, most of the responsibility was always on her shoulders. She had to be able to make calls and avoid all the crap on the ground while making sure none of the DPS pulled the boss off her. It was a lot of work, and not everyone was cut out for it.

But Cassie was.

She could lead a group and was willing to take a hit for the team when necessary. Right now her team was counting on her to go toe to toe with Drago and come out on top. No way would she fucking let them down. Cassie had ice in her veins and lady-balls big enough to choke a hippopotamus.

The door to the dome was right in front of Cassie now. She gave a curt nod to her friends and walked inside. The grass in this area was trimmed like they had brought in the ground crew from Augusta National. The ground looked perfectly flat and perfect for combat. She scanned the manicured grass, but nothing looked out of place. If the lizard-men had rigged the arena somehow, the surprise wouldn't be coming from below her.

The only thing she couldn't be certain of was how or if Drago would use the vine-y canopy above them.

There was no way Cassie would be able to use the vines to her advantage. By the time she scrambled high enough to do anything, Drago would be all over her. Those sharp claws on his hands and feet made him a much better climber, and his size made him faster than her.

Size wasn't everything, though.

Cassie could turn on a dime and duck under a lot of things with ease. Drago would never be able to slow down his bulk fast enough to catch her. Plus, she was getting better at dealing with her inferior reach. It was part of why she had chosen to go with the bō staff instead of a more traditional sword-and-board play style.

With a sword and a shield, she might never get the chance to hit an opponent, which was kind of important for a tank. The last thing she wanted was to be rooted in place. She'd learned a long time ago that there was always someone bigger and stronger than you. Shit, some of those guys on late-night TV pulled buses.

Cassie wasn't built for that, and wearing all that bulky armor would just slow her down. So instead of carrying all that crap, she wore leather and had her custom-made shin and forearm guards. She could block with all her limbs but was still light enough to move quickly.

Her speed and size were what gave her the chance to win.

When Drago entered the arena, the lizard-men around the perimeter started chanting his name. The beast raised his hands above his head and let out a fierce roar that would have made Godzilla jealous. He slapped his chest with one fist, and the men outside did the same.

Cassie watched the door to the arena be sealed shut and tied closed with fresh vines. There was no way she was getting out of this alive unless she won. The odds looked like they were stacked against her, but she'd never been a big believer in odds.

Sometimes you had to make your own luck.

She pointed at her three guildmates as they huddled together to watch her through a gap in the vines. Cassie made eye contact with ShadowLily and nodded in a way that said, "Don't worry about a thang. I've got you."

The lizard king climbed to the top of the dome and held his hands up to silence the crowd. "Drago has been challenged. To the winner goes freedom!" The crowd cheered wildly. "The loser will be sacrificed to appease the Great Worm!"

Soaking up the adulation of his people, the king lifted one hand and pointed toward Drago. "Are you ready?"

Drago roared, and some of the men outside of the dome cringed in fear.

The king turned his attention to Cassie. "Ready to meet your goddess?"

Cassie smirked at the king perched high overhead. "I've already had the pleasure." She shrugged. "Seemed as though she wasn't ready for me to die."

"The rules are simple. Two champions enter, one leaves." Green light started to pool around the king's hands. He brought them in front of his chest, then held them out as if he were cradling something before he broke apart his palms like he was letting water fall back into the basin.

A single neon-green leaf fluttered slowly toward the ground.

"The match will begin when the leaf hits the floor." The king lifted his staff and let out a cry. The drums went silent. The night was so still that it felt like everyone was holding their breath. Every single eye watched the leaf ride the gentle breeze as it fell toward the grass.

The leaf continued its inevitable descent, and Cassie got ready. This was it, ready or not. Drago was coming for her. Cassie made sure her armor was tied tightly in place before digging her back foot into the soft earth. She was ready to move the second the leaf hit the ground.

This big fucker wasn't going to know what hit him.

Drago laughed when the leaf hit the ground. With total disregard for Cassie, he extended his arms toward the barrier. A shield and a spear were lowered through the vines. The giant lizard turned with weapons in hand and snapped his jaws. The crowd grew silent as their champion focused on the tiny human.

It took all of Cassie's self-control not to fall for the bait. Who knew that lizard-for-brains would be smart enough to try to lay a trap? Fighters who rushed into Drago's taunts probably lost quickly. For her, this was a battle of endurance. The best person would be the last one standing.

Not that she didn't want to rush over there and clunk the fucker on the head.

But she was a tank. Her will was made of granite. She would stand like a pillar of earth in the face of certain death. Cassie would not give in to her desire to attack. She would wait for the bastard to come to her, then show him what it meant to be her bitch.

Drago walked forward, and the crowd erupted. Their champion pandered to them for a moment before raising his shield and narrowing his focus on Cassie. He turned slightly so his bulk was behind the giant slab of wood and shuffled toward his target with practiced steps.

The bastard was getting closer, but Cassie wasn't going to let him have all the fun. She twirled her bō staff around her in wicked-looking spirals before tucking it against her back. She extended one palm toward Drago and gave him the classic "bring it on" gesture.

Lizard-for-brains wasn't the only one who could play games.

Three human voices cheered Cassie from behind. She smiled and knew that no matter what, her friends had her back. All she had to do now was be confident in her abilities and trust that this had been set up to test her skills, not make her regret every choice she'd made since coming into the game.

As an avoidance tank, standing in one place might as well have been a death sentence, so Cassie started to circle. Drago matched her, circling with ease and kept his shield aimed at her midsection and his spear raised in his other hand, ready to strike.

This was going to be a long fight if neither of them tried to engage, but the longer the fight lasted, the better it would be for Cassie. That shield looked heavy, and so did all those muscles. There was a difference between being in shape and being incredibly bulky. Bulky muscles were created for short bouts of epic strength, whereas a yoga-like physique had stamina for days.

Cassie reached into her belt and threw a dagger at Drago. The blade slammed into his wooden shield and stuck there like an exclamation point. The giant lizard-man smiled over the rim of his shield as though he'd won some great victory.

Let him think that. Cassie smiled. Her mind was starting to work like Tim's. Her plan was to appear to be less than she was and get Drago to chase her around. Finally, when he was tired, she'd fuck him up. The name of the game was endurance, and she had loads of it.

Drago rushed forward, closing the distance between them in two steps. His shield went out to bash her, but Cassie rolled out of the way. She came up on his side ready, to give him a thumping, only to find the point of spear coming right at her. Her staff deflected the spear thrust and she was moving again.

Despite being so big, the lizard-man was quick. She hadn't thought he'd be able to turn as fast as he had. Maybe he used his tail for balance, which let him recover faster than a human could. Going forward, Cassie would have to keep that in mind. There weren't going to be a lot of opportunities to deliver punishment until Drago got tired.

Keeping that in mind, Cassie started to circle him again, and with each step, she angled herself farther away. She grinned at the lizard, almost laughing at her blade quivering in his shield. If the fucker knew how long it had taken her to learn how to throw that knife, he would have been impressed.

Roaring with fury, Drago charged. His spear slashed forward again and again. Cassie skipped and rolled, using her bō staff to shift the tip of the spear out of the way. There were a few close calls, but so far, she'd been able to keep him off balance, and now his movements seemed to be taking longer.

Cassie scored her first hit when Drago overextended his spear arm. Her staff connected with his wrist, there was a crack like the sound of ice breaking on a frozen lake, and Drago's spear fell to the ground.

Drago roared in pain as he took his shield in both hands and used it like a bat.

Cassie hadn't expected to be assaulted by a wall of wood, not when she was pretty sure the big fucker was down to one healthy wrist. There was nothing she could do to get out of the way. The only thing she had left was to try to roll with the hit.

The shield cracked her in the side, and Cassie flew across the arena. The grass cushioned her fall as she turned it into a roll. She climbed back to her feet after learning what it felt like to get hit by a bus. Drago was smiling at her, and all she wanted to do was rip the smug grin off his face.

People had been smiling at her like that her whole life. When she walked into a room, because she was pretty and tiny, people forgot about her. Well, this shit-licking dragon fucker wasn't going to get the best of her.

The crowd cheered as their champion tossed his shield away. He bent down, picked up his spear with his left hand, and started jogging toward Cassie. She kept her eyes focused on him. It had been easy to keep him away when Drago had the shield, but without it, he could just wrap his arms around her.

Getting smothered to death seemed like a shitty way to go.

It was hard not to sprint forward and meet his charge. She kept circling and adding distance between them. He wasn't nearly as proficient with the spear in his left hand as he had been with his right.

Thankfully for Cassie, that meant she'd done some damage with her lone strike of the fight. If Drago couldn't hold the spear in his right hand, it gave her something to work with.

The king screamed at Drago as his next attack missed Cassie completely. A blue orb fell from the top of the dome, fluttering toward the injured lizard-man. Cassie rushed forward, pulling her hook and chain from her belt. She took aim when the blue orb was fifteen feet away from Drago's outstretched hand.

The hook spiraled through the air, wrapping around Drago's ankle before latching onto the chain. Cassie yanked for everything she was worth and watched Drago stumble to his knees. Dropping the chain to the floor, she sprinted toward the fallen fighter with every ounce of strength she could summon. With a cry, she leapt off the ground, one foot landing on Drago's back as she launched herself upward.

Her hand closed around the glowing blue orb, and power rushed through her. Cassie hit the ground with a smile on her face. Arcs of blue energy ran down her arms, infusing her with a strength she couldn't believe. Cassie ran forward, using her staff like a baseball bat. The running swing hit Drago in the side and sent him flying backward.

Cassie's blows rained down on Drago's unprotected flesh. She heard something break and realized that her staff shattered against the lizard-man's forearm. Getting the staff repaired wouldn't be a big deal, but the weapon's destruction had snapped her out of her battle rage. Looking down at Drago, she realized he was in bad shape. Both his arms were broken, and his ribs were turning black.

Turning her gaze away from Drago, Cassie glared up at the king. "Are you satisfied now, you cheating bastard?"

The crowd grew silent and scrambled off the dome. The ceiling of vines was slowly lifted from the ground. A quick glance to the side showed that her friends' bonds had been cut and they were being herded toward her.

The king appeared at her side. "That was well fought, Champion." He pulled a small token from inside of his belt and pressed it into her palm. "Go forth with the blessings of our people."

Cassie grinned as her quest updated. She'd done it. When they got back to Promethia, she could go to the guildhall and officially update her class and register as an adventurer. Despite the rough start to this quest, things had worked out perfectly.

The smile on her face disappeared as she looked at ShadowLily. The only thing that could have devastated her best friend that much was if something happened to Tim. Cassie ran forward, pulling her into a hug. "Tell me what's going on?"

"Tim's been arrested," ShadowLily said as she choked back tears.

Rounding on JaKobi, Cassie shouted. "What the fuck? We weren't gone that long."

The fire mage held up his hands in surrender. "Jepsom sent the city guard. There wasn't anything we could do."

"I saw them from the inn," Gaston rumbled. "Twenty armed men."

"Well, there has to be a trial or something, right?" Cassie gazed at the two men.

"Not always," Gaston replied uncomfortably.

Cassie smacked him on the chest. "Not helping." She turned toward JaKobi. "Well, wherever the hell he is, we'll break him out."

"That's the thing." JaKobi looked at the ground. "We don't know."

"They can't find him. No one knows where he was taken," ShadowLily replied despondently.

Gaston put an arm around each of the two women and moved them toward the mouth of the cavern. "Let's not press our hospitality. When we get back to the inn, I'll put the word out. We'll know where he is before dawn."

"Then we get to do a prison break." Cassie grinned. "He'll be back in your arms by noon."

ShadowLily smiled at them and picked up her pace. There was a look of grim determination in her eyes that said, "I will get him back, and there is nothing in the universe that will stop me."

CHAPTER SEVENTY-SIX

S leeping in a new place was never easy for Tim.
Trying to get comfortable in prison for the first night was something else altogether. Tim spent most of the night reading the documents Paul had given him. There was a ton of information to review, and he was determined to be ready to strike if he made it out of the prison in time.

Jepsom couldn't win.

Sometime around two AM, he shelved the papers for the last time and leaned his head against the wall. Prison wasn't nearly as rape-centric as he'd been led to believe by late night TV. *Sons of Anarchy* had shone a light on jail that he hadn't needed to see. Although in this case, that could just be the coding. It wouldn't be very good PR if players had too realistic an experience.

The game needed to be tense, not therapy-inducing.

There was no place for a crime like that in the real world, let alone in a game. Thankfully, these developers had decent common sense. While Tim could still get his ass kicked in here, knowing that something else wasn't going to happen to his ass made him feel safe enough to close his eyes.

Tim rested his head against the rough stone wall and wedged himself into the corner. He would be more comfortable lying down, but he'd also be more vulnerable if someone did try to attack him. Slowly, he pushed the thoughts of getting attacked out of his mind and let them wander in a happier direction. Somewhere between dreaming of ShadowLily and a watermelon vodka slide, his mind went blank, and he was dead to the world.

"What in the fuck was that?" Tim rubbed at his eyes, wondering if he'd heard a noise or if he'd simply dreamt it.

A man's wail came again.

Without hesitation, Tim ran toward the noise. He hit a few dead ends, but eventually rounded the corner into what he thought was the right room. The torches in the area had been extinguished so he couldn't see for shit.

Stepping into the hallway, Tim grabbed a torch from the wall just as the awful sound came again. It was a cry he'd expect to hear from a man suffering from delirium or someone stuck in a fever dream. The noise was pure anguish, like the wail a mother makes when she loses a child.

The pain the man must have been in to make those noises pushed Tim into action. He stepped into the room and lifted the torch above his head. As light slowly filled the room, his eyes found two men in the corner. One was lying down, and the other was kneeling over him.

The man kneeling above the other turned to face Tim, shielding his eyes from the light. "Go back to your cell."

Lowering the torch, Tim focused on the man in front of him, trying to make out his features in the flickering light. "Sheriff Hobbs?"

"I said, go back to your cell." The sheriff sneered as he pointed back the way Tim had come. "I'll make sure this prisoner is taken to a healer."

Tim wasn't sure what was going on. There was no reason for the sheriff to be down here. The man had made the point several times that guards don't mix with prisoners except during chowtime. If John Hobbs was down here to help the man, why had he found him kneeling over the prisoner in the dark? Maybe the man on the ground wasn't just a prisoner, maybe he was a victim.

Oh, shit!

Tim took a step back before he could stop himself. If this man was being attacked by the sheriff, he couldn't just leave. Well, he could, but Tim knew he'd feel like shit if something happened to the man and he could have helped save him. Thankfully, the sheriff gave him just the "in" he needed to stay put.

"You might not remember from our brief introduction, Sheriff Hobbs, but I'm a healer." Tim smiled sheepishly, trying to play the part of polite inmate. "I helped cure a man who was suffering earlier. I'm sure I could do the same now."

The sheriff stood up, his eyes flashing briefly in the torchlight as they narrowed at Tim. "I told you to get out. Are you going to follow my orders, or are we going to have a problem here?"

"You won't get any problems from me, Sheriff." Tim made sure to look as if the very idea was an affront to his character. "No fighting, no stealing, no bullshit."

A growl rumbled from deep inside of Jon Hobbs' throat. He moved so that he was standing between Tim and the man on the ground. "I'm going to count to ten."

Tim paused, keeping the torch aloft so he could see the entire room. "By then, who knows how many inmates could be in here?" He pointed to the body on the ground. "He wasn't exactly quiet."

"I'm fairly confident it's just the three of us." Sheriff Hobbs took a step closer to Tim. "And since you've interrupted my meal, I'm entitled to another."

Meal?

So the good old sheriff was the killer, but how? And why would he do it? There didn't seem to be any logical reason for this kind of behavior to suddenly start. Then Tim remembered what Davros had said. The guard had mentioned that Jon had been acting differently since he'd returned from his trip.

Something must have happened to him on his vacation.

"I'm sure if you're hungry, I could probably scrounge up a few stray potatoes." Tim kept the torch between them. He'd use it as a weapon if he had to, but the last thing he wanted was to hit the sheriff with it, only to find himself stuck in the dark.

"You cheeky little shit." The sheriff took another step toward him. "I'll make *you* my fucking potato."

Tim tried not to laugh as he jabbed the torch toward the sheriff. Make me his potato. Who said shit like that?

His one offensive spell was flameburst. Tim started going through the motions as the sheriff continued backing him into the opposite corner. Something flicked out of the sheriff's mouth. Either he had an abnormally large tongue, or there was another mouth in there, just like in *Alien*.

Fuck this!

Tim finished the movements of his spell and let it go by pointing at the sheriff. Flames erupted from his open palm, engulfing the area in front of him with fire. Jon's clothes burned and his hair was gone, but he didn't scream. Instead, he took another lumbering step forward.

This just keeps getting better and better.

Tim's fingers worked through flameburst again as his lips moved in a silent prayer to the goddess. He didn't know what he was facing down here, only that the good sheriff wasn't a man anymore. He was going to need some help to get out of this alive.

The spell was finished and Tim started to lift his arm, only to find it clamped to his side. The sheriff's fetid breath washed over Tim's face like the smell of garbage left in a hot car. "I'd rather you didn't."

Tim's concentration was broken, and the spell fizzled out.

"See, we can be civil," Jon whispered. "But I am still hungry. It would have been better for both of us if you'd just walked away."

"I'm starting to see that now." Even with death on the line, Tim couldn't stop himself from running his mouth.

Sheriff Hobbs knocked the torch out of his hand before spinning Tim around and slamming him face-first against the wall. "So hungry."

Tim heard a noise like someone retching, followed by a slithering sound. He imagined something sliding out of the sheriff's mouth, getting ready to attach itself to the back of his neck. He was about to become Jon's next meal.

Something wet touched the back of Tim's neck, and his body started to grow numb.

"Did you hear that?" someone called.

"Yeah, I think it came from over here," someone else responded.

The sheriff slammed Tim's head against the wall. "I can't wait to taste you." He took a step back. "Or drain you." He giggled. "I can never remember which is better."

Tim turned to face the sheriff, surprised to see that he looked the same as he had when Tim had met him in his office this afternoon. His burnt hair and skin were back to normal. Jon's clothes were still in tatters, but the rest of him looked perfect.

Footsteps echoed down the hall. Tim flicked his eyes toward the door, knowing that whoever was coming had just saved his ass. When he turned to look back at the sheriff, the man was gone.

Like a fucking ghost.

Bending down to pick up his torch, Tim lofted it above his head as his gaze spun wildly, searching for any sign of the sheriff. "Why couldn't he just be a normal serial killer?" Tim groused. It wasn't like the man needed a supernatural edge since they were already imprisoned here. All he had to do was isolate a man, and his chance of getting caught was virtually zero.

Baron and Henry came through the doorway and stopped at the sight of Tim. "What's going on here?" Baron asked as Henry went to check on the man on the floor.

Tim wiped away some of the blood running into his eye. The

sheriff must have slammed his head against the wall harder than he'd thought. It was funny how fear took the edge off pain, or maybe it was the surge of adrenaline that did it. Now that the shock was wearing off, his head hurt more than he'd like to admit.

A quick cast of healing orb cleared Tim's head. "I heard a noise and came to find out what it was." He looked at the ground, unsure of what to say next. If he told these men the sheriff was here and had somehow disappeared, they'd think he was crazy. "I found him like this."

Baron peered at Tim's head. "Bullshit. You don't get a gash like that just walking around. Either you two fought or you ran into something else."

Tim noted that Baron hadn't said some*one* else. Maybe he could test the waters. "I ran into the sheriff."

Henry looked at him. "Down here? Not bloody likely. That fat bastard hasn't come down here in years."

"If he was here with you, why didn't we see him come out of the room?" Baron asked, lifting his torch to make sure there wasn't anyone else in the room with them.

This was the part of the conversation where he was going to lose them. "He just kind of vanished." Tim shrugged. This was going about as well as could be expected.

"How about you start from the beginning, and don't leave anything out," Baron suggested as he pulled a small wooden club from behind his back.

Fuck it. If they didn't believe him and it came to a fight, Tim would pull his daggers and do what he had to. He started his story from when he woke up and ended it when they found him in the room. Henry looked skeptical, but Baron looked intrigued.

"Let me see the back of your neck." Baron motioned for Tim to turn around.

Tim felt the man's fingers brush against his neck. He waited to feel the club smash into the back of his skull, but the blow never came. He turned back around to see a disgusted look on Baron's face.

The inmate was rubbing his fingers together, and there was a clear-ish sticky liquid on them. It kind of looked like when someone covered up a big sneeze, only to find their hand covered in webs of unsightly snot.

Baron wiped his fingers on the floor. "At least that part of your story is true." He shook his head in disbelief. "I never would have guessed it was the sheriff. The man's a little odd, but he's never tried to harm us."

Henry looked at the two men. "I'm still not sold. For all we know, this fucker could be making it all up. Maybe he's the one doing this to us."

Tim pointed at his own chest. "All this started before I got here. And if I wanted you all dead, why would I have healed the guy this morning?"

"Be an easy way to gain our trust," Henry snarled as he stared daggers at Tim.

"Easy now, kid." Baron motioned for Henry to relax. "It might not make sense, but he's telling the truth. What we need to do now is decide what we're going to do with this new information."

Tim looked at their expectant faces, realizing they wanted him to come up with an answer. "The only thing I can think of to keep people safe is for them not to be alone. It was you guys approaching that saved my ass."

"But he left you alive." Henry looked at Tim mistrustfully.

Baron smiled. "Who's going to believe him? Guy had a welt on his head the size of a lemon. Sheriff probably thought we'd do his dirty work for him."

"Let me see what I can do for him, and then we should get some rest." Tim cocked an eyebrow at Baron. "I'm guessing none of these attacks happen during the day."

"No, they don't. Let's get Lenny up, and I'll start spreading the word." Baron joined Tim by Lenny's side.

It was a simple enough thing for Tim to cast cleanse on the man, and Lenny came out of his fevered state almost instantly. He looked around the room, almost as if he couldn't believe his eyes. Tim hit him with a healing orb to make sure he'd be all right, then stood up to leave.

"Find me if there are any issues. Otherwise, I'll meet you back in the vodka room around ten." Tim ducked out the door.

He was lucky Baron was a reasonable man. If the choice had been left up to Henry, Tim would probably be fighting for his life right now. His ability to heal might not have bought him nearly as much leeway as he would have liked.

At least nobody had died since he'd joined the prisoners.

As long as he could keep everyone alive, he had a chance of getting out of this place in one piece. All he wanted was to get back to the inn and fall asleep in ShadowLily's arms. There was something to be said about the simple things in life. When you found someone you couldn't live without, you had to hold onto them and never let go.

Life seemed like it would go on forever, but it was infinitely short.

In his mind, that was what made us such interesting creatures. People lived their whole lives knowing that they were going to die, and yet they gave to each other with such generosity. Sharing one's soul with another was a gift that couldn't be purchased.

He would get out of this and back to ShadowLily. Even death couldn't stop him.

CHAPTER SEVENTY-SEVEN

"Any word?" ShadowLily asked Ernie for what seemed like the hundredth time.

Ernie scowled at her, then seemed to remember that she was on edge and needed to be treated with care. "None of our contacts have reported him being transferred to any of the smaller jails. There are only so many places remaining where he could be. We'll find out soon enough." The innkeeper frowned. "All of the remaining prisons will be almost impossible to infiltrate."

"Then we need access to a lawyer or some way to petition the crown. If Jepsom is behind this, maybe the high priest can stop him." Cassie tried to sound hopeful. "We'll get him back. That asshole can't just do whatever he wants."

Gaston walked into the room and shook his head when they all turned to look at him. "Nothing yet. I've put the word out to see if anybody reported seeing the guards escorting him. If we can figure out which direction they went, we can quickly narrow down the remaining options."

"If Jepsom is behind this, you should probably just pick the worst one and start there," JaKobi muttered and turned his attention back to the book he was reading.

Cassie smacked him on the arm. "Not helpful." She glanced at her bestie, expecting her to look crushed.

"No, he's right." ShadowLily looked around the room. "Jepsom wouldn't just have Tim arrested. He'd want him tucked quietly out of the way." She focused on Ernie. "Is there someplace like that in the city."

Ernie ran a hand through his beard and cast a suspiciously quick look at Gaston. "There is one place."

ShadowLily made a "come on and spill the beans already" gesture.

"They call it 'the Hole.'" Gaston shuddered as he said it. "It's not a very original name, but it's an apt description for the place."

The assassin continued speaking as if he were reliving a traumatic memory. "Only one way in or out. And that's if you make it through the courtyard of armed guards first. Last time I heard, the garrison supported at least forty men. So at the very least, we'd be looking at ten armed men, with thirty in reinforcements only footsteps away."

"How in the fuck are we going to break into that?" Cassie pouted.

"You aren't," said a voice from behind them.

ShadowLily spun, daggers in hand, but paused when she saw a woman in a dress standing there. Her manservant looked like he could cause some trouble, but the lady seemed harmless enough.

"And you are?" ShadowLily tried to keep her voice level, but it might have come across as a little aggressive. She didn't like it when an attractive woman showed up on her turf and started giving orders.

"Lady Briarthorn. Surely you've heard of me." One at a time, she took off her gloves and handed them to her servant. The man also took her coat before the lady glided into the room. She found a chair that looked sufficiently clean and sat with all the grace of a queen.

Ernie and Gaston bowed to her. Cassie just inclined her mug toward the lady before taking another sip. JaKobi was sitting bolt upright. ShadowLily couldn't tell if he knew who Lady Briarthorn was, or if it was her attractive appearance that was garnering the man's full attention.

"Tim's spoken of you." ShadowLily sat across from Lady Briarthorn. She looked the woman over one more time, wondering why Tim forgot to mention she was a stone-cold hottie.

"I should hope so. We've accomplished quite a bit together. He's a rather resourceful young man." Lady Briarthorn gave her a wry smile in a way that said, "See? You don't have anything to be worried about. I'm not interested in your man."

Lucy Briarthorn's look grew more serious. "Thankfully for both of us, the high priest shares my high opinion of Tim, and has tasked me with securing his release."

ShadowLily felt the first genuine smile cross her face since she'd heard about Tim being arrested. "That's great!"

"I have a letter demanding his immediate release, signed by the high priest. Would you care to join me when I go to present it?" Lady Briarthorn watched ShadowLily intently.

"Let's go." ShadowLily moved toward the door. She stopped when she realized no one was following her. "What's the hold-up?"

Lady Briarthorn rose from her chair and turned to face ShadowLily. Her lips were set in a frown. "We can't go until morning. Despite my cajoling, the sheriff has refused to see us until ten."

"By cajoling, she means screaming obscenities at the top of her lungs," her servant quipped.

"Oh, Reggie, I swear I can't take you anywhere." Lady Briarthorn extended her hand toward ShadowLily. "Should I have a carriage sent, or would you like to meet me there?"

ShadowLily looked at Lady Briarthorn's hand, unsure if she

should shake it or give it a kiss. Deciding that kissing her hand might place the wrong kind of boundaries on their relationship, she shook it. "I'll meet you there."

"Then I will see you all tomorrow at ten." She motioned for ShadowLily to follow her to the door. "Tim is handling a time-sensitive issue for us. The high priest is pulling a lot of strings to make this happen. See that Tim comes through on his end of the bargain."

ShadowLily nodded. There wasn't a verbal answer she was ready to give. Until she knew what Tim was up to, she didn't want to commit herself to a course of action. That didn't quite seem to be a threat, but it let her know exactly where they stood.

Tim's get out of jail free card wasn't free.

ShadowLily opened the door for Lady Briarthorn and replied evenly, "See you at ten."

Lady Briarthorn slipped her gloves back on and beamed at her. "Don't take it personally, dear. It's just business." Her eyes twinkled mischievously. "Although Paul does seem a little more worked up than usual."

Lucy stepped outside and climbed into her carriage. She called from the window, "I'll see you in the morning. Don't be late."

As if she'd be late for this. ShadowLily closed the door and turned to face the room. "I don't trust her."

"Never trust the nobility," Gaston retorted. "They'll smile while stabbing you in the back."

"She didn't seem that bad," JaKobi countered with a smile.

"Men," Cassie sighed dramatically. "They'd run headfirst into a wall if it had a picture of boobs on it."

"Don't knock 'em till you've tried them," JaKobi quipped back.

Cassie grabbed her boobs. "Tried 'em." She flipped him off.

"Point taken." JaKobi put his head down and pretended to read his book.

ShadowLily grabbed a beer from the table. "We have to be there before ten tomorrow. Let's just hope Tim's still in one piece when we get there."

Cassie lifted her mug into the air. "To our fearless leader!"

Cheers went up from around the room. ShadowLily hoped Tim knew they would always come for him. That *she* would always come for him.

The tower was bigger than ShadowLily had imagined.

Not that the size of the single tower mattered in relation to the prison. Gaston and Ernie had assured her that the majority of the prison was below their feet. There was one building with a single door that led down into the darkness. If the prisoners somehow made it out of the dungeon, they would exit into the courtyard they were looking at now.

A courtyard surrounded by ten-foot-tall stone walls that was filled to capacity with armed guards.

By the time any rebellion made it out of the courtyard, the city guard would have been notified. The number of men a potential escapee would face would have been insurmountable. The crown would never allow a prison break to happen; it would tarnish their spotless reputation.

Ernie had joked that some of the thieves in the city said the Hole was the safest place in the whole kingdom, even safer than the palace.

In short, without Lady Briarthorn's help or an army, they weren't getting Tim out of prison. Thankfully, the high priest had come through with the help they needed, but there was a cost. Tim was on a quest for the man, something important enough for Paul to exert his will over that of the cardinal.

She didn't like the idea of her man being stuck in the middle of this political cluster fuck. As much as ShadowLily hated to admit it to herself, Malvonis might have the right idea. Getting out of town and keeping out of this shitstorm until it blew over might have been the safest way to go.

Unfortunately for all of them, it seemed Tim was on a quest chain that required him to be here. Maybe he finally got the kill quest, and all of this would be over one way or another. She smiled and thought of how Tim's quests always felt like a classic game. In every game, all the major storylines ended when you killed the big baddie.

Jepsom was definitely a giant fucking baddie.

The bastard might not have green skin or four arms, extra legs, or a really cool weapon, but that didn't make him any less deadly. The scariest part of the entire situation was they had no idea what kind of skills Jepsom actually possessed. All ShadowLily knew for certain was that the cardinal wouldn't have made it to where he was inside of the temple's power structure without being able to intimidate people.

Their little group stopped outside of the gate. A few moments later, a black horse pulled a carriage up alongside them, and Lady Briarthorn exited with the grace of a queen. She walked up to the black iron gate and held out her hand. Reginald placed his walking stick in her palm, and she used it to bang on the gate until someone appeared.

"No admittance!" The guard glared at the group.

"I need to speak to Sheriff Hobbs." When the guard didn't respond, Lady Briarthorn continued, "He's expecting me."

The guard turned and shouted, "Hey, Davros, the sheriff say anything about visitors?"

"Only six times during this morning's briefing," Davros replied, sounding rather annoyed with the man. He waved the guard away from the gate and opened it himself. "Lady Briarthorn, it's my sincere pleasure. Please allow me to show you and your companions to the sheriff's office."

ShadowLily watched the man fawn over Lady Briarthorn and wondered if she'd ever be important enough in the game for people to treat her that way. It must be a crazy feeling to have people know who you are just by seeing you or hearing your name. On top of that, they not only recognized you but also fell all over themselves to give you whatever you wanted.

Must be nice.

It was too bad that kind of fame normally came with responsibilities. You had to make appearances even when you didn't want to. Every time you left the house, it turned into a photo shoot. Maybe it was better not to be so popular. At least you could wear yoga pants at the grocery store without some asshole snapping a picture of you.

Lady Briarthorn could keep the fame. All ShadowLily wanted out of life was to be comfortable. It'd be nice to wake up not having to worry about the future. She didn't need to drive a Ferrari or live on a multimillion-dollar estate. She wanted to be happy and surrounded by people who cared about her.

Sometimes when life was simple, it was perfect.

Their group followed Lady Briarthorn and Davros to the tower and then inside. Before the door closed behind them, ShadowLily noticed men moving to encircle the courtyard. Getting Tim out of here might not be as easy as presenting a letter from the high priest.

If it came down to a fight, there was no way they'd all make it out of here. They'd be better off getting arrested and then leveraging Gaston's lock-picking skills to make a break for it once things settled down. ShadowLily hoped it didn't come down to a fight. Tim and JaKobi hadn't registered as adventurers, and she was pretty sure if Gaston died, he was gone forever.

Now wasn't the time for big setbacks or losing a friend. Right now, they all needed to take large steps toward the future. Being the first to do things and to find new areas or items was the only way to make enough money for all this to be worth it. She wasn't leaving the game with a bigger bill than when she went into it.

Davros motioned to a man sitting at a desk in the main room.

"This is Richard. He will be attending to your needs until the sheriff is ready to see you." He bowed. "If you'll excuse me, I have some duties to attend to in the courtyard."

"Thank you for your assistance, Davros." Lady Briarthorn blessed him with a smile that lit up the entire room.

Davros exited the tower, and ShadowLily stood just behind Lady Briarthorn and whispered in her ear, "The men outside looked like they might be preparing for a fight."

Lady Briarthorn inclined her head to indicate she'd heard what ShadowLily had said. "I have a contingency plan in place." She walked forward until she was standing in front of Richard. The man didn't look up as he furiously scratched notes on a sheet of paper.

"We have an appointment to see the sheriff," Lady Briarthorn declared with the icy impatience of the affluent.

Richard finished what he was scribbling and looked up. He did a quick double-take at all of the people standing before him as if they hadn't been announced moments before. "I've prepared our conference room for you to wait in. The sheriff should be returning momentarily."

"If he isn't collecting the man we've come to have released, there will be hell to pay." Lady Briarthorn glared at the clerk with disgust. "Your sheriff is getting on my last nerve as it is."

"You're preaching to the choir," Richard grumbled as he stood up. "Not that I can do anything about it." He motioned for them to follow him toward the only open door in the tower.

"We've got water and food set up in here." He turned to look at the lady and dropped his voice. "Probably best to avoid it, though."

Lady Briarthorn gave him a curt nod. "Thanks for the tip, and do tell the sheriff to hurry. I have other appointments I must keep today."

Richard looked at her and then lowered his head so he was staring at the ground instead. "I'll do my best."

"I'm counting on it." Lady Briarthorn turned toward the rest of the group. "It looks as though we'll be waiting for a bit. Stay away from the food and drink."

"Never trust prison food," Gaston rumbled as he walked into the room and took a seat.

ShadowLily smiled. It was damn good advice. There were always stories on the news about the quality of food in prisons. While she didn't think prisoners deserved organic everything, they did deserve to eat food that wasn't expired.

That was the burden of our legal system.

If you're going to lock people up, you have to take care of them. And while they didn't need TVs and video games, prisoners deserved access to real food and clean water at the very least. Just don't tell that to the people running the for-profit jails. Because if it comes down to serving you green baloney or spending two more cents to get better meat, they were going to save the two cents every time.

Shit, this jail probably didn't even have simple standards. This was the kind of place where when prisoners died, whoever had them arrested let out a sigh of relief. One less problem for the nobility to worry about when one of their accusers bit the dust.

At least back in the real world, they had trials. They might not always be fair, but they had them. Here in *The Etheric Coast*, it seemed like all you needed to make people disappear was a fat stack of gold. Granted, that seemed to be the case in the real world too. How many people aligned themselves with politicians and ended up dead?

More than she could count on both hands.

ShadowLily sat on one of the available chairs. "What do we do now?"

Lady Briarthorn sat and smoothed out the front of her exquisite dress. "We wait."

"I hate waiting," Cassie grumbled.

JaKobi pulled a book out of his robes. "I brought a little something to pass the time. One thing I've learned in life is that when you deal with a government agency, you have to be prepared to wait."

ShadowLily snorted. "But hey, at least we have snacks we can't eat."

Cassie sat down next to her and put an arm around her shoulders. "Don't worry. Loverboy will be back in your arms before you know it."

"And Reginald should be executing the second part of our plan now." Lady Briarthorn grinned. "They aren't going to know what hit them."

The two best friends shared a look and started smiling. ShadowLily couldn't help but think this wasn't a woman you wanted to trifle with. Lady Briarthorn was the kind of woman you wanted on your side when shit went down.

A little bit of the tension ShadowLily had been harboring since arriving at the dungeon melted. Tim was going to be fine, and with the good lady's help, all of them were going to get out of here in one piece. Sometimes having powerful friends wasn't such a bad thing.

CHAPTER SEVENTY-EIGHT

"Son of a bitch," Tim muttered as he worked out the kinks in his back.

Who knew sleeping on the floor in a video game could make you feel so rotten? It was like that one time he and Xander had gotten so drunk they'd passed out under some bushes on the way home from a party. It'd taken at least three days for his neck to stop clicking.

Sleeping in weird places was something best left to the extremely young. So it shall be written that any child over the age of fourteen who sleeps on the floor will wake up with at least one limb in agony. Tim laughed at his own joke; sometimes, he cracked himself up.

It wasn't his fault if no one else got it.

Tim did a few of the stretches he'd learned from a yoga instructor he'd had a crush on. He might be shit at yoga, but he had a thing for women in phenomenal shape and tight pants—not that he'd be able to hit on them now.

ShadowLily was an amazing person, not just a great ass in really tight pants. She was the kind of woman you'd give up a kingdom for. There was no way he'd even consider cheating on her. Besides the fact that it would hurt her, he liked his penis attached to his body too much to risk it.

His girl kinda had a thing with knives.

Not that he'd blame her for removing his manhood for straying. There were certain things you don't do. One of them was cheating. Tim liked to think that cheaters always got caught. The radio station by his house used to do a thing called War of the Roses, where the station would call and say the caller had won free flowers and ask where they wanted them delivered. Guess how many guys fell into that trap?

Always try to put yourself in the best position to succeed. Find someone who matches your vibe and be happy. For him, life was all about celebrating the good times with the people he cared about. Sometimes you just had to ride the wave.

Big Richie the surfer taught him that. Guy rode a wave right into the grave, but he went out doing what he loved.

But Tim didn't need to worry about the stresses of marriage or divorce just yet. Things were amazing between him and Shadow-Lily, and while they were together most nights, they still each had their own place. It was too early to know exactly where their relationship was leading, but all indications said it was somewhere great.

With his back feeling a little better, Tim made his way out of the cell he'd been sleeping in and toward the common room. Today might be a really long day. They needed to come up with the plan to stop the sheriff. He had absolutely no idea how to do it, but he was confident if they all worked together, they could bring him down.

Baron waved Tim over to his table as soon as he entered the room. "I've got a bowl of slop for you."

Tim peered into the bowl, relieved to find out it was only oatmeal. "Looks ok."

"As far as oats in a bowl go, it's not half bad." Baron swirled his spoon through his oatmeal. "But after a few years, it might as well be that stuff I wiped off your neck last night."

Looking into his bowl, Tim rethought how hungry he was. He shoved the bowl back into the center of the table. "Maybe I'll be hungrier later."

Baron laughed. "Better get used to it, boy. I've been here ten years, and the food's always been the same."

Tim couldn't stop the shudder from running through his body. Having to eat oatmeal every morning for the rest of his life sounded horrible. There were so many great breakfast foods. You could have eggs with just about anything, and the same with pancakes or waffles. Then you got into the fun stuff: sausage, ham, English muffins, hollandaise sauce.

The options were endless.

A life of just oatmeal wasn't a life at all. How could they expect a person to survive on such lackluster fair? It reminded Tim of watching *The Matrix*. Keanu woke up on the ship, and his first meal was protein slop. Imagine going from endless possibilities to gruel. Kinda made a guy wish he'd stayed plugged into the power grid.

Food was the one thing that Tim would allow himself to get plugged into the Matrix for. He loved eating. What he hated about being here was that there wasn't a Joe's. He missed being able to go to his favorite spot and order a meal. He'd been going to the diner for years without knowing it was owned by Sierra's dad. His opinion of the food was solely based on his stomach and not the fact that his girlfriend's dad ran it.

If only they had a Joe's in the game.

Tim smiled as he thought about how much he'd taken breakfast for granted. Now that he was in the clink, he saw the error of his ways. If there weren't more important things to be worried about, he might just sit around thinking about food for the rest of the day. Unfortunately, the sheriff had to be dealt with, and time was of the essence.

"Any ideas after our conversation last night?" Tim watched Baron, wondering who he'd have to kill to get a glass of rumple-berry juice.

"Just that we need to keep a better eye on each other. I've spread the word that we're all going to sleep in the common area and that no one should go anywhere alone." Baron looked at his bowl and pushed the half-eaten mess away. "Not that it will do us any good."

"That's simply not true. The sheriff ran or vanished when he heard just the two of you coming. I think if there were enough of us, we could simply overpower him." Tim shrugged. It sounded too easy, so it probably was. It was more likely he just didn't want to be caught. The longer he could keep up the illusion of being sheriff, the safer the creature was.

"While I've never seen anything like what I saw last night, I think cutting his feeding tube off would probably help." He looked at the mushy oatmeal, thinking about the slime that was on his neck. "If we can grab it."

"Sounds like we'll need bait," Baron mused.

"I don't like the sound of that," Henry said as he joined them at the table with his own bowl of soggy oats.

"I don't know, I thought you liked being tickled by big burly men," Baron tossed out casually.

Tim almost burst out laughing, but a quick glance at Henry told him laughing at the man wasn't a great idea. Henry had been dealt a solid burn; Baron had definitely scored a point.

The red spots faded from Henry's cheeks and he smiled. "Who I let tickle me and how I like them to look is none of your business, you old bastard."

Baron just grinned from ear to ear. "Seems like we found our bait. Now we just have to figure out how to deploy him so we make the catch."

"Spoken like a true fisherman." Tim wondered how a fisherman ended up in this hell hole. Although Baron did seem awfully comfortable coming up with a plan to put one of his own at risk. Maybe he was a pirate?

Oh. My. God. Tim was sitting across from an honest to goodness pirate.

One thing they never talked about in pirate movies was how the men survived. Yes, most of the boats had a selection of dry stores and fresh water, but those only lasted so long. For life out at sea, you needed certain skills. A man who was handy with a fishhook and a blade would be a huge bonus.

It wasn't easy to bring his mind back on track, but Tim managed to do it eventually. He was just about to say something clever when the sheriff walked into the room.

Jon Hobbs focused his eyes on his target and scratched his belly. "I'd like a word."

Tim stood up. "Might as well say it in front of everyone. It's not like they are going anywhere." A few of the men laughed, but Tim felt his heart beating faster. He needed as many people around as possible to make sure he wasn't attacked.

"Out!" the sheriff roared.

People found other places to be and quickly. Only Henry and Baron remained behind. They hadn't seen the sheriff last night, but his appearance today sealed their belief in Tim's story. The man who never came into the dungeons was here, and that was all they needed to know.

Tim looked behind the sheriff and noticed that he'd brought two guards with him. The guards appeared to be on edge. Being trapped in prison filled with men who only ate potatoes and oatmeal didn't seem to agree with them. He would have been nervous too. A sword in this small space wasn't going to do you a lot of good if enough men charged you.

The sheriff, on the other hand, looked calm as a cucumber. "Did you not hear what I said?" He pointed at Baron and Henry. "Get the fuck out of here. I need a word with Tim alone."

"I think we'll stay," Baron replied off-handedly as if he were commenting on the weather. "Our friend here was just telling us the most interesting story."

The sheriff's eyes almost burst out of his head. He focused all his rage on Tim. "Stories are best left for the children at bedtime, don't you think?"

"This was more of a scary story," Tim quipped. "Not suitable for children at all."

"I see." The sheriff's rage melted, replaced by a look of icy indifference. "Nothing to be done about it now. I just hope that these two don't have an accident while you're away."

"While I'm away?" Tim spluttered. The statement didn't make sense. The sheriff wouldn't just let him go, not after what he'd seen. Was the man telling him that he was going to die now? Were Baron and Henry due to meet a similar fate since he told them what happened?

If that was the case, he was going to go down fighting.

Jon Hobbs held up his hands in a disarming manner. "I was thinking about ending this right now, but there is a very persistent bitch upstairs waiting for you, and I believe I've come up with a delicious alternative."

A smile stretched across his face, and he patted his belly. "I'll be seeing the two of you later." Jon pointed at Tim. "Come with me."

The only person Tim knew who was powerful enough to get him out of here was the high priest, probably with assistance from Lady Briarthorn. In the movies, the ladies of this era were all "stab you in the back and simper and preen," but she wasn't anything like that. Tim wouldn't be surprised to find out she could handle herself in a pinch.

Only idiots thought of women as inferior.

Think of how much more we could have accomplished if women had been allowed to help more throughout history. Some of the country's greatest patriots were women, and most of them did it at a time where women were looked down upon. Imagine the courage it took to run an underground railroad when not being escorted by a man when you left the house was considered too forward.

His friends had come to get Tim just like he thought they would, but they'd come too soon. If he left now, the sheriff was going to take it out on these two men. Tim couldn't let that happen, but he also couldn't stay.

He turned to face Baron and Henry, unsure of what to say. Thinking on the fly, he reached into his inventory and pulled out his daggers. He flipped the blades over and handed them to the men, hopefully without the sheriff seeing. "I'll be back for you."

Baron gave him a sad smile as he tucked the dagger into his shirt. He pulled out a small letter and handed it to Tim. "If and only if I'm not around for some reason, get this to Helen Peters."

"I'll see that you get to deliver it yourself." Tim put the letter in his pocket. He knew what was happening. These men expected to die, and he was pretty sure there was nothing he could do to stop it.

Henry tucked the dagger into his belt. He pulled out a small scrap of parchment and placed it in Tim's hand. "Felix Hardgrove." A tear streaked down his cheek.

"I'll see it done." Tim looked at the two men. "I will be back for you."

Quest Received: Dying Declarations

You've been tasked with delivering two letters upon the deaths of the men who gave them to you. There is no more sacred duty than getting the last words of a loved one to the people they left behind.

There is no reward for this quest, you selfish bastard, it's just the right thing to do.

Accept Quest: Yes/No

Tim accepted the quest.

. . .

Tim had meant what he'd said to them. If anything happened to these men, he'd make sure their letters were delivered.

It wasn't that Tim was driven by some bond of brotherhood that formed miraculously after one night. In fact, he kind of disliked Henry. The thing that bothered him was that these men were in danger because of him, and he hated knowing that his actions would lead to their deaths. Sure, the sheriff might have killed them eventually anyway, but he'd helped speed up the process.

The sheriff had to be stopped, but now that he was being set free, Tim had no idea how to make that happen.

"Hurry it up, lovebirds, I doubt the cunt upstairs is waiting patiently. Women tend to overreact to delays." Jon Hobbs huffed with impatience.

Tim shook Baron's hand. "Stay safe."

"I'll do my best." Baron poked Tim in the chest with a finger. "You just follow my instructions."

Henry grinned and slapped Baron on the chest. "Guess I was wrong about him."

"Holy shit, Henry just admitted he was wrong. Now I can die a happy man." Baron wrapped an arm around Henry's shoulders. "Let's get out of here before the sheriff loses his patience."

Tim turned away from the two men to face the smug-faced bastard in front of him. "Lead the way."

The two guards looked relieved as they scurried toward the door like cockroaches trying to avoid the light. The sheriff followed them. Despite his implied impatience, the sheriff seemed happy enough to take his time getting out of the dungeon.

Jon Hobbs' belly rumbled. "As soon as we get this business taken care of, I'm going to need a snack."

Tim shuddered, thinking about what it would feel like to be drained by the man in front of him. He'd seen the after-effects and heard the screams that accompanied a feeding. By all accounts, it was something he never wanted to experience. His gut twisted as he thought about all the men trapped down here with this monster in their midst.

He'd find a way to kill the bastard.

CHAPTER SEVENTY-NINE

J on Hobbs walked into the conference room with the swagger of a Greek god.

Tim couldn't believe that with everything going on, the man felt so confident. Everyone in this room would know his secret soon enough, and then the jig would be up, not to mention the quest Tim had taken to stop him. There was no way he was letting this drop, not when Baron's and Henry's lives hung in the balance.

The sheriff couldn't be allowed to continue feeding on the inmates. Part of Tim wondered if whatever had come back over the mountain could even be considered Jon Hobbs any more. It almost felt like an *Invasion of the Body Snatchers* type thing. Or even worse, maybe it was more of a *The Thing* scenario.

In which case, the entire kingdom might be fucked.

None of that mattered when his eyes locked onto ShadowLily. Tim rushed forward, slamming into her hard enough that they crashed to the ground in a tangle of limbs. It'd only been a day since he'd seen her, but it felt like a lifetime apart. When their lips met, he wanted to stay on that spot of the floor forever.

A very polite cough from above them brought Tim back to his senses.

After disentangling himself from the half-elf, Tim smiled at the rest of the collected individuals. "It's good to see all of you."

Lady Briarthorn inclined her head to the sheriff. "I see that you've honored the high priest's request. Was there a reason we had to wait so long?"

Jon Hobbs leaned back in his chair like a man sipping tea on the front porch. "Oh, these things take time. I also needed to have a private word with the inmate."

"We should have done this last night," Lady Briarthorn fumed.

The sheriff glanced at Tim. "You know, I was just thinking the same thing." He waved away the inquiring looks from the people in the room. "I've concluded the prisoner's exit interview. You're all free to go."

Lady Briarthorn's cheeks burned at being dismissed, but she forced a smile onto her face. "Then we shall do so at once." She motioned for everyone to stand.

Tim waited for the room to clear before staring at the sheriff like Clint Eastwood had done in every film he'd ever made. "This isn't over."

The sheriff leaned forward, placed his elbows on the table and rested his chin on top of his folded hands. "I'd forget everything you saw. You're out, and the men imprisoned here don't deserve your pity. Go and live your life. Let this place be nothing but a dark memory."

He could easily walk out of the room and try the old "out of sight, out of mind" trick.

Unfortunately for Tim, that little mind game had never really worked for him. When there was a problem, his brain gnawed at it relentlessly until he fixed it. He couldn't count the number of nights he'd woken up from a dream about something he was wrestling with. Normally it was something from one of his classes, but every now and then, it was a videogame that kept him up until the first rays of dawn touched the horizon.

You had got it bad when you woke up thinking about the best way to tackle a boss.

The sheriff felt like the kind of problem that would keep Tim up at night until he resolved it. It was mostly because he couldn't deal with him right now. There was nothing he hated more than leaving quests unresolved. It was the kind of thing that came back to bite you.

There was no way he would let what was happening in the dungeon continue. While Tim didn't know what the men in the prison were guilty of, he *was* sure they didn't deserve to be snacks.

"I'll be seeing you," Tim replied as he tipped an imaginary cap to the sheriff. "My guess is it will be sooner than you would like."

Jon Hobbs leaned back into his chair again, a genuine smile on his face. "I'm looking forward to it."

The smug fucker thought he could take Tim in a fight just because he was a healer. Jon would learn the hard way that a monster who faced off with the Blue Dagger Society rarely lived to wreak havoc again. In fact, he couldn't think of one monster who'd escaped death once the guild set their sights on it.

Part of him wanted to say something else, but Lady Briarthorn was waiting at the exit of the tower, and she looked impatient. Tim tapped his hand on the stone and walked out of the room to catch up with the rest of the group.

Just outside the tower, Lucy Briarthorn stopped him. "I'm sorry it took me so long to secure your release." She looked genuinely worried. "Do you have everything you need for tomorrow?"

Tim had formed a rudimentary plan, but there wasn't anything set in stone. Some of what he planned on doing depended on who was in the stands and how Jepsom responded to their initial attack.

"I think I'm good." Tim reached out to shake her hand. "Thanks for getting me out of here."

Lucy gave Tim's hand a firm squeeze. "If you come through for us tomorrow, it will have been well worth the effort. I'll let you see to your final preparations. Have a good day." She dropped his hand and walked to the exit.

Davros caught up to him just before he reached the others. "Sorry about the…" He paused and mimicked punching Tim in the stomach. "No hard feelings, I hope."

Tim was pissed at first, but maybe there was a way he could use this man. "The sheriff isn't what he seems. The prisoners are in danger."

"What do you want me to do about it?" Davros moved a few steps away from Tim as if standing too close to him might get him in trouble.

"Just keep your eyes open, I might need your help when I come back." Tim went to shake his hand but stopped himself. He was sure there was more than one pair of eyes on them.

"No one ever comes back." Davros gave Tim a lopsided grin. "But then again, no one has ever left before." He leaned close before whispering, "If you come back, I'll help you."

Tim couldn't have his inside man watched too closely, but at least he could get a little payback. He took a swing at Davros. His fist connected with the man's stomach. "Fuck you, too."

He leaned over the winded man like he was going to mock him and whispered, "Be ready."

Lady Briarthorn's carriage was already rolling as the gates closed behind them. The rest of the guild formed a half-circle around him. Tim could tell by the looks on their faces they were genuinely happy to see him.

Cassie poked him in the chest. "You had us worried, asshole."

Tim held up his hands. "Not a lot I could do about it. I'm just happy you weren't there when they came for me." Tim looked from his fiery little tank to the woman of his dreams. "Where were you two, anyway?"

ShadowLily wrapped her arm in Tim's and started pulling him

toward the inn. "It's a long walk back. How about we fill you in on our adventure, and then you can tell us what's next?"

"Well, about that..." Tim stopped as ShadowLily put a finger to his lips.

"Our story first," the half-elf purred into his ear.

"And it's crazy. There was a giant lizard, and Cassie kicked its ass." JaKobi doubled over as Cassie punched him in the gut.

Tim chuckled. There seemed to be a lot of stomach-punching going around.

"It's better when I tell it." Cassie brushed some imaginary dirt from her shoulder. "Now that I'm an adventurer."

"Congrats." Tim was excited. Half his party had taken the plunge. It was making his choice easier to see how excited they all were about the opportunity.

"Now listen closely because I'm only going to tell the story once." Cassie paused. "Who am I kidding? You're going to hear it like a million times. So there we were..."

Tim started to tune her out when ShadowLily leaned her head against his shoulder. "It's actually a good story the first time. On listen number fifteen, I started to find it lacking."

He pulled her close and kept walking toward the inn. He felt so comfortable here with his friends that he never wanted to leave. Back in the real world, there were no more dragons to slay or things to conquer, but in *The Etheric Coast*, there were infinite possibilities. Life in the game was whatever you wanted to make it.

People were going to be talking about what he created for years.

It felt so good to step into the inn.

The Blue Dagger felt like home. You know that feeling when you catch a scent and it gives you a huge hit of nostalgia. That was how Tim felt right now. Who knew the smell of stale beer and sawdust would make him feel so comfortable.

All it took was one night in a dungeon to make his little room look like a palace, and there was beer. Potato vodka was okay stuff, but beer was where his heart was. Plus, he could drink a few of them and drive. If he hit the hard stuff, he had to call a ride. One thing he never did was drive when he was drunk.

If Tim went out for a night on the town with the intention of drinking more than a few, he took a cab. The twenty bucks it cost to get from campus to the bars was worth it. He could get drunk with his buddies and not even be tempted to drive. Or if they were at home, you could have just about anything delivered. Why risk hurting someone else or yourself when Taco Bell was only a few clicks away from your door.

The inn didn't have an app, but it had a Liz.

The woman he'd helped out of her previous job had a beer in his hand before he was five steps inside. "Welcome back."

Ernie came out of the kitchen with a tray of food. "I thought you might be hungry." The innkeeper pulled a letter out of his pocket. "Mr. Applebottom left this for you."

He had a beer and potentially good news in his hands. Now all he had to do was figure out a way to get rid of the sheriff and Jepsom. This was a problem that he ran into a lot. He loved the storylines of quests so much he always took on way too many of them. To be fair, Tim thought he'd be in the dungeon for a few days, but things hadn't worked out that way.

ShadowLily dragged him toward a table. "Do you really think your plan for tomorrow will work?"

"I don't know. The only thing we can do is go for it." Tim took a sip of his beer.

JaKobi grinned after taking a sip from his own mug. "Kicking ass and taking names."

"Distraction duty isn't fit for the Destroyer of Lizards." Cassie gazed into her beer as if it would reveal the world's greatest unsolved mysteries.

"Trying out new nicknames for yourself?" Tim snorted. "Is distraction duty good enough for the Lady Who Talks too Much?"

Cassie picked up something from the food tray and threw it at him. "It's a good thing you just got out of prison, asshole."

Tim grinned at her as he started making a plate of food. "I get the feeling this is supposed to be a *mano a mano* fight. My final test before making the first-class change."

"Seems dangerous is all," Cassie replied before starting to put together her own plate of food.

"Like a cage match with a giant ass lizard wasn't?" JaKobi stood up, grinning like a mad man. "You should have seen her, Tim. I would have been shitting myself trying to run away, but Cassie went toe to toe with that monster."

"A man who can shit and run at the same time has many talents." Gaston nudged JaKobi. "Read that on a bathroom stall once."

The fire mage nodded. "Sage advice, my friend, sage advice."

Tim looked around the room and thought about how much fun he was having. Sure there was always tomorrow's fight looming over his head. It was stressful, but knowing that he had these awesome people in his life made it so much better. When the shit hit the fan, his entire guild came running. That was the kind of support money couldn't buy.

The bonds of friendship could be stronger than Gandalf facing down a Balrog.

CHAPTER EIGHTY

T im pushed his bowl of oatmeal away.

The meal reminded him too much of the last one he'd shared with Baron and Henry. Thankfully he had a giant glass of rumpleberry juice and a plate of bacon.

Wasn't life always better with bacon?

Smiling to himself as the salty meat melted in his mouth, Tim looked over his team. Each of them looked calm. Why shouldn't they be? They had conquered every task they'd ever taken on. If he had to be honest with himself, the Blue Dagger Society was pretty badass.

Still, there was that tiny bit of worry worming its way into his skull. Deep down, Tim was a worrier at heart. He liked to have a plan and several backup plans in place for different scenarios that might derail his original options. He didn't like to go into a fight unless there was a possibility of controlling all the variables. He knew all the logistics of today's ceremony.

So he should have felt confident.

Instead, Tim felt worried. There were so many things that could go wrong. If the fight raged out of control, innocent people in the crowd could be hurt. That's why his plan revolved around getting as many people away from the ceremony before his attack as possible.

The only way he'd stand a chance to win was if he didn't have to worry about the crowd. They might just be NPCs, but killing innocent bystanders wasn't something he wanted to do. At least Gaston had been able to replace the daggers he'd given away, so Tim had something he could use to try to kill that bastard Jepsom. Otherwise, he'd have to rely on flameburst, and while he'd dedicated some time to leveling the spell, it wouldn't be the thing that tipped the scales against the cardinal.

Tim wanted this fight to be up close and personal.

He was ready to kill the fucker. Jepsom had gone out of his way to make Tim's life harder just because he'd taken the time to heal a peasant who couldn't afford the temple's services. They say no good deed goes unpunished, and sometimes it was true, but fuck those people.

Tim wasn't going to stop helping others just because people wanted him to stop.

There was a feeling that he got when he selflessly helped someone. You never know what a person's going through; doing something small like covering a dollar when they were short at the register could make all the difference in their lives. A small bit of kindness could be all it takes to make someone's day.

Polishing off the rest of his juice, Tim leaned against Shadow-Lily, his mind already jumping to the business of the day. "Ready to go?"

She winked at him. "As long as you are." She grabbed Tim's chin and forced him to look her in the eye. "We're all going to be there for you. So get out of your own way and just do your thing."

Cassie placed a hand on Tim's shoulder. "We've got this."

"What she said." JaKobi grinned at them as he shoved the last three pieces of bacon in his mouth at once.

Gaston twirled one of his daggers on a fingertip. "The real question is, why don't you want us to do more?"

Tim couldn't put his finger on it. There was no rule that said he had to fight Jepsom alone, but he'd learned to trust his instincts a long time ago. He might be overly cautious, but he was rarely surprised. He was also prudent and didn't want to lose because of his pride.

"Oh, I'm counting on all of you to bail my ass out of the fire when the shit hits the fan. They say no plan survives first contact with the enemy. So if you see Jepsom get the upper hand, feel free to help out." Tim looked around at their smiling faces.

"So much for doing this alone," Cassie chided.

"My pride can take the hit of having help, but not of letting him win." Tim grinned. "So don't wait too long if I'm in trouble." He stood and walked toward the door. "Let's go."

Once their group made it out of the slums, they headed in the direction of the temple. Outside of the massive building, there would be a stage set up and some seating erected for those too wealthy to stand with the huddled masses and one lowly assassin with friends in high places.

The high priest would give a speech, and Jepsom would accept his reward before giving a speech of his own. It was during his speech that Tim planned to make his move. Lady Briarthorn had arranged for him to have a seat in the front row, virtually guaranteeing him access to the cardinal.

As they reached the temple steps, the group split up. Their plan hinged on them not being noticed together. Anyone traveling with Tim could be marked by Jepsom's people and someone might remember a group of five coming to the event together if there was an attack.

And there was going to be an attack of epic proportions.

Jepsom and his reign of terror were going down. Who knew how many lives that bastard ruined by refusing to heal people. Imagine having the ability to cure any disease, to mend any broken bone, and then denying access to the people who needed those treatments. No one should have to die so someone could turn a profit.

He wished there was more magic in the real world. Too many great people died of cancer. That shit was the king of all mother-fuckers. Ryan Reynolds had said it best when he'd simply stated, "Fuck Cancer!" If the choice was to heal what he could or be called a criminal, Tim was going to keep healing.

They had called Rick Simpson a criminal too.

Now he was the hero of a revolution. Tim might not believe you could kill cancer with cannabis alone, but he'd seen too much evidence suggesting it helped to ignore it. If he ever got the Big C, he'd be taking his normal treatments and as much pot as he could handle. If the choice was death or eating a bunch of Rick Simpson Oil, he'd get a penchant for edibles real quick.

It was the logical choice.

Thankfully for him, the cardinal wasn't something he had to fight a long, agonizing battle with. Whatever happened between them would be settled today. Jepsom was a tumor that had latched itself onto the temple, and he needed to be cut out. Once the cardinal had been removed, Paul could run the temple in a way that benefited all the citizens of Promethia.

When you were a healer, you cared about more than just billing or selling certain medications for kickbacks. Wanting to help people live their best and longest lives was a calling. Not everyone was made for it. That was why when people found a doctor who really cared about them, they would stay their patient forever.

Finding someone who cared about your health as much as you did wasn't easy.

That was why Tim tried to spend a little time with each of his patients instead of just throwing a *Healing Orb* at them and taking their money. Part of the process was healing their minds from whatever incident had occurred.

Having a broken arm one instant and a fully functional one the next, wasn't something everyone was used to. Imagine having the mental trauma from a major accident but your body was fine. It took folks time to process their recovery, and he was there to help them with that as well.

With the high priest's and Lady Briarthorn's help, Tim could offer those types of services. Shit, even Ironbeard had given him extra time to focus on his healing. Everything was working out perfectly.

Not to mention his plan to buy out the buildings next to the inn. In his inventory, he held a signed letter for the properties. As long as he had the gold in the account within five days, he'd be the proud owner of every single building he wanted. He didn't know how Applebottom had secured them all, but it always paid to hire the best people for the job.

Sometimes the best cost a little more, but savings in peace of mind were not measurable.

Tim moved through the crowd until he found his seat in front of the raised stage. He sat down and waited for the ceremony to start. It wouldn't be long now until his future inside of *The Etheric Coast* was decided. He'd either kill Jepsom and move on or die trying. There wasn't room for any middle ground.

He fanned himself with the program for the event and casually looked around. He spotted JaKobi and Cassie but not his thief or assassin. Granted, if they were easy to spot, they wouldn't be very good at their jobs. Tim trusted that they were in the right positions and everything was in place.

The next few hours would decide his future, and Tim was ready to embrace the challenge.

CHAPTER EIGHTY-ONE

The crowd quieted as the high priest took the stage.

Paul stepped up to a small podium and looked over the grouping. "The goddess is truly blessed to have so many dedicated followers. Using her light to guide us, we must all strive to be the best versions of ourselves. To truly embrace the divine, one must be not only devoted but compassionate and charitable."

After another review of the masses, the high priest continued, "Let the words of the goddess direct you in all things. Her teachings serve us all. Her words fill us with hope for the future."

Glancing toward the men seated on the stage, Paul motioned to Jepsom. "We've come together today to honor one man who exemplifies the will of the goddess, our very own Cardinal Jepsom."

Jepsom inclined his head to the high priest and offered him the slightest of nods.

Paul smiled warmly as he turned back to face the crowd. "Today, we honor the cardinal for a job well done. With his guidance, our temple has truly become the envy of the continent. Every high priest around the realm is trying to recruit him into their service."

He slammed a fist on the podium. "But I said no! The cardinal is too valuable of a resource for us to part with. The people of Promethia deserve the best."

"Thus, we celebrate the man who thinks of others before himself in every situation. Who would give the very last coin in his purse to help someone in need. A man who would do anything to better the lives of friend and foe alike."

Paul paused for dramatic effect. "I present to you the newly minted Cardinal of the Seven Seals." The high priest started clapping, and the cheering crowd swallowed up whatever was said between the two men before Jepsom claimed the podium.

A smug smile twisted the cardinal's lips almost into a sneer. He looked directly at Tim before turning to face the adoring masses. Tim looked at where the cardinal had been sitting and was shocked to see the high priest sitting next to Jon Hobbs.

Lifting a hand to silence the crowd, Jepsom started to address the gathered masses. "In the spirit of giving, a good friend of mine has asked that I preside over the funeral of two local inmates. I thought it would be appropriate to welcome these men back into the goddess' embrace before thanking you all for this glorious position."

Jepsom's smile turned warm and caring, something Tim wasn't sure the man was able to accomplish until that very moment.

Two caskets were carried onto the stage. Tim felt a sinking sensation in his gut. The sheriff was here, and there were only two other men who knew his secret. Were Henry and Baron in those coffins? He looked away from the two white boxes and back up at the podium. The cardinal winked at him before scanning the crowd with a sorrowful expression on his face.

"The goddess' light shines upon us all. In her eyes, no man is worth more than any other," Jepsom said with just the right trace of self-deprecation.

Tim snorted in disbelief. The cardinal was the kind of man

who'd have your throat slit for scuffing his boots, and he was up there giving a speech about equality. It made him fucking sick.

"These two men might have died in prison, but their light will move on. All of us deserve the chance at redemption." The cardinal paused. He let the tension build for a moment and then continued, "Baron Peters and Henry Hardgrove, I welcome you into the goddess' embrace. May your souls find the happiness in death that they never found in life."

Jepsom lifted his hands into the air, and a beam of brilliant white light shot into the heavens. "The goddess has welcomed them with open arms." The cardinal looked down at Tim with a smile pulled tight across his face before returning his gaze to the admiring crowd. "It is times like this, my friends, that my duties as cardinal fill me with happiness, but there are other times my duties are not so welcome."

The crowd gave a gasp of horror. All of them were eating up this lunatic's bullshit. Tim had heard enough. He took a red cloth from his robes and held it in the air. The little bit of fabric rippled as if on a breeze as he waved it a few times before letting it drop to the ground.

Cassie screamed, "Jepsom is a fraud! Don't listen to his bullshit."

The guards by the stage started running toward Tim's master of distraction. Tim leaned forward in anticipation of the next part of his plan unfolding. He really hadn't expected this part to work, but there was always the chance they would take him by surprise. His eyes moved from the guard's back toward the podium, and he held his breath.

The world around him froze. It was like one of those scenes from *Saved By the Bell* where the main character paused everyone so he could monologue to the camera. "What the fuck?" Tim exclaimed as he looked around for the source of the spell.

A woman appeared out of nowhere and started walking through the crowd in Tim's direction. Her robes were blue, but glowed with a white light. "Not how I'm used to being addressed." The goddess smiled. "But I think I can let it slide under the circumstances."

The goddess seemed a lot hipper than she had the last time he had interacted with her. Tim wondered if the AI who ran *The Etheric Coast* was learning from its interactions with the players and tailoring the game experience to each of them. It would have to be amazingly sophisticated software, but who would want to leave a game where everything seemed made just for them?

Tim wasn't sure if he should stand or bow, so he just remained seated. "Sorry." He winced. Sorry wasn't the kind of thing you said to a goddess. He should have said something like "Please forgive me, your divine worship."

"Yes, that would have been better." The goddess stopped in front of him.

Holy shit, did she just read my mind?

"Yes, but I don't have enough time to explain things now. I'm here to cash in on the favor you owe me." Her eyes said, "Just nod your head so I can give you the details."

There was no way he could deny the goddess. Whatever she wanted him to do, he had to do it. She'd saved Cassie's life, and the only reason he was able to put his plan for the slums in place was because of his work with the temple.

Tim looked into the goddess' expectant eyes and spoke with true eloquence. "Okay." Sometimes he wasn't so great with words under pressure, and he had no idea what else the goddess might want from him. He was already here doing what the high priest had asked him to.

"You can't kill the cardinal," the goddess tried to continue, but Tim cut her off.

"No fucking way." He was pissed. Jepsom had made his life teeter on the edge of miserable since he'd come into the game. If he didn't have such awesome friends, he would not have wanted to stay.

The goddess' eyes blazed with fury but her voice was calm. "You owe me this. It might not make sense now, but all things will become clear in time." Her light started to fade, and the sounds of the world around him started to return. "The choice is yours."

Things were speeding up now. What in the fuck was he going to do? Tim knew he only had seconds to make the decision. The goddess had never steered him wrong. His future, like it or not, was tied to her in ways he couldn't fathom.

"Fuck," he growled. Was he really about to save Jepsom's life?

Jumping up from his seat, Tim pointed to where he thought Gaston might be standing. "Look out!"

When Jepsom saw Tim stand up, he activated the dungeon heart's power and his personal shield erupted around him. The daggers that had been aimed at his back bounced harmlessly away. He stared at the young man and wondered why he had given everything away a moment before he could have taken his revenge.

There was no way Paul would be able to pry the kid from his clutches this time, not after an open attempt on the cardinal's life in such a public place. Tim was going to be punished for picking the wrong side, but not before he murdered that old fool Paul. This was his moment; soon he would be High Priest Jepsom the Great.

He added that last part to the title, but people would remember his name for generations. How could the masses not? He was going to be the greatest high priest who ever lived.

Smiling, Cardinal Jepsom stood tall and looked at Tim with a self-satisfied expression. "There won't be a next time."

The words echoed through his head like a migraine.

Tim looked at the cardinal. He already knew it was true. This had been his one chance to end things, and he failed. Not only had he failed, but he'd been duped into doing it by the goddess. His most likely reward for honoring his promise?

An early death.

Fuck.

Sometimes life was a cold, hard bitch. Tim glared at the cardinal's smug face and flipped him the bird. It was a childish gesture, but it made him feel a million times better. He wasn't going to die letting that asshole think Tim cared about him.

Something landed at his feet, and Tim looked down to find a tiny leather-bound book. White light shone around the edges. Bending down, he picked up the book and opened it. There was an inscription on the first page.

For honoring your promise.

Tim flipped to the next page and saw that this was another spell book. There were two spells listed. He was about to learn how to cast weaken undead and divine light. The second spell looked like some kind of attack spell.

Tim's jaw dropped. He'd be learning both spells at the apprentice level right off the bat. He might be about to die, but he couldn't fault the goddess for providing awesome rewards, even if they wouldn't last for long.

Then it hit him.

Why would the goddess give him this awesome reward if she was going to let him die? You didn't do this kind of thing for someone unless you expected them to live. Maybe he still had a chance.

Tim looked at the stage and took a quick step back. He would have taken another step, but he'd already backed into his chair. His eyes were no longer on Jepsom but firmly focused on the two caskets next to him. Their lids were off, and there was something moving inside the boxes.

What in the fuck was going on?

CHAPTER EIGHTY-TWO

Baron leapt out of his casket.

At least Tim thought it was Baron. The man was the right size, but it was hard to tell with his jaw gaping and some kind of serpentine tube sticking out of it. There were teeth on the end of that thing, and they snapped open and closed.

Tim tried to calm his nerves and thought about the new spells he'd just been given. Seemed like they would be a complete waste if they weren't made for this situation. He started working on the movements for weaken undead. When he glanced to see how long he had before Baron attacked him, he found the monster version of his friend going after Jepsom.

Henry joined Baron a moment later, and the two creatures started slamming themselves against the cardinal's shield. Despite the strength the two monsters had, they couldn't get in. Then a third man landed on top of Jepsom's shield, and it started to buckle. The sheriff had decided to join the party.

Tim wondered what could possibly be driving these creatures to attack Jepsom in the open. This seemed like a "the jig is up" move for the sheriff. There was no putting the cat back in the bag after you landed on top the cardinal with some kind of crazy vampiric feeding tube coming out of your kisser.

Something bumped into his shoulder, and Tim whirled. ShadowLily and Gaston joined him, and he could see Cassie and JaKobi working their way through the screaming crowd.

"I had the perfect throw," Gaston lamented.

Tim put a consoling hand on his shoulder. "I'm sure you did, and I wouldn't have interfered with a master at work if the goddess herself hadn't asked me to."

Gaston seemed mollified, but Tim could already see the wheels in his head spinning with questions. "Let's talk after we take care of our current problem." He pointed at the three creatures trying to crack Jepsom out of his shield like a walnut at a Christmas party.

"What problem?" Cassie huffed. "Those guys are doing the job for us."

It took a second for it to click, but then all the pieces fell into place for Tim. He pulled his bewildered tank into a hug. "You beautiful bastard!"

Tim let go of his perplexed friend and looked at the entire group. "Our job as I see it now is to get these people out of here so we can deal with the three creatures."

"Any chance we can wait until they kill him to help?" JaKobi shrugged when they all glared at him. "I'm just saying. Jepsom doesn't seem like the kind of guy who'd stop trying to kill you because you saved his life."

JaKobi was right, but Tim wasn't sure if that was what the goddess would want. Fuck, when he tried to think about what an actual god might want he had no idea. A god's thoughts and desires might not be comprehensible to a mere mortal.

Fuck it. He was just going to have to do what he thought was right. "No, we go now. We'll deal with Jepsom later. He just told everyone the sheriff was his friend, and the man's up there trying to eat him. Jepsom's going to have plenty of explaining to do."

"Not that it matters now." Cassie pointed at the stage.

ShadowLily snickered. "That's gotta hurt."

The cardinal's shield had finally collapsed, and the sheriff was crouched over him, trying to fend off the other two creatures. It seemed Jon Hobbs wasn't the kind of monster who liked sharing with his friends. It wouldn't be much longer before the other two creatures gave up and started looking for other sustenance.

Tim grabbed Cassie by the shoulder. "Use that big scary voice of yours to get these people to scatter."

Tim turned to the rest of the group and continued, "I've got a spell that can weaken them and one that should harm them, but I can't use them at the same time. That means the three of you have to distract the other one until I'm ready to deal with it."

"What about the big fucker guarding Jepsom?" JaKobi asked.

"We'll let Jepson and the sheriff work out their differences until we take care of the other two," Tim replied with a smile. It wasn't his job to keep saving the bastard's life. At least he hoped it wasn't.

Cassie jumped up on the stage. "Get the fuck out of here!" It wasn't eloquent, but she got the point across. Then she pointed at a guard. "Once these people are out of here, set a perimeter. None of these things can leave."

The guard stared at her blankly. The man was clearly in shock. No one expected monsters to show up while they were just trying to pick up a little bonus pay.

Cassie slapped the guard across the face, breaking the man out of his stupor. "Get to fucking work."

The guard took control of his men and formed a wall to push the crowd away from what was happening on stage.

The sheriff won his battle of dominance over the prize, and Baron and Henry turned away, looking for easier snacks. Tim fumbled through the motions of weaken undead. As he finished the spell, he muttered. "I'm sorry I couldn't help you."

Tim let the spell go, and it hit Baron squarely in the chest. With Baron weakened, Tim started casting divine light. He hoped the spell would be painless for the man, or rather, for the creature that he'd become. He'd promised these prisoners he would deliver letters to their loved ones if they died. Part of him hoped he'd be able to return the letters to them instead of letting them down the way he had.

Putting an end to the sheriff would go a good long way toward easing his guilt.

Tim finished casting divine light, and a cone of pure power darted from his fingertip at Baron. The creature tried to duck out of the way, but the spell hit him in the center of the chest. White flames erupted from where the spell landed and consumed Baron in a single white-hot flash.

Cassie was going toe to toe with the creature formerly known as Henry. Her bō staff was long enough that Henry couldn't quite reach her with his fancy new mouth. Gaston and ShadowLily worked with her, trying to corral and attack the creature at the same time. Tim could see several cuts along Henry's arms and legs. The wounds didn't seem to be slowing the creature down at all.

Tim remembered how infective his *flameburst* had been. The sheriff had repaired the damage almost instantaneously.

Henry erupted in flames as JaKobi entered the fray. Everyone moved away from the flaming creature except for Tim. He kept marching forward. He blasted the creature with *Weaken Undead* and then with *Divine Light*. Henry ceased to exist an instant later.

That left Tim with one last target to destroy.

The sheriff climbed off Jepsom's corpse and roared. Something was going on. Jon Hobbs' clothes ripped at the seams as his arms and legs elongated. It was like he'd turned into the Hulk. Whatever Jepsom had been using to power his shield had drawn the monster toward him, and it seemed the sheriff had absorbed that power.

"Boss fight!" Tim shouted to the rest of his group.

This was going to be fucking awesome!

The sheriff picked up Jepsom's corpse and turned slowly until his eyes locked onto Tim's. The crazy feeding tube sucked back into his mouth. "I told you this wasn't over." He let out a roar and his mouth split open so the snapping jaws of his second mouth could terrify them all.

With the casual flick of his wrist, the sheriff sent Jepsom's body sailing at them.

JaKobi stepped forward, casting flameshield. Jepsom's body flew through the fiery construct and came out as ashes on the other side. JaKobi's spell winked out of existence, and the sheriff sprinted toward them.

Cassie charged forward to intercept the gigantic version of Jon Hobbs. "Asshole!" she screamed as she smashed her bō staff into his leg.

Hobbs shrugged off her attack and shoved Cassie out of the way as he continued toward Tim.

JaKobi hit the sheriff with spell after spell. Jon Hobbs' torso looked like a burnt pincushion. The hilts of twenty throwing knives littered the sheriff's chest like popcorn on the floor of a movie theater. Cassie leapt to her feet and ran forward, striking the sheriff from behind. Jon Hobbs ignored her.

The man was a juggernaut.

Tim cast weaken undead, then he cast it again. The spells were enough to slow the sheriff down, but the third stopped him in his tracks. Using the last of his mana, Tim cast divine light.

The shimmering projectile caught Jon Hobbs in the center of the chest, and he screamed as the fire consumed him. Flakes of his skin floated away on the breeze. After three seconds, all that was left of the sheriff was a bad memory.

Darkness spread across the sky, and a bolt of red energy shot out of the roiling black clouds. The bolt struck the front of the temple and seared an angry red mark on the central pillar.

A voice called from the heavens, "We are hungry, and we are coming for you all."

White light erupted from the temple, banishing the darkness from the sky in an instant. The light gathered in on itself, and the goddess was once again standing before Tim. "The Dark Lord Vitaria has awoken. Will you be my champion in the fight against her darkness?"

Tim looked at his team. One by one, they nodded, letting him know they were all on board with the decision.

Turning to face the goddess again, Tim dropped to one knee. "I will be your champion."

The goddess touched a finger to his forehead, filling his body with energy. "Then rise as a guardian of the light and know that the future of all of Promethia rests upon your shoulders."

"No pressure," Cassie grumbled from behind him.

The goddess ignored the spitfire of a tank and kept her eyes focused on Tim's. "The Dark Lord's wraiths have already infiltrated the city. The sheriff might not be the only one. Find them and end them as you have done here."

Quest Received: Get the Wraiths Out of Here

The Dark Lord Vitaria has decided that now is the right time to conquer the city of Promethia. One of her wraiths has already been unmasked. You are charged with the task of finding the remaining wraiths and exterminating them.

Reward: Staff of Divine Retribution and five gold for each member of your party.

Accept Quest: Yes/No

Tim quickly accepted the quest.

The goddess smiled down upon their group as she started floating into the sky. "Paul will be able to provide you the answers you seek. The future of Promethia rests in your hands. Do not fail me, soldier of light." The goddess turned into a glowing ball and launched into the heavens.

Just like that, she was gone.

"She really does know how to make an exit," ShadowLily said, looking into the sky.

"That's the truth," JaKobi chimed in. "So, what do we do now?"

Tim grinned as he thought about the quests he had to turn in and how they should be enough to push him above level ten. "I've got a few quests to finish, but I'll meet everyone back at the inn and we'll figure out what to do about the goddess' quest."

"Sounds good to me." Cassie slung her bō staff into the holder on her back. "I need a beer after being in my own episode of *The Strain*." She shrugged. "Fighting face-sucking monsters isn't all it's cracked up to be."

"I second the beer comment but am reserving judgment on the monsters. I love a good horror flick." JaKobi grinned. "I mean, who doesn't want to save the world from monsters?"

Gaston raised his hand. "I just want a quiet life. A place where I can drink beer in peace."

Cassie smashed her elbow into Gaston's ribs. "I'm not buying that shit for one second." She smiled at the assassin's wounded expression. "Don't be such a baby. The first round's on me."

Gaston's mood brightened substantially. "Now you're speaking my language."

JaKobi gave Tim and ShadowLily a wave. "See you guys later." He shook his head as he turned away. "I swear, these guys run into the craziest shit," the fire mage mumbled. "I fucking love it."

Tim looked at the woman of his dreams as the guards started coming back into the space to see what happened. "You should go with them. I don't know how long this is going to take."

"Not a chance," ShadowLily smirked. "Last time I left you alone, you ended up in prison."

"At least you know I can satisfy your bad-boy craving," Tim responded with a flirty grin.

"The only thing you're bad at is staying out of jail," ShadowLily ribbed him.

Tim's grin got even bigger. "I'm going to take that as a compliment."

ShadowLily slapped him on the arm. "Not everything I say is a sex thing."

He couldn't stop himself from laughing but he gazed pleadingly into her eyes. "How about this one time? You gotta let me have this one."

"Fine." She put her hands on her hips and glared at him. "Sex was included in my previous statement, but it's not much of a compliment. I only said you weren't bad at it, not that you were great."

"But I *am* great, right?" Tim needled as they kept walking.

"Well, you're pretty good," she agreed reluctantly.

"A win's a win," Tim grinned from ear to ear. "Speaking of winning, as soon as we wrap this up, maybe we could do that one thing?"

"You want me to put on the pants I wore to the Stiff Tart again, don't you?" ShadowLily shook her head in mock disdain.

Tim only smirked at her. "See, you get me." Tim wrapped an arm around her as they headed toward the temple. "That's why we're perfect for each other."

ShadowLily paused and turned so she was looking directly into his eyes. "You really think so?"

"I do."

"Me too." She gave him a quick kiss and started pulling him toward the temple. "Let's get this over with. I've got a hot date and some tight pants to wriggle into."

"I'll do my best to make it quick." It was all Tim could do to not start running toward the temple. Getting back to the inn was now his highest priority.

CHAPTER EIGHTY-THREE

Now that he was out of combat, Tim's notifications were going crazy.

He pulled ShadowLily to a stop as they entered the temple. "Let me take care of a few things before we see Paul."

She nodded her head and started pulling up her own notifications. "Just let me know when you're done."

"Will do," Tim replied as he started looking over the data.

He'd almost hit level nine and still had a few quests to turn in. He'd be level ten by the end of the day for sure. A smile spread across Tim's lips as he thought about his team's future. They were almost at the point where things were really going to take off. The future was looking bright.

Tim pulled up his first notification.

Quest Completed: Something Wicked This Way Comes

You have discovered what was plaguing the prisoners and put an end to it. Not all of the prisoners survived, but at least the immediate threat has been curtailed.

Reward: Three gold coins

He'd give every one of those coins back to have Baron and

Henry alive again. Tim would have wished them back to life for the simple fact that he wouldn't have to deliver their letters. It was one thing to know you were responsible for someone's death, and another thing entirely to have to explain your failure to their loved ones. Not that he had a choice now.

Those letters would get delivered.

No matter how much it hurt, it was his duty to get the last words of the sheriff's victims to their family members. So Tim would do it, and after stepping away from the situation for a few days, he'd re-examine every last bit of what happened to make sure those same mistakes were never repeated.

Maybe there wasn't anything he could have done. It wasn't like he could have stayed in jail, not with Lady Briarthorn outside demanding his release. Knowing their deaths were not his fault didn't make him feel any less guilty or the two men any less dead.

Without his new spells, Tim knew he wouldn't have been able to stop Jon Hobbs. The man had survived being immolated by JaKobi and having his chest filled with knives. Alone in the dark and without his new spells, Tim wouldn't have stood a chance.

There was a part of him that would always feel guilty about what had happened to Baron and Henry. Maybe he could talk to the high priest about doing a monthly healing in the Hole. It wouldn't bring the two men back, but it would ease his guilt. There was something to be said for paying penance. It helped keep the wound fresh so you would never forget what you were fighting for.

In this case, all of Promethia was on the line. Baron and Henry had been the first casualties of war, and their sacrifices wouldn't be forgotten. He'd deliver the letters, and make sure their families knew what they'd done.

Tim brushed away the **You've Reached Level Nine** notification.

He would worry about assigning his stat points after talking to Paul. With all his notifications taken care of or minimized, Tim turned toward ShadowLily. It felt kind of weird coming out of a fight without leveling at least one skill.

"Probably because those new spells were already apprentice level," Tim mumbled to himself.

ShadowLily dismissed whatever she was looking at. "Did you say something?"

Tim smiled as he looked at the most beautiful woman in the world. He didn't feel like explaining his thoughts about the fight, so he tried to get them focused on the next task they had to complete. "Let's go."

Walking deeper into the temple, Tim found one of the boys to escort them to Paul's chambers. As they walked through the dark and winding passages, he thought about what had happened over the last few days. Things hadn't gone exactly as expected, but in the end, everything had worked out.

At least, everything he could control.

What he couldn't control were monsters sent here to feed off people. Tim wasn't even sure what the bastards did. Jon Hobbs certainly wasn't sucking the blood out of the men, so the sheriff must have been feeding off of their essence somehow. That was some scary shit.

Hobbs had looked just fine in the sunlight too.

Monsters not being able to walk around in daylight was the thing that normally saved humans' asses in supernatural situations. It was a huge advantage to only have to worry about being attacked during half the day, and it was an added bonus if sunlight killed the monsters.

The sheriff had stood in broad daylight without so much as a blemish, as did Baron and Henry. That meant these wraiths could be hiding anywhere. Hobbs had been one hungry bastard, though, so maybe the way to track these new monsters was by looking for victims of their feedings.

Finding the wraiths and eliminating them was a problem for another day. Tim still had plenty of work left to do before he could move on to the next task. There was a conversation with the high priest to be had and two letters to deliver before he could focus on the goddess' new quest.

Not to mention a district to revitalize, his job at the forge, and the healing shack. Tim's dance card was pretty full without having to track and hunt the wraiths, but he'd find them. Once Promethia was secure, they could take the fight to Vitaria.

Their runner dropped them off outside of the high priest's chambers. Unlike every other trip Tim had made to visit the high priest, the large golden doors were open. With Jepsom out of the way, Paul seemed more confident in his security.

"The hero of the day returns." Paul clapped as he stood up and walked toward Tim. "Your ability to take control of the situation and save the day was very impressive."

Tim shook Paul's hand. "I was just doing my part."

"And humble. Most heroes are braggarts by nature. They seek out the jobs that will put them in the spotlight." Paul dropped Tim's hand and smiled warmly. "But not you. The goddess truly shines within you."

"I wouldn't go that far." Tim stopped when ShadowLily elbowed him in the ribs. "But her light does guide me."

"As it does for us all." Paul motioned for Tim to join him by the throne. The high priest started digging around in the chest behind his chair. "I believe a reward is in order."

Quest Complete: Wrath of the goddess

Cardinal Jepsom met his untimely end, and while it wasn't done by your hand, his death wouldn't have been possible without your influence on the events leading to the deed. You've also managed to stoke the embers of peoples' beliefs into righteous flames of faith for the goddess' salvation.

Reward: Fifty gold coins.

Paul smiled as he handed Tim the giant sack of coins. "I've also restored your privileges in the temple and awarded you the rank of Honorary Brother. If ever you find yourself in need, the temple will always be a place of refuge."

"Thank you for doing your duty to the realm and the goddess. I am sure you have plenty of questions, but in the aftermath of the attack, I have a lot of work to do. If you need help with research or just general information, seek out Brother Colton in the library. If anyone can shed light on what's happening now, it's him."

Tim shook Paul's hand again. "Thank you." He paused after letting Paul's hand drop and quickly added. "Before I go, I wonder if you have the time to consider a simple request."

"If it's in my power to do it, it will be so." Paul's eyes bored into Tim with feverish intensity.

"Without the help of the two men Jon Hobbs murdered for his attack today, I wouldn't have made it out of the Hole. I was wondering if you could grant me some kind of special dispensation so I could heal the inmates once a month."

Tim looked at the floor, not sure why he was seeking validation for his idea and not just the approval to carry it out. "It would be a nice way to pay back the memory of two men who tried to do the right thing."

"This is why I like working with you." Paul beamed. "You are always coming up with new ways to spread the goddess' light. I will help you get the documents you need, and I would be honored to preside over the services of the two men."

"Thank you," Tim replied. He pulled Paul into a heartfelt hug. "Having their loved ones honored by the temple might bring their families some peace."

Paul waved away Tim's thanks. "It is the least I can do." He clapped his hands, and one of his personal guards stepped forward. "Please show them out."

"Right this way." The guard pointed toward the door and led Tim and ShadowLily out of the temple.

CHAPTER EIGHTY-FOUR

Completing Paul's quest had made Tim level ten.

All he had to do before becoming an adventurer was pick his advanced class, but there would be time for him to worry about that task after completing his last open quest. The delivery of his first letter to a very gruff and unimpressed Felix Hardgrove hadn't gone nearly as well as Tim would have liked.

Snatching the letter and slamming the door in Tim's face wasn't exactly warm and fuzzy.

While a warm and fuzzy response wasn't exactly what he'd been expecting, he was caught off-guard by the abruptness of the entire interaction. Given the news Tim had to deliver, he was willing to give Felix a pass. He didn't know how police and doctors could constantly deliver bad news to grieving families and not be broken. Tim had only done the deed once, and it was enough to make him want to crawl into bed for a week and live on a diet of ice cream and pizza.

Now they were halfway to Helen Peters' house, and Tim was preparing himself for a tough conversation. Maybe getting the Jehovah's Witness treatment earlier had been a blessing in disguise. At least he didn't have to explain himself and deal with the aftermath.

Nothing sucked the fun out of the room faster than a death.

Tim stopped at the edge of the path leading to a small cottage and pulled ShadowLily into a hug. "Thank you for staying with me."

"Are you sure you don't want me to come to the door?" the half-elf asked as she watched him with concern.

"I'll be fine." Tim scuffed his boots in the dirt. "I just have to pull off the Band-Aid."

ShadowLily spun him so he was facing the door. "Then do it."

It was just the kick in the pants Tim needed to get moving. He started walking up the well-maintained path toward the house. ShadowLily was hanging back by the gate, so he had the space to handle the delivery himself. The warm and fuzzy feeling he was getting right now was from the knowledge she'd be right there waiting for him no matter how things went.

Life was so much better when you had at least one person you could always count on.

Tim stopped in front of the door, his heart racing. There was really no good way to deliver bad news, and drawing it out only made it worse for everyone. So did lingering on someone's doorstep. No one liked it when a random stranger was hanging out in their front yard.

Taking a deep, calming breath, Tim knocked on the door.

A few minutes later, a plump middle-aged woman opened the door a crack. Peering out of the opening, she gave Tim a quick once-over. "Can I help you?"

Tim dug deep into his emotional toolbox and managed to generate a weak smile. "My name is Tim. I'm a friend of Baron's."

"There's a name I haven't heard in ages." Helen Peters opened the door a bit wider. "What's that old rapscallion have to say for himself?"

The smile vanished from Tim's face. "I hate to be the one to have to tell you this." He took his eyes off of hers and looked at the ground. "He's dead."

Helen looked shaken but not taken off-guard. "You know, I always thought I'd see him again."

"I was with him the day before he passed. He gave me a letter." Tim fished the letter out of his cloak and handed it to her. "I'm not sure what kind of life Baron led before I met him, but he was a friend to me when I needed one, and he died fighting for the people of Promethia."

"That doesn't sound much like the Baron I knew." Helen eyed him suspiciously.

Tim wasn't sure what to say. His brain defaulted to sarcastic whenever he was nervous or in trouble. His mouth opened, and the words came tumbling out. "Well, he *was* in prison at the time."

Oh, shit! Here he was delivering a death notification, and now he was cracking fucking jokes. Was he the worst person in the world?

"That sounds more like him." Helen slapped her thigh as she laughed. She looked up, the glimmer of a memory lighting her gaze. "But you say he died doing something good?"

"He died trying to save all of us from a threat. The high priest is going to preside over his services." Tim smiled warmly. "No matter his faults, in the end, he was a good man."

Tears streaked Helen's cheeks. "That he was, young man, that he was." She clutched the letter to her chest. "Thank you for coming to tell me."

Tim gave her a little bow. "It was my pleasure to do this for him. If you ever need anything, you can find me at the Blue Dagger Inn."

"That place in the slums?" Helen questioned.

"The very one." Tim laughed. "It might not seem like much yet, but we're working on it."

Helen patted him gently on the arm. "I doubt I'll need anything, but if I do, I promise to call on you." She gave him one last smile and went inside to read the note.

Tim turned and walked back down the path. He felt lighter than he had when they reached Helen's home. She seemed like such a sweet lady. Tim wondered if Baron had gone off to make his fortune only to never return. There was a story there somewhere, but it wasn't the right time to ask.

ShadowLily wrapped an arm around him as he drew closer. "That seemed to go well."

"It did. I get the feeling they hadn't talked in a while, but it was one of those relationships that no matter how long it had been since they saw each other, it was as if only a few minutes had passed." Tim pulled ShadowLily against him. "It might sound sappy, but I don't know what I'd do if you just disappeared and I had no way to find you."

"I'd burn down the world to find you?" ShadowLily said with a hint of anger in her voice. It was the kind of tone that implied anyone who fucked with her man better get the hell out of dodge, and quickly.

Tim laughed. "Maybe start with something a little more subtle."

"Said no one ever." She stopped him and looked into Tim's eyes. "Haven't you seen *Taken*, you've got to be on top of this shit before it's too late."

"The next part is very important. They are going to take you," Tim intoned in his best Liam Neeson impression. "I like to replace the word *take* with *tickle*, though."

ShadowLily started to sprint away from him. "Oh, no, you don't."

"The next part is very important," Tim yelled as he chased after her. "I am going to tickle you and there is nothing you can do about it." He held his hands up fingers extended. The digits twitched slightly in anticipation of touching woman-flesh.

"Buahahahahaha!" Tim roared as he started chasing her toward the inn. He might not get her now, but eventually, she'd let her guard down, and the tickling would begin.

EPILOGUE

Mornings sucked.

Seriously, was there ever a good time for it to be morning? Tim thought as he rolled out of bed. The only time anyone looked forward to mornings was if there was a new release of some kind. Otherwise, the world would like to sleep in until a respectable hour.

Tim looked at the empty half of the bed and realized that maybe he just wasn't a morning person. Was enjoying mornings a conscious decision? Could he wake up one day and just attack the day like one of "those people?"

He took his first lumbering steps toward the door and smelled the coffee waiting for him on the other side. Liz was an amazing person. Tim would sing her praises until the end of time for always knowing when he was going to wake up and having that sweet dark cup of roasted delight ready.

He'd heard tea drinkers refer to coffee as bean water. If that were the case, they were just drinking tree leaves. Those snobby bastards didn't even have the sense to brew them properly. There was a whole art to crafting the perfect cup of coffee. Tim's personal setup looked like a science experiment gone wrong, but the product was divine.

Oddly enough, he wasn't opposed to a good cup of tea. Tim never claimed to be coffee-exclusive, not unless it was the first drink of the day. Sure, a good dark tea had some pick-me-up, but nothing rocked the house like a cup of joe with a shot of his second-favorite bean for an extra jolt. Expresso was like the kicker on a football team. He was important. You couldn't win without him, but most of the time, he just rode the bench.

He wasn't even sure if they had expresso here, but it took him about five minutes of explaining for Liz to figure out what he wanted and find it. The woman was like a wizard when it came to anticipating their needs. The coffee waiting outside of his door in the morning was just one example.

Tim never realized how important it was to get the first cup of coffee down on the way to the bathroom. He'd always been a set the coffee maker and get dressed kind of guy. Then it was coffee for breakfast as he ran out the door. Not at the Blue Dagger.

He had his first cup down before he sat down to take his morning sabbatical.

By the time Tim climbed into his bath, the coffee almost made him feel like a human being again. He hated to admit it, but he might be slightly jealous of the get-up-and-go types. His bed might as well have been his sanctuary. He only wanted to leave it when absolutely necessary.

That meant his relationship, food, work, and raiding were the only things standing between him and the sleep he craved.

Even now that his work was going to be kicking ass full-time, there still wouldn't be enough hours in the day for napping. Four hours a day at the forge, and another four in the healing shack, plus a nightly run of some kind with the group was leaving him a little ragged.

Maybe it was just that he hadn't settled on a new class yet? There were so many good options. Did he want to push on as a straight healer, or did he want to be a little more adventurous? It had been a few days since Jepsom died, and his life hadn't slowed down one bit.

He'd settle on a class before he had the meeting with his case-worker. Apparently, becoming an adventurer meant he had to pause his life in-game to sign a new contract. At least he'd be able to set up access to the currency market.

From the marketplace, he could sell his gold to people for real-world currency, and from there, it was a few simple steps to get that money to his parents. He'd feel a lot better telling his parents about his decision after he sent them some money. Nothing made your choices look better than success.

There was so much to do, and he was just getting started. His project in the slums was underway, with Mr. Applebottom over-seeing the details. A few of the buildings would be ready by the end of the month.

That meant it was time to put his market kiosk into play. Once people started coming for the market, it would be easier to get the prices he wanted for rent on the newly refurbished structures.

With renters in place and his percentage from the kiosk, getting more gold should never be a problem. He leaned back, letting the warm water ease the tension in his muscles. He loved the thirty minutes he took for himself every morning. It was the only time he got to let his mind wander.

A buzz sounded in Tim's head and pulled him right out of the tranquility zone.

Could people not wait until a decent hour to contact him? And why the fuck had the message buzzed through his filters? Tim sighed in frustration as he pulled up his user interface. The first thing he saw was a reminder to pick his class. Dismissing the window, Tim moved onto his messages. He had a priority message from Jeremy.

Wow, he hadn't seen Jeremy since his first day in the game. Not since the man had pointed him toward the inn and said something funny to him. What was it his guide had said? The words didn't immediately come back to him, so he decided to open his new message and find out what he wanted.

Message Received From Jeremy:

I've got someone who wants to meet you. See you in five.

Eat a Fish!

"What does that even mean?" Tim closed the message and climbed out of the bath. Regardless of the daring it took to try to come up with a cool new catchphrase, he wasn't sure "eat a fish" was ever going to catch on. Sure, maybe if you ran a fish taco truck and needed a cool slogan, but otherwise, it just seemed kinda weird.

Despite the friendly feel of Jeremy's message, Tim wondered if he was doing another job for NPC Corp. If the man was working for the company, it wouldn't pay to keep him waiting. He finished drying off and equipped his clothes.

Getting dressed in an instant was never going to get old.

Walking into the main room of the inn, Tim motioned toward his cup and then at Liz. She nodded, and he set it on the counter before heading to the door. He had to admit that living at the inn had its perks.

Tim opened the front door and stepped onto the street before he stretched his back. Jeremy was leading a man he'd never seen before toward him. Part of Tim was jealous that he'd never be able to rock an afro the way Jeremy did. The man had a certain 70s funk about him that was cool as fuck and definitely couldn't be replicated.

The man walking next to Jeremy was about forty. He had a wide, solid-looking frame, and his arms rippled with thickly corded muscles. The guy had on the same starting tunic Tim had been given when he entered the game. Maybe it was the man's first day in Promethia. It was kind of awesome that new people were starting to play every day. The more popular the game was, the easier it would be to make money.

The two men joined him on the porch. Jeremey pointed to the man next to him. "This is Joe. Joe, this is Tim." Jeremy gave Joe's hand a brief shake. "Good luck to you." He turned and headed back the way he'd come.

Tearing his gaze from Jeremy, Tim looked at the man in front of him, wondering what this was about. Something about his face looked incredibly familiar, but he couldn't place it.

Joe stuck out his hand. "It's good to see you again, Tim. I trust you've been taking good care of my daughter."

Holy shit!

It was *that* Joe. Sierra's dad was in the game, and he was here right now. They hadn't discussed what they would tell their parents about their relationship. It just seemed too weird. How did you say, "Hey, Dad, we fell in love in a videogame, and we will be making a life for ourselves here. It's cool, trust me."

Thoughts of what would happen if Joe found out they were basically living together rattled around inside his head loud enough that it took him a few moments to respond. "It's good to see you too, sir. Sierra is in good hands with me." It was overly formal, but he found it was always best to be exceedingly polite in situations where he was terrified.

Sierra's dad wasn't a gamer, he was a cook. What was he doing here?

"Good to hear." He clapped Tim on the shoulder. "Anywhere we can talk in private for a minute?"

Tim wasn't sure how private Joe wanted their conversation to be. He'd obviously come to Tim before Sierra, so something was up, but he had no idea what the man wanted. He hoped it wouldn't be a morning lecture about sex before marriage. Then there was Sierra to think about. She was probably inside training with Gaston, so taking Joe into the inn was out.

That left one place for him to go.

"Follow me." Tim waved to Joe as he set off around the side of the building. He opened the shack and motioned for Joe to join him. Once they were both inside, he closed the door and waited for his unexpected guest to say something.

Joe looked at him for a moment, and then in a rush, he blurted, "I sold my restaurant."

"What?" Tim was shocked. Joe's was an institution. The fucking diner should be a landmark, not something that was bought or sold.

"I couldn't bear the thought of my girl growing up in here and missing all those memories. I don't care where we spend our time together as a family. Being with one another is all that matters." Joe looked at Tim. "I just don't know how to tell her."

Tim was still trying to play catch up. "Wait, you sold your restaurant?"

"Yeah." Joe looked a little bummed about it. "Got a hell of a price from some corporate assholes who wanted the location for some crappy chain." He shrugged. "Thought I could open a restaurant in the game. Things can't be too different."

"You're going to need someone to help you adjust. Some of the things here have different names." Tim smiled sheepishly. "Although you could always just go to the market and point at the things you want."

"Should be fun?" He leaned forward, looking a little worried. "First, I'm going to need some new clothes." Joe's face turned almost ashen. "Do NPCs even eat?"

This was one thing Tim could answer easily. "They sure do, and they like to drink." He started to get excited about the idea. "But I'm also sure there are plenty of people here who would kill for a taste of home."

"I'm counting on it." Joe wrung his hands. "Feeding people is what I like to do. All I have to do now is find a place and set up shop."

"Just so happens I might be able to help you with that, but first, we need to let ShadowLily know you're here." Tim put a hand on

Joe's shoulder. "And get you some clothes. I can't have my girl-friend's dad showing up in a smock."

"Ah, so it's 'girlfriend' now." Joe watched Tim intently.

"Yes, sir."

Joe let Tim suffer for a few more seconds before he started to laugh. "I'm pretty sure I called it before you left."

Tim just nodded. It was funny how parents could see things before their kids did. It must come with experience.

"What I'd really like to do is cook her favorite meal for her." Joe smiled as he thought about it. "God knows, she can't go a week without eating a plate of chicken parm."

Chicken-fucking-parmesan!

"How would you feel about cooking enough for a group?" Tim started thinking about how much the entire guild would appreciate a real meal, especially after weeks of stew.

He paused when he realized he was trying to hijack Joe's moment with his daughter. He held up a hand to stop Joe before he could answer. "Sorry, it was a stupid idea. This moment is about you and Sierra."

"You remember she was in the restaurant before she left with a booth full of her friends? I wouldn't mind cooking for a few of her new ones. Not to mention, it's really just as easy to cook for twenty as it is for two." Joe smiled. "As long as you have a kitchen I can use."

Tim had access to a kitchen, all right. "Let me go and set things up with Ernie. Then I'll find ShadowLily and take her out until tonight. We'll come back to the inn, and you can lay it on her."

"That sounds like a good plan, but why is she here? Doesn't she have her own place?" Joe watched Tim like a dog eyeing a stray burger at a barbeque.

"You'll have to ask her that tonight." Tim opened the door, prepared to run. "Give me about fifteen minutes before you head inside."

Joe nodded, keeping his steely gaze focused on Tim.

Secrets weren't his strong suit, but Tim would have to try his best. His hand closed on the door to the inn, and he smiled. "I've got this."

"Today was such a blast." ShadowLily grinned as she yanked Tim toward the inn. "But I'm hungry. Why couldn't we stop and get something to eat?" the half-elf questioned as she picked up her pace.

"I told you, we've got a guild dinner tonight. If you don't like the food, don't eat anything, and we'll go out afterward." Tim grinned. "Or I could order some of those little cakes you like."

"Petit fours." She stopped walking, savoring the thought of her favorite mini-cake snack. "I can sit through anything for a box of those sweet, sweet delights."

"Good to know for when I have to ask you to do something you don't like." Tim pulled out an imaginary pen and paper to take a note.

"Just promise me it isn't stew. Liz picked the cook already. By now, he should be able to make more stuff." ShadowLily sighed. "I never knew how good I had it, being able to eat at my dad's restaurant."

Tim grinned as he pushed her toward the door. "I made Liz promise we would have something else tonight."

"That's sexy talk." ShadowLily pushed open the door to the inn and paused in her tracks. "What's that heavenly smell?"

She spun. "It smells just like home." She gave him an accusatory glare. "What'd you do?"

"He didn't do anything." Joe came out of the kitchen, wiping his hands on an apron.

"Dad?" ShadowLily paused for a second as she let his presence register. Once she realized it was really him, she rushed forward and pulled him into a hug. "What are you doing here?"

Joe hugged her back and took a step back so he could give her a solid once-over. "Changed your ears," he mumbled before returning his gaze to her eyes. "I sold my place. Couldn't bear the thought of being away from you for so long."

ShadowLily started to grin. "And what's that I smell?"

"Only your favorite," Joe replied swiftly.

Tim motioned for everyone to head to the tables. "Tonight, we feast like gods!"

"Hear, hear," the room shouted back.

Tim looked at their growing band and couldn't have been happier. It was nice that Sierra and Joe were going to get to spend more time together. Ok, so maybe he was more excited about the food possibilities that had just come back into his life, but you could be happy for more than one reason at a time, right?

Things were starting to come together in the best possible way. They had a new quest to look forward to and new monsters to hunt. *The Etheric Coast* was just as fresh today as the first instant he stepped into the game. He took a drink of his ale and smiled. Tim wasn't sure what would happen next, but he knew they'd be ready for it.

The Blue Dagger Society was ready for anything.

List of Tim's Current Stats and Skills.

"Tim" Level ten magic user

Primary Stats
Strength 12
Endurance 12
Dexterity 16
Intelligence 16

Wisdom 30
Perception: 5
Vitality: 3
Revitalization: 3
Luck: 5

Tim also has two undistributed stat points.

Notable Gear

Circlet of Wisdom +1
Simple Dagger of Dexterity +1 (X2)
Level Ten Class Change Token
Boots of Wisdom +2
Robe of the Everlasting: Wisdom +3
Belt of Wisdom +2
Gloves of Wisdom +2

Skills

Healing Orb: Apprentice rank nine
Dodge: Novice rank two
Flame Burst: Apprentice rank three
Cleanse: Apprentice rank seven
Appeal to the Goddess: Novice rank one
Infiltrator: Novice rank three
Small Blades: Apprentice rank six
Throwing Knives: Apprentice rank two
Sneak: Apprentice rank three
Night Vision: Novice rank five
Back Stab: Novice rank seven
Weaken Undead: Apprentice rank one
Divine Light: Apprentice rank one

Healing Storm: Novice level one

Open Quests
Get the Wraith Out of Here

The story is far from over. Tim and his companion's adventures will continue in The Etheric Coast Book 2!

The story continues with book two, The Trials of Tristholm, available now from Amazon and through Kindle Unlimited.

Grab your copy here.

AUTHOR NOTES - BRADFORD BATES
DECEMBER 9, 2019

I always start by thanking my wife. Without her help, inspiration, and steadfast belief that I can do this, none of these books would exist.

This was a fun series to dive into. I've been a gamer since the eighties, and have really enjoyed watching the integration between literature and gaming as it's progressed over time. The marriage of two such beautiful things was bound to happen because, at its heart, every game tells a story.

There were a couple really cool things that happened during this book, and one of them was getting to spend some time working with Michael Anderle. The way Michael digs into a story and can communicate what he feels while reading it really helped me grow as an author. I would call the opportunity to work with him, life-changing.

Now that the sappy stuff is out of the way, I have more people to thank. I'd like to start by thanking Nat, who read the first book and gave me some priceless feedback. I'm not sure if I'm supposed to name my beta readers by name or not, so I won't. But thank you for all of your feedback. I take those notes seriously, and the books change because of them.

My editor Lynne put in the real legwork on these titles. There is no way to put into words how much work she had to do.

Yep, it was that much.

Now it's time to dim the lights, turn on the PlayStation, and get back to work. Cough cough, I mean the computer and writing. Cough cough. "Sorry honey!" Turns off the PlayStation but keeps the dim lighting for eerie writing.

Happy Gaming!

AUTHOR NOTES - MICHAEL ANDERLE
DECEMBER 10, 2019

Thank you for reading our story and then continuing to our *Author Notes* as well!

Right now, I'm at the same resort (The Pacifica in Quivera, Cabo San Lucas), where I coined the term 20Booksto50k® I would use later to name a Facebook group I created to help Indie Authors.

Four years ago, I was getting ready to release the fourth book in my *Kurtherian Gambit* series. Four years later, I'm about to release my first collaboration with Bradford Bates.

Four years ago, I had no idea who Bradford was (and to be fair, he had no idea who I was, either.) But creating the Facebook group and helping other authors ended up being the catalyst for Bradford and me to meet.

During our time creating the world for this story, I asked Bradford about his background and what he did before (and during) his writing career. From those questions, we figured out his knowledge of business and used those aspects of what he knew about business to help shape our protagonist.

Now, both of us are game nerds. We both grew up loving

games, and perhaps if we had been born a generation later, we might have wished to make our living in games (like those on YouTube today.)

However, we didn't.

But, we have one thing going for us, which is age and experience. So, we thought about what sucks with MMORPGs (Massively Multiplayer Online Role-Playing Games) and decided it was the NPC class.

Usually, Non-Player Characters are scripted (often poorly) and can't really change the game too much. So, we decided to see what would happen if a future game company (that makes a ludicrous amount of money) decides to provide employment for humans to come in and BE NPCs in the game.

But, there is a hitch. *There is ALWAYS a hitch.*

And that is what this tale is all about.

We hope that you enjoyed this story. If you did, please consider providing a review, which helps the next reader consider purchasing the book, too. If you happened to love a different story, consider giving THAT author a review.

All books need more reviews!

Ad Aeternitatem,

Michael Anderle

BOOKS BY BRADFORD BATES

Ascendancy Legacy

The Arena

Jar of Souls

Guardian of the Grove

Demon Stone

The Rising Darkness

Redemption

Ascendancy Origins

Rise of the Fallen

Butcher of the Bay

Night of the Demon

The Bozley Green Chronicles

Possessed

The Galactic Outlaws

Forced Compliance

Genetic Purge

Smuggler's Legacy

Fortune Hunters

Star Talon

Lost Signal

A Galactic Outlaws Story

The Marchenko Incident

Smuggler for Hire

Origin Ice

The Fairy of Salem

Witching Hour

The Wild Hunt

Standalone Titles

Crimson Stars

CONNECT WITH THE AUTHORS

Connect with Bradford Bates

Facebook:
https://www.facebook.com/bradfordbatesauthor/

Twitter:
https://twitter.com/Freetheblizz

Website:
http://www.bradfordbates.com/

Connect with Michael Anderle and sign up for his email list here:

Website: http://lmbpn.com

Email List: http://lmbpn.com/email/

Facebook:
www.facebook.com/TheKurtherianGambitBooks

ABOUT BRADFORD BATES

Bradford Bates is a full-time author, husband to an incredible wife, and father to four furry rescue dogs. He lives in sunny Phoenix, Arizona, trying to not melt in the oppressive heat of the summer. When he isn't busy writing the next book, you can find him playing video games and watching scary movies.

www.ingramcontent.com/pod-product-compliance
Lightning Source LLC
Chambersburg PA
CBHW020223110726
47898CB00004B/1121